ISBN 978-0-276-44281-0

www.readersdigest.co.uk

The Reader's Digest Association Limited, 11 Westferry Circus, Canary Wharf, London E14 4HE

and in Canada
www.rd.ca

The Reader's Digest Association (Canada) ULC, 1100 René-Lévesque Blvd. West, Montréal,
Québec, H3B 5H5 Canada

For information as to ownership of copyright in the material of this book, and acknowledgments, see last page.

# of love & life

Three novels selected and condensed
by Reader's Digest

The Reader's Digest Association Limited, London, Montreal

CONTENTS

The Secret Life of Evie Hamilton

Catherine Alliott

The perfect wife and mother, that's what Evie Hamilton always strives to be. Married to successful, handsome Ant and mother of high-achieving Anna, up to now her biggest worry has been whether or not she can fit in a manicure before she collects Anna from her clarinet lesson.

But Evie's comfortable existence is about to change, and she will have to reappraise everything in her life.

1

JUST RECENTLY I find that whenever I enter a church, not only does my heart sink, but I'm invariably late. Today was no exception.

As I crept in, a few heads near the back swivelled to smile sympathetically. I made to slide in among them, but my sister-in-law up near the front was having none of it. 'Down here,' she was mouthing theatrically, beckoning me on like an Italian traffic policeman.

Dutifully I gathered my hymn book and handbag, and hastened, head bowed, down the aisle. As I hurried along, I inadvertently looked up and caught the eye of my brother by the altar, in his occasional capacity of churchwarden. He gave me a huge wink.

'We were worried about you,' Caro hissed as I squeezed in beside her. Everyone in the pew shoved up a bit. 'You're so late!'

'Sorry,' I muttered, and craned my neck past her to greet the rest of my family, such as it was. Beside Caro, my mother and stepmother had both leaned forward to smile: Felicity, my stepmother, elegant in a taupe chenille jacket and vanilla silk skirt, and my mother, startling in leopard-print leggings, a pair of tangerine trainers and matching headband. She blew me an extravagant kiss.

'What's she come as?' I muttered to Caro as I sat back.

'Don't,' she moaned, closing her eyes. 'She looks like she's out on day release. As if the minibus has just dropped her off!'

I suppressed a smile and turned my attention to the vicar, encouraging us in carrying tones, to support the young people being confirmed today, and to applaud them in this, their momentous decision.

I smiled. Jack, my nephew, one of the teenagers in the front pew, had the grace to turn and flash me a grin. When he'd cycled into college one day to see us and I'd casually enquired as to his motives, he'd replied in surprise, 'Oh, you get terrific presents. Hugo Palmerton got a diving watch.' As I'd raised faintly startled eyebrows he'd rushed on, 'And obviously I believe, and all that stuff. And it's a good idea if you want to get married.' He nodded sagely. 'Saves a lot of hassle.'

I had an idea he was confusing confirmation with baptism, but grasped the general sentiment. Getting confirmed was a rite of passage. He was at a particular stage on his greasy pole, as I, I supposed, was on mine. There was a time when I used to go to church for weddings, Saturday after Saturday, and then christenings, Sunday after Sunday. Now it appeared to be First Communions. Next, I imagined, with a jolt of surprise, it would be . . . yes. Well. After all, there'd been one of those already, hadn't there? Dad's. One box ticked. One box that had gone up the aisle, containing a supposedly hale and hearty man, in this, our village church, while we'd all sat in this family pew, shocked and silent: the remains of the Milligan family.

Family pew. An anachronism, of course, but one that Caro maintained rigorously, referring to it loudly, as Mum and Granny never had, as if we were the ancient descendants of some aristocratic lineage, instead of impoverished farmers who'd managed, by the skin of their teeth, to hang on to a certain amount of dubiously infertile land.

Caro leaned in to me now. 'No Ant?'

'No, I told you, he's taken Anna to a clarinet exam.'

'Ah, yes,' she said vaguely. She had a faraway look in her eye, as if in some dim, distant conversation I *had* mentioned it, when in fact I'd made a point of ringing her and apologising profusely.

'Does she still enjoy it?' she whispered incredulously.

'Loves it,' I hissed back, as we were enjoined, at that moment, to get to our feet and sing hymn number 108.

Yes, that was always the implication, wasn't it, I thought as I added my low warble to Caro's reedy treble, that my overstimulated, hot-house flower was wilting under the pressure of academia and music exams and pushy parents, while her 'brood', as she always referred to them—as if three were a cast of thousands—got out into the fresh air and had a 'proper childhood'; as if, somehow, Anna's was *improper*. My blood simmered away for a bit, but then, as the hymn came to rest in a green and pleasant land and we were bidden to pray, I tried to, not have green thoughts, but pleasant ones.

After all, she was not only my sister-in-law, she was my oldest friend.

I was guiltily aware that at one point 'oldest' would have been substituted by 'best'. Certainly years ago, at school, we were pretty much joined at the hip and lived in each other's houses, which was probably where the trouble had started. She'd taken one look at my rambling old farmhouse in its idyllic setting, observed the big family meals in the farmhouse kitchen, the laughter, the sense of history, and thought: I want some of that. I can almost remember the look in her eye as she'd stood at the kitchen window one day after lunch, watching Tim, huge, burly and kindly, with his father's shock of red hair, bowling at a tree stump in the back garden. She'd wanted him too, and she'd got him. And if I'm honest, I thought, I'd looked at her orderly family, her uncluttered town house with its state-of-the-art appliances, her quiet teacher parents, and thought: And I'll have some of that. Of course, I didn't marry her brother—that would have been too neat, and apart from anything else she didn't have one—but my eyes, shall we say, were opened to an urbane, civilised lifestyle.

When, some years later, I'd met Ant, tall, tousled, slightly myopic in his John Lennon glasses, an Oxford academic I'd found in a bookshop I was working in, everything slotted into place. Caro got her heart's desire, and I got mine. In fact, Caro, even more so, because when Dad died, suddenly in his sleep and, it transpired, intestate, Caro got the farm too. She almost hadn't, actually, because everything naturally went to Felicity, but Felicity wouldn't hear of it. No, no, the house and land should go to Tim. It was what Dad had always said he wanted, what would have happened if he'd flipping well bothered to write it down. Felicity took sufficient from the estate to buy herself a small house in town, and left the bricks, the mortar—the acres—to Tim and Caro. Caro had got her farm, her land, the whole bucolic bit.

As I had got my bit, I thought, as I watched Jack come back from the altar. I'd got my academic: my sensitive, clever Ant, who had become a don at the tender age of twenty-nine. And so I'd become a don's wife. We had a house in college, in Balliol, looking out onto the grassy quad complete with gates and porter; we had like-minded friends on our doorstep—other dons' wives with babies, with whom I pushed prams. Life was sweet.

But then Ant had gone one step further. He'd written a book. Not a dry, academic tome, but a rather accessible biography of Byron, about whom he was a bit of an expert and whom he regarded as a bit of a dude. Which was how he'd portrayed him, in an accessible way that had caught the public's eye, and, more importantly, the eye of a daytime television programme, which promoted him. He became something of a success, and Anthony Hamilton, a rather obscure English professor from Oxford, became Anthony Hamilton, best-selling author. Which wasn't entirely in the script, as far as Caro was concerned.

Oh, it wasn't the fame she envied—I knew she got a vicarious thrill out of being his sister-in-law—no, it was the money. Not a great deal, but enough for us to move out of the college house to a large Victorian villa on four floors in that academic mecca, Jericho. Bills were paid, credit cards sorted, and Anna's school fees, which frankly we'd struggled with, became a doddle. And Tim and Caro couldn't even afford school fees. There was no money in farming now, not unless you had a thousand acres or a private income, and even with the extra Caro made from holding wedding receptions in the garden they were still very short. So they'd had to send their three to the local comp.

I shifted in my pew. Yes, their three. To my one. After all, I'd been quite good about that, hadn't I? OK, not in the early days. Not when Jack had been swiftly followed by Phoebe and Henry, and Anna by not a sausage. The despair, the sadness, the seething jealousy had threatened to overwhelm me then, but later . . . well, later, Ant and I accepted it. And she, Anna, was so lovely.

'Are you going up?' Caro nudged me. 'For Communion?'

Our pew was filing out from the other end and I got up and followed Caro, Mum and Felicity. Up on the rostrum, Tim was dutifully helping with the Communion wine. I knelt at the altar rails, and as he approached me with his chalice I felt those terrible church giggles I'd felt years ago; every Sunday, in fact, in this church, as Tim did his damnedest to make me laugh. I determined not to look up at him now. As he put the cup to my lips, he affected a thick Irish brogue.

'De blood of Christ, my child,' he wheedled softly.

No. I would not lose it. And I was fine, actually, until, as I sipped, Tim whispered in mock alarm, as if I'd taken a huge gulp, 'Steady!'

Doing the nose trick with the Communion wine is pretty unforgivable, and as I returned, chastened and wine splattered, to my seat, Caro was frowning darkly. I knew she thought I was a bad influence on her husband. As I bent my head to pray, I recalled a friend's comment when Caro had married Tim. 'How lovely, so you're gaining a sister.' Why, then, years later, did I have a sinking feeling I'd lost a brother?

Shocked by my impure thoughts, I resolved, as we all filed out ten minutes later, to be more sisterly. More . . . supportive.

Caro turned to me, a defensive look in her eye. 'You're coming back to the house?'

'Of course.' I smiled.

'Good.' She beamed, clearly imagining, I realised with a jolt, that I might not. 'We haven't done much in the way of catering, just a glass of sherry and some sandwiches. Of course, we would have done lunch,' she said, scurrying down the path, 'but it gets so expensive, doesn't it?'

Ah, there it was: the first reference to penury. Plenty more where that came from. She hurried up the lane to the farm where our land—her land—adjoined the churchyard. Stick thin as ever, she bustled along and I followed, just as I'd followed her to lessons or PE.

In my not terribly strenuous efforts to catch up with her I passed Mum and Felicity, loitering by the church gate, looking furtive.

'Coming?' I called cheerily.

Felicity glanced over her shoulder. 'Er, no.'

'No?' I stopped in my tracks.

'Well, the thing is, Evie, we've got tickets—have *had* tickets, for ages—for a choral concert at Christ Church. We told Caro at the time, when she arranged this, but you know what she's like.' Felicity looked genuinely fearful, while Mum grinned, enjoying herself hugely.

'Oh, I think we just tell her to piss off, don't you?' she said, puffing on a ciggy. 'After all, it's Jack's party, and he's not fussed, are you?'

'Go on, you ravers, off you go.' Jack appeared behind us, putting an arm round their shoulders. 'Like the leggings, Granny. Got a fag?'

'Yes, darling.' Mum went for her handbag. 'Here, I—'

'No she *hasn't*,' hissed Felicity. 'Caro will freak. Now come on, Barbara, we're in enough trouble as it is. Let's get going.'

As they drove away, Jack and I turned to join the straggle of people making their way down the lane to the farm. Caro, having gone round the back of the farmhouse, flung open the front door from inside.

'Come on, Jack, you're supposed to be welcoming everyone!'

'Coming,' he called.

I went through the sagging, five-bar gate at the front. I could already see a gaggle of people through the sitting-room windows: family friends, neighbours. People who'd tell me they didn't see enough of me these days. Maybe even Neville Carter's parents, I thought with a pang. That rocked me for a second; then I took a deep breath and picked my way in my heels through the filthy yard.

'Evelyn! Oh my God, I haven't seen you in ages.' I'd just taken the few steps required to cross the narrow hall, and duck under the low door into the sitting room, when my arm was seized. An overweight woman in tight white trousers, tight pink sweater, and an even tighter perm, beamed delightedly at me, her face glowing. She reminded me vaguely of a girl I'd been at school with, Paula someone.

'It's Paula! Paula Simons, remember?'

'Gosh. Of . . . course. How are you?'

'Really well, thanks. Have you brought your husband?' Her eyes roved past me, hopefully.

I smiled. 'No, he had to take our daughter to a music exam.'

'Oh, shame.' Her mouth drooped. 'I brought a book for him to sign. Hey, Kay. Kay, look, it's Evelyn *Hamilton*!'

Another pink-faced middle-aged woman materialised, and this one I really didn't know except . . . oh heavens, Kay Pritchard. Suddenly I was nine years old again in the school cloakroom, giggling hysterically. I wondered if I was as changed as Paula and Kay: so . . . old?

'Oh, *Evelyn*! Oh God—is he here?' She glanced around excitedly.

'He's not, I'm afraid. Will I do?'

'Oh.' She pouted. 'Well, you'll have to, won't you?' She gave a tinkly laugh. 'But I want to hear all about it. Did he really go to bed with a different woman every week?'

This, a reference not to Ant, but a Georgian dramatist, whose biography he'd just written and which was currently being serialised, pre-publication, in the *Daily Mail*. Ant referred to it disparagingly as his 'Bodice Ripper'. The whole thing made us cringe a bit, actually. After all, he was a serious biographer, it wasn't usually the sort of thing he did, but the publisher had offered a big advance. To be fair, there was really only one steamy chapter, which, naturally, the *Mail* had chosen . . .

'And you're living in Jericho now, I gather?'

'Well, on the edge.'

'Yes, but *still*.' They looked at me admiringly. I wondered vaguely what they were doing here, these women, then remembered with a jolt they were also Jack's godparents. It occurred to me that none of Anna's godparents stemmed from my school days. They were all friends Ant and I had met together. Well, not quite true. They were Ant's friends, from Westminster, or Balliol. Not Parsonage Road Comprehensive. I wondered, uneasily, what that said about me. That I'd simply moved on? Or reinvented myself? Didn't sound very nice.

Across the other side of the room I noticed Tim standing awkwardly by the fireplace, resting one leg. He'd had a hip replacement a couple of months ago after years of pain, which was supposed to make a new man of him. I thought he looked worse. I'd have loved a quick chat, but Caro, looking harassed, swept by with a plate of egg sandwiches and I realised I should offer to help. But that would mean circulating, and I'd already spotted Neville Carter's parents in the other room, which would mean talking to them and . . . oh, for heaven's sake, Evie.

I seized the plate of sandwiches from Caro's startled hand and marched across the hall into the dining room. The Carters were clutching an orange juice apiece and looking so *old*, I thought with a lurch as I greeted them. To my relief, Mrs Carter smiled.

'Evelyn.' Her face relaxed. 'How are you, dear?'

'I'm fine, thanks, and you? Hi there, Mr Carter.'

He nodded wordlessly at me, shaking his head as I offered him a sandwich. Much less friendly, I thought, my chest tightening.

'Oh, you know, we keep busy. Our Eileen's married now, of course. She's pregnant too. Expecting in March, did you know?'

'I didn't! How marvellous.'

'And the garden keeps us very busy.'

'Yes, the garden's been a great comfort to us,' Mr Carter said quietly.

'Yes.' I caught my breath. 'I can imagine. Although,' I went on bravely, 'no, I can't really imagine at all.'

There was a silence. Mrs Carter put a hand on my arm. 'Well, you had a sadness too, dear. You lost your dad.'

I smiled, acknowledging her graciousness. Losing a parent was ghastly, of course it was. But it wasn't the same as losing a child.

Happily Mrs Pallister from next door approached and I took it as my cue to remove myself. I went down the passage to the kitchen, ostensibly to refuel my plate, but actually, to take a moment.

The kitchen still looked pretty much as it always had done, which was a comfort: the old range was still *in situ*, the oak table still sat squarely in the middle, and the station clock Dad had salvaged from a disused railway yard ticked on above the window seat I used to curl up on with my books. I went to the seat, kneeling on the faded chintz cushion, leaning forward to rest my hands on the sill as I gazed out.

The bumpy, erratically mown lawn tumbled down to the stream at the bottom: in the paddocks beyond, Caro's pink and white marquee, a permanent fixture, flapped prettily in the breeze on the other side. Sheep were encouraged to graze round it and the huge oak tree spread benign limbs above it in the sunshine.

It all looked idyllic, but I knew the reality. Knew about stumbling out there in January in a dressing gown and wellies, stumbling over frozen ruts to crack the ice on the troughs for the sheep. Knew that, just yards from this window, behind that barn, rusting old machinery lurked menacingly, like sleeping dragons, ready to trip the unsuspecting. I knew the Steptoe and Son side of farming; all of which was kept from Caro's brides, of course. They saw none of this as they tripped down the lane behind the hedge, fresh from the church, the congregation following on foot—no cars, that was the draw—through a pretty white gate, and straight into the bottom meadow.

'Bucolic Betrothals' Caro advertised as in the local paper, and then some blurb about olde-worlde charm and England's rural past, which was where all this belonged, of course: the past. It should have been sold years ago, the farm, when Dad died. Not that I'd wanted any money. I agreed with Felicity: it was Tim's inheritance, as it was with all farming families, from father to son. But Tim could have bought himself a little business, set himself up. Keeping it was like hanging on to the trappings of an empire, for all the wrong reasons.

'They can't sell it, it's part of them,' Ant would say.

'Well, it's part of me too, and I had no problems leaving.'

'Ah, but you always had your head in a book. Never looked out of the window, let alone went outside. Never let it get to you, the land.'

It was true, I thought as I made to go back. I'd never really troubled the great outdoors. Too busy trying to leave. All that fresh air and I couldn't breathe. Unsettled, I went into the sitting room.

'Evie.' Caro plucked at my sleeve, brandishing a plate of vol-au-vents. 'Have you had one of these?'

'I have, thanks, delicious.' I took her aside. 'But listen, Caro, I'm going to have to dash quite soon. Ant and I are going out to dinner tonight.'

'Don't worry,' she said gently, to my surprise. 'I know how it is. We all have commitments, and these summer weekends are a nightmare. Everything seems to come at once. It was sweet of you to come.'

'Thanks, Caro,' I said gratefully. 'I'll just say goodbye to Tim.'

'Oh, don't worry, I'll tell him you've gone,' she said, taking my arm.

We emerged on the doorstep in the sunshine. Suddenly I remembered my promise to Anna; wondered if this was a good time. 'By the way, Anna's got a bit of a bee in her bonnet about riding at the moment.'

'Oh?'

'She's had quite a lot of lessons now and I just wondered . . . well, she's terribly keen to join the Pony Club and you're on the committee, aren't you? So I wondered . . .'

'But she doesn't live round here. It's all done locally, Evie. Neighbouring farms, that sort of thing.'

'I know, but I thought she could cycle.'

'Where?'

'Um, here. It's only about twenty minutes—well, half an hour. Or she could get the train. At weekends. Not every weekend, obviously.' I was rapidly losing my nerve. My palms felt a bit sweaty. 'But now and again I thought she could come across. Have some fun with her cousins.'

Caro folded her arms. Her chin retracted slowly back into her neck. She surveyed me through narrowed eyes.

'Right,' she said thoughtfully. 'So you want me to pick her up from the station on a Saturday morning, take her to the rallies, give her a bed for the night, and then drop her back at the station the next day?'

I flushed. 'Well, no. That sounds—'

'You want to cherry-pick your bits of country life for her. You don't actually want to live here, but you want her to reap the benefits.'

I stared at her, horrified. Suddenly I saw red. 'Caro, I did live here, remember? This was my home. And no, I don't mean to pass the buck. I'll come across, do my share, take the children to shows or whatever.'

'Oh, really?'

'Yes, of course.'

'OK,' she said suddenly, 'you're on.' Her eyes glittered. 'You tack up the ponies, muck out the lorry, drive it to shows in the pouring rain— splendid. I'd like to see more of Anna. And you too, Evie. You're on.' She challenged me with her eyes.

'Right. I will.' I swallowed. There didn't seem to be much more to say. After a moment I turned and walked uncertainly to the gate.

'But don't forget,' she called sweetly after me, 'she can't come to Pony Club unless she has a pony!'

I stopped a moment in the muddy yard. Blinked rapidly. Then I took a deep breath and marched on up the lane, fury mounting. Just when I thought we were getting on so well, she had to get all chippy again. And, boy, was her resentment close to the surface. Scratch it and—*whoosh*— did she erupt. Because that was what it was, I decided angrily as I stalked on to the car. Resentment. Anna had her cool town life—plays, concerts, friends nearby—and her kids didn't have any of that, so she was damned if Anna was going to have a bit of something hers had in spades.

Well, we'll see about that, I thought.

'**S**he's infuriating!' I stormed to Ant the next morning, chucking bowls in the dishwasher. 'I thought she'd be pleased to have Anna around, have her more involved in the farm. I certainly didn't think she'd jump down my throat like that.'

Ant folded up his paper calmly. 'Now why do I suspect you're being slightly disingenuous? Surely you knew there was every possibility? Caro is one of life's throat jumpers.'

'Yes, but why?' I wailed. 'She never used to be.'

'Because she's sensitive. For obvious reasons. And tackling her in the middle of her party was not the most subtle of manoeuvres.'

'It wasn't the middle of her party, it was at the end, when she was being uncharacteristically sweet and I was lured into a false sense of security. Oh, *morning*, sleepyhead. You're cutting it fine.'

Anna had slipped into the kitchen via the basement stairs and slunk into position at the table, shoulders hunched, eyes half shut. 'Not really, there's no assembly this morning. Who was being sweet?'

'Caro,' I said shortly. 'At Jack's party.'

'Oh. Did you ask—'

'Darling, how was the exam?' I said quickly. I hadn't had a chance to talk to her the previous night: Ant and I had gone out for supper soon after I'd got back and she'd been asleep when we'd got in.

'Fine.' She yawned widely and sloshed milk on top of some Golden Nuggets. As she began to scoop them into her mouth and the sugar kicked in, her eyes opened a bit. 'I was nervous in the Schubert, though. Probably played a few bum notes.'

'Didn't sound like it from where I was sitting.' Ant crossed the kitchen to put his mug in the sink.

'Could you hear?' She turned to look at him.

'The walls at the Royal College are notoriously thin.'

'Oh. What about the Beethoven? A bit too slow?'

'It's supposed to be slow. It's a moody old piece by a moody old bugger contemplating slitting his throat.'

She laughed and I glowed as I cleared up around them, enjoying the musical banter. It was all Greek to me, just as it was when they talked poetry and Latin and, well, Greek.

Anna got up to put her bowl in the sink and I watched as they leaned languidly against the stainless steel together: both tall, fair-skinned and blond, Ant's springy curls turning slightly grey at the temples, Anna's hair much straighter, more flaxen. Athletic, their figures might be described as, not small and solid like mine, and they both had straight noses and wide-apart blue eyes. She'd got his temperament too—calm, unruffled—and definitely his brain. So what had I brought to the party? You might well ask. Ant would be kind enough to say an impulsiveness to temper his natural caution. I might say, not a lot.

As I popped a slice of bread in the toaster, half an ear on what they were saying about Schubert, I marvelled how I never really made sense of it, but I enjoyed listening. A culture vulture, my father used to call me, when, instead of watching *Grandstand* with the rest of the family, I'd be found lying on my bed with my nose in a book. Not the sort of book Ant and Anna read, I might add, but a light romance. Any sort of book was highbrow to Dad, and the fact that I read all day persuaded him I was clever. That I then messed up my A levels and ended up going to secretarial college was therefore a bit of a surprise all round. Not that he minded. On the contrary, he was pleased I was 'acquiring a skill'. But I hadn't used it, had gone straight into Bletchley's Books on the outskirts of town as a sales assistant. Dad wasn't convinced about that, but I loved it. Loved the feel and smell of the books, loved the people who used to come in and pore over them with their long scarves and their owl glasses. One of whom, of course, was Ant, who'd lost his copy of *Sir Gawain and the Green Knight* and had come in to replace it.

'*Sir Gawain and the* what?' I'd said. 'Is it a fairy tale? Maybe in the children's section.'

He'd laughed. 'I wish it was. No, it's like deciphering Chinese.'

Later, when I'd ordered a copy and boggled at the hideously difficult Middle English, I'd blushed. But it was all part of the learning curve. And after all, that was what I was doing here: acquiring the habits of an Oxford undergraduate without actually doing any hard graft. Naturally I had a bike, and long dark hair, and a scarf of indeterminate origin with the stripes going lengthways, and I'd cycle round the city with a basket of books on the front, hoping the gaggle of Japanese tourists on Magdalen Bridge would think I was the real McCoy. I'd once—laughingly—said as much to Ant, and he'd roared.

'Oh, no, no one would ever take you for one of those St Hilda's girls.'

'Why not?' I'd said, hugely offended.

'You're much too pretty.'

I didn't quite know if I was mollified. Probably. But I wouldn't have minded being both. Like Anna. Pretty and clever. I watched now as she went through the open French windows, pausing to stroke Brenda, our West Highland terrier, who was asleep on the lawn, then going to the wall at the far end where her bike was parked. She turned back suddenly. 'So what did she say?'

'What?'

The washing machine had embarked on its final spin behind me.

'Caro. What did she say?'

I caught this, but cupped my ear, pretending I couldn't hear over the noise, which she acknowledged with an impatient shake of her head. I watched as she pedalled off in her dark blue Oxford High uniform.

'See you later.' Ant kissed my cheek.

I leaned on the open frame of the French windows in my dressing gown and watched him go: crossing the garden to get his own bike. As he went through the back gate into the alley, he met the postman and took the letters from him, brandishing them at me to let me know he'd got them. I smiled and nodded back. These days they were nearly all for him, anyway. Not just the bills—I could barely manage the milk bill—but readers' letters too. When the publishers had sent the first few Anna and I had hooted with laughter.

'Fan mail!' she'd spluttered. 'My God, Dad, like a pop star.'

But it gave us a flavour of things to come, of the number of people who'd come to listen to him give a reading in New College and the sheer volume at the reception in the adjoining room afterwards, as we'd stood clutching glasses of warm white wine: quite a lot of dusty academics—colleagues, many of them—but also plenty of perfectly normal people too, and that was the clincher. To be celebrated among one's peers was crucial, but to have breached the gap between these hallowed, honey-coloured walls and entertained the man on the street was something else. Joe Public's recognition was secretly craved by the high-minded, for only that brought fame and fortune.

And I'd been so proud, *so* proud, standing there beside him in my new wraparound dress, laughing later with Ant as I recalled how someone had asked politely, 'And what do you do?' and I'd replied thoughtlessly, 'Oh, nothing.' 'Nothing will come of nothing,' the bearded cove had murmured before moving on, and I'd shrugged, used to quotes being flung at me in this city, used to people being surprised I didn't teach, or write, secretly knowing Ant did enough for both of us.

But there'd been jealousy too, at his success. There'd been those who'd said Ant had sold out, betrayed Byron, in his flagrant depiction of him as a 'yoof culture' figure. But as Anna said, it was all bollocks, because if Byron had been alive today he'd have loved it. Would have turned up the collar of his leather jacket and given an interview to *Hello!*, unlike Wordsworth, who'd have headed for the Lake District in his anorak. And herein lay the rub. The fact that Byron would have been cool and Wordsworth a geek came as no surprise to anyone in the English Department: it was that someone had thought of saying it, of stating the obvious, that they didn't like.

So we'd been careful, in the face of this potential envy. Or rather, Ant had been careful. I, on the other hand, had gone shopping. House-hunting, to be more precise. Recalling that, I cringed now as I scooped up my breakfast tray, making for the stairs. Oh, we'd agreed we were *moving*—the college house was only rented and we needed to buy—but what we hadn't quite established was where. As I nipped up the stairs now to the ground floor, I passed the double doors into the drawing room—drawing room, God, we never thought we'd have one of those—following the curved, French-polished rail up to my bedroom.

But this wasn't the house I was cringing about, no. It was the one off the Banbury Road in Westgate Avenue with the six bedrooms, the acre of garden, the music room, the—God help me—orangery. I remember looking round it, and then the next day, breathlessly dragging Ant and Anna there, verbally incontinent with excitement.

Ant had thrust his hands in his pockets and jingled his change nervously. 'For just the three of us? It doesn't seem right. It's not . . . us.'

'It's too far from where we've come from,' Anna, young, but terrifyingly articulate, had commented.

Suddenly it was as clear as day. This house took us out of quiet, muted, university-professor land and into loud, cushy, fat-cat suburbia. Suddenly the wall-to-wall white carpets were vulgar, the orangery a joke. And I hadn't known. Not immediately. It had had to be pointed out to me by my intrinsically tasteful husband and child.

We'd headed straight back into town, and then the following day had seen this place. Tall, terraced, with a little iron balcony, still close to our friends, still with integrity. I paused at the landing window now, looking out at our walled garden, elegant and leafy. Yes. It suited us, I thought, going on to my bedroom. Was right up the Hamiltons' street.

I smiled and hopped back into bed with my toast and the papers.

When Ant and I had been married only a few months, he'd left for work one morning then popped back ten minutes later, having forgotten a student's essay. He'd found me back in bed with a box of lime creams, a cigarette and *Cosmo*. I'd been as mortified as if he'd caught me with a naked man, but Ant had roared with delight.

'It's why I love you,' he'd said, kissing me. 'Because you're not up and dressed, beavering away trying to write the next *Madame Bovary*, like everyone else in this city. You just enjoy yourself. You embrace pleasure.'

These days my tastes had changed, and tea and toast accompanied the *Daily Mail*, but I still read the important bits: the 'Femail' section in the middle, the diets, the detoxing, the fashion—I didn't skimp. This being Monday I also shimmied through the local paper too, glancing, out of habit, at the houses at the back, when an ad in the livestock column caught my eye.

For Sale. Beautiful grey Connemara pony, 14.2 hands, 6 years. Very willing, a great character. A teenager's dream. First to see will buy. £1,000.

I stared in disbelief; read it again. Oh. Oh, how marvellous! Right here, in front of my nose. It was fate. A thousand pounds, I was sure, was pretty reasonable. I feverishly read the address. Parkfield Lane.

Which was off the Woodstock Road. Just a few minutes away!

I straightened up in the crumpled bed. Never in a million years had Caro imagined I'd actually *buy* a pony when she'd sent her taunt sailing across the yard. She knew I didn't know a thing about horses, and yet . . . what could be so hard? I peered at the ad again. 'A teenager's dream.' Well, I had a teenager and she had a dream—perfect. My hand was already straying towards the phone on the bedside table when it stopped. Hang on. It was one thing to think, I'll show her, and quite another to march into her farmyard leading a horse. I swallowed. Well, OK, I'd talk to her and we'd sort this out like . . . like friends. If Caro really meant Anna needed a pony for Pony Club, then fine, we'd get one, but if she'd meant over her dead body, we'd forget it.

On the other hand this pony might go quickly. It was clearly a winner, and my sister-in-law was a busy woman. She never answered her mobile and I'd have to go to the farm to track her down, and while I was canvassing her opinion some other lucky teenager would have bought it. Whereas if I just presented her with a *fait accompli* . . . In another moment I'd plucked the phone from the bedside table and dialled the number.

'Hello, yes, I've just seen your ad in the local paper . . .' Ten minutes later I'd agreed to meet a man in a stable yard off the Woodstock Road, who'd promised me a mare so well trained she'd wandered into his kitchen only yesterday, quiet as a mouse, without him even noticing.

I'd had a rather unsettling vision of a horse, perched on a stool at my granite breakfast bar, calmly reading the paper and demanding cereal, but agreed that my daughter and I would most certainly be there on Saturday morning, early, to meet this equine paragon. Then I put the phone down and flushed with horror. Lord, what had I done?

I quickly dialled Caro's number. Tim answered.

'Oh, Tim.' I flooded with relief. 'I was, um, ringing to thank you both for yesterday,' I lied. 'Such a lovely day, and all that delicious food!'

'Well, it was good to see you. How did Anna get on?'

'Oh, fine. She said it was easy. I mean—not bad.'

'Grade seven, Caro tells me!'

'Um, yes. Tim, is Caro around?'

'She's not at the moment. She's down at the yard with Harriet.'

'Harriet?'

'The blind pig. She has to hand-feed her.'

I blinked. Caro was already up and hand-feeding her blind pig, while I was sitting up in bed in my Cath Kidston nightie.

'Right. Yes, well, speaking of animals, Tim . . .' and off I skittered, it all coming tumbling out, ending up with '. . . I mean, we obviously haven't got anywhere to keep it, so I just sort of wondered—'

'Of course you can,' he boomed, interrupting me. 'God, we've got too much grass here for our own horses, one more won't make any difference. And if it lives out it's no trouble at all. No mucking out stables.'

'Well, that's what I thought,' I said eagerly. 'And obviously I'd pop over and—you know—check it occasionally.'

'Oh, Caro can do all that. She has to sort out the others.'

'Oh, no, I don't want Caro doing anything,' I said quickly. 'It's my responsibility. But I just wondered, if it needed—I don't know—its feet picking out or something and I couldn't get there, maybe Jack . . .?'

'Jack's your man, or Phoebe. And how lovely to see more of Anna. The kids will be thrilled.' I knew he was genuinely pleased. 'Caro too,' he added.

'Er, actually, Tim, she wasn't.'

'What?'

'Thrilled. I sort of broached it with her yesterday, and she was a bit . . . you know.'

'Was she? Well, yesterday was a stressy day, Evie. But don't you worry. You get your horse and we'll give it a home. Anna can come at weekends, get the train over. Caro will pick her up. I must fly now, hon.'

I put the phone down guiltily. I'd gone round Caro, hadn't I? But not deliberately. It wasn't my fault Tim had answered, was it? I'd ring her again later, when Tim had already broken the news to her.

Right now, though, I needed to hustle. Maria would be here at ten to clean and I hated her to find me in bed.

2

DAYS PASSED and Friday found me cycling to meet Ant for lunch, under a cloudless sky, treats from the deli for the weekend safely stashed in my basket, long dark hair streaming out behind me. I'd suggested cutting my hair recently but Ant had looked so upset, I'd left it. But perhaps I should tie it up, I wondered as I cycled behind a lady with an elegant grey chignon. She turned left under the arch into Trinity and I smiled to myself. That was what I loved about this city: you never quite knew who you were cycling behind, or sitting next to on the bus: a scientist working on the next cure for cancer, or an astrophysicist sending rockets to Mars?

'Probably some poor devil off to restock the KitKats in the staff canteen,' Ant would scoff.

'Nonsense, you can tell. They have that vague, eccentric look, like they don't know what day it is.'

'Ah, like your mother.'

He had me here. Mum rarely knew what day it was, sported a wispy grey ponytail and a charity-shop wardrobe, yet didn't have a scholastic bone in her body. Felicity, on the other hand, my stepmother, looked as if she'd just stepped off a yacht in Saint-Tropez and was, in fact, a biology professor at Keble. 'I rest my case,' Ant would say smugly.

I smiled as I neared the end of their road: Mum and Felicity's. When Dad died, Mum had told her about a house that was coming up at the end of her street. Felicity had bought it immediately. No one had been terribly surprised when, after Tim and I both got married, my mother left my father. They had always had a tempestuous relationship. Mum had come to loathe the farm—the mud, the wet—and Dad hated what he called her spiritualistic crap.

Mum was heavily into alternative remedies. Reflexology, aromatherapy, you name it, she'd tried it. The final straw for Dad had been her plan to set up a holistic medical centre at the farm.

'I'm not denying there's something in all this alternative bollocks,' he'd roared. 'What I *am* denying is that your mother is in any way, shape or form qualified to administer it!'

One unseasonably clement day in October, after just such a heated exchange, Mum walked all the way into Oxford—no mean eight miles—to visit her sister. She telephoned Dad to say that since it was so far, she thought she'd stay the night. The following morning she rang to say she thought she'd stay a few days, because Cynthia, her sister, was under the weather. A few days had turned into a few weeks—and then she never came back. If Tim or I enquired, Dad would say vaguely, 'Your mother? Oh, she's still at Cynthia's.' And if we rang Mum and asked when she was thinking of returning, she'd say, 'Oh, when Cynthia's a bit better, I expect.'

The truth was that it suited them. Mum was back in the city where she belonged, and Dad was happy with the farm to himself, no frustrated housewife wanting him to sit crosslegged listening to his inner music. Dad lived like a slob, wore the same clothes every day and left washing-up in the sink in a tottering pagoda. They were both happy for the first time in years, and life became remarkably peaceful.

Inevitably, though, as time went by, they both became lonely and then came what Tim and I nervously referred to as 'the courting phase'. Mum embarked on a series of jaw-droppingly unsuitable boyfriends—all of whom predictably came to nothing—and Dad moved in Felicity.

I have to say, in the beginning Tim and I were slightly wary of Felicity, simply because she was so palpably not Dad's type. He'd met a few women through Rural Relations, a country dating agency—primarily rosy-cheeked women with trousers held up with binder twine—but Felicity was tall, slim, ravishingly good-looking and highly intelligent.

'What does she see in Dad?' I wondered to Caro over a cup of tea. She'd bristled slightly, Tim being very like his father.

'Well, he's tall, good-looking and not entirely impoverished, with a farm and three hundred acres—what's not to see?'

Some weeks later Dad had invited us all to Sunday lunch, to meet Felicity properly. We'd tried not to boggle as we spotted napkins on the table and a vase of flowers in the middle, and then sat down to a starter—a starter!—with Dad at one end in a freshly laundered shirt, Felicity at the other, looking nervous. And actually, because of her slight unease, I'd warmed to her instantly. We all had, even Caro.

'She's just what your father needs,' she'd declared when she'd rung me later for a post-match analysis. 'An intelligent woman with a no-nonsense approach to lick that farmhouse into shape.'

It was true, Dad and Felicity were a brilliant team. In no time at all she'd cleared the house of clutter, redecorated, and even attacked the garden. And she was fun to have around; pleasant, friendly but didn't try to ingratiate herself too much, just cheerily invited us to lunch most weekends. Dad adored her.

In time, Felicity included Mum in her invitations too, asking her first one Christmas, for lunch. 'So that everyone can be together, and you and Tim don't have to flit from house to house?' she'd asked me anxiously. 'What d'you think, Evie?'

'I think it's a brilliant idea,' I'd said. 'If she'll come.'

To our surprise, she did, and an unexpectedly jolly Christmas Day was had by all. The first for many years, I'd thought. Yes, Felicity had been the cement our family needed, and no one had been surprised when she and Dad eventually tied the knot and Dad had bounded around the farm like a new man. Which was why, one bright August morning, it was such a shock that he was a dead man.

Grief-stricken as we all were, we knew immediately it was Felicity who needed help. After the funeral she retreated to the farmhouse, hunkering down for days. We'd worried and rallied, Caro and I bringing lunch to the farm on Sundays, trying desperately to keep some semblance of normality going, some cheerful banter as she sat, toying listlessly with her food. After a few months it was no real surprise when, one Sunday, she announced the house was too big for her and that she was moving to 47 Fairfield Avenue, down the road from Mum, who, at number 16, had inherited Cynthia's house when she'd died. Over time, proximity and a shared past they forged an unlikely alliance. Tuesday nights found Mum in Felicity's sitting room at the backgammon board, Thursday night was book club night, and on Sundays, if they weren't with Caro or me, they lunched together in town.

I smiled now as I cycled past Mum's little terraced house at one end and pedalled towards Felicity's more substantial property at the other. Were they there today, I wondered?. If Felicity wasn't teaching, in all probability yes, but I wouldn't stop.

I pushed my bike through Cornmarket, pedalled on along St Aldate's, and swung a left down a little alleyway to the tiny trattoria Ant and I favoured, slightly crummy but off the beaten track.

How lovely, I thought, to have a husband who still wanted to have lunch with me. For years, on alternate Fridays, because he only had one lecture, I'd cycle in and have a bowl of soup with him at Lorenzo's.

'I might even catch the end of your lecture,' I'd called this morning as Ant, as ever, took the letters from the postman as they passed at the back gate.

I hadn't made it, of course. Too busy making huge decisions at the cheese counter and Ant was already at our favoured table when I arrived. He was reading as usual. When I'd first known Ant and we'd lunched in here, he'd invariably be reading a slim volume of poetry. More recently it was an essay, as he tried to catch up with some marking, and I saw him tuck just such a paper hastily inside his jacket pocket as I sat down opposite him. I thought how tired he looked. The end of term couldn't come quickly enough. I folded my arms on the table and leaned across.

'Just another few weeks and we'll head off to the sun. Tuscany again, perhaps?'

He gave me an odd, tight little smile and polished his spectacles, and I experienced a mild inner panic, rather as I had done when I'd shown him the house off the Banbury Road.

'Or Devon,' I said quickly, sitting up. 'Only joking. I just thought we'd agreed Anna might like San Gimignano—'

'No, it's not that. I think it's a good idea, she would. No, it's . . .' he licked his lips, 'something else.'

My stomach lurched. Suddenly I realised he didn't just look tired, he looked white. White and stricken. Oh God, was he ill?

I reached across the table and took his hand. I was vaguely aware that the elderly couple beside us had paused in their conversation.

'Ant?' I could hear the fear in my voice. 'Ant, what is it, darling?'

I saw him swallow. Then his eyes met mine. Those kind blue eyes. They looked scared.

'I had a letter this morning.' He reached inside his jacket. Took out the piece of paper I'd just seen him tuck away. 'You'd better read it.'

I took it from him, mutely. It was handwritten in an immature hand on plain A4 paper with no address at the top; just an email address.

Dear Dr Hamilton,

There is no easy way to tell you this so I've decided to keep it short. OK, here goes. Many years ago, you knew my mother. You met her in Oxford and had a relationship with her. She didn't live in Oxford, she lived here, in Sheffield, and after a while, she came back. I was born in September 1990. As I said, this is not an easy letter either for you to read or for me to

I looked up. Felt my mouth open, the blood desert my face. I stared at Ant's face, also bloodless. My head screamed *no*. But I couldn't speak. I glanced back down. Dumbly, found my place.

. . . for you to read or for me to write. But I knew one day I would, when I was seventeen, which I'm about to be. If you would rather not reply to me, I understand. But if you would like to meet me, I would really like to meet you. I could come to Oxford, if you like. I have enclosed my email address, but not my home address, because I still live with my mum and it wouldn't be fair on her. She does know I've written, though.

Yours sincerely,
Stacey Edgeworth

It was some moments before I found my voice. When I did, it sounded strange. 'A child? You have a child?' I stared at him, stupefied.

He shrugged hopelessly. 'I don't know. No, I didn't think so. But you've read the letter. And—you know, I was young. One had relationships. Sometimes brief. I just don't know . . .' He seemed dazed.

I licked my lips. Tried to think straight. 'When did it come?'

'This morning. I met the postman.'

Yes. Yes, he did. I looked down at it again. The words blurred before my eyes. He had a *child*. By someone else. My head spun.

'So this—this name—Edgeworth. Do you recognise it?'

'Well, yes, vaguely, I suppose. I used to drink in the King's Head, and there was a barmaid there. Blonde. Quite attractive. One night we all ended up down by the river, pissed, and I walked her home. We . . . ended up in a field, somewhere.'

I stared at him. Pissed in a field didn't sound like Ant. But then, as he said, he was young. He looked young now. Young and frightened.

'Ant,' I cleared my throat, 'did you make love to her?'

His eyes widened as if registering the enormity of this. 'Yes, I did.'

'And so then,' I was feverishly trying to assimilate facts, 'then you didn't see her again, and she went back to Sheffield—'

'And then, years later, I get a letter from someone who says she's my daughter!' he blurted out, wide-eyed. 'I mean, bloody hell!'

We stared at each other. I was aware that the elderly couple beside us were gripped, risotto congealing on their plates, but I was beyond caring. Suddenly I felt my blood rising. Oh, no. Over my dead body.

'It's a nonsense,' I said wildly. 'Some . . . some girl comes down from the North to work as a barmaid in Oxford, gets a summer job, gets laid—a lot, probably—and then, years later, with a child to support, gets her to write to you. This is—oh!' A light bulb went on in my head. 'Oh, Ant,' I gasped, 'it's the books!'

'What?'

'The books. She's seen them in the shops! And then—yes—then sees you on telly, of course!' Ant had been on a daytime television programme recently. 'Yes, there she is, doing her ironing in the front room, telly on, and there *you* are, and she thinks, hang on a minute. I remember him. Famous author, eh? Anthony Hamilton . . . *Oi! Stacey!*' I cocked my head up some imaginary stairs. '*Get down 'ere!*'

'Wait,' said Ant nervously. 'I'm not so sure. I mean, what if she's *always* known, and now that the child's grown up they've decided to—'

'Quite a coincidence, don't you think?' I squeaked. 'You were only on the show last week!'

'Yes, but still . . .' He swallowed.

Fear was gripping me, but I wouldn't have it. Wouldn't. Another daughter? Anna's sister? My husband with two children? Oh, no.

'Look,' I said fiercely, warming to my theme, 'this has opportunism written all over it, Ant. This is a scheming adventuress after—'

'What?' he blurted suddenly. 'After what, Evie?'

'Well . . .' I flustered, 'after money!'

He slumped back in his seat. 'Come on. We're not that rich.'

'But if she slept with you on a one-night stand she probably slept with twenty others! The child could be anyone's daughter, anyone's!' I swept my hand around the restaurant to demonstrate mass culpability. A hush fell. I had a pretty captive audience.

'But what if it's not?' he hissed. 'What if she's mine?'

Mine. That word pierced me. 'DNA,' I said suddenly. 'That'll settle it. Let her come, Ant. Let—let Felicity, sort it out. Bring it on, I say.'

He nodded. 'Yes. Yes, you're right. Of course. And Felicity would know someone. Know the right people.'

You bet she would. At the back of my mind I also knew that this mother-and-daughter team would have worked that out too; would know that we'd do that. Which meant they had to be fairly sure of themselves. I caught my breath. I knew Ant was thinking it too.

I looked at the letter. I wanted to burn it. We sat in silence, our bowls of minestrone cooling undisturbed.

'You're right,' Ant said at length. 'It's probably a mistake. But, Evie, if it turns out . . . if . . . you know, Stacey is my daughter—'

Stacey! I took a slug of wine at the very *name*. It went down my chin. As I seized my napkin and mopped furiously, my neighbour's liver-spotted hand crept out to reclaim, what was, after all, his glass of Chianti.

'I mean, if she is,' Ant went on, anguished, 'then obviously . . . obviously I'll have to acknowledge her. It's only right.'

'Of course,' I said brightly. 'Of course, we both will.'

I cycled home in turmoil, my mind racing. Oh, it was preposterous. Preposterous. It couldn't be true, I thought, freewheeling down the alley behind our house and walking the bike in quickly through the back gate. I glanced round warily at the house. Might she just turn up? Don't be silly, Evie. But . . . it could happen, couldn't it? There could, one day, be a knock at my door, and there she'd be: this teenage girl.

'Yeah—me name's Stacey. I've cum for me da'.'

I scuttled down the garden to the French windows. I let myself in and shut them very firmly behind me—locked them too. After all, there was practically a veiled threat at the end of the letter—'I could come to Oxford, if you like', as in, Watch Out!

The phone rang, breaking into my ghoulish thoughts. I snatched it up gratefully, but my voice wouldn't come.

'Evie?' It was Caro. 'Evie, are you there?'

'Yes,' I managed. 'Hi, Caro.'

'God, you sound awful. Have I caught you at a bad time?'

The worst. 'No, I was just—eating. Went down the wrong way.'

'Oh, right. Well, listen. Been meaning to phone you all week. Tim tells me you're dead set on getting this horse, so to avoid any misunderstandings I just wanted to set out a few ground rules.'

I sank my head into my hand, massaging my temples, cradling the receiver with the other. 'Well, no, not dead set, really,' I mumbled. 'It's probably not such a good idea. Too much trouble for you.'

'Nonsense, one more mouth to feed won't make any difference. And anyway, Tim informs me it's a *fait accompli*,' she finished crisply.

I massaged harder as I dimly registered the row they'd no doubt had: Caro shrieking that she was rushed off her feet as it was; my brother taking a stand, talking of family, duty, of helping his little sister. Normally I'd be falling over myself to apologise, but I just nodded mutely into the receiver, imagining the letter like a lead weight in Ant's breast pocket, burning a hole in his heart.

'So if Tim says it's final, it's final, so there we are. Now, for God's sake don't go and buy one on your own. Take someone to see it, OK?'

'OK,' I muttered dumbly.

'I'll come, if I can, but the next few weeks are jam-packed with weddings, so God knows when I'll get away. But for heaven's sake, if I'm not there, make sure it lives out so we don't have any mucking-out to do, and that it's good in traffic. And even *more* importantly, make sure it's got a snaffle mouth. You don't want some Arab in a gag, do you?'

A white-robed sheik, staggering, bound and gagged through the desert, sprang confusingly to mind. 'No,' I agreed.

'Just make sure it's safe, OK?'

Safe. Safe sex. Always wear a condom. Or not, as the case may be.

'And don't look at anything described as a "fun ride"—that's shorthand for goes like a train—or "a proper character"—which means it bucks. But as I said, I'll come with you in a few weeks' time. Just as soon as I can get away from this sodding wedding fiasco.'

I remembered my manners. 'Um, how's it going, Caro?'

'Oh, swimmingly. I've got potential brides bowling up my drive at an alarming rate, but their ghastly mothers are all nightmares. Last week one discovered the groom's family had invited more guests than her side *and then blamed me*. Said I should have spotted it! I kicked her in the end, had to pretend I had a twitch.'

'Good, good,' I said distractedly.

'I mean they're not *all* ghastly, don't get me wrong. The Asians are heaven, lovely big families all smiley and *so* well behaved. Never any fornicating in the bushes, and never any sick to clear up, either.'

'Um, look, Caro, I'd better go, but thanks for . . . you know.' I'd stopped listening to her because I'd just realised something. While she'd been prattling on I'd been thinking about the letter and about the girl being seventeen. I'd done the maths instantly, of course I had, and felt safe. I hadn't known Ant then. But that distracted me from when the child had been born—September 1990. She was still very much sixteen, wouldn't be seventeen till later this year which meant—and here I got to my feet, slowly replacing the receiver as Caro said good-bye—yes, of course. The child couldn't be Ant's. Simply couldn't. Because if it was her seventeenth birthday in the autumn, she'd been conceived—I did some rapid mental arithmetic—the previous January: which meant I'd been going out with Ant. Going out for some time. Not only that, we'd been engaged.

I'd had to order Ant's copy of *Sir Gawain and the Green Knight*. We didn't stock such esoteric titles in Bletchley's: we were just a tiny independent, albeit on three floors, but each the size of your average front room connected by rickety stairs. It was all very charming and Dickensian, and appealed to my romantic notion of how a bookshop should be, even down to the musty smell of Jean's cats, who stretched out on shelves, adding to the ambiance. I think the customers bought into the whole nostalgic bit too, liking the fact that they could settle down in a faded armchair with a book and not be asked to move on. Comfy chairs were a rarity in bookshops back then, and in a way it put us ahead of our time, even if the reality was that they were there for Jean, our fifteen-stone manageress, who liked to pause mid-floor for a breather. A couple of other things gave us the edge too: we were on the fringes of the city where a lot of students lived, we had a larger than average art and architecture section, and also a contemporary music section, which was popular. We stocked the usual fiction, of course, and pretty much all the classics, but not, as it happened, Ant's request.

'They usually get that from the university bookshop,' Jean told me as she overheard me ordering it on the telephone. 'Who was it, a student?'

'He looked a bit older than that. Anthony Hamilton? Local number.'

'Oh, *Dr* Hamilton. One of the youngest dons in the English Department. On a bit of a meteoric rise. Well, he must have dozens of those in his stock cupboard. I can't think why he's getting it from us.' She pulled a not altogether friendly face. 'Perhaps he fancies you.'

'I doubt it,' I said quickly, knowing any single man who came in here had to fancy Jean. Ant was over eighteen and therefore ripe for the cull.

'Well, he's terribly attractive, don't you think?' She pouted provocatively. 'Wouldn't mind getting stuck in the stock cupboard with *him*.'

Jean, a divorcée, who bore an uncanny resemblance to Sybil Fawlty, had a slightly desperate air and a *double entendre* for every occasion.

Nevertheless, I spent the next few days pouncing on every parcel that came in, just in case Jean or Malcolm should get to it first, and practising exactly what I would say on the telephone when it did arrive. In the event, of course, it was desperately prosaic.

'Oh, hello, Dr Hamilton?'

'Yes?'

'It's Evie here, from Bletchley's Books. Just to say, your copy of *Sir Gawain* arrived this morning.'

'Oh, thanks very much. I'll pop in and get it.'

'Okey-doke, bye!'

As I put the phone down a hot flush swept over me. Okey-doke? When had I ever said that? But at least I'd got my name in—all part of the plan. And what a deliciously deep, modulated voice he had. 'Thanks very much. I'll pop in and get it,' I purred.

'Get what?' asked Jean, appearing at my shoulder, frowning.

'Oh, nothing,' I flustered, hurrying away.

Over the next few days, I hardly left the shop. Whenever the door opened my head pirouetted, and I spent a lot of time in Health and Harmony, which was right at the front on the ground floor, with an excellent view of the street.

'Having trouble breastfeeding?' enquired Malcolm, my lovely gay colleague, who was watching me dust Miriam Stoppard's *Pregnancy and Birth Book* for the millionth time.

I giggled. 'Not as such.'

'Something more serious?' He raised an eyebrow as *The Pain of Infertility* was flicked over now.

'How would I know?' I sighed, resting my feather duster a moment. 'I could be as fertile as the River Nile or as barren as the Gobi, I've no idea. No one's ever tested my tubes.'

'Well, as long as you're not hanging around here waiting for blue eyes,' he said gently, 'because I'm afraid you've missed him.'

'Oh!' I swung to face him.

'Came in ten minutes ago while you were in the loo. I was all for running to get you, but Jean blocked my path and served him herself.'

'But she knew—'

'Of course she did, but she doesn't want her pretty young assistant being chatted up by one of the dons, does she? Here, my sweet,' he delved into a shelf and plucked out a copy of *Anger Management*. 'Read and learn.'

Bitterly disappointed, I dusted on in silence. Later that morning I slipped to the café next door to drown my sorrows in cappuccino. When I came back, Malcolm ran up, eyes shining. 'Good news or bad news?'

'Bad.'

'He's been in again, and you missed him.'

'Damn!'

'But the good news is, he's coming to the poetry reading on Saturday night. Took a leaflet and everything, and—get this, poppet—asked if we all had to be there.'

'Oh! D'you think he meant—'

'Well, he surely didn't mean *moi*, munchkin. I'd have known.'

Saturday couldn't come quickly enough. Normally I avoided readings like the plague. Being only a small bookshop we didn't attract the likes of Jeffrey Archer or Jilly Cooper; instead, some unknown local author would shuffle in off the street in a duffle coat, their book in a Tesco carrier bag. Given the spotlight, though, these usually timid souls would become expansive; droning on and on. Poetry readings were the worst. Some bearded type would read banal or incomprehensible verse, as everyone sat round in hushed, respectful silence. The audiences were generally embarrassingly small too—the poet's girlfriend, his mother, and a cluster of loyal friends.

This one looked like being no exception. The poet was female, and although I don't think I've ever seen a picture of Joan Baez, I imagine it's what she'd look like. She took my hand limply, murmuring something that sounded suspiciously like Emmylou Harris.

'Evie Milligan.' I smiled back, determinedly upbeat, and determinedly miniskirt-clad too, with sparkly earrings and lip gloss.

My job had been to arrange a not-too-intimidatingly-large circle of chairs round a solitary 'throne' where she would sit and recite, and to which I led her now. 'Is this all right?

She frowned. 'I think I'd like everyone sitting on the floor.'

I blinked. 'Right . . .'

Half an hour later Emmylou was sitting crosslegged on a beaded cushion—model's own—surrounded by twenty or so similarly intense-looking supporters—not a bad turnout, actually.

'They're all girls,' I hissed to Malcolm, one eye on the door. Dr Hamilton had yet to appear.

'Oh, yes, didn't you know? She's one of us. Well, one of them,' he added sniffily. 'I prefer my gay female friends to be of the lipstick-lesbian variety, glamorous and witty. This is the other end of the spectrum. The hairy-toed right-on brigade. Eh up, here's the Führer.'

Jean, flushed and slightly tipsy—she was always in charge of the warm white wine—was making her way centre stage. 'Ahem! Good evening, ladies and gentlemen. Well . . . ladies. Lovely to see so many of you here, and may I say how delighted we are to have Mary-Lou with us tonight. Emmy . . . lou, as many of you know, is a local poet. I hope you'll listen quietly—' what were we, six?—'as Emily reads from her latest collection entitled *Women in Chains*.'

'Oh my,' groaned Malcolm in my ear, before sliding away to hide behind Crime and Thrillers, the better to roll his eyes at me and make me laugh. I determined not to look at him, but actually, even if I did, I knew I was too disappointed to laugh. After all that, after all my devotions to hair and make-up, not to mention a new skirt and chain belt from Dorothy Perkins, he hadn't turned up. I listened miserably as Emmylou's reedy, self-important voice rang out strident and forceful.

> 'Rise up!
> Rise up and speak of the tyranny of machismo,
> The unequal struggle,
> Of weary loins and sagging dugs,
> Of flesh parting company with bones—'

I took to pushing back my cuticles, while Malcolm, out of sight of Jean, stuck his fingers in his ears.

She paused after poem one, and Malcolm removed his fingers and looked hopeful. But it got worse. Emmylou produced what looked like a homemade recorder, which she proceeded to blow into just as the door opened and Anthony Hamilton, tall, slightly shambolic, came in. He glanced around, found my eyes and smiled. I instantly blushed.

Jean, all jangling bosom, was bustling to find him a seat—not cross-legged with the squaws, I noticed, but on a plastic chair at the back. He looked uncomfortable perched alone and aloft beside Jean.

'This next poem,' Emmylou informed us gravely, 'is called "Maud and Diana".'

Well, that sounded all right. A bit like Hinge and Bracket? Except it wasn't maiden aunts and it wasn't all right either, because Maud and Diana were a couple of little minxes who couldn't keep their hands off each other. My face got pinker with every toe-curling line. I risked a glance at Malcolm, who looked highly diverted, while Jean patted her perm nervously, trying hard to look like a broad-minded woman who was used to poems of this nature being read in her shop, instead of a lonely, frustrated one who simply worked in a bookshop to meet men, as, I realised with a jab of horror, I did, and as I knew Malcolm did too.

'"Diana and Maud found their epiphany that night",' Emmylou declared to the assembled throng. '"Hearts sang. Minds rejoiced."' Her eyes roamed the room and found mine. '"Vaginas throbbed."'

In the startled silence that followed all I could think was, *why is she looking at me?* It was too much for Malcolm. He gave a snort of derision and legged it to the fire escape. I'm ashamed to say I followed hot on his heels. On the wrought-iron staircase, Malcolm and I clutched one another, hiccupping, snorting; even Anthony forgotten.

'You pulled!' gasped Malcolm.

'No!' I shrieked back. 'D'you think?'

'Oh, for *sure*, hon. She's hot for you. She wants her epiphany.'

We dissolved into giggles. Malcolm lit two cigarettes and handed me one. 'Here, hon. Suck on this.'

'I take it this is where the staff take their ciggy breaks?'

I swung round to see a tall, quietly amused figure in the doorway, tapping the end of his own cigarette on a packet of Rothmans.

'Oh.' I struggled for composure. 'Well, not really. It's just—you know—a bit hot in there. But we must go back.'

Dr Hamilton lit up and blew the smoke over my head. 'I wouldn't worry. I think everyone needs a drink after that.'

'Has she finished?'

'Apparently.'

'Well, thank the Lord,' Malcolm said with feeling. 'I'd better go and charge the Lambrusco glasses. Lovely to meet you, incidentally.' He extended a hand and flashed a dazzling smile. 'Malcolm Harding.'

'Anthony Hamilton,' said Anthony, smiling and shaking hands.

'What *is* going on out here?' The fire door swung back and Jean appeared, looking like Brünnhilde, glowering furiously. 'Malcolm! The white wine, please. And, Evie, what on earth are you doing luring our guest out here?' Oh, she *had* to be vulgar, didn't she?

Malcolm came to my rescue. 'Evie doesn't feel very well. She was getting some air.'

'Well, she'd better go home then, hadn't she?' Jean snapped sourly. 'Go on, Evie, go and get your bus. Malcolm and I will manage tonight. Dr Hamilton, shall we?' She opened the door to usher him back in.

'Actually, I ought to be going too.' He turned to me. 'If you're not feeling well, I'll give you a lift. Where are you going?'

'Um, just past Magdalen Bridge,' I stuttered.

'Oh, perfect, I'm at Balliol. Just round the corner.' Nowhere near. He smiled at Jean. ' Thank you so much. It's been a very enjoyable evening and, um, very . . . informative too. So sorry I've got to fly.'

Jean looked ready to spontaneously combust. Malcolm ushered her away like a nurse with a mental patient, pausing only to turn and flash me a meaningful, delighted grin.

My heart was pounding, and naturally I couldn't think of a thing to say as I walked with him to his car. Happily, his *savoir-faire* gene was more developed than mine.

'Feeling better?' he enquired as we got in and put our seat belts on.

'Much. I'm afraid poetry readings tend to have that effect on me.' I couldn't believe I was in his car.

'You're not a fan then?'

'What? Oh, no, I love poetry. It's just . . . not that particular type.'

'What type do you like?' I realised he was interested. Damn. But luckily I knew the names of some poets. Crikey, I lined up their volumes often enough. 'Oh, you know, Keats, Sylvia Plath, Pam Ayres, that sort of thing.'

He smiled. 'Fairly eclectic.'

'Oh, yes, I like the Eclectic Poets.' Possibly a group, like the Romantic Poets, whom I'd heard of.

He laughed. Why? No matter. Here I was in his car, looking at his terribly attractive square profile. Heaven.

'You must be in clover, working in a bookshop. Ample opportunity.'

To pick up square-jawed men? No. 'Well, *quite*,' I enthused, coming to. 'I'm always reading. I read copiously.' Good *word*, Evie.

'Novels?'

'Oh, *novels*,' I gushed. 'Can't get enough of them.'

'And what d'you like?'

I took a deep breath and wondered, fleetingly, if I could bluff my way, literarily speaking, for the next ten minutes or so. Happily some invisible divinity whispered sense in my ear and I decided against it. 'Contemporary fiction,' I said quickly. 'I'm a big fan of E. J. McGuire.'

'I'm not familiar with him.'

'Her,' I corrected. 'Oh God, she's terrific, you must try her. She does these brilliant sort of thriller things, really tense and creepy, and you have absolutely no idea how it's going to end up or who's done it.'

'Sounds like Poe.'

Like . . . poo, did he say? I blinked. 'Well. Obviously it's not to everyone's taste,' I began, 'but—'

'Edgar Allan. You know, Victorian melodrama.'

'Oh! Right. Yes, well, maybe. And actually it is quite melodramatic, now you mention it. But I rather like that. And there's always a terrific twist at the end, which you don't see coming.'

'I must look out for E. J. McGuire. Left here?'

'Yes, then down on the right.' He stopped the car. I turned to him, flashed a winning smile. 'And I must look out for Poo. Poe!'

He laughed; turned in his seat to face me, his arm crooked over the back of it, eyes shining right into mine. Wow. I took a deep breath.

'Would you . . . like to come in for coffee?'

'I'd love to,' he said. 'Or maybe even a drink?'

'A drink!' I said joyfully as if he'd hit on the Holy Grail. Too joyful. Calm down, Evie. I got out of the car. 'But I have to warn you,' I prattled on nervously as I led him down the street, 'I'm three storeys up, so you might need oxygen rather than vodka by the time you get there.'

'I stand warned.'

Further talk was made impossible, as for the next few minutes, we struggled up six flights of steps. I led on, wishing my skirt wasn't quite so short and hoping I didn't have a ladder in my tights.

I was rather dreading our entrance to the flat. Health and Safety hadn't thus far been alerted, but I fervently wished I'd had a quick clear-up before I'd left. Here he was, following me into what would doubtless be a fairly revolting . . . oh . . . my . . . God.

The kitchen, which one encountered fairly promptly, given that the hall was the size of a napkin, was spotless.

I spun round in surprise. 'This is unreal. Someone's tidied up!'

No piles of washing-up in the sink, no midden of newspapers on the table; no broken cupboard doors spewing forth cartons of soup, pasta, Pot Noodles. The lino wasn't sticky, I noticed, testing it tentatively with the soles of my shoes. Suddenly, the sitting-room door opened and a blonde in a pink dress flew out.

'Oh, Anthony. This is my flatmate, Caro.'

'Hi.' She looked flushed and anxious, and shot him only the briefest of glances. 'Evie, my mother's here!' she whispered in terror, pointing back over her shoulder at the door she'd slammed.

'Oh, no!' Christ, no wonder she'd cleared up. Caro's mother was a terrifying woman, formidable, critical and probing, the headmistress at the local high school. 'We'll go,' I said quickly. 'Grab a drink in town.'

'Good idea.' Caro hustled us towards the door.

'Oh, but surely . . .' Ant looked perplexed.

'She's a Buddhist,' I told him firmly. 'Doesn't approve.'

'Doesn't touch a drop,' agreed Caro. 'And really hates anyone who does.' She swung the door wide and ushered us out.

As she went to shut it behind us, though, I peered back round. 'You washed up,' I said in awe. 'Must have taken hours.'

For weeks now, Caro and I had blithely skirted the remains of a particularly gruesome dinner party—casseroles burnt black, mashed potato caked onto pans, all growing penicillin, forcing us to fill the kettle at an excruciatingly awkward angle.

'I threw it away,' she confided softly, glancing over her shoulder.

I giggled. 'You *didn't*?'

'I bloody did. I couldn't face it. It's all in the dustbins outside. You can get it out, if you like,' she added with a defiant grin. 'See you.'

'Is she serious?' Ant asked as we tripped down the stairs.

'Oh, definitely. Caro and I have a very simple approach to clearing up. Most of our stuff is shoved under beds, or even . . . damn.' I stopped. 'I need some ciggies. Won't be a mo.'

I bounded back upstairs, fishing the key out of my coat pocket. Opening the front door and darting through to my bedroom, I hissed '*Fags!*' at Caro, who was still in the kitchen. She was bending over the tiny table, which, I noticed, was laid for two, lighting a candle. I stopped in surprise. Turned. Her pink dress was very short and her thick blonde hair tumbled over her shoulders into, what I now realised, was quite a spectacular cleavage. As a blast of Rive Gauche rocketed up my nostrils, I was aware of Ant, appearing in the doorway. I folded my arms. Cocked an eyebrow. 'Your mother?'

She flushed. Blew out the match. 'Ah.'

'Hasn't she bloody gone yet?' boomed a familiar voice from behind the sitting-room door.

I froze. Then my head rotated slowly towards it. In another moment I'd crossed the kitchen and flung the door wide. A naked man faced me, stretched out on the goatskin rug in front of the electric fire, hands locked behind his head. Although the face was very familiar, it wasn't one I was used to seeing round these parts. Neither were his parts. He sat up languidly, casually flipping a corner of the rug over to cover them.

'Oh, hi, Evie.' He grinned. Then he looked round me. 'Who's this?'

'This is Anthony,' I said evenly. 'Anthony, this is my brother, Tim. We pretty much like to keep it in the family.'

Chronologically speaking then, we all by and large leapt off the starting blocks together, Tim and Caro, Ant and I. All got away at the same time. Tim and Caro, as we know, had a minuscule head start, but it didn't take Ant and me long to catch up. And from the word go, it was a success. We made a good team, the four of us. We drank in pubs together, cooked suppers together, went bowling, saw films. We raced round town in Ant's terrible old Citroën, and even went on holiday in it together, Ant driving,

Caro navigating—naturally—through the Dordogne and right down to the coast, while Tim and I giggled in the back.

It was on that holiday that Tim asked Caro to marry him. I remember them coming back from the beach one day; Tim looking sheepish, Caro unable to resist blurting out, 'We've got something to tell you.'

To this day I can remember my heart dropping like a brick through water. My best friend and my brother—of course I was delighted, of course, but . . . it wasn't me. I hated myself, still do, but I had a lump in my throat as we toasted their happiness.

'How exciting! Oh, I'm *so* pleased!'

And the thing is, even as I was gushing, I knew there was a bit of Caro that knew what I was thinking, because we'd known each other for donkey's years and talked about boys and weddings and what our bridesmaids would wear, and what our children would be called and all the silly things girls aren't supposed to talk about as they're doggedly pursuing their careers but do. So as she's telling me breathlessly about the village church, and the marquee at the farm, she knows too that I also want the village church, and a marquee at the farm. She knows my insides are curdling, but she can't help it. And why should she? She's getting married, she's first, she's won. And her eyes, when they look at mine, are full of happiness and shame. And I'm galvanised. I will be next, I will!

That night, after Ant and I'd made love, he held me close. 'Lovely for Tim and Caro,' I murmured into his shoulder. Yes, I know, a bit obvious, but I happen to think it's a fairly primeval urge women have, after about the age of twenty-five, to get married.

'Hm,' he murmured sleepily. 'They'll be good together.'

I took a deep breath. 'So . . . how d'you think we'd check out? As a team?' Blimey, Evie.

After a moment, Ant rolled over on top of me and propped himself up the better to look at me. The moon, through the open window, lit up his face. Thoughtful. Sincere. My heart began to palpitate. Oh my God . . . this was it. His eyes searched my face, my hair, then—'*Got it!*' He thwacked the pillow, spun round and sat up, showing me a squashed mosquito in the palm of his hand. 'This bloodsucking parasite was about to take a slurp from your cheek. Night.'

Tim and Caro got married in the autumn. And it was lovely, of course it was. It was in the village church, naturally, right beside our house, on a fine October day, and I was chief bridesmaid in a midnight-blue velvet dress, and Ant was an usher, devastatingly handsome in a morning coat. Caro looked radiant in ivory silk, with tiny blue velvet bows sewn just above the hem and velvet ribbons hanging from her bouquet, which was cream rosebuds. The reception was held in a marquee in the garden, with lashings of pink champagne, and then a rather pissy disco, before the happy couple went off on their honeymoon.

And then the next weekend, while Tim and Caro were still in Venice, Mum and Dad, having surprised themselves by making peace for the wedding, or at least an armed neutrality, decided to have a break from the farm, and go on holiday to Crete, where they had an almighty row in a taverna and were thrown out but that's another story. The one you need to know is that Ant and I moved in to look after the farm for them that weekend, and that was the weekend Neville Carter died.

Eighteen years ago, on October 12, 1989. And eighteen years later, here was I, in my basement kitchen in Jericho, knowing I had to remember. Knowing it was important.

The Carters lived across the road from us and, knowing I was house-sitting at the farm, had popped by. 'Evie?' Mrs Carter called up the stairs, 'Evie, are you there?'

I'd run down, flushed, from the bedroom, pulling down my T-shirt.

'Evie, would you mind, dear, only I've been called into work'—Mrs Carter was a district nurse—'and I wondered, could you have Neville for me? I'll only be an hour or so.'

Damn, I remember thinking. 'Of course, Mrs Carter.'

'He can play outside, if you're busy. Just keep an eye.'

And Neville, narrow, weedy, pinched-faced, not an attractive boy, had sidled inside. He was eight, not a baby, not necessarily needing to be watched all the time, and—oh, I didn't want to remember any of this—and I'd said, 'Neville, will you really be all right in the garden?' when she'd gone.

'Yeah.' He shrugged.

And back I'd leapt up those stairs, to Ant, in bed, and Neville had wandered off: first to the swing—I remember glimpsing him out of the window—and then out of sight, to that bit of the stream we'd all been warned about as children, where the water flows much faster, darker, and oh . . . so ghastly. So ghastly later. Ant, ashen-faced as he and Maroulla, the wife of our farm worker, dragged him out: me, weeping, shrieking on the bank, the parents, Mr and Mrs Carter, arriving. My parents then, getting a flight back from Crete, pale beneath their tans, shaken. Telling the truth about what we'd been doing, the horror on my father's face, the shame on Ant's; his gentle, kind, intelligent, wouldn't-hurt-a-fly face that had killed a child.

And afterwards, we'd cried together, cringing, guilty figures at the funeral. The whole village was there, looking at me, who they knew, with a mixture of pity and surprise, and looking at Ant with mistrust. The man they didn't know, who she'd been upstairs with.

Ant had taken time off work and we'd drunk in anonymous pubs where people didn't know us, drinking too much, always there for last orders, our guilt and our shame binding us. And then one of those nights, walking back, full of alcohol, he'd asked me to marry him.

To give me my due, if I was to be afforded any, I'd said no. No, I said, we were too highly strung and emotional right now. Let's wait. But he'd insisted. Said it was all he wanted. And, let's face it, he knew it was all I wanted. Knew that that day, as we'd been fooling around in the farm-house, I'd been angling again . . . saying how lovely Tim and Caro's wedding had been, how happy they'd looked.

I felt the blood rush to my face now as I gazed at the wisteria on the garden wall. While I was angling, Ant had—I forced myself to remember this, as I never had before—looked awkward. I felt a jab of horror. Had gently untangled himself and said, 'Evie . . . I'm not sure.'

I shut my eyes. Well, lots of boyfriends weren't sure. And I hadn't pushed it. Hadn't said, but, Ant, we've been going out for months now, as long as Tim and Caro, and I badly want a baby and she's going to beat me to it. No, of *course* I hadn't said any of that, and only even frac-tionally thought it. It was only because I was forcing myself now, years later, to be so ruthlessly honest that these thoughts were surfacing. But now, now this letter had come and was making me think, what if Neville hadn't died? I knew it was important; knew we'd become closer, but had it changed *everything*? Had Neville dying changed the course of my life? Surely it was always on a trajectory to marry Ant?

I felt panicky, leaned heavily on the work surface. And now—a child. By another woman. Conceived around that time. A barmaid, he'd said, a passing fancy, but nevertheless, a release from me. From my nagging. I pressed my fists to my temples. A child. And so—and this I had to really make myself do—and so think back to the moment before we'd heard the scream from Maroulla, who'd found Neville floating face down; think back to what Ant had said a few seconds before the scream had changed our lives.

'Evie . . . there's something I've got to tell you.'

Up to now, it had been ruthlessly erased from my memory. I'd never said—weeks, months later—what was it, Ant? What was it you had to tell me? That was my shame. That I'd pretended he'd never said it. Or that I'd never heard.

I let go of the slate worktop. Took a deep breath. Exhaled shakily. But as I went to leave the room, I looked around. Wondered what else I'd pushed. He hadn't really liked that Welsh dresser I'd found in the antique shop in Woodstock; had thought it olde worlde, cutesy. But there it was. Hadn't really liked the yellow walls, thinking them too bright, a little challenging over the morning paper. But there they were. And here I was too. I bowed my head and left the room.

3

'MUM! THERE'S A GUY on the phone wanting to know if you're coming to look at his skewbald!'

I sat bolt upright in bed. His what? I hadn't slept a wink until about four in the morning, when I'd finally taken a pill, so now, here I was, groggy, swaying and full of toxins. 'Oh,' I croaked. The horse. I swung my legs out of bed. 'Tell him we're on our way!' I quavered.

Ant's side of the bed was empty, I noticed. I got up tentatively and tottered off to find my clothes, listening to Anna's voice on the phone, downstairs in the hall. 'Yes, I'm so sorry . . . Oh, did she? Oh, my mum's *hopeless*, yes, we're on our way!'

She mustn't know, was my overriding thought as I pulled on my jeans. She mustn't know that this was anything other than a normal day. I clutched my T-shirt and sat down suddenly, remembering last night. Last night, when Ant had come home, quite late, and I'd confronted him.

'You see?' I'd said, with a mixture of fear and triumph. 'See, Ant, it can't be your child. We were going out together, even engaged!'

And then I'd watched his face turn grey as I knew it would; watched him crumple, defeated, into a chair, his gentle eyes pained. I'd listened, as he explained that yes, it could be his. That this had indeed happened while we were going out together, this thing with the barmaid—a one-night stand—because he'd felt so trapped. Felt he was going insane.

'When, exactly?' I'd whispered. 'When had you felt so trapped?'

'After lunch, at your parents' house,' he muttered. 'One Sunday. When Caro told us she was pregnant.'

My mind skittered back, foraging. But I remembered. Caro and Tim had been married for about three months, Ant and I engaged for one. Caro announced she was pregnant; everyone was delighted. Dad hastened to the cellar for a bottle of champagne, and I was genuinely thrilled, because, after all, I was getting married soon, so no sicky feeling inside, not like when she'd got engaged before me, and delighted for Tim, *really* delighted for Tim, so then why, oh why, on the way home in the car, had I casually wondered what he thought of me coming off the pill? Ant? After all, we were getting married in a couple of months, so even if I got pregnant immediately, it wouldn't show. And it might take us ages.

Ant had cleared his throat. Then he'd reminded me, gently, that we'd thought we'd wait a year, hadn't we? Have a year of fun—which we badly needed in the circumstances—and enjoy being young-marrieds. And I'd said, yes, but, Ant, I'm not getting any younger. I'm twenty-six, for heaven's sake, and you're thirty! I'd pressed it, fired up by a few glasses of wine, thinking, golly, at least I'm *asking*. And then finally: 'Whatever you want, Evie.' Wearily. Like a punchbag. And later that evening, when we were back at his rooms in Balliol where I was pretty much living, he'd gone out. For quite a long while. And I'd been a bit scared. Knew I'd been out of order. Later in bed, I'd apologised.

'I'm sorry, darling, I'm going too fast. Forget it.'

He hadn't answered.

'**S**o you went out and shagged a barmaid!' I shrieked last night. 'Christ, Ant, how many times? Once? Twice?'

'Once!' he roared, fists clenched. 'I told you—just once!'

Ant never raised his voice. Never. Instead of being shocked, I shouted back, wondered how many other bastard children he had. Finally, Anna had burst into the kitchen in her nightie, wide-eyed and scared.

'What? What's going on?'

Ashamed, we assured her nothing; scared ourselves now, in case she'd heard anything. And now, here she was again, bursting into my bedroom, her eyes like dinner plates.

'Mum! Come *on*. I said we'd be twenty minutes!'

I hurriedly found some shoes and brushed my teeth, then I followed her downstairs and out to the car, shutting the door on Brenda, who wanted to come with us. My head was swimming and I felt nauseous.

'D'you know where we're going?' Anna asked accusingly as I got in.

'Um. No. Hang on.' I got out and tottered back inside for the directions. When I returned, I fumbled with the ignition and off we went.

'What were you and Daddy rowing about last night?' she said, before we'd even got ten yards down the road.

'Hm? Oh, nothing really, darling.'

'Nothing! You were screaming and calling him a bastard and Daddy was shouting. I hardly call that nothing.'

'Oh, it was just . . . a silly thing. About holidays. You know I always want to go abroad and your father likes Scotland. That was all.'

'Oh.' She looked slightly mollified, but not entirely convinced.

'Where is Daddy, by the way? Have you seen him this morning?'

'He's in the garden. Reading.'

'Ah.' Reading. Always his refuge. His escape. From me? I took a deep breath. Come on, Evie, get a grip. 'Now, anyway,' I turned a bright smile on her, 'this *pony*. How exciting! I wonder what colour it is.'

'It's a skewbald, he said on the phone.'

'What's that, then?'

'Brown and white.'

'Oh.' I blinked. 'I could have sworn the advert said it was grey.'

She shot me a withering look. 'It's down here on the left, according to your bit of paper.'

'Here?' I blanched at the somewhat unpromising urban landscape.

'Yes, look , it says, "After the Shell garage."' She waved the piece of paper in my face.

We were bowling along the Woodstock Road and I obediently swung a left, down a street lined with terraced houses. I slowed down and peered at the directions as she held them up in front of me. This looked like an industrial estate. At length, though, we wiggled round a few bends and then we achieved a track, which led, in turn, to what could hardly be described as a stable yard. More like a collection of sheds with corrugated-iron roofs, and a mobile home standing gauntly in their midst. We came to a halt and Anna and I ventured forth gingerly.

I wasn't really dressed for this, I realised, having stuck my feet into the first shoes that had come to hand: a rather expensive pair of beaded flip-flops I'd bought in Italy. I'd ruin them, I thought, as I picked my way through a mucky yard.

A small, scrawny man in baggy trousers, braces and a flat cap came to meet us. A practised smile revealed an unusual dental arrangement.

'Mr Docherty?'

'Tha's right.' In a slow, singsong Irish brogue. 'You'll be coming after the pony.'

'Exactly. But remind me, Mr Docherty, what colour is the pony?'

'What colour will you be wanting?' Quick as a flash.

'Oh. Well. It doesn't really matter, I suppose. It's just that, well, in the advert you said grey, and my daughter thinks you said skewbald, so—'

'Ah, well, you see the grey one, she was after being sold, but the skewbald now, she's a rare beast. A grand mare altogether. You'd go a long way to find another mare like that, may the Good Lord crack me legs from under me if it isn't so.'

Still smiling, he jerked his head to a young lad, who went sullenly towards a stable and led the horse out.

It was indeed brown and white, and bigger than I'd imagined: rather thin and rangy too. But it had a kind, somewhat sleepy eye, I decided. The mare raised her tail and evacuated copiously out of her rear end a stream of rather evil-looking green slime. Perhaps she was nervous. She wasn't the only one.

'Right. What d'you think, darling?' Christ. In the recesses of my mind I remembered Caro telling me to bring someone along. But we were here now. I deferred to my daughter.

'She's lovely,' she said, stepping forward to pat her, her eyes aglow with owning a pony—any pony.

'Yes. Yes, she is, isn't she?' I agreed. I quite liked the idea that it was a she. Mares were more docile, weren't they? Than boy horses? This one was so docile she was nodding off. 'She'll be a bit keener when she's ridden, I suppose,' I hazarded. 'She looks a bit sleepy.'

'Ah, faith, she's aisy goin', this one is. But if it's keen you want, you won't find a fleeter mare in Oxfordshire,' said Mr Docherty.

'And does she jump?' asked Anna, shyly.

'Jump? Jees, she'll leap that brick wall as soon as look at it.' He pointed to a dry-stone wall behind us. 'Leapt clean out of the yard the other day, right over the five-bar gate. Shown a clean pair of heels, too.'

'But she's—you know—quiet too, is she?' I said, alarmed at the prospect of her leaping round Caro's yard. 'You know, easy to handle?'

'Ah, she is that.'

It occurred to me, suddenly, we might be under scrutiny here ourselves. A friend of mine who'd wanted to get a dog from a rescue home had been startled to find an earnest young woman in her sitting room with a clipboard, asking pertinent questions—and sometimes impertinent ones—about her domestic set-up: grilling her as to her suitability. The fact that she lived in town and was a divorced mother of three apparently didn't go down too well.

'We're married,' I said quickly. 'My husband and I.' Anna looked at me in astonishment. 'And although we live in the city, we'd keep it—her—at my brother's place. Church Farm in Daglington.'

'Caroline Milligan's place?' A shadow crossed Mr Docherty's face.
'That's it. D'you know it?'

'I do. Get that currycomb and look sharp,' he snapped to the boy.

'What's her name?' asked Anna as the boy began grooming her.

'Molly Malone. But we call her Molly.'

'Oh, sw-eet!' Anna, overcome with emotion, put her arms round her neck and kissed her. For some reason, I found this profoundly moving. My eyes misted up. A girl and her pony. First love.

'We'll take her,' I said decidedly. 'Do you deliver?'

The boy turned to hide a smile, and even Mr Docherty had the grace to cough. 'You'll be wanting your lass to ride her first? Or even Barney here to hop on. Show her paces?'

'Oh. Yes.' I coloured. Anna was glaring at me, shocked. Was that how it was done, then? I'd never bought a horse before. 'Yes, good idea. Barney . . . and then Anna. Oh, and what about her legs?'

Still smarting from my gaffe, I had a notion I should be feeling them. I hastened forward to run my hand expertly down a large hairy back one, but my sunglasses slid off my nose and clattered onto the concrete, which startled the horse, who stepped back and smashed them, as I, to avoid her rear end, stepped smartly into her slimy green poo in my flip-flops. I stared in dismay as it squelched up between my toes.

'Her legs are clean,' Mr Docherty assured me smoothly.

'Oh, good.' I nodded, disinclined to take the investigation further.

In another moment, the lad had got a saddle and bridle on her, and vaulted onto her back. He gave the pony a hefty kick. At this his mount jolted off at a rather unsettled pace, through the open gateway and into a ragworty paddock. We watched as he went round and round in circles: first walking, then trotting, then that faster thing . . . marvellous. I felt I was on the set of *Rawhide*. He came back and slid neatly off, handing the reins to Anna.

'All right, darling?' I looked at her anxiously.

She looked a bit nervous, but got on carefully. I felt so proud as I watched her trot off. How brave! A strange horse! I watched her do a careful up-down, up-down trot, immaculate in her yellow jodhpurs, shiny boots and velvet hat, but I was only half watching. I'd spotted a water trough just along the fence line, and unable to bear the poo-between-the-toes feeling any longer, nipped off to dunk my foot.

When I got back, she seemed to be going quite fast, I'd say a gallop, and Mr Docherty was shouting, 'Pull her up now, gurr'l!' but Anna's eyes were shining, cheeks pink, as she careered unsteadily back to us.

'Yes?' I called up to her.

'Yes!' she said breathlessly, elated and excited.

'Marvellous.' I beamed at the man. 'A thousand, you said?' The boy looked astonished, and Mr Docherty anguished, as it presumably crossed his mind that he could have asked twice as much, but he was quick to point out that yes, that was indeed the price, but minus the tack.

'Ah. And how much is the tack?'

'Five hundred.'

'Five hundred!' I looked at the saddle, rather dirty and grey, and the tatty old bridle. 'Good grief. I had no idea.'

'Ah well, you see, it's all in the workmanship,' he said.

'Yes, yes, of course. We'll take it,' I said firmly, writing out the cheque on an upturned bucket, which had been hastily provided.

'And did you say you would deliver?' I persisted, as Mr Docherty pocketed the cheque.

'Ah, we will. Wednesday morning I'll pop her in the lorry and bring her round, just as soon as the cheque's cleared. I'll tek her straight to your brother's place, will I?'

'Yes, please. Oh, and if there's no one about—'

'Ah, no need to trouble anyone. I'll pop Molly straight in a stable, will I?'

'Um, yes. Why not?' I certainly didn't want Caro disturbed and Tim would be relaxed about that. 'You can't miss the stables.'

'I dare say the boy and meself will make them out.' He touched the peak of his cap, in a rather sweet, old-fashioned gesture, as, I felt, in a gentler age, a horse dealer might.

A horse dealer, I thought with a start as we drove out of the yard. Is that what he was? That sounded a bit—you know—dodgy. But I was pretty sure we hadn't paid over the odds. And even if we had, Anna had got her dream, a pony. And she might need a few dreams, I thought wretchedly, if her little world was about to be shattered.

As we drew up outside the house, it was in time to see Ant shutting the front door behind him. He locked it carefully, pocketed the key, then turned to come down the steps, pausing to pick up a large suitcase.

'Where's Daddy going?' said Anna.

My mouth dried as I watched him descend the steps. 'Wait here.'

I parked chaotically, then dashed across the street, nearly getting mown down by an Alfa Romeo, with an alfa Romeo at the wheel.

'Oh, for *fuck's* sake!' he roared fruitily, but I ignored him, climbing over the bonnet and running to Ant.

'Where are you going?' I gasped.

He stared impassively at me. 'To your mother's.'

'My mother's?' Even in my distress it seemed an unlikely bolt hole.

'Don't you remember? We're going for lunch there today.'

My mind cleared. 'Oh!' Yes, of course, lunch. 'But—the suitcase . . .'

'It's not. It's that old Z-bed we had in the attic. She wants to borrow it for this reiki thing she's doing.'

I gazed down at it; saw that he was right. The collapsable bed. I felt my heart slow down. As he looked at me I realised he was suddenly alive to what I'd been thinking. A wave of shock passed over his face.

'But, it's huge,' I prattled on, trying to gloss over my horrific assumption. 'What were you going to do—drag it there or something?'

'No, I was going to put the seats down in the back of my car and meet you over there,' he said evenly. 'I tried to ring you, but your phone's off. I assumed you and Anna had already gone on. It's nearly one o'clock, you know.'

'Is it? No, I didn't. We've been to see that pony. Anna wanted to—Oh, darling.' She'd materialised beside us. Ant and I rallied simultaneously. 'Look, Daddy's taking Granny the Z-bed. We're going there for lunch!'

'We may as well use your car, now you're here,' Ant said. 'Bigger boot.'

'Good idea. And, Anna, you run up and change. Chop chop, Granny will wonder where we are and lunch will be on the table!'

Felicity was already at Mum's place when we arrived. The pair of them were standing outside, looking at the front door.

'It's just a bit misleading,' Felicity was saying anxiously, turning as she heard us. 'I think you should wait.'

'Wait for what?' I asked.

'Your mother wants to put up a brass sign, about being a reiki practitioner,' she explained nervously.

I boggled at the little brass plaque Mum had in her hands: BARBARA MILLIGAN, REIKI THERAPIST.

'Of course she should wait! Christ, she's not even qualified yet!'

'I'm more than halfway through,' Mum said defiantly, clutching her plaque to her breast. 'So I'm a practitioner in progress. And one woman in my class is already seeing students. At half-price, of course.'

'Well then, she's stupid,' I snapped, all the pent-up emotion of the last few days being taken out on my mother, who, if not stupid, was certainly foolish. Three years ago it had been homeopathy, until she'd realised the course took four years. Then she'd switched to aromatherapy, and now this. I found her inability to focus on anything for more than ten minutes intensely irritating, perhaps because I recognised elements of myself in her and dreaded ending up like that.

'It's just ridiculous, Mum,' I stormed. 'You can't go around pretending you're a doctor when you're not!'

'I don't think Barbara was going to do that,' soothed Felicity.

'Of course she wasn't,' said Anna, staunchly. 'You're just practising, as in, having a go, aren't you, Granny?'

'That's it,' said Mum. 'D'you want to see my room, Anna love? Ooh, thank you, Ant, that's just what I need. Bring it down, would you? We're in the basement.'

She turned to descend the little outside staircase that led to the basement. The others clattered obediently after her, Mum chattering on about how marvellous it was for the surgery—*surgery!*—to have its own entrance. Anna turned at the bottom and shot me a warning glance up the stairwell: *Don't* be mean. Oh, right, so we were supposed to encourage her in this, were we? Just as we'd all knocked back the Bach flower remedies and said, 'Oh, yes, so much better, Barbara'?

Mum proudly unlocked the door at the bottom trilling 'Ta-dah!' as she swung it back. We followed her inside. What had been her basement junk room, full of detritus, had been transformed into a pink parlour. Womb music warbled low and candles glowed on every conceivable surface. In a corner on the floor, what looked like a baby bath was full of pebbles, water trickling over them by way of a sort of Heath Robinson pump. I picked up a little leaflet on the side, which told me that Metaphysical Therapy and Self-Development Counselling was also available at this establishment. I could feel myself getting crosser and crosser as the others wandered round, exclaiming and marvelling.

'Just here, Barbara?' Ant was saying, as he and Anna unfolded the bed in the middle of the room on some sort of plinth. Much kinder than me, I thought miserably, watching them assemble it. But then she wasn't their mother, was she?

'I'll be the first patient!' announced Anna, quickly sitting on the bed. 'Come on, Granny, heal me! Reiki style!'

My mother was instantly all puffed-up importance and twiddling beads. 'Well, I'll have to have absolute quiet, obviously,' she said gravely. 'And the lights dimmed. And no audience. Go on, off you go!'

As we left them alone and went to go upstairs, I shut the door behind me and glanced back. Through the glass in the door I saw my mother, eyes shut, God help me, laying her hands on Anna's head.

Ant put a sympathetic hand on my shoulder. 'It's—'

'*Don't* tell me it's harmless!' I snapped.

Later, of course, after a large glass of wine, I relented and went down. Made myself available to Mum's healing hands.

'She likes you to go a bit dreamy,' Felicity whispered to me as we passed on the staircase, she having been the last patient. 'Oh, and you're supposed to feel her hands go hot when she gets to the trouble spots, which of course they don't, so just pretend. I'll put the spuds on.'

This only served to send my blood pressure rocketing, so that by the time Mum—a white coat over her Monsoon dress and cardi—got to work on me, having first fannied around changing the CD in a ghetto blaster that I recognised as being an old one of Anna's, and having washed her hands theatrically with surgical soap, I was about to pop.

'Now, darling, just relax,' she said. I shut my eyes tight, knowing it was the only way forward, but not before I'd seen Mum shut hers too, and look a bit hypnotic. Her hands were hovering over me like a pair of metal detectors. The force was with her.

'Hommm . . .' she started low and portentous, like a Buddhist monk.

After a bit more humming and hovering, the hands eventually arrived, homing in on what she clearly believed to be my trouble spots. They came to rest on my shoulders, then slipped down my arms.

'Where is the pain, my child?' she breathed gustily.

'In . . . my . . . head,' I muttered back with studied irritation and in all truthfulness. I really didn't need this. Mum's hands came to rest on the top of my head. Hot hands, I thought in surprise as I lay there, slightly taken aback.

'Ah, yes,' she whispered, 'it is in your head. I can feel it. Feel your pain. Can you feel the heat?'

I opened one eye carefully to look at her. Her head was thrown back, mouth slack, eyes shut, trancelike. 'Yes,' I said uncertainly.

'I can too,' she breathed. 'Yes. It's channelling through. Transferring.'

Transferring. Blimey.

'I feel it flowing right through me now,' she gasped.

'Where does it go?' I muttered, still eyeing her.

'I store it for you,' she gulped, wincing as if in pain. 'Take it from you, and then—out! Out! Into the ether!'

The hands were cooling now, and suddenly, her eyes sprang open. She stepped back. 'Phew.' She blinked. Looked exhausted. 'Better?' She peered anxiously at me.

I sat up, swung my legs off the bed and shrugged. 'So-so.'

'But you felt the channelling? Felt the transference?'

'A bit,' I admitted grudgingly.

She smiled. 'And in time, you'll feel it more.'

I watched as she bustled round the room, taking off her white coat and hanging it up, blowing out candles now that her last patient had been seen, pausing occasionally, to touch her forehead, as if still a bit weak from her exertions. Then I noticed, as she bent down to blow out the last candle on the floor, that her cardigan fell forward on one side, as if it was weighted down. 'Mum, what's in your pocket?' I said sharply.

She straightened up and swung round, her hand shooting into it protectively. She looked defensive. 'Nothing.'

'Oooh, *Mum!*' There then ensued a rather unseemly little tussle. I was the victor. My right hand was held aloft, and in it was a warm, squidgy object. 'A *hand*warmer!' I spluttered. 'Bloody hell, Mum!'

'Only to get it going,' she hissed. 'Sometimes the transference needs a bit of jump-starting.'

'**S**o mean,' said Anna later, as we drove home, 'to plonk it down on the kitchen table like Exhibit A. Poor, *poor* Granny!'

She hadn't been poor so much as utterly defiant and unrepentant, I thought. Had kept spouting the rubbish about jump-starting, and everyone else had agreed, and I'd been *incandescent* with irritation.

'But can't you see you're just encouraging her?' I'd spluttered, as Felicity—who always cooked, whether lunch was at her house or Mum's—put a roast chicken on the table. 'She's only going to hoodwink some poor susceptible student out of their grant—it's immoral!'

'But if they go away feeling better, so what?' Anna had demanded. 'I bet you felt better when you stood up, and I know I did. So what's the difference?'

I'd opened my mouth to protest, looked to Ant for support, but he'd just shrugged noncommittally, and I wondered if he, like me, was wondering what our very blessed daughter had to feel better about.

That night, in bed, after Anna had sloped off to her room, after Ant and I had gratefully turned in, we'd held each other close.

'We have to face this together, Evie,' he whispered. 'Otherwise it'll tear us apart.'

I'd nearly wept with relief. He was right. So right.

'What shall we do?' I whispered, hanging on to that 'we' for dear life.

'I must write to her. But I'll show you the letter first. No secrets. And, Evie, if she wants to meet me, then I have to do that. You must see that.'

He drew back on the pillows to look at me; his face was racked with anguish, and I thought how dreadful this was for him, and I'd only thought it was dreadful for me.

'Yes,' I whispered, knowing he was right.

'She has to know who her father is. And that's all it'll be, I'm convinced. To set eyes on me. She'll have her own father, I'm sure.'

'Yes,' I said quickly. Because I'd thought of that too. Hoped that. *Clung* to that. But . . . maybe some drunken reprobate? Some unemployed wastrel? And maybe she'd set eyes on Ant and think—wow. Who wouldn't? Think—mm, yes, please. But, then again, why shouldn't she? He was her father, after all. I dug deep for courage. Knew I was going to need it.

'But if not . . .' Ant was saying, picking his words with care, 'if she doesn't have her own father and she does want to see something of me—of us—'

'*Us?*' I gasped, sitting up. 'Steady, Ant, I'm not sure I can—'

'OK,' he agreed hastily, knowing he was going too fast. 'No, OK then. Just me.'

We both lay down again, uncertainly. Instinctively and simultaneously we reached out for each other's hands; held on tight.

Wednesday morning at nine o'clock sharp, Caro was on the phone.

'What the hell d'you think you're playing at? I've got some strange horse in my field kicking seven bells out of the children's ponies. Phil says he saw a lad unload her from a trailer at practically dawn! Said she belonged to a Mrs Hamilton and he'd been told to deliver her!'

I shut my eyes. Shit. Hadn't I rung her? I'd certainly left a message on Tim's mobile . . . Bugger.

'Caro, I—I'm terribly sorry,' I faltered. 'I completely forgot. I did leave Tim a message, on his mobile—'

'Which he never bloody uses!'

'And the boy was supposed to put her in a stable.'

'So she is yours?' Caro screeched incredulously.

'Yes, Anna and I bought her the other day. I meant to—'

'You bought her on your own? Without taking anyone? Without ringing me? Are you totally and utterly out of your mind?'

Yes, it felt like it, recently, most of the time.

'Where did you get her from?'

'Lenny Docherty. He's got a yard just off the Woodstock—'

'Lenny the Liar!' she said with a spectacular hiss. 'Oh God, Evie, he'd sell his own grandmother!'

This was so like Caro, I thought, fury mounting, to take against Molly simply because she hadn't been consulted. 'Right, I'll come and sort her out then, shall I? Come and move her, if she's annoying the ponies.'

'If you can catch her,' Caro scoffed. 'Phil and I have been running round after her since seven o'clock this morning. We'll have to lasso her to bring her in. And then where am I supposed to put her?'

'Well, I—'

'Oh, for God's sake, I'll manage. Just bring Anna over here after school, OK? I want to make sure she can ride the wretched thing.'

'Right,' I said obediently.

There was no one about when Anna and I got to the farm. I roamed around the garden yelling, 'Caro!'

'There!' Anna spotted her, down by her marquee on the other side of the stream. She was walking strangely, bent double like a gorilla, with a bucket in her hand. We hurried down the lawn and leapt across the water via the steppingstones to join her.

'I'm so sorry, Caro,' I panted as we followed the grassy path through the cow parsley, carefully mown for her brides, 'really sorry. I'll sort Molly out. Oh Lord, what's happened to the marquee? Here, let me.' Caro, still bent at the waist, was working her way along the pink and white canvas, wiping it down with great sweeping strokes. I picked up the bucket to move it closer to her. 'Yuck.' I dropped it abruptly. 'Smells like—'

'Puke, which is exactly what it is.' She straightened up to look at me. 'We had a hooray wedding here yesterday, against my better judgment, and after they'd bonked their way round the bushes, they were sick in the herbaceous borders. Some hero sprayed the marquee with it too.'

'Oh!'

She picked up her bucket and marched off to attend to another hot spot. '*And* there was a punch-up on the dance floor,' she said grimly. 'And when Tim waded in to sort it out, he ended up with a split lip!'

Why did she do it? I wondered as I followed her across the stream, Anna behind us. For the money, of course, but—was it worth it? We set off back up the grassy slope of the garden at a brisk pace.

'And now Marcia Wentworth-White at Harrington Hall has decided *she's* doing weddings too so no doubt all my lovely Asians will flock up there and no one will come here except the fucking gentiles!'

Ah. So that was it. Might explain her bad temper on the phone.

'But surely Marcia will charge more? I mean, Harrington Hall—you'd be much better value for money.'

'That's what I'm hanging on to,' she said. 'That they'll price themselves out of the market. We'll see. Pigs.' She stopped in her tracks.

'The Wentworth-Whites?'

'No, I've got to feed them, but yes, the Wentworth-Whites are actually, especially him, no manners at all. Frightfully nouveau.' She turned and headed off down towards the sties. 'Anyway, I'm going for the gay market.' She jutted her chin out determinedly. 'I'm convinced it's the way forward. Here, Boadicea! Here, Crackling!' She rattled her bucket at the pig pen as we approached. Five enormous sows suddenly appeared from nowhere and charged at us. Anna and I backed away nervously.

'Actually, you can help,' said Caro.

Help? In what way? Nothing practical, I hoped.

'If you distract them,' she went on, 'I can get to their trough at the other end.' She handed me the sick bucket. 'Here jiggle this.' I recoiled in disgust. 'Oh, don't be silly, they'll eat anything.'

They surely would. The pigs were huge and threw themselves convulsively against the netting as I jiggled nervously, and as Caro ran away. 'Where are you going?' I bleated.

'To pour feed into their trough down the other end,' she shouted. 'But they tip it over so I've got to right it first. Now jiggle the bucket!'

I jiggled furiously, nose averted, as down the other end of the pen, Caro stole over the fence like a burglar and quickly righted the trough, poured in the rations, just as the pigs, realising they'd been had, turned and charged. Caro nipped back over the fence just in time.

'What would they do if they caught you?' asked Anna, awe-struck.

'Eat me, probably,' panted Caro, brushing herself down.

'So . . . why d'you like them?' Anna whispered.

'Oh, it's all part of country life, isn't it?' Caro beamed. 'And anyway, they've always been here. Your mum probably used to feed them!'

I think we all knew this wasn't true. Mum had kept pigs, but Maroulla and Mario, our farm workers, had looked after them.

'Where's Harriet?' I asked, peering into the pen. 'The blind one?'

'In a stable next to the house so I can keep an eye on her. Anyway, less of the pigs—we've got other fish to fry, haven't we?' She beamed at Anna and put an arm round her shoulders. 'Now, this *horse*!'

Anna smiled delightedly back, and Caro led her off to the stables. I caught her eye briefly, thanking her. Caro might sound off on the phone to me, but she wouldn't rain on Anna's pony parade if she could help it: she was fond of her niece, and I blessed her for that.

'I caught her, finally, with Phil's help,' Caro said from inside the loose box, putting a bridle on Molly. 'Quite frisky, isn't she?'

'Not when we saw her,' I said. 'Oh, look, Anna, isn't she sweet?' Her nose was poking over the door and I went to stroke her. 'Oh!' Her ears went back and she bared her teeth. 'Not very friendly!'

'She didn't do that when you saw her?' Caro led her out.

'No.'

She gave me an arch look as she put the saddle on. 'Disgusting tack. Presumably he threw it in for free?'

'Um. Yes.' I flicked Anna a look.

'Hm,' said Caro, who'd seen it. 'Paid through the nose. Thought so.' She pulled the stirrup down. 'Come on then, Anna, hop up.'

Anna took the reins and Caro gave her a leg up.

'We'll take her in the sand school,' Caro went on. 'I'd have put Jack on her first, but they're not back from school yet, and—oh!'

Anything else she might have said was lost in the wind, as Molly, feeling Anna's weight on her back, charged out of the yard, snatching the reins from Caro's hand, heading for the wide open spaces.

'SIT UP!' roared Caro as Anna bounced around like a ball bearing in the saddle. 'Don't lean forward!'

We raced after her, my heart in my throat. 'Oh God,' I gasped, as Molly, spying ponies in the next field, rocketed full pelt towards all that kept her from their society: a four-foot hedge. How Anna stayed on, I'll never know, but as Molly soared through the air, she soared too, lost both her stirrups, but still landed with a thump in the saddle.

Meanwhile, to our right, behind another hedge, the school bus had stopped. Dozens of children's eyes widened in astonishment as they watched the rodeo show unfold, Anna's cousins among them. Molly was now precipitating down a bank in her determination to reach her new equine best friends, who, having encountered her already today, were unconvinced they wanted her company, and were cavorting round their field tossing their heads, necks arched, nostrils flared. Molly, perhaps believing this antipathy had something to do with her human baggage, gave an almighty buck, thus discharging Anna, and sending her flying through the air, landing with a bump on her bottom.

'ANNA!' I screamed.

Her cousins by now had descended the bus and were flying, horrified, across the field to the scene of the disaster. From different points of the compass we all arrived as one.

'Anna! Oh, darling, are you all right?' I flew to her side.

'NO!' she screamed.

She was in floods of tears, but even I could see that the alacrity with which she stood up and brushed herself down meant, thank God, only pride was bruised, and perhaps her bottom. I wrapped her in my arms and she sobbed piteously on my shoulder. She didn't think she had a pierced lung, as Phoebe helpfully suggested, or that her clavicle, which Henry insisted snapped like a wishbone, was impaired. We all fussed round her until, at length, her sobs turned to gulps. A suggestion of strong tea was made by Jack, and Anna nodded stoically, consenting to being led away to the house by her cousins.

'Put lots of sugar in it, Jack,' commanded his mother. 'I'll come in a minute but I need to sort this bloody horse out.'

'D'you want me to come too?' I called after them as they led her away, but Anna turned and shook her head vehemently.

'You flew that hedge,' Jack was saying to her, admiringly.

'I couldn't have sat it,' Phoebe agreed. 'I've been wanting to jump it for ages, but Mummy won't let me.'

I blessed them for bolstering her. Anna limped off, Caro strode up to Molly. She was quietly grazing nearby as if butter wouldn't melt, and consented to having her reins seized without a murmur.

'This is *not* a first pony!' she seethed. 'I can't believe you bought her!'

'When we saw her she was as quiet as a lamb, so docile!' I wailed.

'Drugged,' snapped Caro.

'No!' I breathed, shocked.

'Quite probably.' She led Molly back towards the stables. I stumbled after her. 'And this mare'—she stopped abruptly to stick her thumb in the side of Molly's mouth and peer in—'is four if she's a day. Brought over from Ireland and drugged to sell. It's disgraceful. We'll send her back immediately.'

When we got to the yard she threw Molly in a box. Then she whipped her mobile from her jeans pocket, and punched out a number. 'Mr Docherty? It's Caroline Milligan here.' And she was off. Giving it to him straight, and in no uncertain terms. Letting him know he was a liar, a thief, and that her sister-in-law's cheque must be returned immediately. This, Mr Docherty clearly declined to do, no doubt informing her in slow, undulating tones that the cheque had been cleared, the transaction made, the deal struck, with both parties seemingly satisfied.

But Caro wasn't finished. 'Except that this mare has been drugged,' she hissed. 'And unfortunately for you, it shat on my sister-in-law's foot, and that shit is still on that shoe, Mr Docherty, and I shall have it tested forthwith for traces of promazine.'

A surprised silence greeted this. Finally, Mr Docherty found his voice. A compromise of sorts was reached: Caro agreed she would return the horse to save him the effort, and he, in turn, would return the cheque. She snapped her phone shut with a satisfied click.

'How did you know about the shoe?' I yelped.

'Anna told me. Together with a hysterical account of you feeling fetlocks and attempting to buy a horse unridden. No malice intended, of course.'

Of course, I thought, following her to the house. There never was.

The children were munching cake when we got to the kitchen. No plates, so crumbs everywhere, and trails of tea where they'd dripped one tea bag after another to the bin, like so many snails, along with pools of milk, which they were incapable of pouring without spilling. Caro pointed this out as she bustled round, putting the cake on a plate, wiping surfaces, admonishing her offspring. Anna's equilibrium had clearly returned, though, and she was laughing at Jack's impersonation of her face as she hit the ground. Then they all shuffled off to the play-room to watch interminable reruns of *Friends*.

Caro shut the door on them and put the kettle on the Aga for us.

'Look,' I said wearily, 'let's forget this pony business. Anna probably isn't quite up to owning one yet, and I can see it's going to be a lot of hassle for you. We'll go back to having lessons at the riding stables.'

'Nonsense,' said Caro, flicking through her address book. 'She's set her heart on it now. And anyway, you've promised.' She gave me a look that suggested *she* wasn't the sort of mother to go back on her word. 'You just went about it the wrong way, that's all. If only you'd listened to me in the first place, we wouldn't be in this mess. Ah, here we are. Camilla Gavin.'

Why did I let her talk to me like this? As if I was a child?

'Who's Camilla Gavin?' I asked meekly as she punched out a number.

'She's the ex-District Commissioner of our Pony Club. A terrifying woman, but she does have some terrific ponies. Pamela Martin told me she'd be happy to let one go out on loan.'

'On loan!' I perked up. 'You mean I don't even have to buy it?'

'No, but you have to look after it, scrupulously. It'll probably be quite old, so it'll feel the cold, and it's bound to be kept in. There'll be stables to muck out, rugs to change . . .'

'Oh, but that's marvellous. If I don't have to buy it—and yes, of course I'll look after it! I'm not working, after all . . .'

I ignored her pointed, 'Quite.'

'Excellent, Caro. Definitely ring her.'

'Which is precisely what I was going to do before you went charging off to Lenny the—Camilla? Camilla, it's Caroline Milligan here!'

I sank guiltily into my tea as her voice went up an octave. She whin-nied on in the secret language of horsy women, asking about laminitis, clipping, boxing, proficiency in traffic, but in the nicest possible way, of course, because this was clearly a woman Caro looked up to.

'Oh, he sounds *orfully* sweet!' she was saying in a voice she'd never used at school. 'Yes, I *do* remember, came second in the crorss-country!'

When had we become these two women? I wondered, as, phone still clamped to her ear, Caro wiped the sink. When had we stopped throwing away the washing-up? When did we start noticing the dripping tea bags, and when would they, our children, start noticing too, and become different people? Long may they drip, I thought vehemently, because if I found her so changed, how did she find me? Arrogant? Aloof? That seemed to be her constant theme.

As I listened to the gales of laughter coming from the playroom, I mourned our younger selves. When did Caro stop being the first person I'd go to in a crisis, the sort of crisis I had now? When did we stop borrowing each other's clothes, giggling over the Cathy and Claire page in *Jackie*, lying on the floor and doing up each other's jeans with the hook of a coat hanger?

'Oh, Camilla, I *know* he's a poppet . . . Well, that's *orfully* kind of you. Are you sure? Tack as well? . . . Golly, if you *could* pop him over . . . sooper!' Caro laughed down the phone. 'Well, mother's clueless, orbviously—haw haw!' Thanks, Caro. 'But daughter's mustard keen . . . Yes, *really* light hands . . . *Soo* sweet of you . . . Ya, you too. Toodle-oo!' My eye was twitching manically as she put the phone down with a decisive click. 'There. Sorted. She's bringing him over Saturday week and you can have him on a renewable yearly loan.'

'But why would someone do that? Why not just sell him?'

'Because she's attached to him and she doesn't want him falling into the wrong hands. Doesn't want someone like Lenny Docherty getting his hands on him and selling him for dog meat.'

Just then Tim limped in. It was a relief to see him.

'Evie! What a treat!' He swooped to kiss me. I beamed. Someone was pleased to see me.

'What's Lenny Docherty got his hands on now then?' he said.

'Nothing, happily. Evie bought a horse from him, but don't worry,' she added hastily, as he turned to look at me in horror, 'it's going back.'

'You bought a horse from Lenny the Liar?'

'Well, obviously I didn't *know* he was a liar.'

'Come on, Evie, he was dealing dodgy horses when you lived here—where have you been?'

His incredulity was quite hard to take, actually.

'Well, clearly on another planet,' I said with a fixed smile.

'Clearly! I can't believe you're so stupid sometimes.'

He sighed and left the room. I held it together until he was safely in the downstairs loo. And then burst into tears.

Caro was beside me in seconds, swooping to my side, astonished. 'Gracious, it's not that bad, it's only a pony!'

'I-it's not that,' I gulped, gasping for breath, 'it's e-e-everything!'

In another moment she'd kicked the kitchen door shut and had a chair pulled up beside me and an arm round my shoulders. 'Everything?'

Was it me, or was there a tremor of excitement in her voice?

'It's all such a mess, Caro! And I'm not supposed to talk about it but it all wells up inside me and sometimes I think I'm going to burst!' As I paused to wipe my face with the back of a trembling hand I saw her forehead furrow, genuinely concerned now.

'What?' she said anxiously. 'Is it Ant? Is he having an affair?'

I shook my head. 'No, he's not, but he was, did have one—well, a fling—and I just can't—just can't seem . . .' I dissolved again.

Caro swung me round to face her, both hands on my shoulders. 'He had an affair? Ant?' I could tell she was flabbergasted. Happily we heard the front door slam as Tim exited stage left. 'But—but that is *so* unbelievable! He's just not the type! When? Recently?'

'No,' I looked up; managed to confine myself to some hiccupy shuddering. 'No, years ago. Years and years ago, a month after we got engaged.' I felt terribly calm suddenly, having said it. And flat.

Her eyes roved back, rolling away the years, remembering. 'Oh, well, I suppose . . . I mean, an awful lot was going on then—'

She meant Neville. And it struck me that other people had wondered at us marrying so soon after, when I hadn't.

'It was probably just a flash in the pan. A sort of desperate last sowing of wild oats, before settling down for good.'

'It was. It was a one-night stand, with a barmaid.'

'Oh, well, there you are! What are you getting so upset about?'

'Caro, there's a child. She wrote to us, the other day. Said she wanted to get to know her father.'

She caught her breath. 'No! And he didn't know?'

'Had no idea! Why should he? A quick roll in the hay, never sees the girl again—why would he?'

There was a highly charged silence as Caro digested this. She didn't take her eyes off me. I watched them turn from horror to steel. Then: 'How do we know it's true? I mean, some barmaid from—where?'

'Sheffield.'

'Sheffield! Who gets up the duff, having slept with God knows how many men—'

'Exactly,' I said quickly. 'And sees Ant's picture on his latest book.'

'Is that how she—'

'Yes! Well, no. I don't *know*, for sure, but you can imagine—'

'Of course you can!' she agreed emphatically. 'God, you can just see it, can't you? A single mother and her daughter, scheming together, writing to him, some—some Sharon—'

'Stacey.'

'Stacey! Eh up, Stacey lass, let's see if we can't get soom brass outa him.'

'You think?' I said anxiously, loving her.

'Oh, for sure! Oh, this has scam written all *over* it, Evie.'

'That's what I thought. But, Caro,' I struggled with the bald facts, 'Ant doesn't see it like that. He thinks that she could be his, and if she is, well then, he wants to do the right thing. Wants to acknowledge her.'

'What, bring her into the family?' Caro squeaked.

Anyone would think we were the Windsors. 'Well, yes. Introduce her to Anna.' My face twitched involuntarily at this.

'Christmas, birthdays,' Caro breathed, a faraway look in her eye, as both of us, I know, had a mental vision of Christmas, which was always at the farm: everyone crowded in the dining room, next to Ant a dumpy, peroxide-blonde girl, a Myra Hindley lookalike, with hard, probing eyes, glinting as they eyed up the silver candlesticks, the crystal glasses. Caro's face darkened. 'Over my dead body!'

'That's what I thought,' I gulped. 'When Ant told me.' With that same steely determination.

'My dead body and yours too then,' she said grimly.

Later, when we'd both calmed down a bit, we walked round the garden, discussing DNA, the fraud squad, getting them arrested, maybe even a court order to stay away.

Tim approached, loping across the lawn towards us.

'Don't tell him,' hissed Caro. 'He'll look on the bright side.'

It was true, he would. And would probably agree with Ant that she deserved to be heard. He looked a bit sheepish. 'Sorry, Evie.'

'What?'

'About the horse. I was a bit . . . you know.'

'Oh! Oh God, don't be silly, Tim. Couldn't matter less. Anyway, I deserved it. I'm a fool. Always have been.'

'No, that's my province.' He grinned and limped off.

I wondered vaguely what he meant by that as he ambled away. 'His hip doesn't look great,' I said.

'Never does at this time of day. He's been on it too long. I keep telling him to rest it, but he won't. But it is getting better.'

I nodded. 'And he's fit?'

'Oh God, is he? Strong as an ox. Hasn't deterred him in the bedroom, either. There was I thinking, oh joy, three months off games, but not a bit of it. The moment he was out of hospital he was chasing me round the bedroom on crutches. We became very familiar with "SPOD".'

'SPOD?'

'"Sexual Problems of the Disabled", a little booklet they helpfully provide you with when you leave hospital, complete with illustrations. I tell you, there are positions in that book you wouldn't attempt if you were able-bodied, let alone disabled. Made my eyes water.'

I giggled.

'I keep reading articles about men being too stressed and exhausted to make love to their wives,' she went on, 'and here I am, with the most stressed-out, exhausted hop-along cripple imaginable, who *still* wants to try the illustration on page thirty-two!'

I laughed. 'You'd be worried if he didn't.'

'I expect you're right. And Ant's the same, isn't he?'

''Fraid so,' I said, forcing a smile. I felt sick at his name, and she saw and squeezed my arm. But it wasn't just that. Ant wasn't the same, these days. This was all such a shock, of course. Put us off our stride.

Nevertheless, when Anna and I left the farm, and when I'd dropped Anna off at her piano lesson, it was still on my mind and I found myself heading to Marks and Spencer. Up the escalator I glided, then into the requisite department. I hovered there, in Lingerie, fingering the white cotton briefs, but secretly eyeing up the black silk on the next rack. Occasionally I bought a pretty bra, but never anything overtly sexy, *certainly* never black, which I somehow associated with sin. A bit grubby. But . . . men liked that, didn't they? I took a deep breath.

Half an hour later, back in the safety of my bedroom, and feeling like a tramp and a whore rolled into one, I took the black lacy bra and knickers—with red bows on, for God's sake—from the bag. Too much. What would Ant say? Well, he'd love them, of course he would. And it was only M&S, not Ann Summers. Oh—and a suspender belt. I'd never in my life worn one before. I whipped off my clothes and put my new purchases on; didn't actually know how to put the suspender belt on. Oh, round the waist? Really?

I tiptoed furtively to the mirror that faced the end of the bed. Stared. How extraordinary. I looked completely different. Like, well, like a woman in a magazine! Lordy. And my flesh looked so . . . wanton.

'Hi!' Up the stairs.

Christ! He was home. And six in the evening was not the moment. I threw on a wraparound dress and was just tying it up as he came in. 'Hello, darling!' I said overbrightly.

'Hi.' He seemed almost not to notice me.

'Ant? What's wrong?' My mouth dried.

'Nothing.' Flatly. 'No, nothing's wrong. It's just she—Stacey . . .' he paused to let the requisite shock waves rip through me at her name, 'she emailed me. She's going to come. One Sunday.'

'She . . . emailed you?'

'Yes. We have done that, once or twice. Quicker, obviously.'

'Obviously.' Except I didn't know. Didn't know she had his email address. I knew he had hers. My heart quickened.

'She got mine from the college. Left me a message. I had to answer it.'

'Of course. Did she say which Sunday?'

'No. Just . . . sometime soon.' He took my hand. Deadly serious. 'Evie, you know what this means. If she's coming, we have to tell Anna.'

Do we? my head shrieked. Why can't we just tell her to sod off?

'Yes,' I agreed.

'And, Evie.' He swallowed. 'I'd like to do it, if you don't mind. Alone. I'd like to . . . explain to her in my own way.'

Without me. I was to be excluded. Why? What did he want to say to her that he couldn't say to me? Didn't want me to hear?

'But, Ant,' I licked my lips, 'surely this is all going much too fast? We don't know anything yet. Don't even know if she's yours!'

'Oh, she's mine, all right,' he said quietly.

4

'HOW DO YOU KNOW?' I felt faint with fear, light-headed.

'Evie . . . I haven't been entirely straight with you.'

Oh God. 'You mean . . . it went on much longer?' I whispered.

'No.' He looked surprised. 'No, it only happened once. But . . . she wasn't a barmaid. She was working in the pub, yes, for a few weeks, for a bit of pocket money, but . . .' He paused. 'She was a student.'

'One of yours?'

'Yes.'

Not a barmaid. One of his students. Clever. An Oxford undergraduate, the kind of liaison he'd always, *always* frowned on.

'How old?' I croaked.

'Eighteen. She was in my English poetry group, so I saw her—obviously in lectures—but on a one-to-one basis too, in tutorials. And that was her special interest, nineteenth-century poetry. The Romantic Poets. Byron in particular.'

Byron. His speciality. A shared interest. 'Very bright?' I whispered.

'Yes. Very clever.'

That hurt. Oh, that hurt. And there I'd been, pedalling round Oxford on a bicycle pretending to be clever.

'Pretty?'

He looked at his feet. Silly question. Gorgeous. Your worst nightmare, Evie. Ten years younger, razor sharp, drop-dead gorgeous.

'Don't answer that,' I snarled. I fought for breath. Then composure. 'What happened? How did it . . .?'

He made a helpless gesture. 'How do these things happen? Slowly. Imperceptibly. It was all . . . so unspoken. So . . . pure.'

I nearly vomited; put my hand to my mouth.

'I noticed her quite soon. It would take a very unobservant teacher not to. She stood out. But not in an obvious, Hedda Gabler way . . .'

I pressed my nails into my palms. Always the literary allusions. He knew I didn't know who the sodding hell Hedda Gabler was.

'More in a Jade Goody sort of way?' I snapped.

He frowned. 'Who?'

'Forget it,' I muttered. 'Go on.'

'Well, as I say, nothing happened. Nothing tangible. It was just . . . well, I realised I looked forward to our tutorials. I found myself poring over her essays, marvelling that her interpretation was so like mine . . . And sometimes, in lectures, I'd find myself just looking at her, directing the lecture at her, embarrassingly. In tutorials, I had to sit a long way away from her, over by the window, looking out at the quad to concentrate. And then when we walked to lunch, sometimes our arms would brush together and I'd feel—'

'Yes, I get the picture, Ant!' I shrieked. 'You fancied her!' For an intelligent man he was remarkably stupid.

'It wasn't like that. I mean, I didn't just feel a sexual desire—that's what I'm trying to explain. What I felt more, was . . .'

Oh, *Ant*. I shut my eyes. Spare me. Spare me Love. He didn't even know the word he was grappling for. 'Something more cerebral?'

'Yes.' He looked at me, surprised. 'Yes, that was it.'

No, Ant. No, it wasn't.

'I . . . couldn't stop thinking about her. I knew it was wrong, dreadful. She was so young, so impressionable.'

I felt prickly with sweat. 'Why didn't you break up with me?'

He hung his head. 'I meant to tell you. To be honest with you. Not to break up with you. After all, I knew it was hopeless. She was a student.'

'So you kept your options open. You couldn't have her, so—hey, let's just stick it out with good old Evie.'

'No! No, Evie, I loved you. We were so good together, *are* good together. I knew this was just a passing infatuation, I tried to put her from my mind. And once I did try to tell you about it.' He looked at me, pleadingly. 'At the farm. In bed that afternoon, just before—'

'Yes, yes, I know.' That terrible day. Minutes before Neville Carter had drowned. *Evie . . . there's something I've got to tell you.*

I went to the window in our bedroom, the pretty little one, like a porthole, with the circle of stained glass in the middle. My arms were folded tightly round me as I gazed out to the street.

'And then, when Neville died . . .' Ant paused.

'You felt you owed it to me? To marry me?'

'No, of *course* not, Evie. But we were so . . . so in it together. And suddenly, what I felt for—for Stacey's mother—seemed so frivolous, in the light of what had happened. It felt so wrong. I'd elevated it in my mind to something courtly and noble, and all at once it became . . . fancying a student. Suddenly I was the sort of man who let children drown while I shagged my girlfriend—oh, and meanwhile, lusted after my pupils. It was a wake-up call.' He began to blink rapidly. 'But I didn't just marry you because it was the right thing to do, Evie. I married you because I loved you, and realised I'd been temporarily diverted.'

I stared at him. He clearly believed that. I didn't, but he did.

I swallowed. 'OK, Ant. Canter me through the next bit.'

'You and I got engaged, and then a few weeks later I went out for a drink one night. I ended up at the King's Head.'

'Did you know she was working there?'

'Yes.'

'And you stayed till closing time and walked her home?'

'Yes.'

'And it was a mild night and you walked down by the river, past Magdalen Bridge . . .' I breathed in deeply. 'You felt trapped. You felt you were getting married out of force of circumstance, and you felt you had unfinished business and you finished it, in a field.'

He hung his head.

'Did you feel it was finished, Ant? Is that why you never saw her again?'

'I . . . yes. I felt terrible. Worse. So I decided—we, decided, we talked about it—that that was it. I switched my tutorial with her and she stopped taking my lectures. Changed to Metaphysical Poets. And then a few weeks later, she just wasn't there any more. I asked another student, a friend of hers, casually, in the cloisters one day, and was told she'd gone home. Was homesick, or something, thought Oxford was too much for her. I hoped she'd transferred to a northern university.'

'And you never checked? Never found out?'

'No.'

'And have you thought about her since?'

'No!' He turned, almost frightened. His eyes were wide, pleading. 'I mean, once or twice, obviously, but no, I've been happily married to you, Evie, ever since.'

I walked back to the bed. My legs were a bit wobbly. I needed to sit down. 'What was her name, Ant?'

As I said it, I saw something pass across his eyes. Something wary.

'Isabella,' he whispered. 'Her name is Isabella.'

I flinched as if I'd been struck. I stared at him, horrified.

'Isabella? Anna *Isabella*? You called our *child* after her?'

'Evie, look. It wasn't like that. I just liked the name, I . . .'

I needed something to throw. I picked up the first thing that came to hand. A jar of moisturiser, as it happened. L'Oréal, because I'm worth it. I hurled it at his head. Happily he saw it coming, ducked, and it went flying through the window behind him with a spectacular smash, glass flying everywhere, sailing out to the empty street below.

I wasn't far behind. Not through the window, obviously, but seizing my bag and my car keys from a chair, I ran from the room, down the stairs and into the front hall, just as Anna, who'd walked back from her piano lesson, was coming up the stairs from the kitchen, having come in via the back door. She gazed at me, astonished.

'What's wrong?'

'Ask your father!' I snarled. I exited via the front door.

Outside in the street I stood for a second on the pavement, holding my head. I had to, actually: thought it might come off. Anna *Isabella*. How dare he? Furious, I hastened to my car and flung myself inside. I wrenched the gear stick into reverse and shot backwards, too fast, into another car. Shit. Sweat breaking out in beads all over, I leapt out to assess the damage. Not much, a dent to mine and a tiny one to his, but only the bumper. I bent down and tried to rub the scratch off the one behind. Bugger. Bit worse. Best left, Evie. I turned to scurry back to my car, but my way was barred by a dark-haired man. He looked like that football manager, José whatsisname, and just as furious.

'Is this yours?' He held up a piece of broken china pot.

'Oh. Yes, where did you—'

'On the back seat of my car. It smashed through the rear window.'

'No! Oh, how *awful*.' I swung round to scan the cars in the street. 'I'm *so* sorry, which car?'

'That one, behind you. The one you've just reversed into.' He pointed, green eyes blazing, to what I now realised, when I wasn't looking just at the bumper, was really rather a smart locomotive. Slightly old-fashioned—perhaps classic was the word I was groping for—and very sleek. Only not so sleek now, with a huge gaping hole in the back window, glass and cream all over the back seat.

'Oh Lord. I—I'm terribly sorry,' I faltered, appalled. 'You see I was having an argument, and I threw the pot, and—'

'You could have killed someone!' he spluttered.

I swallowed. 'Yes. And I'm really very sorry. It's not like me at all. You see, my husband and I had a row and—'

'I couldn't care less about your squalid domestic violence,' he spat. 'What does concern me is my bloody car!'

I drew myself up to my full five foot three. 'We do *not* indulge in domestic violence. My husband and I are civilised people—'

'If he was the Archbishop of Canterbury I couldn't be less interested. Just get your insurance details, right now, lady.'

'Ooh . . . there is *no* need—' I stopped. Those green eyes were quite intimidating. Rattled, I turned and hastened to my car. I rifled in the glove compartment and found the relevant bits of paper. I wrote it all down on the flap of an envelope, marched back and handed it to him.

'You'll be hearing from me,' he snapped.

'Can't wait,' I snapped in reply, matching him now, glare for glare. I stalked to my car. As I started the engine, I realised my wraparound dress had unwrapped itself. I'd been trading insults with him with one black bra cup showing and half a pair of pants with red bows cheekily on display. *Bugger*. I lifted my bottom from the seat to rewrap my dress and my foot slipped off the clutch. The car stalled, lurched forward and into the one in front. *Shit*. I froze, horrified. Oh, thank the Lord, it was Ant's. Feeling hot and fumbly now, I rearranged my dress and restarted the car, but as I glanced in the rearview mirror, Green Eyes was watching me. I buzzed down my window and stuck my head out. 'It's *my* car, *actually*, so mind your own business, OK?'

He shook his head in naked disbelief. I childishly stuck my tongue out, then I faced front and shot off, kangarooing elegantly out of my space and into the traffic, narrowly missing a car coming up behind me.

Bloody man, I seethed as a horn blared angrily in my wake. Yes, and you can sod off too. I glanced in the mirror to check the first one was out of sight. Yes. Good. I took a deep, shaky breath, and as I did, he and his poxy car shuffled right down my deck of worry cards and instead, my debacle with Ant shuffled effortlessly to the top. 'Oooh . . .' I shrank down in my seat and exhaled at the wheel. This was all getting far too horrible. *Far* too horrible. He'd felt trapped. Felt he had to marry me. And all the time, all the time he'd been in love with someone else. Someone younger, clever, beautiful . . . Someone, who perhaps he'd have pursued, married even, if it hadn't been for Neville.

A few spots of rain splattered the windscreen. I gazed numbly through them into the traffic. No. No, you're wrong, Evie. You're over-reacting. There's nothing to say he would have even gone out with her. And anyway, it was *years* ago. Move on. It's history. Except . . . it wasn't. Not when there was a child. Living proof. This would never go away, never. They'd always be with me, this Isabella—I almost retched—and her daughter, Stacey, and somehow I felt it was my fault. That God was punishing me for forcing Ant's hand.

I was heading, I realised, towards the ring road. I was instinctively going home, to the farm, which, even after all these years, I knew I still regarded as such. I swung the car all the way round the next round-about and headed back. I couldn't go to the farm. Couldn't tell Caro this. And I couldn't go home, either. Ant would be telling Anna. And she'd be horrified—a *sister*? He'd have to deal with the fallout. My heart ached for her, but I also knew, if I was there, I'd make it worse. I'd scream too, point a finger, shout—*your bloody father!* In my heart I knew that Ant could make it—if not better—as good as it could be. I had to let him try, at any rate. We owed that to Anna.

So this was where I'd go, I thought suddenly. I swung a sharp right, amid another blare of horns, past the University Press and carried on, turning into one of the side streets. The familiar winding road, with its charming crooked houses and shopfronts painted every colour of the rainbow, soothed me. I felt my bones relax as I swung into a cobbled yard at the back of one particular shop.

The sign on the familiar glass door said CLOSED but I knew better, and as I pushed on through I felt I'd come home.

'Oh Lordy be. What brings you here, flower? When you've been avoiding your old friends previously.'

I forced a smile and shut the door behind me. The lights were off, so the shop was in comparative darkness, but I could just make out the owner of the voice through the open door at the back. He was sitting in his office, legs propped up on the desk, peering at me over his glasses, a book he'd been reading, by the light of an Anglepoise, in his hand.

'Not avoiding, Malcolm. Just pressures of life, really.'

'Call it what you will.' He swung his legs down and got up to greet me. 'I'm impervious to snubs, as you know. Notoriously thick-skinned.'

I smiled again at this blatant lie. Cinders, Malcolm's aged golden retriever, thumped her tail in greeting on the floor as I passed, and as her master held out his arms, I stumbled the last few steps into them, managing to knock his glasses off.

'Oops, careful, hon. These are my three ninety-nine specials from Boots—Oh, what's *wrong*, sausage!'

At this point, and in all probability due to the lovely hug he'd just given me, I collapsed on Malcolm's shoulder, soaking his Thomas Pink.

'*Well*,' he said emphatically later—ten minutes or so later, in fact— patting my hand as he put the mug of strong, sweet tea he'd made in front of me. 'Well. I can see that it's a *shock*, my sweet, yes. But this is the worst it'll get, I guarantee. It won't get any more dramatic than this.'

'You don't think?' I gulped, installed now in his leather chair.

'No,' he consoled, shaking his head as he perched on the edge of his desk beside me. 'She won't impinge on your life. Oh, initially, of course, and out of interest—who wouldn't?—but she'll have her own life. She's not suddenly going to decamp and live with you, is she?'

'I suppose not,' I said uncertainly.

'You're imagining the worst. Thinking that life as you know it is over. That the whole cosy Ant, Evie, Anna bit . . .'

'Yes!' I wailed.

'. . . is shot to bits, and it's not. And how much better that she's not some grasping tart's offspring, but that of an educated woman? Not some trashy bairn turning up on your doorstep demanding money?'

'I suppose,' I agreed doubtfully. 'Bit more of a threat, though.'

'Is that what you're worried about?' Malcolm said kindly. 'That just as you would have felt threatened by her mother seventeen years ago, you'd feel threatened by her daughter now?'

I nodded mutely, damp eyes trained on lap.

'You've got your own smart, pretty daughter, chicken,' he chided.

'Yes. I suppose. So it's just me, then, who's not. I'm the odd one out.'

I glanced up quickly, then back into my lap, but with time enough to see his fine, sculpted features, which were still delicate and arresting, but these days fretted with fine lines, looking anxiously at me.

'Evie, Ant loves you for what you are. For who you are. You've got to stop living your life wishing you were someone else.'

I sneaked a look into those wise grey eyes. 'You're right,' I conceded, and I knew he was. I was the one with the problem, the one who felt I wouldn't match up.

'He *loves* you, Evie, you know that. You don't doubt that, do you?'

'No.'

'Well, then.'

A silence descended as we sat there together in his little back room. At length, Malcolm shifted off the desk and slipped into the other leather chair opposite me, while I sat in Jean's chair. We still felt it was Jean's, Malcolm and I. Jean's room. In those days the walls had been relentlessly magnolia; Malcolm had painted them a smart navy blue, added a few choice pieces of furniture.

He broke the silence: 'You've got the love of a good man, Evie, even if it does come with complications. Hang on to it. Spare Ant your righteous indignation. He made a mistake. There were consequences. He has to deal with it. Help him. Don't fight him.'

I swallowed. He was right. As he usually bloody well was. And I'd do that, I determined, when I got home. Later. I'd let Ant talk to Anna, and then I'd help too. We'd sit down as a family. Talk about it.

'And maybe,' I blurted out, 'well, maybe Stacey and Isabella could become our friends? Maybe we could all help each other?'

'Easy, tiger,' said Malcolm nervously. 'There's a way to go before you're all holding hands and heading off to Center Parcs together.'

I nodded, but I felt happier. I took a deep breath, looked around properly. 'You've bought a new computer.'

He scratched his head sheepishly. 'Had to, really. You've got to move with the times, haven't you?'

I blinked. Malcolm was usually a Luddite, like me. I frowned and peered into the main body of the shop, which was almost, but not quite in darkness now, the low summer sun just making it through the bow window and glancing off the books on the top shelves. 'Something's happened out there too,' I said suspiciously. A new carpet, I realised, had been laid, and the wall space above the shelves was now a rich dark red, not Malcolm's usual navy blue. It made a nice change. 'You'll be competing with Poo-Face soon. His walls look a bit like that, don't they? How is he, anyway?'

Poo-Face was Malcolm's arch rival: an ex-media type who, a year ago, had bought the toy shop next door and turned it into a bookshop. It had had Malcolm spitting tacks. 'Next door! Direct competition!'

'Calm down, Malcolm, it's not competition. It's different.'

It was, in fact, completely different. I knew because I'd popped in to do the recce. The new shop specialised in military history, with none of the paperback chart toppers or thrillers that Malcolm stocked in copious, gaudy numbers as he tried, desperately, to compete with the giants roaring at him in the High Street. It was run by a man who I'd never met, having only encountered an assistant, but whom Malcolm had christened Poo-Face, on account of the nasty smell under his nose.

'What?' Malcolm glanced up from thumbing distractedly through a new Frederick Forsyth as I strolled off to look.

'I said, how's Poo-Face?'

'Oh . . . he's not so bad, actually.' I turned back to stare at him. He scratched his chin. 'We've . . . well, we've sort of joined forces.'

'Really?' I frowned. 'Merged?'

'Yes. Did you not notice as you came in?'

I glanced back round, went quickly to the front room, where, I suddenly realised, to my left there was a bloody great hole. An archway had been cut in the dividing wall, which, in my frantic, snivelling state, I'd failed to notice as I'd hurried past. And the new carpet swept right on through into next door. 'Oh!' I yelped in alarm. Jumped back into Malcolm's patch. 'Malcolm, I don't believe it!'

'I had to, Evie.' He'd got up to join me now. 'Those huge chains with their massive discounts—I simply couldn't compete. He approached me one day, asked me to have lunch.'

'No!'

'He put a proposal to me and here we are. My highly commercial shop with a children's section and cards and wrapping paper, and his highly intellectual one with History, Art and Philosophy.'

'And?' I was agog.

'And . . .' he said cautiously, 'if last month's takings are anything to go by, it works. I've got my loyal customers and he's got his, but when they've got their new Napoleon biography, they pop in here for something for the wife. A Joanna Trollope, maybe. My clients go in there for their dads on Father's Day.' He shrugged. 'So far so good.'

'Crikey.' I was astonished. 'Oh, Malcolm, I'm thrilled.' I know the last time I'd been in, which was a couple of months ago, he'd been worried sick. It must have been just before he was approached.

'So what's he like?' I asked, gripped. 'I mean—d'you get on?'

'He's rather attractive, actually.'

'Oh—is he . . .?'

'No, no, dead hetero. I just meant easy on the eye. And he's not nearly as arrogant as I thought.' His mobile rang. He drew it out of his jeans pocket and looked at it. 'Talk of the devil. He's supposed to be relieving me tonight—in the nicest possible way. We're stock-taking, and the shop is closed, but I'm allowed out. Got a date.'

'*Have* you? Oh, Malcolm, *good*. I'm so pleased. Anyone nice?'

'D'you know how much like a mother you sound? Hang on.' He was reading a text. Suddenly he threw back his head and laughed.

'Says he'll be here in a mo. Apparently he got held up by some middle-aged tart in Miss Whiplash knickers who threw a jar of sexual lubricant at him she was so desperate. Oh, here he is now.'

I glanced round in horror as the door opened, and pocketing his mobile, in swept Green Eyes. I gaped. 'Oh God.'

His face darkened as he registered me. 'Jesus.'

Malcolm raised his eyebrows. 'Shall I invoke the Holy Ghost?' He glanced at me, then back at him. 'You two know each other?'

'I'll have you know,' I seethed, 'that my underwear, up until today, has never been anything other than snowy white and my *moisturising* cream has never been used for anything other than lubricating my face!'

'Then you've got problems,' he drawled. 'A cross-Channel swimmer would be pleased with the level of heavy-duty emollient you sport.'

'Oh!' My jaw dropped. 'How dare you?'

'I dare because I've just scraped it off the back seat of my car.'

'Whoa, whoa!' Malcolm sprang between us, palms up, like a referee between a couple of prize fighters. 'Easy there, Evie. Steady, Ludo. Now *clearly* something untoward has gone on here and you two have got off on the wrong foot, but there's no need to—'

'I'll say it's the wrong foot, and the wrong side of two hundred pounds to clean the upholstery too, which I'll charge you for.'

'For a bit of cream on the seat? Oh, you stupid, pathetic man with your stupid penis extension.'

'Evie!' Malcolm's eyes were thunderous now. 'She's not been well,' he explained nervously as he hustled me to the door. 'Family troubles.'

Once outside in the fresh air, I held my head again. 'Oh God.' I shut my eyes. When I opened them, Malcolm had lit a cigarette for me.

'I've given up.'

'It's like riding a bike. Just suck.'

I did. After a few drags, it all came flooding back. Heaven.

'Sorry,' I muttered again. 'So sorry, Malc. The thing is, I've got all men in the same category at the moment.'

I handed him back the cigarette. He took a deep drag. 'Go home, poppet. Go home to Ant and Anna and make it work, hm?'

As I drove home, I thought about what Malcolm had said. Don't blow it, Evie, I urged myself, you're very close to the edge right now.

Back at the house, all was quiet. Ominously quiet, I thought, as I shut the front door softly behind me. No teenage daughter throwing the contents of her bedroom down the stairs and herself after it, gathering it all in her arms and slamming out of the front door. But wait: soft music from the drawing room. I pushed open the door.

Ant was sitting by the window in semidarkness as he listened to Mahler's Second Symphony. The saddest. He looked up and gave a wan smile as I came in. 'Hi.'

'Hi.' I stole across the room and slipped in beside him on the sofa. He put his arm round my shoulders. I felt every fibre in my being relax; begin to hum with relief. I felt so safe. I laid my head on his chest.

'How was it?' I whispered into his blue checked shirt.

'Averagely ghastly. Her father is the devil incarnate. Either that or Don Juan. Apparently I've ruined her life.' His voice quavered.

I sat up. I knew I had to be strong. 'That's just shock talking, darling. She feels as if, all the time, something's been going on behind her back. And she feels betrayed. She's bound to be frightened too, because she thinks everything will change, but it won't. Initially she'll have to adjust to this person actually existing, but her life, our life, will go on the same as ever. Me, you and Anna.'

'Who have you been talking to?'

'Malcolm.'

He smiled. 'Good old Malcolm.' He sighed. 'Let's hope he's right.'

'Where is she?'

'In her room.'

'I'll go and see her. This is a big shock,' I promised him. 'Give her time. She'll come round.'

'Have you?' His eyes, when they found mine, were vulnerable.

I swallowed. 'I'm getting there.'

I went upstairs and knocked on her door. 'Anna? Can I come in?'

There was a rustle within. After a moment, a piece of paper came under the door: *I don't want to talk about it.*

I went to my room and found a pen. *Not even to me?* I wrote back.

Especially not to you, came back the missive.

Oh. Right. I could feel myself bridling involuntarily. Why especially not to me? What the hell did I have to do with it? Anger and resentment, which I'd so painstakingly quelled for the last half-hour or so, resurfaced. After a moment, I gave myself a little shake, went through to the bathroom. I turned the bath taps on full and reached for a bottle, shaking in a good dollop of Chanel bath oil. Oh—and what about these? I took a box from the cupboard. Candles. I was bemused that so many of my girl friends gave me them as gifts, but they obviously used them. When? I'd asked once. Oh, in the bath, with all the lights out. Oh. Right. Why? Well, to relax. Ah. It seemed a bit cheesy to me: something Mum might do. But while the bath ran, I lit the candles. Golly. Just *lighting* them was soothing. Perhaps there was something in this.

I padded back into the bedroom for the radio and fiddled around for some soft music. I *would* be soothed. The bath was well back from the French window and I left the curtains open. Lit some more candles, then turned James Blunt up, so that what with his crooning and the roar of the taps, I didn't hear Anna come in.

'Oh! Darling.' She looked around the flickering room, surprised. Her face was pale; tear-stained.

'What are you doing?'

'Just trying to relax. Get some karma. Like you always tell me.'

'Oh. Right.' She put the loo lid down and sat on it heavily. 'I'm not going to meet her,' she said in a cracked, defiant voice to the carpet.

'You don't have to, darling.' I swooped to hug her, but she quickly turned a rigid shoulder to me. I perched on the edge of the bath.

'Then why did he bloody well tell me?' she cried, looking up.

'Because you had to know, my sweet. We all had to know.'

She stared at me. Her eyes were bright, anguished. 'The whole thing is just gross. And I mean—what will my friends say? If I suddenly produce this—this *sister*, called *Stacey*, from nowhere? Who talks differently to me, *looks* different to me, all crop tops and piercings.' She was conveniently forgetting she'd wanted her ears done. 'What do I say?' she wailed. 'Oh, this is my father's love child. I can't bear it!'

'That won't happen,' I said quickly. 'You don't have to meet her.'

'I just feel so jealous,' she whispered, 'even though I've never met her,' she gazed down at the carpet again, 'that he's got someone else. It must be awful for you, Mum,' she quavered. 'You were engaged.'

Ah. Right. I could see she thought this a terrible betrayal. And yet, frankly, if it hadn't been for the circumstances, for Ant feeling pressurised by Neville, that bit wouldn't bother me. Oh, initially, yes, but I rather agreed with Caro; once I'd got over the shock I'd think—well heavens, it was a long time ago and OK, we were engaged but we weren't married and an awful lot of water has flowed in seventeen years. But in a scrupulous, fourteen-year-old mind, being engaged, or even going out with someone and cheating on them was a terrible treachery. Her eyes filled for me, for what she saw as my pain, and I took advantage of it: in that moment, I knew I could reach her. I swooped to hold her and she clung to me as I folded her in my arms.

'It's fine,' I whispered into her sweet-smelling blonde hair. 'Imagine this from her point of view. Here we are, this well-off, educated Oxford family, and there she is, an outsider, looking in.'

'Which is where I want her to stay,' she said harshly. 'Looking in. It's all because he's written a book, I bet! Just because he's well known, she wants to meet him!'

This wasn't my Anna talking. She was upset. And yet I'd felt the same.

'And I don't feel I know Daddy at all now,' she blurted, getting up and turning round to face the street, arms tightly folded. 'Don't feel I know this man who gets students pregnant. I mean, God, it could be one of *my* friends in a couple of years' time. It's so debauched of him!'

'He was young,' I soothed, hating that she thought of him so. I turned to switch off the taps, wearily untying my dress, slipping it off.

'Youngish. Thirty, *and* he was engaged—' She turned. 'Bloody hell.'

'What?'

She was staring at me. 'What are you wearing?'

'Oh!' I grabbed a towel. I'd forgotten about the underwear. 'Just something I . . . threw on. I was feeling a little insecure in the light of your father's revelation. Felt like—looking attractive.'

She reached out and yanked my towel away. 'It's sad,' she said. 'You look minging. Like a singing telegram.' She turned the light on to get a better look. 'Where did you get it, Ann Summers?'

'Certainly not. Darling, turn the light off, the curtains are open.'

'No, Mum, you need to look at yourself.' She took my shoulders and swung me round to the full-length mirror. 'You need a reality check.'

'Turn it off!'

I wriggled out of her grip and lunged for the light cord, but she got there first, holding it out of my reach. I hastened to draw the curtains, and as I reached up to grab them both, hands outstretched, I saw a man across the street turn before he put his key in his front door. I whipped the curtains together smartly, but not before I'd caught the unmistakable features of Poo-Face, and the astonishment in his eyes.

I spun round flat against the wall. Oh dear God. Here I was in my knickers again. I shut my eyes and gave a little moan. Anna, flicking me a last withering look, flounced out. 'Arrgh!' In a few swift motions I had ripped off the hateful garments and jumped in the bath.

So what? So flaming what? I sank down under the bubbles. In the scheme of things, that unpleasant man couldn't matter less. What *did* matter, right now, was keeping my family together. Being strong when they needed me. What was that Kipling quote? If you can be strong when all around you de da de da . . . keep your head when something

something . . . then you'll be a man, my son. OK, not entirely appropriate, but still. I squared my shoulders in the bath. I could be a woman. More like a tigress, perhaps. What was that other one? About the tiger? Burning bright, in the something of the night. Blimey, I could do this; throw out literary allusions if I felt like it. Perhaps because I *felt* like a tigress in the face of someone threatening my brood.

Days passed. Ant was quiet and withdrawn, while Anna bolshed around defiant, not speaking to her father. We coexisted, the three of us, albeit rather tensely, but after a few days, less tensely, I thought.

I overheard them talking at breakfast one morning, Ant tentatively suggesting a choral concert in Christ Church Cathedral that evening. I was ironing in the utility room next door. I heard Anna mumble noncommittally, but at least answer him, which she hadn't done for days. I strained to hear more, wondering if I dared hope for some thawing. Because, if so, now was the time to execute my plan.

To my astonishment they did go to the concert together—an early one, six o'clock—and when they returned, and Anna had gone to do her homework, I cornered my husband, back in the utility room.

'Ant, I have a plan,' I said quickly, shutting the door behind us.

'Oh?'

'Yes. What I thought was, we need to face this head-on, don't we? It's no good pretending it doesn't exist. That . . . Stacey . . . doesn't exist, so instead of waiting for her to call,' which obviously I was, jumping whenever the telephone rang, 'I've decided we should invite her here, properly. Ask her to tea or something, to meet the three of us.' I beamed. 'I've written to her.'

His eyes widened.

'Oh, no, I haven't sent it,' I said quickly. 'I wouldn't do that, not without consulting you. But don't you think it's a good idea, darling? To—you know—confront our demons?'

'I don't think of Stacey as a demon,' he said slowly, 'but I came to the same conclusion. We shouldn't just wait for her to appear, we should invite her. I've emailed her. She's coming tomorrow.'

'Oh!' Tomorrow. And he hadn't even told me. What would I wear? I can't *believe* I'd thought that. Tomorrow. 'You didn't tell me.'

'I was just about to. I only sent it today, on a whim, really. Before I knew it I'd pressed SEND. But she emailed straight back. We're meeting in Browns for lunch. Her mother's coming with her.'

'She's *not*!'

'She's only sixteen, Evie. She needs some moral support.'

'Yes,' I croaked. Blimey, what *would* I wear? 'What about Anna?'

'I asked her this evening as we walked to Christ Church. She wants to come—grudgingly.'

'You asked her before me?'

'Only because I had the opportunity; it's the first time she's talked to me for days. I was coming back to talk to you.'

'Oh. Right. So . . . five of us.' My head spun. 'I'd better book a table.'

He looked surprised. 'Well, four. I don't think . . . well, it wouldn't be appropriate, would it?' His eyes were kind, gentle.

It took me a moment. 'You mean . . . for me to come?'

'Well . . . Look at it from her point of view. She wants to meet her father and her sister. She needs her mother there. I don't think—'

'No, no, quite right.' I was surplus to requirements. They were all blood relatives. And I was hyperventilating. I gave an approximation of a smile, lips blurring, cheeks wobbling. 'Good plan. Good luck, darling.'

'You don't mind?' he asked, worried. 'That you won't be there?'

'Noo, not in the slightest. Blessed relief, actually. Oops, too much coffee on a middle-aged bladder. S'cuse me, darling, need the loo.'

And off I slipped, down the corridor, shutting the lavatory door behind me. This was all about making Stacey feel comfortable. What would I bring to the party?

I sat up and stared blankly ahead. Banks of framed photographs faced me by the loo door: Anna at prep school in her reception class, then in Year One, Year Two and Year Three. Ant had made me stop at that stage, pointing out, quite sensibly, that we'd need to extend the loo to accommodate every single year. So I'd restrained myself until this year, Year Nine, and now there was Anna in the netball team, Anna in the hockey team, Anna in the lacrosse team. There was also Ant at university, Ant in the cricket team. I either wasn't in any teams, or hadn't been to the sort of school that took photos and put them in frames. The latter, I think. There was even Ant as a fledgling don with his first lecture group. My heart began to beat fast. His first *lecture* group? I peered wildly at the names below. I'd never read them before—why would I? It took a few moments. But then I found her. Miss I. T. Edgeworth. Fourth name on the second row, so fourth face along . . . oh! That one. The doe-eyed blonde with the big smile. The beauty. Isabella, who'd been in my loo for—ooh, years now. Whom Ant probably looked at every day of his life and thought . . . what? What did he think?

My heart began to accelerate. I felt it a terrible betrayal. Ant had known she was here, among us, and I hadn't. Did he smile affectionately at her, wonder where she was? Or did he—and this sent my heart into overdrive—did he know where she was? Had he known all along?

Suddenly the blood surged to my head. In one deft movement I hoicked the picture off the wall and marched with it back to the kitchen. Ant had emerged from the utility room and was standing at the sink. I flung the photo down on the kitchen table.

'Take it to work,' I hissed. 'Put it in your loo there, look at it as you do your trousers up, or pull them down, but don't keep it here!'

And with that, fists clenched, and for the second time in not very many days, I slammed out of the house. I got in the car and drove off, too fast, and without my lights—*stupid* Evie, I flicked them on as someone flashed me—I went hot. What was I trying to do, kill myself? I slowed down. And when my phone rang, I pulled over to read the text. It was from Ant.

I won't go. We won't go. I love U more than anyone in the world, Evie. I'm just trying to do the right thing. Struggling to do the right thing. But if it means losing you I can't begin. Please come home. Ant x

I took a deep breath. Read it again. Then my thumb got to work.

Darling. I love U too which is why I'm behaving so badly. I'm scared. But of course you must go, with Anna. And Stacey must have her mother. I WILL get there. I WILL be fine. I just need time. Back soon. LOL Evie xxx

I sat there, in the dark, head back on the headrest, staring at the stars. All of us are in the gutter but some of us are looking at the stars. Blimey, another one. I'd say Chrissie Hynde, but Ant would laugh and say Oscar Wilde. I took a deep breath. Let it out. Was there something wrong with me? One minute I was offering tea and biscuits to Ant's daughter, the next I was hurling pictures. It was being wrongfooted that sparked me off. Thinking I was in control, and the next minute, knowing I was so patently out of the loop it sent me careering off track.

I drove through the city to the other side of town, past the Bodleian and New College, the mighty spires of Trinity looming over me. Usually I revelled in their majesty, but tonight I hated them. Hated Oxford. I hated the brains, the power; felt threatened. Suddenly I wished we lived in Streatham. Or Middlesbrough. Somewhere where I could saunter down the high street, swinging my Topshop handbag—somewhere where I belonged. Not here. I felt these buildings harboured people who were capable of remarkable harm. I felt Oxford and its inhabitants turn on me, their contorted, sneering faces leering aggressively, like some nightmarish Hieronymus Bosch painting.

And yet, and yet . . . I ducked down a tree-lined side street, then another, pulled up outside a familiar little house. Not this inhabitant.

Mum was wearing a lime-green jogging suit with a pink stripe down the side. The tangerine trainers clashed violently.

'Oh! Hello, love.' She was eating a Cadbury's Creme Egg and had some down her chin. She sucked her finger. 'What brings you here?'

'Can't a girl pay an impulse visit on her mother without getting the third degree?' I regretted it the moment I'd said it. Always the confrontation. I could see her back go up as I followed her down the hall.

'Of course she can, but these days it's increasingly rare, that's why I asked.' She stalked into the sitting room. I followed.

'Sorry, Mum,' I said meekly. 'Sometimes my mouth says things my brain has absolutely no idea about. I didn't even mean it. How's things?'

I sat down heavily. A dogeared paperback was spread-eagled on the arm of the sofa. I picked it up. 'Good book?'

'Terrific. Mavis Brian's latest. You should read it, you'd love it.'

It occurred to me that I would. I glanced at the title. *The Miller's Child*. All clogs and shawls and smouldering romance. Years ago I'd have devoured it, reading one after the other that Mum passed on to me: sagas, historical romances. But then, I maintained, my tastes had changed; become more literary. Not like Ant, of course, not Chekhov—but certainly Jane Austen instead of Georgette Heyer. It occurred to me I didn't read for pleasure any more. I read to better myself.

'Where's Ant?'

'Oh—at home. Working,' I added quickly to avoid suspicion. 'The house was a bit quiet so I felt like popping out.' I sank my head back on a soft leather cushion.

'Do you like Ant, Mum?'

She stared at me wide-eyed. 'Of course I do! Why d'you ask?'

I flushed under her astonished gaze. Why had I asked? I did my best to answer. 'I suppose . . . well, you're very different.'

'I suppose we are. But he's true to himself. I like that.'

As Mum was. Which Ant liked. And as I wasn't, it occurred to me.

'He's got another child,' I blurted, and even as I said it, I knew I wanted to tarnish him. To disenchant her. 'By a girl he once taught.'

'Yes, I know. Anna told me.'

My jaw dropped. Eyes popped too, probably. 'When?'

'A few days ago. She dropped by after school on her bike. Told me all about it. We had a long talk.'

'Oh!' I was flabbergasted. 'Why didn't you tell me? Ring me?'

'I figured Anna might not want me to pass back how she felt. Thought maybe she'd come here to offload.'

Yes. Yes, she was probably right. And Anna often did come here; she liked seeing Mum. In fact, she sometimes talked to her more than . . . well. It was often the way, wasn't it, I told myself stoically. Skipping a generation. I gave my head a tiny shake to regroup.

'How is she?' I had to ask how my own daughter was?

'Not great. Threatened. Jealous. Scared.'

'Makes two of us.'

She patted my hand. 'You're bound to be. But, Evelyn, don't make this too big. She's only a child, this Stacey. Imagine if it were Anna.'

'How could it be Anna!'

'Easily. Imagine if he'd married her, not you. Left *you* pregnant. And you'd brought Anna up alone. For sixteen years.'

I gazed at her. Her grey eyes were steady. 'She's done very well. To get this far without inconveniencing you. She could have made your life very different. But they left you alone.'

I went quiet. 'They're having lunch tomorrow, at Browns.'

'I know. Anna just texted me. Browns is a good idea,' she went on. 'Neutral ground. Neutral territory.'

And I'd suggested tea at home. On my territory, in my smart town house with its challenging art on the walls and its antique furniture giving us—or me—the edge. I swallowed. 'I flounced out,' I muttered. 'I mean, just now. For the second time in days.'

'You've a lot to flounce about. Where did you flounce the first time?'

'Malcolm's.'

'Ah.' She smiled. 'An excellent choice. Discreet, too. I saw him yesterday. He didn't mention it.'

'Oh?'

'Yes, I popped in to see his ritzy new shop. He offered me a job.'

'Did he?' I boggled.

'Just a couple of mornings a week. Only he's quite busy now he's joined forces with that other chappie.'

'So what did you say?' I said impatiently. I couldn't help feeling a bit jealous. Mum had been offered a job, in *my* old shop, by *my* friend. But . . . I wouldn't want it, would I? Malcolm knew that.

'Hm? Oh, I said yes, in theory. The only thing is, it's Mondays and Fridays, and Mondays I usually do meals on wheels with Felicity.' Her brow puckered anxiously. 'I was wondering, darling . . .'

'Me?' Do charity work? I was taken aback. But why? Why surprised? Mum did it. Felicity did it. Even Caro, the busiest person in the world, rattled a tin outside Waitrose occasionally for Save the Children.

'Of course,' I muttered.

'Oh, darling, *would* you? Just till I find a replacement. I know you're terribly busy, and I could ask Jill Copeland because she only works at the library three days a—'

'No. No, it's fine, Mum. I'm not terribly busy.'

She looked surprised to hear me say it. But it was true. I didn't have a job. I had one child at school all day. A Portuguese lady who cleaned my house. I did nothing. Who was I?

I said goodbye to Mum and went down the path to my car. Who was Evie Hamilton? Ant's wife. Anna's mother. But now, recent events were questioning my exclusive rights to even those claims.

I drove home, staring blankly at the rain on the windscreen. They defined me, Ant and Anna. And now, two other women claimed they defined them too. I couldn't see my way through. Oh. Wipers. I felt panic rising as I watched the blades swish hypnotically in front of me. I wanted to get back quickly to my house. Stake my claim.

I swung into my road. The rain was torrential now, beating its outraged tattoo on the car roof. My eyes scanned the road, desperate for a space. Many of the houses were divided into flats, so the road overflowed. Ours wasn't, of course. Divided. Ours was one of the few original houses, I used to think smugly. Smug! That's who I was. Smug Evie Hamilton. A trophy wife. *Trophy* wife? I blanched as I shot across the road to the opposite side where I'd spotted a space. I lined up to parallel park. God, that suggested Ivana Trump or Victoria Beckham, with beautifully coiffed hair, polished nails, expensive clothes, whereas my roots needed touching up, my nails were bitten to the quick and these jeans had been on for three days. I couldn't even get *that* right, I thought with a flush as I swung back into my space. At least, I thought it was mine, but someone, while I'd been glancing down at my grubby jeans, had backed in before me, from the opposite direction. So that as I reversed, quite fast, and without really looking, I heard that horrible, familiar crunch of metal on metal.

I slammed on the brakes and stared, aghast, in my rearview mirror. The headlights of the car behind went out. A door opened. I shut my eyes and prayed hard. Oh dear God, no. I'll jiggle tins outside Waitrose. I'll jiggle my *tits* in Waitrose. Just please, don't let it be him.

I opened one eye a fraction and saw a pair of jeans strut towards my open window. Then he crouched down until his face was proximate with mine. 'Bloody hell,' I heard in disbelief. 'Bloody hell—you again!'

I sat bolt upright. 'That was *my* space and, what's more, you saw me backing into it!'

'Like hell it was your space. You just barged across from the wrong side of the road, and then kept on reversing straight into me!'

'I was committed,' I hissed.

'Doesn't surprise me. Give me the name of the asylum and I'll tell them to take you back.'

'To the space! And anyway, how come you are always in my street?' I hissed again.

'Because I *live* in your street,' he hissed back.

'Since when?' I snarled.

'Since two months ago, if you must know,' he snarled back.

We were nose to nose now, snarling and hissing like tomcats, our eyes centimetres apart. His were flecked with gold; greeny gold. His black hair flopped into them. He looked like a dark lion.

I jerked away smartly and, without thinking, opened my door, which since he was crouched behind it, sent him flying backwards.

'Shit!' he barked as he sat down in a puddle.

'Sorry,' I muttered, climbing out. 'Sorry . . . here . . .' I attempted to help him up, but he swatted away my hand in horror.

'Never mind me, what about my car!' he roared.

'Oh Lord. Oh heavens. I really am terribly sorry.' Blinking through the driving rain we both gazed, aghast, at the crumpled remains of his car. The boot was almost entirely concertinaed in. Even by my standards it was not good. 'That's *dreadful*.' I hastened across. 'I had no idea! I mean—I only *tapped* it.'

'Then you don't know your own strength,' he snapped. 'Let alone your own horsepower. Now kindly take your monstrous vehicle away so I can repark what remains of my car!'

I had to park flipping miles away, of course. And then walk back, in the rain, sodden, to my house. I went up the front steps and shut the door behind me. Then I turned off the hall light, knowing, as I passed the dark sitting room and went upstairs, that Ant and Anna were in bed. The bedroom was in darkness, but Ant was still awake.

'Hi,' he whispered. 'Problem? I heard shouting outside.'

'Oh. Crashed the car. My fault.'

'Ah.'

Ah. Just ah. You see? It was indicative of how guilty he was feeling that he didn't hit the roof. Didn't sit up and go, '*What? Again? Bloody hell, Evie!*' May as well go for it. A good day to bury bad news.

'Second time in a fortnight.'

There was a pause. 'Right.'

'Same car, too. I mean, I've hit it twice now.'

I heard him swallow. Then: 'Irritating.'

'Yes, isn't it?' I got into bed.

'But then again, keeps the insurance claims simpler.'

'That's the way I looked at it. Night.'

'Night.'

I turned over and lay there, staring at the wall in the dark. His back was to mine and I knew he was wall-staring too. After a while, a tear slowly trickled down my nose. 'Ant,' I gasped, 'thanks for your text.'

He turned over. 'Thanks for yours.'

In another moment we were in each other's arms, clinging on.

5

THE FOLLOWING MORNING dawned bright and sunny; a sunny Saturday, and the one, as we all conveniently tried to forget as we ate boiled eggs in the kitchen, on which Ant and Anna would be meeting the love child. I kept a bright smile going and some buzzy conversation, and was glad when the phone rang. I lunged and seized it first.

'Evie, hi, it's Caro. Just to let you know Heccy will be here at ten.'

I frowned. 'Heccy? Who the hell's Heccy?'

'The horse, you goon. Hector. Camilla Gavin's pony.'

Oh damn, I'd forgotten. 'Caro, I'm sorry. Anna's going out today.'

'Out? Evie, I *told* you he was coming today.'

'Um . . .' I got up, walked into the drawing room and shut the door. 'Caro,' I hissed, 'she can't. She's meeting thingy today, with Ant.'

'His bastard?'

'Yes!'

'Blimey. And you're allowing that?'

'What can I do?' I wailed. 'He has to meet her at some point, and Anna has to, so they're going to Browns and—oh, I don't know.'

'Browns!' There was a silence as Caro digested this. 'Actually,' she said thoughtfully, 'it might be a good idea. When some lardy peroxide tart and her chain-smoking daughter turn up and hardly know how to hold a knife and fork, Anna will die. She'll never want to see them again.'

I wasn't up to telling her we'd moved on from Barmaid With Foundling country, and were firmly in Beautiful Undergraduate land.

'Anyway, you'd better come. Camilla will want to see some representation from your family, or she'll wonder where her horse is going to.'

I wasn't sure a horse who needed to know who Our People were was entirely what this family needed right now, but Caro was a very persuasive woman and I dutifully trotted upstairs to dress.

I wasn't the only one changing. I couldn't help spotting Ant had his cornflower-blue shirt on, the one that matched his eyes, and that Anna changed three times. She finally settled for studied casualness in skinny white jeans and a pale blue peasanty smock. She looked gorgeous. I told her so as I went out. 'Good luck,' I whispered.

'Thanks. What are you going to do today?' she asked anxiously.

'Meet Hector. You know, your horse.'

'Oh!' Her brow puckered. 'Will it matter I'm not there?'

'Of course not! I'm just going to pop him in a stable and thank the owner.'

'Oh. OK. Take Brenda, or she'll be all on her own.'

'I will,' I promised, bending to scoop up the dog.

Caro was waiting in the yard as I drew up to the farm. 'Come on, quick,' she muttered. 'She's here.' I scuttled to her side, leaving Brenda circling hysterically in the car. Sure enough, a ruddy great lorry trundled down the lane and turned into the yard.

'Camilla!' Caro called in the hearty voice she reserved for her hearty friends. 'You made it!'

'Only jarst. Tyre wars flat. Had to bloody change it!' A formidable-looking blonde with a weather-beaten face jumped athletically from the cab. She slammed the door on two obedient fox terriers. They didn't move a muscle, unlike Brenda, who'd stopped circling and was now eating the car seats.

'Camilla, this is my sister-in-law, Evie. Camilla Gavin.'

'Hi!' She strode across and flashed me a smile. Nearly broke my fingers as she shook my hand. 'You're the mummy, ya?'

'That's it.'

'And where's the gel?' Camilla looked around brightly, in that slightly vacant way overbred people have.

'Oh, she's—meeting someone,' I said quickly.

Camilla frowned. Looked piqued. 'Eau. I rather wanted to see her orn him. See how she sits.'

She walked round to the back of her lorry and began flicking catches and bolts back. She reached up, and with a deft heave-ho tug on a rope, had the ramp down before you could say Jack Robinson.

'Oh, she sits beautifully,' I assured her. 'Got a lovely little . . .'

'Seat,' put in Caro, helpfully.

'And hands?'

'Yes, she's got hands.' Heavens. What a question!

'Are they light?' Camilla turned to me impatiently.

'Oh, yes! Terribly light. Hardly weigh a thing!' Had I missed that in the Penelope Leach book? Who weighed their child's hands?

She gave me an odd look but, happily, disappeared into the depths of her lorry. Moments later she reappeared, leading an immaculate, but disconcertingly purple horse: purple coat, purple leggings, purple ribbons in his tail. I could just about see, under the purple head collar, its head, which was dazzlingly beautiful, with huge eyes.

I drooled quickly. 'Ooh . . . isn't he lovely! He's blond!'

'Palomino. Welsh crorss.'

'He doesn't look cross. Or Welsh. He looks lovely!'

'J'a ride yourself?' She tied the pony to a bit of binder twine on the side of the lorry and was busy whipping off rugs, expertly fixing the saddle to his back.

'A bit. I mean—I used to. As a child.'

She'd popped the bridle on and turned to face me, legs astride, hands on hips. 'Want me to run through your wardrobe?'

I gaped. Visions of her powering, in slow motion and in jodhpurs, through the rails of my extensive fitted wardrobe, sprang confusingly to mind. 'Not . . . unless you . . .' I waved my hand vaguely.

'Think I will. Hang on. Just take these orf. Should have done it first, of course, but wanted to show you how they work.'

She turned and removed Hector's purple legs, which, I realised, stood up by themselves and were made of polystyrene.

'Oh my God—*thigh* boots!' I squealed.

'Travel boots.' She shot me an icy look. 'Velcro, see?'

'Ah, yes. Right.'

She disappeared into her vast lorry, only to reappear with a wheelbarrow, piled high with blankets. She set it down with a thump.

'Right.' She proceeded to toss the blankets on the ground, one at a time. 'Stable rug, turnout rug, summer sheet, fly sheet, sweet itch rug, all-weather turnout rug, sweat rug and thermal. Got it?'

I gaped. 'Blimey. He's got more clothes than me!'

She treated this with the contempt it deserved, gazing at me steadily, hands on hips. I realised she was still waiting for an answer.

'Oh! Got it.'

'And this is his hood.'

He had a hood? A horse with a hoody? 'What, for when he goes mugging?' Quite amusing, I thought, but her eyes were like flints.

'For when it gets a bit chill. Goes orn like this, see?'

'Righto,' I agreed meekly.

'Now.' She reached into the wheelbarrow again. 'Jumping boots, overreach boots, crorss-country boots, exercise boots, competition boots, brushing boots, more travel boots, support boots . . .' and so it went on until I was beginning to long for dear, scruffy, wild-eyed Molly, who wouldn't have worn a stitch in her life.

'Next.' In a trice she'd bundled it all back in the barrow again. 'Personal hygiene.'

I guiltily clamped my arms to my sides. I was a bit warm.

'You pick his feet out every day, and you brush him down, ya?'

'Ya.'

'Then you clean his eyes and his hoo-ha with a damp sponge, but you must also clean his sheath.'

I stared at her. I had a vague understanding of what that word meant, but I hoped I was wrong. 'Sheath?'

'Because it gets a bit crusty, hm?'

Oh dear God.

'So like this, with a wet wipe . . .' She flicked out a wipe from her pocket, bent under his tummy and . . . I couldn't watch; pretended I was rubbing my nose with my fingers, but also couldn't help peering through with morbid fascination as she took hold of his . . . *thingy* . . . which was *whopping* . . . pulled it right down, then pushed back . . . oh, gross. Even Caro's 'soopers' were fainter now as Camilla swabbed it down. Poor *chap*. Did he want that done to him?

'And eyes before hoo-ha, orbviously,' she said, lifting up his tail and peering in intrusively. 'Don't want any muck on the sponge.'

'No,' I agreed faintly, making Hector a promise. Not only wouldn't I touch his sheath, but never would I touch his hoo-ha, either.

'Want to hop on?' She swung about, legs planted, beaming broadly.

'N-no.' I cringed. 'No, I'm fine, honestly.'

'I'll do the honours then.' She'd sprung up into the saddle. 'Manège?' She looked enquiringly at me. I gaped.

'Evie,' I croaked. Had she forgotten my name?

She looked impatient.

'Yes, yes, in the manège, sooper,' twittered Caro.

In a trice they were off: Hector and Camilla, trotting away towards the sand school, Caro trotting behind. After only a moment's hesitation, I too was scampering in their wake.

Camilla trotted efficiently round the sand-manège. Even to my untutored eye this pony was cool. All archy neck and high knees and pointy toes. She came to a halt in the middle of the school. 'OK?'

'Sooper,' I whinnied, tossing my head.

'Right.' She vaulted off smartly. She was taking the tack off now, busily putting a head collar on. Everything this woman did was at breakneck speed. 'Caro, where are you putting him?' she barked.

My sister-in-law jumped to attention. 'Oh, I thought in the front paddock. With Pepper, Phoebe's pony.'

The paddock got the seal of approval and Camilla led Hector away to be set free in his new home. Caro and I followed and leaned on the gate to watch as Pepper, Phoebe's pony, trotted up inquisitively.

'Gets fed twice a day,' came a voice from behind us. We swung round to see Camilla's departing back, returning to the yard. No sylvan scene-gazing for her. Caro and I scuttled after her. 'Meadow mix, chaff, and I find a little sugar beet goes a long way if he's tucked up. Obviously he comes in at night.'

In? Tucked up? Visions of Hector beside me in bed sprang alarmingly to mind. 'What?' I gaped stupidly as we followed.

'Of course,' Caro said quickly, eyeing me, then jerking her head meaningfully towards the stables. Happily the moment was lost on Camilla, who'd marched to the cab of her lorry to ferret in the glove compartment. 'Drew up a little agreement.' She was striding back to me now, a piece of paper in her hand. 'One year's loan to you, all shoeing and vet's bills your shout. He's due a tetanus next week, incidentally. Eau, and not to be ridden by anyone other than your daughter. OK?' She handed me the paper and a pen. I signed dumbly.

'Get him in at eightish. Quick rub dine and rug him up well, and then put him ite again at seven o'clock in the morning, sharp.'

Seven? Seven in the morning? Was she mad? I hadn't even opened my eyes. She was vaulting back into her cab. She slammed the door on us, energetically winding down her window.

'Eau, and when you catch him . . .' She started the engine; was revving it up and yelling at me as she manhandled the gear stick. 'JARST NUTS!' she bellowed. Then she vroomed out of the gate.

'Just nuts to *you*, dear,' I muttered, as Caro and I watched her go.

'Pony nuts,' said Caro faintly. 'In a bucket. When you catch him.'

'Oh,' I nodded, equally faintly, back. 'Right. Rude woman. As if I'm going to fanny and fart-arse around a horse like that—worse than having a husband!'

'Oh, much.' Caro glanced round, surprised I didn't know.

'An invalid husband, at that. Feed him twice a day, change his clothes . . . At least I don't have to clean Ant's cock. I am *not* doing that.'

'She'll check!' Caro squealed. 'I swear, she's going to do spot checks.'

'Let her. She'll find a dirty but happy horse. And seven o'clock in the morning—dream on.' I went to let Brenda out of the car.

'Oh, I get it. *I'm* going to have to do it, aren't I?'

'No, no, Caro, of course not,' I soothed, instantly contrite. 'I intend to do everything,' I informed her. 'I just rather object to her giving me a schedule, that's all. I mean, what's wrong with nine o'clock in the morning? Hector might like a lie-in, for heaven's sake.'

'Well, the later you leave it, the more poo you have to muck out, you realise that? Added to which—Oh, hello. Look who's here.'

Jack, Henry and Phoebe were shuffling warily out of the barn that housed the ping-pong table.

'Has she gone?' whispered Phoebe.

'Yes, well done, you've missed her.'

'God, that was close,' said Jack, shuddering. 'We were literally in the middle of a rally and we heard her voice. Phoebs got under the table. You might have warned us, Mum.'

'I deliberately *didn't* warn you because I was *hoping* one of you might hop on that pony of hers.'

'What, with her watching? No way.'

'I wondered where you lot were.' I gave Jack's shoulders an affectionate squeeze. 'Thanks for the moral support, guys.'

'You didn't need it, you were awesome,' he assured me.

'I loved it when you said thigh boots,' giggled Phoebe.

'Well, why on earth would a horse want those?'

'And you should see what her kids wear,' put in Henry. 'They've hardly got shoes at all!'

'All right, Henry, that'll do,' muttered Caro. 'She is a bit slapdash with them,' she admitted to me.

'Mum, there's a woman waving at you.'

We followed Jack's narrowed gaze to a silver BMW, parked just outside the gate. A fat woman in a lilac blouse was waving a bit of paper out of the passenger window, a furious look on her over-powdered face.

'Oh my God,' muttered Caro. 'Mrs Goldberg.'

'Who?'

'The mother of the bride last week. The strictly kosher wedding from hell, when the loos overflowed, the caterers she'd insisted on booking let us down and Tim and I ended up doing the food ourselves.'

'I hulled six hundred strawberries,' put in Henry, grimly.

'I'm not paying this!' she screeched, venturing forth from her car while her husband sat, staring stonily ahead at the wheel. She was picking her way towards us in a tight white skirt and lilac heels. 'Not any of it! My Michelle had to spend a penny in the bushes when she was caught short—in her wedding dress!'

'Your Michelle was so pissed she couldn't find her way up to the house where the rest of the guests were using the house loos I'd so graciously provided, when your wedding party thought it would be oh so funny to block the Portaloos with party poppers.'

'And the food was a disgrace. You roasted a pig!' she squealed.

'Because you didn't provide any food! And the non-Jewish contingent wolfed it down with alacrity. There was none left, you know.'

She shoved the bill in Caro's hand. 'Well, I'm not paying it,' she said savagely. 'Take me to court for all I care. I'm not paying a penny!' And with that she turned on her lilac heel and stalked off.

'Good God. What a nerve,' I said, gaping.

'Oh, yes,' Caro said wearily, watching her go. 'Unbelievable nerve. And unbelievably common too.'

'Yes, she looked it.'

'Well, that too, but no, I meant not unusual. That sort of behaviour. Before the wedding, when they come to look at the venue: couldn't be nicer. Then they go a bit steely when they're organising the food, trying to shave money off, and then the moment something goes wrong they turn ugly. Really ugly. I think that was our worst one yet.'

'No, the worst one was when someone died on your bed,' Henry reminded her.

'No!' I gasped in horror.

'Dad didn't know he was there, right, and got into bed with him—'

'All *right*, Henry!' Caro fixed him with a look.

'Good heavens,' I said somewhat inadequately. 'Well, I won't be adding to your workload, Caro. I will be here tonight to get Hector in, and back at seven in the morning to put him out again.'

She sighed and picked up the barrow handles. 'Oh, don't worry. I'm here. I can do it this evening.'

'And I always muck Pepper out and feed her, so I could feed Hector, too,' said Phoebe eagerly, knowing her cousin would be pleased.

My heart warmed to both of them. 'You're sweet, both of you. But I'll definitely be here in the morning. I'm going to jolly well do my best.'

Yes, I would, I thought as I drove home. At least this morning had taken my mind off what was happening in town. I glanced at my watch. Yes, right now. One o'clock. Upstairs in the bedroom, I sat hunched

and watchful at my dressing table, which had a view of the street, so I'd
see them coming. I sat, and I waited.

I was still sitting there, when, an hour later, at half past two, my
hands sweaty on my lap, I saw them coming down the street. They
were laughing and joking. My heart plummeted. The key went in the
door and I heard their voices in the hall. Not hushed, but bubbly, buoy-
ant. I went to the top of the stairs.

'How did it go?' I managed.

'Oh, hi, Mum.' Anna smiled up at me, eyes shining. 'Actually it was
fine. They were great.'

My heart, which, as you know, had already plummeted, slipped
through my shoes and tumbled down the stairs.

'Good. Well, that's good.' I executed a tight smile.

Ant was watching me anxiously as I slowly descended, hand on the
rail in case I fell, knowing he had to temper our daughter's enthusiasm.

'It went much better than we expected,' he explained.

'Stacey—Anastasia—is really sweet and really good fun and soo
pretty, Mum. Really tall, with this long blonde hair—she was spotted by
Storm Models in the mall in Sheffield—and she's really clever too. She's
here because she's got an interview at Trinity, and she's only sixteen!'

I couldn't speak.

'And Bella—that's her mum—God, she's *soo* nice, just your type.
Really sweet, you'll really like her, and she's a writer. You know those
historical romance books Granny likes? Bella Edgeworth—that's her!'

I stared as if I didn't recognise her. Bella Edgeworth? Yes. Yes, I'd
vaguely heard of her. Anna was clattering through to the kitchen now I
followed dumbly, Ant behind me. Anna filled a glass and glugged noisily. 'She used to work in a bank, Bella, and she started writing one day,
under the desk, and got the sack. She was really upset 'cos she had no
money, and a baby, of course, but then she was like—right, damn it,
and she wrote this book. Finished it in six months, sent it off and it was
published! Isn't that an amazing story? Just like J. K. Rowling.'

'Amazing.'

'And now she's written four more, and Stacey wants to write as well.
She's going to read English, which Dad's so pleased about, aren't you,
Dad? At his old college too. How cool is that!'

'And you didn't feel—' my voice was strained, 'a tiny bit jealous?
This—this strange *person*, sort of—invading your territory?'

'D'you know what I felt, Mum?' She put down her glass. 'I felt—how
amazing. I've got a sister. I honestly, *honestly* didn't feel a twinge of jealousy, and I *so* thought I would. Thought I'd want to kill her, but I didn't.'

Her brow puckered in an effort to explain. 'Maybe if she'd been pushy, or cocky, but she wasn't. She was worried, nervous. She was trembling, wasn't she, Dad? But not at the end. At the end we were all laughing.'

Laughing. And I was finding it hard to breathe.

'I felt . . . d'you know, I felt almost guilty? That here she was, Stacey, sixteen, with no father, and I'd had Dad, my dad—*our* dad—had his love all those years, and she hadn't.' Her guileless eyes filled with tears. 'And I also thought—there we'd been, sisters. I'd had a *sister*, Mum, and I'd not had the pleasure of it. Always been an only child.'

'You said you liked being an only, all the attention, the love—'

'I know, but today I was like—God, all those wasted years.' She took another gulp of water. I honestly feel . . . I've found her.' She brought those astonished blue eyes back to me. 'Found a sort of . . . missing link.' She gave her head a bewildered shake. 'I can't explain it, Mum. Maybe it's because she looks so like Dad. Maybe that makes it easier.'

Easier! Don't faint. Don't faint.

'And it's odd, because if you'd told me that before, that she looked so like him, I'd have said that would have made it worse. But *we* look alike too. We look like sisters!' Her face was alight, on fire. 'Don't we, Dad?'

Ant looked up slowly. 'Yes. You do look alike. Anna, you've got a clarinet lesson later. D'you want to have a go at that Schubert?'

'No, it's OK. I know it pretty well.'

'Anna, go and do some practice! Your father and I want to talk!' I yelled, fists clenched.

She looked at me astonished. 'You knew this was going to be hard for me—I thought you'd be pleased I liked her!' Her face buckled as she pushed past Ant and ran out. I made to follow her down the hall.

Ant caught my arm. 'Let her go. You'll make it worse.'

I turned to face my husband. 'So,' I whispered, raising my chin, 'it all went swimmingly.' I didn't want to be this hard, sarcastic person.

'No, but it went better than I expected. Anna's young, Evie. Everything's either brilliant or awful. She's high at the moment but she'll come down. She'll realise that the situation is still complicated.'

He was right. The voice of reason, as ever. Anna wanted everything to be all right. Children do. Eternal optimists.

'But it is more complicated?'

'Of course it is. But essentially they're nice people. Who thus far haven't wanted to invade our lives. And who feel . . . very nervous . . . about doing it now. But the fact is, Stacey has an interview at Trinity, and it looks very much as if she'll get a place. How could she be in the same town as her father and not say anything?'

I nodded. Yes, I could see that. I sat down shakily.

'Was she . . . is she, very like you?'

'Enough not to bother with DNA.' He sat opposite me.

'And . . . nice?'

'Yes. You'd like her. You'd like them both.'

I knew what was coming. 'You want me to meet them.'

'Well, that's what you originally wanted, Evie. Or, we could just leave it at that, if you like. They certainly aren't asking for more. For any integration. Stacey just wanted to meet me, set eyes on me.'

'Of course she did.' In spite of my jealousy I knew this to be true.

'And now—well, now, I don't feel I can just leave it. Walk away.' He looked at me pleadingly. 'Do you see that?'

'Yes,' I whispered. How odd it would be if he didn't feel that. What sort of a man would that make him? 'How did it feel? Seeing Stacey?'

He caught his breath. 'Indescribable, Evie. Imagine meeting your child after all these years, knowing she'd grown up without you. I felt shame. But Bella was at pains to point out that I couldn't have known, she hadn't told me. Because . . . well, obviously . . .'

I nodded. Because he was engaged to marry me. But still, she could have done. Other women might. Other, less educated women.

'And love,' he said suddenly, astonished. 'Which completely took me by surprise. After all, she's a stranger—Stacey. But I felt . . .'

'Love?'

'Not love,' he said quickly. 'But—a definite pull, something strong.'

I nodded, staring at the wall above his head. The big question. Pull it out, Evie. Pull it out. 'And how did it feel, seeing . . . Bella?'

Something flickered in his eyes. I caught it just as he tried to mask it. It killed me.

He sighed. 'OK. Fair question. I felt . . . something leap. But it was a nostalgic pull, to do with memory. With the past. Not the here and now.'

He was always going to be honest. I knew, if I asked, I had to accept the consequences. As I folded my arms protectively he struggled to get it all out. 'And of course she is very beautiful, and she's—'

'OK!' I said breathlessly, holding up my hand. I shut my eyes. 'Enough. I know I asked, but . . .' I froze a smile. 'You didn't think—I wish I'd married you, wish I'd stayed with you and Stacey all these years?' I blurted out in a rush, shocking myself.

He looked horrified. 'Of course not. Although, of course,' I saw him plucking up the courage to be honest again and almost put my arm over my eyes, 'the fact remains we have an unbreakable tie.'

I gulped. 'Yes.' Damn. Should have put that arm up.

On Sunday we took Anna over to the farm where she spent the day falling in love with Hector. The following morning, however, it was my turn, so as promised I drove to the farm. All was quiet; all was still. The hens had been let out and were pecking in the dirt. A faint mist was lifting, rolling up like a fleecy grey blanket over the vale, but still shrouding the hills beyond, where the cows, having spotted Tim's pick-up rolling towards them with their hay, lowed in Pavlovian response.

At the sound of my car door shutting, Megan, the old sheepdog, came lumbering up. As I stroked her bony head, I made out Tim's pick-up, coming back through the mist in the distance.

Sounds of activity were coming from a stable further along the row of loose boxes. I put my head over a door in time to see Phoebe adding the finishing touches to Pepper's immaculate bed. 'Morning, Phoebs.'

'Oh, hi. You're here!'

'I am indeed.' I grinned. Oh, ye of little faith.

'I put Hector out for you with Pepper 'cos he'd have got all stressy on his own. I was just going to start on your stable.'

'You will not! Look, I'm all wellied up and ready.'

'Cool. You know where the muck heap is, don't you?'

'Of course. Don't forget I lived here, Phoebe!'

'Mum will be pleased you're here. I'll go and tell her.' And off she went, bounding away to tell Caro. I thought what a sweet girl she was and how I didn't know her well enough. We should get the children together more. All five of them, now. I seized a pitchfork and steadied myself on it. Took a moment. Yes, how would the cousins take to Stacey? With alacrity, I should imagine. I could just see Jack's eyes lighting up as this prospective Storm model sashayed into their yard. Well, good. That was good, Evie, wasn't it? Excellent. Taking the fork firmly in both hands, I marched off to muck out.

My, what a lot of muck, and all sort of spread around the place. Not in neat piles. It was as if the wretched horse had tap-danced in it. Oh, well. I set to work, wrinkling my nose in disgust as I balanced one load of ordure after another on the end of a wobbly pitchfork and plopped it in the wheelbarrow. Yuck. Urgh . . . I tried not to retch.

I began to get used to it. My barrow was full, but the stable still didn't look anything like Phoebe's. I popped next door. Nothing like. Hers was neat and tidy, a flat bed of sawdust banked up slightly round the walls and finishing in a neat line about three foot from the door, revealing a strip of clean concrete. Right. I beetled back, banked up the sawdust round the walls and swept a clear strip of concrete between the bed and the door. There. I stood back. But no, because—there were still lumps of doodah everywhere. Small lumps that—I seized my pitchfork—fell through these wide prongs. I hastened next door. Did Phoebe's stable have . . .? No, no little lumps. So how . . .? Ah. I hastened to the tack room: found a smaller fork with narrower prongs. Hurried back. No. The little bastards still dropped through. I threw down my fork and hurried up to the house, skirting round the back to the kitchen window, where . . . I couldn't quite believe what met my eyes. It was like something out of a TV commercial. Three children in school uniform sat at a scrubbed farmhouse table, while Caro, strapped into a Cath Kidston pinny, fried bacon and eggs at the Aga. How unlike my own chaotic, much smaller, household, where Ant and Anna foraged for themselves in a cupboard, found cereal if they were lucky, while I, when they'd gone, nipped back to bed to read secret copies of *Hello!* and eat chocolate. I was a terrible mother. Terrible. I banged on the window.

Caro turned. 'Oh, well done, Evie!' she shouted. 'Phoebe said you were here. I couldn't quite believe it!'

God. They *really* thought I wouldn't.

'Well, I'm not making much headway, I'm afraid. Lots of really annoying little ponky poos keep slipping through my fork.'

'What?' She cupped her ear and lunged to turn the radio down.

'*Tiny bits of shit!*' I yelled, as a rather glamorous blonde turned from where she'd had her back to me in the shadows. She gazed in wonder.

'Oh, this is . . . Alice,' breathed Caro, going pink. 'One of my brides. Getting married in the autumn. Phoebe, go and speak to your aunt.'

I must have made a tremendous spectacle: sawdust in hair, red of face, shouting obscenities through the window. Perhaps they'd pass me off as the mad aunt. Pass me off? I *was* the mad aunt. On a rogue impulse, as the young woman gave me a dazed nod, I rolled my eyes up into my head in an insane manner. She looked startled. Happily Caro missed it, but Phoebe giggled as I bent to whisper in her ear. She whispered back; saw my eyes widen as she divulged her advice.

'But you don't have to,' she said quickly. 'I'm just fussy.'

I gazed at her in wonder. 'Me too,' I whispered. I hastened off.

Back at the stables I located said bucket in said tack room and found said Marigolds at the bottom covered in . . . ugh. Face averted I slipped them on, and then crouched in my Armani jeans, arms outstretched, I picked one up . . . dropped it in the wheelbarrow . . . picked one up . . . dropped it in. Just grass, I told myself, nostrils clenched.

Twenty minutes later, barrow now brimming, I stood and gazed around. Immaculate. You'll get there, I told myself as I sped back down the lanes. It's all a matter of practice. And you a farmer's daughter, a little voice in my head said. What had I been doing with my life while my sister-in-law held breakfast meetings—which I now realised that little tête-à-tête had been, both women finding a window of opportunity before they started work, proper work. What had I been doing? Reading trashy mags and eating lime creams, that's what.

But I was focused now. I was going to Malcolm's shop, to get the low-down on Bella Edgeworth. I sped towards town; parked in the little cobbled yard at the back. Good: just Malcolm's car. Quietly opening the shop door, I glanced through the archway to my right . . . but no sign of Poo-Face. In fact, the whole shop was empty and still in semidarkness, save for Malcolm. He peered over his specs as I came in. Beamed.

'Darling! You're up bright and early. What a treat.'

'Malcolm.' I shut the door and hastened towards him urgently. 'Malcolm, have you heard of Bella Edgeworth?'

'Yes, of course I have.' He took his glasses off. 'She writes those lovely Victorian romance books. All crinolines and petticoats. Why?'

'Lovely? I thought they were more sort of . . . throwaway and trashy.'

'Well, they're not highbrow, but they're certainly very charming.'

Oh God. Like her probably. 'Sexy?'

'No throbbing members, if that's what you mean. I've got some here. Why?' He got up and went to the shelves to peruse.

'Because she's the sodding ex-girlfriend, Malc. With the child!'

'Oh!' He turned in astonishment, stared at me. 'How *thrilling*. Oh, Evie, d'you think she'd do an event for us? She's awfully popular.'

'Malcolm!'

'No, no, sorry. Silly me,' he said quickly. He snatched a couple of books from the shelves and hurried back with them. 'But you must admit, quite exciting. And so much better than a Doreen?'

'You mean, if one's fiancé is going to shag another woman and have a love child, much better that she's beautiful and famous?'

Malcolm scratched his chin thoughtfully. 'Ye-s. Yes, I think that's exactly what I mean,' he declared defiantly. He flipped open the back cover of one of the books. 'Oh!' A young woman of quite astonishing beauty was revealed. Her hair was long and blonde, her eyes doe-shaped and limpid, her cheekbones high, her lips full.

'AARGHH!' I collapsed into his chair and brought my forehead down dramatically onto the counter.

Malcolm bustled away into his back room. A few minutes later he returned with his usual remedy: hot and strong. I raised my head weakly from the counter. 'Two sugars?' I whimpered.

'Three. One for the nerves.' He patted my back. 'Now listen, flower. I know you're in a bad way, but would you do me a humongous favour? I'm supposed to be taking Cinders to a doggy-training class in five minutes, and your ma is supposed to be relieving me here, only she's a bit late. You wouldn't hold the fort for *moi*, would you? Till she comes?'

I shrugged resignedly. 'Sure. Why not?' I rested my head on his counter again. 'I have no life. Nowhere to go. I am a zero.' I gazed down at my thighs. 'If only I were a size zero too, like Bella Edgeworth. Go.'

'Thanks, hon.' He straightened up. 'We're running over The Three Commandments again today. D'you want to hear them?'

I raised my head wearily. 'I know you're going to tell me anyway.'

'First you say—"Sit!" Then you pat your dog and say, "*Good* sit." Then you say, "Down! *Good* down." Then, my favourite,' his face twitched with suppressed mirth, '"Come! *Good* come."' He giggled.

Annoyingly I could feel my mouth twitch.

'I just dissolve. No one else does, though. I did catch American Cocker's eye last week. He gave me a very knowing smile, which I thought was encouraging, *n'est-ce pas*?'

I shrugged. '*Peut-être*.' I sipped my tea weakly.

'And don't torture yourself with those books, hm?' He went to pick them up, but I slapped my hand down on the pile.

'Leave them,' I said savagely. 'Torture is what I want right now.'

He shrugged. 'Whatever,' he said peevishly. 'But don't slit your wrists in my shop, hon. It wouldn't be good for business.'

And with that, he was away, whistling for Cinders. I watched them go. Cinders, it occurred to me, was not only pushing twelve, but also the most obedient dog in Christendom. Puppy-training classes? I smelt a rat.

I slumped right back in his chair, head lolling, eyes shut. After a moment, I reached out a hand and drew one of the books towards me. I opened the back cover gingerly, peered at the photo. Worse. Much worse. Older than in the previous picture, but more sophisticated. Eyes wild, I read feverishly:

> Critical Acclaim for Bella Edgeworth
> 'Brilliant! Witty and compelling' *Scotsman*
> 'A wise, funny book, beautifully written' *Daily Mail*
> 'What a find! Who is Bella Edgeworth? I want to have her
> babies!' Mark Cox, *Daily Express*

'Arghhhh!' I roared again, dropping the book like a hot coal. Fists clenched, I sprang from my seat and jumped on it. Then I kicked it, as hard as I could, to the back of the shop, and my bare toe in its flip-flop caught the edge of the counter. I screamed out in agony, '*Shitshitshit!*' Clutching my foot, and hopping across to the chair, I collapsed into it. And then, predictably, I burst into tears.

It was quite a noisy outburst, with a fair amount of shuddering, but I got relatively quickly to the hiccupy stage, coughed a bit . . . then froze. Coughed? I wasn't coughing. A deep throat-clearing noise came again. 'Who's there?' I sat bolt upright.

Out of the shadows, halfway down the shop, and from behind the archway, came a tall dark figure. He was frowning at his shoes.

'Oh. You! How long have you been there?'

'Well . . . a while, I suppose.' He looked up, defensively. 'I came in through the back. My office has a door to the yard. You and Malcolm were talking, and it seemed inappropriate to announce myself. But then, when you were . . . you know.' His brow puckered. He looked uncomfortable. 'Just now. I couldn't just sit there and listen, so . . .'

He really did look uncomfortable. 'No, I understand.' I gulped. 'Well, then,' I forced a bright smile. 'There you have it. The mad woman who parades in kinky underwear at her bedroom window, throwing lubricant at cars before reversing into them, is married to a man who's ex-girlfriend is not only beautiful and famous, but has recently pitched up with his love child. No excuse for such terrible histrionics in a bookshop, I agree, but perhaps at least it goes some way to explaining it.' I used my sleeve to wipe my nose. Saw snot. Attractive.

He shrugged and moved cautiously my way. 'It . . . fills in a few gaps.'

I nodded bravely. 'That's her,' I said bitterly.

He picked up the book on the floor. 'Bella Edgeworth. So I heard.' He looked inside the back cover.

'If you whistle, or say "tasty", I will go outside and torch what remains of your car,' I snarled.

His mouth twitched. 'Well, it's a hire car—mine's at the garage being fixed—so help yourself.' He put the book down. Looked at me. 'You all right?' His determinedly brisk tone betrayed kindness.

I nodded wordlessly, my face full of snot and tears.

'I met her, actually. At a literary festival. In Cheltenham, last year.'

I glanced up. 'Is she a whore?' I gasped hopefully.

He threw back his head and barked out a laugh. 'No, I don't think so. Not that I noticed. But then, maybe I wouldn't.'

'Why not? She's gorgeous, isn't she? And single. Are you married? Not that that appears to matter,' I added bitterly.

He smiled. 'I'm not married. I was.'

'Divorced?'

'Widowed.'

'Oh,' I said. That put my petty problems into perspective, didn't it? 'I'm so sorry. Really.'

'Thank you.'

A silence ensued. He was standing in front of the counter, and I was behind it. His legs were long and slim. Good legs, actually.

'Here, why don't you . . .?' I swung the other chair behind the counter round to face him.

'Oh. Thanks.' He came and sat beside me. Another silence.

'D'you mind me asking . . . I mean, how did she . . .?'

'She was killed by sniper fire in Uzbekistan.'

'Good God. A soldier?'

'No, a photographer. For *Le Figaro*. She was French.'

'Gosh. How brave. Like Kate Adie? Dodging bullets?'

'Or not, as the case may be. But actually, that was me. I mean, I was Kate Adie, the reporter.'

'Oh my God, how romantic. So how come—'

'I'm running a bookshop?' He shrugged. 'I carried on reporting for a year or so after Estelle died, but then I didn't really have the stomach for it. Thought if I saw another teenage Iraqi boy shot as he threw a stone, or another truckload of young British soldiers ambushed and blown up by grenades, I'd jump on a grenade myself. Time to move on. Leave it to the young and the unembittered. Running a bookshop had always appealed. I like books.'

'Me too. It's what I used to do. I mean, work here. With Malcolm.'

He looked surprised. 'I didn't know that.'

'No reason why you should.' I regarded him. He seemed intent on his shoes. Funny, I'd always thought him arrogant. Maybe shy. It was very quiet. 'Don't you miss . . . being abroad? In Afghani . . . Paki . . .'

'Uzbekistan?'

'That's the one.' I flushed.

'You mean, do I miss the action?'

'I believe I do.'

'Sometimes. But it's Estelle I miss. And it wouldn't be the same. Not seeing her face in the pack of photographers as they rolled into town.'

I gulped. He had a way of telling it like it was. Painting a picture. Reporting, I suppose.

'Had you been married long?'

'Five years.'

'Children?'

'No. The lifestyle wasn't conducive to children. Wasn't fair. We wanted them, though. When she died . . . well, she was pregnant.'

'Oh God, I'm so—'

'So you see,' he swept on, 'our lives would have changed anyway. It seemed like the right thing to do. Settle down a bit. Buy a house. Get a steady job. And obviously to get a penis extension.'

My hand flew to my mouth. 'I'm so sorry!'

'Don't be. It amused me. And maybe you were right. Maybe I was an older man in a cool car cruising for chicks. It made me think.'

Older. Was he older? Not than me, surely.

'Well, under the circumstances,' I blustered, 'who can blame you if you were? You must be lonely.'

'No, no.' He got to his feet suddenly and I realised I'd gone too far. 'No, I'm very busy. Life's . . . very full.' He walked to the shelves and realigned some books unnecessarily. 'Lots of friends, lots of plans.' His profile was to me now. A strong jaw, strong nose. I could see him in Baghdad, head down, running across sniper-watched streets; his beautiful French wife, camera round her neck, racing along beside him. Was that how it happened? I wondered. Was he running ahead of her, heard her cry out, turned to see her crumple, fatally wounded in the dirt? His stony profile didn't invite enquiry.

On a gust of wind and eau-de-something-strong, my mother burst into the shop, jogging. 'Evie! What are you doing here?'

'Waiting for you. Malcolm had to pop out, so I said I'd hang on. You were supposed to be here ten minutes ago.' I glanced across to the shelves, but Ludo had melted into his half of the shop.

'I know, I'm sorry, but I decided to run, and it's further than I thought. But, darling, you're supposed to be with Felicity.'

'Felicity?' I frowned.

'Yes. Remember you said you'd do meals on wheels for me? She'll be waiting for you at the Civic Centre.'

I stared at her. 'Bugger!'

'Felicity! I'm so sorry!' I yelled out of my car window as I pulled up in the Civic Centre car park.

She was already loading what looked like dozens of polystyrene boxes from a stainless-steel trolley into the back of her old green Subaru. She glanced up in relief. 'Oh, Evie. Thank heavens.'

'What can I do?' I got out and hurried across to her.

'Well, there are about ten more of these boxes on another trolley in the kitchen.' She jerked her head back towards the town hall, a crumbling stone affair behind us. 'But if we go together, we can carry them, and then we won't have to wheel the trolley out and back. We'll be out of here in a jiffy.'

Together we swung her empty trolley round and hurried it through the back door. In a vast, operating theatre-style, stainless-steel emporium, we found the remaining boxes. I took half.

'So what have they got today?' We hurried to the car.

'Oh, all sorts. Nothing as simple as one meal for all. They all have something different,' she said, as we loaded them into her open boot. 'Different dietary requirements. Some are no pork, some are no fowl or no fish, some have to be puréed—no teeth—and some, no beans or onions,' she raised her eyebrows, 'for obvious reasons.'

'Oh. Right.'

'And the coloured dot in the corner of the box tells you what's what. Here's your crib sheet.' She shoved a piece of paper in my hand. 'I'll drive since it's my car, so you pop in with the meals, OK?'

She was already in the driving seat, strapping herself in. Thank heavens I hadn't let her down. I beetled round the other side and strapped myself in beside her.

'They're all elderly, obviously,' she was saying, glancing in the rear-view mirror and reversing out smartly—note to self: use rearview mirror more—'and they're always the same. The complainers complain, the sunny ones are sunny, some haven't seen anyone all day—or all week, even—so you might have to linger a moment, OK?'

'Yes, fine,' I mumbled. I felt humbled. I did nothing. Nothing. No committees, no charity work. Ah, yes, back to you, Evie. As usual.

She frowned at my tone; glanced across. 'What's up?'

I shrugged. 'Oh, just thinking how good you all are.'

She gave me a look. 'I'm not good, Evie. And don't feel guilty about your own lack of Good Works either.' She swung the car round a mini-roundabout and headed off down a suburban street. 'You have your own problems at the moment.'

'Mum told you?'

'She did.'

I sat up. 'And what do you think?'

We'd pulled up outside a row of tiny bungalows. After a moment, she said, 'I think that if I'd had one child, I'd be the happiest woman alive. If it turned out I had two, like Ant, I'd be delirious.'

I gazed at her. I'd never thought of it like that. 'And if you were me?'

'I'd look at it as one and a half. Which is still better than one.'

I swallowed. It occurred to me that Felicity, like Stacey, was an outsider who had integrated into our family. And what a success that had been. All the lights went on. I felt alive suddenly, electric: yes, look what Felicity had done for our family. She'd made us. Completed us.

'You're right!' I said, eyes shining as she got out of the car. I hurried round to join her at the boot. She handed me two polystyrene boxes. 'You're right, Felicity. I'd never thought of her as an asset!'

'Well, one step at a time. You've yet to meet her, but you're getting the idea. Now. This one for Mrs Carmichael at number six—no fowl— and this one for Mr Parkinson, see the blue spot, no red meat, next door. He's quite a distinguished old boy. Just to give you a flavour, when he filled out his original order form, under "Any Special Dietary Requirements", he put, "Red meat and good claret."'

I grinned. 'Good for him! So what's he getting?'

'Lentil stew and rice pudding. He's got gout.'

'Ah.'

As I beetled up the path to his door, I wondered briefly if he'd prefer to be gouty and take his pain relief in the form of a very fine Fonseca '66, or to be pain free and sucking lentils. Mine was not to reason why, though, and anyway, I was miles away. My heart was still up there, at three thousand feet, soaring through the stratosphere.

Next door, a wary, toothless old woman—puréed—and then next door to that . . . I hastened back to the car as Felicity kerb-crawled along . . . a nice old couple who chortled with delight when I told them it was lamb stew today.

'All right?' shouted Felicity through the car window.

I ran towards her. 'Yes. I'm getting the hang of this. What's next?'

'No fowl, number ten. No lumps, number sixteen,' she barked.

'Right.' I went round to the boot; set off with my booty.

Two minutes later I was back. 'OK. Go again!' I yelled.

'Mrs Mitchell has a stiff drink on the dot of twelve every day, and since we're late,' Felicity consulted her watch, 'she'll be away with the fairies by now. Chopped liver, red dot. And Mrs Mason next door is black dot.'

I ran to the boot and hurried up the path, delivering to an old dear who was clearly flying. I put the box down, but as I made to leave, she stopped me by way of sticking an arm in my path, a glass of what was patently neat gin in her hand.

'Definition of a teetotaller?' she demanded.

'Someone who knows their day isn't going to get any better?'

She threw back her head and cackled in delight, letting me pass: cheering me on my way as she knocked back the rest of the tumbler prior to settling down to her liver and bacon. Good on yer, girl.

Next door, a frail figure with a vacant expression opened the door in a diaphanous nightie. She stared at me and my purple box in wonder. 'Oh dear,' she whispered. 'I keep forgetting if I've had lunch or not.'

'That poor old soul,' I said to Felicity as I got back in the car. 'Should she be on her own?'

'What d'you suggest, a home? She'd hate it. Now. Two to go. Mr Bernstein, no pork, pink spot, and Mrs Partridge, purple spot, everything puréed.'

'Right.' I tumbled out again as we stopped. Ran round to the boot. Two boxes left. One black spot, one green. I frowned. Shouted through the car to the front. 'Sure it's pink and purple?'

'Positive.'

I opened the green box. Sniffed. Pork. Oh Lord. Opened the black one. It was very far from puréed.

'Er . . . Felicity, I think I may have boobed.'

'Oh God,' she groaned. 'What did you give Mrs Mason?'

'Well . . . purple. Isn't that no beans, no onions?'

'No! Black is no beans—and Mr Clarke at number sixteen?'

'Oh God—yellow. Oh, Felicity, I think I've got them muddled!'

'Quick, get in.'

We roared off back to number sixteen. Felicity got out with me and we ran up the path as one; leaned on the doorbell. As Mr Clarke came to the door, napkin tucked in under his chin, knife and fork in hand, Felicity slipped past him into the sitting room. 'Hello, Mr Clarke, have you eaten it yet?'

'What?' He cupped his ear.

'HAVE YOU EATEN LUNCH?'

'Not yet, just about to. Looks delicious.'

He shuffled past us through an archway to a tiny dining room and sat down in front of a full plate. Felicity lunged and whipped it away.

'It's not. But this is.' She gave me a nod and I quickly replaced the fish with the pork. Together we raced out.

Felicity was already a few doors down, ringing the doorbell. I took a short cut across the tiny front garden, to join her.

'This could be disastrous,' she muttered, leaning hard on the doorbell again. 'Mrs Mason has the sort of flatulence that could propel a small moped. You've just given her puréed beans, onions and prunes.'

'Oh shit.'

'You bet. No plumbing in the civilised world could accommodate what she might evacuate.'

Finally, after three more mighty rings, she came to the door beaming vacantly in her diaphanous nightie, a few telltale stains down the front.

'Hello, Mrs Mason, have you had your lunch?' breathed Felicity.

'Yes, delicious,' she said, beaming. 'And prunes for pudding. Lovely!'

'Good, good,' purred Felicity nervously. 'Well, jolly good, Mrs Mason. Just checking you enjoyed it.'

'It made a nice change, thank you, dears.' She went very red in the face suddenly. Her flimsy nightie floated up at the back. *Vrrrrrp!*

'Mrs Mason,' Felicity was rooting around in her handbag, 'take a couple of these pills with a glass of water, hm?' She punched out a couple of tablets from some silver foil.

'What are they, dear. Sweeties?' She gazed at them in wonder.

'Yes. Sort of. But take them right now, hm?'

'Oh, I *will*. Thank you, dear!' And her face began to turn pink again, her nightie wafting up, as she shut the front door.

'But what about the last one?' I wailed. 'Mrs Purée?'

'We'll go to McDonald's and get her a strawberry milkshake and some ice cream. She'll love it. Oh, and a few chips to suck. Perfect.'

'Right,' I agreed faintly.

When we'd delivered the fish to its rightful owner we did just that, and Mrs Purée did indeed seem to love it. One satisfied customer at least. Albeit with quite a lot of sugar and additives inside her.

'I'm so sorry, Felicity,' I muttered as we drove home.

'Oh, don't worry, it's easily done,' she said, smiling. 'Your ma's got them muddled up once or twice too.' She was consulting her watch. 'Well, we may have been a bit erratic, but at least we were quick. I'm in bags of time.'

'For?' I turned my head wearily towards her. I was exhausted.

'I'm delivering a lecture at Keble in ten minutes.'

Of course you are.

Later, much later, on the other side of Oxford, a typically quiet evening unfolded at number 22 Walton Terrace. I was sorting through a pile of odd socks at the bottom of the laundry basket in front of the tiny television in the sitting room. Anna was in the far corner on her computer, Ant was in his study. After a bit, he came through to join me. 'I've just had an email from Stacey. She's asked us all up to Sheffield, after the summer holidays. At half-term, for a couple of days.'

'To stay with them? In their house?'

'Yes.' His eyes were steady. Kind. My heart began to pound.

'All of us? Or just you and Anna?'

'All of us. What should I say?'

I took a deep breath. 'Say yes. Yes, we'd love to come.'

He smiled, leaned forward and kissed me. 'Thank you, darling.'

6

THE HAMILTON FAMILY were driving north. The early hours of the morning had been stormy; now, mid-morning, the heavy rain had eased but the wind hadn't. Ant and Anna were in the front listening to Brahms and chatting about birdwatching, and I was in the back reading old copies of *OK!* and sucking Werther's Originals.

We'd been lulled by the summer holidays, then distracted by the new term, then, as half-term approached, it had taken a frantic few days to get us to this ostensibly cosy, familiar point. Not withstanding the nervous flutterings of my heart, there had also been Hector, our new dependant, to deal with. Years ago, of course, I'd have rung Mario, Dad's farm worker. Dear, wizened old Mario, with his round walnut face and his eyes that all but disappeared when he smiled, and his wife, Maroulla. Originally from a poor village in Andalusia, they'd come across to work at the Triumph factory, planning to stay for five years and take the money back to Spain. Instead, they'd lasted one at Triumph, missed working on the land, come to the farm and stayed for ever. Mario had died just after my father, and Maroulla had moved out of the cottage to live with her daughter. Whenever I thought of Maroulla now I felt guilty, because I knew she'd recently moved to a nursing home and I hadn't been to see her.

Instead I'd called Caro and arranged to pay Phoebe to look after Hector.

As one lush field gave way to another, punctuated by a few dreamy-looking sheep and enclosed by neat dry-stone walls, I frowned.

'Are we nearly there?' I really was the nine-year-old in the back. And actually I needed the loo too.

'Very. The next village.'

I blinked. 'But I thought they lived in Sheffield.'

'No, close by. Their village is eight miles outside.'

'Down here, Daddy.' Anna was navigating, a printed-out email in her hand. 'And then left at the postbox, apparently . . .' Ant swung the car obediently, 'and then down the hill into the village . . .'

I gazed in wonder. By now the rain had dried up, and a bright blue sky had been offered by way of apology. Down the bottom of the hill, in a fold, an adorable little village came into view. A huddle of grey slate roofs grouped around a skinny church spire; a river warbled and rushed through the middle of the village. Beyond, the toppling steepness of the hills rose up as a backdrop, painted with a smudgy green brush, and just a daub of purple heather.

'Just the other side of the church, Daddy, the very next house.'

Set back slightly from the lane was a detached, but compact, grey stone house. It was twin gabled and symmetrical, and the discreet wooden sign on the gate bore the legend THE OLD RECTORY. It opened automatically, sensing our car bonnet, and as we crawled across the crunchy gravel under the roomy shade of a splendid old beech tree, the sun, with a flash of cussed brilliance, picked out the mellow stone façade of the house, complete with pretty wooden porch.

As if this paralysing sight weren't enough, the front door opened and there, on the doorstep, were mother and daughter. Both were tall and slim, with long blonde hair, and wearing jeans, T-shirts and big anxious smiles. Gorgeous. For some reason it was the mother my eyes flew to first, with those fabulous cheekbones I recognised from the photograph: full mouth, flawless pale complexion and teeny tiny figure. I gulped. Your average nightmare.

Ant and Anna were already out of the car, embracing, kissing, exclaiming. I hurriedly got out to join them.

'Evie, this is Bella. Bella, my wife, Evie.'

I flashed a manic smile. 'Hi!'

'We're so glad you've come,' Bella said eagerly, meeting my eyes. 'You've no idea what this means to us.'

It was a simple little speech, but heartfelt, unrehearsed, unlike so many of mine, and consequently disarming.

'It's . . . lovely to be here,' I managed.

'And this is Stacey.'

I turned, properly, to the daughter. Wide nervous blue eyes gazed at me. She was so obviously Ant's child it took my breath away.

'Hi,' she whispered, averting her eyes to the gravel.

'Hello, Stacey.' I smiled and held out my hand.

Bella ushered us inside, me, gushing nervously about the proportions of the wide hall, Bella, thanking me for my compliments as I secretly marvelled at the two girls, drifting to each other's side, smiling shyly. Sisters, I thought with a lump in my throat and I realised Bella was watching them too, eyes bright. I glanced at Ant, but his eyes were full of such extraordinary pride and astonishment, I had to look away.

We followed Bella through to the kitchen: a square room with a terracotta floor. French windows were flung open onto a sunny terrace and garden. I prattled away nervously, admiring everything, which wasn't difficult—even a bantam hen that had wandered in, and which Bella shooed out, clapping her hands at it: tiny hands, I noticed, with translucent skin. Ant was quiet, as was his wont.

'Have you been here long?'

'Not really.' She brought a tray of coffee to the table with a plate of cakes. 'Two years. We'd always wanted to live in the country, and we drove out here one Saturday afternoon, didn't we, Stace?' She glanced across at her daughter but she was deep in whispered conversation with Anna. 'Saw this place, fell in love with it.'

She flushed and I flushed and then Ant did too.

Falling in love. Brought up, inadvertently, and really quite early on in the proceedings. I saw Ant watching her and tried to interpret his look. It was one I wasn't familiar with. Or had I just not seen it for a while?

'Well, I can quite see why,' I rushed on approvingly, knowing, with an aching heart that I liked this girl, with her quick nervous manner, her obvious efforts to please me, and her blushing highly strung daughter; knew they were entirely my type: the sort of people who, had I met them first, I'd come rushing home to enthuse to Ant about. 'Oh, you'll love them, Ant, they're a stunning mother-and-daughter act, clever, pretty, sensitive,' as one does when one is secure in a relationship, knowing they would pose no threat. I very much wanted to assist, not to hinder relations, which surprised me enormously. Pleased me, too.

'Your garden's beautiful,' I was saying, getting up to admire it.

Ant was talking to the girls on the terrace as Bella and I strolled out onto the lawn; damp and shiny and strewn with curling yellow leaves. A cherry tree planted centrally enjoyed sole occupancy, its skinny grey branches scantily clad now. Round the trunk was a circular wooden seat, which I admired.

'Except I hadn't realised my tree was so fat, and look, it doesn't meet!' Bella wailed, showing me where a six-inch gap prevailed.

'Looks like the zip of my jeans on a bad day,' I commented. 'You need someone to knock a piece of wood in there for you,' I advised, and as I said it, I knew I meant a man, a husband, an Ant, which of course she'd been without all these years.

'I . . . want to thank you so much for what you've done today.' She looked at me, eyes huge in a pale face. 'You have no idea how much it means to Stacey. To both of us. And a lot of women wouldn't have done it. Wouldn't have come. I think you've been tremendous.'

My eyes filled with tears and I wanted to tell her I hadn't been tremendous. That up to now I'd been filled with jealous loathing.

'It hasn't been easy,' I admitted. 'I have to tell you, Bella, when I first heard about you and Stacey I wanted you both burned at the stake.'

'I can understand that,' she said quickly. 'I'd feel just the same.'

'So . . . did you feel the same? When you heard he'd married me? And you were left holding the baby?'

She narrowed her eyes at the untamed hills beyond. 'No,' she said slowly, 'I didn't hate you, because I knew your claim to Ant was more valid than mine. The fact that I got pregnant was immaterial. And immature and stupid. But . . . I resented you the cosy family life. Which I didn't have. I had a bit of a struggle.' She sat down on the rickety seat.

I sat beside her. 'What happened?'

'I came home when I knew I was pregnant. I was terrified.'

'Of your parents?'

'No, no, my dad was brilliant. Shocked, but brilliant. My mum died when I was little, so he'd brought me up. He works at the Vodafone factory, down at Sutherton. He just took it in his stride and gave me all the support I needed. We lived with him for six years, Stacey and I.'

'He must have been very disappointed about Oxford.' A factory worker. His only daughter. Beautiful and bright. Ticket to ride.

She smiled. 'You'd think so, wouldn't you? Me, an only child, getting out of our tiny council house to the dreaming spires, and then made pregnant by a don. Most fathers would bustle down south, rolling up their sleeves and brandishing a meat cleaver, but he's a remarkable man, my dad. He was completely with me when I decided not to have an abortion. Told me a human life is more magnificent than any degree. And he has to be right, doesn't he?'

I followed her gaze to her daughter, Anastasia, older than Anna but not as confident, desperately shy. Not the type I'd envisaged at all.

'Yes. He has to be right.'

'And he's a great believer in what goes round comes round.' She flattened her vowels to mimic a broader accent. 'Things 'ave on 'abit of comin' right in the end, pet.' She smiled.

'And he's right, they have,' I said slowly. 'Your books . . .'

She shrugged. 'Came about because I didn't want to work in a bank and put Stacey in childcare. They've paid for all this. And I love doing it.'

'He must be very proud.'

She smiled. 'Brimming. You'll meet him tonight. He's coming for supper.' She looked at me anxiously as if to check this was all right.

I smiled. 'I'd like to meet him.'

Her father was a great bear of a man, who, when he'd squeezed through the doorway, seemed to fill the small kitchen, his arms full of flowers as he exploded out of a hairy tweed jacket several sizes too small for him. Ant had followed the girls into the room and Bella turned to make the introductions: I could see she was wondering how to do this.

'Hi, I'm Evie.' I stepped forward, smiling and proffering my hand. 'And this is my daughter, Anna, and my husband, Ant.'

Bella shot me a grateful look and muttered, 'My dad, Ted.'

The two men's eyes met and they shook hands. I realised, with a start, how hard that must be for Ted: to shake the hand of the man who'd got his teenage daughter pregnant. He must have hated him. And no one ever hated Ant. I saw the colour shoot to his cheeks, in this moment of . . . well, shame. Again, not something he was familiar with.

'What lovely flowers!' I said, breaking the moment and seizing a jug from the middle of the table. 'Shall I put them in water for you, Bella?'

'They're for you, luv,' Ted said gruffly, handing them to me. 'I know you're stayin', like, so I thought you could put them in your room.'

'Oh. Thank you.' I was taken aback.

'No, thank you. It's a rare and fine thing you've done for us here today.' His pale blue eyes swam a bit. I took the flowers, touched; aware of quite a few eyes on me.

The evening slipped on. For slip, read well oiled, for Bella forgot to put the vegetables on, which prolonged the cocktail hour, and also people were nervous, so by the time supper was finally on the table, I, for one, was flying. The table was a long thin slab of oak, and to prevent us being miles apart, Bella had seated three down each side, with Ted and I opposite one another, then the girls, then Ant and Bella. Eventually three conversations developed. And I got on famously with Towering Ted. His voice boomed out as he talked, mostly about his daughter, and how all his colleagues at work bought her books.

I smiled. 'You must be very proud.'

His eyes filled as he seized his wineglass. 'You'll never know, lass.'

The girls, who'd managed craftily to recharge their glasses while we weren't watching, shrieked and laughed at each other across the table, while Ant and Bella fell into a quieter conversation at the end. I strained to hear as I pretended to listen to Ted. What were they talking about? I heard Stacey's name. Yes, of course. Their daughter. The bizarreness of it hit me. I lunged for my glass. God, this was surreal. I needed help. I seized the wine bottle and topped Ted up—rude not to join him—so that by the time Ant and I climbed the stairs to bed in the pretty spare room, me carrying the vase of flowers precariously, I was plastered.

'Aren't they lovely, Ant? My flowers?' I demanded. I crossed the room, sloshing water on the carpet and setting them unsteadily on the chest of drawers, right beside a vase of roses already put there by Bella. I blinked in surprise. 'Blimey. Looks like a bloody florist's in here.'

Shutting my eyes was a mistake. 'Shit,' I gasped, rocking back abruptly on my heels. 'Head spin. Nurofen, Ant. Fast. In my bag.' I staggered back to sit on the edge of the bed.

Ant found some. As I glugged gratefully on the glass of water he put to my lips, gulping down the pills, I allowed myself to be laid back on the pillows. Tucked in. 'Sleep,' he said firmly as he straightened up.

Just before I blacked out, I whispered hoarsely, 'I've done well though, Ant . . . haven't I? Been good?'

He kissed my lips. 'You've been very good.'

The next morning I awoke in terrible, terrible pain. After a few minutes I managed gingerly to open my eyes, to peer at the clock. Ten o'clock. Ten o'clock! Oh Lord, quite late. I sat up slowly. Ant's side of the bed was empty. Were they all downstairs having breakfast?

I staggered to the loo, found some more Nurofen in my bag, guzzled them down. Then I got dressed. As I went to go downstairs, I glanced back and realised I hadn't drawn my bedroom curtains, which looked a bit slutty. I waddled back in and swept them aside, and that's when I saw them. In the middle of the garden, sitting on the circular seat round the cherry tree. Bella and Ant. And why not? I thought as I instinctively ducked back behind the curtain. Why not sit and chat? So why was my heart beating so fast? So furiously?

I watched, fascinated, from behind the curtain. Their heads were close together, and they were deep in conversation. But I couldn't really see . . . I glanced behind me to our open suitcase: Ant's bird book and binoculars were stuffed in the side pocket. I seized the binos . . . and . . . golly, amazing. It was as if the pair of them were right in front of me. Ant's head was cocked as he listened intently to Bella. She seemed to be struggling to explain something, and then he spoke . . . and then they looked at each other without speaking for a moment. As they gazed at each other, a lock of hair fell forward into her eyes. Gently, and in an unbearably sweet gesture, Ant reached out and tucked it back behind her ear.

'Eh up, twitcher!'

I swung round in horror. Bella's father was in the open doorway.

'Oh!' A *curtain* twitcher. 'Oh, no, I was—I was watching the birds!'

'Aye, like I say, a twitcher. A girl after my own heart. I come here sometimes to do just that. What 'ave you seen then, luv?' He peered keenly out of the window. 'Tit,' he muttered.

Tit? I cringed. What, me? Or her?

'Some kind of tit. Probably a great tit. You can see its yellow under-parts, look.' He handed the binoculars back to me. 'In the cherry tree, just behind your Ant. See?' I was grateful for the possessive article before my husband's name, and of his guiding hand.

'Yes, I see it now,' I breathed. 'Very pretty. Lovely.'

'Aye, and tha's what we need to keep focused on, eh?' he said gently. 'The lovely birds.' His eyes were kind as they held mine a moment. 'Well, anyway, luv, I'm away. Just popped up to say goodbye to you. Thought you might be up by now.'

'Yes, I . . . overslept a bit. Goodbye, Ted.' I went to peck his cheek but he'd already enveloped me in a huge bear hug.

'Goodbye, luv,' he said gruffly.

And then he was gone. I watched as he reappeared below, through the French windows into the garden; saw Ant and Bella stand up to say goodbye as he approached, bag in hand. And he saw nothing peculiar, Terrific Ted, as he'd become in my mind, in the two of them sitting under the tree together, and she didn't get up with a start. I watched as he took his leave. How I envied him. I wanted to go too. The look Ant had given Bella as he'd tucked her hair back had pierced my heart. It spoke volumes. Because I knew Ant wasn't given to gestures like that.

On an impulse I darted to the bathroom, threw my toothbrush into my handbag and went downstairs. Ant and Bella were strolling up the garden with Ted, making for his car at the front. They saw me and stopped. Waved. 'Hiya!' called Bella.

'Hi!' I called back. I tripped across the lawn to join them. She was looking particularly lovely, I noticed, in a white pin-tucked peasanty top, a tiered denim skirt and floppy suede boots. What teeny tiny legs she had poking out of them. 'Um, where are the girls?'

'Oh, they went into town after breakfast, caught the bus. Stacey wanted to show Anna around. I hope you don't mind?'

'Oh, no, not at all. It's just . . .'

'Is everything all right, darling?' Ant looked concerned.

'Well, not entirely. I've just had a call from Caro,' I lied. 'It's—Hector.'

'Hector?' Bella frowned.

'The horse,' Ant explained.

'He's really bad,' I said. 'Been terribly sick all night.'

'Can horses be sick?' wondered Ant, aloud.

There was a reflective moment as we all tried to remember if we'd seen horses quietly vomiting at the side of the road. Dogs, perhaps . . .

'Nay, luv, you mean colic!' said Terrific Ted, galloping to my rescue.

'That's it! Very bad colic. He might die. *Is* dying. I must go, Ant.'

Ant scratched his head. 'Really? I mean—is there actually anything you can do? Surely Caro's the best person. Or the vet . . .'

'Oh, they've called the vet, he's been there all night, but I'm responsible for him, you see. I must go.'

'She's a grand woman, your wife,' announced Ted suddenly in a broken voice. 'She's all heart. If it was a tiny kitten, maybe even a mouse, you'd go, wouldn't you, luv?' He regarded me keenly, this living embodiment of Francis of Assisi.

I didn't know what to say. 'Yes,' I croaked.

'We'll all go,' Ant said decisively. 'I'll ring Anna.'

'No! I'll get the train. And don't tell Anna Hector's so ill, just say— he's caught a cold, or something. But honestly, darling, I really can't dump this on Caro.'

Ted was gazing at me dreamily now, loving me. Ant looked uncertain, but I could tell he was halfway there.

'There are trains to London from Sheffield, surely? And then on into Oxford . . . straight from Paddington. Where's the bus-stop?'

'No, no—' began Bella.

'I'll drop you, luv,' said Ted, gruffly. 'I live in town. I'll give you a lift.'

'Oh, perfect.' I beamed. 'Thank you so much. And thank *you*,' I turned to Bella, on a roll now, 'for all your hospitality and everything. Bye, darling!' I sang to Ant. 'Bring my things with yours.' I patted his cheek as I got in Ted's car. 'You stay till Tuesday as planned—have fun!'

And off we purred, Terrific Ted and I, with Bella and Ant standing together on the crunchy gravel drive, waving us off uncertainly. When they were out of sight and I could legitimately wave no more, I turned and rested my head on Ted's sheepskin headrest. Shut my eyes.

'Oh God, what a nightmare,' I whispered.

Happily Ted was too busy leaning out of the window calling his own goodbyes to catch my heartfelt aside.

'Good.' He smiled, facing front. 'That went well. And as I say, it's all down to you. You made it work.' He reached across and squeezed my hand, giving it a little shake.

'Nonsense,' I murmured absently as we drove on up the lane. My head lolled sideways on the rest and I blinked out of the window. It was a heavenly morning, touched with frost, gilded with sun, and now that we were out of the shelter of the valley, the landscape spread about us frigid and ghostly white, the sky above as blue as the Costa Brava's.

'She's a lovely girl, your Bella,' I said at length.

He swallowed. Reached for his hanky. 'Aye.'

O Lord, here we go.

'I'll bet she has masses of men chasing after her, doesn't she?'

'Oh, aye, she's had her fair share of admirers, if that's what you mean.' It was very much what I meant.

'And any,' I persisted nosily, 'that she's tempted by?'

'Aye, she's had a boyfriend these last three years. Mike Hathaway, a local solicitor. They split up six months back. He buggered off.'

'Oh. Shame. Did you like him?'

He shrugged. 'I did, but I don't now. Like to punch his lights out.'

Right. Things were obviously done slightly differently in Yorkshire. We drove for a bit in silence, Classic FM gently easing our path.

'He's a grand chap, your Ant,' Ted remarked.

'Yes, he is.' I licked my lips, dug deep for courage. 'Although I don't suppose you thought that seventeen years ago.'

He shrugged. 'He was young. He made a mistake. We've all done that, haven't we? And he's more than made up for it now. He could have run too, couldn't he? But he didn't. And don't forget, he didn't know about Stacey. Who knows what might have been?'

My throat constricted. What Totally Truthful but verging on the Tactless Ted was saying here, whether he realised it or not, was that Ant might have stood by Bella and Stacey. Might? Would. So where would that have left me? High up on the stale bun shelf, that's where.

We drove on in silence, both lost in thought. When we'd left the bypass and negotiated a sprawling city with a startling juxtaposition of old and new architecture, which had even my distracted eyes swivelling round, we pulled up at the station.

'Thank you, Ted.' I leaned across and kissed his cheek.

'My pleasure, luv.'

With the sort of luck that is never habitually on my side, a train bound for the south was waiting, and at Paddington, another spookily convenient train whisked me to Oxford in record time. It gave me a few hours to reflect on why I had left Yorkshire in such a tearing hurry, and then to come to the startling, but alarming conclusion that, as usual, I'd not only acted impulsively and foolishly, but also imprudently. What had I really been afraid of back there in the Peak District? The sparking of Ant's latent emotions for Bella, or the sparking of all sorts of unattractive emotions in me, all sorts of jealous outbursts I'd have bitterly regretted later? I let out a low sigh. The latter, I suspected.

But I was here now. Could hardly go back, could I? Of course I couldn't. I walked out of the station. But by the same token, I couldn't go home either. Now that I was here, I knew I didn't want to be alone, imagining the rest of my family in that idyllic rectory in Yorkshire. Two minutes later, I was in the back of a taxi bound for the canal and Malcolm's company, which, right now, I decided, I badly needed. I knew he wasn't working today.

I hastened along the dusty towpath by the side of the meadow behind Worcester College, the sun glinting on the water and the long-boats slumbering peacefully at its edge. I could see Cinders, lying on her side, asleep in a sunny spot, beside Malcolm's very idiosyncratic barge: navy blue with red and yellow tulips painted in bold sprays. Quite the prettiest, I always thought.

As I knocked on the window, a freshly washed blond head and an eager smile popped out of the trap door. 'Oh.' His face dropped. 'It's you.'

'Oh, thanks.'

'Sorry, petal.' He clambered out on deck and came to greet me. 'It's just I was expecting someone else.' He peered down the towpath.

'A date?'

He sighed. 'I thought so. He should have been here an hour ago, though.' He glanced ruefully at his watch. 'And anyway, I've promised to relieve Ludo in the shop at five, so he's too late,' he said petulantly. 'Ah, well, it was only going to be Earl Grey. Can I interest you? You look a bit peaky.'

'So would you if you'd been sitting on a train for hours.'

'Where from?'

'Yorkshire.'

'Ah. The wicked witch of the North. Well, come on down.'

I followed him down the steep wooden ladder, ducking low to achieve the main cabin. 'She's hardly wicked. In fact quite the opposite.' I sat down heavily. 'She's Snow White. Sweet, beautiful, kind, success-ful—oh, Malcolm, how can he not fall in love with her again?'

'You've left him there?' He blinked. 'Interesting decision.'

'I panicked!' I pleaded. 'Thought, I've got to get out of here. It's just so weird, Malcolm!'

He shrugged. 'Well, you've got to leave them to it to some extent. See how it plays out.'

'You think?' I said eagerly.

'No, I'm just trying to say the right thing. It's what friends do.' He eyed me as he poured. 'But I don't doubt Ant for one moment.'

He didn't doubt Ant. No one ever did. Ant could do no wrong. Ant would never tenderly brush hair out of another woman's eyes. I mean, how familiar was that? Or perhaps it wasn't? Impulsively I unleashed a lock of hair from behind my ear and let it fall over my face.

Malcolm glanced up. Didn't notice. I flicked it forward more so it flopped over one eye.

'You haven't admired my tea set. It was my granny's.'

He was talking to my one visible eye for crying out loud: the one that wasn't curtained with hair. In desperation I plucked a socking great clump from the top of my head and flopped it right over my face.

'Evie, why are you doing that?'

'What?'

'Why is your hair all over your face?'

'Is it? I hadn't noticed.'

'Yes, you need to sort of . . . you know. Push it back.'

'Go on then.'

'What?'

'Push it.'

'Me? Why?'

'Because I'm holding my saucer.'

'Well, put it down.'

'Malcolm.' I clenched my teeth. 'Push my hair back!'

He stared. 'Oh, for heaven's sake.' He reached forward and brushed it clumsily off my nose. 'There.'

'Was that so difficult? *Why are you wiping your hand?*'

'I'm not!'

He was, though. On his trousers.

My shoulders sagged. 'You're right.' I nodded miserably. 'It is a very familiar gesture, isn't it?'

'What is?'

'Brushing hair out of someone's eyes. It's what Ant did to Bella. I watched from the bedroom window.'

'Oh!' His face flashed with recognition. 'Oh, no, not at *all*. It's just— well, you know how fastidious I am, always washing my hands. I've practically got that disease housewives get—oh!' He froze, mid-sentence, eyes wide. 'Did you hear something?'

The boat suddenly gave a terrific lurch. I clutched my tea.

'Helloo?' a voice called. 'Anyone at home?'

Malcolm's face lit up like a torch. 'It's him!' he breathed. He got to his feet, radiant suddenly, smoothing down his hair. 'Evie, you must go!'

'All right, all right,' I grumbled.

Malcolm flung the trap door wide and scampered up the ladder with me following in his wake. As I emerged in the sunlight, it was to see the most beautiful black man I'd ever clapped eyes on.

'My, but this is pretty,' he was saying admiringly, glancing around the boat. 'Very *Swallows and Amazons*. Sorry I'm late, I had a bit of a crisis.'

'No, no, not at *all*.' Malcolm was beaming and squirming delightedly.

'Sooty had a difficult stool,' he informed us.

'Sooty?' I asked.

'My dog,' he explained, and I followed his gaze to where a little black spaniel puppy was leaping delightedly round an indifferent Cinders. 'Quite fun calling her in the park. I'm afraid I couldn't resist it.' He flashed me a wicked grin. 'Clarence Tempest.' He held out his hand. Was he really gay? What a shame.

'Evie Hamilton,' I murmured, basking in his dazzling good looks.

'And she was just leaving,' purred Malcolm, hustling me away.

'Oh, don't go on my account,' Clarence said, smiling.

'She's not, she was going anyway,' Malcolm assured him with a pussycat smile, ushering him down the steps to his lair. I grinned and made my way down the towpath towards the bridge. Two minutes later, Malcolm was panting beside me, holding my arm. 'Evie, do me a favour. Stand in for me at the shop for an hour? I promised Ludo I'd be there. He wants to go to his sister's party and I promised—please, hon!'

'Oh, all right. Although I'll be hopeless. I haven't worked in years.'

'No one comes in. It's late-night shopping but they're all too busy buying three for two in Waterstone's. Thanks, luvvie. What d'you think, by the way?' he couldn't resist adding, eyes shining.

I grinned. 'He's gorgeous, Malcolm.'

'Isn't he just? He's on sabbatical from King's in London, doing an exchange at Corpus Christi. Teaches law. Imagine, beautiful *and* clever! Aren't I lucky!'

'You certainly are.'

I needed to take a very deep breath before I pushed open the door. My last meeting with Ludovic Montague, as I now knew him to be, had been of a fairly highly charged nature. Let's face it, I'd made a complete fool of myself. And for some reason, what he thought of me mattered, I realised with a start. So now I would be brisk and efficient, not tear-stained and needy.

'Well, hello.' He looked up from behind the counter.

I smiled. 'I've come to relieve you. Malcolm asked me to step in. He's entertaining.'

'Ah.' He took his glasses off. 'Would that by any chance be Clarence from puppy-training group?'

'It would.'

'And is poor Cinders still lying through her teeth about her age?'

'Is that what he's doing? Passing her off as a puppy?'

'Hasn't he told you? He saw this doggy group through the window of the church hall in Cardigan Street—or, more particularly, saw Clarence—and after weeks of lusting and steaming up the window, minced in with Cinders declaring she was nine months old.'

'I can just see him,' I giggled, relieved we were exchanging light-hearted banter, 'prancing around after Clarence, poor old bemused Cinders at his heels.'

He grinned. 'You look better,' he commented shortly.

I wasn't. But I wasn't going there. 'I am,' I lied. 'Much. We've just been up North to visit Bella Edgeworth and her daughter. Who's lovely, actually. They both are. And we all got on terrifically well, so that's marvellous, isn't it?'

'Marvellous,' he echoed faintly.

Damn. Why had I embarked on this? I hadn't needed to.

'So.' I joined him behind the counter and straightened a pile of books efficiently. 'Just another hour or so, is it? Till we shut?'

He wasn't deflected so easily. 'So, what—you made a flying visit?'

'What? Oh, yes. Well I did, but Ant and Anna are still there. Lots of things to discuss, naturally. And I felt a bit . . .' I tried to gather myself, 'well, superfluous, really!'

I stuck the exclamation mark on the end for courage, but the sentence rocked me nonetheless. Superfluous. Ludo stayed motionless on his stool beside me. Arms folded. Watchful.

'Well, no, not superfluous,' I went on as he watched me dig my hole. 'But the sisters, Stacey and Anna, wanted to get to know each other.'

'And your husband and Bella Edgeworth?' he asked gently.

'Needed to talk,' I managed. 'About their daughter.' A silence ensued. It hung there, waiting to be filled.

'I trust him implicitly,' I said, apropos of absolutely nothing.

He gave me a steady look. 'Good.'

'Even though,' I couldn't quite believe I was doing this, 'even though I'm sure he likes her very much. And it would be odd too,' I blundered on, flying kamikaze now, 'not to be attracted to anyone else at all, other than one's spouse, during the entire course of one's marriage.' Who was one, the Queen?

'It would,' he agreed, ever watchful.

'Were you ever?' I fumbled on, keen to dodge the spotlight. But what a *question*, Evie. She was dead!

'No.' Shortly.

'No, of course not,' I said quickly. 'I think I meant now. Yes, I'm sure I did. Now you're not married.' Worse?

'You mean, have I been attracted to anyone since Estelle died?'

'Yes.' I cringed.

'Only once.'

'Oh.' Something of a result. 'What happened?'

'Nothing. Nothing's happened. I mean—not yet.'

'She doesn't know?'

He didn't answer. As we looked at one another, a lock of hair worked itself free from behind my ear. He reached forward and gently pushed it back off my face.

A silence spread out around us. I recovered first.

'Right.' I got up with a start. 'You must . . . go to your party.'

'I must. It's a bit of a late engagement party. My sister's getting married at the end of the week. It's a drinks thing.'

'I see.'

I didn't really. I was miles away. Had he meant me? Or was I imagining things? I turned, quite boldly, and his eyes snagged briefly on mine. I quickly turned to the books on the shelves.

'Have you got secrets and lies?' asked a voice in my ear.

'Certainly not!' I spluttered. I turned to find a middle-aged woman frowning at me. She looked disconcerted.

'I think we have, actually.' Ludo swept by me to the Young Adult section. 'It's by Ian Atkinson, isn't it?'

'Quite possibly. It's for my grandson.'

A few minutes later, her purchase made, she hurried from the shop. Which left just Ludo and me. He glanced at his watch.

'There's only fifteen minutes till closing time. We may as well shut up shop, it's so quiet.' It was as if nothing had happened.

Wordlessly, I gathered my bag and scarf, and waited as he locked the till, then I followed him outside.

'How did you get here?'

'I walked. From Malcolm's. I came down by train, you see.'

'I'll give you a lift home.'

'No, no, I can walk.'

'Don't be silly, I live opposite you.'

'But you're going to a party.'

'That's where it is. I live with my sister at the moment.'

'Oh.' There didn't seem to be any answer to that, so I followed him mutely to a blue hire car and we drove through the backstreets of

Jericho. As we approached my road, his road, I glanced at him.

'How come you live here? You haven't always lived here?'

'No, I was renting a flat in Summertown before, but my sister's going to live in Scotland when she's married, so I'm taking over her flat. It seemed sensible to move in now. I'd have had to fork out another year's rent in Summertown. I've only been here a few months.'

We drew up outside my house. It was dark and uninviting. Across the street the lights shone; through an upstairs window a party could be seen silhouetted and in full swing, walls practically vibrating.

'Come and have a drink. It'll do you good. Do *me* good.'

'D'you think? I mean . . .'

He grinned. 'In light of what I've said? Look, Evie, I realise I've shown my hand, but I'm not going to jump on you. I'm not fifteen.'

I smiled into my lap. Nodded. 'No. I know. I'm sorry.'

'No cause for alarm. I believe it's what's called an idle crush.'

An idle crush. Well, I'd had a few of those in my time, who hadn't? I remembered a heavenly Latin teacher at Anna's school who I'd fondly imagined declining a few verbs with—but nothing more. I felt relieved. Flattered. I took a deep breath. 'I'd love a drink.'

The party was indeed at full tilt. Plenty of bright young things were packed in like so much human lasagne, knocking back champagne, shrieking and braying at each other in a high-ceilinged room.

'They look about nineteen,' I shouted over the din, accepting a glass of champagne from a passing waiter.

'Twenty-five-ish,' he shouted back. 'Alice was an afterthought. Ten years after my little brother Ed. Ah, here she is—Alice, this is Evie.'

'The bride.' I smiled as an attractive blonde with very pink cheeks swayed towards us in a pissed fashion in a plunging black dress. She looked vaguely familiar. 'Congratulations!' I shouted.

'Oh, we've met!' she squeaked. She reached out and clutched my hand. 'Don't you remember?' She staggered a bit. 'Oops.'

'We have?'

'Yes—you were having trouble with your poos!' she yelled.

I flushed. It was true, I did suffer spasmodically from constipation. Had news of it reached this side of the street? 'Really?' I gasped.

'Little annoying ones you had to pick up in your hands.'

No. I was pretty sure I'd never . . . 'Oh!' It dawned. 'Hector's! The horse,' I hurried to reassure Ludo, whose eyebrows were gently raised. 'I was mucking him out, and your sister was in the kitchen and—oh, you're getting married at the farm!'

'That's it.' She beamed happily. 'Caroline Milligan's place. It's absolutely fabulous—well, you *know*. You keep your horse there.' She waved her champagne glass at me and some spilt down my jumper.

'Yes, I used to live there, actually. It was my home.'

'Really?' Her bloodshot eyes widened. 'Gosh, how could you bear to leave it, it's *idyllic*. Angus and I just love it.'

'Well, it was my childhood home. It's my brother's now, he farms it. He's married to Caro, she's my sister-in-law.'

This was too much for Alice at this time of night, with the amount she'd shifted. She tried gamely to make sense of it. 'Caro is married . . .' she yelled, 'to a farmer?'

'That's it,' I shouted back, feeling weary. 'My brother, Tim.'

'Is he a farmer too?'

I remembered why I hated these stand-up-and-shout parties. Ludo's sleeve had been plucked and he'd half turned away to listen politely, head down, to what a tall, very beautiful redhead in a green halter-neck dress had to say in his ear.

'Can I just say,' Alice had found my ear too and was slurring into it, 'how thrilled we all are. Mummy and Daddy. Ed and me.' She rocked back on her heels, chin disappearing into her neck.

'Thrilled?'

'Yes, since Ludo's met you—he's a different person. You've no idea!' She flung her arms wide, champagne flying again. 'Oops—sorry!'

'Oh, no,' I shouted. 'You've got this wrong. I'm married!'

'Yes, I know, and he knows you're happily married, it's just—well, he never thought, after Estelle, he was capable of feeling anything, ever again. The fact that he can, even if it's not to be, is just a miracle.'

'Are you sure you're not exaggerating?' I shouted. 'I've met him about three times. I smashed up his car. Twice!'

She nodded. Lurched backwards. 'That's right,' she yelled. 'He met Estelle when she reversed into him in Sainsbury's in the Cromwell Road. That's what's so spooky. *And* she was engaged to someone else. He'd married her within three weeks! That's Ludo for you! Take it from me, he's got you firmly in his sights. This is no idle crush! Oh, s'cuse me. *Clemmie!*' she shrieked as a girl in a tiny white dress fell through the door. I hastily downed my drink. Shit. I must go. Three *weeks*.

I began to thread my way towards the door. I glanced over my shoulder. Ludo was still talking to the redhead; I'd just slip away.

'Evie!' I jumped out of my skin. Felicity had my arm. She followed my gaze. 'Rather gorgeous, I agree,' she yelled. 'Half these young girls are lusting after him.'

That hadn't escaped my notice as we'd walked in.

'Felicity. What are you doing here?'

'You mean at my age?' She laughed. 'I used to teach Alice. Rather a bright little thing when she could get up for lectures. But not a patch on her brother, apparently,' she yelled in my ear. 'I mean, brains-wise. Not my department, though, a historian.' She nodded in Ludo's direction. 'Bit of a legend by all accounts.'

Christ. Another bloody brilliant Oxford scholar. A legend. Why did I always pick them? Pick? No. I hadn't picked. Not remotely. I must go.

'Felicity, shield me, would you? I'm going to squeeze out.'

She blinked. 'Sounds dramatic. But listen, Evie, before you go, have you seen Maroulla?' Her eyes were anxious suddenly.

I went hot. 'No, but I keep meaning to. Damn, I keep forgetting.'

'No, no,' her hands were fluttery, 'I'm not saying you should. I mean—well, the thing is, Evie, she's so gaga now, I went the other day. And it'll just upset you.' She looked agitated.

'Is she? Oh God, how awful, *poor* Maroulla.' I stopped still. She'd been like a second mother to us when we were little. The thought of her gaga in a home somewhere was ghastly.

'I will go,' I determined, edging door-wards again and whipping my phone out. 'I'll put the address in here. It's Parsons Road way, isn't it?'

'Yes, but, Evie, I wouldn't, because—'

'Bugger, who's this?' My phone tinkled. 'Oh—Caro.'

In Carluccio's with Tim when Camilla rang. Wants to see Hector NOW. And you told Phoebe he could sleep rough. Thanks a bunch. On my way. Caro.

I gazed at the text in horror. Then I punched in Caro's number. She answered immediately. 'Caro? I'm back in Oxford,' I shrieked.

'I thought you were in Yorkshire?'

'I was, I'm back. It's a long story. What's the problem?'

'The problem is bloody Camilla Gavin. She's just rung to say she's on her way back from the sales in Newmarket, and she's passing our gate and wants to see Hector and give him a carrot. At this time of night! Which means she'll go to his stable and find it empty!'

I shut my eyes. Oh, blinking heck. She'd see Hector sleeping in the paddock with his lady friends, which was what he loved most, with a nice cosy rug on, which, when Anna and Phoebe's enthusiasm for mucking out had waned, had seemed the obvious solution.

'Right,' I quaked. 'I'll go over. Unless, of course, the children . . .?'

'Phoebe's at a sleepover and the boys are on a school trip. And I'm in Carluccio's because it's my bloody birthday.'

Her birthday. Oh God, I'd forgotten. 'Happy birthday,' I said weakly, massaging my forehead with my fingertips. 'Of course I'll go, Caro.'

'Well, I'd get down there fast, if I were you. She's just leaving Newmarket now. Don't forget, Pepper's in season so Hector's pretty sexed up at the moment. He might be a bit bolshie about coming in.'

'Not a problem,' I croaked. 'Don't you worry, Caro.'

I pressed the over-and-out button. When I glanced up, Felicity had been nabbed by a young man with a high, academic forehead. Ludo, on the other hand, was at my elbow. 'Problem?'

I gazed up into his eyes. The greeny-yellow flecks in them were glinting. 'What's your experience with sexed-up horses?' I whispered.

He returned my gaze steadily. 'Extensive.'

'You're lying.'

'Of course. But how else am I going to keep a grip on your company tonight?'

I took a deep breath. 'Come on,' I said grimly. 'We're leaving.'

'Where exactly are we going?' Ludo asked, not unreasonably, following at a more leisurely pace as I hurried down the stairs and across the street to my car.

'To my brother's place. The farm, where your sister's getting married. It's where this wretched horse is.' I turned the ignition, and because I'd left the car in gear, we kangarooed elegantly down the road.

He clutched the dashboard in mock terror. 'The horse with the unnaturally small faeces? Christ, steady.' He braced himself against the door as I picked up speed, wheels screaming as I took the corner.

'The very same.' The car righted itself. 'And the voracious sexual appetite that keeps him out in the field with the ladies, and not in the stable where he belongs, and where the woman who owns him thinks he is right now, and is hotfooting it to come and check.'

'Now? In the middle of the night?'

'Oh, Ludo, you have no idea.' I passed a harassed hand through my hair as we sped towards the ring road. '*No* idea. These horsy women are unbelievable. Particularly this one, Camilla.'

There was a silence as he sensibly let me negotiate a roundabout in peace, his white-knuckled grip on the upholstery the only giveaway.

'We're here,' I announced some minutes later, as, having belted at record speed down the lanes, I swung the car round the stone gatepost, only just grazing it. We came to a halt in the stony drive. 'Come on, the yard's over here.'

He followed as I marched off round the side of the house.

'So, presumably you grew up with horses?' he said, looking about as I disappeared into the tack room and emerged with a head collar.

'No, it was only ever Dad's thing. I was much happier with a book.'

'Ah.' He smiled.

'Mills and Boon,' I said tartly, before he got too excited. 'Right. Now you hold this . . .' I handed him a bucket with pony nuts in it, 'and when we're in the field, rattle it loudly to make a noise. When he comes across I'll try and nab him.'

'Got it.'

I ignored him. It occurred to me he'd become remarkably skittish since his earlier revelation, not quite the brooding, dour chap of yester-year. Was this him turning on the charm? If it was, I had to admit, it was rather attractive. And it was forcing me into a shrewish, exasperated role I knew wasn't attractive at all. But then, that was the point, wasn't it, Evie? I shut the feed-room door.

'Had much success with this method in the past?' he asked.

'Not a lot, but it's dark, so we might surprise him.'

'Right. But essentially,' he glanced in the bucket, 'we're counting on his physical appetite triumphing over his sexual one?'

'Yes, I suppose,' I said impatiently. 'Whatever.' Whatever. When had I ever said that? But it sounded quite good. I should have dropped the T.

'Mind if I take a couple more of these?' He turned to grab a pair of head collars hanging over a stable door.

'Wha'ever.' I strode off, pleased with myself, towards the paddock. I let us in. 'Now. They're usually down by the river. Jiggle your nuts.'

Ludo's face in the moonlight lit up.

I swallowed. 'Just . . . shake them,' I muttered. 'Hector!' I called, striding down the hill. 'Hec-torrr!'

'Aren't you just alerting him to our presence?' whispered Ludo, beside me. 'I thought an element of surprise was part of our plan?'

Bloody man. I didn't answer him, but he had a point.

We advanced river-wards, like a drummer boy and his army of one, I thought. Sure enough, as we marched down the grassy slope, we saw Hector standing under the willows with his two grey mares lying at his feet in an idyllic, pastoral scene, like a Stubbs painting.

'How cosy is that,' muttered Ludo. 'Three in a bed. But hasn't he had the snip? He can't be a stallion.'

'No, a gelding, but Caro reckons he might be a rig.'

'What's that?'

'A stallion who's had the op but it hasn't quite worked. He's lost most of his tackle, but he still gets the urge.' I was quite glad it was dark.

'Blimey. Poor bastard.'

'Now. You rattle, and I'll go round the back.'

'Hang on.' He stayed my arm. 'Can I just try something? Wait there.'

I folded my arms. Whatever it was, it wouldn't work. Recently, possibly because he wasn't coming in at night and being handled much, Hector had turned rather feral. Gone was the biddable Hector, and in his place, a thuggish Hector, with a very muddy hoody. He'd be in a mall soon, sipping Red Bull straight from the can.

I watched as Ludo put his bucket down and stole across to the pliant, sleepy mares. Within seconds he'd got a head collar on each. Ludo ignored Hector and led the mares to me.

'You've done that before.'

'Alice had a pony. But it's common sense. Or sexual psychology. Never chase a man. Ignore him, and he'll come running. You'll see.'

He challenged me with his eyes. I turned away abruptly and walked off, taking the mares with me. Annoyingly, Hector, who'd initially bolshed off towards the river, had turned, and was even now following us to the gate, albeit at a wary distance. 'Shall I have a go at getting him now?' I asked, realising I'd lost control in so many ways.

'No, let him suffer. Wait till he's desperate. Don't tell me you've never kept a man at a distance, Evie? Made him wait?'

I clenched my teeth. I certainly wasn't going to tell him I'd always done the chasing. We'd reached the gate and Ludo went ahead to swing it open for me. I led the mares through, one on either side.

'Now?' I glanced back. Hector was hovering anxiously.

'No, take them up to the yard. We'll teach him a lesson.'

Feeling like a pliant old grey mare myself, I dutifully led them away into the night. When we got to the stables I waited on the hardstanding with them. A few moments later, Hector appeared out of the darkness looking pretty worried. The ponies all whinnied to each other in relief, and Ludo popped Hector in a stable. Then he jerked his head at me and the mares. Clearly I'd morphed into the sort of woman who understands the jerk of a man's head, because I instantly turned and led the bemused mares back to their field.

Back in the yard, Ludo was propped up against a stable door, looking impossibly handsome and pleased with himself. 'Are we done here?'

'Not quite. Wait in the car. I won't be long.' I disappeared into the tack room to get a bucket of water and a sponge. Please go.

'Why, what happens now?'

I was inside Hector's stable now, bolting it firmly behind me. I wondered if I could do this in the dark. There was a stable light, but I certainly didn't want to turn it on. 'Oh, I've just got to change his rug,' I muttered, whipping off the muddy one and seizing the little purple number from a hayrack. I slipped it on him. 'Amongst other things . . .' I was buckling him up underneath.

'What other things?'

'Um . . . give him a wash.'

'A wash? Here—look, there's a light.' He flicked it on, just as I'd crouched down with my bucket and sponge and teased out Hector's . . .

There was a highly charged silence as I determinedly finished what I'd set out to do. After a while I couldn't bear it.

'Please wait in the car,' I whispered.

'You're kidding,' he drawled breathlessly. 'I wouldn't miss this for the world. Do you do this to all the boys?'

'It's Camilla,' I hissed, red-faced. 'She insists. She'll check.'

'I've changed my mind about Camilla,' he said after another long pause as he watched me. 'I love her. I want to have her babies.'

'Shut up, Ludo, and pass me that hoof pick.'

'I love it when you talk horse,' he moaned as I pointed to the pick.

'Just belt up and—oh. Shit!' I stood stock-still in the middle of the stable. Listened. 'She's here!' The unmistakable sound of thundering tyres and hissing air brakes filled the night, as the lorry surely rumbled through the front gate. A cab door slammed. 'Quick, turn off the light.'

Ludo flicked it off, and in an instant I was out of there, the stable door shut and bolted behind me. I looked around wildly, quivering with indecision. Too late, her heavy footsteps came earthshakingly towards us. Fi-fi-fo-fum . . . There was only one way into the yard, and she was coming through it. We were trapped.

'In here,' Ludo muttered.

Quick as a flash, he'd bundled me into the adjoining stable. We scuttled to a far corner and crouched down, Ludo's arm clamped pseudo-protectively round my shoulders, but I knew better. I glared at him and tried to shake him off, but he clamped himself even harder, a finger to his lips, enjoying himself hugely, not remotely scared.

There was the sound of a bolt shooting back on Hector's box. Then the stable light went on, and . . . instead of Camilla's usual clipped, posh bark, came breathy, treacly tones: 'Oh, Heccy Heccy, wath he a lubberly, lubberly boy then? Wath he? Kissy kissy, Hec. Brrr . . .!'

Sounds of a horse being open-mouth-snogged ensued. Or something horribly similar. I couldn't look at Ludo. Memories of Tim in church threatened. I bit my cheek and thought hard about Gordon Brown.

'Hath she been picking out your feet?' Pause while she checked. 'No, Mumma,' came a high-pitched, tremulous lisp. 'She hathn't.'

It was too much for Ludo. He snorted. I shut my eyes tight.

'Who's there?' The unmistakable tones of the real Camilla Gavin rang out from next door. She was out of Hector's box in a trice, working her way along the line of stables, happily away from us. We heard her kick in the doors, one by one. 'Come on—come out! Bloody gypos!'

She marched back our way, towards the only box she'd yet to kick in. As she opened the door and simultaneously flicked on the light, Ludo seized my face in his and kissed me very hard on the lips.

'Good *God*,' she spluttered.

I pushed Ludo away and sprang to my feet.

'What on *earth* are you doing?'

'Well, excuse me, Mrs Horse-lady,' Ludo drawled. 'This is Evie's family home. One might just as well ask what *you're* doing here, interfering with horses in the middle of the night. But since you ask, I came to check out the lighting for my sister's wedding here. Found Evie checking old Hector's rug—she's that fussy about his layers. The fact that I backed her into a stable and stole a kiss is really none of your business.'

'Good gracious.' She gaped. 'Evie, are you all right?'

'Yes,' I whispered pathetically, hanging my head. It wasn't hard.

Ludo sauntered past her, hands in his pockets, out into the yard. He turned to flash her a grin, then strolled off into the night. When he'd gone, she turned to me, aghast.

'What a *dreadful* man! Is he a Gypsy?'

'Quite possibly. Some sort of vagrant.'

'A very well-spoken one. Perhaps a drug addict? From the varsity?'

'Perhaps.'

'*Are* you all right? You should have slapped his face!'

'I . . . was about to.'

We stared at each other. I had a nasty feeling she wasn't entirely convinced. Could go either way. 'Would you like me to put another rug on Hector?' I asked unctuously. 'I was worried he might be cold.'

It was the right move. 'No. No, I've felt behind his ears, he's fine.'

'Good, well, if you're sure . . . I'll be off then.' I slid past her nervously in the stable. Out of the door.

'Good for you for checking on old Hector!' she called after me.

'Not a problem!' I trilled back, throwing myself into the car. I roared out of the drive, wheels spinning in the mud. A few hundred yards down the lane, Ludo was sauntering along. I slowed down, leaned across and threw open the passenger door as I stopped.

He hopped in, grinning. 'I thought that went rather well.'

'Really. Except that when she's given it some thought and finds out who you really are, she'll realise we've duped her, and then it'll be all round the village: Evie Hamilton, found snogging in a stable with a man half her age.'

'Being assaulted in a stable,' he corrected me, 'by a man surely only a few years younger than herself. How old are you, anyway?'

'None of your business.' I suppressed a smile and drove on fast towards town. That shut him up. The driving, I mean. Occasionally I heard him utter a profanity under his breath as we took a corner. When I drew up outside Ludo's house, his eyes were shut.

'Dare I look?'

'Idiot. We're here.'

'Thank the Lord.' He looked at me. Watched me, rather. Fondly. Consideringly. 'Fun, though, wasn't it?' he said lightly.

'Yes,' I agreed softly. 'It was.' I sat, motionless, in the warm focus of his regard. The silence hung around us.

'Night, Evie.' He leaned across to kiss my cheek, but instead, his head dipped, and his lips brushed my neck. It was the gentlest of touches but the most electrifying.

As the blood surged under my skin, I knew I desperately wanted him to kiss me properly. The thought shocked me. 'Ludo—'

'Shh.' He put his finger on my lips and I saw in his eyes he'd read both emotions. The desire, and then the shock. 'Don't panic,' he told me quietly. 'But don't go away.' And then he got out of the car.

7

THE FOLLOWING MORNING, Caro was on the phone before I'd even opened my eyes. 'Are you all right? Camilla said you'd been assaulted in a stable!'

I propped myself up on one elbow. Switched the phone over to the other hand. 'Caro, it's a long story and it's only half past seven.'

'And I've been up for an hour and I'm armed with a coffee. Tell.'

I sighed, but knew better than to argue. When I'd finished there was a long silence.

'So he did kiss you?'

'Yes, but purely in the line of duty.'

'On the lips?'

'Yes, OK, on the lips, but—'

'Tongues?'

'Certainly not!'

'Just asking. Was it nice?'

'Caro!'

'It was!' she breathed ecstatically.

'Goodbye!' I snapped, putting the phone down. *Was it nice?* What a question! I got in the shower cubicle, turning my face up to the jet of hot water. *Was it nice?* I washed my hair vigorously, then got out, found a towel and wrapped it round me. Walking slowly to the long mirror and towelling my head at the same time, gazed critically at my face, with its still-creamy complexion, rather too full lips. Kissable lips, Ant used to say. I stared. Yes, OK, it was nice. Very nice. Especially the one I hadn't told her about. I towelled myself dry and got dressed. Giving myself an inward shake and reminding myself of certain friends of ours involved in unseemly midlife crises, I went downstairs to make a cup of tea.

The house was very still, very quiet. Unnaturally quiet: no Brenda, of course. Caro was looking after her at the farm. I went to the calendar on the side of the fridge: flipped over the page. Tuesday the 23rd. Ant was going on a book tour in the West Country on . . . the 26th. Oh. So pretty much the moment he got back. I wouldn't see him. Not properly, anyhow. I certainly wouldn't be able to talk to him properly. Hear about Bella and Stacey. As much as he'd tell me, anyway. As much as he'd tell me? We'd always told each other everything. But then, I wouldn't tell him about last night, would I?

The phone rang, making me jump. I snatched it up. 'Hello?'

'Hi, it's me.'

'Ant!' I sat down abruptly, flooding with relief. 'Darling, how are you?'

'I'm OK.' He sounded guarded. My chest tightened.

'Good,' I said lightly. 'And Anna?'

'She's fine.'

I licked my lips. This wasn't right. Didn't sound right.

'So, when are you coming home?'

'Well, there's been a bit of a hitch. The publishers have just rung to say that the rep who was taking me on the book tour in Devon is ill, but they've managed to cobble something together with the rep up here and he's going to take me to Harrogate, Leeds and Ripon instead. So I'll stay here, if that's all right?'

'With Bella?'

'Yes, it makes sense.'

Was he telling me or asking me? 'Of course. And Anna?'

'Well, Anna says she's got some Pony Club rallies, so I'm going to put her on the nine fifteen to London. She'll be on the train to Oxford around twelve o'clock. I'll get her to ring you en route, OK?'

'Yes, OK.'

We said goodbye and I put the phone down. Gazed at the wall. The longcase clock in the corner ticked on.

Anna got off the train just after one o'clock and walked towards the barrier looking deliberately nonchalant.

'How was it?' I slipped round the barrier to greet her.

'Fine,' she said with studied boredom. 'I was in bags of time at Paddington, so I had a hot chocolate in Pret A Manger.'

I smiled and took her bag as we walked along. Now that would hit the spot. Having a hot chocolate in London, alone, at fourteen. I opened the car doors and she got in. Odd how, in such a short space of time, she looked different. Thinner. Taller.

I went to put the key in the ignition. Dropped it. 'My God—you've had your ears pierced!'

'I know.' She twisted a tiny gold stud in her ear. Guilt mingled with brazenness flooded her face.

'But—'

'Dad said I could. Chill, Mum, I'm fourteen. I had this done as well.' She pulled up her T-shirt and a tiny gold stud winked at me from her tummy button.

'Anna!' She met my eyes, defiant. Suddenly I knew what she was doing. I fumbled for the keys, started the engine.

'I suppose Stacey's liberally pierced, is she?' I said, trying to keep my voice steady.

'Well she's seventeen, so why not? But as it happens, no.' There was real aggression in her voice. Her face looked pinched. Older.

'Where did you have it done?'

'Claire's. And no, it won't go septic. I've put surgical spirit on it.'

Breathe, Evie. Breathe. It's hardly a tattoo. Nothing permanent. She was texting on her mobile now. Stacey? Either way, she wasn't paying attention to me. I fought for composure.

'So how was it, oop North?' I said with studied lightness.

She shrugged. 'You were there.'

'Yes, but yesterday. Did you have fun with Stacey?'

'Yeah, it was good.'

'Did you go out at all? Meet her friends?'

'No.' She turned incredulous, you're-such-a-loser eyes on me.

'So what did you get up to last night? What did you do?'

'Stuff.'

'Did you all have supper together?'

'Who?'

Blood from stones. 'You and Daddy, with Bella and Stacey.'

She swallowed. Stared out of the window. Didn't answer.

'Anna?'

She turned back. Her eyes were bright. 'Look, Mum, you're going to have to ask Dad about this. I promised, OK?'

I nearly crashed. 'Promised what?'

Silence.

'Promised *what*, Anna?'

I stopped the car. Right there on the Banbury Road. The back end swung round in surprise. 'PROMISED WHAT?' I shrieked.

'I can't tell you, OK?' she shrieked back. 'I can't!' And with that she burst into tears, got out and began to run.

'Anna!' I caught up with her and seized her. Gripping both her shoulders, I shook her hard. It's no excuse, but I was very frightened. She wrenched herself free, face streaming with tears.

'Ask Dad, OK?' she yelled in my face, her own, red and contorted.

'Anna, this is ridiculous,' I breathed. People were watching.

Tears were filling my eyes now, and she saw it. Saw my anger was over. 'I can't,' she said miserably. 'You'll find out. I can't.'

Every fibre in my being turned to ice. We stood staring at each other. I held out my arms and she walked into them. We held each other close. Then we walked back to the car together and drove home.

Later that afternoon, she found me sitting at the kitchen table in the fading light. My mobile flickered feebly in my hand. I'd thrown it at the wall when an anonymous voice had informed me for the tenth time Ant's mobile was switched off.

Anna stood in the doorway. 'I've just spoken to Phoebe. You know this Pony Club thing is a three-day event? She says why don't I stay there. At the farm. It's happening in next door's fields.'

'OK. I'll drop you over there.'

'Tonight?'

'If you like.'

Even though it didn't start till tomorrow. I saw relief flood her face.

I didn't go in at the farm. Brenda was in the yard with Megan, and came wagging towards us, jumping straight on the back seat when I opened the door. I just dropped Anna off, with her overnight bag and her jodhpurs and hat, and some chocolates for Caro, telling Anna to let her know I'd got the dog. Normally I'd always pop in, but I knew Caro would take one look at my face, drag me to the sitting room, shut the door on the children, and then the floodgates would open.

Ten minutes later found me walking along the canal towpath. It was dark, but Malcolm's boat was always lit up like a Christmas tree, making it easy to find among the other barges. As I approached, I saw Cinders and Sooty rolling around together in the grass. I stopped. What might I be interrupting? I hesitated.

'Well, hello.' Malcolm's voice, not discernibly displeased, hailed me.

I hastened on, encouraged, and saw the pair of them, sitting in wicker chairs on deck, wrapped in overcoats, scarves and blankets.

'Clamber aboard, m'hearty.'

'You're sure? I'm not interrupting?'

'Certainly not,' said Clarence, standing up to offer me a hand. 'In fact you're just the girl I need. I'm trying to piece together the jigsaw that is Malcolm's life, and all I'm getting at the moment is sky. I feel you might be a crucial corner.'

Malcolm beamed, thrilled that Clarence was bothering to piece him together, and I sat down relieved in a spare wicker chair. The water lay inky around us, and the stars twinkled down from the velvet heavens.

Malcolm got up to pour me a glass of Chablis, and Clarence confided, 'If you're wondering what we're doing out here in the middle of October, I get horribly seasick down below.'

I giggled. 'But it's hardly moving.'

'I kid you not. Malcolm's cabin makes me feel like I'm being tossed around on the high seas.'

'That might be a problem, then?' I ventured.

'Nothing we can't handle. And Sooty loves it.'

We glanced across to where Sooty was chasing Cinders in mad, frantic circles in the grass. 'Look at Cinders go!' I marvelled.

'I know,' agreed Malcolm. 'New lease of life.'

As two pairs of eyes gazed gooily at their dogs, I realised a little sea-sickness was not going to be insurmountable.

'So what brings you here, sugar?' asked Malcolm breezily, knowing full well it had to be a major catastrophe, but begging me, with his eyes, not to rain on his romantic, starlit parade. Which I wouldn't.

'I need a job, Malcolm. I've decided I don't do enough. And I think and imagine far too much, when what I actually need is occupation. But the thing is, all I've ever done is sell books. So I was wondering . . . well, I wondered if you needed anyone in the shop. I badly need to work.' My voice was in danger of quavering and I sank into my wine.

'I wondered when you'd get bored with your gilded cage,' said Malcolm lightly.

I glanced up. 'You think that's what it is?'

He shrugged. 'I think you lead an enviable, cushioned existence. Which would be enough for many women. But you're brighter than the average monkey, Evie. And you can't just be the supporting act.'

I swallowed. 'Even though it's what I've always been.'

'You've changed, Evie. You've grown up.'

I wasn't quite sure what he meant by that. I could feel Clarence watching me. 'And it's not just me,' I said, instinctively dodging the spotlight. 'Ant and Anna would be pleased too, I'm sure.'

Malcolm frowned. 'You're doing it for them?'

I ducked and weaved some more. 'Of course not. I'm just saying . . . well, obviously I'm doing it for me. For self-esteem, and—oh, give us a sodding job, Malcolm.'

He smiled. 'Now that the shop's so much bigger we could do with the extra help, and you're a good bookseller, Evie. Good with people.'

I glowed. 'Thank you.'

'But this isn't to be some dilettante stance which you chuck in after a couple of months when your family life is back on track, OK?'

I gulped. 'Absolutely not.' I meant it. 'So when can I start?'

'As soon as you like. Your mum does Tuesday afternoons now, and Sundays and Mondays are quiet, but Wednesday to Saturday would be good.'

'Perfect,' I said firmly. 'But can I have Friday off because Anna's in a pony club competition?'

'Of course. And you don't have to do every Saturday,' he said kindly. 'We tend to rotate them, Ludo and I.'

I nodded. 'Um, Malcolm, that's the only tricky bit, actually. Ludo.'

'I thought he'd forgiven you for trashing his car?'

'He has. The problem is, Malcolm . . .' I took a deep breath, 'Well, the problem is, he fancies me.'

Malcolm stared at me. Suddenly he threw his head back and roared with laughter. 'Don't be ridiculous, Evie!' He turned to a bemused Clarence. 'Ludo's hot,' he explained.

'Oh, thanks!' I spluttered.

'No, but he is, hon, isn't he?' he pleaded, eyes brimming with ill-disguised mirth. 'He's young and he's fit and—'

'Sounds just like Evie.' Clarence smiled loyally.

'Oh, no, he's *much* fitter than Evie!'

'Malcolm! He's not even that much *younger* than me, *actually*. Anyway,' I went on doggedly, albeit through clenched teeth, 'it would be better if I did my shifts with you, rather than him.'

'What, in case he ravishes you in Fantasy Fiction?' he snorted. This struck Malcolm as unbearably funny. Clarence and I waited patiently as he rocked about, clutching himself. 'Oh God,' he moaned, 'marvellous. Absolutely priceless. Yes, sure, whatever you want, Evie. Ludo's mostly there at the beginning of the week, anyway.'

'Thanks for the drink.' I stood up.

'You're going?' Clarence got up too as I drained my glass. We both studiously ignored Malcolm, bundled in his rugs, sniggering weakly.

'I am. I shall leave you in peace. I wouldn't want Malcolm to have a hernia. But thanks, Malc.' I prodded my incapacitated friend with my toe. 'You're a star.' He raised a weak hand in recognition.

'My pleasure, hon. You've made my evening.'

If I were to put my motives for going back to work under a mental microscope, I'd probably conclude that I'd wanted to impose some control on my life: that it seemed to be spiralling away from me; that this was a stab at self-preservation. But whatever my motives, what I hadn't bargained on was enjoying it. Remarkably, though, those first couple of days in Malcolm's shop were the happiest I'd had for some time.

Initially, of course, I was ridiculously nervous, thinking I couldn't begin to get to grips with the new computer system or the credit card machines. But within moments of Malcolm showing me, I was away. I remembered why I'd done it for so long; why, when friends said, 'But isn't it just like being a shop assistant?' I'd smile, knowing it wasn't. Particularly in a small shop like this, where people came for help and advice, and often with only the scantest shreds of information.

'It's red,' one faintly harassed woman said, as she glanced back at her car outside on a yellow line, fairly vibrating with children.

'Red,' repeated Malcolm, patiently.

'And quite big.' She demonstrated with her hands as she turned to shake her head furiously at the wild animals in the Discovery.

'What's it about?' Malcolm prompted gently.

She turned back distractedly. 'Battles. Wars.'

Malcolm steered her through to Ludo's side. 'Military history? A new one?'

'Yes!'

Getting warmer.

'Been reviewed?'

'Yes. My husband read about it at the weekend, said he'd like it.'

'What paper does he read?'

'*The Sunday Times.*'

'*The History of the Crusades* by Victoria Clark?' Malcolm plucked a large red book from a pile on a round mahogany table.

'Oh! That's it. Oh, you *are* clever.'

She glowed, paid, and left the shop at racing speed, waving her keys furiously at her brood. I too looked admiring. 'Nice work.'

He shrugged.

Then came some browsers—students, mostly—then more women and children, which was right up my alley as Anna had read a lot of the books they were after, and I was able to guide and enthuse accordingly. Then an elderly woman, in a long brown coat, who smelt of spearmints. She plucked a Catherine Cookson from the shelves and shuffled to the counter. 'I've found one I haven't read!' she declared.

Malcolm picked it up. 'Joan, you've read this.'

'No, I've never read one with a windmill on the front.'

'Ah, but they've repackaged them. Changed the covers. This one,' he reached under the counter, 'is this one.' He produced another book.

She stared, dismayed. 'I've read that.'

'I know. Sorry, pet.'

'Oh. Oh, well.' She turned to go.

I nipped round the counter. 'Um, Joan, have you tried Lyn Andrews? She writes lovely period romances, very Catherine Cookson.'

She took the book I'd plucked from a shelf behind me. 'I don't know . . .'

'Try it,' I urged. 'And if you don't like it, I'll give you your money back.'

Behind me I heard Malcolm moan low and drop his head like a stone on the counter. He banged it up and down, Basil Fawlty-style.

'All right,' she said, brightening. 'I'll take it.'

'Hon!' Malcolm wailed when she'd left. 'I'm not running a charity.'

'Trust me. She'll be back.'

'Indeed she will,' he muttered darkly.

Sure enough she was. The next day. 'Read it in a day!' she declared. 'In the bath too. Has she written any more?'

Some were harder to please. One tall, haughty-looking woman with a nose a great deal of breeding had gone into, wanted a light romance for her niece. I offered her the best-selling chick-lit title.

'Has it got any sex in it?' she demanded.

'None at all,' I assured her.

'Well, that's no good, is it?' she snapped and left the shop.

'Never fall for the niece ruse, hon,' Malcolm murmured. 'Point her in the Anonymous direction, next time. She wants to get horny.'

The shop was a friendlier place than I recalled in Jean's reign. Most people knew Malcolm by name; some came to buy, some to browse, and some, it seemed, just to chat. One or two curled up on the sofas upstairs for hours, read books they didn't buy, and even spilt coffee on them, brewed for them by Malcolm in his kitchen.

'Don't you mind that they don't buy?'

He shrugged. 'They're students—no money. They make the place look busy and tell other people about it, who do buy.'

I watched him go carefully back upstairs balancing a tray of Nescafé. He was a sweetie, Malcolm. But sweeties didn't make money.

'Oh, there's no money in it. But it's a nice place to be, isn't it? And isn't that what life's about? Having a nice time?'

He had a point. And with only a houseboat and a dog to run, what did Malcolm need with money? I sensed, though, that he was distracted, these days: his eyes were permanently on the door, looking for Clarence to come in, which he did, every lunchtime, whisking Malc off to Bertorelli's or somewhere equally smart.

'How come Clarence is so rich?' I asked one day.

'He inherited it. He's a trustafarian. Close your mouth, Evie, it's not becoming. Here he is. Can you see my spot?' He raised his chin anxiously as a sleek convertible Mercedes drew up outside.

'Hardly. Just keep your chin resting pertly in your hand all lunchtime. You'll be fine.'

And off he went, frisky with excitement, leaving me in charge of a shop and two dogs for a couple of hours, which I loved.

I wandered round, trying not to think too much, passing the time with customers, managing not to dwell too much on my own problems. Managing not to go there. Up North.

After Anna's little outburst on the Banbury Road, I knew, of course, that something reasonably monumental had happened. And initially, I'd rung, of course I had, nearly broken my phone in the process. Something had stopped me calling The Old Rectory—pride, maybe— but the very next morning, on my first day at work, I'd tried again, hoping to get Ant on his mobile. His answering machine was on. I left a message. No reply. I sent a text. I know you can't talk, but Anna was very upset when I picked her up yesterday. What's going on? LOL E x.

I got an equally measured one back. I'm sorry she was upset. Can I please tell you when I get back? LOL Ax.

I read it again. I felt my blood rise. My thumb got to work. No. Tell me now. If you think I'm going to sit here and stew while you . . .

While he what, Evie? I stopped. Scrubbed out my rant. Some quiet wisdom, something very un-Evie Hamilton stole over my soul. Something in my daughter's face in the Banbury Road, which I couldn't quite put my finger on. I looked at his text again. He'd asked if I could please wait. Asked politely. And implicit in that, I realised in a sudden rush of blood to the head, was Trust Me. And Ant was an honourable man. I mustn't lose sight of that. I went about my work with a dawning sense that something bigger than the personal happiness and well-being of Evie Hamilton was going on here.

The next day, I got another text. I've booked Carluccio's for Friday night. LOL Ant x.

Carluccio's. Where we always went for major chats. The biggies.

I texted back: Fine.

That night, I was woken by the sound of a sash window sliding up. Still in the folds of a disappearing dream I groped groggily for the clock in the dark. Ten past two. I lay there listening. A creaking noise from below, in the kitchen. I sat bolt upright. Soft footsteps were stealing round down there. I jumped out of bed and threw on my dressing gown. It occurred to me that I'd forgotten to lock the kitchen window. Footsteps crept towards the foot of the stairs. I prickled with fear. Panic button. I knew we had one under the bed. I dived underneath. But it was pretty crowded. Over the years I'd stashed a lot of rubbish behind the valance, and I couldn't get to it. Couldn't reach the button.

The footsteps kept coming up the staircase, creeping . . . then stopping. The door softly opened. He was in the room. I put my fist in my mouth to stop myself screaming. I heard him first at the chest of drawers, scooping up the loose change Ant kept in a saucer. Then drawers opened softly, but didn't shut. Next I heard him at my dressing table, rustling in my jewellery box. I stared, wide-eyed into the darkness, nerves as taut as violin strings, when, improbably, awfully, the mattress above me sagged heavily as the springs gave way. My eyes bulged in the darkness. He'd got in my bed. This was beyond my stunned intelligence. A tramp? A vagrant? I lay there, rigid with horror. Then he cleared his throat. I slowly took my fist out of my mouth. 'Ant?' I said, mostly under my breath.

'Yes?' came back a cautious response from above.

It still took me a moment. I scrambled out of there and darted to the light switch by the door. As I illuminated the room and swung about, we stared at one another in astonishment.

'Where did you spring from?' he gaped, sitting bolt upright in bed.

'Under the bed!' I gasped.

'Why?'

'Because I thought you were a bloody burglar, that's why! What are you doing here, Ant?'

'I live here!'

'Yes, but you were coming back tomorrow.' Fear had sucked the air from my lungs and I sounded as if I'd inhaled a helium balloon. 'What were you doing in my jewellery box?'

'I wasn't in your jewellery box, I was putting my watch down.'

I stared at him in disbelief. 'How did you get in?'

'Through the door.'

'But the window. I heard it—'

'You left it open. I shut it.'

'Why didn't you ring?'

'Because it's the middle of the night. I didn't want to wake you.'

'But you must have known I wasn't in bed!'

'I assumed you were at the farm or something.'

'Oh, Ant . . .' I flew to him. Threw my arms round his neck and he held me close. 'I was so scared,' I breathed in his ear.

'I'm sorry, I'm sorry, I'm sorry,' he whispered back.

We held on tight like that for a minute. Eventually I drew back; sat opposite him on the bed. 'Why are you here?'

'Because when I got your terse little text, I suddenly realised what you might be thinking. I knew I had to come back.'

My text. What had I said? Fine. Yes, a bit terse, but then I'd felt terse. 'What's this about, Ant?' I managed.

'It's about Bella. But it's not what you're thinking. She's very ill.'

His eyes were sad, I realised. Some distant wave of comprehension was gradually building out at sea, slowly approaching.

'Define very ill.'

'It's terminal. She's got cancer. She's dying.'

He watched me absorb it: watched the wave break over me and throw me onto the beach.

'She *can't* be,' I heard myself say eventually.

'She is,' he said.

'How long?' I whispered. 'Until . . .'

He made a helpless gesture. 'No one knows, exactly.'

'But . . . isn't there something they can do?'

'It's cervical and it wasn't caught in time. Wasn't picked up.'

Cervical. The silent killer, they called it. 'She doesn't look ill,' I said.

'She's very thin.'

Yes. Yes, she was thin. I remembered those tiny legs protruding from her denim skirt and disappearing into floppy boots.

'And very pale,' he added.

'Yes,' I conceded numbly, recalling her pale, anxious face. I remembered feeling ruddy and hulking beside what I imagined to be her ethereal beauty. And I remembered Ted's face too, when I'd commented in the car on how lovely she was. How the tears had welled up again. No wonder. His daughter. His *grand*daughter.

'Stacey!' I breathed. 'Oh my God—does she know?' I asked stupidly.

'Of course. From day one.'

Yes. Of course she knew. Questions were muscling through the wall of shock now, in no particular order. 'When did she tell you?'

'Bella? The second day we were there. You were still asleep upstairs.'

I stared at him. 'Under the cherry tree? On that little round seat?'

'Yes.'

'You pushed her hair back.'

'Did I?' He looked startled. Then bewildered. 'Maybe. I don't remember. Perhaps I felt I had to . . . you know, do something.'

'Oh, Ant.'

'What?'

'You should have taken her in your arms!' I roared. 'Held her close, held her tight, my *God*, Ant!' I gazed at him. What kind of uptight emotionally repressed academic was he?

He shrugged helplessly. 'I didn't know what to do, what to say. I needed you then, Evie. You'd have known what to do.'

'You should have stopped me going home, told me! Oh Lord,' I breathed. I remembered them waving me off. So brave. And Ant, smiling, waving too, playing a part. What planet was he on? But what did it matter: the girl was dying. 'Is that why they asked us up there?'

'Yes. Mostly.'

'So Anna knows? Which is why she's so upset?'

'Yes. I told her. She was terribly shaken.' He took a deep breath. 'One thing I did do, when Bella and I talked later, with the girls, which I shouldn't have done without consulting you, and the reason I needed to talk to you face to face, and didn't want Anna saying anything first . . .' He stopped, hesitating.

I frowned. 'Is?'

'Is I promised to look after Stacey.'

'Well, of course.'

'No.' He swallowed. Didn't meet my gaze. 'Not just keep an eye.

Really look after her. For ever. With us. Live here with us. I'm her father, Evie. She needs me. Bella asked me. And I said yes.'

My heart thudded. Which is all it took. A heartbeat. I'm ashamed it took that long. 'Yes, of course.'

'Yes?'

'Yes,' I repeated.

He looked at me. I glimpsed fear vanishing from his eyes. Then they filled up. 'Oh, Evie.'

He let out a breathy sigh.

'What did you think I'd say?'

'I didn't know. I'm really appalled to say, I didn't know. But I should have known. But . . .' he struggled, 'she's mine, after all, not yours. And Anna's too, of course, and we thought—'

'Anna thought I'd say no, too?' I remembered her face in the car: challenging, defensive, gold earrings glistening aggressively.

'She came back from town that day with Stacey and you'd gone, so she assumed you'd flounced off home, couldn't hack it. You told me not to tell her about Hector . . . But then later, when she found out about Bella—well, she assumed you'd say . . . well, it's a big ask.'

I was shocked. They both thought that I wouldn't bring up someone else's child. And actually, if he'd asked me when he'd first got the letter, yes, I might well have said forget it. A big ask. Was it? It didn't feel like it now. What—that shy, sweet, seventeen-year-old girl? With no mother? Oh, no. She had to come here. Did they think I was a witch?

'Evie,' he took my hands, reading me, 'what you fail to realise is that an awful lot of women, regardless of how nice Stacey is, would not want their husband's child in the house, let alone living with them.'

I gave this some thought. Put like that . . . 'And what *you* don't realise,' I said slowly, 'in the spirit of full disclosure, is what I thought was going on. That in my darkest moments, I thought I'd lost you. Give a child a home? Oh, Ant, there's no comparison.'

We sat facing each other on the bed. After a moment, I laid my head on his shoulder. He drew me in close.

'I know you don't know exactly, but . . . weeks? Months?'

'Months. Maybe weeks. She's in and out of the hospice. Ted's not good. Not good at all. Stacey's being unbelievable, but Ted—'

'But surely Stacey might have gone there?'

'Well, of course, he would have had her like a shot. Wanted to have her. But he could see . . . well, we all talked about it—'

'Did you?' Blimey. Anna. What a very grown-up conversation. No wonder she looked older.

'And Bella was very firm. Ted's a tremendous grandfather, always will be, but she wanted a proper family for Stacey. A young family, and when Stacey got the interview at Oxford—'

I inhaled sharply. 'It was a no-brainer.'

'That's when they wrote. Bella said they agonised for ages, thinking it wasn't fair on me, on you, but knowing too, at the end of the day . . .'

'She had to do the best for her child. She did the right thing.'

'I'm so glad you think so, Evie.' He couldn't mask his relief. His hand closed over mine and he squeezed it, summoning up something else. 'And I'm so, so glad I'm married to you.'

I couldn't help but smile. That was huge, coming from Ant. We sat there on the bed together, exchanging sad little smiles, holding hands. At length, I stood up.

'Where are you going?'

'To ring Bella.'

'It's the middle of the night.'

'She'll still be awake. And she'll be waiting for me to call.'

8

THE FOLLOWING MORNING I drove to watch Anna in the final day of her pony competition. You couldn't have scripted the day. It was one of those hazy golden ones with just a faint breeze, which might just as well be August. As I turned into Ed Pallister's farm, just down the lane from ours, it occurred to me that Bella Edgeworth wouldn't wake up to too many more mornings like these. I locked the car and made my way towards a far-flung field, full of circling ponies in the distance, reaching in my bag for my sunglasses in defence of the low sunshine and much else.

We'd talked at length last night, Bella and I. And when I'd finally come back up the stairs to bed, I'd repeated it all pretty much verbatim to Ant. I told him first about her treatment. 'It makes her pretty sick.'

'Oh.' His eyes widened slightly at me. 'I didn't know that.'

'Didn't you ask what she was on? Talk to Ted about it?'

'I tried but he got so upset. He's very emotional, Ted,' my husband informed me gravely, as if perhaps I didn't know. 'Blew his nose a lot.'

I smiled. 'I'll talk to him. He'll have to come and stay often, certainly at the beginning, so that Stacey's got an ally, a friend. Bella agreed. I thought he might come on holiday with us.' I switched the bedside light off.

'Right,' I heard Ant say faintly.

We carried on talking quietly in the dark, or I did. He listened. Familiar roles. I told him how, initially, Stacey had said she'd like to live with her granddad, stay up north with her friends, maybe not even go to Oxford at all. They'd argued. Stacey had talked of getting a job, doing a secretarial course. Bella had had to push.

'She's terrified of being without you,' I'd said to her mother on the phone.

'Of course she is, but the thing is, Evie, Dad would just give in to her—and that would be such a waste. And I'm running out of time here. I'm having to edge her on all the time, persuade her.'

'But her reservations are understandable. We're strangers, effectively.'

'Of course you are, and she loves her granddad very much, and doesn't want to leave him alone with his grief, and I understand *all* of that, and there's an element of me that says—oh, let her be, Bella. Let her have a year off at least, she's so young. She could apply next year, or even the year after, but an even bigger bit of me knows she wouldn't.'

'What, wouldn't reapply?'

'Not without me there to push her, no. I just need to know she's on track before I die,' she said with an air of desperation but not a hint of martyrdom. 'Is that so selfish of me?'

'Not at all,' I said slowly, 'and you're the best judge. Presumably you're equally certain once she starts her degree she'd enjoy that too?'

'Oh, she'd love it, that's entirely my point. She'd never look back.'

'OK, so now that she's met us, how does she feel? About coming?'

'Much happier. As long as she knows *you're* all happy, that's her biggest angst. She doesn't want to impose.'

'She won't be imposing. Ant would love to have her. Anna would love to have her. I'd love to have her,' I said, with a truthfulness that surprised me. 'But it all has to be done softly-softly.'

'Otherwise she'll feel bamboozled, I know. I'm so worried she'll get the next train back and I won't be there to stop her.'

'I'll stop her.'

I heard her swallow. 'Oh, Evie . . .' she managed.

'And anyway, she won't do that,' I rushed on, saving us both. 'As long as everything's done sensitively, with patience—'

'*Endless* patience, which is a lot to put on you, a lot of pressure. She's going to be desperately grief-stricken, she's got no idea.' Her speech was coming rapidly now, as if she really were running out of time. 'I know she hasn't properly got her head round that. It'll be awful for her, and pretty grim for you too, picking up the pieces, walking on eggshells when she's down, depressed, which she can be, occasionally, even at the best of times, let alone when—'

'No, it won't be grim,' I interrupted firmly. 'It'll be fine.'

I'd heard her wobble over the last few minutes as I sensed she hadn't wobbled very publicly before. By adopting a position of strength, I'd allowed her to lean, invited her to be weak for a moment. And I understood all too clearly that most of the time she was being strong for Stacey, and for Ted, resolutely persuading them this was the best course of action, when, in reality, she had doubts—of course she did—about uprooting her child at such a cataclysmic time.

And as I informed Ant now, in bed, of the reality of what it would really be like, which Bella hadn't burdened him with either, he blinked rapidly. 'It's not going to be easy,' he said with a hint of misgiving.

'No, it's not. But it's not going to be impossible either. Trust me, Ant. It'll be fine.' Which is what I'd said to Bella. Trust me. Odd, how I had no fear about this. Ask me to take an exam and I'd come out in a muck sweat, but help an emotionally insecure teenager who's recently lost her mother? Cope with her grief, the fallout when Bella had gone? I'm not saying it would be a walk in the park but I'd roll up my sleeves without trepidation. And I needed a challenge. Except . . . my eyes widened slowly to the wall in the dark . . . I already had one. Shit. 'I've got a job,' I announced. I told Ant about the shop.

'Right. I'm delighted. Um, did you enjoy it? I mean, the two days you've done there?'

'I absolutely loved it.' The passion in my response surprised even me. Loved being useful. Except now that Stacey was coming I'd be useful in my more familiar, maternal way: my supportive role. The one I still felt was instinctive, biological. I hesitated.

'Don't even think about it,' he said. 'If you love it, do it. You'll need a distraction. Something for you. Don't even think about chucking it, Evie.'

I lay down quietly impressed. Quite forceful, for Ant.

I went on through the fields following the post-and-rail fence that bordered the farm, past the cottage Maroulla and Mario had once had, now occupied by Tim's farm worker, Phil, and his girlfriend, Carly. Carefully skirting piles of manure, I arrived at the gate to the main horse arena. Vast horseboxes and lorries, which, by virtue of their cargo, were allowed to progress here while lesser pilgrims like me had to stop short in the yard, were parked in neat lines just proud of the collecting ring, which was cordoned off with white tape. There were lots of fat little girls on thin ponies and lots of thin little girls on fat ponies: apparently Norman Thelwell's house had backed on to just such a field. Despite the numbers, almost the first person I saw was Anna. She'd tied Hector to a fence post and was sitting crosslegged on the grass beside him, iPod in her ears, texting away on her phone. She looked up as I approached. Her face, which a moment ago had been a blank, teenage canvas, suddenly became watchful, apprehensive. I gave her a broad smile, a little nod. I watched relief flood her face. She got up with just the merest tinge of uncertainty, pulled her earplugs out and came towards me tentatively, eyes searching my face.

'Really? Have you talked to Daddy? Have you—did you—'

'Yes, yes and yes. What a lot of doubting Thomases I've got. Did you really think I wouldn't?'

She flew the last few steps into my arms. I gathered her to me.

'Well, you might have said no, why shouldn't you?' she demanded, brushing her eyes roughly with her sleeve. 'She's not yours, after all.'

'No, but she's yours. And Daddy's. And that's good enough for me.'

We laughed and she hugged me again.

'And she's lovely, Mum, isn't she? Really sweet. You'll love her.'

We linked arms and walked back towards Hector.

'But, Mum . . .' she hesitated. 'She's not like my other friends.'

'What d'you mean?'

'Well, she's not—you know—like Chloe and Poppy. Not . . .' she struggled to explain; looked worried, as Ant had looked worried last night. About reality dawning. Not posh, was what she meant. Not flicky-haired and clued up and rally rally nice. So much the better. But in their desire to make it work, my family had forgotten these minor details and were handing them to me now, no—*dropping* them at my feet, hoping I'd pick them up, as I'd picked up behind them all my life: scooping toys into the toy box, wet towels from the bathroom floor to rails.

'Of course she's not like them, and that's very refreshing. And after all, the majority of students at Oxford don't actually come from within a twenty-mile radius of here, or from public schools. And although she's coming to live with us, that's where she's going. To the university.'

'I suppose,' she said in some surprise.

'We'll make it work, Anna, you'll see. Everything's going to be fine,' I assured her, as women have assured children for years, and then, even if it killed them, made sure it was. We sat down on the ground together.

As Anna pulled at the grass, she told me how we were going to redecorate the spare room for her—no—she sat up straight, eyes bright—she and Stacey would redecorate it together, paint it lilac, or apple green.

'Number one five two!' sang out the nasal loudspeaker. 'Number one five two to the collecting ring now, please.'

'Ohmygod—that's me!' She fled to untie Hector. 'Quick, Mummy, my hat.' I ran round picking things up. See? Scooping.

'Are you enjoying it?' I asked.

'It's OK, but there's so much standing around and so many bossy women. And hardly any boys do it, either.'

'Right. Where are your cousins, then?'

'Oh, Jack and Henry don't do this. They only hunt. Phoebe's around somewhere, but she's giving up Pony Club next year too.' She leapt into the saddle and trotted away. 'Oh, by the way,' she called, turning back. 'My ears have gone septic!'

Excellent news. I made a mental note to get some witch hazel on the way home. To scoopeth some more.

I followed at a slower pace, and by the time I'd got to the ring, the last competitor had finished and Anna was cantering in. She set Hector at a fence of coloured poles, which he cleared easily, then another, and another, but then I think she missed one and had to go back and do it again, and then the last one she knocked flying. She cantered out, laughing. 'Whoops!' she yelled as she flew past me.

'Seven faults, for competitor number one five two,' the loudspeaker informed us.

'Abysmal!' came an even louder voice to my left. I turned to see Camilla striding towards me, fists clenched. A small boy was trailing in her wake. 'Seven faults! She didn't line him up at *all*.'

'Oh, Anna won't mind,' I assured her.

'I mind!' Camilla exploded. 'That's my pony, and half of Orxfordshire are watching!'

'Yes, but it's only a bit of fun,' I said nervously.

'That pony jumps ite of his skin in the right hands, and now look at him. Ruined! *And* I think there's more to what went on at your sister-in-law's yard the other night than meets the eye.' I quaked nervously under her gimlet gaze. 'I don't think you've been bringing that pony in at all!' Oh, *that*. 'His ears are filthy!'

'So are your son's.'

'What?' she gasped.

'Just a hunch. And no, you're right, he hasn't been coming in. He's been frolicking in the fields, footloose and fancy-free.'

'Oh! Just like you with that—that man!' Ah. Spoke too soon. 'Gypsy, my foot. He's got that bookshop in Jericho, *and* I've seen him again today, hanging arind, up to no good. Well, that's it, Hector's coming home. You're not to be trusted.' With men, or horses? I wondered. 'I shall be collecting him forthwith.'

'You do that. And if Anna still wants a pony, I'll buy her one, and we'll treat it with care, but like an animal.'

'And if that tack isn't cleaned to within an inch of its life I'll want to know why,' she ranted on, ignoring me. 'That breastplate is brand new. It's Dobson and Farrell!'

I leaned towards her. Put my nose close to hers. 'You can stick your Dobson and Farrell breastplate where the sun don't shine, Camilla. You don't frighten me.' And with that I sauntered off, sticking my hands in my pockets, wishing I could whistle.

'Evie.'

I stopped; realised in a flash what she'd meant about seeing that man again. For here he was, strolling towards me in jeans and a white T-shirt, looking so devastatingly handsome it fairly took my breath away. I was fairly sure I could resist him, but I kept my eyes firmly on the horse manure, just to be on the safe side.

'Ludo. What the devil are you doing here?'

He grinned. 'I'm checking out the noise level for this afternoon's shindig.' He jerked his head across the hedge to where Caro's pink and white stripy marquee was flapping in the breeze in the distance.

'Oh! Is it today?'

'Three o'clock. I was just casting a weather eye over the booze supply when I saw—heard, more like—this malarkey going on over the hedge. I'm not convinced loudhailers and strident women yelling is quite the ambiance Alice had in mind, but I gather it finishes at three.'

'Who told you that?'

'Some very forceful women in the secretaries' tent, one of whom I recognised from our encounter the other night, but all of whom could quite easily have led the Charge of the Light Brigade . . .' He shuddered.

I giggled. 'Camilla and cronies. She said you were here.'

'She clearly couldn't *quite* place me until it was too late. Kept peering at me, head cocked, eyes narrowed, rather as she peers down the barrel of her shotgun, I imagine.'

I laughed. Then a silence prevailed. We both regarded the ground with interest.

'You look different,' he observed, at length.

'I am different,' I said in surprise. Then I remembered why. I sighed.

'Ant came back late last night. Bella Edgeworth is dying, Ludo.'

He blanched in astonishment. 'Shit. Of what?'

'Cancer. And she wants us to bring up her daughter.'

'Christ alive.'

I shrugged. 'She's Ant's daughter, too. And she's seventeen. Hardly a child.'

'Right. Blimey. Still—heavy. And you said?'

'I said yes. We all said yes.'

A shadow crossed his face. 'Right.' He gave me a slightly rueful, lop-sided smile. 'Which gives me a no.'

It was my turn to blanch. Had he really . . .?

'No, no,' he went on quickly, seeing my face, 'I don't mean that. You're quite right. I always knew it was a no. I shouldn't have said that.'

I didn't know what to say. He smiled, a proper smile this time. Took my hand. 'I have a theory about you.'

'Oh?'

'Actually, it's more about me. Some men find women who pick badly, attractive. I've decided I'm the opposite. I find myself inconveniently drawn to women who pick well. Who love their husbands. Who are in a happy place. It's what I lost, you see.' He looked at me searchingly, willing me to understand. I did. In an instant.

'Yes, I do see.'

'I'm aware that I could bag a single young girl, like the ones at Alice's party, but I want someone who knows how to make a commitment.'

'Not much of a commitment if I go off with you.'

He laughed shortly. 'No. Not much of a commitment. But then, at one point, you thought you were losing him. And I'd lost my wife.'

I shook my head sadly. 'It's too neat, Ludo. Promise me you won't go looking for young widows? Just wait. The right, gorgeous . . .' I searched the sky for words, '*joyous*—young girl, will come along, unattached and unencumbered, and will make you happy again. You'll see.'

He remained unconvinced. 'It wasn't just the attachment kick.' His eyes were full of mischief. 'I also really fancy you.'

I laughed. Blushed a bit too. 'Right.'

'As I said in my note.'

'What note?'

'With the flowers.'

'What flowers?'

'You didn't get the flowers?'

I shrugged, at a loss.

'I only sent them for a laugh. I was a bit pissed, actually; thought I'd try a different tack. A rather cheesy, obvious one. And only because I knew your husband wasn't at home.' It dawned on us collectively. 'Oh shit.' He whipped out his phone. 'Don't worry, I'll call them.'

I waited anxiously as he walked round in small circles, talking on his mobile. After a moment he snapped it shut. 'They hadn't gone. They're still in the delivery van and they're ringing the driver to say hold fire.'

'Oh, thank God.'

He smiled. 'Why, what would he have done, punched me?'

'No, of course not. Ant's a gentle man. But he's quite . . . possessive.'

'I don't blame him.' He held out his arms and I walked into them.

'Bye, Evie.'

'I'll see you in the shop,' I muttered into his neck.

'I know. But you know what I mean.'

'I do. Bye, Ludo.'

We squeezed each other and then, after a long moment, I pulled back. Eyes averted, I walked away. With a bit of a lump in my throat. As I went, I saw Anna tying up Hector again, watching me with her mouth open. It occurred to me to go and explain, and then it occurred to me not to. I put my sunglasses on and walked to the car feeling slightly sad for the loss of something I'd never even had. But I felt, too, as if things were finally slotting into place. I was squaring away, as my dad would have said, and even though I was pretty sure my heart would always falter when Ludo walked into a room—well, that wasn't too terrible, was it? And if, too, I really had been the antifreeze his atrophied heart had needed after Estelle, then I was glad. And proud. And very flattered. I smiled. A secret smile, down at my shoes. But as my path took me, for the second time that day, past the little brick and flint cottage, my smile faded and I became less pleased with myself. Less proud.

I got into my car. Don't kid yourself, Evie. Be that good woman. Square away some more. I started the car, headed back towards Oxford and St Michael's Hospice.

I rang the bell. A tired, fragile-looking woman opened the door. I explained who I'd come to see and she led me down a corridor, pointed to a door, and disappeared.

Maroulla was in the bed at the far end, eyes shut, mouth open. Her once-brown face was faded, her eye sockets hollow. I sat on the grey plastic chair beside her. I gazed at this once-energetic, noisy woman, who'd chased Tim and me round the garden with a stick.

'Maroulla.' I lifted her limp hand off the bedclothes. Her once-dark, but now yellowing eyes focused on my face.

As recognition dawned, a weak smile materialised. 'Evie?'

'I'm sorry I haven't been before.' I really was. She gazed at me, her eyes not wavering from my face. 'I should have done.'

'You busy,' she said, giving my hand the faintest squeeze. 'As it should be. Family . . . Anna . . . how is my Anna?'

'She's well, thank you. And lovely. Riding her pony.'

'And Ant?' she asked.

'Ant's fine.'

'Good.' Her eyelids were closing. I watched as the lids slowly came down like parchment shutters. 'He no blame himself, no?' Her eyes had flickered opened again.

I realised she'd gone back in time. Way back to Neville Carter, the boy Maroulla had found in the river and never forgotten. In some small, non-specific way, I still thought about it every day. I knew Ant did.

'You theenk is why he marry you.' She looked directly at me. I was aware of a brightness behind those deceptively cloudy eyes.

I sighed. 'I did, Maroulla. But I was young, then. Insecure. I don't think so now.'

'Good.' She smiled. 'He no panic buy.'

Panic buy. Maroulla's English, dodgy at the best of times, was sometimes unnervingly spot-on.

'How are you, Maroulla?'

'I die. And good job too. Time to see Mario.'

I smiled. 'You reckon he's waiting for you?'

'Of course.' She gave a ghost of a smile. 'He be cross I so late.'

I grinned. Yes, he probably would. If Maroulla was fiery, Mario was more so. I had the feeling she was rather looking forward to it.

'And your father too. He good man. He be there. He good master.'

'Maroulla . . .' I hated it when she was the forelock-tugging tenant.

'And he make good sex love too.'

'Dad?' My eyes popped. Good Lord. Feudal rights?

'No. Mario. And I know what he say when I see him.' She tapped my arm with a bony finger, wide awake now. 'He say—you keep it safe? Because I take photos.'

'What photos?'

'In village shop.'

She'd lost me. 'The photocopier in the village shop?' I hazarded.

'Yes, ten pence each. Right rip-off.'

'Oh. Of what, Maroulla?'

'Of thees. Mario say keep it safe, but when I die, who knows? I can't keep it safe no more, can I? So I geev one to Tim, yesterday. And Felicity when she come.'

'Tim's been here?'

She was pushing herself up her pillows, opening the drawer by her bed, rummaging. 'Of course. He come one time every week.'

'Does he?' I was appalled.

She pulled out a piece of paper and gave it to me. 'There. You read.'

'What is it?'

'I no know, I no read.' No, of course she couldn't. Not English, anyway. 'But he make us watch, and sign it. And when I ask Mario, he say very important paper, but he no read either. So I clean office every day, and your father, he so very untidy, and many things get lost in there, and I worry. So one day I open drawer and find paper, and I take to rip-off shop to copy.'

I gazed at her a long moment. Then down at the paper. An A4 sheet bearing a photocopy of a piece of notepaper. In my father's scrawling hand, I read:

This country is a complete and utter disgrace. More crap from Defra, more unwarranted restrictions on my land, more outrageous demands from Brussels and piss-poor market prices. Felicity, my darling, I have no option but to leave the whole bloody shooting match to Tim. Farm, land, money—everything. You always said you'd be happy going back to your flat in college. You have your work, and Evie has Ant to provide. I can't saddle Tim with the bricks and mortar and not the wherewithal to run the place. It will break him, as it's surely breaking me.

 Your loving husband, Victor Milligan, February 27, 1999
 Mario Rodríguez, February 27, 1999
 Maroulla Rodríguez, February 27, 1999

I read it again. Looked up slowly. 'He asked you to witness this?'

'Yes, see there.' She tapped her signature impatiently.

'So where's the original?' I breathed.

'*Qué?*'

'The first one he wrote, from the notepad.'

'Back in his drawer, I tell you.'

'You put it back in his desk?'

'Yes, his desk. In special folder.'

But we'd gone through his desk when he died, Felicity and I. We'd taken that whole, chaotic room apart. There'd been nothing. He'd died intestate, nothing at all. I exhaled. 'And Tim's seen this?'

'Yesterday, when he come. He lose blood. In his face. Whiteness.'

'Oh. Right.' I swallowed.

She frowned, worried. 'I do wrong?'

'No, no, you did right, Maroulla.' I forced a smile; made myself talk some more. Then she looked tired. I kissed her papery cheek as, simultaneously, her eyes closed. I slipped away.

Just a scrap of photocopied paper, I thought as I shut the front door. February 27. Six months before he died. The end of a long hard winter, never a good time in farming. He'd written it in a fit of pique, but later, after Maroulla had copied it and put it back, he'd destroyed it. That was why we hadn't found it. 'Flog the bloody place,' I'd heard him say to Tim. 'It'll be a millstone round your neck.' And Tim would smile, say nothing, knowing . . . what? That he didn't mean it? Or he did mean it?

I drove home, unsettled. Something Felicity had said at Alice's party, about how I shouldn't see Maroulla, how she was gaga, reared up at me. But she wasn't really, was she? Just old. I inhaled deeply. No. Forget it, Evie. It's nothing. Tim hasn't reacted, so it's clearly nothing.

Caro rang me on my way home, breaking into my thoughts, making me jump. 'I've got a police car up my backside so I've got to be quick.'

'Well, I'm driving too. What is it?'

'I'm completely stuck in traffic. In about twenty minutes I've got a wedding reception in the garden and I'm not going to make it.'

'Oh Christ. Alice Montague.'

'Exactly, and I can't get hold of Tim. Can you get there for me, please, Evie?' She sounded desperate.

'And do what?'

'Not a great deal, just organise the children to park the cars—the boys know where—and then sort of stand around looking charming.'

'OK,' I said doubtfully.

'You're a star, because I have absolutely no idea when I'm going to get back, and I've got Leonard with me and he's a bore,' she hissed.

Leonard. I had an idea he was an elderly uncle. I hoped his hearing wasn't too acute. 'Where is he?'

'In the back. Thanks, Evie, bye.'

Right. I could do that. I hadn't entirely planned on seeing Ludo quite so soon but I certainly owed Caro. And she'd sounded all right, hadn't she? Not in any way pissed off about anything Tim had told her? Or shown her? No. So forget it, Evie. Another little inward shake.

And a wedding would take my mind off things, I decided. But I really must change. I parked creatively outside the house and nipped up the steps. The door was double-locked so Ant wasn't at home. Must have gone into college. As I went in, a heavenly smell wafted up the passageway. Mmm . . . I pursued it to its source in the kitchen. Two dozen roses at least, bright red, sitting plumb in the middle of the kitchen table. My heart began to quicken as my eyes snagged on a white card on the end of a long green plastic stick. No envelope. I read:

Dear Evie,
Can't stop thinking about you in your Miss Whiplash underwear.
Isn't it time it had another outing?
Love and heavy breathing, Ludo. xx

Oh blinking blithering hell. The message hadn't got through. Ant must have taken delivery of them. I went hot. Pulse racing, I scrambled in my bag for my mobile. His phone was switched off. I left a breathless message about needing to speak to him urgently, to, um, explain, erm, the underwear thingy, which was just a silly joke, a message that even to my ears resonated with guilt. I had to find him. I seized a piece of paper from the kitchen pad and wrote in large capitals: THIS IS NOT WHAT YOU THINK! I CAN EXPLAIN!—and left it on the flowers.

Then I hurried out of the front door. I vacillated on the bottom step. Hang on. Where was I going? To Balliol? Where he may or may not be? And what would I do when I got there, barge in on a tutorial? No. Of course not. I'd look ridiculous. And guilty. I must wait. Explain later. And meanwhile, exhaust all other possibilities. Because if, say, he wasn't in college, where might he be? Was there anyone he'd confide in? Mum? Quite possibly. I sat down abruptly on the bottom step and rang her.

'No, darling, I haven't seen him. Has something happened?'

'No, everything's fine. It's just—if he does ring or call by, would you tell him I'm at the farm? Caro asked me to step in for her at a wedding.'

'I will, but I'm going there myself soon. Are you OK?'

'I'm fine.' I hesitated. 'It's just . . . Ludo sent me some flowers as a joke, and I'm worried Ant might get the wrong idea.'

'Ludo? Oh, I doubt it, Evie. He's much too young for you. Ant will know that.' She laughed.

Loyal, my mum. But on another level, encouraging. I tried the shop. Ant might look for me there. Clarence answered.

'Malcolm's at Alice's wedding. Ludo invited him and sweetly asked me to the reception too. I'm just shutting up here for him before going across. D'you want me to give him a message?'

'No, don't worry, I'm going there myself in a minute. I'm looking for Ant, actually. He hasn't popped in, has he?' I said casually.

'Not that I know of. But if you're going, why don't we go together?'

Good plan. Safety in numbers. I leapt back up the steps and into the house to change. Bafflingly, all the clothes I'd been planning to wear had shrunk in my wardrobe, so after struggling out of some linen trousers and yelling 'You bastards' at them, I'd thrown on a caftan, a look I knew was fashionable again, but perhaps not the way I'd interpreted it: over beige culottes and with a pink straw hat. I slid by the shop just as Clarence was locking the door.

He looked delicious in his morning coat and was kind enough to give my attire only the briefest of glances. In fact he was so smiley and chatty I relaxed, and as we drove along, on the wings of an impulse, I ran the roses up the flagpole again. And the sexy note, which involved explaining the scantily clad siren at the window. I cringed behind the wheel as I awaited his response. The first stone. He laughed.

'Well, I haven't met your husband, but from what Malcolm tells me he's a rational, intelligent man. He'll surely wait to hear your side of things? Before he jumps to any conclusions?'

'Yes,' I breathed happily. 'Yes, he will.'

When we finally arrived at the farm, the congregation was already drifting out of the church, following the bride and groom. Alice, beautiful in ivory silk, white roses scattered in her blonde hair, on the arm of her new husband, was leading the procession down the narrow lane.

We waited for everyone to pass by, a happy, smiling throng. I spotted Felicity in the crowd, in a pale blue suit and hat, talking to Malcolm. She looked lovely. *Was* lovely, I decided, banishing impure thoughts. As the last of the guests strolled by, I swung the car into the yard. I got out and, with Clarence following more sedately, hastened round to the back of the house where I found Jack

'Jack, I'm supposed to be helping. Did you manage to park the cars?'

'They park themselves in the churchyard. Mum gets stressy but it always goes like clockwork. She rang and said you were coming but there's no need, honestly. No offence.'

'No offence taken. This is Clarence, by the way.'

'Hi, Clarence.' They shook hands.

'So, waitresses?' I swung round, taking a few steps down the lawn and shading my eyes against the sun towards the marquee. I spotted Ludo, looking devastatingly handsome in the receiving line.

'The waitresses have got trays of champagne and some orange juice.'

'Well done. Canapés?'

'Not yet. Mum usually lets them have a drink first. Canapés in half an hour.'

'Right. Well, it looks like you've got it all under control, Jack.' I smiled back at him. 'D'you get paid for this?'

'Dream on. Mum's far too tight. And, actually, it's just as well she's not here, she wouldn't like that.' He jerked his head across the hedge to the lane, where the last of the horseboxes were sneaking out, dripping straw and poo in their wake.

'Anna must be about somewhere, then,' I said.

'She was, but she and Phoebe went to a friend's house in the village.'

'Oh, right. I don't suppose Ant's here, is he?' I asked nonchalantly.

He shrugged. 'Dunno. Dad might know. He's inside.'

'Is he? I thought he wasn't here?'

'Yeah, he's around somewhere. See you.' He loped off, weary with interrogation, towards the marquee.

Actually, Ant could be with Tim, it occurred to me. Perhaps they were ensconced in the study? Deep in chat? About me? I went to go in, then remembered Clarence. But he'd already spotted Malcolm, who was coming up the garden to meet him, looking rather radiant in his morning coat. I saw their eyes shine at each other as they shared a moment. I'd just got my foot in the back door when I saw Caro's car draw up in the yard. She leapt out almost before the car had stopped.

'Everything OK?' she called anxiously, bustling across.

'Perfect. The cars are parked, and everyone got from the church to marquee without incident.'

'No wretched horseboxes dropping poo in the lane from next door?'

'No,' I lied, 'and now everyone's drinking champagne.'

'Excellent. I'll go down.' From just inside the back door she snatched a pink jacket and hat, which she slung on now over her denim skirt.

'Keep them there for emergencies.' She grinned, deftly swapping her boots for slingbacks. 'Is your mother here yet? She was going to help me with the pigs.'

'Haven't seen her, but she did say she was going to—'

'NO, NO, THIS WAY!' she yelled suddenly. She ran towards the hedge, calling over it to some latecomers. 'Through the gate at the end of the lane, look . . .' She beetled off, arranging her face brightly.

I went inside to find Tim. All was quiet downstairs, so I went up. The children's doors were open, revealing exploding bedrooms, unmade beds and still-closed curtains. I went on down the corridor to Tim and Caro's bedroom door, which was shut.

'Tim?'

'Come in.' My brother's voice, subdued.

I poked my head round. He was lying on the bed in old jeans and a checked shirt. His gun was by his side. I stared, appalled.

'What are you doing?'

'Cleaning my gun. Why?'

'Oh!' I clutched my heart dramatically, as I went in, shutting the door behind me. 'I thought . . .'

'What, I was topping myself?' He sat up with a struggle. 'Not quite there yet. But I can't even clean my gun without sitting—or lying down—now.'

'Oh, Tim.' I came and sat beside him. 'Is it very painful?'

'Very,' he said, grimacing. 'But I'll get there. Hundreds of people walk around with artificial hips, don't they?'

'They do, but they don't farm.' I regarded him. He returned my look.

'I don't farm either, Evie. Oh, I've got a few cows, and we grow a bit of wheat and dutifully get it harvested, but d'you know how much I got for it this year? Twenty-three grand. I have to pay Phil, obviously, because I can't do all the combining myself, and Steve, who comes to help in August, and d'you know what their wages come to?'

I didn't answer.

'Fifteen grand. Which leaves me eight grand to run the place and to feed a family of five for a year. Ha!' He threw back his head and gave a cracked laugh to the ceiling.

'Which is why Caro does all this,' I soothed, waving my hand out of the window.

He sighed. 'Yes. But she's run ragged.' He gave me a twisted smile. 'It's not great, Evie, seeing your wife run herself into the ground, having your house overrun with people . . .'

'Well, not actually *in* the house.'

'Excuse me?' He cocked an ear theatrically.

Voices drifted up from downstairs. 'They come in?' I boggled.

'To use the loo.'

'But the Portaloos—'

'The Portaloos get busy—or blocked—so they come up here. Don't forget, nearly everyone we entertain in our splendid house and grounds is pissed. They don't give a toss that it's your house.'

We heard the sound of a loo being flushed down the passage in the children's bathroom. Then more footsteps tripped towards us and a loo seat banged down, next door in Tim and Caro's en suite, which could also be accessed via the corridor. I let my jaw drop incredulously.

I smiled. 'But things will improve,' I assured him. 'Your new hip will click in soon and then you won't need Phil.'

'And get to keep all of the twenty-three thousand pounds? Gee whiz.'

'Well, maybe—maybe wheat prices will improve?'

'And maybe a whole heap of money will just drop out of the sky, just as if—ooh, I don't know, as if Dad didn't die intestate after all, and in fact the chunk he left to Felicity should have gone to me, to run the farm. Keep the place going.' He gave me a steady look. I gazed back.

'Right,' I said eventually. 'I wondered when we'd get to that.'

'You know?'

'I went to see Maroulla this morning.'

'Ah.' Another silence prevailed. 'Well,' he said lightly, 'it's all been spent now, I imagine. So it's academic.'

'You think?'

'I don't know, Evie,' he said wearily.

'But I mean . . . is it legal?'

'This bit of photocopied paper?' He shifted on his side and brought it out of his back pocket. 'Who knows? But, as far as *we* know . . . it was what Dad wanted. Which, actually, is the point, isn't it?'

'Yes,' I said slowly. I paused. 'But . . . where's the original?'

'Well, somewhere along the line, someone may have . . .' he was carefully avoiding using Felicity's name, 'disposed of it, I suppose.'

'Not knowing Maroulla took a copy.'

We glanced guiltily at one another. Guilty, because we couldn't believe we were thinking it. Saying it. The loo flushed next door.

'Or,' I said quickly, 'Dad may have chucked it. Changed his mind.'

'Exactly. Didn't want to cut out his wife, which is quite a major thing to do. And on that note . . .' Tim heaved himself off the bed and hobbled to the window . . . 'what's that godawful noise?'

A terrible banging was coming from the yard below where Caro had left her car. 'What the . . .?' Tim turned and marched, quite quickly for a man with a gammy leg, down the stairs. He shot back the bolts on the front door and went out. I was on his heels. Something—or someone— was crashing around inside the trailer behind her car.

'Oh God—it can't be Caro's uncle, can it?' I gasped.

'Lionel?'

'Yes, she went to get him.'

'Did she? But why would he be in the trailer?'

'I've no idea, but she said he was in the back. Oh, poor man!'

Giving me a startled glance, Tim unfastened the clasp and loosened the ramp. But before he could lower it, it came smartly down of its own accord, with a bang. An enormous, hairy orange pig stampeded down it, and raced past us. 'BLOODY HELL!' roared Tim, swinging about. 'That's not Lionel, that's Leonard! The boar! Come to service the pigs!'

We watched, aghast, as the pig galloped joyously down the garden. It crashed through flowerbeds and made for the river, just as Phil, Tim's farm worker, came running up the lawn towards us.

'There's a barney going on in the tent!' he yelled. 'You'd better come!'

'Oh fuck.' Tim started hobbling down the lawn. 'Phil! Get that pig!' he roared, as the pig, thwarted by the stream, veered left. Phil raced after it.

'Dad! Quick!' Jack, looking appalled but enthralled, was waving his father on with a huge arm from the mouth of the tent.

As Tim and I reached the entrance to the marquee, it was to find a frustrating bank of backs blocking our way. The majority of the guests had shrunk back to the sides of the tent to create a clearing on the dance floor. Not, we realised as we muscled through, to give the happy couple room for a first waltz, but for another couple, Caro and Felicity, the latter pale and trembling, the former the colour of her pink hat and jacket, to take centre stage. Caro was directing a ferocious diatribe at her step-mother-in-law, the gist of which, if one sifted through the scorching profanities, was that she considered her to be a dirty, low-down, conniving thief. Felicity's mistake, I gathered later from those closer to the action, was to interrupt, albeit in a low, quavering voice. At which point Caro took a swing at her. Felicity ducked and Ludo leapt in to restrain Caro in a half nelson. At this identical moment, my husband made his entrance. With a dramatic leap he pulled Ludo off Caro, swung him round to face him, and landed his own punch on Ludo's jaw. It sent Ludo tottering back in astonishment and onto his bottom. As a collective gasp went up from an already captivated crowd, Caro delivered a mighty slap to Felicity's cheek. It was at this salient moment that the pig chose to enter the arena at racing speed.

He careered round the dance floor like a bull in a ring, knocking people off their feet, sending champagne glasses flying, upending tables. He was huge, bewildered and terrifying. Women ran shrieking for exits. Men shouted orders to each other to corner him. One fell on him, attempting to wrap the pig's head in his coat, but Leonard was surprisingly nimble. Bucking like a bronco, tossing the coat off his head and the fifteen-stone man from his back, he broke out of the circle.

Through the mayhem I caught a glimpse of Felicity, looking dazed, sitting at the side of the marquee on a chair. Caro was sitting a few seats along from her, slumped and spent. She reached out and caught my arm as I ran past her. 'She took our money,' she muttered up at me.

I shook her off and, ignoring the pig too, raced to the scene of another crisis. Just to the right of the dance floor, my husband, looking nothing like his quiet, gentle self, was, to my horror, squaring up to Ludo again. Ludo had his palms up, doing his best to dissuade him.

'*Ant!*' I screamed, racing up.

As he swung round, even I could see I was the oil this fire didn't need. His eyes met mine with glittering aggression. Happily, Clarence, on my heels, had sized up the situation, and in an instant had plucked me as a cat would her kitten, by the scruff of the neck, and flung me at Malcolm, while in another he'd got between Ant and his target.

Unfortunately, at this exact same moment, Leonard decided to leave the dance floor and pick a fight with Clarence. Clarence neatly side-stepped the charge on his legs, pushing Ant out of the way too, where-upon Leonard charged the top table instead.

'GET THAT PIG OUT OF HERE!' roared Tim, brick red in the face.

Younger members of the male guests took up the challenge. Shimmying out of their jackets they hurled them at Leonard like mata-dors, and themselves afterwards, a strong smell of testosterone in the air. Perhaps past beaus were among the gallant young men who attempted to rugby tackle the pig into submission, but Leonard was strong, and very angry now. He slipped, he slithered, he evaded cap-ture. And the awful thing was, he'd spotted the cake. One could almost see the thought processes whirring. Could something so tall, so white, so patently unlike swill in a trough, smell so delicious? He cantered steadily towards it as yet more shirtsleeved heroes flung themselves in his path, until a cry went up. Not a human cry, but a loud, desperate, porcine honk. It stopped him in his tracks.

We all swung round; Leonard too. There, at the entrance to the mar-quee, sat Mum, revving a quad bike. A small trailer was on the back, and inside it, honking her heart out, was a very horny Boadicea. She'd smelt Leonard, and she wanted him. For a moment Leonard hesitated. The cake was big, but this girl was hot. And what's more, other potential girl-friends, hearing Boadicea's cry, were baying for him in the background. Once more, the wheels of his piggy brain were visible. Food . . . or sex? Sex . . . or food? How many male hearts did not go out to him? Offer their sympathies?

Boadicea, sensing indecision, dug deep and gave one lusty primeval bark; a bark full of longing, a bark he couldn't resist. Leonard trotted hypnotically towards her. He went to the back of the trailer, where Henry, Mum's accomplice, was poised, ready with the tricky little assignment of opening the cage door and letting Leonard in, but not Boadicea out. He hadn't grown up on a farm for nothing, though, and the operation went faultlessly. Within seconds, for the benefit of the entire wedding party, the pigs were united, in every sense.

The crowd went wild: cheering, whooping and clapping. It seemed Mum's inspired insight into the male psyche had saved the wedding.

After all, the cake was still standing, the broken champagne glasses were quickly swept up, chairs righted. Leonard and Boadicea were driven away, up the hill to where the rest of the sows were waiting, honking furiously.

Meanwhile, back at the marquee, the wedding reception was recovering its equilibrium. Bridesmaids' tears were mopped, the top table was relaid, and Alice, being a game girl, rose to the occasion, and did not sob that her wedding had been ruined, but roared with laughter, along with friends, about what a hoot it had been; what a day.

My day, however, continued on its remorselessly unamusing course. Ant, whom I'd taken my eyes off for one minute, had gone. I ran this way and that, cursing myself for being so stupid as to let him out of my sight. Then, suddenly, I glimpsed him, sitting on the riverbank beside Clarence. Ant was clearly giving a great deal of attention to what Clarence had to say. Clarence saw me. He stood up and jerked his head meaningfully. 'He's all yours,' he murmured.

He sauntered away towards Malcolm and I sat down uncertainly beside Ant. He stayed staring at the water, shoulders hunched. The silence deepened. Then Ant turned and gave me a lopsided smile.

'It appears I've made a complete tit of myself.'

I breathed again. 'Oh, I wouldn't say that,' I warbled.

'Those flowers. That note.' He shook his head, bewildered. 'I'm afraid I just saw red. But Clarence says he just saw you through the bedroom window across the street. Still. Quite a familiar thing to write.'

'I know. I'm sorry.'

He shrugged. 'Not your fault. And then I rang Anna, to see if she knew where you were, and she said she'd seen you hugging some man at her gymkhana, and that one of the girls, some horsey woman's daughter, had been spreading rumours that you'd been seen snogging him in a stable. I flipped, I'm afraid.'

'Oh no, Ant, it wasn't like that. I—'

'I know,' he interrupted wearily. 'Clarence explained that too.'

Did he? I boggled. Did Clarence know about that?

'I don't dispute that you are blameless, Evie,' Ant went on carefully, 'but the fact remains that this man clearly has designs on you.'

I couldn't help but smile. At his appalled face. His horror. 'Is that so extraordinary?' I asked.

'Well, no,' he said, momentarily disconcerted. 'But—he seems to have pursued you relentlessly!'

'He has,' I agreed. 'But don't forget, Ant, at the time I thought you were entranced by Bella Edgeworth.'

'So you encouraged him?'

'No, I didn't encourage him. In fact, if you ask Malcolm, I think you'll find I only agreed to work at the shop if our shifts didn't coincide.'

Ant nodded gloomily. 'I know. Clarence said. Red roses,' he spat. 'What a cliché.'

I smiled. 'That's how I knew they weren't from you.'

'I don't do clichés,' he said defensively.

'Or flowers, come to that.'

He frowned. 'Haven't I ever sent you flowers?'

'You picked me some buttercups, once. When we were in Devon.'

'I don't remember that.'

'I do.'

He blanched. 'OK. Maybe I haven't been great in that department.'

'I've no complaints.'

'But . . .' he hesitated. 'A little bit of romance . . .?'

'Is quite good for the soul,' I agreed softly.

'So . . . were you tempted? He's young, handsome, virile, no doubt. And clearly besotted with you.'

'I was flattered,' I said finally. 'But I didn't fall in love with him.'

'No, I can see you didn't. Although, I think he did with you.'

I blinked, baffled. 'God knows why. I mean, look at him.' He followed my gaze to where Ludo, handsome, smiling and crinkly-eyed, was entertaining Alice's young friends just outside the tent. 'And look at me. A middle-aged housewife. Fading looks, marshmallow for brains—'

'Big heart,' he interrupted, giving me his steady look. I met his blue gaze, knowing he wanted to kiss me. But I had a confession.

'About my heart, Ant,' I said slowly. 'I think I should tell you . . . in fact, it's only fair to tell you, I've been very jealous of Bella Edgeworth. The thing is . . . I'm not sure that if Bella were to make a miraculous recovery, I'm not sure I'd be so magnanimous. I have a nasty feeling that the reason I'm welcoming her daughter—your daughter—so graciously into my home is because her mother is not going to be around. When you told me she was dying, a tiny part of me felt sort of relieved. You should know that, Ant, before you wander round this city telling everyone what a generous, big-hearted wife you have.'

'I think we should also remember,' he observed at length, and was it me or did his mouth twitch, 'that only a small part of you thought that.'

'Well—'

'And that many women wouldn't have admitted to it. Let me tell you, Evie, if everyone examined their motives so minutely, it wouldn't be a pretty sight. I too have a confession to make. If that man was found dead in a ditch tomorrow, I wouldn't be crying my eyes out either. In fact I might be dancing on his grave.'

Rather shocked, I followed his gaze to Ludo, who was welcoming an elderly couple to the party, but not before shooting an anxious glance over his shoulder in our direction.

'Instead of which,' Ant got to his feet, 'I have to go over and apologise for hitting him.' He took my hand and helped me up too. 'It's not a question of being good, Evie, it's a question of behaving well. It's what we do that counts; not how we feel. We can't control what goes on in our hearts, but we can help how we behave. And with that bit of cod philosophy out of the way, I shall go and shake the bastard by the hand.' He grinned sheepishly at his feet. Turned to go.

'I love you, Ant.'

He turned back, surprised. 'I love you too.' His eyes widened. His arms opened too and I walked into them. 'More than you'll ever know.'

We kissed, then, like lovers do. Not like a thoroughly married couple. And then Ant turned away and strolled along the riverbank, back towards the marquee.

I made my way to the house. I was pretty sure this would have replaced the marquee as the venue for the continuing saga of any Milligan family dramas. Sure enough, as I made my way upstairs towards Caro's bedroom, I met my nephews, quietly exiting it.

'We took her a cup of tea,' whispered Henry, tiptoeing wide-eyed down the corridor towards me. 'Is it a nervy breaky, Evie?'

'Oh, no, she's just upset,' I assured them, shooing them downstairs. As I opened the bedroom door and Caro rose, rigid from the waist, from her pillows to stare at me, hair vertical, eyes seemingly rotating.

'She took our bloody money!' she blurted out. 'I was in there,' she pointed a quivering finger to her en suite bathroom, 'on the bloody bog, when I heard you and Tim talking about it—couldn't believe my ears! I couldn't believe you were both so calm about it. I went straight down to knock her front teeth out!'

'You only slapped her though, didn't you?' I said nervously.

'Tragically,' she muttered, flopping back on her pillows. 'Must be my upbringing. Couldn't make a fist. I wish I bloody had, though.'

The door opened softly and Felicity stood in the doorway: very pale, very shaken, her hat at an unusual angle. I flung myself on top of Caro as she rose up from the marital bed like The Thing From the Swamp.

'*Arrrrghhh!*' she shrieked.

'Caro! Pull yourself together!' I yelled. 'Felicity, I'm not convinced this is the moment,' I squealed over my shoulder.

Suddenly Caro flopped submissively back into the pillows again. 'Let her come,' she said darkly. 'Let's see what she's got to say for herself. Bring it on, I say. I hope you've got a good lawyer, Felicity. You'll need one.'

I cringed. Oh, this was horrible. Horrible. They were such friends.

'Yes, you're quite right,' Felicity whispered, coming—rather bravely, I felt—to stand at the end of the bed. Her lipstick was smudged, her pallor deathly. 'I did take your money.'

Oh Lord. I crumpled inside. Felt Caro stiffen beside me, as, simultaneously, Tim appeared in the open doorway.

'But not immediately. I didn't know about that letter,' she glanced at me, then round at Tim, 'until well after your father died. Like you, I assumed he died intestate. Evie and I took that room apart, didn't we?' I nodded enthusiastically. 'File by file, box by box, and we found nothing. And then I moved out and you moved in,' she looked steadily at Caro, 'because even though it wasn't written down that you should have the house, I knew it was what Victor wanted. He'd told me so. But I could have stayed. First or second wife, the house was legally mine.' Caro looked less sure of herself. Tim's face was hard to read.

'So when did you find the letter?' I prompted gently.

'Almost a year later, when I'd been at my house in Fairfield Avenue for a good nine months. I went to MOT the car. Found the logbook in the bureau, together with the grey plastic folder with all the documents. Inside was the tax certificate and the latest MOT, and tucked behind that, the piece of paper.'

I remembered Maroulla telling me she'd put it back, when she'd copied it, in a very important-looking folder, with certificates.

'It was a beautiful summer's day, I remember it vividly, and I was happy. For the first time for ages, I felt my life was getting back on track. I had this dear little house, my job; I felt I could go on without Victor. Then all of a sudden, my life came to another juddering halt. I felt sick.' She looked, for the first time, directly at Caro. 'I was nearly sixty years old. I was alone. I had no children, no family. And soon, no house.'

'You could have gone back into college,' Caro muttered.

'Could I? Those flats are fought over tooth and nail, as Evie knows, and in my college they were all allocated. Maybe I could have pulled rank, but how much rank did I have? I was no longer head of the department. I was a part-timer, working three days a week. Might the powers that be not gently suggest that actually, maybe I should think about retiring, instead?'

'Well, then you could have bought a one-bedroom flat off the Cowley Road!' said Caro savagely. 'Lived according to your means!'

Felicity lowered her head. Didn't answer.

'What did you do with the letter?' I asked.

'I put it back in the top drawer of my desk. Under lots of papers. Buried it, like a dog would a bone. But almost hourly, I'd dig it out again, and stare at it. Have to sit down. It was dated six months before his death, but I couldn't decide what state of mind he'd written it in. I didn't know if it really was his last wish, or just a whim, late one night, after half a bottle of whisky. Had he wanted it to happen? If I'm honest, he'd said to me once that leaving Tim the farm with no money was a millstone round—'

'Of course it was!' shrieked Caro, rising up from her pillows again. 'It left us impotent, and working so hard. We struggled day and night, while you sat watching, *knowing*, in your pretty Queen Anne house with its terrace and its wrought-iron railings, not only with your salary from the university but with Tim's inheritance as well!'

Felicity swallowed. 'Yes,' she nodded, 'yes, that's true. But my salary was my due, Caro. I worked for it.' Her voice quavered. 'And my husband's money, I'd *thought* was my due. We all agreed, didn't we?' She glanced around beseechingly. 'Tim and Caro should have the farm, Evie—well, not much . . .'

'I didn't need much,' I said hastily.

'And I'd receive whatever money—'

'But that was before you found the letter!' Caro exploded. 'And you say you didn't know how to read it—well, I don't believe you. You saw in that piece of paper that Victor Milligan wanted his son to carry on the farm for the next generation, for Tim, and then Jack, and then maybe Jack's son, to do the same. That you weren't important in the scheme of things; that set against a barrage of history, against the pull of the land, you were nothing. You were just the wife!'

'And so are you,' said Tim, quietly. It was the first time he'd spoken. Caro opened her mouth to object, but his face silenced her. He limped into the room. 'How much money did he leave? I forget.'

'Almost two hundred thousand,' said Felicity. 'Which I put down as a deposit on the house.'

'Not a great deal.'

'Not a great deal!' squealed Caro. 'Believe you me, my darling, two hundred thousand pounds would go an awfully long way to—'

'Not a great deal *in the scheme of things*,' he interrupted, deliberately using her words. She closed her mouth.

'But still, quite a lot for Dad to have?' I suggested. I remembered at the time being surprised it was there.

'It was his sinking fund,' said Tim. 'Grandpa made most of it in the good days, but Dad never touched it, the idea being that one day, hopefully, he'd buy more land with it, make the farm viable.' He turned back to Felicity. 'Did you ever consider showing us the note?'

'Many times. I was in agonies. I knew it was deceitful, but as every day went by, well, the awful thing was, it got easier. I still had to live with myself, of course—'

'But you had your charity works to salve your conscience,' Caro said bitterly.

'Perhaps,' Felicity agreed. 'Trying to be the person I knew I wasn't.'

'But not a bad person, Felicity,' I said quickly. She shot me a grateful look. Caro shot me a venomous one. 'I can see how it happened, how Felicity got herself into the pickle. No one knew about it, she was the only one who had the letter—'

'Apart from Maroulla, as you discovered when you went to see her in the hospice, which must have given you a *really* nasty shock,' interjected Caro. 'But then again, Maroulla was dying, wasn't she, Felicity? So soon, no one would know. Marvellous.' She folded her arms grimly.

There was a silence as we digested this. But I could feel my blood rising. 'OK, Caro, tell me something.' I turned to her. 'If you found a letter in the study, tucked, ooh, I don't know, behind a picture maybe, written in Dad's hand, saying that actually, he wanted to leave the whole shooting match to Felicity, that there was no point struggling on with the farm any more, that Tim would be flogging a dead horse, what would you have done? Hand your house back to Felicity and move back to the leaky little bungalow in Rutlers Lane? And let's, just for the sake of argument, say that as you stood in front of the fireplace reading the letter, the fire was alight? What would you have done, Caro?'

I fixed her with my eyes. She looked back defiantly, but I knew Caro. Knew she'd protect her family's interests, her children's, at all costs. I knew about the indomitable strength women have in that department, had felt it myself very recently.

'Well, I'd like to think—' she began disingenuously.

'*Bollocks!*' I roared. There was a silence. Caro and I glared knowingly at each other. She looked away first.

'I'll sell up, and then you'll have your money, Caro,' said Felicity quietly. 'Every penny.'

Tim cleared his throat. 'Felicity—'

'No,' she held up her hand; shut her eyes, 'I mean it. It's what I should have done years ago. And, you know, it'll be a relief. The guilt has weighed very heavy on my shoulders. I'm very, very sorry.'

We all looked at our hands. Even Caro looked uncomfortable. Tim spoke first. 'Thank you, Felicity, but there's no need. Even with the money, it's still not enough to keep us going here. We'd still have to sell up.'

I glanced at him, shocked.

'We'd already decided that, hadn't we, darling?' he said gently, turning to his wife. Caro looked in real pain now. Suddenly I understood where all this anger had come from. And possibly been misdirected.

'Look at me,' he appealed to us. His legs, we knew without looking, were splayed from various operations. 'This isn't a farmer. This isn't a man up to working the land.' Even his wife didn't have the gall to gainsay this. 'This is a man who needs a desk job,' he finished bitterly. 'I can't do this any more.'

He limped to the window and gazed out. It occurred to me that no amount of money would have found a way round this, his disability. Looking at Caro, I felt she knew this too. There was a resigned inevitability about the slump of her shoulders on the pillows. I also believe, in her heart, she knew that even if Felicity had come round, waving the scrap of paper, Tim would have screwed it up, said—forget it, Felicity, we can't possibly take your money on the strength of this. What's done is done; we are where we are—silencing, in one glance, the protests of his outraged wife. I don't say that simply because I know my brother, because he's a nice guy, but because it seems to me that if people behave well, it encourages others to do the same.

Yet when people behave badly . . . I looked at Felicity. She was not one I'd associate with human frailty, but fear is a powerful motivator, and once it had gripped her, once she'd found her whole future dropping away from her, and failed to rush round here, I could see how it became harder to do it. And as the years slipped by and as life went on, so the whole wretched business would have faded into the background. But maybe around the time Henry had been bullied at school and his parents had tried but failed to afford a private one for him, maybe as Tim had come in from the fields, yet again well after dusk, shattered, maybe the guilt had closed in on her then and she'd had trouble going to sleep. Maybe after all, as she'd said, it hadn't been worth it.

Footsteps padded down the corridor and the next face to pop round the door, wreathed in smiles, was Mum's.

'Oh, *here* you all are. I wondered where you'd got to. There's a terrific band playing in the marquee and Alice says we must all come and dance. You're missing all the fun.' As her eyes swept round the room, over our faces, her expression changed. 'What's going on?'

I saw real panic pass through Felicity's eyes. She glanced fearfully at Caro. Felicity valued Mum's high opinion very much. Her best friend.

Caro got off the bed. 'Nothing,' she said shortly. 'I just felt a bit peculiar and came up for a lie-down. Then Tim came in bellyaching about his hip, and the next thing I knew, the whole bloody family was in here.'

Three people flashed her grateful looks. 'Now come on,' she said briskly, 'we've got tea and cake to serve yet. And what a relief we *have* got cake, thanks to you, Barbara, and no thanks at all to Leonard.'

'Yes, although thanks to Leonard,' said Mum following her out, 'all your sows have now been serviced.'

Caro stopped in her tracks in the doorway. 'All of them? I was going to separate them. Let him have two at a time.'

'But Henry said Mum wants them all done at once.'

'Did he, by jingo? Which means in six months' time six sows will produce up to fifteen piglets apiece, which means . . . ninety piglets. Oh, splendid.' She looked a bit faint. Then something in her face lightened. She threw up her arms. 'So what? What the hell do I care? It certainly won't be *me* sloshing the swill in the trough, will it?'

9

BELLA EDGEWORTH died in March. The funeral was held in the village church next door to her house in Yorkshire, and the Hamilton family were among the mourners. The tiny church was heaving and we fairly raised the rafters. Then we listened as two of Bella's best friends read: first from Genesis Chapter One, and then her favourite Shakespeare sonnet, the one about the darling buds of May. Bella had been thinking of Stacey, I thought as I listened. Didn't want anything that would set her daughter off. Just a few gentle reminders of what a beautiful world it still was out there.

Stacey didn't read, but back at the house, where we all gratefully went for tea and sandwiches later, she got up on a kitchen chair and said a few words, blushing to the roots of her blonde hair: about how her mum would have liked to see everyone in her kitchen like this. How pleased she'd be to see us admiring her garden. How Stacey wished she was here, but knew she was no longer in pain, and that, however sad it was to lose her, she, Stacey, was glad she was no longer suffering. Those of us who'd held it together in church for Stacey's sake completely lost it now, myself included.

Ted, beside me, mopped furiously with his huge white hanky. Stacey looked her grandfather firmly in his damp eye and thanked him for all he'd done, for the rock he'd been. Then, to my surprise, she introduced Ant as her father, Anna as her half-sister and referred kindly to Anna's mum, who'd offered her a home in Oxford. It wasn't, she went on, that she was deserting her Yorkshire friends and family: she'd always be a Yorkshire lass, it was just that her mum, Bella, had wanted her life to move on, and for her to get to know her father properly. It was a straightforward speech, but it told everyone precisely what the score was. It didn't exactly spare Ant's blushes, who, as everyone turned to peer at this Johnny-come-lately, went puce. It ended with a glass of champagne raised—'To Mum. The best a girl could ever have. My world. My everything.' It was the only bit where Stacey's voice cracked.

'To Bella!' we all roared, to cover it, as she was helped down from her chair by Ant. Then the teacups were put away and out came the wine.

Stacey was hugged by school friends with whispered assurances she'd done 'really really well', then, likewise by teachers, and neighbours and friends of Bella's. I felt very proud of her. I waited for my turn to come and told her so.

'Was it OK?' she asked anxiously. 'Not too schmaltzy? Mum and I felt something should be said before I just sort of—disappeared. We also thought it might stem the flow of—oh, didn't you know?' She broadened her accent: 'There's a father. Oh, aye, 'e's finally cum out the woodwork. Didn't want to know 'er when she was a bairn, but now she's going to college, now she's proving herself to be an asset . . .' She rolled her eyes meaningfully. I laughed.

Despite Stacey's brave words, it was surely the longest day of her short life, and towards the end of the afternoon she looked very tired. There were more brave words though, as we said goodbye.

'I thought I might use Anastasia when I'm at Oxford. What d'you think?' She coloured up as she said it.

'I think it's a good idea. It's a lovely name. What did your mum think?' I could have kicked myself. Already looking for back-up, the first time she'd turned to me.

'It was her idea. But I don't know. I don't want people to think I'm . . . you know, reinventing myself, or anything.'

This time I didn't miss a beat. 'That's just another word for taking life by the scruff of its neck. There's nothing wrong with that.'

She looked pleased, and relieved. 'Although,' she hesitated, 'I might still be Stacey at home.'

This last word wasn't lost on me either, and as we drove away from that mellow stone house, I felt moved and humbled beyond belief. What a privilege it was going to be to have her, I realised. I made a silent promise to her mother. I know she's rare and valuable. I know what we have here. I shall cherish her accordingly.

Six months later and Stacey was beside me again. Yet again we were surrounded by bottles, yet again we were preparing for a party, only this time, it was of a very different nature. Together we heaved clanking boxes into the boot of the car outside the farmhouse, preparing to take them to an occasion I don't think any of us had seen coming.

'Where's Anna?'

Stacey grinned. 'Still dithering about what to wear.'

'Come *on*, Anna!' I yelled back at the open front door. 'We're going!' No response. '*Anna!*' Eventually she appeared at the doorway with a big box of Hula Hoops, her only responsibility.

'And don't forget to lock the door,' I called to her.

It was odd, I thought, how, since Stacey had arrived, Anna had slipped effortlessly into the role of little sister. I watched as she tried to lock the front door while balancing the box of Hula Hoops on her knee. She seemed happy to let Stacey play the part of elder statesman, while she, rather refreshingly, became the hopeless kid; predictably, she dropped the whole lot onto the yard.

'Sorry!' She looked up helplessly as Stacey and I went to help.

Happily the packets weren't too disgusting as the yard had recently been resurfaced, and we brushed them down and slung them back in the box. Yes, amazing what half a hundredweight of crunchy gravel did, I thought as I followed the girls back to the car. Amazing what had happened to the farm full stop.

Ah yes, the farm: which had to be sold, that much was certain; everyone, even Caro, agreed. And she hadn't messed about. A frightfully up-market estate agent called Peregrine had admitted it was worth a fortune, Mrs Milligan. Pound signs rotated in Caro's eyes as she personally, elbowing Peregrine out of the way, oversaw the bidding war that got under way. The victor, Mick Arnold, a local property developer, eventually paid way over the asking price.

'Twenty-five per cent more!' squeaked Caro excitedly when I popped round one morning for a coffee. 'Which means we can afford the house

I've seen with the walled garden. Six bedrooms! *And* a Chalon kitchen.'

'Good.' I was thrilled for her. Knew it was genuinely what she wanted now. Knew that, when she'd crossed the line that meant leaving the farm, she'd done it in a leap. Landed on the other side without looking back. It was what Tim and the children wanted too.

'Have you seen the new house?' I asked the children.

'Not yet. But I know where it is,' Jack told me. 'Miles Jackson lives in the same road.'

'Oh, it's terribly convenient,' gushed Caro, pouring out coffee at the Aga as Tim came in. 'The children can even walk to school. It's literally just off the Banbury Road, in Westgate Avenue.'

'Oh, we looked there.' I turned, surprised, as she delivered a mug of coffee to me over my shoulder. 'But Ant thought it was too grand.'

'Not for us it's not,' snorted Caro, sitting down at the far end of the table with an enormous Designers Guild samples book.

I laughed and picked up my coffee. 'Good old Mick Arnold.'

'And look what he's doing to the place,' said Tim in awed tones, unrolling plans and spreading them on the table in front of me. 'All the barns are being converted,' he explained, running his finger across the drawings, 'and they all look out onto a courtyard in the middle, here.'

I went cold. 'What—you mean like a sort of complex?'

'Well, there'll be six of them in all, oh, and a couple of flats.'

'Right.' I swallowed. 'And the farmhouse?'

He unrolled another sheet. 'Oh, the *house*. Blimey, Evie, you've no idea. It's going to be tarted up beyond belief. Every bedroom gets an en suite, and then they're digging down to make an indoor cinema.'

'Christ. And what's this?'

Tim peered. 'Not sure. Think it's a fountain.'

'It is,' affirmed Caro. 'They're doing a sort of mini-Versailles in the yard. Very tasteful, apparently.'

'Yuck.'

Tim grinned as he rolled up the plans. 'Yuck, but he's paying through the nose for it, Evie.' He looked me in the eye. 'And it's only a pile of bricks and mortar, after all. Not hearts and minds.' He gently jerked his head to his children at the other end of the table, all leaning eagerly over Caro's shoulder, picking wallpaper for their teenage bedrooms.

Yes, it was only bricks and mortar, I thought as I left that day. Before I got in the car, though, I stood in the yard where the fountain would be. Gazed at the 300 acres of land, which no doubt would be parcelled up too, eventually, and sold as individual plots for yet more desirable homes; more ribbon development in the Oxfordshire countryside. I narrowed my eyes to the familiar view: the rolling hills, the swaying chestnuts, no longer with a marquee flapping in the foreground. I supposed they'd still leave the willows standing, and the stream would still run through the valley as it always had done—you can't stop a stream, can you? And people had to live somewhere, didn't they?

I said as much to Ant that evening, with forced jollity: telling him about mini-Versailles; making a joke of it as Caro had. Told him progress was good, and it was time the farm moved on.

'What, and become unaffordable executive housing?'

'Well, affordable to some.'

'Yes, but not the people who live in the village who need it. Londoners, second homers. City boys with fat bonuses. And you call that progress.'

The following day Ant came home from work looking thoughtful. 'Would you hate to live at the farm again?'

I turned slowly from the sink where I'd been washing up. 'No . . .'

'Could you even entertain it?'

My heart began to pound. 'You're not seriously suggesting . . .'

'Why not? We could do it up. Put a new kitchen in, solve the damp, redecorate. What d'you think?'

I thought a lot of things. But I didn't want to get excited.

'Can we afford it?'

'Yes, but not easily. Mick Arnold's offered a fortune, and we'd have to match it.' He was talking quite fast now. 'This place will be worth quite a bit, though, being so central, but we'd probably need two salaries. So in answer to your question, yes, we could afford it, but only if you work. Which is what you tell me you want to do.'

'I do,' I said soberly. Then blinked. 'Gosh. Sounded like a vow.' And in a way, it was. To begin a new life. 'Oh, Ant,' I breathed.

'I wasn't convinced you'd want to. You're such a townie.'

I laughed, taken aback. 'Yes, I am, aren't I? But once I was a farmer's daughter. And d'you know what? I've done the city. Oxford was such a challenge when I was growing up, those flipping dreaming spires waving at me over the treetops—come on, Evie, d'you dare? But I've got to grips with it now, and I'd like to go back to the sticks where I belong.'

It was a surprise to hear myself say it, but it was true. And I no longer felt a fraud here, either. I'd fought my battles in this town, and now I was very much looking forward to going home and curling up in the window seat with a box of lime creams and a Georgette Heyer. I wondered if Caro felt that way about going back to town. Tossing her swill buckets over her shoulder and kicking off her wellies as she went.

'Caro—' I started.

'I know,' said Ant quickly. 'We'd be doing everything to the farm they'd ever wanted to. I know, Evie, that bothers me. We'd have to square it with them first, obviously, and I'm not sure—'

'No,' I interrupted impatiently, shaking my head, 'I mean yes, we will have to square it with them, but I think she'll be fine.'

'You do?' Ant looked surprised, but I didn't just think, I sort of knew. It was over fifteen years since Caro and I had been passionate about our futures, and over time, our ancient desires had become unrecognisable, even to ourselves. I'd seen Caro turn round and blink in astonishment the other day, as she'd glimpsed her new self in her lofty, spacious, state-of-the-art kitchen; in fact, I'd seen her gawp. It seemed to me it wouldn't matter how many terracotta tiles we put down in that farm, she still wouldn't want it.

'I'll ring her later, sound her out. But as long as *you're* sure, Ant.' It was my turn to interrogate him. 'It's further into college—'

'I know, but I'm working at home more now. Doing more writing.' He looked young, excited. 'I can work in your father's old study. French windows open to the garden, the stream . . .' He turned. His eyes caught sharply on mine.

'No, no demons,' I said quickly. 'You?'

'No. Not now. Too long ago.'

Which was how, some months later, I came to be standing in the not so muddy yard of my childhood, waiting for my girls. Happily they'd been enthusiastic about the move, talking parties in barns, barbecues by the stream. They'd already worked out the buses into town, one of which, these last few days, Anna had started taking into school. Stacey, meanwhile, was still enjoying the end of her last, long, seemingly endless summer holiday, waiting for her new term to begin.

'You're such a loser,' she told Anna now, who was giggling as she trailed yet more packets of Hula Hoops out of a box that had clearly burst its bottom. 'Shame the pigs have gone. They'd love these.'

Ah yes, the pigs. Happily no longer with us, and happily, not ninety of them either, only eight. Leonard turned out to be all gong, no dinner, and only Boadicea produced a litter. Caro had disclaimed all responsibility. She had, however, been kind enough to tell us about a lovely little slaughterhouse near Thame, which absolutely everyone went to— rather as if she were recommending a new bistro.

So, no pigs now—even Harriet, Caro's blind pig, had passed away in her sleep one night—but lots of restful sheep, thanks to Ed Pallister next door, who was leasing the fields, pathetically grateful for the extra acres. We didn't sell the land to him, though. Ant and I owned every blade of grass, and in a ridiculous, romantic way, I wondered if Tim's boys might want it back one day. Caro, naturally, was keen on this idea. She'd gripped my arm, eyes shining. 'Oh, *yes*, wouldn't that be wonderful? I mean, obviously I'm thrilled you've got it and not Mick Arnold, but if Jack could have it back one day . . .' She'd been showing me round her new house at the time, and the children were with us. Jack, who'd recently confided his ambition to be a stockbroker and live in Docklands with a horny blonde, shot me a horrified look.

'Henry, even,' she mused happily, as Henry, behind her, slit his throat with his finger and fell quietly to the blond wood conservatory floor.

Yes, I reflected, as the girls and I finally set off; once the stress of the farm had been removed, Caro had indeed become a different person. When Felicity had sold her house and taken a year's sabbatical at the University of Toronto, where her sister lived, writing Tim and Caro out a large cheque, Caro had promptly stuck it in an envelope, determined to return it. Tim and I, with a lot of eye rolling, had snatched it back. 'It's what she wants, Caro. Don't throw it back in her face.'

'I'm not! But I feel awful!' she wailed.

'Bit late now' sprang to mind, but I didn't say it. I sighed. 'Look, Caro, we are where we are. Write Felicity a big thank you, with an offer to come and stay whenever she's in Oxford. You've got six bedrooms in that house. Tell her one of them's got her name on it.'

'Yes. Yes, I will.' Her face lit up like a born-again Christian's. 'I'll put "Felicity" on the door.'

Tim and I exchanged weary glances. So exhausting when everyone wanted to be good.

She wasn't through, either. Two days later, she and Tim came to see me. 'OK, we're keeping the money, but we're sharing it with you.' She handed me a cheque.

'He was your father too,' said Tim firmly, as I opened my mouth to protest. 'It's your inheritance as well. Fair's fair.'

I shut my mouth. If I'm honest, it had quietly occurred to me. I gazed down at the cheque in my hands. 'Thank you.'

As I pulled up outside the shop now, Caro was waiting for us. She looked stunning in chocolate linen trousers and an ice-blue cashmere wrap top, happily not stick thin any more, but with a wonderful curvy figure and fuller face.

'You're early!' I wailed, as I got out.

'I know, but I thought I'd help you set up.'

'You're a guest, Caro, you don't have to do that.'

'Nonsense, many hands and all that . . .'

'Where's Tim?'

'Here.' She jerked her head as he came down the road. 'He went to park the car. What about Ant?'

'He's got a meeting, but he'll be along later.'

'Now, what can I do?' Tim appeared, rubbing his hands.

'You could set up the trestle table at the back of the shop—I've left it leaning against a wall in there—and take some boxes in. Girls, go with him and line up the glasses on the table.'

They disappeared, the three of them, carrying a box of booze apiece, and then Tim came back for more, nimbler on his pins these days now he wasn't on them twenty-four hours a day. He was selling agricultural machinery, a rep; getting out to all the many farms around here, which, as he said, meant 'seeing all my mates but not doing the sodding donkey-work. I wave bye-bye as they stand in the shit admiring my company car.' He pointed it out to me now as he came back for the final box of lemonade, parked just down the road: a brand-new silver Saab.

At the back of the shop the girls had laid the table. Stacey was attacking the lemons. 'Mint for the Pimms?' She glanced up.

Oh. I darted back to the car. As I came back with it, though, I paused a moment midway through the shop; took a second to gaze around. Yes, the duck-egg blue really *had* worked, I decided. Cheered the place up no end; made it more sophisticated. I'd been nervous of going down that route, since I certainly didn't want to alienate Malcolm's old customers. I needn't have worried. As the door opened behind me, I turned to see a clutch of his elderly regulars come in, bang on the dot of six o'clock. I spotted Joan of the long brown coat and spearmint smell among them as they hurried past to the back, keen to be the recipients of the first drink. Anna and Stacey were going to have to pour fast.

A few more early birds appeared, and then the man I was most worried about, who breezed in on a gust of wind with Clarence.

'Darling!' He sashayed across the room to kiss me, then clasped his hands in delight. 'What a triumph!'

'D'you really think so, Malc?' I said nervously. 'Not too girlie?'

'Oh, it's *girlie* all right, but that's what makes it work, don't you think, hon?' This, hon, not directed to me, but to Clarence.

'I agree—thank you.' He took a drink from Stacey, who'd approached with a tray. 'You've done a superb job, Evie.'

I relaxed: these boys had taste, and I was pretty sure I'd know if they were fibbing. I enquired about London life, which, they assured me, was working out well. Some months back, Clarence, having completed his sabbatical at Magdalen, had headed back to King's, leaving Malcolm desolate. Until Clarence had asked him to come with him, that is.

'What, to visit?' Malcolm had told me how the conversation had gone. Malcolm was a very good mimic and he'd acted out the parts, jumping to one side to be Clarence, and affecting his deep, treacly tones, then jumping back to play himself, in a high, silly voice.

'No, to live,' Malcolm growled, a.k.a. Clarence.

'What, with you?' (High squeak.) 'In Little Venice?'

'If you can bear it.'

'But . . . what about my boat?'

'It's not called Little Venice for nothing, Malcolm. I'm sure a mooring can be arranged. If not, it can be our country retreat.'

'Can Cinders come too?'

'Sooty would be distraught if she didn't.'

Malcolm, adopting an even higher falsetto: 'You're asking me to move in with you?'

'That's . . . the general idea.'

Quite a lot of jumping up and down on the spot was re-enacted for me then, together with excited flapping of hands. 'But what about the shop?' squealed baby bear. 'Which is where you come in, flower.' Malcolm had turned to me then, in something more like his normal voice. 'Ludo wants to sell up too. He's going back to journalism.'

'Is he?' I'd flushed at his name.

'Oh, yes, didn't you know? Says he needs to get back to where the action is. He went back to London last week.'

'Oh.' I felt a pang. Of regret, I suppose; but I was pleased for him too. 'It's the right thing for him,' I told Malcolm.

'Of course it is. He was wasted here. But the *shop*, dear heart . . .'

The shop. I moved around it now, feeling strangely weightless. It—and the renovation—had been paid for with Dad's money, of course. Would he have approved? I gazed around. I think so. The money was going to support a family business, and that, I believe, would have pleased him. Oh, it could have gone straight into the bottomless pit of renovating the farmhouse, but Ant had said no. Use it for something definitive, something to remember him by: something for you. Use it to take out a mortgage on the shop. My shop.

'What d'you think?' I asked him now as he approached.

'Terrific.' He smiled down at me. 'You're terrific.' He bent his head to kiss me, and at that moment Ludo walked in, together with Alice and her husband, Angus, and a very beautiful Asian girl.

'Ludo!' Ant and I sprang apart. He and Ant lunged to shake hands, somewhat overheartily, and then Ludo and I pecked cheeks as if we were encountering molten metal.

'Hi.' He stepped back smartly as I did too. 'This is fantastic.'

'You think?' I wasn't really listening: I was looking at the fashionably crumpled linen jacket, the crazy red and white print shirt.

'For sure. It's taken it out of the last century and brought it hurtling into this one.' He saw me clocking the new wardrobe. 'Oh. Sunita bought me these.' He grinned, that lovely old tigerish smile. 'Sunita— Evie,' he said. 'Sunita wanted to bring me out of the last century too.'

I laughed. 'About time too. It's lovely to meet you, Sunita.'

'It was nice of you to invite me,' she said with a secret smile, and I knew, in an instant, she knew. I caught a glimpse of surprise in her eyes now. Ah, but you see, Sunita, I thought, excusing myself politely, you don't have to be a spring chicken to make hearts beat faster.

I moved on round the room, revelling in being among friends, family, on this, my opening night; a blissfully balmy, late summer's evening. I spied Ted, talking to Stacey, and went to say hello.

'You're sweet to come all this way,' I said, pouring him a drink.

He knocked it back in one. 'Don't be soft, I wouldn't have missed it for the world. You've done a grand job here. And look at all the support you've got.' His eyes roved around, marvelling at the crush. 'If all these people buy their books here, you're quids in!'

'Well, let's hope they do,' I said nervously. 'I'm rather counting on people's loyalty to their small, quirky, local bookshop.'

'Aye, well, as that lovely lady over there was saying earlier, that's the charm o' the place.' He nodded across the room. 'Its quirkiness.'

'That's my mum,' I said in surprise. 'Weren't you introduced?'

'Not properly, like. I just muscled in on the chatter, then someone else nabbed her. Your mum, eh?' He looked in surprise: from me back to her. 'I can see it now. Same smile. Same generous spirit too, I'll warrant.'

'Oh, no, she's much nicer than me. Come and meet her properly.'

I led him across the room and introduced them. Yes, Mum did indeed look rather lovely, I thought, as I left them chatting. The girls had persuaded her to cut off her ponytail and have her hair done properly, with a few highlights, which made her look years younger. In fact, everyone looked lovely this evening, I decided. Anna and Stacey were with the boys behind the bar, Phoebe too. She saw me looking and smiled across. Then, after a moment's hesitation, she came over. 'Um, Evie? You know you said to Mum that one day Jack or Henry could buy the farm back from you?'

'Yes?'

'Would you say the same to me?' Her colour rose up her neck. 'If one day I wanted to, would you give me first refusal too?'

I put my jug down. 'Phoebe Milligan.' I put my arms round her and hugged her tight. 'With the greatest pleasure,' I whispered in her ear.

'Thank you.' She beamed at me. 'It's just, I thought I might go to Cirencester after school. You know, agricultural college. Learn how to do it properly. And, who knows, one day . . .'

'Who knows in*deed*,' I said, delighted.

It was warm in the room, and I threaded my way through the noisy, baying throng to the front to open a window. I propped open the double doors too, hooking them both back on the wall, then wandered outside. I wanted to be at a vantage point where I could look back and see it all properly. I strayed across to the other side of the road. As I turned on the opposite pavement to look back at the shop, my heart contracted a moment, then kicked in.

Brightly lit and buzzing, juxtaposed by its darkened, quiet neighbours, it looked quite the place to be this Friday night. Voices sang into the night, up into the skyline of treacle-coloured Cotswold stone. My eyes roved critically over the shopfront. Two shopfronts seamlessly merged by a set of double French doors, painted off-white, the detail picked out in the same duck-egg blue as the interior. Either side of them, on the pavement, sat two lemon trees in round, leaded pots. I hadn't been able to resist.

'They'll get nicked,' Malcolm had warned, the moment he saw them.

'I'll bring them in at night,' I'd retorted.

'You'll get lazy, you'll leave them, they'll get nicked,' he'd repeated.

'We'll see.' I'd smiled, and he had too, at my enthusiasm.

My eye travelled up now above the windows, to something I hadn't been able to resist either. Across the hoarding, in pale lemon scroll the name of the shop had been picked out in bold, swirling letters:

Hamilton and Daughters

I smiled. Raised my glass. 'Here's to us,' I said softly, into the night.

Catherine Alliott

It was a cold but bright day in London when I travelled from the Reader's Digest offices in Canary Wharf to meet Catherine Alliott on the other side of town. Over the last few years we have featured several of Catherine's books in Of Love and Life: *A Crowded Marriage*, *The Wedding Day*, *Olivia's Luck* and *A Married Man* and, although I was due to interview her, it felt far more as though I was going to catch up with an old friend, which is also how I feel when I settle down to read one of her books. As usual, Catherine looked wonderful—cool, calm, and very trendy—but then she has two teenage daughters to keep her on her toes!

As we chatted about our respective families and life in general, I discovered that Catherine, who has always been something of a technophobe, has finally joined the twentieth century and set herself up on email, mainly to keep in touch with her three children, who are all away at boarding school. 'Apart from the children, I'm guaranteed at least one email a day,' she said. 'My son set up Dr Dictionary for me, which sends through a word of the day, with its definition. I love either finding a new word or patting myself on the back because I already know it.'

Catherine has now published ten bestselling novels and usually writes a book every two years. 'Although without the children around, I do find I have more time and, you never know, the next one could be finished sooner.' But life at Catherine's

Hertfordshire home is still busy as she has an aviary and a menagerie of animals to look after: cows, sheep, Bantams, chickens, two Labradors, and a Border Terrier. 'We had a cat but it ran away because our Border Terrier was making its life a misery. It's probably found itself a much more relaxed home in the village.'

When Catherine first started writing, her heroines were always single, looking for the right man and living in flats. 'But life moves on and over time my heroines became young marrieds and then young marrieds with kids.' What hasn't changed is that Catherine says her characters still let her know how the story will turn out. *The Secret Life of Evie Hamilton* marks a slight departure as this is the first of Catherine's novels in which the plot arrived before the character. 'I started with the idea of someone receiving a letter, completely out of the blue, giving them news that totally tears their world apart. It happened to someone I know, and the repercussions of that letter affected their whole family. It was too good an idea not to pursue and I absolutely loved writing the novel.'

Jane Eastgate

A few of Catherine's favourite things

Favourite TV programmes?
Spooks. But why on earth did they have to kill off Adam? Oh, and *Silent Witness*. I just love Harry Cunningham. And *Strictly Come Dancing*, of course.

Favourite holiday destinations?
France. Italy.

Favourite films?
Truly, Madly, Deeply. I loved *Mamma Mia*—but then, who didn't? We walked out of *Quantum of Solace*.

Favourite book?
Just finished *Reading in Bed* by Sue Gee, which I really enjoyed.

Favourite food?
Pasta.

Favourite shop?
My local farm shop. I'm always buying pet food, especially sheep pellets—what a glamorous life!

Favourite cities?
London. Paris.

Favourite clothes?
Anything from Joseph. I spend my days mainly in wellies/dressing gown or wellies/jeans, so anything other than that.

Favourite flower?
Primrose. Also the middle name of one of my daughter's.

Favourite guilty pleasure?
All the green triangles from the Quality Street tin.

The Fleece

Silvino's

LYON'S TEA

The
Accidental
Time Traveller

SHARON GRIFFITHS

Journalist Rosie Harford is having a very unsettling day. She's had a flaming row with her boyfriend, Will, and now, on her latest assignment, has been duped into entering the TV set of *The 1950s House* on a local housing estate. But if this is reality television, where are the cameras? Why is her mobile phone suddenly dead? And, worst of all, why has Will been transformed into a devoted family man called Billy?

CHAPTER ONE

'YOU ALL RIGHT, LOVE?'

The taxi driver was looking at me oddly as I scrabbled in my bag. Mobile . . . iPod . . . notebook . . . Dictaphone . . . everything but my purse. Ah. There it was, right at the bottom, of course. I pulled a tenner out—I think it was a tenner—and pushed it through the window. Just peering in at the driver really hurt my neck.

'Here. Thanks. Keep the change.'

'Are you *sure* you're all right?' he asked, swiftly folding the note into his wallet. Maybe it had been a twenty.

'Yes. Fine. Fine.'

But I wasn't. Not really. And it got worse. As the taxi roared off—no one likes to hang around The Meadows longer than they have to—I stood swaying on the pavement. My head was thumping, my eyes were hurting and I couldn't stop shivering. It was one of those Mondays when I swore I would never drink again. Or have a row with Will . . .

Right. No time to think about that now. I tried to get myself together. I was here to do an interview for *The News*. Mrs Margaret Turnbull had been one of the first people to move into The Meadows when it was built fifty years ago in the days when it was the Promised Land. Bit different now. You're lucky to come back and find your car still there. Even luckier if it's still got its wheels.

But *The News* was doing a special supplement to mark the Meadows' fiftieth birthday. One of the big TV stations was apparently planning a reality programme where people have to pretend to live in the past— *The 1950s House*—and that was going to be in The Meadows too. So I had spent the morning in the dusty little library at the top of *The News* building, reading through the bound files of yellowing newspapers from the 1950s—stories of new roads, new houses, flower festivals, pageants, mysterious deaths, and adverts for cigarettes and washing machines, and lots of housewives prancing around in pinnies.

Meanwhile, back in the present I leaned on the gatepost as my head swam. Tidy gatepost. Neat path and pretty garden with tulips, primroses and violets. This was one of the nicer bits of the estate, and a very posh front door showed that Mrs Turnbull had bought her council house. Through the window, I could see a grey-haired lady in trousers and a sweatshirt watching out for me.

But as I walked up that path I realised something was very wrong. My eyesight had gone haywire. The flagstones seemed a long way away. It was hard to find them with my feet. Everything was at odd angles. My head was swirling. I wanted to shake it to clear it, but my neck wouldn't work properly. There was a pain in my eyes. This wasn't a hangover, this was something else. I was ill, really ill. I got to the front door, pushed my hands out in front of me and somehow rang the bell.

I suddenly wished that Will and I hadn't argued, that we'd said goodbye that morning with a kiss instead of sitting in the car in strained and sulky silence. I wished . . . then everything went black.

Things had started to go wrong on Sunday. As well as living together, Will and I work together too—he's the paper's deputy news editor—and so a weekend when neither of us is working is a bit of a treat. After a good Saturday night out with Caz and Jamie we had a lie-in, and then Will had gone to play football and I'd pottered round the flat and sorted out the washing. Just my washing—Will does his own.

Caz and I got to the pub at the same time. She was wearing a jacket I hadn't seen before, black and fitted, with fancy frogged buttons. Very romantic. 'Love the coat,' I said, as we made our way to the bar. 'New?'

'Don't be daft.' She laughed. 'This was in the charity shop reject box, because it had a stain on the bottom. So I chopped that off and found the buttons on eBay.' Clever girl, Caz. A real eye for what looks good.

With that, Jamie's car pulled up outside. Will was in the passenger seat. Just that glimpse of him through the pub's small window made me smile. Even after all this time together, I still got so excited to see him. He and Jamie breezed in, smelling of fresh air and full of the joy of victory. We got our drinks, ordered some food and bagged the last table.

So, everything was fine . . . until Leo and Jake came over.

But it wasn't their fault. Not their fault at all.

'It's OK. We're not stopping. We've just called in for some Dutch courage,' said Jake. 'We're off to lunch with Leo's parents. We have some news for them.'

'News?' Caz and I immediately sat up straight and took notice.

'We're getting married!' said Jake. 'Or civil-partnershipped anyway. Midsummer's Day. Old Shire Hall. Marquee in the rose garden. Lots and lots of champagne. Lovely music. Lovely people too, if you'll come.'

Caz and I jumped up and hugged and kissed them both. Will and Jamie stood up and clapped them round the shoulders in a manly way.

'Can I get you a drink to celebrate?' asked Will. But no, Leo's parents were waiting. They didn't want to be late. It was an important day.

'Good luck!' we yelled as they went out.

'Well,' said Jamie, after they'd gone. 'What's the form for a woofter wedding then? Do we have to wear pink?'

'Don't be so silly,' said Caz. 'It will be good fun. And it's great they can do it. Makes sense with tax and money and all that sort of thing.'

'But that's not just why they're doing it,' I said. 'I think it's lovely. Public declaration and all that.'

'Do you really?' asked Will. The sharpness of his tone surprised me.

'Well, yes,' I said. 'I mean, they're obviously devoted to each other and it's great that now they can tell the world.'

'Yeah, guess so,' said Will, but he looked as though he wanted to carry on grumbling. Then our food arrived and we got stuck into eating. Drinking too. Afterwards we walked round to Caz and Jamie's place.

'Yes!' went Will, as soon as we walked in. 'Oh, that is just beautiful!'

Jamie laughed. 'Pretty neat, isn't it?' I was behind them, pulling my boots off, so I couldn't see at first what all the fuss was about. Then I padded into the sitting room and saw it was a TV set, one of those huge plasma jobs. It was hanging on the wall like a picture. Caz raised her eyebrows in a 'Don't blame me, it's one of his toys' sort of expression.

'That is just mint!' said Will, standing in front of the set with his tongue practically hanging out. Jamie switched on some motor racing. It looked as though the cars were racing from one end of the room to the other. Impressive, but too much. Much too much. I went through to the kitchen to help Caz dig out some ice cream. More wine too.

'It's his latest toy,' she said.

'Don't you mind?'

Caz shrugged. 'It's his money.'

'Gerrin there!' Will was yelling at the TV like a kid.

We took the wine and the ice cream back into the sitting room and I curled up on the sofa. My throat was a bit scratchy so I could kid myself the soothing ice cream was medicinal. Then Will said, 'I think we should get one of these TVs, Rosie.'

'In your dreams. We haven't got that sort of money. If we had, we'd be living in a bigger flat.'

This was a sore point. Our flat was actually mine, and it was tiny, which is why I had been able to buy it. When Will—and all his stuff—had moved in a few months earlier, the plan had been we'd try and save to buy a bigger flat together. We needed more space. We didn't need a couple of thousand pounds' worth of television.

'Don't even think about it,' I said crossly. Suddenly Will had that slightly sulky expression that he has when he doesn't get his own way. But then Caz came downstairs, holding a photo and giggling.

'I was sorting out some stuff at my mum's, Will,' she said, 'and I found this.'

'Oh my God!' said Will. 'The outdoor activities week in Year Eleven!'

Oh, yes. Will and Caz were at school together. They even had a bit of a fling at one time, long before I knew either of them.

Actually it was quite a funny photo. They must have been sixteen years old and were on an outdoor week in the Yorkshire Dales, all climbing, canoeing and gorge-walking. Caz was wearing one of those enormous geeklike cagoules. But she had the full make-up on: three different shades of eye shadow, blusher and lip gloss.

In the picture she was gazing adoringly up at Will. Jamie snatched the photo from him. 'I bet you were hell for the teachers,' he said—and he should know; he teaches in the local comp—'sneaking off to the canoe store for a quick snog. They all do.'

Caz and Will looked at each other very quickly and almost blushed.

Caz grinned. 'Thank goodness you don't choose your life partners at sixteen,' she said. 'Bad enough working with you, Will, let alone having to live with you. Don't know how Rosie manages it.'

'With difficulty sometimes,' I said, laughing. But I felt a small pang. I had fallen for Will the moment I'd arrived at *The News*, where he was already a senior reporter. He had to show me round on the first day and I knew, just knew, that he was the one for me. We were both slightly involved with other people at the time and as soon as we untangled ourselves, that was it. It was as if we had always been together.

But we hadn't. And Caz had known him since they were eleven years old. They had a past: experiences, memories, daft jokes I couldn't share. And sometimes, just sometimes, I felt a twinge of jealousy.

Jamie and Will started playing on the PlayStation. 'What about Leo and Jake then?' asked Caz. 'I bet that will be a brilliant day.'

I laughed and started to say something to Will, but he was still gazing at that bloody television screen.

'Look, Will, you've only just got your new car,' I said, as Caz passed me more wine. 'That's a nice new toy for now.'

'Well, you're the one who wanted to go to New York.'

'And you're the one who spent a fortune in Nieman Marcus,' I snapped back. 'How many cashmere sweaters does one man need?'

'Children, children,' said Jamie. You could just hear him with Year Seven, though at school he probably wouldn't have the lager can in his hand. 'Have you not thought that perhaps if you didn't buy new cars and fly halfway across the world for a long weekend, you might just be able to buy a bigger flat, or even a little house? Unless, of course, your subconscious is telling you to spend your money on fun and toys instead of being grown-up and sensible and salting it away for your future.

'Strange, isn't it,' he went on, 'that the only people in our group who are getting married are Leo and Jake? Takes a pair of gays to set the rest of us loose-living reprobates a good example.'

'Me, I don't see the point of being married,' said Caz. 'We're fine as we are, aren't we, sweetie?' she said, patting Jamie's knee. 'We don't need a posh frock and a piece of paper. It might be different if we wanted kids, I suppose. But Jamie sees enough of kids at school.'

'And what about you?' I asked.

'Not a maternal bone in my body,' she said, laughing. 'Anyway I'd be an absolute disaster as a mum.'

Jamie looked baffled. 'I always thought girls wanted to get married. You know, waiting for their knight in shining armour to come along and sweep them off their feet, rescue them from dragons.'

'We can fight our own dragons, thank you,' I said.

'See?' said Jamie to Will. 'This lot have made us redundant.'

'Yeah, well,' said Will, now quite drunk, 'maybe Leo and Jake have got something to prove. They want to settle down and play house.'

Then, just like that, as if it wasn't really that important at all, he dropped the bombshell that nearly destroyed my world.

'As for me,' said Will, 'there's not much point in tying myself to a house if I'm not going to be around long.'

I was so shocked I gasped. 'What do you mean? Where are you going?'

'Well, nowhere at the moment. But I might do,' he said, looking sideways at me. 'I might go out to work in Dubai. Mate of mine out there says they always want English journos. Plenty of money, easy lifestyle.'

Dubai? This was the first I'd heard of it. 'And is that what you want?

Plenty of money and an easy lifestyle?' I snapped.

'Well, it's what we all want really, isn't it?' he said, taking a gulp from his can and sprawling back into the armchair.

I was furious. I was also drunk, which didn't help. I had thought Will and I were pretty solid. Maybe even permanent. Wrong!

'Look, Rosie.' He put down his can. 'I just mean—'

'Forget it!' I snapped again.

'Coffee?' said Caz, very brightly.

'No, no, I don't want coffee,' I said. 'I think I want to go home.' I marched out into the hall, wriggled my feet into my boots and left.

Will came after me and I didn't know if I was pleased or not. I could hear his footsteps but he said nothing. His long legs meant he soon caught me up. He walked alongside me, looking straight ahead. And we walked like that, in silence, all the way to the flat. My flat.

When we got in, I turned to him. 'Are you really going to Dubai?'

'Who knows?' He shrugged. 'It's just a thought, a possibility. You can come too, if you like.' He hunched his hands into his pockets.

'If I like? *If I like?* You make me sound like an optional extra! I thought we had a future together.'

'Did you? Did you really?' Those big brown eyes flashed. 'If you think we have a future together,' he said, 'why is it that all I ever hear is what *you* want? *You* want the bigger flat. *You* bought the bigger sofa, without mentioning it to me. *You* pay the bills and tell me how much to cough up. Fine, fine. It's *your* flat after all, as you keep reminding me.'

I was stunned. 'I don't feel like that. I thought—'

'What did you think? Come on, tell me. I really want to know.'

'I was frightened,' I said. 'I didn't want to be dependent on you.'

'Why not? Don't you trust me?'

'It's not like that. No. It's nothing to do with trust. It's just that . . . Well, I don't know. We've never talked about the future, not really.'

And we hadn't. We'd planned holidays and weekends away but no more than that; not grown-up, till-death-us-do-part future.

'Well, let's talk about it now. Come on, Rosie, what do you want from me? From us?'

'I don't know.' And that was honest. I had sometimes daydreamed of being married to Will, of having him there all the time. He was the only person I've ever daydreamed like that about. But I had never told him. Because there were times that the same dream could terrify me. Will wasn't exactly husband material. I mean, he was nearly thirty and he still acted like a big kid. Away from work all he and Jamie cared about was football and drinking and playing computer games.

'You don't know?' he repeated, still waiting for my answer.

I looked up at him. 'Will, I love my job and I'm just beginning to get somewhere. I want to see how far I can go.'

'Fair enough. You'll go far, Rosie. We both know that.' Full of angry energy, Will was pacing up and down the tiny sitting room. 'But I don't know if I'm part of your plan. Frankly, Rosie, I haven't a clue where I am with you. You want everything your own way.'

'But it's not like that . . .' I was struggling to find ways of saying what I thought. And then he nearly floored me with his next question.

'Tell me, do you see yourself having children?'

'Hey!' I tried to joke. 'You can't ask questions like that at interviews!' Will wasn't laughing. 'I want to know.'

'Well, yes, since you ask, one day, probably,' I said. I'd daydreamed about that, too. A boy and a girl, with Will's blond hair and big brown eyes. But not yet. 'What about you? Do you want children?'

'Maybe, one day. Depends.'

'Depends on what?' I asked. 'On whether you can fit it in between the PlayStation and the plasma TV? You've got to be a grown-up to be a parent, Will, not an overgrown bloody kid yourself.'

Of course it all went downhill from there. We both said too many things that shouldn't have been said. I called him spoilt, immature and childish, among other things. He called me a selfish, unthinking control freak, among other things. In the end I went off to bed and I could hear Will impatiently flicking through the TV channels, until he finally went to sleep on the sofa. My new sofa.

And me? I lay in bed and tried to rerun the row. Did I really want to be married? Yes, of course. Maybe. But now? What if Will went to Dubai? What if I went to London? What if?

My head was thumping. I hardly slept, and in the morning it was worse. We drove to *The News* on Monday morning in Will's car, in silence. I'd been hoping to crawl to my desk and just plod through the day, but the editor, Jan Fox, known to all as The Vixen, spotted me.

'Rosie! A word, please!'

The Vixen was standing at her office door, eyes glinting, coppery highlights shining. In one hand she held a large sheet of paper, on which the perfect scarlet nails of the other hand were lightly drumming. It was not a happy drumming.

I realised that the piece of paper she was so obviously hacked off about was a proof copy of the next day's feature page. A feature on childcare, one I'd written. My heart sank even further. Happy Monday.

'Do you realise,' she said, shooting me one of her fierce looks, 'how incredibly young and silly this makes you sound? It's written as though everybody in the world has a responsibility to look after children, with the sole exception of their parents.'

'But I was just quoting from the reports and the government—'

'Yes, I know you were.' She sighed. 'I wonder about your generation sometimes. You must have had it easier than any other in the history of the world and it's still not enough; you're still asking for more.'

I just stood there, longing to get to the Ibuprofen in my desk drawer.

'OK, I've marked up some ideas. Get that done. And then there's something else I want you to have a go at.'

Just what, I found out at the morning conference.

The news editor, picture editor, chief photographer and others all crowded into The Vixen's office, with mugs of coffee and piles of notes balanced on their knees. Will was there, but not looking as polished as usual. I don't know if he was trying to catch my eye, but I just kept staring at the photos of all the old editors on the wall above him: George Henfield, fat and bald; Richard Henfield with his pipe.

We'd whizzed through the plans for the following day's paper and much of the week's ideas, but The Vixen was still talking. 'Right,' she said. 'Now what about The Meadows? It's fifty years since the first families moved in and I think we should have a good look at it. At the time it was revolutionary: homes of the future, the perfect place to live.'

'They must have been desperate,' muttered Will.

The Vixen, of course, heard him. 'Will, you haven't a bloody clue, have you?' she said in withering tones, which cheered me up.

Will tried to score some Brownie points. 'We've done quite a lot on the way the school's improved,' he said. 'We've had a few interviews with Rosemary Picton, the new head teacher, who's working miracles.'

'Yes,' said The Vixen briskly, 'and I'm sure we'll be back to her. An amazing woman. But, as you know, they are using one of the houses on The Meadows for a new reality TV series, *The 1950s House*, so we need a good look at why people were so pleased to move there. What it was like at the beginning. Why it went wrong in parts. Why other parts are flourishing. We'll want to take a look at life in the 1950s. It could make a series of features. The Meadows seems a good place to start.'

By now I'd finished gazing at the old editors and was working my way round all the awards that *The News* had won under The Vixen. Suddenly I heard her mention my name. I sat up and tried to take notice.

'Rosie? Are you with us? I said I think this is something for you. If you wait afterwards, I'll give you some contacts.'

She always had contacts. I swear she knew everyone in town, not to mention the country. As the others picked up their notes and went back to their desks, she scribbled a name for me.

'Margaret Turnbull was one of the first people to move into The Meadows, and she's lived there ever since. Nice woman, good talker. She's actually Rosemary Picton's mother. When you've met Margaret you might get an idea of why her daughter's so determined to help the children of The Meadows. Anyway, here's her number.'

Dutifully, I rang Mrs Turnbull and arranged to see her later that afternoon. Then I made a huge mug of camomile tea and took a notebook up to the bound-file room, where all the back copies of *The News* are stored in huge book-style files. I settled down in the dusty little room. I didn't want to talk to anyone. Not even Caz and certainly not Will.

I felt so rough. My shoulders and neck hurt from poring over the old volumes, and my hands and feet were so cold. Bugger! My car was still in the car park at the Lion. So that's when I ordered a cab and went off to see Mrs Turnbull. Well, I thought she was Mrs Turnbull . . .

CHAPTER TWO

DESPITE THE PAIN in my head, I managed to open my eyes. The woman who came to the door wasn't the same as the one I'd seen through the window. Come to that, the window wasn't the same. Nor was the door.

I slumped against the door frame, my head swirling, trying to make it out. What I really wanted to do was just slide down the wall and lie down . . . but the woman was asking me something. 'Are you the girl from *The News*?'

'Er, yes, I am,' I said. It was about the only thing of which I was sure.

'Well, you'd better come in.'

I dragged my body together and followed her into a dark hallway. Something very odd here. I was sure that this sort of house didn't have that sort of long, dark hall, or the sort of kitchen it led to, which had one of those cast-iron stoves, a bit like an Aga. I could feel the warmth, which was wonderful. But there was a strange smell. It took a while for me to realise it was coal and soot.

'Here,' said the woman, 'sit down.' There was a cat curled up on the rocking chair by the stove. 'Shoo, Sambo,' she said, pushing him off. 'I'll make you a cup of tea,' she said to me. 'You're as white as a sheet.'

I felt as if everything in my head had slid down to the back of my scalp and was made of lead. Never mind trying to make sense of what was going on. But at least I was starting to warm up. The cat, Sambo— Sambo!—jumped delicately back onto my lap and curled round. I rocked gently, feeling the warmth of the fire and of the cat. I could even begin to attempt to make sense of my surroundings.

The woman wasn't as old as I first thought. Probably only in her fifties. She was wearing a heavy woollen skirt and cardigan, a checked apron and the sort of slippers that not even my gran wears any more. In the middle of the room was a big table covered with a dark green velvety cloth. Against one wall was a dresser stacked with plates and jugs. Above the range was a wooden clothes rack covered with sheets and pillowcases and what looked like old-fashioned vests and underpants.

As the woman moved round the room between the dresser, the table and the range, it was like watching a film. She set out a tray with proper cups, saucers and plates, wrapped a cloth round her hand and lifted a huge black kettle off the top of the stove and poured boiling water into a little brown teapot. From a hook by the range she lifted a tea cosy like a little chequered bobble hat and popped it on the teapot. She went into the scullery and came back with a fruit loaf, cut a chunk off and put it on a plate in front of me. Then she passed me a cup of tea. It was strong and sweet—both of which I hate normally—but I drank it and could feel the warmth going through me.

'I'm sorry about this, Mrs Turnbull,' I said.

'Oh, I'm not Mrs Turnbull,' she said.

'Oh my God,' I said, and tried to stand up. 'Then I'm in the wrong house. I *thought* something was wrong. Look, I'm really sorry. I'd better be on my way. Is it the house next door?'

'Sit down, girl,' she said, not unkindly. 'I'm Doreen Brown. If you're Rosie Harford from *The News* then you're in the right place. I've been expecting you. Your trunk's upstairs.'

'Trunk? What trunk?'

'The things you'll need for your stay, of course. They sent it round from your office this morning.'

I gazed at Mrs Turnbull, who was now Mrs Brown, and tried to follow what she was saying. I promised myself I would never drink again.

Where was I? Why was I apparently staying here? I took deep breaths and tried my best not to panic.

By now I'd had two cups of tea and I suddenly realised that I really needed the loo. I couldn't deal with this on a full bladder.

'Upstairs, along the corridor, down a few steps and on your right.'

The bathroom was freezing. There was black-and-white checked lino on the floor and the bath was huge with claw feet, a small brass tap and a big chrome one. The room smelt of old-fashioned, rose-scented soap.

I got my phone out of my bag and tried to ring Will. I know we'd had a row, but this was really weird stuff. There was no signal. More than that, the phone was dead, as if the battery had gone. I sat on the loo and felt wretched. The loo paper was horrid. Nasty scratchy stuff. And the loo had one of those big iron cisterns and a chain.

This house seemed so old-fashioned. Couldn't have been touched for fifty years. I had to get out. I stood up quickly. Too quickly. My head swam again and I leaned against the door. I mustn't panic, I told myself.

I washed my hands, splashed some cold water on my face and made my way back downstairs, holding on to the banisters. I would explain to the woman in the kitchen that, sorry, I had to go. And as soon as I was outside, I would phone Will and ask him to come and get me. And if my phone didn't work, I would walk towards town. Even The Meadows must be safe enough in daylight. There might even be a phone box. I would be all right once I was out in the fresh air . . .

I made it into the kitchen but collapsed back into the rocking chair. I would just sit here for a while and get my strength back. My eyes lit on a calendar on the wall. There was a picture of the Queen looking very young. The calendar didn't look old or as though it had been sitting in a junk shop for fifty years. It looked new in a 1950s sort of way.

I stood up. My head didn't swim. Good. I went through into the scullery to find Mrs Turnbull or Brown or whatever her name was.

'Look, Mrs . . . er, Brown. I think I'd better be on my way,' I said. 'I was meant to be meeting a Mrs Turnbull so I think I'd better get back and check with the office. Thank you so much for the tea—'

'Oh, you can't go yet, pet,' said Mrs Brown. 'You're meant to be staying. Anyway, Frank and Peggy will be back soon. Supper won't be long.'

Meant to be staying? Who were Frank and Peggy?

'I'll just get some fresh air, if you don't mind.'

'Carry on, dear.'

I picked up my bag and walked back along the hall. My head felt a bit better now. I'd tried to be polite about it, but I would just have to walk out. Strange. I was sure that when I'd walked up the path there'd been a modern white door, but here was this heavy wooden thing with stained glass at the top. I turned the handle and opened it.

Everything was different. Instead of the wide road of The Meadows with its rows of semidetached houses and front gardens, parked cars and abandoned vans, the door opened directly onto a narrow, cobbled street. No cars. No people. I stepped back into the house and shut the door again quickly.

I walked slowly back to the kitchen.

'Mrs Brown . . . did you say my office arranged this visit?'

'That's right. And a young man brought your trunk round this morning. That's why I knew you were coming. All arranged with the editor.'

The editor. I thought back to the morning conference. What exactly had The Vixen said? I'd been feeling so lousy that I hadn't really been listening. Something about The Meadows, of course, that's why I was here. And a reality TV programme. *The 1950s House* . . .

It couldn't be, could it? When she'd talked about people living in a 1950s house for a TV programme, she hadn't meant me, had she? She'd mentioned research. That's why I'd spent the morning in the bound-file room.

Was I taking part in one of those reality TV shows? I looked around for the cameras. Was I being filmed now?

But how had they got me here? And how was outside completely different? It must have been something to do with that taxi driver, I supposed. Maybe the path up to the house had been a stage set and that's why it had sent my eyesight funny. A trick, just projected on a wall or something. It seemed a bit over the top, but then for *I'm a Celebrity* they parachuted people into the jungle, didn't they?

'All right, dear?' said Mrs Brown. 'You've got a bit of colour back. You just sit there for a bit while I get supper ready.'

Feeling calmer now I thought I'd worked this out, I sat on the rocking chair. This must be *The 1950s House* and The Vixen must have volunteered me for it. I wondered what the rules were and was just wishing I knew more, a lot more, when Mrs Brown called out, 'There we are. Here's Frank and Peggy. Right on time.'

Frank was clearly Mr Brown, middle-aged in a thick suit, specs and moustache. He smiled at me and said, 'Well, you must be Rosie.' He shook my hand. A nice handshake.

'And this is Peggy,' said Mrs Brown. Peggy was about my age, maybe a year or so younger. She had curly blonde hair and a pleasant, open face that darkened when she saw me.

'Hello,' she said. That's all, and went to hang up her coat.

'So,' I said brightly, 'are we all in this together then? All play-acting in the 1950s? Did you enter a competition to get here? Or were you just volunteered by your boss, like I was?'

There was a silence. Peggy stood and looked at me as if I'd totally lost it. Mrs Brown came wandering out of the kitchen with a baffled expression and her hands in oven mitts. And Mr Brown took off his jacket and his tie, swapped his shoes for slippers and put on a cardigan.

I realised I must have said something wrong.

'Oh, sorry,' I said. 'Aren't we allowed to mention it's a programme? Do we have to pretend all the time that we're in the 1950s? I mean, I don't even know if it's like the *Big Brother* house and we're all competing against each other, or if it's just to see how we get on. Do you know? I mean, how did you get here?'

The silence continued. Finally, Mr Brown said, 'We've rented this house since before the war. That's why we're here. You're here because our Peggy asked us to have you to stay, on account of you were working on *The News*. No more than that can I tell you.'

Right, I thought, that explains it. We have to pretend at all times that we are in the 1950s. These three were clearly 'in character' in a big way. No sneaking back to the twenty-first century.

'I see,' I said and tried to enter into the spirit of the thing. 'Since before the war?'

'Yes. Peggy was just a toddler and now look at her.'

I did. She glared at me.

'Now then, young Rosie,' said Mr Brown. 'Tell me all about America.'

'America?' I said, not knowing what he was talking about. 'Well, I've only been there twice, once to New York and once to Flor—'

'Now, girl, don't be silly. I know you must be American, wearing trousers like that.'

I was dressed perfectly normally for work. Black trousers and a stretchy, silky top.

'Never mind about that now,' said Mrs Brown. 'She's got plenty of other clothes in her trunk, I expect.'

'Well, she can't wear those to work,' said Peggy with sarcastic satisfaction. 'It might be all right in America but it won't do here. No, Mr Henfield won't stand for that. No women in trousers in the office.'

'Mr Henfield?'

'Richard Henfield, the editor of *The News*,' said Mrs Brown. 'Peggy's his secretary,' she added proudly.

Henfield . . . Henfield . . . I remembered The Vixen's office, the wall with the photographs of all the editors of *The News* that I'd gazed at in conference. Somewhere I'm sure there was a Richard Henfield.

'Does he have a moustache and smoke a pipe?' I asked. 'I think I've seen his picture somewhere.'

'Well, you would,' said Peggy. 'He's very well known.'

'Never mind that now,' said Mrs Brown. 'Peggy, come and mash the potatoes for me.' She took a big casserole dish out of the stove and put it on the table.

'This looks special for a Monday,' said Mr Brown, rubbing his hands.

'Well, seeing as we have a visitor,' said Mrs Brown.

So I didn't dare say that I don't really eat red meat. I didn't want to seem like one of those whingeing contestants, so I ate it up, and it was really quite good. Afterwards, from another compartment in the stove, Mrs Brown produced a rice pudding. I couldn't remember when I'd last had rice pudding that hadn't come out of a tin.

'Does your mother like cooking, Rosie?' asked Mrs Brown.

'Yes, I think so. She doesn't bother much when it's just her and Dad, but when my brother or I go home . . .'

'Oh, don't you live at home? In digs, are you?'

'Digs?'

'Digs,' she said again. 'Lodgings.'

'Oh, no. I have my own flat. It's small, but there's secure car parking.'

'Your own flat and a car?' said Peggy, accepting another helping of rice pudding. 'All I can say is it must be very nice to be American. I hope you can manage to slum it with us.'

She really didn't like me.

'Look, really, I'm not American.'

'Well, you talk like one.'

'Do I?' The Browns all had quite strong local accents. I didn't think I had much of any sort of accent really. I wished they didn't keep thinking I was American.

I offered to help with the washing-up, but Mrs Brown was adamant.

'No, Frank will help me tonight, for a change. You two girls go and watch the television.' That sounded like a good idea. A bit of goofing in front of the box was just what I needed. Some chance. The TV was a huge box affair with a tiny screen showing a programme about ballroom dancing. There were a lot of tiny grey figures in grey dresses and grey suits waltzing across a grey ballroom.

Of course, they didn't have colour TV in the 1950s.

'Anything on any of the other channels?'

'What do you mean?' asked Peggy. 'There's only this one.'

'Haven't you got ITV yet?'

'The one with adverts? They've got it in London, but we haven't.'

Right. I looked round the room, trying to spot where the cameras were. The mirror above the fireplace—that could be a two-way job with a camera on the other side. I looked straight at it and smiled.

Mrs Brown came in, picked up a bag from behind the armchair and took out some knitting. This was going to be a riveting evening.

'If you don't mind, I think I'd like to sort myself out,' I said.

'Of course, dear. What was I thinking of?' said Mrs Brown. 'Peggy, take Rosie up to her room, will you, please, pet?'

Clearly, Peggy didn't want to be dragged away from the grey delights of television, but, sighing heavily, she led me up the narrow, dark stairs, along a narrow, dark landing to a small, icy-cold room. It had been quite nice in front of the fire in the sitting room, toasting my toes, but once you went out of that room, the temperature plummeted.

'Here you are,' she said. 'It's really my brother Stephen's room, but he's in Cyprus.'

'Oh, lucky him,' I said, thinking of bars, beaches and clubbing.

She stared at me. 'Two soldiers were killed there last week.'

'Is he a soldier then?'

'Doing his national service, isn't he?' she said, and left me to it.

It was a bleak little room. Lino on the floor and a rug at the side of a narrow bed covered with a shiny green quilt. There was a chair and a wardrobe, and a bookcase with lots of football annuals and Biggles books. There was a trophy of a cricketer and some model planes, and that was about it. The only clothes in the wardrobe were a school blazer and a few old jumpers. Our Stephen was hardly a style icon.

I looked around for cameras. Nothing obvious. Would they give us privacy in our bedrooms? They didn't in the *Big Brother* house, did they? If there was a camera here, it had to be in the cricket trophy, I decided. Or maybe the model planes . . . I picked them up and put them in the wardrobe. That felt a bit safer. Now I could look in that trunk beneath the window.

A proper, old-fashioned trunk, and on it were my initials, RJH— Rose Jane Harford. I lifted up the lid. Clothes! So this is what I was to wear. I rummaged through them excitedly. Oh, I do love clothes.

I tried to remember what clothes they wore in the 1950s. I thought of Grace Kelly in *High Society* and Audrey Hepburn in *Funny Face*. Or even Olivia Newton-John in *Grease*. Oh, yes. In my mind's eye I was already jiving with John Travolta, his hand on my nipped-in waist . . .

To my deep disappointment, there were a couple of heavy woollen skirts, one of which had a matching jacket, some cotton blouses and hand-knitted cardigans, and a pair of Capri pants in thick navy cotton.

There was a dressing gown that looked like my granddad's. Oh, and the underwear! The bras were made of white cotton and looked as though they were designed for nuns. I bet Grace Kelly never wore anything like those. Knickers too—white cotton. They were dreadful.

There was a serviceable raincoat and a bright red jacket like a duffle coat. I quite liked that. It had a matching beret too. I hung the dressing gown in front of the blotchy wardrobe mirror, just in case of cameras.

A very functional sponge bag contained a toothbrush, a round tin of bright pink toothpaste, a facecloth, a bottle of White Rain shampoo and some cold cream. And at the bottom was a boring brown leather handbag. I opened it to find a funny little purse containing money. But not money I knew. There were some orange notes that said ten shillings and green ones that said one pound. Also lots of big, heavy coins.

I put the jacket on. It was so cold in there. Out of the window I could hear the sound of rushing water. There must be a river. I looked out, but the streetlights were so dim I could see only the faint outline of some trees and a bridge. The view could wait till morning. I presumed I would still be here in the morning. I felt very unsettled and lost.

There was a knock on the door. Mrs Brown. 'Rosie, I'm making a cup of tea. Or you can have cocoa. Come downstairs and get warmed up.'

Cocoa! Such excitement, I thought as I went down into the kitchen. In the dim light, Mr Brown was sitting in the rocking chair, reading a copy of *The News*—the old broadsheet version, of course, very authentic. But there was someone else in there.

A small girl was sitting at the table surrounded by exercise books. Judging by the dirty dishes near her, she'd also polished off the remains of the casserole and the rice pudding. She was wearing one of those old-fashioned pinafore dresses they had in the St Trinian's films—a gym-slip?—a grubby school blouse and a stringy tie. Her mousy, greasy hair looked as though it had been hacked rather than cut. And she had specs: the ugliest specs I've ever seen.

As she looked up at me, I realised she was older than I had first thought—probably about eleven or twelve—and that behind those horrid specs she had a measuring, challenging expression.

'Are you the American?' she asked.

'I'm not American,' I said, already weary with that assumption.

'This is Janice,' said Mr Brown. 'She's very clever, doing well at the grammar school, and she comes here to do her homework.'

I must have looked a bit puzzled by this because Janice said simply, 'I've got seven brothers. Two of them howl all the time.'

'Her mum cleans the post office where Doreen works,' said Mr Brown.

With that, Peggy came into the kitchen and, to my surprise, gave the grubby little girl a smile. Peggy looked really pretty when she smiled.

'Hiya, kid,' she said. 'Shall I wash your hair for you?'

'Oh, yes, please, Peggy!' said the little scruff.

She bundled her books into a satchel and soon she was on a stool, kneeling over the big white stone sink in the scullery, while Peggy shampooed her hair and rinsed it using a big enamel jug. She wrapped it in a rough kitchen towel and then combed it out for her.

'If you like, I'll trim the fringe a bit for you,' said Peggy, and went to get her mother's sewing scissors. She snipped away, turning Janice's head this way and that. 'There, see what that's like when it dries.'

It was already starting to fluff up in the warmth of the range. It looked so much better, shinier.

'Now, Janice, it's time you were at home and in bed.' Mrs Brown had come into the kitchen. She took a scarf out of a drawer. 'Put that over you. You don't want to be walking the streets with wet hair.'

'Right-o, Mrs Brown,' said Janice, gathering up her satchel. She smiled hugely at Peggy. 'It's lovely, Peggy. Thank you. See you tomorrow.' She slid out of the back door, small and scruffy and smelly.

'She can't help it,' said Mrs Brown, noticing my expression. 'Terrible family. Father's out of work half the time. Mother's a willing little woman but has no idea really. All they seem able to do is make babies. There are seven boys and Janice, and two of the boys are simple. Still, Janice got into the grammar school, so let's hope it helps get her somewhere. She deserves a chance, poor scrap. Right. Tea or cocoa?'

I chose cocoa, said my good nights and took it up to bed with me. Then I undressed, put on the big dressing gown, scuttled to the bathroom, scuttled back, popped the dressing gown back over the wardrobe mirror and got in between the icy sheets. I reached for my notebook.

Day One in The 1950s House

Very cold but headache better and at least I realise what's going on. Clearly, our reactions to a new situation must be part of The Test. Must find out how long I'm going to be here for.

Find video-diary room.

Find cameras. Smile at them.

Be nice to everyone.

Peggy—a test?

Have noticed that all Big Brother, *I'm a Celebrity etc TV shows are never won by the loudmouths, but by the quiet, pleasant ones.*

I tried to ring Will again, but my phone was still dead. That made me feel really alone. But then there was a knock on the door.

'I thought you might like a hot-water bottle,' said Mrs Brown, handing one over. 'Are you sure you're all right?'

'Yes, fine, thank you!' I said brightly.

The hot-water bottle was warm and squidgy. I shoved it down between the sheets and, as I wriggled down between them, with my feet nice and warm, I clutched my phone, the way I used to clutch my woolly, cuddly cat when I was little. I was asleep in minutes.

The next day, my first on *The News*, 1950s style, had started badly. Someone must have taken my clothes while I was in the bathroom. I thought of going down to demand my things from Mrs Brown, but then I remembered the golden rule of reality TV which is Be Nice, Smile. So after a wash—I couldn't even have a bath because there's only one loo and that's in the bathroom and people kept banging on the door—I got dressed in my 1950s clothes.

Everything itched, scratched and dug in. Dressed in the skirt suit I felt trussed up like a turkey. My suspender belt (when did I ever think they were sexy?) threatened to ping at any minute. And my hair! No shower, no dryer, no mousse, no straighteners. All I could do was comb it. Great. No wonder people in old photos look miserable.

The day got no better. My usual breakfast was yoghurt and banana. Here it was porridge and boiled eggs. By the time I'd eaten it I felt so weighed down I thought I'd never lift myself off the chair. And the coffee came from a bottle that looked like gravy browning.

To make it worse, Peggy and I had to do the washing-up.

'You can wash,' said Peggy, handing me the porridge pan, with its burnt-on bits. 'It makes sense for me to wipe up and put away because you don't know where anything lives.'

'You could show me,' I said, but knew as I said it, there was no point.

Do you want to know what I think of the 1950s so far? Well, porridge pans really piss me off. Nonstick hasn't been invented yet. Neither has washing-up liquid, just disgusting green soap. You have to scrape the congealed porridge off with a knife and then you have to scoop great blobs of it out of the plughole. That is so disgusting.

And Peggy is a pain. I am trying hard to be nice to her and smile a lot (for the cameras, which I haven't found yet) but it's really tricky.

'Are these clothes all right for work, Peggy?' I asked.

'Very suitable,' she said.

'Do your clothes make you itch?'

'Of course not,' she said. 'Come on. Time to get a move on.' She handed me an Oxo tin. I must have looked blank because she said, 'It's your sandwiches, for your dinner.'

Off we went. Peggy led the way. (She must be part of the team setting the challenge.) We went through some narrow streets and across a market square. (It's clearly a film set.) There was very little traffic, just a few old cars. (The sort they always have in period films.) And a delivery boy on a bike. (They always have that as well.) And there was a milk-man with a horse and cart (which I thought was taking it a bit far, but that might have been where the camera was hidden, so I gave the horse an extra nice smile).

'Is it far to *The News*?' I asked, wondering how we'd get to the industrial estate.

'No,' she said. And that was it. No chatty, girly conversation. But I remembered my winning ways and smiled and tried again.

'Have you worked there long?'

'Five years.'

'So what's the editor like?'

At this she went pink. 'He's a wonderful man!' she said vehemently.

Bit of a giveaway, wouldn't you say?

But now we were at *The News*. It was a really old timbered building, with leaded windows, right in the centre of town. The funny thing was that it looked just the same as it did in the old pictures we have hanging at reception in the industrial estate. There were some big gates at the side, leading into a yard where I could see old-fashioned delivery vans. I don't know how they'd done it, but it was very clever.

As soon as we walked in through the door, Peggy changed character and was all smiles and 'good mornings'. She led the way upstairs.

Well, it was a newspaper office, but not as I knew it. The place was chaos. A warren of small rooms, each one crowded with heavy wooden desks piled high with papers. The windows were small and grubby and almost obscured by heaps of papers and files.

Health and Safety would have had hysterics at the stacks of yellowing newspapers on the floor, in corners and on windowsills. Especially as everyone seemed to be smoking. One stray fag end in that lot . . .

Peggy led me into an outer office, hung up her coat and knocked reverentially on an inner door. 'Good morning, Mr Henfield.' She was almost simpering. 'I've brought Rosie Harford.'

Richard Henfield looked exactly like his photograph. That was a nice touch, I thought. Middle-aged, specs, moustache and pipe.

'Ah, yes, you're with us for a few weeks.'

'Apparently,' I said with a smile. There *must* be a camera in here.

'So, tell me what you've done.' He leaned back in his chair.

'Well, after my degree, I did a diploma in journalism and worked on a weekly paper. For the last few years I've been a general reporter and now I'm a features writer, specialising in social and consumer issues.'

'Well, aren't you a clever little girl,' he said, gazing at my boobs.

Really! My fingers itched to slap his pompous, patronising, sexist face. But I smiled.

'Better see what you can do then,' he said, standing up to put his arm round my shoulders—not nice, he smelt of stale tobacco and sweat—and led me back along the corridor and into one of the smoky rooms, where an oldish man in a trailing overcoat was sitting with his feet on the desk reading a paper, while a woman talked on the telephone. Two other men were picking up their coats as if on the way out.

I removed myself from Henfield's arm.

'Is Billy about?' asked Henfield.

'Assizes,' said the man with the paper. Seeing me, his beady eyes lit up and he gave me and Henfield his attention.

'OK, Gordon,' Henfield said. 'This is Rosie. She has a degree and a diploma and knows all about business and social issues.' He said it in a sarcastic, mocking tone.

'Very fancy,' muttered the woman behind him, putting the phone down and lighting a cigarette.

'She'll be here for a few weeks and no doubt she has many talents to reveal.' He leered. 'And a lot to show us.'

He and Gordon gave each other knowing glances and then both looked me up and down, when Peggy came along simpering, 'There's a phone call for you, Mr Henfield,' and off he went.

'Smarmy bugger,' muttered the woman. Then she added, 'I'm Marje, by the way. Well, let's see what you can do then.'

'Anything,' I said, desperate to get stuck into a decent story.

'Kettle's over there,' said Marje. 'No sugar for me, two for him'—pointing at Gordon who'd gone back to reading the paper—'and the cups need washing. Down the corridor at the very end.'

Did I have a sign saying 'skivvy' stuck to my forehead?

Gordon was the news editor. 'You'd better follow Marje around,' he said as he took his tea. 'She can show you the ropes. There's a couple of golden weddings you should be able to manage between you.'

Golden weddings! I hadn't done those since my early days. But off I went dutifully with Marje to walk to the old people's houses.

'Have you been on *The News* long?' I asked, with the little breath I had left. Marje was setting a cracking pace.

'Since the war,' she said. 'I was on the switchboard and when all the men got called up there was only me and old Mr Henfield left, so I started doing everything.'

The war again.

'Young Mr Henfield, the one who's editor now, was in the army, along with Gordon and most of the others. John, the chief subeditor, was in the RAF. Billy and Phil were just a bit too young, lucky for them. But they've done their call-up and their fifteen days since.'

'Fifteen days?'

'Yes. Two years' national service and then fifteen days every year for three years. Don't they do that in America?'

'Oh, yes,' I said vaguely. 'Something very like.'

I was really getting into this 1950s thing. But it was a bit worrying that everyone else seemed to have done so much research. Maybe they'd had more notice than I had.

Walking along, I could see that the TV company had been very thorough. There were so many little shops: butchers, a couple of bakers, a fishmonger, two bookshops, lots of tobacconists, a wool shop, toy shop, baby-clothes shop, a couple of chemists, a china shop, ironmongers. No supermarkets, but grocers' shops like Home and Colonial, and Liptons. To be honest, it all looked a bit run-down.

Then I smelt it . . . coffee. Proper coffee.

'Oh, Marje, can I really smell coffee?'

'Probably. Silvino's is just round the corner.'

'Silvino's?'

'Italian coffee bar.'

'Oh, glory be. We haven't got time, have we? Just for a quick coffee?'

'No time. Sorry,' said Marje, and we hurried on to the first golden wedding. Nice couple. George the photographer turned up to take their picture when we were there. He was only a young lad, in a baggy suit that looked far too big on him, but he seemed to know what he was doing. And he had the staff van, which meant that Marje and I could squash into the front seat and get a lift to the next golden-wedding couple. Eric and Bessie had met in the church choir and still sang in it. They said the secret of a happy marriage was never to let the sun go down on a quarrel. Bessie looked smug and Eric tried to pinch my bum.

I suppose they were all extras. There seemed to be an awful lot of them. I didn't realise that the TV company had such a huge budget.

Afterwards, while George went off on another job, Marje and I walked back to the office and I remembered about my Oxo tin. I opened it and found a brown paper bag. Inside that was a sandwich made with doorsteps of good white bread, filled with something that smelt a bit odd. I took a tentative bite. It had a sort of fishy taste. Then I remembered my gran's kitchen cupboard and those little jars. Fish paste. I was eating a fish-paste sandwich.

Marje had to show me how to type up a story. What a chew! There was this mucky black paper, carbon paper, that made a smudgy sort of copy. You had to put three pieces of paper together, with two bits of carbon between them, and roll them into a typewriter. It was so heavy. You really had to bash the keys. And you couldn't delete mistakes!

'Bet you wish computers were invented,' I said to Marje.

She looked at me blankly. She was very good at pretending to belong to the 1950s.

'Well, quick and easy to type, correct your mistakes, spell check.'

'Spell check?'

'Yes, it corrects your spelling for you.'

'That's handy if you can't spell. How does it do it?'

'Um, I don't know really. But that's before you start on the Internet.'

'The which?'

'Internet. You can find anything you want to know in seconds. About anything. Facts, figures, famous people, shopping. You can go on the Internet, find things and buy them.'

'How does it do it?'

'I don't know, but it's wonderful. And—'

'You don't know much, really, do you?' said Marje. 'Especially about spelling.' She turned back to my chaotic-looking copy and carried on marking up my typing mistakes. 'Here.' She handed the piece back. 'You'd better type it again or the subs will go mad. See you tomorrow.'

I typed up the golden weddings again and, because there were no messengers around, and because I was curious, I took it along myself to the subs' room. The subs, all men, were smoking pipes or cigarettes and sitting round a long table, marking up the copy for the printers.

One of the men looked up from the piece of paper he was writing on and whistled at me. Another sat back in his chair. Soon all six of them were staring at me. The first said, 'Well, hello, girlie. Who are you?'

'Rosie Harford. I'm here for a while as a reporter and features writer.'

'Features writer, eh? We used to have one of those, but the legs fell off,' said one young man. They all laughed uproariously.

An older man leaned across the desk. 'Well, Rosie, you've certainly got rosy cheeks. Rosie by name, rosy by nature. If I said you had a beautiful body, would you hold it against me?'

More sniggers.

'Watch yourself,' I said. 'That's sexist language.' They looked shocked for a moment and then the laughter started again.

'Sex, is it?' said one. 'Well, if you're offering.' He grinned at the others.

'No, I am *not*,' I said and banged the copy down on the table. 'And certainly not with you.'

I slammed the door behind me, but could still hear their laughter. Pigs. Idiots. Stupid ignorant men. Bugger! I realised it was probably a test, to see how I'd cope. Well, I'd really blown that, hadn't I?

Flustered and feeling stupid, I went back into the newsroom. Gordon was there, talking to another man. A tall man with sleek blond hair, standing with his back to me under the yellowing light.

I recognised him instantly even in the shabby, unfamiliar clothes. I would have recognised him any time, anywhere. The set of his shoulders, the angle of his head, the gesture with his hands as he explained something to Gordon. Oh, I knew them all.

Will! I was so happy I nearly let out a yelp of excitement. If Will was here, then I could cope with anything, from sexist subs to fish-paste sandwiches, scratchy underwear and no showers.

'Will!' I said, going towards him. 'Will! Thank God you're here!'

Will looked round. He looked surprised. He looked at me as though he'd never seen me before in his life.

CHAPTER THREE

THE SILENCE SEEMED TO HANG heavy in the air above the heaps of newspapers, the jumbled files and scuffed desks. I had stopped breathing. I was just waiting for Will to respond, to laugh, to step forward and hug me, but he didn't. There wasn't a hint, not a glint of recognition.

When I saw that blankness in his eyes, my whole world shifted, as though the very earth I was standing on had been hollowed out from under my feet. Without him, there was nothing to cling to. Nothing.

Gordon was looking at me oddly. 'Billy,' he said to Will, 'you haven't met Rosie, our temporary girl, have you? From America or somewhere.'

There was a little spark in Will's eyes and then he smiled—oh that smile!—and held out his hand. 'How do you do, Rosie,' he said. 'Welcome to *The News*.'

I looked at him, expecting an acknowledgment, a little secret smile, anything. But no. I shook his hand. That's when I had another shock. His hand was rough. Not at all like Will's. I looked up at him, puzzled. There were other differences too. His haircut, of course. Very 1950s, short back and sides. But his face looked older, more hollowed and angular. I wanted to touch his cheek, follow those bones and hollows with my fingers, but he was looking at me as if I were a stranger.

Why did he blank me like that? I sat down at my desk, a copy of *The News* propped up in front of me, while I tried to work it out. Yes . . . we were in this 1950s house, where no one must know how close we were. We must pretend to be strangers. Then, secretly, we can work together to sort out what we should be doing and do it. But we mustn't let on.

It was the only explanation I could think of, and I clung to it.

I knew I had to speak to Will alone—ideally somewhere out of reach of any possible cameras. But I needed to stay in the office so that I could watch him, catch him when he left. Looking at him bent over the typewriter instead of a computer, with the same fierce expression as he thought of the next sentence, and then the half-smile as he bashed it out, that was the Will I knew. Even if here he was wearing baggy grey trousers and a shabby shirt instead of a stylish suit.

I watched and waited. Brian, the night-news editor, came in and was introduced to me. At last he and Gordon went out to see Henfield. Will and I were alone in the newsroom and I had to seize my chance.

'Will,' I said, standing opposite him in the dusty yellow light.

He didn't react immediately, just looked up vaguely, as if puzzled.

'Will!' I hissed. 'What's this all about? Do you know what's going on?'

He looked at me, baffled. 'Sorry, er, Rosie. I'm not sure I know what you're talking about. I'm nearly finished here. Have you done all your stuff? It's time to go home.' He looked back to his typewriter, typed a few more words, pulled the papers and carbon out of the machine and folded them over. 'Have you sent your stuff along? If you give it to me, I'll drop it off with the subs for you on my way out.'

This was hopeless.

'Will! We've got to have a plan, work out how we're going to deal with this. Do you know who the other contestants are? Where are the cameras? And is there a video room? We've got to find out.'

Now he was lifting his jacket—a heavy, shapeless, tweedy sort of jacket with pens in the front pocket and leather patches on the elbows—off the back of the chair and easing into it. 'Sorry, Rosie,' he said politely, 'I don't think I know what you want. Have a word with Gordon. Or if it's cameras you're interested in, talk to Charlie, the chief photographer, or young George. Anyway,' he said, picking up the papers from his desk—and that was another difference, his desk was absolutely immaculate and tidy, very un-Will—'I must be getting a move on. I promised my wife I'd be home early. Good night.'

I stood there, looking at his desk and the seat that he had left. He'd promised his wife he'd be home early. *His wife*? No. I couldn't believe it.

I was still in the office when Brian came back in. 'Still here, Rosie?'

'Tell me,' I asked. 'Will, Billy. Is he married, do you know?'

'Billy? Oh yes, love, a real family man. Got a couple of kiddies too. Three of them, I think.' He smiled. 'You're wasting your time there, love.'

Billy. Will. A real family man. Married. Three kids.

No. *No!* I gathered up my stuff and headed out of the building and back 'home' through town. My mind was going crazy. Will couldn't be married. Not my Will. Three kids? My skin went clammy with panic.

Calm down, I had to calm down. Think. I tried to think of all the possibilities. This was all pretend. Yes, that's what it was. It was just another challenge. I had my breathing almost under control. A challenge on a reality TV show. Somewhere in a viewing gallery there were people watching me and laughing themselves silly at my overreaction.

Will couldn't say anything in the office. There were cameras in the office. That's it. Of course. I'd have to get him outside. Somewhere where there weren't cameras. Somewhere where we could talk properly.

I was calmer now. It began to make a sort of sense. But I couldn't forget that blank look. It had seemed so genuine. Could Will be that good an actor? I tried to shrug the memory from my mind.

It was a test, that's all, just a test. Right now, what I needed was a drink. A large vodka would hit the spot. Or a rich, red Merlot. Just the thought of it cheered me up and made life seem almost normal. I went out into the street and up into the marketplace, where all the shops were already shut up for the night. There were no off-licences, no wine bars, no restaurants and no burger joints. Didn't anybody ever eat out? There were plenty of pubs, though. Some of them looked a bit rough.

The Fleece, however, looked terribly respectable. I bowled into one of the side bars, which was full of smoke and smelt strongly of beer.

I made my way past the tables and headed for the bar. It was quite full and I needed a big fat chap to move his chair so I could get past.

'Excuse me,' I said. 'I'd like to get past, please.'

'You can just bugger off,' he replied, and turned back to his drink.

'There's no need for that!' I said crossly.

'There's every bloody need. You shouldn't be in here,' he said, still not moving. The man with him laughed—not a nice laugh—and some of the other men joined in.

I wasn't going to be bullied. 'I have every right to be in here,' I said.

'No, you haven't. Now get out.'

I looked over at the barman. Surely he would do something.

'Sorry, miss,' he said, 'but you're not allowed in here. This has always been a men-only bar. You'll have to go.'

'You can't have bars that are just for men! It's illegal.'

'Yes, you can, miss, and this is one of them. Will you go now, please?'

What else could I do? With my face bright red, I pushed my way past all the tables and out into the corridor. Another test. I tried not to let it worry me. Opposite I saw a door marked LOUNGE BAR. That would be all right. I walked in, trying to calm myself down.

This room looked much nicer. Comfortable chairs, horse brasses, a log fire and an air of quiet calm. And there was a woman here—a middle-aged couple were sitting in one of the corners beneath a picture of a hunting scene. I walked up to the bar and perched on one of the stools. There was a different barman, older. He was wiping glasses.

'A large vodka and cranberry juice, please.'

He carried on wiping glasses. I waited for a moment.

'Excuse me,' I said in my Like-I'm-here-can't-you-see-me? sort of voice. 'May I have a vodka and cranberry juice, please?'

This time he did at least bother to look up.

'You on your own, madam?'

'Yes, and I'd like a large vodka and cranberry juice, please.'

'Two things, madam,' he said. 'First, we haven't got any Russian drinks. And second, we don't serve unaccompanied ladies.'

'This is ridiculous,' I said, getting really angry now. 'If you haven't got vodka, then give me a large glass of Merlot.'

He leaned forward menacingly and said, 'I'm not giving you anything, madam.' Then, in a fierce undertone, 'This is a respectable establishment. We don't want your sort in here.'

My sort? What did he think I was? A tart touting for custom?

And then it dawned on me. That's precisely what he *did* think. The idea was so ridiculous I started to laugh, despite myself. I slipped off the stool and made quite a good exit. But outside I was shaking. It was ridiculous but it was also insulting. I still hadn't got a drink. And Will had got a wife. Not a good day.

I desperately needed to talk properly to Will. This was a challenge too far, no joke. I blew my nose on the silly lace-edged hanky I'd found in my jacket pocket and headed back to the Browns'. I wasn't sure of the way but I strode out purposefully and kept my head held high and my expression determined. I even tried to smile—just in case those cameras were watching.

The next morning we marched into work together, Peggy and I, umbrellas up against the suddenly fierce spring rain, neither of us in the best of moods, neither of us saying a word.

At breakfast Peggy had been a real pain, obviously more than normal as even her dad kept asking her if she was all right, but she only snapped back at him. Anyway, his mind was on other things and Mrs Brown was worried about a friend who was having some problems.

'I'll pop round to give her a hand later. At least I can make sure the kids get a decent meal. You two can fend for yourselves. There's some ham in the pantry and some cheese and I'll pop a couple of potatoes in the oven for you so they should be baked when you get home. And there's some of that treacle tart left.'

'Right-o, Mum,' said Peggy, 'but I might be going out anyway.'

'That's nice, dear. In by ten o'clock, mind.'

I expected Peggy to sound off. *In by ten o'clock!* She was twenty-six, not sixteen, for heaven's sake! But she didn't say anything. Staggering. On the other hand, if Peggy is another contestant then maybe it was a test for her and she's better at not overreacting than I am.

We arrived at *The News* offices still in silence, and as we got to the front door, both of us sort of stopped and took a deep breath before we went into the building. I glanced across at Peggy. There was a hint of a smile and fellow feeling, but not enough for me to ask.

I wasn't sure about all this at all. If this was a reality TV programme then I should have had some rules, some instructions, some guidelines, some clue about what was going on.

I took a deep breath and went into the reporters' room, bracing myself for seeing Will. As I hung my coat up, I took a quick look around, oh, so casually . . . but he wasn't there. I let out a huge sigh. I'd been holding my breath so hard that my chest hurt.

Gordon was talking to the other reporters, Alan, Tony and Derek, allocating jobs. 'Billy's over in the district office today, chasing something up, so you can do his jobs,' he was saying to Alan.

'Anything for me?' I asked, keeping a desk between me and Gordon. I was careful not to stand too near to him. Already he had a habit of getting closer and 'accidentally' brushing against my bum or breasts. I felt like hitting him, hard, but remembering I had to be all teeth and smiles, I had, so far, restrained myself.

He looked up at me as if wondering who the hell I was.

'If she does all the shorts today, why doesn't she do the Prettiest Village feature tomorrow?' asked Marje quickly, lighting a cigarette. You only ever saw this woman through a cloud of cigarette smoke. 'I've booked a photographer but I've got a lot on.'

Gordon looked at me again. 'I suppose so,' he said grudgingly, 'if you've got other things to do, Marje. I suppose if she makes a mess of it, you can do it on Friday.'

The condescension of the man!

'Right,' I said, all brisk and businesslike. 'What does this involve?'

'You tell her, Marje,' said Gordon, and went back to his desk.

'Well, now it's spring,' said Marje with a wry glance through the tiny grubby window at the rain outside, 'it's time to start our village feature. Simple idea: go along to one of the prettier villages, lots of lovely pictures and maybe a few words with the oldest resident, squire, lady of the manor, vicar, that sort of thing. Anything newsworthy or interesting. We might dig up a few stories for the rest of the paper while we're at it. I was going to start with Middleton Parva. You all right with that?'

'Fine,' I said. 'How do I get there?'

'You can team up with George and take the van. But Charlie's out with it most of today. So can you just sort out those short pieces first?'

'No problem,' I said.

The door opened and an oldish woman came in carrying a narrow wooden box full of brown envelopes.

'Rose Harford?' she said, looking at me.

'That's me.' I went up to her, like a child going to Santa.

My present was a brown envelope full of money. I was getting paid for this: £8 12s. 6d. to be precise. In my normal life that would buy a couple of coffees and a sandwich, but judging by what I'd seen of prices, it would buy quite a lot here. I put the money away in my purse.

I'd just started my list of NIBs (News In Brief—mainly jumble sales, meetings and talks) when a messenger looked round the door.

'Billy in?' he asked. 'His missus is downstairs.'

Will's wife downstairs? An opportunity too good to miss.

'I'll pop down and tell her,' I said, getting up quickly.

'Suit yourself,' said the lad. He walked off, whistling. My heart was banging as I clattered down the stairs. Will's wife. What would she be like? What sort of girl would make Will give up his freedom? Closer to the front office, I slowed down. Did I really want to see who he'd chosen, who he had children with? How was I expected to play this? Too late: despite myself, I was pushing through the door.

There were only two people in the scruffy reception area: a woman and a small child. The woman was wearing a workaday brown coat. She had her back to me, leaning down to talk to the child, yet there was something familiar about her. The hair was the wrong colour, the wrong style but . . . She turned round.

'Caz!'

This time, I didn't get the blank look I had had from Will. Instead Caz's face lit up. 'Hello!' she said. 'Are you the American? I've heard about you. I'm Carol, Billy's wife.'

Caz? Married to Will? Somewhere in the universe, someone was playing a very sick joke on me. And it couldn't be Caz and Will, could it? The two people closest to me in the world wouldn't do this to me, would they, not even as a joke, not even for a reality TV programme?

'You? You're really married to Will?' I heard the catch in my voice.

'Married to Billy. Yes, for eleven years and counting. Is he in?'

'No, sorry. He's had to go out to one of the other offices.' How did I manage to answer so calmly and politely? Eleven years? Will was still at school eleven years ago.

'Oh well. It's not important.' She smiled and turned to leave.

'Can I give him a message?' I wanted to talk to her. I needed to know more.

'No, it's all right.' She hesitated. 'Well, yes, go on then. Tell him I've got a job. Next term, when this one'—she indicated the little girl who was staring up at me with a shy smile—'starts school, I do too. I'm going to be a school cook. They told me today. Isn't that grand?'

Her face was alight with happiness. This was Caz pretending to be delighted about being a school cook? Caz whose idea of sophisticated cooking was putting a bit of parsley on a ready meal? We needed to talk, away from the office, away from any cameras.

'That's brilliant!' I said, entering into the game, for it had to be a game. 'Why don't we celebrate? Look, I've got half an hour to spare. Why don't we go to Silvino's? My treat? I've just been paid.'

This world might be pretend, but at least the coffee would be real. And I guessed Gordon wouldn't miss me from the office for half an hour. Caz—in true Caz fashion—hesitated for less than a split second.

'Oh, yes, if you've got time,' she said, then turned to the little girl. 'Well, Libby, isn't this turning out to be a good day?'

With Libby holding firmly onto Caz's hand, we went across the marketplace to Silvino's, squeezing past women with bags of shopping and dripping umbrellas. The menu was strong on tea cakes and buns and buttered toast, but the smell was of proper Italian coffee.

'Right,' I said, once we'd ordered, and Caz was undoing Libby's coat buttons for her. 'Come on, Caz, tell me what this is all about.'

'What? The job? Well, it—'

'No, not the job, this reality TV thing. Where are the cameras? What are the rules? Who else is in it? Who's running it? Were you just dropped in it too? How do we get out when we want to?'

The smile faltered on Caz's face. She sat back from the table, put a hand on Libby's arm as if to protect her and looked at me warily.

Then I noticed that, just as Will didn't look exactly the same as Will in this place, Caz, or Carol, didn't look quite like Caz either. Her hair was a different colour. Well, that's no surprise. Caz has been colouring hers for so long that not even she can remember what colour it was originally. But Caz's hair is always shiny, whereas this Carol's hair looked a bit dull and as though it needed washing. Caz's never looked like that. Then, this Carol had slightly crooked teeth and the beginning of wrinkles round her eyes and on her forehead. And now she was looking at me as if I were a stranger—suddenly, I wasn't so sure . . .

I put my head down. 'I'm sorry. It's just that you and Will—Billy—look very like my closest friends back home. And it's such a shock to discover that maybe you're not them after all.'

'Oh, you poor thing!' said Carol, in such a Caz-like way that I was sure it *must* be her. 'How awful, especially if you're feeling homesick. It's such a long way from America. Are they nice, these friends?'

'The best, the absolute best.'

'Well, let's just hope Billy and I will do instead,' she said in a wonderfully cheering, normal sort of a way. 'Now, come on, drink your coffee.'

She was treating me as though I were the same age as Libby, and for some reason, I began to feel better. Whether she was Caz or Carol, I needed a friend. I began to relax a little, though the thought of Caz being married to Will was too horrible to consider. If the two people closest to me were married to each other, where did that leave me?

Even if this were pretend, I didn't like it. At the very least the pair of them must have ganged up to play this trick on me.

Yet here was Caz, sipping her coffee, her eyes huge over the rim of the cup. No longer looking worried, she now seemed concerned only for me. Just as if it were me and Caz as we had always been. Maybe she knew there were cameras in here.

'Oh, look,' I said, 'they've got music here tomorrow night.' On the wall was a handwritten notice: *Saturday Night at Silvino's. The Skiffle Cats!*

'Yes. There's another room with an entrance from the side alley. Silvino's has got a jukebox in there and the kids listen to records in the evenings at weekends.'

'Will you go and see the Skiffle Cats?'

'No, that's for kids, not for people like me.' Carol looked wistful. 'Tell you what. I'll be in town on Saturday. I could meet you, say, at the cross at elevenish and we could get what we want and then go in the back room with the kids for a coffee and some music. What do you say?'

'Yes, great. Why not?'

'Well, that's settled!' Then Caz/Carol turned to Libby and said, 'We'd better go and do some shopping, otherwise none of us will eat tonight. See you Saturday, Rosie.' She did up Libby's coat buttons again, took her hand and manoeuvred through the crowded tables.

I paid the bill and dashed back to the office, teetering between gloom and a strange almost-happiness. The thought of shopping with Caz/Carol made me feel more cheerful than I'd done since I'd got here.

Will/Billy didn't come back to the office. All through the afternoon, every time the door opened and anyone came in, I geared myself up to see him; then every time it wasn't him, I slumped again. In the end, I went home early for my ham and baked potato.

Middleton Parva was a separate village. Amazing. I just thought of it as the bit by the ring road where the new B&Q and Tesco were. But we went out of town, past fields and off the main road and down a country lane to get to it. George's driving was erratic to say the least.

'Hey, hang on! You're on the wrong side of the road!'

'Sorry!' yelled George. 'Habit. Think I'm in Germany still. That's where I learned to drive, when I was doing my national service.'

'You were in the army?'

Honestly, he didn't look old enough.

'How old are you, George?'

'Twenty.'

'Did you break any of the Fräuleins' hearts?'

'No.' George grinned. 'We didn't do much of that sort of fraternising. Plenty of drinking though! Those Germans know how to drink.'

Somehow, we got to Middleton Parva. And as we did, so the sun came out. It was really pretty. There was a proper village green with trees, a pub at either end, a couple of little shops and a post office, and a very attractive church. This couldn't be a film set, could it?

While George went off to scout for pictures, I went to the post office and struck gold straight away. The postmistress's family had been running the place since the days when mail came with the stagecoach, so that was a nice easy story to write up. Then I found the vicar and we talked about the history of the church while George took pictures.

'What now?' he asked.

'The lady in the post office said the Royal Oak was run by a cockney, a chap who came here as an evacuee during the war. No doubt he'll have a tale to tell. Shall we go there?'

'A pub will do me fine. We'll get a drink while we're there.'

The Royal Oak was low and squat and old-fashioned. It had small windows, and beams that made it look as though it had grown up out of the ground. The Rising Sun, on the other side of the green, was a flash new place with a car park.

We went in through the tiny low door of the Royal Oak. Inside there were flagged floors and a small log fire. Two old men, smoking pipes, were playing dominoes. They looked up when we went in. 'Afternoon,' they said, and went back to their game.

Since we'd walked in, I'd been waiting for someone to shout at me, or say they couldn't serve me. Instead, the cheerful young landlord was saying, 'Right, sir, and what can I get you?'

'Pint of bitter for me, please,' said George.

'And for the lady?'

I hesitated. Apart from the beer pumps, the stock on the shelves looked pretty limited.

'No vodka, I suppose?' I laughed, as if I were making a joke.

'No, this is Middleton, not Moscow, miss.'

'Sorry, I don't know what to have.'

'She's American,' said George, in explanation.

'Right, darling. Why not have a shandy, or a drop of local cider?'

'Cider. That sounds fine. Yes, please.'

The landlord disappeared for a moment and came back with a large enamel jug. He placed a half-pint glass on the counter and lifted the jug. Cider poured from it in a long arc and fell, perfectly on target.

'Cheers!' I said. I took a sip and nearly choked. 'This is strong! What's in it?'

'Apples, mostly,' said the landlord. 'And a few dead rats, of course.'

I trusted he was joking, but, boy, was that cider good. I remembered I'd left my Oxo tin at the office. 'Any food on? Sandwiches?'

'The missus can make you a sandwich if you like. Ham or cheese?'

We both chose ham and while the missus was making them, I told the landlord why we'd come. He was happy to talk, and George took a nice picture of him leaning on the bar. By the time the sandwiches came, we'd just about finished.

George and I took our sandwiches—and a second drink—over to a table by the tiny window. The sandwiches were made of proper thick bread with black crusts, masses of butter and chunks of delicious home-cooked ham. They were brilliant.

'Did you go into the army straight from school, George?'

'No. I was a messenger on *The News*, and then I used to help Charlie with the developing and printing. I told them that when I got called up and so I got to work for the information unit. I worked with the army photographers, so when I came back Mr Henfield took me on as a proper assistant for Charlie. I think Peggy put in a good word for me. You're lodging at her house, aren't you? She's nice, isn't she? She was always kind to me when I was a messenger. She'd say that there was no reason why I shouldn't be a photographer. She's got a lovely smile.'

I have to say this was a completely different view of Peggy from the one I had. But then I remembered how nice she was with Janice, and I didn't say anything. Young George clearly had a bit of a crush on Peggy.

'Do you like it on *The News*?'

'It's good, yes. And I like driving the van. I'm going to get a car of my own one day. I'll have a proper wage soon when I'm twenty-one.' He glanced out of the window. 'Ah, looks like Henfield's popped out for his lunchtime drink. That must be his car parked over at the Rising Sun. There aren't that many two-tone Hillman Minxes round here. Maybe he's meeting one of his floozies.'

Floozy! I thought my granddad was the only one to use that word!

'Goes in for floozies, does he?'

'One or two. Another drink?'

'George, you've had two. You'll be over the limit.'

'What limit? I drive better after a drink or two. One for the road?'

As he was getting the drinks—and that cider was good—I gazed out of the window. A real old-fashioned country bus pulled up on the other side of the green and a young woman got out and hurried across to the Rising Sun. There was something familiar about her . . . Yes, no doubt about it. It was Peggy—who should have been at work—rushing into the pub. The pub outside which Richard Henfield's car was parked. She vanished through the door just as George came back with the drinks.

So Henfield liked his floozies, did he? And he and his secretary just happened to be in an out-of-the-way country pub at the same time. Interesting. Very interesting.

CHAPTER FOUR

Day Six in The 1950s House

If that's where I am. I'm not sure of anything any more.

If this is the 1950s House, why wasn't I briefed about it? Interviewed, insured, given explanations and introduced to it?

It's more than just a house and a newspaper office. It's a whole town, not to mention the countryside around it. Middleton Parva was no film set. And no TV company would pay for so many extras. I haven't seen any cameras. No one's mentioned a video room.

None of the other people seem to be contestants. Mrs Brown was expecting me. My trunk was here. Everyone seems to think I'm here for a few weeks. But where's 'here'?

It's not really the 1950s, is it?

After I'd written that, I seized up. I couldn't get air in and out of my lungs. As I tried to breathe, I tried to get my brain to work.

I had thought this was a reality TV show, yet nothing, absolutely nothing, backed that up. This wasn't a single house or even a single film set. This was an entirely different world, a world locked in the past of fifty years ago. I ran to the window and beat my hands on it as if it were the bars of a cage. It was eight o'clock in the morning on a Saturday morning off. I couldn't have gone back in time, not really back into the 1950s. But where was I?

All I knew for certain was that I wanted to be home, with Will's arms round me, and his mouth whispering in my ear the way he did when I had nightmares. Because this was turning into a real nightmare.

I was still leaning with my head against the cool of the window, taking deep breaths, trying to control my panic, when Peggy came in.

'You all right?' she asked, not unkindly.

'Yes, no . . . oh, I don't know.' But then I had a thought. 'Peggy, you know you asked your mum if I could come and stay here? Well, who arranged for me to come and work on *The News*? You're the editor's secretary. It must have been arranged through you.'

'Yes, it was.'

'Well, how?'

This was it, I thought, I'm getting close to the truth now. If I knew who'd organised my trip, the clothes and everything, then I'd know just what was going on. There'd be correspondence, letters about it.

'We had a phone call from Lord Uzmaston's office. I've never met him, but Mr Henfield has. He's been to lunch at Uzmaston Hall.' She said this with pride. 'He owns *The News* and quite a lot of other papers.'

'What did he say?'

'Oh, it wasn't *him*. He wouldn't ring himself, would he? It was a man, a young man, I think. Just said that they had a reporter who needed a temporary job and that we were to fit her in. I can tell you Mr Henfield wasn't happy, not with the idea of a woman reporter. But you've got to obey orders, haven't you? Especially when it's the owner.'

'Was there any correspondence? Any confirmation in writing?'

'No. Nothing at all. It was all most irregular. They asked if we could find her—you—accommodation. And I thought of our Stephen's room, it being empty. But before I said that, I asked how much they would pay. And the man said, "Whatever is usual. It would be easier if you pay it direct from your office."'

'Oh, and do you?' I realised, to my shame, I hadn't actually given a thought about whether I should be paying rent out of my £8 12s. 6d.

'Yes, I take it out of the petty cash and Mr Henfield signs a chitty.'

'And no one's come back to you? Asked anything about it?'

'No, which was a bit worrying really. But everything seems to be fine. Why? Who were you dealing with?'

'Tricky to explain,' I said, which was the understatement of the year really, or maybe even fifty years. One more thought occurred to me.

'Peggy, why did you suggest I should stay here? Was it to get your mum a bit of extra cash?'

'No, not really—though I suppose that was part of it.' Peggy looked embarrassed. 'No, I thought it would be fun.'

And that really surprised me. If Peggy thought it would be fun to have me here, why has she barely said a word to me since I arrived? She was still standing in the doorway with an armful of laundry. She looked almost concerned.

'Are you all right?' she asked again.

'Yes, yes, fine. Really,' I said, too baffled to say otherwise. But at least I had a plan now. Somewhere to start. Once I was back in the office on Monday, I could talk to the person Peggy had spoken to and see who had arranged things.

'Here,' said Peggy. 'I've brought you a clean sheet and some pillowcases. We change the beds on Saturdays.'

'Only one sheet?'

'Put the top one on the bottom and the clean one on the top,' she said with exaggerated patience. 'And if you bring the dirty sheet down and any white cotton things, I'll put them in the washing machine.'

After she'd gone, I made the bed. Tricky job with sheets and blankets, but I straightened those sheets so there wasn't a crease or a wrinkle to be seen. If only my life could be as neat and tidy.

I gathered up the laundry and took it down to the scullery and put it into the funny little washing machine. In the background, the radio—a huge thing the size of a fridge—played children's songs: 'The Teddy Bears' Picnic', 'There Once Was an Ugly Duckling' . . . and something about pink and blue toothbrushes.

The washing machine didn't rinse. Well, it did, but first you had to empty the sudsy water out and put clean in. Peggy took the dirty hot water and threw it across the back yard and then scrubbed the yard with a big brush. This was meant to be a lazy Saturday morning . . .

I wanted to ask Peggy about her visit to the Rising Sun, but she was looking pretty grim-faced so I thought I'd better leave it for now.

Later on, we had to get the clothes out of the washing machine and put them through the mangle thing at the top. It was hard work turning that handle as it squeezed the water out.

'Careful,' said Peggy. 'A girl from school went to work in the laundry and she put her hand in the mangle. Got all broken and crushed.'

'Horrid!' I said. 'I hope she got some compensation.'

Peggy looked at me blankly.

'You know, a payout for her injury,' I explained.

'Course not. She should have been more careful, shouldn't she?'

Peggy took the washing down the small, steep back garden to hang on the line, while I used the last of the water to mop the scullery and kitchen floor. Then I had to dash as I was meeting Caz.

The town was busy. I thought uneasily that the crowd couldn't all be extras. There were a few young men and one or two very bent old men on sticks making their way between the market stalls, but otherwise it was a world of women clutching baskets and shopping bags.

And there were children everywhere, many as young as seven, on their own and equally laden with shopping bags. They stood in the queues at the stalls and seemed to cast a keen eye over the limited number of vegetables, confidently pocketing the change.

Was it safe for these children to be out on their own? Shouldn't someone be looking after them? I was still wondering about it when I spotted Carol standing on the steps of the market cross.

Carol or Caz? I stopped. Was she my friend from my real twenty-first-century life, playing a nasty trick on me? Or was she Carol, a young mother of three, whose life was half a century different from mine?

She was talking to a young boy and handing over a couple of bags of shopping to him. He was about ten or eleven years old and the image of Will. He was wearing short trousers, long socks and a hand-knitted jumper, and he glowed with health. Will's son. Just like the boy I'd imagined in my daydreams. He gave me a quick grin as Caz greeted me.

'Perfect timing. I've just finished the shopping. Right, Pete, go straight home, mind. Your dad wants you to help him. Now scoot!'

The boy duly scooted, even though he was weighed down with all the shopping bags.

'Right,' said Caz. 'Let's go and look for some material. Will and I have got a posh do to go to next month and I must have something to wear.'

Will and Caz, posh do? I knew it couldn't be the real Caz saying this. I must stop thinking of her as Caz and think of her as Carol instead.

Carol was already leading the way to the far end of the market, where there was a clutch of fabric stalls. Great bolts of cloth lay out on the trestle tables, mostly woollen and tweedy mixtures, ginghams and flowery cottons. Carol stopped at a stall where the bales of cloth glinted with the richness of velvet and taffeta.

'Now then, Mrs West,' said the cheerful stallholder, 'looking for something special today are we?'

'Yes, please,' said Carol, reaching in and pulling out rolls of cloth.

'Have you got something in mind, then?' asked the stallholder.

'Yes,' said Carol, 'but I won't know until I've seen it.'

'Well you're turning my stall nicely upside-down,' said the man.

Then I saw it. Right at the bottom of the pile was a narrow roll of taffeta in a wonderful rich colour that hovered between a deep dark red and black. It would be just the thing for Carol.

'That's the one!' I yelled and tried to grab for it. All the rolls shifted slightly and I thought the whole lot would come down, but the stall-holder held them back with one hand, while shuffling the dark red taffeta out with the other. He pushed it across to Carol, who unrolled a bit and held it up against her.

'Perfect!' I said. 'That's definitely the colour for you.'

Carol grinned, then unwound the fabric from its roll. 'Not much left there,' she said, pursing her lips. 'Don't know if I'll be able to make anything of that. No,' she continued, making a show of putting it back and walking away, 'I'll have to look for something else . . .'

'Go on,' said the man, 'you can have it for eighteen bob.'

'Hang on!' Carol had grabbed another roll end from under a heap. It was a creamy cotton with a deep pink design. 'Look, here's another roll end, neither use nor ornament to anyone.' She looked at him challengingly. 'You can throw that in buckshee, can't you?'

'Not on your nelly,' said the stallholder, 'but go on, give us a quid for the lot.' Carol had a pound note out of her purse like lightning and the man wrapped the material in a sheet of thin brown paper. Soon we were heading for Silvino's, with Carol clutching her purchases.

As we approached the café, I could smell coffee and hear the sounds of music beating out from a jukebox. Just like in those old American films! Inside it was smoky and crowded, with people mostly in their mid- to late teens or early twenties. Their faces were bright and lively, but otherwise they were a drab-looking crowd.

The kids went up to a hatch that presumably opened into the main café and placed their orders, mainly for Coke or milk shakes, it seemed.

As we ordered our coffee, the jukebox started playing 'See You Later, Alligator', and the kids were dancing and everyone was singing along.

Carol was drinking her frothy coffee from the shallow Pyrex cup and swaying to the music. 'You know, when we get our new house, I'm going to get a wireless. Maybe even a television.'

'A television? You haven't got one?'

'No electricity.'

'No electricity?' I was thinking about what it would be like to live without electricity. I mean, a two-hour power cut can cause chaos.

The kids were crowding round the jukebox and 'Rock Around the Clock' came on again.

'Time I was on my way,' said Carol. 'We have to have dinner early on Saturday. Billy goes to the match to do the football report for *The News*.'

'Oh, right,' I said. 'Well, I guess I'd better be getting on home.'

'No need for that,' said Carol. 'Why don't you come and have fish and chips with us? Might as well, unless'—and she looked suddenly shy—'unless you've got anything better to do.'

'No, fish and chips with you would be great,' I said.

We joined the end of the queue outside the chip shop until it was our turn to wait in the greasy steam and sizzling noise for our order. The woman behind the counter wrapped everything in old copies of *The News*, and Carol produced a string bag and shoved them all in.

We carried on walking. I didn't recognise this part of town. The streets were smaller and darker, many of them were just potholed mud tracks. On the corner of one of the streets a group of about half a dozen twelve- or thirteen-year-old boys were gathered round a lamppost. On the other side of the street was an old advertising sign that had come loose. It swung back and forth on two screws—driven by the stones the boys were throwing at it.

'Yeah! I win! I win!' yelled one of the boys, who had managed to hit the exact centre of the board.

Instinctively I'd drawn in on myself. Gangs of thirteen-year-olds are never good news, especially when they're bored and they've got pockets full of stones. I was busy hurrying along, when I realised Carol had stopped. What's more, she was challenging the boys. Was she mad?

'Hey, you lot!' she said. 'Haven't you got anything better to do? What would your mothers say if they could see you now? Or your dads?'

To my utter astonishment—when I dared to look up—the boys looked abashed and embarrassed. 'We weren't doing any harm, Mrs West,' said one.

'No, not now, but you soon would be if I know you lot. Now go and find yourselves something useful to do.' And she started walking again while the boys shuffled a bit then ran off down the road.

I was lost in admiration. 'You know, Carol, I wouldn't have dared speak to them like you did.'

'What?' She looked at me, astonished. 'But they're only kids, Rosie. Surely you can deal with a bunch of kids?'

'Well, no, actually, we can't. Where I come from, they'd beat you up, have your purse off you soon as look at you.'

'Then you're off your heads if you ask me,' said Carol. 'Come on, here we are. Home sweet home.'

At the bottom of a narrow lane, beside a stream, was a derelict mill and a tiny cottage.

'Oh, isn't that pretty!' I exclaimed.

'You wouldn't think so if you had to live here,' said Carol.

Inside, the rooms were small and dark. Carol went through to a kitchen and then out into a back garden that spread up the hill. It was huge. And there was Will. Will in baggy army trousers carrying an old window, with young Pete hanging onto the other end.

'Careful now, Pete,' Will was saying. 'Just bring it round to the side of the house, next to the other one.' The two of them manoeuvred it carefully into place and looked at it admiringly.

Carol called out, 'Dinner's ready. Come and get your fish and chips!'

Pete dragged his eyes away from the window frame and came running down the path. 'Can we have them in the paper, Mum? Not on plates?'

'Course you can,' said Carol. 'Save on washing-up. We'll eat out there, pretend we're on holiday. Where's Davy?'

'Gone round Rob's on his bike. My bike.'

'I know, dear, but it's too small for you now,' said Carol. 'Come on, Libby.'

The small girl who'd been with her in the office was crouching intently over a small patch of earth. 'I'm planting lettuces,' she said.

'And we've been building a cold frame,' said Pete, jumping up onto the low wall and reaching for his chips. 'Dad and I have built one half and we've got the framework and bricks ready for the second half.'

'Good boy,' said Carol. 'Here you are, Billy.'

Will/Billy wiped his hands on his trousers, took the fish and chips that Carol handed him, then perched on the wall, looking out over his garden, a man who was competent and capable with practical things.

'I didn't have you down as a gardener. I don't know why,' I said, though I did know why—because I couldn't imagine Will gardening.

'My dad always had an allotment. I kept it going during the war. We Scouts were always busy for the war effort—digging for victory, firewatching, collecting scrap metal.'

Carol was giggling. 'He was a good Scout,' she said, 'but if he'd remembered to Be Prepared, we wouldn't have had Pete, would we?'

So that's why . . . Caz had been pregnant and that's why Will had married her. That's why they were married so young. Even as I worked it out, it hurt. Caz's giggle and Will's answering grin, their shared complicity—not to mention their shared lives and shared children—cut me out. They were the couple. I was the outsider.

Billy ruffled Peter's hair affectionately. 'Wouldn't be without him.'

I ate my fish and chips and tried to take in this new Billy. At the end of a long working week, he had spent a morning doing hard physical work and yet he looked really happy.

'Right,' he said, screwing up the fish-and-chip paper. 'Come on, Pete. We've got time to get that window fixed before I have to go to the office.'

Pete gobbled the last of his chips and the two of them went back up the path. I could see Billy explaining the job to Pete as they fastened the old window to the framework on the wall beside the shed. Billy did one bit, then handed the tools to Pete, who did the next while his father stood and watched approvingly, just making an occasional suggestion, or holding the boy's hand steady. Then they tested the frame, lifting it up and down and laughing, pleased with their work.

'Tea's made,' called Carol.

Billy strode down the path with his arm round Pete's shoulders. 'I'll just get a wash before I have that tea,' he said, going inside.

I could hear the sound of water running in the kitchen behind me.

He was having a wash at the kitchen sink! And he came out wearing his work trousers and tweedy jacket and tying his tie.

'Right, see you later,' he said, drinking his tea quickly. 'Pete, make sure you put the tools back in the shed, please, and I'll go and earn my corn.' He nodded towards me. 'Nice to see you, Rosie.'

'He seems very grown up,' I said, staring after him.

'Billy? Of course he's grown-up, you daft ha'porth. He's twenty-nine years old and if that's not grown-up I don't know what is.'

I thought of Will and Jamie playing table football, of them drooling over the motor racing. Twenty-nine? Grown-up? Not always.

As instructed, Peter was carefully putting all the tools back in the shed. Libby had abandoned her lettuce planting and was busy with a battered dolls' pram, tucking her charges in under blankets.

'Tell you what, let's make a fresh pot of tea,' said Carol.

I followed her into the kitchen and, once my eyes had adjusted to the gloom, took a good look around. Above the low ceiling was a clothes rack covered in folded ironing, just as at the Browns'. There were two armchairs on either side of the fire, and an alcove of books.

There was a table covered with a cloth, and a cheap metal cupboard with plates and cups and a few packets of food—I could see a tin of peas and a packet of Puffed Wheat, and on a drop-down shelf, a loaf of bread and a dish of butter.

Against one wall was a big stone sink with a wooden draining board, scrubbed white, with a mirror above it. And on a shelf alongside were a couple of mugs. One held a family of toothbrushes and another held a shaving brush. So this is where Billy shaved in the morning. I thought of Will and our power shower and his shelf full of gels and foams. The big tin bath I'd seen outside, I realised, was their bath . . .

Beneath the sink was a gingham curtain, hiding pots and pans, I presumed. And on top of the stove was a big covered pan.

'Something nice cooking for supper?' I asked.

'No! Billy's underpants boiling.'

Oh God, definitely too much information. 'When we move I'm going to have a proper electric wash boiler, maybe even a washing machine. You can get one on the never-never.' She looked wistful. 'Tell me about America, Rosie. Tell me about the things you have.'

'I'll tell you about my friend Caz,' I said. 'The one who's just like you.'

'OK.' She settled down happily with her cup of tea.

'Caz lives with a teacher called Jamie.'

'What, just lives with? They're not married?'

'No.'

'And he's still allowed to be a teacher?'

'Well, yes.'

'Didn't think the parents would like that. Not a good example.'

'Half the parents aren't married either.'

'Oh, well. Funny place, America. So what's their house like?'

'It's a Victorian terraced house.'

'What, an old-fashioned thing, not a nice new one?'

'With four bedrooms, two bathrooms—'

'*Two* bathrooms? Blimey, I'd be happy just to have one!'

'And it's all decorated in whites, creams and beiges.'

'Sounds boring.'

'Not really, because they have wonderful paintings on the walls.'

'Paintings? They must be rich, these friends.'

'No, as I said, Jamie's a teacher and Caz works with me on the paper.'

'Have they got a telly?'

'Yes, Jamie's just bought a big one. The colours are really sharp.'

'Colours? You've got TV in colour?'

'Yes, and we can have over a hundred different channels to watch.'

I told her about Caz and Jamie having a car each, how they went skiing at Christmas and were planning to go to Thailand in the summer.

'Have they got any kiddies?'

'No. I'm not sure if they want any.'

'Well, you get what you're given,' laughed Carol, 'even if the timing's not quite right. But I wouldn't be without them.'

Libby had come in, sucking her thumb and carrying a doll in her other hand. She snuggled into Carol, who put her arm round her.

'And what about Billy?' I asked, my heart thumping.

'He's a good dad,' said Carol. 'Works hard, brings his pay home.'

'And you're happy?' I hesitated but had to ask. 'You still love him?'

'Love him?' Carol laughed. 'We've rubbed along for a long time now and he's a decent man. Never hesitated about getting wed and been a good provider ever since. He earns the money and looks after the garden. And I look after him and the kids and the house. And when we get our new house, we'll all be made up, won't we?'

'Where is your new house going to be?'

'Up at The Meadows.'

'The Meadows?'

I thought of that vast estate where joy-riders terrorised the streets and then made bonfires of the cars they'd stolen. The wrecks sat in the streets for weeks, blending in with the other rubbish dumped in front gardens of houses with boarded-up windows sprayed with graffiti. Litter blew in the wind and aggressive young girls sat on walls, chain-smoking, while their babies sat ignored in buggies.

'Yes, it's going to be great up there. The houses are lovely, really lovely. They've got big windows so they're all light and airy and we'll have a bathroom and three bedrooms and there's a kitchen, with a proper cooker and a sitting room with a back boiler. And you can have a bedroom all on your own, Libby. Won't that be lovely?'

There was a crash outside the door. A small boy came bursting through. He looked just like Carol but with Will's big brown eyes.

'Hi, Mum. Is there anything to eat? I'm starving!'

'Then you should have been home for your dinner. I'll get you some bread and jam—but will you look at the state of your clothes! I think we'll get you in the sink and wash you down.'

Time for me to leave.

'I'd better be going, Carol. Thanks for the fish and chips and the tea. Maybe we can have a coffee again in town if I can get out of the office.'

'Smashing.' But she had already turned to Davy.

I let myself out and walked back through town to the Browns' house. By this time, I was desperate for the loo, but Peggy was in the bathroom. I waited a while, then finally I had to bang on the door.

'Peggy, could you hurry, please? I'm desperate!'

Eventually, she flung open the door and came out surrounded by billowing clouds of steam.

'Good grief! It's like a sauna in here,' I said, getting past her. I'd never known that bathroom so warm, and I could have sworn she smelt of booze. But that was just daft. Peggy wasn't the drinking type.

Sunday morning started with church. Surprisingly, I knew the first hymn, sort of. 'Praise My Soul the King of Heaven'—I've sung it at weddings. But then I dropped my hymn book and people glared at me.

As for the sermon . . . it was so riveting that I started counting pieces of stained glass. If that was what church was like, no wonder everyone stopped going. And yet, maybe something got through. Not so much the service, but the building itself. And the thought of all those people, going back hundreds of years, who had come here to worship, to say the same prayers. In a way, I could almost feel them there around me.

And it gave me a chance to think about Will, or rather Will as Billy, a family man. Would Will be like that if we had a family? Would he take responsibility? Billy had taken responsibility since he was seventeen, when he became a dad. At eighteen, he was married, a father and a soldier. Is this what they mean by making a man of someone? I thought of the way Billy was passing on skills to his son. Oh God, I wanted to cry.

As soon as we got home, Mrs Brown changed out of her Sunday best, rolled up her sleeves and started on the lunch. This was a big deal. Peggy was trying to read the *News of the World*, but not for long. Mrs Brown had us both peeling potatoes and chopping. She had the cloth off the kitchen table and was making pastry.

'Rosie, can you go down the garden and pick some rhubarb, please?' she asked.

The back garden was steep, narrow and treacherous, a sort of series of terraces leading down to the river, which went rushing past below. It was easy to see from the debris on the steps that the river had been halfway up the garden recently. I went up and down those slippy steps, along the little patches of garden and couldn't see anything looking like rhubarb. I was so long that Peggy came to look for me.

'I can't find it, sorry,' I said.

She just gave me a withering look and marched over to a big upturned metal bucket. She picked it up and beneath it were some long, thin, pink sticks of rhubarb with large, pale green leaves.

'Well, how was I meant to know it was under a bucket?' I said.

'Where do you think rhubarb grows?' she said, very sarcastically.

I wanted to say 'in a long polystyrene tray just on the left when you go into Sainsbury's', but thought I was probably wasting my breath.

The meal was like something out of *A Christmas Carol*. Mrs Brown produced the meat, Mr Brown carved it. We were all meant to say ooh and ah . . . Gosh, it would have been so much easier for us all just to go to the pub. The only excitement came when I said, ever so casually, to Peggy, 'Do they do good food at the Rising Sun?'

She gave me a filthy look and said, 'How should I know?'

'Oh,' I said. 'I thought you might have been there on official business, with the editor maybe.'

'Well, I haven't,' she snapped, banging down a rhubarb pie on the table. She looked really upset and a bit pale. I'd clearly touched a nerve.

Finally, when we were all too full to move, we had the washing-up to do. It took hours. It was like the porridge pot only much more of it, all cleaned with a bit of wire wool and some grey powder.

And that was it. That was the excitement for the day.

I went up to my room and lay on my bed. Sambo followed me up and lay beside me, purring happily. I tried to make sense of it all.

I am no nearer to working out where I am or why I'm here but I'm beginning to think that it can't be a reality show. There are no cameras,

*no rules, no video room. You can recreate a house, a newspaper office,
a street even, but not a whole town.*

*Then there are the people. Carol and Billy are like Caz and Will would
be if they had been transplanted to the 1950s. I mean, Caz has always
said she doesn't want children, but here she is with three of them on whom
she dotes. I can't think of Will and Caz as a couple. But Billy and Carol
seem a real partnership, working together for the kids. If they'd had to,
could Will and Caz have worked it out like Billy and Carol?*

I thought of the hymn we'd sung in church that morning. There was
a line in it: 'Dwellers all in time and space'. We are all dwellers in time
and space. We think we're restricted to one little place, but what if we
can move around in it like astronauts in the weightlessness of space,
bobbing here and there without much control over where we go?
Could I really, actually, be in the real 1950s?

It was a terrifying thought. So terrifying that I had been refusing to
consider it. But now I had to face it. I had time travelled. In a way,
mindblowing as it seemed, it was the only thing that made sense.

Panic surged through me. If I stayed here, I'd be older than my
parents. But no. Deep breath. This wasn't a full-scale exchange, just a
time-trip, a holiday in another age. I had to believe that. It wasn't for ever.

CHAPTER FIVE

On Monday morning I felt a lot calmer. Part of me was still bewildered,
but I clung onto the fact that everyone said I would be here for just a
few weeks. So the other part of me was curious, excited almost. After
all, I thought, it could be a great story . . .

I practically ran into the office. I was actually looking forward to work.
I went into the reporters' room expecting to be greeted by Gordon's
demands for tea. But he wasn't there. Instead Billy was standing with the
big diary in front of him, marking up the stories.

'Hello, Rosie,' he said, pleasant and friendly but still like a stranger.
'Nice to see you on Saturday.'

'Yes. I enjoyed meeting Peter. He's a great lad, isn't he?' Gosh, I was
making conversation like an old granny with the vicar.

'Not bad,' said Billy, but he looked pleased. 'Right,' he went on, 'Gordon won't be in for a week or two. He's broken his leg. Fell downstairs apparently—while stone-cold sober, before you start! He's in the Victoria Infirmary and they won't let him out until he's mastered the crutches. So I'm taking over the desk for now and I've had to reorganise some of the jobs. Alan, you'll have to get to the council planning meeting today. It's the day they decide on the ring road. That's a must. Tony's down at the petty sessions. Derek's gone to an accident. Marje—I've got you down for the duke and duchess opening the new school. OK?'

'Fine by me,' said Marje.

'What about me?' I asked.

'Dan and Doris Archer are opening the flower show in the Shire Hall, but that's at lunchtime, so if you can get on with some shorts—'

'What, off the radio show? *The* Dan and Doris? Gosh, my mum would be jealous. She loves *The Archers*.'

'Not a patch on *Dick Barton*,' muttered Marje. 'They're all yours.'

First I had a phone call to make. Making phone calls was tricky because there were only three phones in the office, none of them on my desk. And everything had to go through the operators downstairs. You couldn't just dial a number, you had to wait for them to put you through. The upside of this was that often you didn't even need to know the number you wanted—just left it up to the operators.

I waited until the office was quiet, then I went over to Gordon's desk, took a deep breath and picked up the phone. There was a quick click and a voice said, 'Switchboard!'

'Could you put me through to head office?' I said briskly.

'Who is that please?' asked the switchboard operator suspiciously.

'Rosie Harford. I need to speak to Lord Uzmaston's secretary.'

'Oooh, right you are,' said the operator and, many clicks later, I was speaking to another operator who sounded as though she was on Mars.

'This is Rosie Harford on *The News*. I would like to speak to the person who arranged my attachment here.'

'Have you a name for that person, caller?'

'No, I don't. Sorry.'

'Right, I'd better put you through to Lord Uzmaston's office.'

This was promising. The phone was answered by a posh-sounding woman. I went through my request again.

'Yes. That would be our Mr Simpson.'

'May I speak to him, please?'

'Unfortunately not. He is away from the office for two weeks.'

'Does Mr Simpson have a secretary? There must be somebody . . .'

'That would be myself. If I don't know about this . . . arrangement, then I'm afraid nobody will. You will have to speak to Mr Simpson.'

And she put the phone down. Great. Two more weeks before I could get any further with this mystery of where I was and why I was there.

Which gave me another thought. I started dialling my parents' number. Maybe they could put things right. It was a moment before I could remember the string of numbers—I was so used just to clicking 'Home' on my mobile. But it didn't matter. I hadn't got past the area code when a voice interrupted. It was the switchboard lady asking bossily, 'Which number do you require?'

'It doesn't matter,' I said, deflated. I decided to make some tea. I was just leaving the office to fill the kettle when the phone rang.

'Newsroom,' I said.

'This is Ron Neasham, the newsagent in Friars' Mill,' said a voice. 'Do you know what's going on down here?'

'No, I don't, Mr Neasham,' I said. 'Should I?'

'Well, there's police here with dogs. I think a kiddie's gone missing.'

'A missing child? Are you sure? They didn't say anything to us when we made the calls this morning.'

'I think it's just happened. You'd better check it out.'

'We certainly shall, Mr Neasham. Thank you.'

I'd just put the phone down when Billy walked into the office.

'Missing child in Friars' Mill, apparently,' I said. 'Someone called Ron Neasham rang to tell us there's a lot of police activity there.'

'Good bloke, Ron,' said Billy. 'Used to be one of our van drivers so he often passes us snippets. Odd that the police didn't mention it, though.'

'That's what I said.'

Billy looked round the empty office. 'Look, you get down to Friars' Mill and find out what you can. Ring me when you've got something.'

'Right.' I'd grabbed my bag and was out of the office before he could change his mind. I'd miss Dan and Doris, but what the hell—there'd be another fifty years to catch up with them.

Friars' Mill was about two miles out of town. Which would take me forty minutes to walk. Then I remembered that George was nearby waiting to take Dan and Doris's picture. I dashed out and pushed through the crowds to find him.

'Are they here yet?'

'Just arriving,' said George.

'Then just take a picture as quick as you can and let's get out of here.'

With that, Dan and Doris arrived looking a lot more like actors than a farmer and his wife. As they went up the steps to the Shire Hall, they stopped halfway to wave at the crowd and a small child shoved a toy lamb at them. Brilliant. George got them perfectly.

Soon we were bundled in the van and heading for Friars' Mill. There was something about the name that kept niggling at my brain. I knew it from something but I couldn't recall what. Anyway, the place I went to with George was in the country. There was a green, a river with a weir, a duck pond and a row of small cottages. There were a couple of black cars parked on the green and I could see two policemen, dressed in old-fashioned uniforms, talking to someone on a cottage doorstep.

Inside the corrugated-iron hut that was the newsagent's, Ron Neasham was busy marking up a ledger. He looked up eagerly when he saw George and his camera and realised who we were.

'It's the little girl from the big house, the housekeeper's daughter,' he said, keen to tell us all he knew. 'She set off to school this morning as usual, about half past eight. Then her mum went down there about half past ten to take her to the dentist and she wasn't in the school. Apparently, when Joyce Williams—that's little Susan's mother—was asking if anyone had seen her, Charlie, one of the little 'uns, pipes up that he saw her being pulled into a van by an old man.'

'What! Well, why didn't he say anything before?'

'Little lad's only five years old.'

I was scribbling in my notebook as he spoke.

'Well, when she heard that, the headmistress got onto the police and they came right out. They're up at the house now, and those two over there have been going from door to door asking people what they've seen. As far as I can tell, no one's seen anything, apart from the lad.'

'And if he's only five, he could be making it all up.'

'Maybe. If you want to talk to the man in charge, I think he must be up at the house.' He pointed out an impressive gateway at the far end of the green. 'That's the entrance. The house is half a mile up the drive.'

'Thanks, Ron.' I pushed the notebook into my bag. 'You're a real star.'

'Just like to help the old firm, you know,' he said, looking pleased.

I got George to take a picture across the green with the policemen in the background. Then we went up the drive to The Grange. It was a big house, not quite a stately home, but pretty impressive all the same. The drive swept round in front of well-tended lawns. I could see a tennis court, and what looked like stables and a paddock.

'Better find the tradesmen's entrance,' said George, and we turned up past two small cottages and stopped in a back yard where there was a big black car and a young policeman guarding it.

'Press,' I said confidently. 'From The News. Is the chief inspector about?'

'He's in there. But I don't think—'

'Thank you,' I said, and I went in, with George following.

We went into a room full of old coats and welly boots and dog baskets, and along a passage until we heard voices, which we followed to a huge, high-ceilinged kitchen. As we stood in the doorway, a young woman almost ran towards me. 'Have you found Susan?' she asked.

'No, I'm sorry. We're from *The News*. Someone rang to tell us what had happened,' I said quickly, before the chief inspector could throw us out. 'They thought we could help.'

'Help? How could you help?' An older woman, grey-haired, very erect, was standing by an Aga. She was clearly the lady of the manor. I learned later she was Caroline Cavendish.

'My apologies,' I said, as politely as I could, to the housekeeper. 'I'm sure the chief inspector has told you that nearly every child who goes missing wanders back, safe and sound, in a matter of hours.'

Joyce clutched her hanky, sniffed and said yes, he had said that.

'But, as a sort of safety net, if we had something in tomorrow's paper, and if we had a picture of Susan, then by six o'clock in the morning you could have a hundred thousand people on the lookout for her.'

'She's right,' said the chief inspector. 'The press can be very useful on such occasions.'

I turned to him. 'Are you having a press conference?'

The police chief looked blank. 'Press conference?'

No, of course no press conferences. No reconstructions, handout pictures, interviews for TV and radio. I spotted a picture on the dresser. Clearly a school photo, a little girl with blonde plaits and a gappy grin, arms folded above an impressive-looking encyclopaedia. 'Is this Susan?'

'Yes,' said her mother, snatching the photo and holding it close to her.

'Maybe,' I said gently, 'you could just let George here borrow it for a moment and he could take a photograph of it, a copy of it. You can have it straight back. And while you're doing that, George, perhaps the chief inspector and I can just go outside for a moment?'

Outside, the detective recapped on the details of the case. 'Little Charlie thought Susan was waiting for him, you see, when a grey van appeared and a "fat man" got out, shouting. This man dragged Susan into the van and roared off. The boy's only five, but he seems quite sure and quite consistent. He thinks the van came from the woods.'

'Who lives in The Grange?'

'Mrs Cavendish you've seen. Husband Colonel Cavendish is up in London during the week. There's a daughter at boarding school and a son, Jeremy, up at Oxford, though he's home for the holidays. He went to see friends in Upper Middleton last night, presumably stayed the night and isn't home yet. The Cavendishes don't own a grey van.'

'So what happens now?'

'Well, I still think that Susan will turn up by teatime. Amazing the number of kids who remember to come home when they're hungry.'

'And if she doesn't?'

'If she doesn't, then in view of the evidence of the little boy, we'll start a full-scale search. But I'm sure it won't come to that.'

'Thanks, Chief Inspector.'

I went back into the house and spoke to Susan's mother, Joyce. Susan had never missed a day at school, nor been late. She was doing well, wanted to be a teacher. She would be home soon, wouldn't she?

Down the drive I could see a policewoman coming up, firmly holding onto the hand of a small boy, no doubt Charlie. By now it was a quarter to four. Nearly teatime. Let's hope Susan would get hungry.

George and I were just getting into his van, when I saw a young policeman running up the drive. 'Sir, sir!' He was calling to the chief inspector, who was just going into the gardener's house behind the policewoman and little Charlie. 'Sir, we've . . . we've found a body.'

'Oh, no,' said the chief inspector. 'Not Susan.'

'No, sir, not Susan. We think it's Jeremy Cavendish. He's been shot.'

I was out of the van in a flash. But the chief inspector held up his hand and his former friendliness vanished under an air of grim authority. 'You must leave now, please.'

I needed to talk to Billy anyway, and George had to get his pictures printed. We raced back to *The News* and I bounded up the wooden stairs. Billy was talking to someone on the phone, writing in his notebook as he listened. I waved to get his attention. He brought the call to a quick but very polite end, and turned to me. I told him what had happened, as quickly, clearly and as professionally as I could.

Billy took it all in, then said, 'Write up the story of the missing girl, but don't mention the body until we get official confirmation.' He turned to the other reporter in the room. 'Derek—have you got your bike here?'

'Of course.'

'Right, get yourself up to Friars' Mill. Don't annoy Watkins, but try to get the gen on this body. They're going to have to open an inquest, so there's bound to be an ID. We need to know exactly what's going on.'

'But it's my story,' I said.

'Yes, Rosie, I know, and I'm not taking it away from you. This is a team effort. You get your stuff written up as quick as you can.'

I typed as fast as I could, with all that fiddly carbon paper. I had just finished when I suddenly remembered.

Back before all this strange Narnia-type adventure had happened, when I'd been sitting in the bound-file room, going through all the copies of *The News* from the 1950s, there was that small, sad paragraph. A sixteen-year-old girl had died in the river below the millpond at Friars' Mill. I remembered it because the verdict had been Accidental Death, but something about the way it had been written had made me think it had really been suicide.

'Friars' Mill,' I said to Billy. 'Wasn't that where a young girl drowned recently?'

'Yes,' said Billy. 'I was at the inquest. She was only sixteen. What we didn't say in the paper was that she was pregnant. It was pretty clear that she'd killed herself, but the jury decided to spare the family's feelings and say it was Accidental Death.'

'Pregnant and abandoned?'

'Yes.'

'Do we know who the father was?'

'No, it didn't come out in court. A friend of the dead girl said that her boyfriend came from a good family. Something about him being a student but refusing to give up his studies and marry her because his family wouldn't approve. Wouldn't even consider it.'

'A student? Good family?' I looked at Billy.

'Jeremy Cavendish?' he asked, looking back.

'That would explain why she did the deed in Friars' Mill, wouldn't it? On his doorstep. Who was the girl? Can you remember her name?'

Billy frowned. 'Amy something. Amy . . . Amy . . . She was a farmer's daughter, lived the other side of town, I think. Oh'—he banged the desk in frustration—'if only I could remember her name!' He started turning the pages of the big, bound, back copies that lived on a shelf at the end of the newsroom.

Meanwhile, I ran upstairs to the library. This consisted of shelf after shelf of brown envelopes packed with curling cuttings. First go I grabbed a fat envelope marked 'Friars' Mill' and shook the cuttings out onto a desk. There were stories about garden parties at The Grange, about archaeological digs, about the leek show, the spring fair, an over-turned milk lorry and the WI planting daffodil bulbs. Nothing yet about a sixteen-year-old girl 'accidentally' falling into the river.

'Rosie!' Billy had come upstairs. 'I've remembered. She was Amy Littlejohn. Her father has a farm about two miles from Friars' Mill.'

'A farmer would have a gun, wouldn't he?'

'Yes. Of course we could be barking up completely the wrong tree . . .'

'Of course,' I agreed. 'But it does seem to fit. So what shall we do?'

'Phil's the reporter on night shift. He's already in. We could send him up to have a look around. Or'—he grinned; it was a real Will grin—'we could borrow his motorbike and go ourselves.'

'What are we waiting for?' I said.

Five minutes later, I was perched on the back of the borrowed bike and Billy was speeding out of the yard in search of the story.

It was a long time since I'd been on the back of a motorbike—not since I briefly had a rocker boyfriend when I was about fifteen—and it's amazing how vulnerable you feel without a helmet. And uncomfortable, too, when you're wearing a skirt and stockings.

As we roared round bends and along the narrow country roads, I wanted to wrap my arms round Billy, hold him tightly, bury my head in his shoulder. Instead, I just hung on as lightly as I could.

The roads were getting bumpier now and Billy was driving more slowly, searching through the gloom. 'Right, I think that's it.'

We got off and Billy tucked the bike in a gateway and pointed across the road. 'I think that's Littlejohn's down there.'

A short, steep, muddy track twisted down into a hollow where there was a small farm. Even in the fading light it looked grim. The house had once—long ago—been whitewashed, but was now dirty and mottled. A heap of logs lay scattered across the mud-covered yard along with bits of abandoned machinery.

Billy was already wriggling his way through the fence. 'Come on. We'll have a better view from here.'

He took my hand—it was wonderful to feel his hand on mine—and guided me into the field. We heard a dog give a few muttered barks.

'Look!' said Billy. Below us, tucked into the shelter of one of the barns, was a van, a small grey van. 'Coincidence?' said Billy drily.

A light went on in the house: a soft, dim glow. From an oil lamp, I realised. Someone was carrying it across a room, and for a second I saw two shadows. A big one and a small one. The small one had plaits . . .

'Billy, that must be Susan. What shall we do?' I hissed.

'It could be a perfectly normal farmer and his daughter or grand-daughter,' Billy said calmly. 'We have no reason to think it's Susan. Only a string of coincidences. On the other hand, if that *is* Susan, we can't abandon her. We need to get help. There was another farm about half a mile back. They might have a phone. You go there and call the police.'

'Can I take the bike? If there's no phone I can get to town quickly.'

Even in the dark I could see Billy's grin. 'Can you ride a motorbike?'

'I think so.'

'Well, be careful, girl. Here.' He handed me the key and I turned to go back down the slope. As I did, I slipped and gave a yelp. Below us, the dog went mad. It was as if he were saying I *thought* there was someone up there and now I know. I could hear his chain rattling.

The door of the farmhouse was pulled open. In the doorway, with the light of the oil lamp behind him, stood a giant of a man. In his hands he had a shotgun, which he was pointing up towards us.

'Who's there?' he yelled. 'Show yerself, before I set the dog on you.'

'Run!' hissed Billy at me. 'Run!'

But the farmer had started crossing the yard. 'Stay where you are,' he said, his gun up at his shoulder.

I stood next to Billy. Soon the farmer was just a few feet away from us. 'Get down to the yard,' he said, pointing at us with the gun.

We slithered down the slope. In the yard, the dog ran towards us, growling. The farmer motioned us into the house and into the kitchen, where the big range across the far wall was dead and cold. In the dim light I could see newspapers heaped on a chair. A bit of machinery lay in pieces on the table. Beside it was a heap of cartridge cases and an almost empty whisky bottle. And in the corner, on a wooden settle, sat a small girl with blonde plaits. She was sobbing.

'Susan?' I asked. 'Susan?'

The little girl looked up at me, terrified.

'Will you shut that bloody row!' yelled the farmer.

'She's frightened,' said Billy, in a reasonable, noncommittal voice. 'She's cold too.' Billy was taking off his jacket. 'Can we just put this round her? Just to warm her up a bit? It might stop her crying.'

The farmer grunted. Billy took this as assent and threw the jacket at me. I went over to the settle and wrapped the jacket round Susan. She clung to me and I sat down next to her, wrapping my arms round her, partly to comfort her and partly to keep her warm.

Her sobs quietened but I could feel her trembling.

'There, that's better, isn't it?' Billy said to Littlejohn. 'She's only a little girl after all. Why did you bring her here? Why the gun?'

The farmer was still pointing his gun at us. 'She saw me.'

'Saw you?' asked Billy, still calm and in control. 'Did that matter?'

'She saw the van coming down the track from the woods. Anyway,'— he suddenly jerked the gun back up again so it was pointing straight at Billy—'what are you doing here? I've seen your face before. You're the reporter from *The News*. You were in the court, weren't you?'

'That's right, Mr Littlejohn, I was. It was a very sad occasion. I was very sorry for your loss.'

'Amy was a good girl, you know. Ever since her mother died . . .'

'Was that a long time ago?'

'Amy was only nine when Megan went. She tried to look after her mother, tried to look after me . . .' He was still pointing the gun at Billy. 'Megan had cancer,' the farmer said, as if trying to make Billy understand. 'She was a long time dying.'

'It must have been a terrible time. For you as well as her.'

Littlejohn gave Billy a sharp look. But Billy seemed quite open, honest and straightforward.

'So then it was just you and Amy?' asked Billy, his eyes never leaving Littlejohn's face.

'Ay, and Amy did her best. I wasn't much good, I know that. The girl needed her mother. She was a young woman and I didn't realise. One day I was watching her putting coal on the range. She looked just like my Megan did when she was carrying Amy. I knew then.'

'That she was expecting a baby?'

Littlejohn nodded.

'So you were angry with Amy?'

Littlejohn looked astonished. 'No, not with Amy. Ay, she'd been foolish right enough. But, no, I wasn't angry with her. I was angry with that stuck-up, cowardly lad she'd got involved with. And when he told her he wanted nothing more to do with her, nothing to do with his baby, that he didn't want his Mummy and Daddy to know—then I was really angry.' He slammed the table with one hand and bits of machinery clattered about. Susan whimpered and clung even closer to me.

Despite my fear, I was beginning to feel sorry for Mr Littlejohn. But even more sorry for Amy. Then curiosity overtook me. How on earth did a little girl from this neglected farm get to meet the likes of Jeremy Cavendish? I must have asked the question aloud because Littlejohn looked at me and said, 'The Hirings.'

The Hirings? For a minute I was lost, then I remembered that The Hirings was the name for the annual fair in the town. Everyone went to The Hirings, all ages, all backgrounds. Easy to see how Amy and Jeremy could have bumped into each other there.

'So what happened?' Billy asked in a low, coaxing voice.

'I wanted that Cavendish to come here and face me like a man, but he wouldn't come. So I was going over there after she told me, that night. I wanted to go to see him and his precious Mummy and Daddy, but Amy cried and sobbed and made me promise to wait till morning when I was calmer. So I promised.

'Next morning she was gone. I looked all over and she was nowhere. And then they came and told me they'd found her in the river . . .'

Tears were streaming down his unshaven face. 'He broke her heart. And I could never forgive him for that. He never turned up at court, did he? Didn't have the decency to do that for the girl he had wronged. Just wiped his hands of her and got back to his precious studies.

'Then, last night I'd been in the Blue Bells at Barton, and as I came through Witton I saw him. Gone midnight it was and he was leaving the Lion, laughing, happy as you like, with some of his friends. Now that's not right, is it? You can't go ruining someone's life and then go laughing. Not when a girl and her baby are drowned in the river.

'So I followed him. I knew which way he'd go. I waited till he was alongside the woods, then I drove up and got him. Didn't even put up a fight. He whimpered like a dog and I shot him like a dog.

'I was there in the woods, thinking about Megan and Amy and what had happened. Then I realised it was well past dawn. I took the track through the woods. Nobody uses it. But then the little girl saw me. So I picked her up. I shouldn't have done that, I know, but I didn't want her telling everyone that she'd seen me. I'm sorry I frightened her, but I was never going to hurt her.'

He looked at me. And despite it all, I felt sorry for him again. He was a desperate man driven by despair. He nodded his head at Susan.

'Why don't you take the little lass back to her mother now?'

Billy nodded at me. I took hold of Susan and practically carried her out of the house into the darkness of the yard. The dog growled, but made no attempt to come near me.

I stood out there, hardly able to breathe.

'Right, Susan,' I said as brightly and encouragingly as I could. 'We're going to walk up this track to the road and then see if we can find our motorbike. All right?'

She sort of nodded, and we trudged up the mucky track, Susan still wearing Billy's jacket and blowing her nose on the handkerchief she'd found in his pocket. Then I heard the sound of cars coming slowly along the road. As the first one rounded the corner, I snatched the hanky from Susan and waved it. The cars stopped, and in the light from the headlamps I could just make out the shapes of police uniforms.

'Chief Inspector! Am I pleased to see you!' We bundled Susan into the car. 'Billy's still in the farmhouse with Littlejohn, who's confessed to killing Jeremy Cavendish. He's just let us go. He's got a gun, but I don't think he's dangerous.'

With that a gunshot rang out. The sound echoed and bounced round the farmhouse in the little dip. The dog barked wildly and we could hear it running round the yard, the chain clanking.

I gasped, 'Will!' and started to run back, but the chief inspector grabbed me. 'Stay there!' he snapped. 'Look after the girl!' And he and the other policemen swarmed down the hill.

Susan was curled up on the back seat of the car. She was rocking herself back and forth and making small whimpering sounds. I leaned into the car and stroked her arm.

'There, there,' I crooned. 'You'll soon be home, back with your mum.' And all the time I was trying to look past her, down the hill.

At last the farmhouse door opened and a small gleam of yellow light fanned out in front of it. I could see a figure in the doorway, illuminated in the lamplight. It was impossible to see who it was. Then the figure moved forward. He was tall and slim, in shirtsleeves . . .

Billy. It was Billy. Thank you, God. Billy was walking out of the house. He was safe. In the yard, he was quickly surrounded by policemen. I could see him talking to them, pointing back inside the house. They went in and he walked slowly up the hill towards me. As he reached the car, I stretched out my free hand towards him. I just had to touch him. He got in and leaned back against the leather upholstery.

A policeman drove us back to The Grange, where Joyce Williams hugged her daughter and took her into the house.

Then Billy told me that Littlejohn had shot himself. I started shivering and Billy put his arm round me, companionably. I grasped his hand. I wanted to hold his face in my hands and kiss every hollow of his cheekbones in gratitude that he was here, alive.

He smiled at me, and, as his eyes held mine, for a moment I thought I saw my emotions mirrored in his. But then gently, wearily, he eased his hand out of mine, putting a distance between us, and we just sat like that in the back of the police car as they drove us into town.

'G'night,' said the policeman, as he stopped to let us out in front of *The News.* 'I'll read all about it in the morning.'

'We've got to write it first,' laughed Billy, taking my hand to help me out of the car. We went into the yard, past the vans and the newspaper hoist and in through the back door, to the shabby back staircase. Billy stopped at the foot of the stairs and put his hands on my shoulders.

'You were terrific tonight,' he said. 'The way you looked after the kid and calmed her down.'

'You were pretty fantastic yourself,' I said.

'We must be a great team, then, mustn't we?' He smiled down at me. 'Come on! We've got a story to write. We'll make the last edition if we're quick.' And he was bounding up the stairs. I trailed behind, my legs suddenly heavy with fatigue and disappointment.

The next morning, everyone wanted to know what had happened. Even Peggy was quite chatty and she made me a cup of tea while I told her all about it. I'd just got to the bit where Billy had calmed Littlejohn down, when Leo walked in.

Leo! I thought back to when I'd seen him the day before all this began, in the pub with Jake, arm in arm, laughing.

'Leo?' I asked. He looked at me blankly, and it was Will and Caz all over again.

Peggy jumped up from her desk. 'Hello, Lenny!' she cried. 'I've got a pile of books here for you.' She turned to me. 'This is Lenny. He does a lot of our book reviews. He reads an awful lot.' She giggled. 'That's why he has no time for girls.'

'That's why, is it?' I said, putting my foot in it big time. Well, I mean, when Peggy said that he had no time for girls, I thought she *knew*.

Lenny went white, then red, and gazed at me. Then he picked up his briefcase hurriedly. 'I'll see you later, Peggy,' he said.

'What about—?' But Lenny had gone.

'Well, what's the matter with him?' Peggy sniffed.

Later, when Billy and I were checking the page proof of our story, I said, 'Billy, can I ask you something?'

'Mmm?' He was drinking a cup of tea while reading the proof.

'Tell me, is it acceptable to be gay around here?'

He looked at me a bit blankly. 'Well, er, of course it is. You can be as gay as you like. Laugh, sing, you don't have to be gloomy.'

Now it was my turn to look blank. 'No, not gay like that, I mean *gay*.'

Blank look.

'Gay as in homosexual.'

A faint light began to dawn in Billy's eyes. 'You mean like er, like . . .' He was clearly a bit embarrassed.

'I mean one man loving another man.'

'Well it's against the law for a start.'

Was Billy blushing?

Of course. Homosexuality was illegal until, oh the 1960s, I think.

'But even though it's illegal is it still, well, all right?'

Billy was definitely blushing now.

'Well, er yes, there are people you know, who are . . . But, well, you don't make a song and dance about it. Now, can we just get on, please?'

He was *so* embarrassed. I wondered whether it was because he was talking about gays, or just because he was talking about gays to a woman. But it looked as though I had dropped Leo/Lenny right in it.

I was just thinking about that when Phil, the reporter on night shift, came in. 'Have you got your motorbike back?' I asked.

'Yes, thanks. I think the police have more or less finished there now.'

'What are we going to do about a follow-up?'

'Follow-up?' Both Billy and Phil looked at me blankly.

'Yes. I mean this has been a terrific story, but shouldn't we be getting more background about the Littlejohns? What led up to this tragedy, etc, etc? And see how Susan's coping? And her mum?'

'I don't think so,' said Billy. 'Let's allow them to get on with it in peace now.' He took some papers and walked out of the office.

'Look, Rosie.' It was Phil's turn to look a bit embarrassed now. 'Tonight's my last day on nights. Would you like to come to the flicks with me on Thursday?'

I looked at him. I was still thinking of follow-ups, and he was asking me out. A date! It was ages since anyone had asked me for a date. Because of course, I was with Will. But not here I wasn't. I smiled.

'Right, yes. OK, Phil, that would be really nice. I'd like that.'

When I got home, everyone wanted to know about the kidnapping and the murder. So I had to tell the story all over again.

'Well, I don't care what anyone says,' said Mrs Brown firmly. 'All this started when that silly girl got herself in the family way.'

'But she didn't get herself pregnant on her own, Mrs Brown,' I said. 'She must have been desperate if she killed herself.'

'She drowned herself in Friars' Mill, didn't she?' asked Peggy quietly.

'Yes,' I said. 'Cavendish had presumably said he'd stand by her, and when he didn't she shamed him by killing herself almost on his doorstep.'

'Ha! There's a lot of girls have trusted a fellow and look where it's got them. Silly girl. Look where it's led to,' snapped Mrs Brown.

And that's when I opened my big mouth.

'If only they'd been sensible,' I said. 'If only she'd been on the pill.'

'Pill?' asked Peggy sharply.

'Yes, you know, the contraceptive pill. No, actually you probably don't, do you? There's a pill that stops you getting pregnant. And if—'

'That's quite enough of that, thank you,' said Mrs Brown. 'I've never heard of such a thing. I will not have that sort of talk in my house.'

'I'm very sorry, Mrs Brown,' I said contritely. 'I didn't mean to upset you. It's just that where I come from we talk quite openly about—'

'Enough!'

At that moment, Mr Brown pointed out that they had more important matters to discuss. 'We'll soon be saying goodbye to this house, then,' he said, rattling the newspaper.

The dramatic events at Littlejohn's had overshadowed the council meeting that Alan had been to cover. The plans for the bypass and new inner ring road had been approved, Mr Brown told us.

'Well, that's it, then,' he said. 'Just as well we never got you that fancy kitchen you wanted. The whole street's coming down and all of Watergate and Fisher Quay.'

'Oh, but they're lovely old buildings!' I said. They were an interesting collection of higgledy-piggledy, timbered buildings overlooking the river. True, they were a bit dilapidated but they must have dated back centuries and were a real part of the town's heritage.

'Get away with you!' said Mr Brown scornfully, as Mrs Brown passed him a cup of tea. 'The quay's been a right warren of slums ever since I was a lad. Terrible place, only good for rats and thieves. Pull the whole lot down as far as I'm concerned. We'll get one of those new houses they're building up at The Meadows. They're what I call proper houses. Nice and light with big windows. And they won't have the water and rats flooding into the cellars every time there's a bit of rain. They'll be all new and modern, with a proper garden and all.'

'What about you, Mrs Brown?' I was trying hard to get back into her good books. 'Won't you miss this house?'

'Not a bit. I want a nice new house without damp in the walls or cracked old cupboards and shelves that you can't keep clean however hard you try. And no more blooming mice. And a front garden! Oooh, it'll be lovely to have a front garden, not to walk straight in off the street with every Tom, Dick and Harry staring in your windows.'

I looked at the proposed plan as shown in *The News*. It showed the inner ring road sweeping over a new bridge and alongside the river. It looked familiar. Of course! That's how the town used to be until just before I'd started on *The News*. The area alongside the river now had smart new bars and restaurants, and an arts centre. Funnily enough, they'd called it Fisher Quay. If only they'd kept some of the original buildings . . . In my time we were desperate to hark back to the past. But here the Browns were longing for the future. They seemed to think that everything could only get better, that the future was new and exciting, a great big present just waiting to be unwrapped.

And who was I to disillusion them?

CHAPTER SIX

I WAS JUST ON MY WAY back to the office, dodging through the stalls of the market, when I saw a familiar figure in her brown coat. Carol was struggling with a basket, a string bag full of vegetables, and a brown paper carrier bag as well.

'Here, let me take one of those.'

'Oh, thanks, Rosie. I got carried away with carrots and potatoes!'

I took the string bag from her. 'Libby not with you?'

'No, she's playing at a neighbour's house so I thought I'd take the chance to dash into town. You been doing anything interesting?'

'An exhibition at the town hall. Very boring.'

'Look, I can manage from here, if you've got to get back to work.'

'No, it's all right. They're not expecting me back yet anyway.'

'Fancy a cuppa?'

'Why not?'

We walked companionably on, carrying the shopping between us.

Inside the house, in the kitchen, Carol moved the kettle from the hearth and put it on the fire. She gave the coals a quick poke and soon they were glowing and the kettle steaming.

'Ugh! What's that?' A large bowl on the wooden draining board seemed to be full of blood. Carol looked surprised. 'Hearts, soaking for supper. Haven't you had them? Got a bit of stuffing for them. Very tasty.'

She made the tea and put the pot down on the table. I sat down, with my back to the bowl with the hearts in. Despite the gloom, it was a cosy kitchen. There was a jug of daffodils on the windowsill, a brightly coloured rug in front of the fire, and patchwork cushions on the chairs.

On the arm of the chair next to the table was a library book.

'Oh, who's reading *Lucky Jim*?'

'Billy. He's really enjoying it. Says I'll like it when he's finished.'

'It's one of Will's favourites.'

'Tell me about this Will, then,' she said, pouring the tea.

'Well, he's very like Billy. Amazingly like.'

'Are you going to get married?'

'I don't know. I'm not sure he's ready for it yet. Not to settle down.'

'How old is he?'

'Same age as Billy.'

Carol laughed. 'Well, that's old enough. Billy and me have been married for eleven years.'

'Yes, but it's sort of different.'

'Is he good to you?'

'Oh, yes.'

'Does he make you laugh?'

'Often.'

'Is he kind, generous?'

'Very.'

'And is he, you know, does he make you go tingly all over?'

'Oh, yes, definitely!'

'Then what are you waiting for, girl, snap him up!'

'But what if he doesn't want to be snapped up?' I put my cup back in its saucer and looked at Carol. I really wanted to know the answer.

'Oh, men do. There's not many men that's happy on their own. They pretend they want to be off with their mates, but really, they just want a family to look after. They want someone they can trust beside them.'

'Where I come from, a lot of men don't get married. Women neither. They might just live together for a while, sort of semidetached.'

'Oh-ho. Try before you buy, is it?'

'No, not like that. It's sort of not thinking too far ahead. Lots of women choose not to have children. They have jobs. Same jobs as men.'

'Someone's got to look after the kids though, haven't they? That's why I'm going to work at the school. Fits in nicely. Don't want my lot to be latchkey kids. Anyway, you don't want to be left on the shelf. If this Will is anything like Billy, what are you waiting for?'

'I really don't know. When I see him again . . .' I imagined Will in front of me. But it was hard, as he kept getting confused with Billy. I shook my head. 'I'm going out with Phil tonight. Just to the pictures.'

'What would your Will say about that? Still, what the eye don't see, the heart don't grieve over . . . But he's a nice lad, Phil. Don't you go leading him on and breaking his heart.'

'That is the last thing I want to do. It's just a night out. But I'd better get back to work. Thanks for the tea.'

'Any time. Enjoy yourself tonight.' She was already wrapping her apron round her, ready to tackle the vegetables and the hearts.

'**O**h, so that's the way it is then, is it?' said Charlie the chief photographer as Phil and I walked out together.

Billy looked up from his typewriter and our eyes met. He frowned, then forced a quick smile. 'Enjoy the film,' he said.

Downstairs, outside on the pavement, Phil hesitated, a bit unsure. Not as unsure as I was. I mean I'd never been on a 1950s date.

'I thought we'd get something to eat at the Odeon,' said Phil.

'Oh, can you eat there?'

'Yes, they've got a café upstairs.'

'Right. The Odeon it is.' The Odeon was a wonderful old cinema. All red plush and gold curly bits. Two huge staircases curved up on either side of the foyer. In the middle was a tiny booth of a box office where Phil bought our tickets. The best in the house—3s. 9d. each, which isn't even twenty pence in modern money. We went up one of the staircases and found ourselves in a café. One wall had windows overlooking the street and the other had windows that looked out over the auditorium, so you could sit there and eat and watch the film if you liked.

The menu offered poached egg on toast, scrambled egg on toast, cheese on toast, beans on toast, sardines on toast, mushrooms on toast, tomato soup, ham sandwiches, cheese sandwiches or egg sandwiches. Right. No low-carb diet here then.

'What are you having?' I asked Phil.

'Poached egg on toast for me.'

'I'll have the same please.'

'And a pot of tea for two,' said Phil to the middle-aged waitress.

'So how did you get to be a reporter, then?' asked Phil.

I told him about my A levels, the degree and the post-grad course.

'You did a degree? Just to be a reporter? And then spent another year learning all about it?' Phil was astonished. 'You must have been twenty-two when you got your first job.'

'Yes. Twenty-two and a half when I started on the *Swaledale Courant*.'

'Blimey, I'd been working seven years by then. Eight if you count all the stuff I did when I was still at school.'

'What, you were writing for *The News* when you were fifteen?'

'Fourteen. Did sports reports, not that there was much sport on during the war. And I wrote pieces about the concerts and the fundraising efforts until in the end old Mr Henfield was asking me to do things official like. Taught myself to type and learned shorthand at evening classes.'

'Have you been on *The News* ever since?'

'Apart from national service, yes.'

'You could make your name in Fleet Street,' I said, pouring the tea and passing him a cup.

'Well, there was a chap in the army. He's on the *Express* now. He says there's a job there for me if I want it.'

'Go for it! A job in Fleet Street! No question. You're young, single. You're a good journalist. Do you want to be on *The News* for ever?'

'No. I mean I like it well enough, but when I was in the army I met all sorts of different blokes, and here, well, here I just meet the people I've always known. That's why it was so great when you came here. You're so different, from the other side of the world with different ideas, a different way of doing things. I really like that.'

Oh dear, he was beginning to look at me. Meaningfully.

'You'd love it in London,' I said quickly. 'All those new people, all those stories. And a real chance to make your name. It could be great.'

'It could, couldn't it?' He grinned. 'Well, maybe I shall.'

He paid the bill, refusing my offer to go halves, and we went in to see the film. It was *Blackboard Jungle* and had music by Bill Haley. But when the film started it was some feeble cowboy film. This was the supporting film, the B movie.

In the interval we had an ice cream and then settled down for the main feature. When the titles rolled and the Bill Haley music blasted out, a group of kids near the front yelled and whistled and tried to bop a bit, but the usherette came down the aisle with a big torch and said loudly, 'Any nonsense from you lot and you're OUT.'

Phil grabbed my hand when the lights came up. 'Come on!' he urged and we scuttled out. Odd, I thought, then I heard a creaky rendition of the National Anthem and those people who hadn't left were standing to attention. Sliding out ahead of us were Lenny and Peggy. They must have been sitting a few rows behind us.

'Well, that's something I thought I'd never see,' said Phil. 'Still, nowt so queer as folk, as they say.' He looked at me in a sort of knowing way.

I smiled quickly, to show I understood, but after my very awkward conversation with Billy, I said nothing. It was dark now, and the town was quiet. I wished I was going home, proper home, wandering along the pavement with my arms wrapped round Will. We could have a nightcap, curl up on the sofa together, go to bed . . .

Instead, here I was with Phil, who was a perfectly nice, decent sort of bloke. But he wasn't Will.

After we left the town centre, we seemed to have the night and the streets to ourselves. The noise of our footsteps echoed along the silent houses, until we got to the Browns'.

'I'm not sure if I can ask you in,' I said. 'It's not my house and . . .'

'It's all right,' Phil said. He paused. 'It's been a nice evening. See you tomorrow then, Rosie.'

'Yes, see you tomorrow, Phil.'

He turned and strode off up the road, leaving me with the key in the lock, wondering about not even getting a good-night kiss.

Phil was straightforward enough. As for Billy . . . it was tricky being alone with him. I found it hard remembering how to behave, hard to behave naturally. Sometimes I could feel him watching me, but when I looked he was always intent on his story on the typewriter. Until one day I was quicker and caught his glance. And what a glance.

We gazed at each other across the newsroom. It was no ordinary look. I could feel myself blushing. At that moment, Phil came in with a bag of currant buns. He bowled a bun to Billy, who batted it away with a ruler. Instinctively I reached up and caught it, to cheers from them both.

'Owzat!' shouted Phil. Billy smiled. An ordinary, friendly sort of smile, which was both a relief and a disappointment to me.

A sort of camaraderie developed. But the real breakthrough came a few days later.

'Phil and I are thinking of going over to the Fleece at lunchtime,' Billy said. 'Fancy joining us?' He was smiling at me.

Phil came and stood alongside him. 'Yes, do come with us, Rosie.'

This, believe it or not, was the first time I had been invited to the pub with the lads. So, yes, I jumped at the chance.

'Afternoon, Jack,' said Phil, as we walked into the small bar. 'Two pints of the usual, and . . . what would you like, Rosie?'

'Cider, please.'

'And a half of cider.'

Who said I wanted a half? But I wasn't going to argue. Phil got some crisps and we all sat in the corner. We had a game of darts and shared the last two curling cheese sandwiches from under a plastic dome on the counter. Billy bought another and then, when the glasses were empty again, I got up. 'My turn,' I said, getting my purse out.

The landlord looked surprised, and Billy and Phil both objected.

'I insist,' I said. 'Where I come from, if we work we pay our turn.'

'Can we accept that?' said Billy, turning to Phil in mock seriousness.

'Do you know,' said Phil, equally serious, equally mocking, 'I think we can.' And they took their pints.

Billy raised his glass and said, 'Your very good health, Miss Harford.'

'Cheers,' said Phil companionably.

I leaned back, sipping my cider, and almost felt I belonged.

Until I went home alone and Billy went home to his wife.

Peggy had beaten me to the bathroom. While I was being helpful and taking out the dishes, she'd nipped upstairs. I could hear the hot water gurgling and could smell Yardley soap and bath salts.

'She's got to make herself beautiful for her young man,' said Mrs Brown equably. 'She seems to be seeing a lot of him these days.'

'That Lenny, do you mean?' asked Mr Brown over his newspaper.

'Yes. Such a nice young man.'

Mr Brown snorted. 'Too bloody nice if you ask me,' was all he said.

'Well, he's making our Peg happy and that's what's important.'

'Doesn't seem very happy to me. Don't know what's got into the girl lately,' said Mr Brown. He looked prepared to put down his paper and discuss it.

Mrs Brown was busy putting her shopping away. 'Oh, you know what girls are like, especially when they're in love,' she said.

'We don't seem to see her smiling much any more,' Mr Brown persisted, but Mrs Brown had disappeared into the pantry.

'Now, Rosie,' she said when she emerged. 'We're off early tomorrow morning. We're going to a christening. What a journey it's going to be. A train and two buses. So you two girls will have to fend for yourselves. There's plenty of rabbit pie left, and mind our Peggy doesn't leave you with all the pots to do.'

I was about to reply when a cheery yell came from the top of the stairs. 'Bathroom's free!'

I went up and was almost knocked over by the smell of bath salts, talc and the scented soap that Peggy had used in abundance. I stayed upstairs until I heard Lenny arrive to call for Peggy. I thought it best, really, that I didn't see him. I didn't want to upset him.

The doorbell rang again. 'That'll be your young man, Rosie,' said Mr Brown. 'Aren't our girls popular tonight? You get your coat, I'll let him in.'

I went down into the hall, where Phil was standing shyly.

'I've got the bike. I thought we'd go out into the country,' he said. 'A pub, perhaps?'

'Great idea,' I said as we went outside. I clambered on the back of the bike. I put my arms round Phil's waist, companionably. I didn't long to cling to him and get as close as I could, not the way I had with Billy.

We went up into the hills that surrounded the town. Then we rode along a ridgeway looking down on the valley below. We came to a few houses and Phil stopped in front of a small pub with a bench outside.

'Cider?' he asked, taking off his big leather gauntlets.

'Yes, please. Can we sit out here?'

'Of course. I thought you'd like the view.'

It was terrific. You could see for miles. I was trying to place the village we were in on the modern map that existed only in my mind and memory. But I couldn't quite reach it.

'Here you are,' said Phil, coming back with the drinks.

'Thanks.' I took a mouthful of cider, still gazing at the view.

'It's the motorway!' I said suddenly.

Phil was looking at me over his pint. 'Sorry. What did you say?'

'Oh, nothing at all,' I said quickly. 'I was just admiring the view.'

What I wanted to say was that I recognised it because I always came back this way from seeing my parents. You come across the view suddenly, just past the Long Edge Services, so it sort of hits you—I always know that I'm nearly home, nearly back with Will. But here there was no motorway. Just a country road and a cluster of cottages.

'What's this village called?'

'Long Edge,' said Phil. I sipped my cider and thought of the narrow road overlaid by the six-lane motorway. This little pub is somewhere under the service station now, all flashing yellow-and-red neon signs and constant traffic noise. It was a hard idea to get my head round.

'Penny for them,' said Phil, smiling.

'What do you think this place will look like in fifty years?' I asked him.

'Probably much the same as it does now,' said Phil. 'It hasn't changed much in the last thousand years, so I can't see fifty making much difference.' He lit a cigarette as though that ended the matter.

'I liked your story about the dog that caught the train,' he said.

I'd done a shaggy dog story about a dog that hopped on a train every day to meet his master coming from work. It was a bit daft.

'Billy reckons you've got a really nice touch with light stories—as well as the big stuff like the Littlejohn piece. He thinks highly of you.'

I wanted to punch the air with glee. I was glad the light was fading so Phil couldn't see me blush, or see the eagerness in my face. We had another drink or two and talked in easy, friendly fashion about work.

Finally it was dark. We still sat there on the bench outside the pub, with the sound of the sheep and the muffled buzz of conversation and clatter of dominoes from the few old men inside. Phil put his arm round me and then he kissed me. Not passionately, but nicely.

And I kissed him back, a bit absent-mindedly, but politely. And we got on the bike and rode down the hill into the darkness, with just a few pinpoints of light from the occasional house. And I thought about the lights and the gantries on the motorway, and it was a bit odd, really.

When we got back to the Browns' house, I hopped off the bike and gave Phil a swift kiss on the cheek before he could get the bike propped up and get me into a clinch.

'Thank you for a nice evening, Phil,' I said, and went quickly into the house and upstairs to bed, where I could devote myself to thinking about Will without any distractions.

Just before I drifted off to sleep I wondered briefly about Peggy's big night with Lenny.

As I lay in bed on Sunday morning I could hear the Browns getting ready for their day out. They were making an early start for their complicated journey. Finally, I heard the front door close and their footsteps receding along the quiet street.

Once I had dressed, I decided I'd go for a walk. I put on my red jacket, scribbled a note for Peggy, and set out. I meandered through the town and found the path alongside the river. Soon, by chance, I found myself on the opposite side of the river from Billy's house. I climbed some steps and sat down on a bench in the shelter of the old town wall. From here I could see that Billy's rows of vegetables, just beginning to come through, had the organisation of a medieval garden.

Two small figures were running round the lower part of the garden. Pete and Davy, I guessed, chasing a ball. Then I saw Billy coming down the path, carrying some sort of rake or hoe. He propped it up by the shed, then, wiping his hands on the seat of his trousers, he intercepted the ball. The two boys' delighted yells of mock indignation floated across the river. I wasn't the only one watching them. Another figure was coming up the steps. It was Carol, who came to a standstill and stood watching them all, while a tiny figure, Libby, clung to her skirts. Then Will moved over to Carol's side and put his arm round her.

It was a tiny snippet of family life. The sort of thing happening in hundreds of back gardens all over Britain. Nothing special at all. And it broke my heart. They were a family, enclosed, happy together. And I was on the outside. I had no place with them. How could I still want Will when he was clearly so happy with someone else? Oh, yes, Billy was attracted to me. But he wasn't going to do anything about it, was he? Billy had already chosen Carol. He had a wife and family, and there was no way I could fit into his plans.

I jumped up from the bench and down the steps, landing awkwardly on the river path below. I'd grazed my hands and knees. But I didn't care. I hobbled home, almost glad of the pain. When I got back to the house I headed straight up to the bathroom. I needed to bathe my cuts and find some other clothes.

At the top of the stairs I paused, frozen. There was someone in my bedroom. I could hear a drawer being opened, then another drawer . . .

There was a phone downstairs in the hall. If I could get down quietly, I might be able to dial 999. I started inching back down the stairs. Then I heard a familiar but desperate voice say, tearfully, 'Oh, where are they?'

'Peggy?' I asked tentatively, coming back up to the landing. I pushed the bedroom door open. All the drawers and the wardrobe were half open with a lot of stuff flung to one side, and my handbag had been emptied out onto the shiny green eiderdown.

Peggy was sitting on the bed. Her face was swollen and blotchy.

'Peggy? What on earth are you doing?'

'Where are they?' she demanded. 'Where do you keep those pills you told me you had? The ones that stop you having babies.'

I remembered our conversation at the kitchen table. The one that her mother had cut short.

'Oh, Peggy, I haven't got them with me. Anyway, you have to take them to *prevent* you getting pregnant.' Suddenly it all became clear. 'Do you think you might be pregnant?'

And with that she began to howl. 'Don't say it!' she shrieked at me.

'Hey,' I said, as gently as I could. 'It's not the end of the world.'

'What do you know about it?' she sobbed. 'It's not you, is it?' She flung herself face down on the bed. 'I don't know what I'll do.'

Gingerly, I put out a hand and handed her one of my little lace-edged handkerchiefs that she had flung on the floor.

'How far gone are you?' I asked gently.

'I've missed one of my monthlies,' she said, not looking at me, 'and the other was due yesterday and it hasn't. . .' She started crying again.

'There's still time for an abortion, just.' Suddenly I remembered the steamy bathroom, the smell of booze. 'Is that what you were trying that afternoon? Hot bath and gin—were you trying to get rid of the baby?'

She sat up. 'I didn't know what else to do. But it didn't work,' she sobbed. 'I don't know who to ask about . . . someone who can arrange things. And I'm scared.' She stared at me, panic in her eyes.

Oh God, it was years before abortion would be legal. What a mess.

'Don't you know anybody?' Peggy said desperately.

'Sorry,' I said. 'Can't help.' And before she could start howling again I asked, 'So . . . the father? Does he know? How does he feel about it?'

'He can't do anything!' snapped Peggy. 'He's married.'

'Oh.' I remembered the way she smirked at the editor, the country bus to Middleton Parva . . . 'Oh, Peggy. It's not Mr Henfield, is it?'

She sniffed a bit and then nodded.

'Have you told him?'

'Yes. He said that I was panicking. That I was just late. And I prayed he might be right.' She had screwed the hanky into a knot.

'Could it be a false alarm?'

'I don't think so. I'm ever so regular normally.'

'Then why . . . ?' I was getting confused. 'If you were still trying to talk to Henfield about it, why were you so keen to go out with Lenny?'

'Richard's married, isn't he?' she hiccuped. 'I knew he couldn't marry me, so I thought—'

'So you thought Lenny might. Is that it?'

She nodded.

'But don't you realise . . . ?' She clearly didn't realise where Lenny's sexual preferences lay, and I didn't know how to begin to explain.

'I thought . . . I thought if Lenny and I, well, did *it*, then maybe . . . but Lenny, well, he, well, almost ran away from me. He said there was no point in us seeing each other again.'

She howled again.

And suddenly I felt very responsible. I'd opened my big mouth and talked to Lenny as if he were Leo. If homosexuality was still illegal, what better way to quash any rumours than by getting himself a girlfriend? And there was Peggy, on the hunt for a man . . .

'Look, if Henfield's the father then he *has* to support you. It's his baby as much as yours. Even if he stays with his wife, he should give you enough money to live. But you must tell your parents.'

'I just want to die.' Peggy flung herself back down on the eiderdown.

'No, you don't. What you want is to be well and happy and have your baby. Lots of women do it where I come from. They have babies all on their own, no man around, and it works.'

And so I went on. We sat there for another hour or more as I extolled the joys of single motherhood. I don't think she was persuaded but she did seem to be listening. Finally she stopped crying and we decided that the next day she would tackle Henfield and persuade him to do something for the child. And then, armed with that bit of provision, Peggy would come home and tell her parents.

'Don't worry,' I said. 'I'll be there for you. I'll help you all I can. Now, I'm going to have to do something about these cuts.'

'Oh, I'm sorry,' sniffed Peggy. 'You should have done that instead of listening to me.'

'That's all right,' I said. 'Why don't you go and have a wash first and then go and get that pie out of the pantry and warm it up? Your mother will play hell if she comes home and we haven't eaten it.'

Peggy nodded and dutifully went off to the bathroom. When she'd gone downstairs, I too hobbled off there and tried to clean myself up. I realised as I sat on the edge of the bath that all the time I'd been talking to Peggy I hadn't given Will a thought. It was the longest I'd gone without thinking of him since I'd arrived here.

Monday morning, and Peggy and I were standing outside *The News* office, both of us waiting to pluck up the courage to go in. I knew why Peggy was so frightened. She had no idea why I was dreading the day.

'OK, now remember,' I said. 'You tell Henfield you want to see him and have a proper talk to him.'

'Right,' said Peggy again. 'Rosie, you've been a real brick,' she said suddenly. 'I'm sorry I haven't been very nice to you, but I thought with you working at *The News* you would realise what was going on and tell my mum. Then it seemed a frightful idea, you staying with us, and I wished I'd never thought of it.'

'Well, yes, now I *have* realised, but it doesn't matter. In fact it's a good thing. I can help you sort it out.'

What was I saying? But Peggy was smiling—not much of a smile admittedly, but it was something.

'Right,' she said. And in we marched.

Billy was sitting with his back to me and the diary open in front of him, talking to Alan and Brian. 'Hiya, kid!' he said, turning round and giving me a wonderful smile. 'Good weekend?'

'Yes, yes, fine thanks.' Should I tell him I'd spent a large chunk of Sunday spying on him and his wife and family? No, I didn't think so either. So I said brightly, 'Shall I make the tea?'

'What a marvellous woman you are, Rosie,' said Billy.

If only he meant it . . . I made the tea and brought it in just as Marje arrived in her normal flurry of hat, scarf, cigarette and shopping bag.

'Ooh, you've made the tea! What a pet you are!' she said, reaching over and taking the cup I'd meant for myself. I went back and got another as Marje had a good cough and wafted the smoke away. Billy and Alan were busy on the telephone. Here was a chance. I'd promised Peggy I would ask, and Marje was the only person I could think of.

'Marje,' I whispered conspiratorially, 'can I ask you something?'

'Ask away, my dear,' said Marje, hunting the ashtray under a drift of yellowing copy paper.

'Well, a friend of mine is in a spot of bother . . .'

Marje looked up at me. 'And what sort of bother would that be?'

'Well the usual one, I'm afraid.' I whispered across the desk. 'You know, young girl, older man, and now . . .'

'Got caught has she?' asked Marje, inhaling deeply on her cigarette.

'Yes. And, well, she's desperate. I don't suppose you know anyone . . .'

I let the idea, the question, hang on the smoky air. I didn't want to have to spell it out, especially not with the men just yards away. Marje had found the ashtray. She put her cigarette in it and came across to me. Then she put her hands down on the desk and leaned over my type-writer until her face was only inches away from mine.

'Yes, as a matter of fact, I do know someone,' she said. For a moment I felt a surge of hope on Peggy's behalf. 'I know someone who promises to "help" young girls. Then the poor girl bleeds like a stuck pig and, if she's lucky, she gets over it. The unlucky ones end up in hospital. The really unlucky ones don't get that far.' Marje's eyes glittered. 'Just tell your friend that she's done what she's done and now she has to live with it. She can put the baby up for adoption. In a few months it will all be over and she can make a fresh start and be more sensible in future. But please, please, tell her not to go near any woman who offers to "help". Not if she wants to live and maybe have more children one day.'

With that Marje went back to her desk.

A few minutes later Billy came over with the diary. He stood there, looking at me with that half-smile on his face, and as he spoke he waved the pen in the air. Such a Will gesture . . . I had to swallow hard.

'So there's the village feature, the preview of the spring flower show and the cheque presentation for the Hospital League of Friends. If you and Marje would like to sort those out between you?'

'Sure,' said Marje. 'I could do the village feature—maybe Somerton— if Rosie does the flower show and the League of Friends.'

'Fine with me,' I said. At least it would get me out of the office.

But first I had to go and see Peggy. She was sitting at her desk.

'Hi,' I said quietly. 'I've spoken to Marje and I'm sorry, but she doesn't want anything to do with it. Says it's better to go ahead, even if you have the baby adopted. Have you arranged anything with Henfield?'

Peggy looked at me glassily. 'He's not coming in today. He rang in. He has to take his wife somewhere. I told him I had to see him, we had things that needed to be talked about. He put the phone down on me, Rosie. He just put the phone down. I don't know what to do.'

'It's going to be all right,' I said as forcefully as I could without yelling. 'Really. We'll talk about it tonight. We'll sort it all out.'

A spotty young man from advertising knocked and walked into the office. 'Mr Henfield about?' he asked cheerily.

'No,' said Peggy and fled from the room. I felt I should go after her, but young George was waiting for me. I grabbed my notebook and my handbag and left.

The flower show was very straightforward. It was their fiftieth, so I spoke to the organiser and got a bit of history. I spoke to the secretary of one of the gardening clubs, and to a nice old chap who'd been a gardener's boy when the very first show was held. George took lots of pretty pictures of flowers and we were back in the office by lunchtime.

I poked my head round Peggy's office door. She wasn't there. Her coat was on the peg and her handbag by the desk.

'Looking for Peggy?' said a girl from accounts, who was putting some papers on her desk. 'I think she must have gone home. I haven't seen her since early this morning. Nobody else has either. I asked.'

'But her bag and coat are here.'

'Maybe she wasn't well and left in a hurry.'

This was worrying. I went and looked in the ladies'. I ran down to reception. I asked the women on the switchboard. They took off their headsets. 'No, she hasn't been in since mid-morning,' one said crossly. 'And she didn't tell us where she was going.'

I ran back up to the editorial floor and bumped into George, who was bringing down the pictures of the flower show.

'Do you want to see these?' he asked, handing me the prints.

'Very nice,' I said, not looking at them. 'George, are you down to do the League of Friends cheque presentation tonight?'

'Yes, seven p.m. in the hospital. Do you want a lift up there?'

'Yes, please. And could we leave a bit early? I need to pop back home on my way.'

'Right you are. I'll see you in the yard at six thirty. That do you?'

'Perfect, George. You're a star.'

I felt an arm round my shoulder. For a second I hoped . . . But no.

'Hello, Phil,' I said as cheerily as I could. 'Ships in the night, I'm afraid. I'm just finishing off these few bits then I'm off to the League of Friends cheque presentation. Exciting, eh?'

'You could make anything exciting, Rosie,' said Phil, and it didn't sound smarmy because he was such a nice bloke. 'Will you be back in time for my break, about nine-ish? I'll buy you a drink if you are.'

'Maybe. I'll see,' I said and blew him a kiss as I picked up my copy to take to the subs' room. I knew Billy had listened to every word. Good.

Peggy wasn't at home.

'Hello, Mrs Brown, just popped in for something I've forgotten. I'll be back later,' I said as breezily as I could.

'Is our Peggy with you?'

'Peggy?' I said. 'I haven't seen her. Though'—oh blessed inspiration—'I think I saw Lenny in the office.'

'Oh, well. That explains everything, doesn't it?' said Mrs Brown indulgently. 'But she'll miss her mince and dumplings. She could have shown a bit of consideration and let me know.'

She muttered on as I dashed up to my room, really just so I could look into Peggy's room. She wasn't there. So where was she? I was beginning to get really worried.

It was raining when we left the hospital; cold, wet, miserable rain. The van rattled back to the office.

'George, are you going to print those up tonight?'

'Yes, they want them for tomorrow's paper.'

I didn't want to go back into the office. With both Phil and possibly Billy still there it was going to get complicated.

'Could you do me a favour, George? Could you look into Peggy's office and see if her coat and bag are still there?'

'Yes, of course, but why? Not anything wrong is there? Not with Peggy?' George looked anxious. I'd forgotten he had a soft spot for her.

'I don't know. But just do that for me, will you?'

He was back in five minutes. 'Coat and handbag still there,' he said. 'Now, will you tell me what's going on?'

'How long will you be printing your pics?'

'Half an hour or so.'

'Well, I'm going to wait in the van. I've got some thinking to do.'

'Is this something to do with Peggy?'

'Just be as quick as you can, will you, George? Please?'

He turned and ran, his skinny little body flying up the rickety stairs. He was back in record time. 'Now will you tell me what this is about?' he asked, settling into the seat as the rain lashed against the windscreen. 'What's happened to Peggy?'

'I think she may be in trouble. Do you know where Mr Henfield lives?'

'Yes. Big house on the hill, other side of town.'

'Can we go there, please?'

George folded his arms. 'Only if you tell me what's happened to Peggy.'

'Not my secret to tell, George. Sorry. But can we go to Henfield's house now, please?'

Reluctantly, he started the engine and we drove through the dark and the rain. George peered at the road, since the tiny windscreen wipers were pretty ineffective, while I kept a lookout for Peggy.

Finally, we pulled up outside a large 1930s house. The place was in darkness, the curtains open as though no one had been in all evening.

'How about you tell me what this is all about now?'

George sounded firm, sensible, adult. And I needed his help. So I told him Peggy's story.

'Poor Peggy,' said George, looking shocked. 'That Henfield, he's a bastard. Sorry, Rosie, 'scuse my language, but he is.'

'I'll not argue with that. But forget about him for the moment. Where can Peggy be?' I asked him. 'Her bag and her coat are still in the office. She's pregnant and desperate. Where would she go?'

'Well, that other girl threw herself in the pond at Friars' Mill, didn't she?' said George. He'd started the van and was turning it round. The little van tore through the night. At Friars' Mill George braked hard, then drove slowly along the road above the mill pool. We could hardly see a thing. Just the trees and the sheet of shining dark water.

'What's that?' George was hunched over the steering wheel, peering into the darkness. 'Over there. Something light.'

I opened the window to see better and was greeted with a swirl of rain. But, yes, I could see something. 'Something white, by the water.'

'Come on!' George jumped out of the van. He moved quickly through the dark and I stumbled after him, small branches whipping my face as I pushed past them. George was now racing along a path towards a patch of white at the edge of the mill pond. 'Peggy?' he shouted. 'Peggy! It's her! Rosie, we've found her!'

Thank God, I thought, thank God.

George had his jacket off and was wrapping it round Peggy, who was hardly conscious. The skirt and blouse that had been so neat this morning were torn and covered with mud. She seemed to have no shoes.

'Come on,' said George. 'We have to get her back to the van, get her into the warm. Rosie, you take one arm, and I'll take the other. Come on now, Peggy, not far. You can do it.'

Between us we staggered back to the van with her between us, slipping and sliding with our burden.

'No,' muttered Peggy. 'Leave me . . . just leave me.'

'Never,' said George fiercely. 'We're not leaving you anywhere.'

We soon had Peggy back by the roadside and, somehow, got her into the back of the van. I climbed in beside her, took my jacket off and wrapped it round her. Then I tried to rub some circulation into her limbs while George drove up to the hospital.

The place was all in darkness, except for a small door with a light over it. A sign said NIGHT ENTRANCE. I rang the bell and George pounded on the door, then we almost fell in as the door opened and a nurse in a dark blue dress and a fiercely starched white cap stood in the dimly lit hallway.

'Well?' she said. Then in a blink of an eye she seemed to assess the situation. She reached for a wheelchair in an alcove, pushed it towards Peggy and expertly manoeuvred her into it.

'She's been out in the rain,' I blurted. 'All day. She's pregnant and the father . . . well the father doesn't want to know.'

'Has she taken anything? Tried to harm herself or the baby?'

'I don't know.'

'Her name?'

'Peggy Brown.'

'Wait here, please.' The nurse disappeared with Peggy along an oak-panelled corridor. I followed. The nurse turned. 'I asked you to wait there,' she said, and vanished with Peggy.

So George and I waited. There was a bench but no coffee machine. The floor gleamed and it all smelt sharply, cleanly, of disinfectant and polish. It was very quiet. Where were the drunks and all the usual chaos of a casualty department late at night?

George was pacing up and down. 'Is she going to be all right, Rosie?' he asked anxiously.

'I'm sure she will be,' I said, though, like the nurse, I wondered if she'd taken anything.

'She's always been really nice to me.'

'Yes, I remember you saying. Helped you get the job.'

'Yes, and looked out for me when I started. She's a really good sort.'

'Yes, George, I know.' We waited. Eventually the nurse came back.

'I'm pleased to tell you your friend is in no danger,' she said crisply. 'Neither is her unborn child. Though whether that will please her I cannot say. She is severely chilled and in a state of shock, but otherwise seems unharmed. We shall probably keep her in for a few days.'

I gave her Peggy's name and address.

'Date of birth?' asked the nurse.

'September the 20th,' said George quickly. 'Same as mine, only she's six years older, so she's twenty-six.'

'Wouldn't it be easier if her parents did all this when they come up? I'm sure they'll be here as soon as we tell them,' I said.

The nurse snapped a folder shut. 'They can visit tomorrow between two and three p.m.,' she said. She must have seen the horrified look on my face because she added, 'Tell them if they telephone between seven thirty and eight o'clock in the morning I shall still be here and will tell them how their daughter is. But I'm sure'—and she almost smiled—'that she'll be home before the end of the week. Good night.'

By the time George dropped me off it was very late, and the poor lad still had to get the van back to the yard and walk home.

'What if we hadn't found her?' he asked, looking frightened.

'But we did, George—and you probably saved her life.'

He looked pleased and then with a final 'Good night' drove off. I took a deep breath and went into the house.

'Peggy?' said Mrs Brown sharply as soon as she heard the door click.

'No, sorry, it's me,' I said, going into the sitting room. The fire had died down, but the Browns were still sitting by it, waiting up for Peggy.

'Where's Peggy?' said Mrs Brown, worry making her angry.

'She's fine. But she's in hospital.'

Mrs Brown leaped to her feet. 'What's happened? Has there been an accident? Why is she there?'

So I told them the whole story. Well, not the bit about Lenny, but everything else. I'd thought about this in the van coming home and I'd decided it would be much easier if they knew before they got to the hospital. If I told them, then at least Peggy wouldn't have to.

When I told them Peggy was pregnant, Mrs Brown gave a little cry, her hand on her mouth. When I told them the father was Henfield, Mr Brown's right hand clenched into a fist and he pushed it repeatedly into his other hand, as if practising for Henfield's face.

When I told them how we'd found Peggy by the millpond Mrs Brown went white. 'Silly, silly girl,' she said. 'I should have known, I should have realised . . .' Her eyes were full of tears.

'She really is going to be all right,' I said. I told them about the hospital and what the nurse had said.

'And the baby?'

'That's all right too.'

They didn't say anything and I didn't know if that was good news.

Mr Brown looked up at me. 'It seems to me that you've done our Peg a great service today, Rosie. If you hadn't looked for her and found her, she could still be out there now'—Mrs Brown gave another small, strangulated cry—'so we are very grateful to you. Thank God you were here.'

Suddenly, Mrs Brown started bustling with the tea tray. 'You'll be wet and cold yourself. I shall make you some cocoa, then you must have a nice hot bath even though it's so late.'

She was busying herself in order not to think, I could see that. As she put a cup and saucer down on the tray, she knocked the milk jug flying. I thought she was going to cry.

'Now now, Doreen,' said Mr Brown soothingly as he came back with a cloth. 'No use crying over spilt milk, is there? What's done's done and now we have to think what to do next.'

I went upstairs and peeled off my wet and grubby clothes. As I had a special dispensation, I ran a bath. I used every last drop of hot water and luxuriated in the warmth creeping back into my bones.

Peggy came home on the bus three days later. Her dad went to meet her at the bus stop.

While he was gone, Mrs Brown fussed back and forth in the kitchen. She had cleaned the house from top to bottom and had prepared the meal with extra care. There were lamb chops and mint sauce. She'd made an apple crumble—Peggy's favourite—with the stored apples. It was as if she were expecting an important visitor, not her daughter.

When Peggy walked in I thought there'd be a big welcome, but Mrs Brown just said, 'You're back then,' and went to strain the potatoes. Conversation was stilted and awkward, with many silences.

'Lovely meal, Mum, thank you,' said Peggy, her eyes pleading for a response from her mother.

'Well, I never trusted hospital food,' said Mrs Brown, getting up and taking a dish out to the scullery, almost unable to look at her daughter.

Peggy and I did the washing-up. 'It's all right, Peggy, I'll do it if you want to put your feet up.'

'She's not ill now,' snapped Mrs Brown. We washed up in silence, suffocated by the atmosphere. Then there was a ring at the door.

George shuffled in carrying a bunch of primroses. 'I brought these for you, Peggy,' he said, blushing. 'I just wanted to know you were all right.'

'Thank you, George,' said Peggy, giving him the first smile I'd seen since she was home. 'That's very kind of you.'

'Yes, George,' said Mr Brown. 'Mrs Brown and I, well, we can't say how much we want to thank you. If you hadn't been there, I don't know what would have happened.'

'Well, it was Rosie really. I just drove the van.'

'We know what you did, and we're very grateful.'

'Well, as long as you're OK now, Peggy.' George was trying to come up with an exit line. 'So I'll see you at work then, shall I?'

'No,' snapped Mrs Brown. 'She won't be going back there. Never.'

'Oh, right. OK, then.' George looked awkward. 'Well, I only wanted to see that you were better, so I'll be going now. Goodbye.' And he fled.

'Well you might have offered the lad a drink,' said Mrs Brown.

'Drink?' said her husband. 'He doesn't look old enough.'

Later, when Peggy was going up to bed, her mother suddenly reached out her hand and put it on Peggy's arm and, with eyes full of tears, she looked at her and said fiercely, 'Don't you ever do anything that stupid again.'

'**D**o you like it?'

Carol was in the reception area at *The News*, taking off her coat to show me her new outfit.

'It's a bit thin for now, but I just wanted to show you.' It was the material she'd bought on the market, which she'd made into a skirt. She was wearing it with a wide, black, patent-leather belt and a fitted white blouse. She looked stunning.

'Did you make that yourself?'

'Yes, of course. The skirt's not as full as I'd like because there wasn't really enough material, but it's all right, isn't it?'

'Great,' I said. 'What a clever mummy you have,' I said to Libby, who was waiting patiently by a full shopping bag. I looked up again. 'Time for a coffee?'

Smiling, Carol shrugged back into her shabby brown coat, picked up her shopping bag, took Libby's hand, and we went over to Silvino's.

As soon as we got there Libby wanted the loo. So while Carol took her I ordered the coffees and sat doodling in my notebook.

'What's that?' asked Carol as she came back.

'It was my favourite outfit when I was a student,' I said. I'd sketched a girl—a very long-legged girl, not at all like me—in my favourite denim mini, a strappy vest, and my lovely, lovely cowboy boots. I quickly drew in the last tiny detail and showed it to Carol.

'What's that?' she asked, peering at the paper.

'My bellybutton stud,' I said. 'It was a little fake diamond.'

'In your bellybutton? You never!' She looked shocked. 'Didn't it hurt?'

I shook my head, smiling.

'And what did you wear on top?'

'I had a lovely little denim jacket.'

'No, I mean on top of this,' said Carol. 'You couldn't go out in this.'

'Yes, I did.'

'But . . . it looks just like your underpinnings!' she said.

She looked so worried that I drew her something a bit less revealing.

'Here's the outfit I wore to my cousin's wedding last summer,' I said, drawing a knee-length, flippy silk skirt and boxy jacket. 'That's a sort of bright peacock blue and the edging and lining'—I scribbled swiftly—'are a jade green. And my shoes, ah, my shoes.' I tried to draw them, but didn't do a very good job. 'They had really high heels. I could only just walk in them and kept sinking in the grass. They were the same jadey colour as the edging on my jacket and across the middle they had little tiny jewels. Well, bits of coloured glass, really, but the effect was good.'

'I would love to have shoes like that,' Carol said.

'You'd be a princess,' said Libby.

'Yes, my love, I would. A real princess.'

That day, Mr Brown went to see Henfield.

'So what's happening?' I asked Peggy. She'd just knocked on the door to my bedroom, where I was putting some ironing away.

'He denied it,' Peggy replied, coming into the room. 'Said there was no proof the baby was his.'

And you couldn't get DNA testing, could you? Not yet.

'What did your father do? What did he say? What happened?'

'There wasn't much he could do. Honestly, I can't believe how stupid I was to get involved with him.'

'Easy to be wise with hindsight. And what will you do? Are you going to keep the baby?'

'I don't know. Don't care really.' She looked down at the small but noticeable bump. 'I keep hoping it's all a nasty dream and I'll wake up and everything will be just as it was. Oh, Rosie, it was awful when my dad came to see me in hospital. He was so upset. I felt I'd really let him down. And as for Mum. She's so ashamed of me. I think she'd have preferred it if I'd, if, well, if you hadn't found me.'

'Rubbish! Don't you dare think that! If you'd seen them on Monday night, they were beside themselves. And when you came home yesterday your mum did your favourite food.'

Actually, I couldn't understand it. I thought that they'd be so relieved Peggy was safe that they would be happy about the baby.

'Mum's written to my Aunty Emily. She lives in London. Mum thinks I should go and stay with her, until . . . until the baby's born. Then I can just have the baby and have it adopted. And no one will know. I can come back home and everything will be just the way it was. But it won't be, will it? There'll be a baby. Wherever it is, there'll be a baby.' She sank onto my bed, looking wretched.

There was no question of Peggy going back to work. Instead she gradually took over the housekeeping. She did the washing and ironing and cooked the evening meal. She would then collapse onto the sofa while her mother or I did the washing-up. Nothing was said, not in my hearing anyway, but the threat of Aunty Emily still hung over the house. Whether Mrs Brown had had a reply yet, I didn't know, but we were all walking on eggshells. Nothing was actually said about the baby, either. It was as if, by not mentioning it, it didn't exist.

The atmosphere in the house had been so heavy that even Janice had kept away, but one day she crept back into the kitchen with her satchel.

'You come in, Janice, and have a cup of tea and some cake,' Mrs Brown said, and she led the child towards the table, her arms protectively round her thin shoulders, as if she could be kind to Janice when she couldn't be kind to her own daughter.

A few days later, Janice was at the table doing her homework, when she started looking at Peggy quizzically. 'Peggy, are you having a baby?'

Peggy went bright red. 'What makes you think that?'

'Well, you look as though you are.'

I remembered she had seven brothers, most of them younger than she was.

'Well, actually, Janice, yes I am. But it's a secret.'

'Well, it won't be a secret for long, will it?' said Janice and calmly went back to the amoeba or Latin, whatever it was.

Mrs Brown must have thought so too. She started producing strange clothes for Peggy to wear. Maybe even her own old maternity clothes she'd dug out and altered. Even by the standards of the day they looked bleak. But they inspired Janice to put her pencil down for a while.

'Rosie, will you tell me about the clothes your editor back home wears?' she asked, pushing a lock of lank hair back behind her ears.

'Well,' I said, 'they are always beautifully cut, stylish without being gimmicky and absolutely immaculate.'

Janice listened attentively, as if she had to memorise the details for yet another test, as if she were saving up the information for future use.

Peggy watched her for a moment, then disappeared upstairs and came down again holding what looked like a tiny leather purse.

'A present for you,' she said to Janice. 'It's a manicure set. Look, there are some nail scissors, some emery boards, and some little sticks to push your cuticles down nice and tidily. See?'

Janice looked, her bright little eyes lighting up her face. 'For me?'

'Yes,' said Peggy. 'Now, go and give your hands a really good wash and I'll show you how to use everything. And if you look after your nails properly then next week I'll let you have some of my nail varnish.'

Janice scuttled off to the scullery to wash her hands and I thought how kind Peggy could be, and how a manicure—however unlikely— seemed the perfect distraction for them both.

CHAPTER SEVEN

'JOB FOR YOU,' said Billy, his eyes dancing with laughter.

I grinned back, relishing the warmth of his smile, the feeling that he and I were about to share a secret joke.

'Sir Howard Castleton,' said Billy, 'is a junior government minister.'

'Isn't he the one who said women weren't safe driving cars because they would be too busy looking in the mirror to check their lipstick?' I interrupted indignantly.

'The very same,' said Billy, his huge smile making him look young and happy, and also making me long to kiss him. Instead, I had to content myself with gazing into his big brown eyes. 'And he's coming here to open the new driving-test centre today.'

'Is he? Well, I'd like to tell him just what I think of him and his crackpot outdated ideas. Everyone knows that women are better drivers than men, much safer, fewer accidents, not so reckless—'

'OK, OK,' laughed Billy, handing me a piece of paper with the details. 'Somehow I thought you'd feel like that.'

'Honestly, he must be living in the Dark Ages,' I rattled on, well and truly on my soapbox now. 'I mean, even in the 1950s. Weren't women driving during the war? They drove cars and buses and lorries . . .'

I stopped. Billy was standing close to me holding a finger to his mouth for silence. Then he leaned forward and put his finger gently to my lips instead. His eyes held mine for one, two, three seconds. He looked as if he wanted to kiss me . . . But he suddenly turned away, went back to his desk. 'He's due at ten o'clock. I've booked a photographer.' He glanced up at me. I was still standing where he had left me, clutching the piece of paper. 'You can drive, of course?' he asked.

'Of course,' I said. 'Passed first time. Bought my own car soon afterwards. No accidents, no insurance claims.'

'I thought that's how it would be,' he said, looking at me and smiling.

I picked up my bag and ran downstairs, out into the spring sunshine, with my hand on my lips, remembering Billy's touch and the expression in his eyes . . .

At the new driving-test centre, Sir Howard Castleton was ushered away by his flunkies as soon as he'd made his short and boring speech, so I didn't get a chance to interview him.

But it didn't matter—because Billy had wanted to kiss me. I almost sang it to myself. Billy had wanted to kiss me. I dragged myself back to work. Concentrate, girl. Concentrate.

The chief examiner said he was pretty sure that, actually, a greater number of women than men passed their driving test first time. He could give me the figures, if I liked.

'Women drivers are the best.' The story would write itself, though I doubted it would do much to stop the flood of women-driver jokes.

'Want a lift back?' asked George.

'Oh, yes, please. Thanks.' I got into the van, still in a dream. Billy . . . But then we were just getting going when I spotted the window display in the Home and Colonial. It couldn't be, could it? Yes, it was. In the centre of the window was a wonky-looking pyramid made up of bottles of washing-up liquid. Squeezy had arrived.

'Hang on a minute, George,' I said. 'I've just got to go in there.' I dashed inside and joined the queue.

When I clambered triumphantly back into the van with two bottles of washing-up liquid, George asked me how things were going at home.

'Peggy's mum looking forward to being a granny then, is she?'

'Not with undiluted joy, no.'

'Is it safe for me to pop round and see Peggy yet?'

'If you take your tin helmet and body armour. Peggy needs cheering up and I know she likes you.'

'Does she? Does she really?' George seemed quite excited.

I went back up into the office, wondering whether Billy would look at me in that magical way again, wondering if he would say anything. But the newsroom was empty apart from Marje at her desk in her little cloud of smoke. She looked up from the notes she was scribbling and asked suddenly, 'Did your friend sort out her little problem?'

'Yes, well no, well, she's decided to go ahead and have the baby.'

'Mmm.' More scribbling, then, 'Is Peggy coming back to work soon?'

'No, I don't think so.' The official line was that she was on sick leave.

'She was quite close to Henfield, wasn't she?'

'Yes, but—'

'Don't worry. I won't breathe a word. Henfield's secretaries have a habit of leaving suddenly. She should have known. Silly girl.'

'You can't blame her!' I said indignantly. 'Henfield shouldn't have led her astray, abused his position.'

'Henfield is a great editor but a swine of a man. She is old enough to know what she was doing,' said Marje, heading down to the subs' room. I shrugged. It wasn't worth arguing about any more.

When I got home from work, George was there, sitting at the kitchen table with Peggy, having a cup of tea. He was there to watch my great washing-up liquid demonstration.

'See. One squeeze and it gets everything nice and clean. No rubbing bits of green soap or using washing powder. Simple, isn't it?'

Mrs Brown eyed it all very suspiciously, but later, after she'd done the tea things she came out into the kitchen and said, 'Well, it works. I'll grant you that. Very clever, but I bet it costs a lot.'

'No matter, Mrs Brown,' I said, feeling like Lady Bountiful. 'I promise you that as long as I'm staying here, I will buy the washing-up liquid. Anything to make life easier.'

'Very nice, I'm sure,' said Mrs Brown. 'Another cup of tea, George?'

George became quite a regular visitor. He even started helping Janice with her homework. But, while the atmosphere at home was gradually getting a little easier, it still wasn't exactly a laugh a minute. I escaped when I could. I went to a jazz club with Phil. It was very smoky, in a cellar that seemed to smell of damp and to be full of teachers from the boys' grammar school. I didn't think I liked jazz, but I enjoyed the evening there. I drank whisky and ginger and felt quite mellow.

I went to the theatre on press tickets. 'Anyone want to go to the Hippodrome?' asked Billy one morning, waving a set of tickets in the air. 'Normal reviewer can't do it. It's a thriller. Any takers?'

'I'll have them,' I said. It had to be better than sitting in at the Browns'. 'Do you think Carol would like to come?'

Billy looked surprised. 'Carol? Yes. I'm sure she would. I'll ask her and let you know tomorrow.'

'Tell her to come early.'

I didn't recognise Carol when she arrived at the Hippodrome. She was wearing a boxy jacket and a pencil skirt.

'Gosh, don't you look smart!' I said, and then worried that I might seem condescending.

'Are they all right? I made them myself. Billy said reviewers get the best seats so I thought I'd better look a bit posh,' she said. 'It's ages since I've been to the theatre. Proper theatre that is, not just the pantomime.'

'Come on. We've got time for a drink.'

Up in the circle bar hardly anyone had arrived. 'Gin and tonic,' I said to Carol, as I brought the drinks over to the table. 'Is that all right?'

'Smashing,' she said, she lifted the glass and breathed in the fumes of the gin. It was so like Caz I had the most dreadful ache for my own life, my real life. For a moment the yearning was a sharp physical pain—that longing to be in a bar with Caz, having a good gossip over a bottle of Chablis. Oh, how I missed it. I felt tears coming. I blinked quickly.

'Strong, isn't it?' said Carol, happily knocking back the gin.

'I'll just get us another. Before the rush,' I said. 'On expenses,' I added so that she would enjoy it even more and not feel obliged to offer to pay. When I came back with them—doubles again—Carol nudged me and nodded towards a woman just coming in. She was removing a jacket to show a fitted dress with a boat neckline.

'What a corker!' whispered Carol. 'Not like her.' She pointed towards a well-upholstered matron.

Soon Carol and I were studying all the people coming in. In the circle bar we had the pick of small-town fashion to gaze at, and here and there would be a dress Carol thought she could copy.

'He's a bit of all right,' said Carol suddenly, gazing at an elegant young man who'd come in with an older woman, 'but no, he's got a moustache. That's no good. It would tickle, wouldn't it?' She started to giggle. It was infectious, and as the second bell rang and we went in to find our seats, we were shaking with silent laughter.

In the darkness of the theatre, Carol sat forward in her seat, totally absorbed in the action, happy and relaxed. Meanwhile, I thought of Billy and felt guilty and miserable. How could I be a friend to Carol when I wanted Billy so much? And I was sure that Billy wanted me as much as I wanted him.

At the end of the evening, we made our way out into the fresh air.

'I've had a really nice time,' Carol said, as we stood at the edge of the town centre where our ways parted. 'Really nice.' She beamed happily.

'It does me good to get out of the house sometimes and away from the kids. Perhaps we can have a coffee soon. If my slave-driving husband will let you out. My treat next time.'

'Great. Yes. Soon,' I said, and managed to smile.

It was as if Billy was playing a game. I'd catch him looking at me, but I wouldn't be able to work out the expression on his face. At other times he would bounce ideas off me.

'I like your American way of thinking,' he would say. 'It's different, fresh. Better than sleepy old England, eh?'

Or he'd hand me a story and go out of his way to be helpful, leaning over my desk, scribbling names and addresses of contacts. It was very much the way Will and I worked together. And although I loved the closeness, if I got Billy to love me, then what about Carol? The kids? So I did what I always do when things are tricky—I went shopping.

Only there weren't many shops. There was a tiny Marks and Spencer, which was full of cardigans and underpants and dreary dresses. There were a number of chichi little shops that sold 'ladies' modes'. One had a fur coat in the window. I think not.

The nearest the town had to a department store was Adcocks, which actually had a pair of jeans in the window. True, they were in a side window under a sign saying TEENAGE FASHION, but it was a start.

I'd hardly got through the door when a middle-aged woman in a black dress came sweeping down on me. 'Can I help you, madam?'

'Oh, yes, please. You have some jeans in the window.'

'Jeans? Ah, yes, the denim slacks.' She wrinkled her nose as though there was a nasty smell. 'Miss Marshall will help you. Miss Marshall!'

Another woman came gliding over and led me through a warren of rooms, up steps, down steps until we came to a room where a display model was wearing a pair of jeans and a peasant-style top.

'Could I see what jeans you have, please?'

'We have those, madam.'

'Is that the only style you have?'

'Yes, madam. Would you like to try a pair? What size are we?'

I wanted to say, 'Well, we're a size ten but I don't know about you, sunshine,' but I resisted. Instead, 'Size ten,' I said meekly. 'And I'd like to try the top as well, please.'

She looked at me, showed me into a tiny fitting room with a wonky chair, and then brought me the clothes. I tried the blouse on first. The cut of the jeans was pretty rubbish, but they'd do. I took them out to Frosty Face and followed her back through the warren of rooms to the till.

Saturday morning was sunny, and when Phil came round and asked me if I fancied a day at the seaside, I leapt at the chance. Just the opportunity to wear my new clothes, perfect for the back of a bike. Though Mrs Brown didn't think so. As I came downstairs in my new jeans she asked, 'Is that considered decent in America, then?'

Mr Brown laughed. 'Of course it is,' he said. 'Those are cowboy trousers. That's what cowboys wear.'

'Not like that, they don't,' sniffed Mrs Brown.

'These are girls' jeans, Mrs Brown,' I said, and gave a little wiggle. And then I felt guilty because Peggy was standing there in a shapeless old skirt.

'Enjoy yourself,' she said. I could see envy in her eyes. I pretended not to.

It was about thirty miles to the coast. Quite a long way on bumpy roads on the back of a bike, but it was just wonderful to feel so free. The sun was shining and spring was well and truly here. We drove straight onto the prom and parked up. I felt like a kid and raced Phil down to the shore. I pulled off my shoes and felt the sand between my toes and the little ripple of waves breaking on my feet.

'Ow! It's cold!'

'Still early in the year,' laughed Phil.

We walked the length of the bay and then put our shoes back on to scramble up a path to the top of the cliff. There was a large corrugated-tin building in a grim shade of green. On one side, in huge white letters, was painted TEAS. Phil went in and emerged a few minutes later carrying a tin tray with two thick white cups and saucers, and a couple of solid-looking scones on plates. He brought it over to the top of the cliff where I was sitting on the grass, looking at the huge drifts of pale pink thrift coming into bloom beside the paths.

'Beautiful, isn't it?' said Phil.

I nodded. And then burst into tears. I don't know why it happened at that particular moment. Maybe because I'd started to relax.

'What's the matter?' asked Phil, looking concerned and frightened.

'I want to go ho-o-me,' I wailed. 'Real home. Where I belong.'

Phil found a nice, big, clean, white hanky in a pocket and passed it to me. Then, after I'd given my nose a good honk, he put his arm round me. 'You're bound to get homesick occasionally.'

'I did at first, dreadfully, but then I thought I'd got used to it. I haven't been thinking about home so much,' I said with a sniff.

And I hadn't. I had got drawn into this 1950s life. Sometimes, home—proper home—seemed like a dream. It was getting further and further away from me. And maybe that was the problem. I was scared of forgetting where I came from, where I belonged, who I really was.

Then the floodgates opened and I started.

'Everything's so different here. I want home and my friends and comfy clothes and proper showers and big televisions and computers and my phone and texting and fluffy towels and garlic and curry and soft loo roll and cars and the Internet. I want everything to be light and bright and white and clean, not scruffy and shabby and smelling of mice. I want creams and shampoos and lotions and mascara you don't have to spit on and my boots and my duvet and my iPod. I want . . . oh I want Caz and my mum and dad. But most of all I want Will.'

I only stopped because I couldn't breathe and cry and talk at the same time. If this was Narnia, of course, there'd be Aslan to guard me. Or a faun or a talking horse. At the very least I'd have a bottle of magic elixir to make things better, or a magic hunting-horn to summon help.

I thought of the words of that hymn again: 'Dwellers all in time and space.' Somewhere I'd lost my way in time and space. I was locked out of where I should be. I wanted to go home and I didn't know how. Panic was bubbling up into my throat, choking me. There must be some way I could get home. There had to be.

Phil was brilliant. He kept his arm round me and at the same time gave me my tea in the big white cup.

'Drink this,' he said. 'It will make you feel better. You'll go home again. Of course you will. Don't worry. Home is still there waiting for you.' His voice was gentle, repetitive, hypnotic. I began to calm down. Took deep breaths. Let his voice murmur on, soothingly.

I looked out at the sea and wondered if it was the same sea I'd seen before. For weeks I'd been battling to find out where I was and why I was here. And I just didn't know if I could any more.

At least I'd stopped howling. I wiped my eyes and sniffed. 'I'm sorry, Phil. You bring me on a nice day out and I just go and cry all over you.'

'Nothing to apologise for. It's all quite normal, quite natural,' Phil said soothingly. 'We used to see it in the army, time and again. Young lads getting on with things, no bother. Then suddenly, for no reason, out of nowhere, they'd be struck by the most awful homesickness. I remember getting really drunk one night because I suddenly missed my dog, of all things. It's bound to happen. Only natural. Don't worry about it. Here . . .' He passed me a scone. I nibbled it, still sniffing.

'So how long are you going to be over here for?'

'That's the trouble. I don't know. But I don't think it's going to be long.'

'Well, that's all right then,' said Phil easily. 'If you're not here very long, then all you have to do is make the most of it while you are. Get your head down and get on with it and you might find you enjoy it.' He smiled at me. He looked so straightforward and cheerful. His pale blue eyes were full of kindly concern and I really wished I could love him.

So we drank our tea and threw the remains of the scones for the seagulls, and then we walked back along the cliff path to the promenade. The turf was springy under my feet and Phil was holding my hand and whistling. The sun glinted on the waves and we seemed to have the whole world pretty much to ourselves. Wherever and whenever it was, it was a very good moment in time and space.

Back on the bike, we took a roundabout route home via a tiny fishing village. There was a pub right down by the little quayside and lots of boats were pulled up on the beach. It was a place of lobster pots and fishing nets. The sort of place so simple and unspoilt that you don't think it exists any more. And I suppose it probably doesn't. We sat on the wall and ate crab sandwiches, drank a beer or two and watched the sun set. Then we climbed back on the bike and came home.

'It's been a lovely day, Phil,' I said when we got to the Browns' house. 'And thank you for being so kind. I'm sorry I was an idiot.'

'Shh, not an idiot. Just normal,' Phil said. He took me in his arms and kissed me gently. 'I don't know who this Will is who you miss so badly. But I think he's a jolly lucky chap.'

Then he went back to his bike and roared off.

'Nearly finished,' I called across to Brian. 'The subs can have this in two minutes.'

There's a strange atmosphere in an office at the end of the day. *The News* was a twenty-four-hour operation. Yet after six o'clock, the atmosphere changed. Unlike the twenty-first century, where office and printing centre were separate, in the 1950s they were in the same building. Evening work was done against a background of the sound of the presses rumbling away in the cavernous press room on the ground floor. Instead of the office and advertising staff in the building, you'd bump into printers in aprons and overalls, covered in ink. Or messengers carrying copy from the subs to the printers. *The News* printed five different editions, and by the time the last edition started printing at about three in the morning, the first edition had been printed, bundled up and stacked onto the fleet of vans that rumbled out into the darkness through the big gates.

Although it was still daylight outside, the light had begun to fade, and the atmosphere in the office was closer, more intimate than in daytime. I finished typing my story, pulled the paper out of the typewriter and separated it into the three copies, making one or two pencil corrections on each sheet in turn.

I could feel Billy watching me. I looked up and saw that he was sitting at his desk reading some story. But I knew he wasn't really reading it. He was waiting for something. Waiting for me. No. He couldn't be.

I checked the corrections and folded the sets of copy paper—story facing outwards—making a show of having finished.

'I'll take those along to the subs if you like,' said Billy, picking up the stories with his own.

'Thanks.'

And yes, I could have picked up my jacket and been down the stairs and out of that building in thirty seconds flat. It was late. I'd finished. I was ready to go home. But I wasn't. And I didn't.

Instead I got my jacket and left it draped across my desk—obvious to anyone that I was still in the building but about to leave—went to the loo and washed my hands. And I waited. All right. I knew I shouldn't have done. But I had to know how Billy felt. Is that so bad?

Billy would be a few minutes in with the subs. Say five minutes, I thought to myself. Five minutes would be about right. And I counted down. Sad, isn't it? But I counted, '300, 299, 298, 297 . . .' standing there by the dingy little washbasin. When I got to 129—still more than two minutes to go—I wanted to change my mind and go back to the newsroom. But I made myself wait.

And it worked. At a silent, triumphant 'One!' I walked back down the corridor and entered the newsroom at the same time as Billy. He went to the coat stand and got his jacket. It was only natural that we should walk down the stairs together and out into the marketplace. Just two colleagues who happened to leave the office at the same time.

But there was a tension in the air—a wonderful, toe-tingling tension, a sense of possibilities . . . just like the time I first met Will. Only then I wasn't sure if he was the man for me. This time round I knew. I'd never been more certain in my life. All the time we were talking I was so aware that it was just the two of us. And I knew he was too.

'Well, the newsroom has certainly changed since you came,' Billy said. 'You look at things differently. It's good. Must be the American way.'

(I had long given up explaining that I wasn't American. After all, it acted as explanation for such a lot of things.)

He was smiling down at me. 'When you talk, well, sometimes I don't know what you're on about—computers, and phones you can put in your pocket, and getting information out of the air—but I like to hear you talk about it. And I like your ideas for the paper. You look forward, not into the past all the time. It's the future we want to be thinking of. I love to hear you talk about it. In fact'—he stopped and turned to face me—'in fact, I just love to hear you talk.'

His words hung on the evening air. The way he was looking at me, you can be sure he wasn't thinking of work. I held my breath.

'Rosie, do you have to go straight home? Shall we . . . ? Maybe a drink?' He looked at me anxiously, and I knew this was more than a quick after-work drink with colleagues.

'Why not?' I said. 'Where?'

And with that there came a shout.

'Dad! Da-ad!'

A small figure on a battered bike was hurtling down a narrow side street and into the marketplace. Oh, no, talk about timing . . .

'Davy! Whoa, careful son!'

The small boy and bike had screeched to a halt with the help of feeble brakes and the toes of his shoes. Round his waist he wore a mock leather, cowboy-style belt with holsters, each holding a toy gun. He sat astride his bike, face bright red, hair sticking up on end, and he had a huge grin on his face. 'Hiya, Dad! I thought it was you.'

Billy was caught off guard, but quickly laughed. 'Well, if it isn't Two-Gun Tex!' he said. 'Howdy, pardner!' He looked at his watch. 'Hey, it's time you were home. Mum will be worried.'

'Yes, I know. I've been to Kevin's, but if I'm with you, that's all right then, isn't it?'

Billy tried to look cross, but didn't make a good job of it. 'Right, then we'd better get home as quick as we can. Come on, cowboy.'

He turned to me. 'Nice talking to you, Rosie. See you tomorrow.'

And with that he went, loping along with one hand on Davy's shoulder as the little boy pedalled down the street. I stood there, staring after him, helpless with frustration. What had Billy been planning? He clearly wanted to be alone with me. Where might it have led? I longed to be with Billy, but part of me was pleased, maybe relieved, that Davy had come along just when he did.

As I pushed open the back door to the Browns' and went into the kitchen, I knew something was up. Mrs Brown was bustling around with the best cups and saucers, white porcelain with a little blue flower, and the place was fizzing with excitement.

'Oh, Rosie! You're just in time! Go on through.'

In time for what? Intrigued, I hung up my jacket on the back of the kitchen door, dumped my bag and walked through to the sitting room.

Mr Brown was sitting in his usual armchair, with a bottle of beer and a bemused expression. Meanwhile, on the sofa sat George, also with a bottle of beer and looking completely at home, while next to him was Peggy, smiling rather tensely. Mrs Brown came through with the tray laden with tea things, including neatly cut sandwiches, a huge fruit cake and a Battenberg cake, with its pink and yellow squares. Gosh. That was a real sign of celebration—a shop-bought Battenberg. She placed the tray on the table, then went to the dark oak sideboard and opened one of the cupboards. From it she took a bottle of Harvey's Bristol Cream sherry and three small gold-rimmed glasses. She poured the sherry into the glasses, then handed one to me and one to Peggy.

'It's like Christmas!' giggled Peggy.

'What are we celebrating?' I asked, bemused by the lightening of the grim atmosphere that had pressed so heavily on the Browns recently.

'A toast,' said Mrs Brown. 'Shall you do it, Father, or shall I?'

Mr Brown waved a hand in her direction.

'To George and Peggy!' said Mrs Brown grandly, raising her glass. 'To their future happiness together!'

The sherry hadn't even got to my lips and I was already choking. 'Together? George and Peggy? You mean . . . ?'

'Yes,' said George, beaming proudly. 'I asked Peggy to marry me and she said yes.' He reached out and held Peggy's hand. He looked young and proud and there were a million questions I wanted to ask him, chiefly, 'Do you know what you're doing?' and, 'Are you sure?' But he looked so pleased that instead I raised my glass of sherry and said, 'Congratulations! I wish you all the happiness in the world!'

Then I recognised the atmosphere in the room for what it was. It wasn't excitement—except perhaps on George's part. It wasn't celebration. It wasn't even happiness. No, it was relief. Sheer, unadulterated relief. A huge problem had been solved, thanks to young George.

Peggy had found a husband. Peggy had found a father for her baby. Respectability and reputation were saved. No wonder the Browns were so pleased. George had ridden to the rescue. No matter that he was six years younger than his bride-to-be, or the couple had never gone out together. He had presented himself as husband material and they had been only too eager to snap him up.

As long as the child was there and the mother was on her own, no one would ever forget that she was a fallen woman, a girl who had sold herself too cheaply. For the rest of her life, and her child's life, she would be labelled as the woman who was loose or foolish. A few might condemn the man involved, but more would condemn her for giving herself too easily, for not ensuring a proper father for her unborn child.

But getting pregnant and getting married, well, that was a different thing. That was just two young people so in love that they couldn't wait. Not ideal, but forgivable. Except that it wasn't George's baby . . .

'Are you sure about this?' I had to ask him as the others busied themselves with plates and finding the big sharp knife to cut the cake.

'Never surer. I've loved Peggy ever since I was about fourteen. I thought she was a great girl. And when I was doing my national service, well'—he gave Peggy a quick sideways glance—'I used to dream about her. She was always the one for me and now I'm the one for her too.'

'But . . . but you're only twenty.'

'Soon be twenty-one. My mum said that as I could do it soon enough without her say-so she might as well give me her blessing now.'

'Permission?' I was floundering here.

'Yes, because I'm not twenty-one yet. But that doesn't mean I don't know what I'm doing. We'll be fine, just fine,' he said firmly.

I went to bed early, and I was sitting up reading *Pride and Prejudice* and wondering idly how Will would look in breeches and a wet shirt, when Peggy knocked and came in. She sat on the bed. I waited.

'I couldn't do it on my own,' she said. 'I know you said you had lots of friends who did. But I just couldn't. And I couldn't give the baby away either.' She put her hands over the bump. 'This is the best way.'

I still didn't say anything.

'George has always had a bit of a crush on me. He's a nice lad.'

It was no good. I couldn't keep my lips zipped any longer.

'If George had asked you out six months ago, six weeks ago even, you wouldn't have considered it. You would have laughed at him for his cheek. And now you're thinking of *marrying* him. Marrying's for ever, Peggy. And what about George? Are you being fair to him? He barely earns enough to keep himself and you're saddling him with someone else's baby. Have you thought about that?'

'Of course I've thought of it!' snapped Peggy. 'I've thought of so much that my head's bursting with thinking! All I know is that this is the best way for me. It's best for my parents too. And it's best for the baby. And as for George . . . No, I'm not madly in love with George, but somehow, he brought me back to this life. I know he cares about me. He always has. And I'm beginning to care about him. Really. And if George looks after me and this baby, I will look after him. I'm going to do my very best to make him happy. I promise that. It's what he deserves.'

I clambered out of bed and hugged her. What else could I do?

Billy was ignoring me and I knew it was because he'd nearly made a pass at me. He hardly spoke to me. And when he did, it was brisk and businesslike. Perfectly polite, but he was definitely avoiding eye contact. Yet sometimes I knew he was looking at me across the office.

I knew he was falling for me, but was trying hard not to, because of his loyalty to Carol. I admired him for that. And I loved his loyalty to his children. He was their father and he took that seriously. It was wonderful that he felt the same as I did. But he wasn't going to do anything about it because he was a married man, a family man. I genuinely admired him for that, even if it made me feel utterly miserable.

I was sitting in the newsroom, typing up a very dull story about Bob-a-Job week (sending small boys to knock on doors offering their services. Paedo fantasy or what?) and trying not to put my head down on the typewriter and weep, when young George came bouncing in.

'All ready for Thursday then, Rosie?' he asked happily, to a chorus of comments from the men in the room.

Word had got round about the wedding and had stunned everybody. Marje had guessed the story but I knew I could trust her to say nothing, so everyone presumed Peggy's baby was George's, which meant he got all the sympathy—and the rude comments.

George took it all, and responded merely by grinning.

Mrs Brown was busy trying to alter a dress for Peggy to wear on the day, letting out seams, moving buttons. 'It's not the way I thought my only daughter would be getting married. Not the way at all.'

'My friend Kate had a lovely dress when she got married, even though she was six months pregnant,' I said chattily as I brought them a tray of tea. 'You can get nice maternity wedding dresses.'

Mrs Brown nearly choked. 'Maternity wedding dresses! Well, really!'

I could have pointed out that Peggy was far from being the only girl in need of such a thing, but guessed I'd be wasting my breath.

'There.' Mrs Brown handed the dress to Peggy, who slipped it on. To be fair, her mother had done a good job. The dress, a pale blue silk, looked pretty and flattering.

'What are you going to wear on top?'

'I don't know. My coat, I suppose.'

Oh dear. Her coat was very fitted and it was some time since she'd been able to do it up. Which gave me an idea. In the window of Adcocks, I had spotted a very nice jacket. It was a mid-blue, short, loose and fastened with one huge button. It would, I thought, go perfectly with Peggy's let-out dress. I wanted to buy it for her.

I went back to Adcocks and tried the jacket on. It was a bit tight across the shoulders for me, but Peggy was narrower there than I was, so that would be fine. And it was plenty big enough in the middle. So I forked out a week's wages for it and took it home.

Janice was sitting at the kitchen table and Peggy was sitting in her dad's chair, sewing. She looked tense and tired, not a bit like a bride only days before her wedding.

I placed the big box ceremoniously on the table. 'This is for you. Open it.'

I grinned and Peggy giggled and looked years younger. She stuck her needle carefully into her sewing, put it down and picked up the box.

'It's from Adcocks!' She unfastened the string and opened the box to reveal a cloud of tissue paper. She removed it carefully, putting it on the table, then took the jacket out of the paper. 'Oh, it's beautiful!' she said.

'Try it on.'

Even over the old jumper and shapeless skirt she was wearing, the jacket looked good. We took it upstairs and tried it against the dress.

'It goes perfectly,' said Janice, who had followed us up. She stroked the jacket and looked in admiration at the big button and the silky lining. 'It's wonderful, isn't it?' she said, almost in awe. 'Very special.'

'Here, Janice, you try it on for a second,' said Peggy, and popped it over Janice's scraggy gym-slip, where it hung like a clown's coat. Her hands and nails, I noticed, were spotlessly clean.

Janice looked at herself in the mirror. 'It would be lovely to have clothes like this all the time. It would be like a fairy tale, wouldn't it?' she said. She solemnly handed the jacket back to Peggy.

'Oh, Rosie, I've never had anything as posh as this. It must have cost a fortune.' Peggy was almost in tears. 'Thank you.'

'You deserve to have something new. It's a special day.'

'Yes, it is, isn't it?' she said, looking determined. 'It's the start of my new life. With George. It will be a good life, Rosie. I promise I'll do my best. It will be worth celebrating.'

Mr Brown obviously thought so too. He came home later and said he'd booked a table at the Fleece for us all after the ceremony.

'But I was just going to do something for us here,' said Mrs Brown.

'It's our only daughter's wedding. We'll do it properly,' he said firmly.

We could have walked to the registry office, but Mr Brown insisted on a car to take us. When Peggy came downstairs in the altered dress and the new jacket, he walked towards her and wrapped her in his arms. 'My little girl,' he said. 'You look lovely.'

She did too. Very smart. And though I say it myself, the jacket was a triumph. I was so pleased. Best of all—from Mrs Brown's point of view—was that you couldn't really see that Peggy was pregnant, especially when she held her bouquet in front of her.

'Something old, something new—that's the dress and jacket,' said Mrs Brown. 'Something borrowed! Quick, Peg, borrow something!'

'Here,' I said, 'borrow my hanky.' It was one of the little lace ones I'd found in the trunk the day I arrived.

'Thanks, Rosie. Now I've got everything I need to bring me luck. And the something blue is my dress and jacket again.'

With that the car arrived and we all bundled into it quickly, while the neighbours stood on their doorsteps calling, 'Good luck, girl!'

The registry office smelled of polish and flowers. George looked nervous, but when Peggy walked in his face lit up.

And so began the ceremony to unite Margaret Elizabeth Brown and George Arthur Turnbull. I realised I hadn't known what George's surname was before. So, officially, Peggy would now be Margaret Turnbull.

Margaret Turnbull . . . Margaret Turnbull . . . The name niggled. There was something about that name that I should recognise . . .

The ceremony was brief. With a bit of handshaking and congratulations, it was all over and we were out in the street again.

'Come on then, Mr and Mrs Turnbull,' said Derek, the best man. He was a pleasant-faced young man with slicked-back hair and a cheerful grin. 'Time for the first drink of your married life!' and he led the way the fifty yards or so to the Fleece.

It was as we were walking into the lounge that I remembered.

Margaret Turnbull was the woman I'd been on my way to interview when I'd fainted and had landed in the Browns' house. I looked at Peggy, smiling now, looking young and glowing. I remembered that brief impression I'd had of an old lady answering the front door.

'I say! Are you all right?' Derek was looking at me anxiously.

'Sit down!' Mrs Brown commanded. I sank into one of the armchairs by the fire. 'You've gone as white as a sheet. Frank! Get Rosie a brandy!'

The brandy hit my system and I could feel its warmth spreading through me. Margaret Turnbull. Peggy. It was too much of a coincidence. My head filled with fog and cotton wool as I tried to work it out. Whatever it was, this wasn't the time and place to think about it.

The brandy and the fire did the trick. Well, they didn't really, but enough to bring some colour back to my cheeks and enable me to join in with what was going on. The last thing I wanted to do was ruin George and Peggy's wedding day.

'That's better!' said Mrs Brown approvingly.

Peggy was laughing. 'You all right, Rosie? Not going to have to plan another wedding are we?'

Everyone laughed with her and the day turned into a party. We were in an alcove off the dining room so we had a certain amount of privacy from the businessmen and old ladies enjoying their lunch. Just as well. George's mum got quite tiddly on a couple of glasses of sherry.

There was a small heap of cards and telegrams, and after the pudding Derek stood up to read these out. The lads from work had sent a card saying, 'May all your troubles be little ones!' which caused huge hilarity.

The last card looked big and fat and expensive. 'This looks a posh one,' said Derek cheerfully, tugging it open. A shower of notes cascaded onto the tablecloth, drifting onto the uncleared plates and bowls.

Mrs Brown gathered them up. 'There's a hundred pounds here! A hundred pounds!' Her eyes were wide with shock. '"With all good wishes, Richard Henfield."'

There was a small silence.

'I don't want his money,' said Peggy quietly.

'Oh, yes, you do, my girl,' said her mother. 'You can buy a lot of baby things with a hundred pounds.'

'Or it can go towards the university fees,' I said merrily.

'Why not?' asked George cheerfully, putting his arm round Peggy. 'Our baby will go to university if he wants. Or she . . . A student with a briefcase and a gown and one of those long stripy scarves.'

George's mum looked at Peggy. 'Twenty-six,' she said. 'That was the age I was widowed.' She was in danger of getting maudlin.

'Well, don't say that too loudly!'

'No, love, I won't. But it will be nice to have a baby in the house. I'm looking forward to that. I'm glad they decided to come and live with me. I wouldn't like to be on my own. Be better when we move, mind.'

Of course, George's house was in the line of the bypass, so Mrs Turnbull, too, had been offered a house at The Meadows. I was doing my sums. If George's dad died when his mum was twenty-six, then she'd be only about forty-two. And I'd thought she was about sixty . . .

The head waiter was bustling towards us with a stand, which he placed alongside the table. Next, he came with a bucket full of ice and a bottle. 'Your wine, sir,' he said to Mr Brown.

'Champagne!' cried George's mum.

'Well, near enough,' said Mr Brown. 'It's fizzy anyway.'

'Oh, I never thought I'd drink champagne,' said Peggy, already giggly.

I caught sight of the label. Not champagne, Asti Spumante. Oh, well. The waiter brought those saucer-shaped champagne glasses and opened the bottle with a huge pop! We stood and drank a toast to the long life, health and happiness of Mr and Mrs Turnbull.

'It's bubbly!' laughed Peggy. 'They go up your nose! Isn't this special!'

As we sipped the fizz, I reached across the table and picked up the cards and the telegrams and idly looked through them. Many of them featured intertwined hearts, pink and pretty and satiny.

I thought of Peggy and Henfield, the scene at Friars' Mill, Amy who had killed herself, and Peggy who'd wanted to. I thought of Will, who I loved, and of Billy who loved his children and sort of loved Carol, but who also wanted me. Love hearts weren't neat and pretty like a sugared sweet, they were like those hearts I'd seen soaking in the bowl at Carol's—messy and bloody, staining the waters all around them.

Soon it was time for the newlyweds to get their train. They were off to stay with Aunty Emily in London and do the sights. A bit different from the trip that had been planned for Peggy before.

We saw them off at the station. Derek had tied a JUST MARRIED sign to George's suitcase and, try as he might, George couldn't undo all the many knots that Derek had tied so devilishly.

'Give you something to do at bedtime!' yelled Derek as the guard blew his whistle and the train started to pull out. George and Peggy leaned out of the window of their compartment and we all waved until they vanished in a cloud of steam.

'Well,' said Mrs Brown with the air of a job well done. 'Let's go home and have a proper cup of tea then, shall we?'

CHAPTER EIGHT

I WAS STANDING in Boots looking glumly at the shelves, waiting for super-strength, conditioning, extra-volume mousse to be invented . . . and lemon cuticle cream . . . and waterproof mascara . . . and summer-glow body moisturiser . . . and whitening toothpaste . . . and . . .

'Hi, Rosie!' I turned round to see Carol standing there clutching a package. 'Home perm,' she said. 'Going round to do my mum's for her.'

'Oh, right.'

'How are you then, Rosie? Still enjoying *The News*?'

What do I say? Do I say, 'Hello, Carol. I'm in love with your husband and I think he might fancy me' or, 'I'd really love it there, Carol, if I could just work with your husband all day and gaze into his eyes.'?

No, you're right, I didn't.

'Fine, fine.'

'I heard Peggy got married to George.'

'Yes, just a few days ago.'

'Well, she's a dark horse, isn't she? Did you go to the wedding?'

'Yes. It was low-key, you know, but very nice.'

I was torn. I longed to have a coffee with Carol and tell her all the details, the way I would with Caz. And I wanted her take on it all too. Carol was good company, kind and funny . . . I wanted her as a friend.

And I wanted her husband.

Carol was smiling at me. 'Got time for a coffee? Look—no kids!'

Well, why not? I abandoned any hope of buying anything I wanted and followed Carol out of Boots. Minutes later, we slid into a booth at Silvino's.

'Come on, then,' said Carol. 'Tell me about the wedding. I didn't even know Peggy was going out with George. She must be six or seven years older than him.' She grinned. 'But he obviously knows what it's all about then. So tell me all about it. Did they have a do?'

'Yes, at the Fleece.' I told her about Peggy's dress and jacket and about the meal and the 'champagne'.

'Ooh,' said Carol, hungrily. 'There's posh. When Billy and I got wed we just had sandwiches and cake at my mum's.' She spooned some of the froth from her coffee in its shallow Pyrex cup. 'Have they gone on a honeymoon, then?'

'Yes, a few days in London. Peggy has an aunt who lives there, so they'll have seen the sights. They're back tomorrow. They're going to live with George's mum. She lives in the line of the bypass, so they'll all be moving up to The Meadows soon.'

'That's good. I like Peggy. It'll be nice having her near. Anyway . . . tada! I've finished the dress!'

The dress she was making to go to the 'posh do' with Billy.

'Oh, great. Does Billy like it?'

'He hasn't seen it yet. I've decided he's not going to see it until that night. It's a shame you're not coming, Rosie. I'm really looking forward to it. They've got a proper dance orchestra, and at the end they have a great net of balloons that come down from the ceiling.' Her eyes were shining. 'Anyway, it's time I wasn't here.' She picked up her shopping bag. 'Maybe Phil could get you an invite to the ball and you could both come with me and Billy?'

'Yes, maybe,' I said, but dismissed the thought. I wanted to keep Phil at arm's length, as a friend. I felt he was beginning to get ideas.

'Are you seeing Phil this weekend?'

'No. Well, we haven't arranged anything.'

He'd asked me out for Saturday night and I'd turned him down. I regretted it now. Without Peggy, the house was already feeling empty.

'Blooming heck! It's raining and I haven't got a brolly!' Standing in the doorway of the café, Carol tugged a scarf from her coat pocket and tied it over her hair. 'Tara, Rosie. Maybe see you in the week!' With her head down, she dashed out into the crowds.

Back at the Browns' house, there was no smell of cooking. Instead, Mrs Brown was looking busy and harassed.

'You can have bacon and eggs and a bit of mash for your supper. I'm making a start on Peggy's room. We're going to be moving soon. The first phase is just about finished up at The Meadows. They'll be allocating the houses. I don't suppose we'll get the first phase, but we'll probably get the second if they want us out of the way to start on their new road.'

Just then, Mr Brown came in, stamping the rain off his shoes.

'You're late, Frank,' said his wife.

'Yes, and for a very good reason. I've bought a car.'

There was a silence.

'You've done what?'

'I've bought a little car, a Morris Minor.' Mr Brown looked very pleased with himself. 'I've been thinking about it ever since it took us all day to get to that christening and all night to get back from it. If we'd had a little car, we could have done it in an hour.'

'Can we afford it, Frank?'

'I had a bit of money put by for our Peg's wedding and, well, in the end that didn't cost as much as I thought.'

'But do you know how to drive a car?'

'Course I do. Learned in the army, didn't I?'

'And have you got it here now?' Mrs Brown darted out to the front, to see if it was in the street.

'No, no. It will take a few days to get the paperwork arranged.'

'Well, well,' said Mrs Brown, finally absorbing the idea. 'Fancy that. A new house, a new baby and a new car, all at the same time. We *are* going up in the world, aren't we?'

'If you want to put it like that,' said Mr Brown, looking pleased with himself. 'Right then, where's my supper?'

The wind and rain had blown George and Peggy in through the door on Sunday evening, their cheeks glowing, their eyes dancing with excitement. Was it the weather or the honeymoon? I wondered.

'Can't stop long, Mum,' said Peggy. 'George's mum will be waiting for us. But I'll come over tomorrow afternoon when you're back from work and tell you all about it. We've had a lovely time. We've seen Buckingham Palace and the Changing of the Guard, and we saw the Houses of Parliament—it's just like on the sauce bottle!'

Over a quick cup of tea and a slice of the sponge cake Mrs Brown had baked that morning, Peggy handed over a little plate with a picture of Buckingham Palace. 'I brought a present back for you, Mum.'

Mrs Brown smiled and put it on the dresser, slap bang in the middle of the shelf. 'I'll put it there so people can't miss it,' she said proudly, 'and I can say my daughter and son-in-law brought it back from their honeymoon in London.'

After Peggy had given her parents a quick hug, she and George dodged back out into the rain.

'It doesn't seem right her not being here,' said Mrs Brown, peering out of the sitting-room window, watching them going down the street.

'Her place is with her husband now,' said Mr Brown.

It had rained all day and it rained all night. The wind whipped along the streets and blew the blossom off the trees. The blossom bobbed on the ripples whipped up on the puddles. As I sat eating my breakfast porridge, the rain slashed angrily against the kitchen window, making the old frame rattle and turning the outside world into a cold, wet blur.

'More like blooming winter than nearly summer. I hope Peggy wraps up well when she comes round,' said Mrs Brown, tugging on a pair of rubber boots and tying a scarf round her head. 'No point in taking a brolly today. It'll be blown inside out before I'm across the doorstep.'

'When you get your new car you'll be able to have a lift to work, or drive yourself,' I said.

Mrs Brown stopped, her hands in midair where she'd been tugging at her scarf. 'Ooh, I couldn't do that. We couldn't use the car for that. Though Frank might. Anyway, I'm off now. Make sure the door's shut really tight when you go out, won't you?'

I finished my breakfast, washed the dishes and did my make-up in the kitchen mirror—powder, lipstick and a quick spit on the mascara. Then, wrapped up nearly as securely as Mrs Brown, I tugged open the front door and launched myself into the storm.

Ouch! The rain slapped me in the face and tugged through my hair.

It was a battle to get over the doorstep, never mind down the street. How I missed my nice, *dry* little car. I would have caught a bus, but there was no direct route between the house and *The News*, so I had to walk, hands in pockets, head bent against the wind and the rain.

'Lovely weather for ducks,' said the receptionist cheerfully as I squelched into *The News*, water dripping off the end of my scarf.

The office smelt of wet clothes and wet shoes, horribly reminiscent of wet dog. It mingled with the smell of musty newspapers and all the cigarette smoke. But despite the damp and the smell, I went up the stairs with that small sense of excitement, that fluttering in your insides that comes from fancying someone you work with.

'Bit damp are you, kid?' asked Billy as I dripped past him, my face bright red with the rain and the wind.

I grinned—if he'd called me 'kid' back at home in our own real time, I would probably have hated it, but here it was great, a sign of comradeship, affection almost . . . I shook my head so the drops flew off and spattered all over the newsdesk diary.

'Just for that,' he said sternly, 'I think I will send you on a nice little door-stepping exercise.'

My face must have fallen because he laughed.

'No, you're OK, I wouldn't send a dog out today. No, Marje is off today, so could you do the Women's Page please, Rosie?'

I groaned. But at least it kept me out of the rain, which got no better as the morning went on. At lunchtime I was still bashing away at my typewriter when Alan came in.

'The river's very high,' he said, peeling off his sodden raincoat and draping it over a chair. 'Sergeant Foster was down there, looking worried. Apparently the civil defence are on standby. They're filling sandbags. It looks as though they'll be needed. It's getting serious out there.'

Billy was pulling on his raincoat. 'Can you run the desk for a while, Alan? I must check on Carol and the kids. If the river's running high, it could be well up towards my house.'

'Glad to, Billy,' Alan said.

But Billy was already gone. I could hear him dashing down the stairs.

'Are you making the tea then, Rosie?' asked Alan as he looked at the work on Billy's desk. Deflated, I turned to get the kettle.

The rain didn't let up. I ate my sandwiches at my desk and was finishing the Women's Page when the electricity went off.

Alan cursed, lit a cigarette and then went groping around in the back of a cupboard from where he produced a paraffin lamp. He cleared a space for it in the middle of all the clutter and lit it. After a few failed attempts it finally got going and cast a cosy glow over the office.

By now the phones were ringing, with reporters and members of the public wanting to know what was happening. Alan was already talking on two phones when a third rang. I answered it. It was Billy.

'Is your house OK?' I asked.

'Probably not for much longer. But we've moved all we can upstairs and Carol and Libby have gone to her mother's. There's nothing more we can do . . . Look, Rosie, can you get Alan? We need to be out and about. The river's burst its banks and people are going to have to be rescued. There are great stories. I've seen George and Charlie, but we need another reporter out.'

'I'll come!' I said. 'Alan has only just dried out. And he can run the desk better than I can.' I let the thought hang in the air.

It took a second for him to make the decision.

'OK. I'm down by the old quay, so get yourself to Watergate and see what's happening there. But be careful! Now, put me on to Alan.'

I interrupted Alan's phone calls, handed him the receiver and fled. Floods! A real story! Worth getting wet for! And Billy had told me to be careful. Adrenaline and happiness were surging round my system.

The receptionist on the front desk looked horrified as I clattered down the stairs. 'You're not going out in this, are you?' she said, and when she saw that obviously I was, she said, 'Well, at least get yourself something sensible for your feet. Haven't you got any wellies?'

'No. Where's the nearest place to get some?'

'Woolies, of course.'

It was only across the road. I dashed in and found some wellies and some thick socks. I went back to *The News* to change and left my soggy shoes in reception.

Down at Watergate it was chaos. The river was over its banks and the road was disappearing. The water was already up to the arch of the bridge and was roaring through in a torrent, bringing branches and debris down with it. I splashed along on what had been a pavement but was now about a foot deep in water. It was lapping near the top of my wellies. I moved away, up higher towards the marketplace.

A policeman in fisherman's waders was standing in the middle of the road directing traffic. A tractor and trailer were ploughing through the water sending up huge waves, but people were wading across to get into the trailer, bringing babies and possessions. A short fat man came waddling out nearly bent double under the weight of a cardboard box full of papers. He dumped the box and went back to his office for more.

Normally, I'd dart in and out talking to people, grabbing a chance and a quote where I could. But it's tricky to dart when you're wading in water in wellies.

A fire engine arrived and a fireman climbed up a ladder and took a bundle from a woman at a window. The bundle shrieked. It was a baby. The fireman took the baby down the ladder and it was handed from arm to arm to the safety of a lorry parked in the shallower water. Then there was a slightly larger bundle, a little girl of about two.

At that point, hooray! George arrived. He got some good pictures and I paddled through the water to the trailer and got the names of the mother, who'd climbed down the ladder, and her children. I tried to write them in my notebook but it was hopeless. So I struggled into a covered alleyway and scribbled down the names of the people I'd talked to, then ripped the already wet pages out of my notebook and stuck them deep down in the pocket of my bag.

Back in the rain, the fat man with the cardboard boxes was shouting at the policeman, who didn't want him to put any more on the trailer as it was fully loaded and ready to go. By now, what had been the road was just part of the river, which was growing wider every second. A group of lads, about fourteen or fifteen years old, appeared. They had their shoes tied round their necks and their trousers rolled up.

'Right, you lot!' bellowed the policeman in waders. 'Make yourselves useful and get along to those houses at the end. See if anyone needs help getting their stuff shifted upstairs. If they want to leave their houses then wave something out of the window so we know.'

The boys splashed off up the waterway, full of excitement and a sense of adventure and ready to help.

My sense of adventure was definitely beginning to pall. Time, I thought, to get back to the office. I'd begun to retreat when I saw a bright red rowing boat coming up what had been the street. The man rowing was doing it competently and confidently, with regular strokes.

'Want a lift?' he yelled across at me. It was Billy.

He brought the boat as close as he could to me and I waded across and climbed in. The boat rocked terrifyingly, but Billy got it steady as he helped me in. 'Do you like it?' he asked, grinning. 'I requisitioned it.'

'Brilliant!'

'The bloke at the boating lake wanted five bob—*five bob!*—for the hire charge, but I told him it was a national emergency.'

I clung to Billy's arm for maybe a fraction longer than necessary and then settled down opposite him.

'Where are we going?'

'I thought we'd have one more look around, see what's going on.' He grinned at me and suddenly I didn't feel cold any more.

It was really weird rowing around the streets. The water was running fast, and every now and then a particularly fierce current would catch us and the boat would swoop and dip. We were on the main road between the marketplace and Watergate when a sudden torrent came. Billy let the current send us down a narrow pathway, one of many that led through Watergate down to the river.

The buildings were narrow, dark and virtually derelict. Suddenly I could see why Mr Brown thought the whole lot would be better off demolished. Perhaps the flood would finish most of them off.

'All right?' asked Billy as I clung to the sides.

'Never been better!' I yelled back at him.

And as I did, I spotted a face at a broken window above us. An old woman was looking out. 'Help me! Please help!' she called.

Billy managed to pull the boat round and tie the rope to the spear-shaped top of a railing—all that showed above the water.

'We need the fire brigade!' I shouted to Billy. 'We can't get her out.'

'And I can't see how the fire brigade would get down here—even if we could get to them in time!' he shouted back.

By now he was out of the boat—rocking it hard in the process—and had pulled himself up onto the railings, one hand holding onto an old light bracket on the wall.

'Pass me an oar up, Rosie,' he called down. I did and, telling the woman to step back, he smashed the rest of the window. He took hold of a bit of blanket that had been stuffing one of the missing panes and laid it across the windowsill to protect her from the splinters of glass.

'Now, what I want you to do,' he said to the old woman, 'is to sit on the windowsill with your legs outside.'

'I can't! I can't!' yelled the woman, who seemed to be wearing a heap of raggedy clothes, her hair escaping from a greasy, untidy bun.

'Of course you can,' said Billy soothingly. He caught hold of the woman and guided her down. 'Pull as hard as you can on that rope, Rosie!' He turned back to the woman. 'Right,' he said. 'Can you just jump into the boat? It's just a step really.'

'No, I can't! I can't!' yelled the woman, clinging harder to Billy. Quick as a flash Billy bundled her into the boat. They landed with a thud and a scream and the boat rocked wildly. I flung myself to one side to try to balance the weight. The boat rocked a bit more, and the woman lay in the middle of it, whimpering, but at least she had the sense to stay still.

'Come on,' said Billy, passing me an oar and untying the rope. 'Let's paddle.'

Once loose, the boat swirled out into the water and, with Billy kneeling at the front and me perched on the little seat at the back, we paddled through the streets. There I was with Billy, working as a real team. Our heavily laden little pleasure craft seemed to sing over the water.

The raggedy woman stopped whimpering and looked up at us paddling. 'Blimey,' she said. 'I've been rescued by a pair of bloomin' Red Indians.'

Billy and I laughed out loud in shared amusement.

Soon we came to higher ground and the boat started bumping along the pavement. A couple of civil-defence volunteers were in a lorry.

'Where are you taking people to?' Billy shouted to them.

'Church hall,' one of them yelled. 'They're doing soup and sandwiches.'

'Ooh,' said our raggedy woman, sitting up. 'I could just do with a drop of soup.'

'Hop aboard then!' shouted the civil-defence man.

The woman bundled up her clothes round her knees. 'Thanks for the lift,' she said to us, before turning conspiratorially to me. 'You hang on to him, love. He's a bit of all right.'

As she waded off, Billy and I laughed, with only a little embarrassment. Then we splashed along the road, pulling the boat behind us.

'Well, kid,' said Billy. 'We certainly have some adventures, don't we?'

My heart did somersaults. 'We certainly do. And it's a lot more interesting than writing Meal Ideas for Busy Housewives. Thinking of which, we'd better get back to the office. I've got a lot to write up.'

'What time is it?'

I pushed my soggy sleeve back up to see my watch. 'Five to six.'

'In that case, I've got a better idea. I'll just make a phone call first.'

He disappeared into a phone box while I stood outside hanging on to the rope of the little red boat.

'Right,' he said, emerging from the phone box and taking the boat rope from my hand. 'Follow me.'

We splashed along for a little way until we came to the steep steps that led up to the old town wall. There was a tapas bar up there in my day, I remembered. Will and I had been there once or twice. But right now, on this rainy night, it was a pub. Billy tied the boat to a lamppost.

'Come on, up the steps.'

The steps were narrow and crumbling. There was no light anywhere, just a dim glow from the window of the pub.

'Jolly good. Bert has got the fire lit,' said Billy, holding open the door for me. The bar was lit by candles and the glow of a coal fire.

'Oh, it's you,' said a voice from somewhere in the gloom behind the bar. 'I might have known it would have to be some daft beggar out in weather like this. Even the dog's got more sense.'

As if to prove it, a small terrier uncurled itself from a chair and came to sniff at my wellies.

'And a good evening to you too, Bert,' said Billy. 'A pint and a half of bitter, please. And may we take a couple of these candles over to the table? We've got work to do.'

'Help yourself,' said Bert. 'Give us a shout when you want another drink or if any more daft beggars come in. I'll be out the back.'

'Right,' said Billy. To me he said, 'They're managing fine at the office, so I thought we might as well write our stuff up here and then we can phone it through. Much nicer, wouldn't you say?'

'I would. I most definitely would.'

So we sat on either side of the table, working by the fire in the glow of the flames and the candlelight. Just us in this strange little world.

'Right, that's me done,' he said eventually. 'I've got the intro and a few bits. The rest I'll do on the phone.'

'Oh.' I really admired the way some people could just write a story off the top of their heads. I was carefully writing out everything. As Billy disappeared outside to the phone box, I concentrated harder. There were so many different stories, all good. I scribbled on quickly.

'OK, your turn with the phone. The copytaker's waiting for you,' Billy said, clearly not even considering the possibility that I couldn't be ready. 'Don't forget this.' It was a torch—well, a bike lamp really. 'You've got to be able to read what you've written.'

Now that's what I call being prepared.

'Thanks.' I wriggled back into my sodden mac, went outside into the rain and clambered down to the phone box at the bottom of the steps. There I started the long process of dictating the stories to the girl at the end of the line. When I walked back into the pub, Billy was getting us some drinks.

'I don't suppose there's any food, is there?' I asked. 'I'm starving.'

'Can do you crisps,' said Bert. 'And pickled eggs.'

'Pickled eggs? Well, thank you, but I think I'll pass on that.'

'Go on,' said Billy, 'local delicacy you can't miss out on. Two bags of crisps and two eggs, please, Bert. My treat.'

'Thank you. I think,' I said.

I have to say that a pickled egg is not my idea of a delicacy. In fact it was pretty gross, *and* it made the crisps soggy. I wasn't a great fan of beer either, but I ate and drank and steamed gently by the fire and just counted my blessings for being here alone with Billy.

'You've done a good job today,' he said, 'as good as many of the men could have done.'

He meant it as a compliment. I tried not to feel patronised.

He was laughing now. 'That old dear was right. You were paddling like a Red Indian. A very wet Red Indian.'

'Was that old woman living there?'

'Yes, there's all sorts of people living in there. It's a warren, and probably not safe really. But I suppose it's better than nothing.'

We leaned back on the bench, cherished the warmth of the fire and talked about the day's work—and the hope our hard-won words would get a decent show in the next day's paper. And I watched the way the firelight showed up his cheekbones and the way his hair went into small curls at the nape of his neck as it dried.

We had another beer. And another. And even in the candlelight I could still see his long eyelashes and his deep brown eyes. And I wanted to bury myself in his arms . . .

'Right, you two! Ain't you got no homes to go to?' Bert was doing things to the fire, closing down at the end of the night sort of things. He took our empty glasses and one of the candles back to the bar.

'OK, Bert, we can take a hint,' said Billy. 'I've left a boat tied up at the bottom of your steps, but I'll be back for it.'

'Boat on my steps! What next?' muttered Bert, wiping down the bar.

We went out by the light of the bike lamp. The rain had stopped and the wind had died down. It was actually quite mild.

'Let's walk along the town walls,' Billy said. 'It's probably quicker, and certainly a drier way home for you.'

Being up on the town walls was a bit like being in the middle of a lake. Vast stretches of water now reflected back the moonlight.

'This is the highest flood since 1888,' said Billy. 'If you could forget about the damage it has caused, it's beautiful in its way. Careful . . .' He grabbed my arm as a pothole suddenly appeared in the path. In my day it was all smoothed and tarmacked, with a safety rail, but fifty years earlier it was uneven and rubbly with a sheer drop to the water below.

Billy didn't let go of my arm. Instead he pulled me round to face him.

'You were a lovely little Red Indian today,' he said. 'I'll never forget you. You were so wet, but you were paddling away. You looked so determined. So'—he hesitated—'so beautiful.'

I knew what was coming next and I did nothing to stop it. He took me in his arms, brought his head down to mine and kissed me, a long lingering kiss that tasted of beer and crisps, and was utterly wonderful.

Oh the joy of it! To be wrapped in Will's arms again, to feel his arms round me, to put my head on his chest and be cocooned.

We kissed again. And again. Each kiss fiercer than the last. It was strange, the clothes were unfamiliar, the scent of his skin was not what I knew, but yet it was still Will, still the man I loved, the man I'd missed so dreadfully. And now here I was wrapped up in him again.

We disentangled ourselves and I looked up at him. He was smiling down at me and his eyes were Will's eyes, laughing and loving. He started to say something and stopped.

'I—' I started, but he put his finger gently on my lips to silence me and I fitted myself back under the curve of his shoulder with his arm round me, holding me against him. We ambled along the top of the wall, with just a bike lamp against the dark, and the only sounds were the lapping of the water and the flump flump flump of our wellies.

We came down from the town wall about fifty yards from the Browns' house. In the darkness of the steps, once again we wrapped ourselves round each other and kissed long and hard.

Billy finally pulled away. He took my face and held it gently in his hands so I was looking up at him. 'I think a lot of you, Rosie. You really are very special. I don't want to, but I could love you, I really could. In fact'—he looked at me helplessly, hopelessly—'I already do.'

It was what I had longed to hear all the weeks I'd been there. I closed my eyes and reached hungrily to kiss him again.

But something had happened. I could feel his hands holding mine. He was taking my hands and removing them from round his neck. I could feel the strength in his wrists as he pushed my hands away. I tried to push against him, but it was no good. He was holding me away from him. 'It's no good, Rosie,' he said, and his face looked desperately sad. 'I am married. I have a wife and three children. I can't hurt them. They have done nothing wrong. They are my responsibility. I can't let them down, not even . . . not even for you.'

I stared at him, not believing what I was hearing. Had I won him only to lose him just a few heartbeats later? One look at the pain on his face told me the answer.

'Carol is a good wife and a brilliant mother. She works hard and we're happy. We *were* happy, until you came along. And we will be again. I think you're wonderful, magical, different from any girl I've ever known. I would love to leave everything and be with you, but I can't. I must stay here with my family and you must go back to where you came from. I'm sorry, I shouldn't have kissed you. I shouldn't have said what I said.'

'But you did! This can't be the end. We're meant to be together, you and I. You're the only one for me. There's no one else.'

Billy looked at me sadly. 'I can't let Carol down. It's not fair, not right.'
And it wasn't. I knew that really, deep down.

'Then why did you tell me you love me? Just so you can snatch it away! That's not fair, Billy!'

'I'm sorry, Rosie,' said Billy, brushing my tears gently away. 'I just wanted to hold you in my arms, to know what it would be like. But I shouldn't have done it. I'm sorry. This has been a magical night and I really do wish . . . but it can't happen. Wrong time, wrong place.'

Wrong time. Wrong place. And how. If Billy and I were meant to be together, it wasn't in the 1950s.

I made myself stop crying. I tried to act casual. 'Well, it was only a kiss. What's a kiss between friends?' I said, though my tough-girl attitude didn't quite work between sniffs. 'It's been a funny old day, funny old night. We'll blame it on the weather, shall we?'

I reached up and kissed him gently on the cheek. He bent down and kissed me in return, the same gentle way.

I swallowed hard. 'OK, I'm nearly home now. Good night, Billy. See you tomorrow.'

He was still holding my hand. As he let go, he rubbed his thumb over mine the way Will always did. That nearly finished me off. I broke free of him and ran the few yards to the house.

'Rosie!' I heard Billy shout. And it echoed strangely over the lake of moonlit water. 'Rosie!' As if it were coming from a very long way away. Another time. Another place.

When I got home the Browns had long since gone to bed. Walking into the kitchen I almost tripped over sacks of potatoes, tins of paint, a clothes horse, an old wash boiler—all things that had presumably been rescued from the cellar when the flood waters had soaked in.

There was a pan of milk sitting on the side of the stove waiting for me. I heated it up, made some cocoa and crept to the cupboard in the sitting room where the Browns kept a bottle of sweet sherry and another of brandy, for medicinal purposes. I definitely needed medicine. It would be months before they got the bottle out. They wouldn't notice. But it didn't calm me.

I went back to the kitchen, wondering what on earth I was to do next. I was more confused than when I had first arrived. There was no future here for me and Billy. He was good and loyal. And—oh bitter, bitter irony—that made me love him even more. He had made promises that he would keep even if his heart wanted to be elsewhere.

But Billy was just Will in another age, other circumstances. And, I realised, quite suddenly, that I could trust Will too. In every way, with my life, my future. Why couldn't I have seen that before? I had built up spiky little barriers all around me, afraid of letting him in, in case he let me down. But there was no need. He wouldn't. I knew that now. Once Will committed himself to me, it would be for life. No question. As I would to him. If only I could get back to him to tell him so . . .

I finally went up to bed as dawn was breaking, but I still couldn't sleep. When my alarm went off I dragged myself downstairs to get a cup of tea. But even wrapped in my dressing gown, I was shivering.

Mr Brown was out looking at the garden. It was a chaos of mud and branches where the river had flooded. Already the water level had dropped right down, but the devastation was clear.

I leaned over the range, trying to get warm. 'You're not going anywhere today, young lady,' said Mrs Brown. 'You're not well. You got yourself chilled with all that trailing about in flood water. Get yourself back up those stairs into bed and I'll bring you up a hot-water bottle.'

She did too. And some more tea. I heard the front door slam a little while later when she went out to work. Then I slithered gently down the pillows and gave up.

I tossed and turned, half slept, half woke, dreamed weird dreams, imagined worse. And sometimes when I closed my eyes I could hear Billy's voice, calling to me from far away. 'Rosie! Rosie! Are you there? Can you hear me?'

Eventually I got up, remade my bed and went and had a bath, which warmed me a little. I had just got dressed when I heard a 'Yoohoo!' from downstairs.

Peggy had arrived.

'I saw Mum and she said you weren't well so I came round to see you. Did you write all the flood stuff?'

She was looking at *The News*. There was our story all across the front page, with George's pictures. 'By our News Staff', it said. I glanced at it. They seemed to have used plenty of it, but it hurt my eyes to read it.

'I think George took most of those pictures,' she said proudly. Then she looked up at me. 'You look awful.'

She poured me some tea and cut a slice of the cake her mum had baked for her homecoming. I couldn't face it and let it sit untouched.

Peggy looked at me, concerned. 'Is it just the chill that's making you feel bad?'

'I don't know.' I was damned if I was going to tell her about Billy. 'I suppose I'm wondering why I'm here, really. What's been the point of it.'

Peggy put down the teapot and gazed at me earnestly. 'I don't know where I would have been without you,' she said. 'Me and my baby and George, we're a family now. And that's thanks to you. If you hadn't turned up . . . if you hadn't got George to come looking for me . . . We're all here for a reason, Rosie, and I think that was your reason. You saved me and my baby.'

Was that the reason? Could that really be why I was there?

When Lucy went through the wardrobe to Narnia, she and her brothers and sister had a mission to save Narnia, the whole world, not just one person. Everyone who ever travelled in time had some great and noble mission. I didn't know why I was there, but I knew all that it had really achieved was to make me realise how much I loved Will. If I ever got the chance to tell him, I would never let him go again.

I was still wondering how to reply to Peggy when we both heard a strange noise out in the street.

'It's a car horn,' said Peggy, and then, with a squeal of excited realisation, 'Dad's got the car!'

She rushed to the front door, where Mr Brown was sitting at the wheel of a little black Morris Minor.

'What do you think?' he asked. 'Isn't it grand?'

Peggy had rushed outside to look at the car. I had sunk onto the bench of the hall stand, my legs seemingly made of cotton wool.

'Oh, there's Mum! Cooeee! Mum!' yelled Peggy down the street.

'Well, will you look at that!' Mrs Brown walked all round the car.

'Can we go for a ride, Dad?' asked Peggy, as excited as a two-year-old.

'Ooh, wait, let me get ready!' said Mrs Brown. She ran into the house, took off the beret that she wore to work and put on a felt hat.

'You don't need a hat to go in the car!' said Peggy.

'It's my first outing in our car. I have to look my best,' replied Mrs Brown firmly.

'Come on, Rosie,' urged Peggy as she climbed into the car, 'you've got to come too!'

I really didn't feel like it, but they were so excited that it seemed churlish to refuse. I stood up and managed to walk to the car. Mrs Brown had to get out again, to push the front seat forward for me to get into the back.

'Right, where shall we go?' asked Mr Brown.

'I know, Dad! Let's go up to The Meadows and see where we're going to live.'

'Right you are, then.' Mr Brown turned the engine on. 'Self-starter motor,' he said proudly, as we chugged off down the road.

In the weeks I'd been working on *The News* I had never yet been up to The Meadows. The estate was slightly above the town, the new road curving round from the end of the old High Street. Squashed in the back of the car, I couldn't see much out of the small windows, though I could feel the car struggling up the hill. Mr Brown turned off onto the bottom road, the first phase of the new estate. There were just a couple of vans parked there as workmen were doing the last of the tidying up.

Peggy and I scrabbled out of the back of the car and I had a shock.

The view from The Meadows was tremendous. You could see down over the town and the old parish church. Although the flood level had dropped you could see the river still overflowing its banks. The bottom half of the marketplace was a small lake, and there were fire engines down by Watergate. 'Still pumping out the flood water,' said Mr Brown.

The road we were standing in was like a scar on the hillside. The gardens were churned-up mud, but workmen were fitting in fences and the houses looked fresh and new.

'Isn't this grand?' said Mrs Brown, walking along. 'Look at the size of those windows! They'll be lovely and light. Proper front gardens, and the gardens at the back are a tidy size. Plenty of room for your vegetables, Frank. And not far to walk into town, Peg. Be a nice walk when you're pushing the pram. And, look, we're almost in the countryside.'

True. At the end of the road was a field, and beyond that some woods.

'I just hope we get some good neighbours,' Mrs Brown said. 'These houses will be wasted on some of those people from Watergate. Bathroom! They wouldn't know what to do with one.'

Peggy laughed. 'Well, there's you and my dad. Then there'll be me and George and his mum. And Billy West and Carol and their three kiddies will be moving up here. So that's a good start.'

I thought of Billy living up here with his family, making a new garden, playing football with his boys, riding his bike down the hill to work, his coat flapping . . . The thought hurt so much, I bent double.

Peggy and her mum walked up the path of one of the houses and peered in through the windows, while Mr Brown poked his toe into the soil in the garden.

'Come and look, Rosie!' yelled Peggy. 'If you look in through this window, you can see into the kitchen and through to the front room!'

I started to walk up the path, but my head was hurting and my legs were like lead. Everything was out of focus. I was ill, I realised, really ill.

'Can we go home please?' I said in as strong a voice as I could muster. 'Can we go home, please? I don't feel very well.'

Suddenly they were all fussing round me, squashing me back into the car. Peggy was holding my hand, rubbing it to get it warm. I knew I was icy cold. I couldn't stop shivering and I couldn't keep my head up. It felt so heavy. As we bumped along in the car, I felt so sick.

The car had stopped, I think. Hands were pulling me, helping me, trying to support me. Voices swirled above my head. They were telling me I'd be all right soon, but I seemed to be falling through all their helping hands. Everything was dark . . . and somewhere in that darkness, Billy was calling to me.

CHAPTER NINE

LEMONS. I COULD SMELL LEMONS. But mixed with something else, something woody. And soap. There was soap in there somewhere too. It was a very clean smell, a familiar smell. I knew I had smelt it before, long ago. But also that it had been near me a lot recently. I realised it had been there, on the edge of my consciousness for a long time.

I knew that it would make me happy. But I didn't know why. And it seemed such a long way away. Maybe I could go towards it? But I didn't think I could reach it. Everything was such an effort . . .

The smell was closer now. I was breathing it in. It was filling my nostrils, my head. Maybe I could reach it if I tried very hard . . .

'Rosie! Rosie! Are you there? Can you hear me?'

If I concentrated very hard, I could open my eyes. I flickered them open. There was someone bending over me. Someone familiar. Billy?

'Rosie! It's me, Will. Can you hear me?'

Will? Of course. Lemons. Will always smelt zingy and zesty of delicious woody citrus. Billy smelt of sweat and beer and newsprint. This was Will. Will! I opened my eyes and smiled at him and he was crying.

'You're back! Oh, Rosie, you're back!'

And then there were all sorts of things going on. People talking, testing, beeps of equipment. But I could still smell lemons and I knew that wherever I'd been, I was back.

I was in hospital. I worked that out. A nice twenty-first-century hospital. It had to be. Mum and Dad were there. But it was Will I had to be sure about. As nurses prodded and poked and measured and tested and asked me how many fingers they were holding up, Mum and Dad were either side of my bed. Mum was holding my hands and Dad was stroking my shoulder. A nurse adjusted one of the many drips that seemed to be plugged into me and gradually I calmed down.

Will, meanwhile, was standing at the back of the room watching me intently. It was hard to keep my eyes open. The light hurt my eyes. But it was Will, not Billy. The well-fitting jeans and polo shirt, the decent haircut, a face less lined, all gave the game away. But even in my dopey state I realised the big difference. Will was looking at me with an expression of pure love. And concern. No guilt. No worry. No thoughts about a wife and children. Here life was simple. I slipped away from the pain and back into sleep. But I knew I was smiling.

It was meningitis. What I had thought was a cold and sore throat meeting a huge Monday-morning hangover after a row with Will, had actually been a very serious illness. Apparently, I'd walked up the path to Mrs Turnbull's and had collapsed at her feet, literally at death's door.

'Mrs Turnbull's house?' I asked, a day or so later when I was well enough to talk and was trying to get things straight in my head. 'Mrs Brown's house in Cheapside where I'd been staying?'

'Cheapside? No,' said Will, exchanging a glance with my mum. 'No. Mrs Turnbull's house at The Meadows.'

'Ah, the new house, George and Peggy's new house . . .'

'Not that new,' said Will. 'It's been there fifty years.'

I think I might have had to go back to sleep again before I could work this one out and ask any more questions. My head was seriously confused. This time, Mum and Dad had gone to get something to eat and I was lying in bed watching the sun set while Will held my hand.

'So I haven't been in *The 1950s House* then?'

'No, you've been here, in hospital. You went a week ago on Monday afternoon to interview Mrs Margaret Turnbull at The Meadows. You were meant to be doing a feature on fifty years of The Meadows. Do you remember that?'

'Yes. I got a taxi because my car was at the pub.'

'That's right.' Will looked relieved. 'And you'd just rung the bell at Mrs Turnbull's house, when you collapsed. She opened the front door and found you lying on the doorstep.'

'No, it was Mrs Brown's house and she gave me tea and cake and I began to feel better. And I stayed there and I thought it was *The 1950s House*, and I was looking for the cameras.'

'No, my love,' said Will, gently. 'You dreamed that. You never went into the house. You never got over the doorstep.'

It was too confusing to argue. I just listened to Will's version.

Apparently Mrs Turnbull had taken one look at me and suspected that it was meningitis. She didn't mess about, but got straight on the phone and told them what was wrong. The ambulance was there in minutes and had whisked me here. If it hadn't been for Mrs Turnbull's quick actions, I would not have lived to tell the tale. Which takes some getting your head round, believe me. As it was, it had been touch and go. I had been in hospital for over a week, they told me, and Will and my mum and dad—and my brother Dan too—had been at my bedside.

'So I haven't been living in the 1950s?' I asked Will.

'No, just nearly dying here in the twenty-first century.'

'And the farmer didn't shoot himself?'

'Not any farmer I know.'

'And there haven't been floods and you didn't borrow a boat from the boating lake?'

'Not guilty. No floods. No boat. No boating lake.'

'And you're not married to Carol? Caz? You haven't got three children?'

Will laughed gently. 'No, last time I looked I definitely wasn't married to Caz and I have no children at all.'

'You're not married to anyone?'

'No, no one at all.'

'And it's all right to love you?'

'It's very all right to love me,' he said, kissing my hand and smiling.

'That's good,' I said and fell back onto the pillows.

The next day my mum was helping me wash, oh so gently sponging me down. I couldn't wash my hair yet, or get in the shower, but already some of the wires had gone.

'Oh, Rosie, I thought we'd lost you,' Mum said as she eased a fresh cotton nightie over my head.

'I felt lost. In my head I've been away for six weeks or more. I thought I was living in the 1950s. I was working on The News but it was all different. It was very real.'

'Of course it would be, you were very ill. Your brain was swollen and you were full of drugs. Being somewhere else sounds very sensible to me. Though I think I would have chosen somewhere more exotic than the 1950s. A nice warm bit of foreign coast might have been nicer.'

'It was . . . interesting. Do you remember the 1950s, Mum?'

'Not much. I was born just after the Coronation. I remember wearing hand-knitted cardigans and your gran wearing a pinny all the time. Except for going to the shops when she would put a hat and coat on.'

'Did you eat hearts?'

'Hearts? Yes, I think Gran used to stuff them. Goodness, if you've been dreaming about hearts, you *have* been having strange dreams.'

And so the days drifted by. I spent a lot of time sleeping, dozing, trying to make sense of what had happened to me. Life in the 1950s had been so vivid. It seemed more real than what was going on around me. I knew I was physically back in the twenty-first century, but I think my head was taking a bit longer to catch up.

Mum, Dad and Will took turns to be with me, though no one stayed the night now. My dad just sat by my bedside and did the crossword.

'It's nice to have you here,' I murmured to him one day, half asleep.

'It's what dads are for, Princess, to look after their little girls, however old they are. And to look after their mums as well. I look after Mum, so she can look after you. It's quite a good system really.'

I drifted back to sleep and thought about it. We got into a routine. Morning was tests and doctors and physio and things, and visits from the consultant, Mr Uzmaston, and the registrar Dr Simpson. Mum and Dad came in at lunchtime to be with me all afternoon. Will came in the evening. He'd been off work all the time I'd been unconscious, but was back now.

I hadn't realised that Mum and Dad were staying at the flat.

'Will insisted,' said Mum. 'After all, he says, it's your flat. And it's much nicer than staying in a hotel. Will sleeps on the sofa. I get a meal ready for him to eat when he comes back from the hospital.'

Strange to think of this cosy domestic life going on without me.

One evening Will took me for a walk. This was a big adventure. We were going all the way along the corridor to a small lounge area that not many people seemed to know about. It had wonderful views over the town and tonight we had it to ourselves. The first time we'd walked there—all of 100 yards—Will had had to bring me back in a wheel-chair. But I was getting good at it now.

'You'll be running along here soon,' he said, as I made my way extremely slowly to one of the armchairs and collapsed into it. I knew I looked a mess and smelt stale, yet here was Will with his arm round me.

'Oh, Will, you're so kind and patient.'

'You've been very ill. You need looking after. I don't think you're quite up to killing dragons at the moment.'

That rang a bell. Jamie talking about redundant dragon slayers. Something about being able to kill my own dragons . . .

'Will, did we have a row just before I was ill?'

'Shhh. It doesn't matter now.' He gently stroked my lank hair.

'We did, didn't we? You wanted to go to Dubai. You wanted a big television. You're not going to Dubai, are you?' I could feel panic rising.

'No, sweetheart, I'm not going to Dubai. Don't worry.'

Suddenly scraps of the row came back to me. Will telling me I was selfish. Me telling him he was a big kid with no sense of responsibility. Was that true? I thought of Billy, who had taken on the responsibility of marriage and fatherhood when he was a teenager, and had made a brilliant job of them. Was Billy just Will in different circumstances? If Billy hadn't had to get married and had had plenty of money, would he have just wanted fast cars and big televisions? I called the gadgets Will had a passion for his 'toys'. But why not? He had no need to grow up. If he was like Billy, then he would grow up when he needed to.

'You asked me what I wanted for the future. If I wanted children.'

Will put his finger gently on my lips. 'There are lots of things to talk about. But not now, not yet. First thing is to get you better. Then we will have all our lives to sort things out. Just a few days ago, the chances of that looked slim. Take it gently, Rosie. We have all the time in the world. And I'm not going anywhere.' Then he grinned and laughed at me. 'And you're not exactly running marathons yet, are you!'

He helped me up and I started the slow totter back to my bed.

Slowly, I got better and I was allowed more visitors. First to come was Caz, who bounced into my room with an aura of fresh spring air around her. When she smiled she showed perfect, even, white teeth. I thought of Carol and her crooked smile.

'Caz, did you ever wear braces on your teeth?'

'Oh God, yes! From twelve to fifteen, *just* the age when you're most self-conscious,' she said, helping herself to some of my grapes. 'Dentists have a lot to answer for. Ruined my social life until I had them off in Year Eleven and I could finally flash my winning smile at Will.'

'And it worked.'

'Oh, yes. However, not for long, which only goes to show that dentists can give you perfect teeth but cannot also be responsible for finding you a life partner.'

'But what if you had? What if you'd got pregnant and you and Will had got married, could it have worked?'

'Well, if I'd got pregnant, I would have got rid of it. The thought of marrying Will aged seventeen . . . Um, no. Let's not go there, Rosie.'

I wasn't giving up. 'Seriously, think about it. Could it have worked?'

'Oh Lordy. Basically I would say no, because Will and I—though I love him dearly as a friend—would drive each other mad. But, I suppose, yes, in a parallel universe sort of way, in your bizarre hypothetical situation, if Will and I had been forced to marry, we might—if we'd both tried hard enough—have made a reasonable fist of it.' She put the grape stalks in the bin and took one of my tissues to wipe her hands.

'One more thing.' I had to ask this. 'I know it's none of my business, but are you sure you don't want children?'

'Not that again!' Caz laughed. 'As sure as sure as sure,' she said. 'Honestly, Rosie, Jamie and I have talked about it a lot, so it's not a whim. We are both adamant.'

I thought of Carol and the way she looked after her children, the way they were pretty much her whole life.

Caz settled down to tell me all the juicy gossip I had missed while I had been ill. But as I smiled and listened, all I could think of was Libby, the little girl with the shy smile and the bright inquisitive eyes who was the image of her mother. Who in this age would never be born.

'**R**ight then, where's my darling girl?' The voice drifted down the garden where I sat on the bench, relishing the early summer sunshine.

'Granddad! Granny!' I hadn't heard them arrive, but now here they were, coming down the path, their arms wide open for hugs and kisses. They looked terrific. Life in Spain suited them. They were trim, tanned and toned. My brother Dan had just collected them from the airport.

'We had to be sure you were all right.' Granny looked worried and, for a moment, old.

'I am, I really am. A bit wobbly still, but getting better all the time.'

'And where's this wonderful young man of yours?' asked Granny, looking around as if expecting to see Will pop up from behind a bush.

'He'll be down later, Gran. He's got to work.'

'We've been hearing all sorts of good things about him.'

'Yup,' said Dan, coming out into the garden, a chunk of cheese in one hand and an apple in the other, 'the man's a hero, a regular Florence Nightingale. Actually, Sis, he must think something of you because let's face it, when you were ill, you looked really crap. I thought sick people were meant to look all frail and beautiful. You looked really minging. Bit better now, though,' he added hastily, as I tried to throw my book at him. 'Almost human.' And he dodged back up the path.

Everyone was laughing, but Gran was holding my hand. 'People die from meningitis, pet,' she said.

'I know, Gran, but I didn't. Thanks to the woman I went to interview. I shall go and see her as soon as I'm back to normal,' I said. 'She saved my life; the least I can do is say thank you.'

Then Mum was calling that lunch was ready. Granddad rummaged through their bags to find some wine they'd brought from Spain, and he insisted that I sit next to him. It was wonderful to be back with my family, safe and loved, listening to their chat.

Shortly after the meal, Will arrived, clutching a bunch of flowers for my mum and a scruffy carrier bag for me. He shook hands with Granddad, had a kiss from Mum, a beer from Dad, a cheerful shout from Dan, and a huge hug from Gran, who made him come and sit next to her while she cross-examined him. He grinned at her and answered all her questions like a lamb.

They were both laughing when she turned to me and said, 'I think he'll do for now, Rosie. He's passed the first interview.' Then she said, in a fake whisper, 'He's lovely, isn't he?'

Soon it was time for Mum and Dad to take Gran and Granddad back to the small flat that was their base in England. Gran stood on tiptoes to kiss Will goodbye. 'And mind you look after Rosie,' she said in mock severity. 'She's very precious to us all.'

'And to me too, don't worry,' he said, walking down the drive arm in arm with her.

They finally drove off, with much waving and blowing of kisses. Dan went off to see his girlfriend, and at last Will and I were alone together. Which is when I remembered the carrier bag. I found it behind my chair, opened it up carefully and peered in. Inside was an ice-cream tub full of soil, in which was a small plant with a couple of tiny green things growing on it.

'Um, lovely. What is it?' I asked.

'Chillies!' said Will proudly. 'I grew them from seed. Bloke I interviewed gave them to me. He makes all sorts of chilli sauces. Really hot stuff. And I planted them—went down with a serving spoon and got some soil out from the base of one of the cherry trees outside the flat. Then I watered them and put them on the kitchen windowsill and they've flourished. See. I'm a gardener, a horny-handed son of the soil. There's a couple more back in the flat, a regular production line.'

'Well, I'm impressed. Eat your heart out, Alan Titchmarsh.'

'Definitely. On the other hand, it's a sort of magic, isn't it? You put a little seed in some soil and then eventually it turns into something you can eat. Pretty cool when you think about it. I might do some more.'

'More chillies?'

'Well, more anything you can grow on a kitchen windowsill.'

I remembered a garden stretching up a slope, planted and tended so carefully. Neat rows, little paths, tall wigwam frames for runner beans.

And a man like Will leaning on his spade, watching his sons helping.

'Rosie, you've got that faraway look again. Still in your dream?'

I shook my head to shake the memory away and smiled. 'Yes, a bit. It still seems so real. Much more than a dream, really.'

'Why don't you write it all out, everything that happened? If nothing else it would make a great piece for the Health page—"Me and My Meningitis". It would be a neat way of getting back into work.'

'Well, that was something else I was going to tell you. I'm ready to go back to work.'

'Rosie, you mustn't rush it.'

'I'm not, but the doctor's said it's up to me now. I've just spoken to The Vixen and I'm going to go back a week on Monday. She says I can do as much or as little as I like until I'm back in the swing of things.'

'If you're sure.' Will was looking worried. 'But it would be wonderful to have you back, to be back to normal.' He lay down on the sofa beside me, pushing his long legs under mine and wrapping an arm round me. 'I've missed you horribly, you know,' he said. 'I don't like it on my own. I miss having you in the flat, miss talking to you, miss your opinions, miss just having you around. Rosie, all this has made me realise that, well, basically, I just don't want to live life without you.'

I lay there in his arms, not looking at him, but gazing out of the windows where I could see the high branches of the apple trees in the garden. I could feel the bones of his chest, the warmth of his skin through his shirt. He was so close to me that I almost felt part of him. I remembered watching Billy go home to another woman and her children. It might have been a dream, but the pain was real.

'The day before I was ill, and we had a row . . . you said you wanted to go away to Dubai or somewhere. Why did you say that?'

'I was angry. Do you really want to talk about this now?'

'Yes, I want things to be clear.'

He took a deep breath. 'Well, it's partly because I don't know what you want. It's as if you have your life planned out and if I can fit in round the edges, then, well, that's fine. But if you've got more important things to do and I don't fit into your plans, then, well, forget it. .

'I mean, I don't want a wife who's a little woman, waiting at home for me. But I don't want someone who's just going to skip off and do what she wants. That's why I thought I might as well do my thing too. Travel a bit, the sort of things I'd planned to do before I met you. I was getting too used to being with you. Working with you, going to the pub with you, cooking, even just goofing out in front of the TV.'

He picked up a strand of my hair and wrapped it gently round his fingers, then stroked my cheek. I could feel my insides tingling.

'It all mattered to me more and more.' He had twisted himself round now, so that he was looking at me. 'I found myself hoping that we would always be together. The problem was I wasn't sure about you. Every now and then you'd just announce that there was something you wanted to do, just as though it was nothing to do with me.

'Then when I saw you in that hospital bed, when I knew there was a real chance that you could die, I felt as though my whole world was knocked sideways. Without you, there just didn't seem any point in anything. Without you, I'm lost. Sad, isn't it? But there you go.

'So that's me, Rosie. I love you and I'm pretty sure I want to spend the rest of my life with you. Those are my cards on the table.'

I took a deep breath. 'I thought if I let on how much I wanted to be with you, that you would run a mile. I wanted my own life, because I thought I would need it when you left me. I thought you wanted no commitment, no responsibility, no putting down roots. I didn't want to let you hurt me, so it was easier to pretend that it didn't matter.'

Suddenly an image of Billy in the garden showing Peter how to build the cold frame flashed into my head.

'Then we had that row and I thought I'd lost you. I realised that more than anything else I wanted to be with you. And I also realised that you could be all those things if you needed to, had to. It's just that so far you hadn't needed to. I mean, I'd never needed to scrape burnt porridge off a pan with no washing-up liquid, or face a gunman, or walk miles, but I know I could if I had to. Like Caz could live without electricity.'

I could feel Will looking puzzled.

'Rosie, what are you talking about?'

'Tricky to explain.' And how. 'But I guess it's just that I've realised we don't know what we can do until we have to. Sometimes we've just got to trust people and take the leap.'

And I knew I could trust Will. He was absolutely rock solid.

He was baffled. 'But what's that got to do with porridge pots and gunmen?' he asked.

'Nothing. Everything. I can't explain. I just know I don't want to live without you. I knew it before, really. Being ill just made me certain.'

Will was still playing with my hair. I could feel his breath, warm and gentle, on the side of my face. All the time he'd been coming down to my parents' house since I'd left hospital he'd been sleeping in the spare room. Not because of any prudery on my parents' part, just that I'd still felt so rough and could hardly bear to be touched. As Will started kissing me, as our legs wrapped round each other, as I took him in my arms and pressed his head close to mine, I knew that had changed.

'So, Rosie, is it you and me against the world? A couple? Are we going to stick together and see how it works out?'

I nodded. 'Somebody told me that you and I were a great team, that things happened when we were together. I think that's right.'

I untangled myself, took hold of his hand and led him upstairs to my bedroom.

'Are you sure?' he asked.

'I'm sure. I'm sure about everything.'

'**O**h, you lovely, lovely computer!' I patted its sleek black casing, as if it were a favourite pet.

There was a snort of familiar laughter behind me. I turned round and The Vixen was standing there smiling.

'Welcome back, Rosie. It's very good to have you back and looking well. But I didn't think you'd have missed your computer that much!'

'I was just thinking'—how could I explain?—'just thinking of what it was like in the old days when they used typewriters and you had to put in paper and carbon paper.'

The Vixen smiled. 'Yes, that's what it was like when I was starting out. Then you'd send your copy to the subs, and then it would go to the typesetters and then the printers. Seems medieval now.'

'Were the subs all men when you started out?'

The Vixen perched elegantly on the edge of my desk. 'Always, until around the 1970s, I think. They'd sit round their table in a fug of smoke— they all smoked pipes—and I used to hate going in there.'

'Oh, so did I! I mean, well, aren't we lucky things have changed.'

'Yes, we are,' said The Vixen, looking at me oddly. 'Oh, by the way, that 1950s house thing isn't going to be in The Meadows. Apparently they're filming it in Birmingham instead. Shame, it would have been fun to have had it on our doorstep. You heard about Margaret Turnbull?'

I had. The old lady I'd been about to interview, who had been so quick to get help for me, was now in hospital herself.

'Yes, I rang up because I wanted to visit her, thank her. But her daughter, the head teacher, was at the house and answered the phone. Said she'd let me know when her mother was up for visitors.'

The Vixen picked up her sheaf of papers and turned to go to her office. 'Anyway, I'm very pleased to see you back, but for heaven's sake, take things gently. Don't push yourself.'

Off she went, her immaculate red bob catching a streak of sunlight streaming in through the windows.

That was the other thing I couldn't get used to—the office was so big and light. There were plants on the windowsills, not piles of yellowing newspapers. True, most people's desks were chaotic, but there were computers everywhere and every desk had a phone. The place was clean and spacious and tidy with carpet—carpet!—on the floor.

Honestly, I never thought I would be so happy to be back in *The News* office. There was a balloon tied to my keyboard and a bunch of roses by my phone. I inhaled their scent and sat down at my desk and switched on my computer. My inbox was full, going back to the day I was ill. So I just deleted the lot. Fresh start.

It was good to be back in the twenty-first century. I'd driven my little car up to the flat at the end of the previous week. And, yes, Will and I bought a new TV. Well, I know we didn't have room, but we soon would have. Because we were house-hunting. We didn't know where we were going in our careers, but we would see what happened. We were a team. We could work things out.

Whether the 1950s was a dream or reality, it left a lingering influence. I went shopping for some new outfits and I thought of Carol wearing the same coat, skirt, jumper and shoes, day in, day out. I certainly thought a bit more about what I bought.

It was wonderful to have waterproof mascara again, all on a double-ended twirly applicator, and not some disgusting little scrap of something that you spat on and then scrubbed at. And the first time I went into Waitrose after I'd been ill, I cannot tell you how wonderful it was. I was in foodie heaven. But there again, there was something about all those stacked shelves that made me feel a bit queasy.

One of the first features I was asked to do when I got back to work was about all the ways we could save energy, save the planet, and save money at the same time. I sat at the computer, looked up all sorts of facts and figures, and then it dawned on me—if we lived now in the way we had in the 1950s, it would solve the problem pretty well instantly. The intro snapped into my head. 'How green was your granny?' I typed and recalled all the things I remembered from the 1950s house.

The piece hit a nerve. I had letters and emails from people remembering how they, their mothers or their grannies used to do things.

'Do you think there's a column there?' The Vixen was asking. 'We're all meant to be recycling more and using less, and reducing our carbon footprint. Not too worthy, though. We might as well try to make it fun. Give it a bit of glitz and glamour. Glitzy green. Just your style.'

'Well, great, yes. Why not?'

'If you run out of ideas, come and ask me. I was a child of the 1950s.'

So, in a way, I couldn't let the 1950s go. Or they wouldn't let go of me. One day I even went up into the bound-file room and pulled out the dusty volumes from the 1950s shelf. I got very excited when I read the report of the great flood. No byline, just 'By our own staff'.

That was it! I thought, carefully turning the pages. That was the bit that I had written. And there was Billy's story. And George's pictures. That was the story we had written up by candlelight in that little pub in the walls, where we ate crisps and pickled eggs. It *had* happened.

For a moment I could smell the old newsroom, the piles of papers, the damp coats, the cigarette smoke. But then I opened my eyes and I was in the bound-file room in a modern building in the middle of a modern industrial estate. And I realised, of course, that I'd probably been reading that story when I was getting ill. That's why it had stuck in my mind. That's why I had dreamed of it. And put myself in it. There was no magic. No time travel. Just a nasty illness and vivid dreams.

I put the huge file back in its place on the shelf and felt somehow disappointed. The flood had seemed so real. I still believed I had lived it, not dreamed it—the little red boat, rescuing the old lady, wading through the flood water dragging the boat on a bit of rope, sitting in the pub with Billy and then walking along the walls in the moonlight . . .

For a dream, it had been pretty powerful. I asked Kate, The Vixen's secretary, if there was a way we could check back on former members of staff. I wanted to know if Billy had been real, or if I'd dreamed him up too. But there was no way of checking, no way of finding out. Even the accounts department had no record.

But Richard Henfield was real, of course. His picture was on The Vixen's office wall. The nice eyes, the weak chin . . .

One day I had an email from Margaret Turnbull's daughter, the head teacher, Rosemary Picton.

> Mother's by no means totally recovered and is still quite confused, but she is much better and we are going to try a spell in her own home, with plenty of care and support, to see how she gets on. We hope that being surrounded by familiar things might help a bit more.

A few days later I went to visit her. Will came with me. We took a huge bunch of flowers, an enormous box of chocs and a bottle of brandy. It felt really odd going up to The Meadows. I could remember the day I came up before, feeling so ill, and also that time—in my dream—when the houses were still bare and the gardens unmade.

'Oh, the view's gone,' I said to Will as we got out of the car. 'You used to be able to see right down to the town and the church and along the river. But now it's gone.'

'It's a long time since anyone could see the river from here,' he said. 'There are all those office blocks in the way. Some of those must have gone up in the 1960s. And the leisure centre and the multistorey car park. I remember all that going up when I was at school.'

We were walking up the path to Margaret Turnbull's house. I took a deep breath and rang the doorbell. I expected everything to go black again, the ground to come up and hit me, or to find myself back in Doreen Brown's kitchen, with the range and Sambo, the cat.

But no. The door opened and Rosemary Picton—scary head teacher of The Meadows School—was ushering us in. She had blonde hair, going grey, and a pleasant, open face. She reminded me of someone.

'How lovely to see you. I'm so glad you've recovered. Mother will be so pleased. Come on in.'

We manoeuvred our way through the tiny entrance hall into a spacious, light sitting room. As well as the big window facing onto the front garden, there was another window in the side wall. The views were still far-reaching and must have been stunning when the house was first built. Mrs Turnbull was sitting in a chair by the window. We went towards her with all our offerings and, as she smiled in welcome, I could see that the right side of her face drooped slightly, but her eyes still held a hint of sparkle. She had been a formidable woman. It was thanks to her that the south side of The Meadows was still a decent place to live—not like the no-go area to the north.

'Rosie!' she said, quite clearly, lifting her left hand out towards me.

I passed the flowers to Mrs Picton and turned back to her mother, taking her hand in both of mine and gripping it hard. 'Mrs Turnbull, I hardly know what to say. Thank you for saving my life! Because you did. If it hadn't been for you . . .' There was a low stool next to her chair and I sat down on that, still holding her hand.

'You . . . better . . . now?' she asked me. The words came out slowly.

'I'm fine. Fine. In fact'—with a quick glance at Will—'I'm better and happier than I was before, than I've ever been. I am very, very lucky. And that's largely down to you. But how about you?'

'Getting . . . there. Getting . . . there.'

'I'm sorry I never did the piece about the fiftieth anniversary of The Meadows.'

A freelance had done it while I was ill. It had been competent enough but, of course, she hadn't been able to interview Mrs Turnbull.

'Very different . . . when I moved in. See for miles. Tried to keep it nice.'

'Yes, you did wonders. This part of The Meadows is still a good place to live. And now your daughter's doing wonders with the school.'

At that moment Rosemary Picton was coming sideways into the sitting room carrying a tray with tea things. She put it down carefully on a low table. 'Best china!' she grinned. 'Mum insisted.'

I looked at the cups and saucers. White porcelain with a little blue flower. There was something familiar about them.

Will, meanwhile, having got up to hold the door open for Mrs Picton, was looking at some of the photographs. The room was full of wonderful local scenes on the walls, and a rack of family photos—weddings, babies, graduations—stood in front of the books on the shelves.

'Of course,' said Will, 'your husband was a photographer with *The News*, wasn't he?'

I looked up, surprised. I hadn't known that before I was ill. I was sure I hadn't known that.

'Yes,' replied Rosemary for her mother. 'He started at *The News* at fourteen and was still working there when he died in 1994. Tragic. He died much too young. He was a lovely man. Both my brothers have followed in his footsteps. Tony works for the Press Association and David's a cameraman with the BBC.'

'Was he called George?'

'Yes, there he is. That's my parents' wedding photograph.'

I looked at the photo she was holding towards me. A boyish young man was beaming proudly beside a slightly older young woman, who was holding a bouquet of flowers very carefully in front of her as if to hide something. She was wearing a dress and jacket, the jacket was loose and stylish and fastened with a single large button . . .

Mrs Turnbull was struggling to say something. 'You . . . bought . . . jacket . . . wedding . . . beautiful . . . jacket . . .'

'What, Mum?' said Rosemary Picton gently. 'No, this Rosie didn't buy your jacket for you. It was another Rosie. You were married long before this Rosie was born. I'm sorry,' she said to me, 'but she does get a bit muddled.'

All my nerve ends tingled. I had so many questions and Margaret Turnbull was in no position to answer them. I looked across at her. For a second there was a flash of knowledge, recognition. 'Yes,' it seemed to say, 'you're right. It *is* me.'

Rosemary poured just half a cup of tea and placed it, without its saucer, in her mother's hand. I remembered where I'd seen those cups before. It was the night of the engagement. Peggy and George's engagement. Mrs

Brown had got them out because it was a special occasion.

I felt frightened, excited. Was this old lady, drinking her tea so carefully, really Peggy? It couldn't be. Could it?

Mrs Turnbull was lifting the cup to her mouth. She took barely a sip and then set the cup on its long journey back to the saucer.

'Mrs Turnbull,' said Will, 'what really impressed me was the way you didn't mess about, didn't hesitate. You knew instantly what was wrong with Rosie. If you hadn't, if you'd dithered, she wouldn't be here now. Rosie means a lot, everything to me. So really I owe you everything too.' He turned the full power of his smile onto her.

Mrs Turnbull smiled with half her mouth.

'It's quite sad really,' explained Rosemary. 'When Mum was young, just about the time my parents were married, she had a friend, an American girl who was lodging with them, who died of meningitis very suddenly. That's why my mother recognised the symptoms. She'd seen them before and always felt guilty that she couldn't save her friend. Always thought that if they'd called the doctor sooner, they might have saved her. Long before there was all the publicity about meningitis, my mother was always telling us the signs to look out for. She knew speed was so important. Funnily enough, the American was called Rosie too.'

'Rosie . . . saved my . . . life,' said Mrs Turnbull. 'Rosie and George.'

'She's never told me the full story,' said Rosemary, 'but she always said that if it hadn't been for this American girl, she wouldn't be here today. And neither would I—that's why she named me after her.'

Rosemary. Suddenly there was a woman of fifty named after me. I poured myself another cup of tea and wished I could have poured a generous slug of the brandy into it.

Will was admiring some of George's photos of Watergate before it was pulled down to make way for the ring road. While he and Rosemary talked about them, I took Mrs Turnbull's hand again. 'Peggy? Is it you? It's me, Rosie. Rosie, the one you thought was American, Rosie who lodged with you. Rosie who came with George looking for you.'

Oh God, if I found it hard to accept that this was Peggy, how on earth would this muddled old lady realise I was Rosie?

'Peggy,' I whispered. 'Peggy. Is it you? Is Rosemary the baby you were expecting when I knew you? Were you happy with George? What happened to Billy and Carol? Did they move up here? Are they still here?'

It was no good. Of course I shouldn't have bombarded Mrs Turnbull with questions. She was confused enough. I would only make it worse. It was my dream. What was I doing, trying to use her to explain it?

Mrs Turnbull was gearing herself up to say something. 'Want to say . . .

happy life . . . wonderful husband . . . best daughter . . . good sons . . . all thanks . . . Rosie . . . Lovely . . . see her . . . again . . .' She reached for my hand again.

I hugged her. 'It's all worked out, Peggy,' I found myself saying. 'Everything worked out. Everything worked out fine.'

She looked tired, but was still trying to smile her lopsided smile.

'I think it's probably time we went, Rosie,' said Will, putting his hand on my shoulder. 'We've exhausted Mrs Turnbull.'

We made our farewells and went to the door. I looked across the room and for a second I could see Peggy again. The young Peggy who was laughing when she came back from her honeymoon, her expression flitting over the lined and wrinkled face of Mrs Turnbull.

'G'bye, Rosie,' she said, and then, 'G'bye, Billy.'

'It's Will, not Billy, Mum,' Rosemary said.

'It's all right. I answer to anything,' said Will, as I tried desperately to see Peggy again in Mrs Turnbull. But she had switched off.

'Thank you for coming,' said Rosemary. 'That's the most lively we've seen Mum since she was ill. You've done her good. You must come again.'

'Thank you,' I said.

But I knew we wouldn't. Peggy—Mrs Turnbull—and I had said our thank yous to each other. I had saved her life and her daughter's. She had saved mine. Peggy would like that. It balanced everything up. The past was over. I didn't belong there. I had my own life to lead, here and now.

CHAPTER TEN

IT WAS A PERFECT DAY. The sun shone and the garden of the Shire Hall was rich with the scent of roses. Leo and Jake, looking incredibly smart in matching morning suits, were posing happily at the top of the steps, while the rest of us waved and cheered and cameras flashed.

It had been a simple and moving ceremony of civil partnership, in which Leo and Jake had promised to love and support and care for each other, and to each help the other flourish and achieve his dreams.

At the end of the service, Leo and Jake had hugged and now here they were on the steps, their arms still round each other's shoulders.

'Now to the important part!' shouted Jake. 'Champagne!'

A little brigade of waiters and waitresses carrying trays of champagne were strategically placed round the garden. We all took it in turns to congratulate Leo and Jake before we moved down the steps into the garden to collect a glass and then gather in little clusters. Somewhere in the background a jazz band played. The air was full of saxophone and laughter, glasses and the pop of more champagne corks.

'Good do,' said Will, helping himself to another glass from a tray offered by a passing waitress.

'It's a lovely day. A perfect day. About as far away from hospitals as you can get, thank God. I know it sounds corny, but I can't think of any other way of putting it—I'm so glad to be alive.'

'Not nearly as glad as I am that you are,' said Will, kissing my nose.

There was a big contingent from *The News*, including The Vixen, who was holding court on a stone bench in the shade of a tree. She glanced up, pushed her designer shades back up her nose, and looked from under her fringe straight at me.

Suddenly I was back in the Browns' kitchen. I *knew* I'd recognised her.

'Will . . . what's The Vixen's first name?'

'Jan, of course.'

'Yes, I know. What I mean is, what's Jan short for?'

'I don't know. Is it short for anything? Janet I suppose. No, hang on, I remember seeing something somewhere. Janice, that's it. I remember thinking she wasn't a Janice sort of person, but she is. Or was.'

I looked at Jan Fox in her sharp designer outfit, her gleaming hair and immaculate make-up, her style and confidence. I remembered the small and smelly girl with the broken specs and the ravenous appetite for food, for learning, for life. I couldn't ask. I just couldn't.

I shivered, and Will put his arm round me. 'All right?'

'Yes, yes. It's nothing.'

A maître d' was summoning us in to eat. There was delicious food, more wine, crackers with jokes and streamers. Leo and Jake both made speeches. Back out in the garden in the early evening the jazz players had been replaced by a band playing hits from the 80s and 90s. The party was now in a blissful mood of post-meal, lots-of-wine relaxation.

Leo and Jake, arm in arm, came laughing up to their mothers, took their hands and danced them gently across the lawn, all four joined together, the mothers delighted at their sons' happiness.

And suddenly they were going. Waiters came round with ice-cream cake, coffee and trays of liqueurs, and there were Leo and Jake at the top of the stairs, blowing us all kisses and getting huge cheers.

'I've got no bouquet to throw,' said Jake, 'but instead I shall throw you my . . . buttonhole.'

And he freed the flower from his jacket and tossed it with a flourish down into the group standing at the bottom of the steps. To my surprise, it was Will who leapt high into the air and grabbed it from above the heads of them all.

'I always was great in the line-out,' he said, amid cheers and cat calls.

There were even more yells when he tucked the flower into the very low neckline of my dress.

'Your turn next!' shouted Jake.

After cheering them on their way, the guests split into little groups, some making leaving noises, others ordering more drinks, a few energetic souls planning to go clubbing.

'What would you like to do?' asked Will as I shrugged into my jacket.

'Well, I don't want anything more to eat or drink.'

'I think we're ready for home. Shall I call a cab?'

'No, let's walk.'

The Shire Hall was in the old part of town, and I knew which way I wanted to go. We slipped through the gardens, then down a path through a small secluded square and along a crescent of lovely Georgian houses, until at last we found ourselves by some steps leading up to the old town walls. The tapas bar was bouncing and people were overflowing up the steps and onto the walls, but after twenty or thirty yards their noise faded into the distance and we were alone.

In the soft evening light we could see along the river and across to the other side. The click click of my kitten heels echoed against the old stones.

'The last time we walked along here I was going flump flump flump in wellies.'

'I don't remember that.'

'Well, no, it wasn't you, not now.'

'Your dream again? My alter ego?'

'That's it.'

There was a bench just where there had been a bench before. New bench, old walls. We sat down and I looked across the river. All the streets of little old houses had gone. Instead there was a block of very expensive apartments, a green open space and a car park.

'There was a little house over there, where your alter ego lived with Caz and the children. The house was very picturesque, but dark and damp and smelly. No electricity. You had a huge garden that stretched up the hill, and you had lots of neat rows of vegetables. And a cold frame that your son helped you build.'

I remembered the togetherness of the little family and the pain of being excluded from Will's life. I couldn't believe that he was here beside me now. I leaned against him, pleased that I had the right to snuggle up to him, to claim him as my own.

'That reminds me!' Will sat up suddenly. 'There was something in the post this morning from the estate agent. The postman arrived just as I was going out to bring the car round. I'd forgotten all about it.'

He pulled an envelope from his inside pocket and ripped it open. 'Don't suppose it'll be any more interesting than the rest of the overpriced doll's houses he's sent us.' He looked. 'On the other hand . . .'

I snatched the details from him and peered in the dying light. I could see a picture of a house, a square-ish, no-nonsense sort of a house, surrounded by gardens. I liked the look of it immediately.

'Three bedrooms . . . two reception . . . original fireplaces . . . needs some work . . . plenty of room to extend.' I read the details out loud, with Will looking over my shoulder. 'Large, well-maintained garden including lawn, orchard and vegetable plot.'

'I think I could take to gardening,' Will said. 'I mean, I've grown those chillies, haven't I? I quite fancy going out and picking nice fresh veg. We'll ring them tomorrow and arrange to take a look, shall we? If it needs doing up we've got the rest of our lives, haven't we? When I'm not growing prize marrows or whatever.'

I was laughing. 'Tell you what,' I said. 'I'll even buy you a shed.'

'A shed! It's a deal!' Will pulled me to my feet and put his arm round me. The bench and the wall and the river, and the memory of that dark, damp, little house faded into the darkness as Will and I walked into our future together.

Sharon Griffiths

How did the idea of time travel first occur to you as the storyline for a novel?
It was when I was thinking about how long adolescence seems to last these days. Many young men in their twenties, or even thirties, still act like teenagers, without any sense of responsibility. Little more than a generation ago, they would have been real grown-ups.

You have two sons, aged twenty-four and twenty-six. Were you thinking of them when you created the characters of Will and Jamie?
I was thinking of my nephew, mostly. I was looking back to when he built an obstacle course for his young nephews and nieces *inside* his sister's house and all of them were leaping over it on rollerblades. He'd even built a ramp over the dog! And I thought: I remember your father at about your age. He was an army bomb-disposal officer. In fairness, my nephew did become hugely successful!

Do you feel that women are now more willing to assume responsibility?
They are much more independent and they don't need men in the same way. I have very clear memories of how utterly different 1950s attitudes to sex and marriage were. When writing the book, I thought: How would modern women cope if they were back in the 1950s, when sex at sixteen invariably meant a

wedding and a baby at seventeen, and precious little chance of a career? They are used to their freedom now and they aren't going to give that up lightly.

Did you model Rosie on yourself when you were a young journalist?

Oh, no, she's much nicer than I am and much more confident.

In the book, she falls ill with meningitis. What sparked that idea?

Well, I've researched meningitis because the doctors thought that one of my sons had it, and then they thought that I had it. In fact, neither of us did, but one of the aspects of the illness is that you do get very, very, vivid dreams, and when people recover, they're not sure what has been happening.

The children in *The Accidental Time Traveller* are given a lot of responsibility and considerable freedom. Is this something you experienced as a child?

Yes. I was born in Pembrokeshire in West Wales, where I lived a 'William and the Outlaws' type of childhood. Both my parents worked and I used to do all the shopping and think nothing of it. In the holidays, from the age of nine, I used to make lunch—bread and cheese, or a pork pie with pickle—and have it ready for my parents when they came in. I'd be left to my own devices all day.

This just wouldn't happen these days. What has changed so radically?

One of the things, and it's a very real worry, is the amount of traffic on the roads. As a child, I used to ride my bike everywhere. But it can't be done now.

You enjoyed being free to roam, but did you also enjoy the discipline of school?

I went to Brecon Girls' Grammar School and I was part of a remarkable year. We reckoned we had the most girls entering university as well as the most girls getting pregnant! And one or two of them did both! After studying English at Bristol University, my first job was with the BBC as a secretary at Radio Oxford.

How did you meet your husband?

I was the only female journalist on a press trip with forty men travelling on a goods train from Ipswich to Glasgow. He was one of the group: a brilliant young journalist called Mike Amos. That was more than thirty years ago now.

You've just celebrated your sixtieth birthday. What does being sixty mean to you?

We went to Paris to celebrate my birthday, taking our sons and their girlfriends, the lot. We had a wonderful time. I'm delighted that I had my first book published this year and am just finishing the second. I had lunch with a Hollywood agent recently, and she was very enthusiastic about *The Accidental Time Traveller*. We'll see . . . But the future is exciting.

Do you hanker after the past at all, particularly the Fifties?

I certainly wouldn't want to go back to that era. My generation can remember the Civil Rights marches when black people didn't have a vote in many states of America. Now they have Barack Obama as their President. This is the start of my third age and I can do anything I like, health and strength permitting. My motto is: 'Get on with life, enjoy it!'

Anne Jenkins

UNDER A BLOOD RED SKY

KATE FURNIVALL

Sentenced to ten years in a Siberian labour camp, Sofia Morozova has learned to exist from minute to minute, from mouthful to mouthful. All that sustains her through the bitter cold and hard labour are the stories told by her friend, Anna: beguiling tales of a charmed upbringing in Petrograd—and of Anna's love for a passionate and handsome revolutionary, Vasily. One day, Sofia vows, she will escape and bring the young lovers together again . . .

1

Davinsky Labour Camp, Siberia
February 1933

THE ZONE. That's what the compound was called.

A double barrier of dense barbed wire encircled it, backed by a high fence and watchtowers that never slept. In Sofia Morozova's mind it merged with all the other hated lice-ridden camps she'd been in. Transit camps were the worst. They ate up your soul, then spat you out into cattle trucks to move you on to the next. *Etap*, it was called, this shifting of prisoners from one camp to another until no friends, no possessions and no self remained. You became nothing. That's what they wanted.

Work is an Act of Honour, Courage and Heroism. Those words were emblazoned in iron letters a metre high over the gates of Davinsky Labour Camp. Every time Sofia was marched in and out to work in the depths of the taiga forest she read Stalin's words above her head. Twice a day for the ten years that were her sentence. That would add up to over seven thousand times—that is, if she lived that long, which was unlikely. Would she come to believe that hard labour was an 'Act of Heroism' after reading those words seven thousand times? Would she care any more whether she believed it or not?

As she trudged out into the snow in the five o'clock darkness of an Arctic morning with six hundred other prisoners, two abreast in a long silent shuffling crocodile, she spat as she passed under Stalin's words. The spittle froze before it hit the ground.

'There's going to be a whiteout,' Sofia said.

She had an uncanny knack for smelling out the weather half a day before it arrived. It wasn't something she'd been aware of in the days when she lived near Petrograd, but out here, where the forests swallowed you whole, it came easily to her. She turned to the young woman sitting at her side.

'Anna, you'd better go over and tell the guards to get the ropes out.'

'A good excuse for me to warm my hands on their fire, anyway.' Anna smiled. She was a fragile figure, always quick to find a smile, but the shadows under her blue eyes had grown so dark they looked bruised.

'Make sure the brainless bastards take note of it,' grimaced Nina, a wide-hipped Ukrainian who knew how to swing a sledgehammer better than any of them. 'We don't want to lose anyone.'

When visibility dropped to absolute zero in blizzard conditions, the prisoners were roped together on the long trek back to camp. Not to stop them escaping, but to prevent them blundering out of line and freezing to death in the snow.

'If they've got any bloody sense, we'll finish early today and get back to the stinking huts ahead of it,' snorted Tasha, the woman on the other side of Sofia. She had small narrow features and a prim mouth that was surprisingly adept at swearing.

'That would be better for you, Anna.' Sofia nodded. 'You could rest.'

'No, I'm doing well today. I'll soon be catching up with your work rate, Nina. You'd better watch out.'

Anna gave a mischievous smile to the three other women and they laughed outright, but Sofia noticed that her friend didn't miss the quick glance that passed between them. Anna struggled against another spasm of coughing and sipped her midday *chai* to soothe her raw throat. Not that the drink deserved to be called tea. It was a bitter brew made from pine needles and moss that was said to fight scurvy. Whether that was true or just a rumour spread around to make them drink the brown muck was uncertain, but it fooled the stomach into thinking it was being fed and that was all they cared about.

The four women were seated on a felled pine tree, huddled together for warmth, kicking bald patches in the snow with their *lapti*, boots shaped from soft birch bark. They were making the most of their half-hour midday break from perpetual labour.

All around, as far as the eye could see, stretched dense forests of pine trees, great seas of them that swept in endless waves across the whole of northern Russia, packed tight under snow—and through it all they were attempting to carve a road. Dear God, but road-building was wretched. Brutal at the best of times, but with inadequate tools and temperatures of thirty degrees below freezing it became a living nightmare. Your shovels cracked, your hands turned black, your breath froze in your lungs.

'*Davay!* Hurry! Back to work!'

The guards crowded round the brazier and shouted orders, but they didn't leave their circle of precious warmth. Along the length of the arrow-straight scar that sliced through the trees to make space for the new road, a collective sigh of resignation rose like smoke in the air as the brigades of women took up their hammers and spades once more.

Anna was the first on her feet, eager to prove she could meet the required norm, the work quota for each day. 'Come on, you lazy . . .' she muttered to herself.

But she didn't finish the sentence. She swayed, her blue eyes glazed, and she would have fallen if she hadn't been clutching her shovel. Sofia reached her first and held her safe, the frail body starting to shake as coughs raked her lungs. She jammed a rag over Anna's mouth.

'She won't last,' Tasha whispered. 'Her bloody lungs are—'

'Ssh.' Sofia frowned at her.

Nina patted Anna's shoulder and said nothing. Sofia walked Anna back to her patch of the road, helped her scramble up onto its raised surface and placed the shovel in her hand. Not once had Anna come even close to meeting the norm in the last month and that meant less food each day in her ration. Sofia shifted a few shovels of rock for her.

'Thanks,' Anna said and wiped her mouth. 'I'll be fine now.'

Sofia gazed hard into her friend's sunken eyes and what she saw there made her chest tighten. Oh, Anna. A frail wisp of a thing, just twenty-eight years old. Too soon to die, much too soon. And that moment, on an ice-bound patch of rock in an empty Siberian wilderness, was when Sofia made the decision.

I swear to God, Anna, I'll get you out of here. If it kills me.

The whiteout came just as Sofia said it would. But the guards paid heed to her warning, and before it hit they roped together the crocodile of ragged figures and set off on the long, mindless trudge back to camp.

As the prisoners made their way through the trees, Sofia and Anna pushed one exhausted foot in front of the other and huddled their bodies close to each other. This was an attempt to share their remaining wisps of warmth, but it was also something else, something more important to both of them.

They talked to each other. Not just the usual moans about aching backs or broken spades or which brigade was falling behind on its norm, but real words that wove real pictures.

Early on, Sofia had worked out that in a labour camp you exist from minute to minute, from mouthful to mouthful. You divide every piece of time into tiny portions and you tell yourself you can survive just this small portion. That's how you get through a day. No past, no future, just this moment. Sofia had been certain that it was the only way to survive here, a slow and painful starvation of the soul.

But Anna had other ideas. She had broken all Sofia's self-imposed rules and made each day bearable. With words. Each morning on the two-hour trek out to the Work Zone and each evening on the weary trudge back to the camp, they put their heads close and created pictures, until the delicately crafted scenes were all their eyes could see. The guards, the forest and the unrelenting savagery of the place faded, like dreams fade.

Anna was best at it. The stories were all about her childhood in Petrograd before the Revolution, and day by day, month by month, year by year, Sofia felt the words and the stories build up inside her own bones. They packed tight and dense where the marrow was long gone, and kept her limbs firm and solid as she swung an axe or dug a ditch.

'Anna,' Sofia urged, holding on to the rope that bound them together, 'tell me about Vasily again.'

Anna smiled, she couldn't help it. Just the mention of the name Vasily turned a light on inside her, however wet or tired or sick she was. Vasily Dyuzheyev—he was Anna's childhood friend in Petrograd, two years older but her companion in every waking thought and in many of her night-time dreams. He was the son of Svetlana and Grigori Dyuzheyev, aristocratic friends of Anna's father, and right now Sofia needed to know everything about him. *Everything*. And not just for pleasure this time—though she didn't like to admit, even to herself, how much pleasure Anna's talking of Vasily gave her—for now it was serious.

Sofia had made the decision to get Anna out of this hellhole before it was too late. Her only hope of succeeding was with help, and Vasily was the only one she could turn to. But would he help? And could she find him?

A quiet and thoughtful smile had crept onto Anna's face. Her scarf was wrapped round her head and the lower part of her face, so that only her eyes showed, narrowed against the wind. But the smile was there, deep inside them, as she started to talk.

'The day was as colourless as today. It was winter and the new year of 1917 had just begun. All around me the white sky and the white ground merged to become one crisp shell, frozen in a silent world. Vasily and I had come out for a walk together down by the lake on his father's estate, just the two of us, wrapped up well against the cold.

'"I'll build you a snow sleigh fit for a Snow Queen," he promised.

'You should have seen him, Sofia. His eyes bright and sparkling as he watched me climb up among a sycamore tree's huge branches that spread out over the lawn like a skeleton. He didn't once say, "Be careful" or "It's not ladylike", like my governess Maria would have.

'"You'll keep dry up there," he laughed, "and it'll stop you leaping over the sleigh with your big feet before it's finished."

'I threw a snowball at him, then watched as he carefully carved runners out of the deep snow, creating the body of a sleigh with long, sweeping sides. At first I sang "Gaida Troika" to him, but eventually I couldn't hold back the question that was burning a hole in my tongue.

'"Will you tell me what you've been doing, Vasily? You're hardly ever here any more. I . . . hear things."

'"What kind of things?"

'"The servants are saying it's getting dangerous on the streets."

'"You should always listen to the servants, Annochka," he laughed. "They know everything."

'But I wasn't going to be put off so easily. "Tell me, Vasily."

'He looked up at me, his gaze suddenly solemn, his soft brown hair falling off his face.

'"Do you really want to know?"

'"Yes, I'm twelve now, old enough to hear what's going on. Tell me, Vasily. Please."

'He nodded pensively, and then proceeded to tell me about the crowds that had gathered noisily in the Winter Palace Square the previous day and how a shot had been fired. The cavalry had come charging in on their horses and flashed their sabres to keep order.

'"But it won't be long, Anna. It's like a firework. The taper is lit. It's just a question of when it will explode. My parents refuse to listen to me but if they don't change their way of living right now, it'll be . . ." He paused.

'"It'll be what, Vasily?"

'"It'll be too late."

'I wasn't cold in my beaver hat and cape but nevertheless a shiver skittered up my spine. I could see the sorrow in his upturned face. Quickly I started to climb down, swinging easily between branches, and when I neared the bottom Vasily held out his arms and I jumped down into them. He caught me safely and I inhaled the scent of his hair, all crisp and cool and masculine. I kissed his cheek and he held me close, then swung me in an arc through the air and gently dropped me inside the snow sleigh on the seat he'd carved. He bowed to me.

'"Your carriage, Princess Anna."

'My heart wasn't in it now, but to please him I picked up the imaginary reins with a flourish. Flick, flick. A click of my tongue to the make-believe horse and I was flying along a forest track in my silver sleigh. But then I looked about suddenly, swivelling round on the cold seat. Where was Vasily? I spotted him leaning against the dark trunk of the sycamore, smoking a cigarette and wearing his sad face.

'"Vasily," I called.

'He came over but he didn't smile. He was staring at his father's house, three storeys high with elegant windows and tall chimneys.

'"Do you know," he asked, "how many families could live in a house like ours?"

'"One. Yours."

'"No. Twelve families. Probably more, with children sharing rooms. Things are going to change, Anna. There are people out there, millions of them, who will demand it."

'"Are they the ones on strike?"

'"Yes. They're desperately poor, with their rights stolen from them. You don't realise what it's like because you've lived all your life in a golden cage. You don't know what it is to be cold and hungry."

"They can have my other coat," I offered. "It's in the car."

'The smile he gave me made my heart lurch. It was worth the loss of my coat. "Come on, let's go and get it," I laughed.

'He set off in long galloping strides across the lawn, leaving a trail of deep black holes in the snow behind him. I followed, stretching my legs as wide as I could to place my fur boots directly in each of his footsteps, and all the way I could hear the wind tinkling in the frozen trees. It sounded like a warning.'

Sofia sat cross-legged on the dirty floorboards without moving. The night was dark and bitterly cold as the temperature continued to plummet, but her muscles had learned control. She had taught herself patience, so that when the inquisitive grey mouse pushed its nose through the rotten planks of the hut wall, its eyes bright and whiskers twitching, she was ready for it.

She didn't breathe. She saw it sense danger, but the lure of the crumb of bread placed on the floor was too great in the foodless world of the labour camp, and the little creature made its final, fatal mistake. It scurried towards the crumb. Sofia's hand shot out. One squeak and it was over. She added the miniature body to the three already in her lap and carefully placed the crumb back on the floor.

'You're very good at that,' Anna's quiet voice said.

Sofia looked up, surprised. In the dim light she could just make out the restless blonde head and delicate pale face on one of the bunks.

'Can't you sleep, Anna?' she asked softly.

'I like watching you. Besides, it takes my mind off'—she gestured about her with a loose flick of her hand—'. . . off this.'

Sofia glanced around. The wooden hut was crammed with a hundred and fifty undernourished women on hard communal bunks, their snores and moans filling the chill air. But only one was sitting with a precious pile of food in her lap. Though only twenty-six, Sofia had spent enough years in a labour camp to know the secrets of survival.

'Fancy roast rodent?' Sofia asked Anna with a crooked smile.

'*Nyet*. No, not tonight. You eat them all.'

Sofia jumped up and bent over Anna's bunk. 'Don't give up, Anna,' she said fiercely. 'You've got to eat whatever I catch for you, even if it tastes foul. If you don't eat, how are you going to work tomorrow?'

Anna closed her eyes and turned her face away into the darkness.

'Anna,' Sofia said angrily, 'what would Vasily say?'

She held her breath. Never before had she spoken those words or used Vasily's name as a lever. Slowly Anna's tousled blonde head rolled back and a smile curved the corners of her pale lips. Sofia didn't miss the fresh spark of energy that flickered in the blue eyes.

'Go and cook your wretched mice then,' Anna muttered.

'I'll catch one more first.'

Anna's hand gripped Sofia's. 'Why are you doing this for me?'

'Because you saved my life.'

'That's forgotten,' Anna whispered.

'Not by me. Whatever it takes, Anna, I won't let you die.'

Sofia sat back against the hut wall, shutting her mind to the icy draughts, and let Anna's words echo quietly in her head.

That's forgotten.

Sofia pulled off the makeshift mitten on her right hand, stitched out of blanket threads and mattress ticking, and lifted the two scarred fingers right up to her face. She could just make out the twisted flesh, a reminder every single day of her life. So no, not forgotten.

It had started when they were taken off axing the boughs from felled trees and put to work on the road instead. The prison labour brigades were not told from where the road had come nor where it was headed, but the pressure was hard and unrelenting.

Sofia had reached such a state of exhaustion that her mind was becoming foggy. Her world became nothing but stones and rocks and gravel. She piled them in her sleep, shovelled grit in her dreams; hammered piles of granite into smooth flat surfaces till the muscles in her back forgot what it was like not to ache with a pain that sapped her will-power. Even worse was the ditch digging. Feet in filthy water all day and spine fixed in a permanent twist that wouldn't unscrew.

'Can any of you scarecrows sing?'

The surprising request came from a new guard. He was only in his twenties and with a bright intelligent face. What was he doing as a guard? Sofia wondered. Most likely he'd slipped up somewhere in his career and was paying for it now.

'Well, which one of you can sing?'

Singing used up precious energy. No one ever sang. Besides, work was supposed to be conducted in silence.

'Well? Come on. I fancy a serenade to brighten my day.'

Anna was up on the raised road crushing stones into place but Sofia noticed her lift her head and could see the thought starting to form. A song? Yes, she could manage a song. Yes, an old love ballad would—

Sofia tossed a pebble and it clipped Anna's ankle. She winced and looked over to where Sofia was standing three metres away, knee-deep in ditch water. Her face was filthy, streaked with slime and covered in insect bites and sweat. Sofia shook her head at her friend, her lips tight in warning. *Don't*, she mouthed.

'I can sing,' came a voice.

It was a small, dark-haired woman in her thirties who'd spoken. The prisoners close by looked up from their work, surprised.

'I am an . . .' The woman corrected herself. 'I *was* an opera singer. I've performed in Moscow and in Paris and Milan and—'

'Excellent! Warble something sweet for me, little songbird.'

The woman didn't hesitate. She threw down her hammer with disdain, drew herself up to her full height, took two deep breaths and started to sing. The sound soared out of her, pure and heart-wrenching in its astonishing beauty. Heads lifted, the smiles and tears of the workers bringing life back into their exhausted faces.

'*Un bel dì, vedremo levarsi un fil di fumo sull'estremo confin del mare . . .*'

'It's *Madame Butterfly*,' murmured a woman. She was hauling a wheelbarrow piled high with rocks into position on the road.

As the music filled the air with golden enchantment, a warning shout tore through it. Heads turned. They all saw it happen. The woman had dropped her barrow carelessly to the ground as she'd stopped to listen to the singing, and now it had started to topple. It was the accident all of them feared, to be crushed beneath a barrow-load of rocks as they plunged over the edge of the raised road surface.

'Sofia!' Anna screamed.

Sofia was fast. Knee-deep in water, her reflexes had her spinning out of the path of the rocks. A great burst of water surged up out of the ditch as the rocks crashed down behind her.

Except for one. It came crunching down on Sofia's right hand, just where her fingers were clinging on to the bank of stones.

Sofia made no sound.

'Get back to work!' the guard yelled at everyone, disturbed by the accident he'd caused. Anna leaped into the water beside Sofia and seized her hand. The tips of two fingers were crushed to a pulp, blood spurting out into the water in a deep crimson flow.

'Bind it up,' the guard said, throwing Anna a rag from his pocket.

She took it. It was dirty and she cursed loudly. 'Everything is always dirty in this godforsaken hole.'

'It'll be all right,' Sofia assured her, as Anna quickly bound the scrap of cloth round the two damaged fingers, strapping them together, one a splint for the other, stemming the blood. Then she put the injured hand first into her own glove and then into Sofia's wet one for greater protection against knocks.

Sofia looked at the bulky object as though it didn't belong to her any more. They both knew infection was inevitable and that her body lacked sufficient nutrition to fight it.

'Back to work, you two!' the guard shouted. 'And no talking.'

'Don't you dare even *think* that you won't come through this.' Anna commanded. 'Now get on that road in my place and haul stones. At least they're dry.' Anna seized the shovel from where it had fallen and set to work in the water.

After that, Sofia became ill. They'd both known she would but the speed of it shocked them. The injured hand was worse, and Sofia's skin had grown dry and feverish. Her work rate was too slow to earn anywhere near the norm and, even though Anna fed her friend pieces of her own meagre *paiok*, the fever made her vomit.

The opera singer had been shot. You don't break the rules, not where everyone can see. The guard learned the same lesson but his was a harder one: he was forced to face an execution squad made up of his own colleagues. Sofia shuddered when she recalled how close Anna had come to bursting into song that day on the road.

'Here, this will help.' Cradling her friend's hand gently, Anna had started to unwind the slimy piece of rag that bound it.

Sofia didn't even open her eyes. She was lying on the bed board, her breath fast and shallow. She hadn't worked for days and in this camp if you didn't work, you didn't eat.

'Sofia,' Anna said harshly, 'open your eyes. Show me you're alive.'

With a huge effort, Sofia opened her eyes.

The sight of the hand was almost too much to bear. It was a black and swollen piece of rotten meat with great splits between the fingers, wounds that oozed foul-smelling pus.

'My poor Sofia,' Anna breathed. She brushed a hand over Sofia's burning forehead, sweeping the hair off her face. It was soaked in sweat. 'This will help,' she murmured again, 'it'll make you well.'

She wrapped a poultice of green and orange lichen round the hand, working it in between the fingers and up the skeletal wrist. As she did so, though she was gentle, Sofia shuddered. Anna slipped a strip of shredded leaves mixed with butter between Sofia's cracked lips.

'Chew,' she ordered. 'It'll help the pain.'

She watched like a hawk as Sofia's jaw slowly attempted movement.

'Anna.' A raw whisper. 'Where did this come from?'

'It doesn't matter, just swallow it. There'll be more tomorrow.'

The leaves were followed by a nugget of pork fat. Sofia's cloudy blue eyes had fixed on Anna's face with an expression of confusion and then, as understanding abruptly dawned on her sluggish mind, it changed to one of despair. She moaned, a deep, bone-aching sound that made Anna flinch. There was only one way a woman prisoner could lay her hands on medicine and the guards' pork fat in this camp and they both knew what it was. Her good hand reached across and clung to Anna's wrist.

'Don't,' Sofia hissed. A tear slid out, creeping across her cheek and down to her ear. 'Don't do it any more, I beg you.'

'Sofia, I want a friend who is alive. Not one rotting in the stinking pit of corpses they dump in the forest.'

'I can't bear it.'

'If I can, you can,' Anna raised her voice in an outburst of anger.

Sofia stared at her friend for a long time.

'Now,' Anna said fiercely, 'eat this.'

Sofia opened her mouth.

Two years and eight months had passed since that day. Yet the memory of it still had the power to rip something open inside Sofia and make her want to shake Anna. And hug her, hug her to death. From where Sofia was sitting on the floor waiting for the next over-adventurous mouse to venture into the hut, she could see the blonde head tossing from side to side on the crowded bed board. She could hear the coughs despite the cloth jammed over the mouth.

'Anna,' she whispered, 'I haven't forgotten.'

She dipped her forehead to her knees. *Whatever it takes, Anna.* Vasily had to be the key. Anna had no family and she was far too weak to make the thousand-mile journey through the taiga, even if she could escape from this hellhole, so there was only one answer. Sofia would have to find Vasily and hope he would help. *Hope.* No, that was far too weak a word. *Believe.* That was it. She had to believe that first, she could find him, and secondly that he would be willing to help Anna even though he hadn't seen her for sixteen years—and if she was brutally honest with herself, was it likely he'd risk his life?

She lifted her head and grimaced. Put like that, it sounded an insane and impossible idea, but it was all she had to cling on to.

'Vasily,' she breathed, 'I'm trusting you.'

The risks were huge. And of course there was the small matter of how she herself would escape. Hundreds tried it every year but few made it more than a *verst* or two. The tracker dogs; the lack of food; the wolves; the cold in the winter. In the summer the heat and the swarms of black mosquitoes that ate you alive—they all defeated even the most determined of spirits.

She shivered, but it wasn't from the cold. A part of her tired brain had just caught a glimpse of something that she'd almost forgotten.

It was freedom.

'I'm leaving,' Sofia announced.

'Leaving where?'

'Leaving Davinsky Camp. I'm going to escape.'

'No!' Anna cried, then looked quickly about her and lowered her voice to a small whisper. 'Please, Sofia, stay. It doesn't make sense. Why leave now? You've done five years already, so it's only another five and you'll be released.'

Only another five. Who was she fooling?

She tried tears and she tried begging. But nothing worked. Sofia was determined and for Anna it felt as though her heart was being cut out. Of course she couldn't blame her friend for choosing to make a break for freedom, to find a life worth living. But . . . it still felt like . . . desertion.

For a while they didn't speak because there was nothing left to say that hadn't been said. Anna coughed into her scarf, wiped her mouth and leaned her head back against the wall.

'I'm fearful for you, Sofia.'

'Don't be.'

'Fear is such a filthy stain rotting the heart out of this country, like it's rotting my lungs.' Anna struggled for breath. For a while they said nothing more but the silence hurt, so Anna asked, 'Where will you go?'

'I'll follow the River Ob, then head west to Sverdlovsk and the Ural Mountains. To Tivil.'

That came as a shock. 'Why Tivil?'

'Because Vasily is there.'

Anna felt the sick hand of jealousy squeeze her guts. It made her want to strike out, to shout and scream *Nyet!* How dare Sofia go to Tivil? Anna thrust her hands between her knees and clamped them there.

'Vasily?'

'Yes, I want to find him.'

'Is he the reason you're escaping?'

'Yes.'

'I see.'

'No, you don't.'

But she did. Anna saw only too well. Sofia wanted Vasily for herself.

Sofia looked at Anna intently and then sighed. 'Listen to me, you idiot. You said that Maria, your governess, told you about Svetlana Dyuzheyeva's jewellery.'

Anna frowned. 'Yes. Vasily's mother had beautiful jewels.'

'She told you,' Sofia continued slowly, as though speaking to a child, 'that Vasily buried some of the jewels in the church in Tivil.'

'So it's just the jewels you're going for?'

'No, not just the jewels.'

'Vasily too?'

'Yes, for Vasily too.'

Anna shuddered and started coughing again. She hunched over her scarf, pressing it to her mouth, fighting for breath. When it was over, she looked flat-eyed at Sofia.

'Take good care of him,' she whispered.

Sofia tilted her head to one side. For a while she said nothing, then she reached out and pulled back the scarf from Anna's mouth. In silence they both studied the blood stains on the cloth. Sofia spoke very clearly and deliberately.

'There's only one reason I'm leaving here. Using the jewels and with Vasily's help, I will come back.'

'Why in God's name would you want to return to this stinkhole?'

'To fetch you.'

Three words, only three. But they changed Anna's world.

'You won't survive another winter here,' Sofia said quietly. 'You know you won't, but you're too weak to escape. If I don't go to fetch help for you, you'll die.'

Anna couldn't look at Sofia. She turned her head away and fought the onrush of tears. She felt the sickening weight of fear and knew it would be there inside her for every second that Sofia was gone.

'Sofia,' she said in a voice that she barely recognised, 'don't get yourself eaten by a wolf.'

Sofia laughed. 'A wolf wouldn't stand a chance.'

2

The Ural Mountains
July 1933

THE DOG. That's what Sofia heard first. The dog. Then the men.

Coming closer, too close, with belly-deep whines, teeth bared and tongue loose, thirsting for the taste of blood. It set Sofia's own hackles rising into sharp spikes of fury.

But how could she be angry with a dog? The animal was only doing what it did best, what it was bred to do. To track its prey.

And she was its prey. So they'd come for her at last. She shivered.

She had been watching the evening sun slide away from her along the curving line of the trees, transforming the greens to amber and then to a fierce painful red. She was standing in the doorway of a cabin. She'd found it in a small clearing that was hidden way up on the northern slope of the forest, deep in the Ural Mountains.

It had taken four never-ending, hard, grinding months as a fugitive to reach this point. She'd scuttled and scrambled and fought her way halfway across Russia, travelling always southwest by the stars.

Her escape from Davinsky Camp had proved even more dangerous than she'd expected. It was a dull damp day in March with a mist that swirled among the trees like the dead drifting from trunk to trunk. Visibility was poor. A perfect day to join the ghosts.

She and Anna waited until the *perekur*, the smoke-break, which gave her five minutes. Sofia stood in a huddle with the other women from her brigade and saw Anna watching her, taking in every last detail, saying nothing. The idea of leaving Anna behind felt absurdly like treachery, but she had no choice. Even alone her own chances of survival were . . . She stopped her thoughts right there. Minute by minute, that's how she would survive.

She stepped closer to Anna and said quietly, 'I promise I'll come back for you. Anna, wait for me.'

Anna nodded to her. That's all. Just a nod and the look that passed between them. A moment frozen in time with no beginning and no end. A nod. A look. Then Anna left the huddle of women and hurried over to where four guards were standing around a brazier and smoking. One guard was holding a German Shepherd dog on a chain.

Anna skirted the dog warily. She was to create the distraction.

'Look!' she shouted. Heads turned towards her. 'Look there!' she shouted again, this time pointing urgently at the line of pine trees behind the guards.

'What?' All three guards swung round, raising their rifles.

'Wolves!' she warned.

'How many?' asked one of the men.

'*Tri*. Three. I saw three,' Anna lied. 'It could have been more.'

'Where?'

'There's one!' Anna screamed. 'Over there.'

A rifle shot rang out. Just in case. The dog and its handler were running closer to the trees. The prisoners all watched nervously. Sofia seized the moment: everyone's attention was focused on the forest to the north of the road, so she turned to the south and began to move. The trees were fifteen metres away. Her heart was hammering in her chest. *Don't hurry, walk slowly.* She cursed the ice that crunched noisily under her boots. Ten metres now. Another rifle shot rang out in the still air and Sofia instinctively ducked, but it wasn't aimed at her. It was followed by a string of bullets that ripped through the undergrowth on the north side of the road, but no howls lifted into the mist.

'That'll scare the hell out of the creatures,' one guard declared with satisfaction and lit himself a cigarette.

'OK, *davay*, back to work, you lazy scum.'

There was a murmur of voices, and quickly Sofia lengthened her stride. Three more steps and—

'Stop right there.'

Sofia stopped.

'Where the hell do you think you're sneaking off to?'

Sofia turned. Thank God it wasn't one of the guards. It was the leader of one of the other brigades. Sofia breathed again.

'I'm just going to the latrine pit, Olga. I'm desperate to—'

'Don't. We both know the nearest latrine is in the opposite direction.'

'That one's overflowing, too disgusting to use, so I—'

'Did a guard give you permission?'

'Of course not, they're all busy watching out for the wolves.'

'You know the rules. You can't leave your work post without permission from a guard.'

'Look, I really am desperate, so please just this once—'

'Guard!'

'Olga, no.'

'Guard! This prisoner is running away.'

The ground was still packed tight with the last of the winter ice. Every thrust of the spade made Sofia's bones crunch against each other and she muttered under her breath at the guard, a thick-set man who stood watching her with a rifle draped over his arm and a grin on his face.

She had been ordered to dig out a new latrine pit as punishment and it was like digging into iron. It could have been worse, that's what she kept telling herself. This punishment was for not requesting permission before stepping away from the road because, thankfully, none of the guards believed the brigade leader's story that she had been trying to escape. The punishment for an escape attempt? A bullet in the brain.

The latrine, which had to be three metres long and one metre deep, was set no more than two paces beyond the edge of the trees. Near the end of the day, when the mists were stealing the branches from the trees, a young, dark-haired girl was made to come and help her as punishment for swearing at a guard. As they worked side by side, in silence except for the metal ring of spades, Sofia attempted to catch sight of Anna on the road, but already her brigade had moved on, so she was left alone with only the girl and the guard.

The sky was beginning to darken and the rustlings on the forest floor were growing louder, when the girl suddenly pulled down her knickers, straddled the new latrine pit they'd dug and promptly christened it. The guard's grin widened and he ambled over to watch.

That was the moment. Sofia knew it as clearly as she knew her own name. She stepped up behind him in the gloom, raised her spade and slammed its metal blade on to the back of his head.

There was no going back now.

They came after her with dogs, of course. She knew they would. So she'd stuck to the marshes where, at this time of year, the land was waterlogged and it was harder for the hounds to track down her scent.

Time and again she heard the dogs come close and threw herself down on her back in the stagnant water, her eyes closed tight, only her nose and mouth above the surface. She lay immobile like that for hours in the slime while the guards searched, telling herself it was better to be eaten alive by biting insects than by dogs.

As she travelled through the taiga, she found a railway track, its silver lines snaking into the distance. She followed it day and night, till eventually she came to a river. Was this the Ob? How was she to know? She knew the River Ob headed south towards the Ural Mountains but was this it? She felt a wave of panic. She was weak with hunger and couldn't think straight.

She lost track of time. How long had she been wandering out here in this godforsaken wilderness? With an effort of will she forced her mind to focus and worked out that weeks must have passed, because the sun was higher in the sky now than when she had set out.

She almost drowned when she was stupid enough to take a short cut by swimming across a tributary of the river where the currents were lethal, and five times she came close to being caught with her hand in a chicken coop or stealing from a washing line. She lived on her wits, but as villages started to appear with more regularity, it grew too dangerous to move by day without identity papers, so she travelled only at night. It slowed her progress.

Then disaster. For one whole week she headed in the wrong direction under starless skies, not realising the Ob had swung west.

'*Dura!* Stupid fool!'

She cursed her idiocy and slumped down in a slice of moonlight on the river bank, her blistered feet dangling in the dark waters. Closing her eyes, she forced her mind to picture the place she was aiming for. Tivil, it was called. She'd never been there, but she conjured up a picture of it with ease. It was no more than a small sleepy village somewhere in a fold of the ancient Ural Mountains.

'Oh, Anna, how the hell am I going to find it?'

Yet now, at last, she was here. In the clearing among the silver birches, the mossy cabin warm at her back, the last of the sun's rays on her face. But it seemed that just when she'd reached her goal, they were coming for her again. The hound was so close she could hear its whines.

She ran.

Seconds later two men with rifles and a dog burst out of the tree line, but by then she had already put the hut between them and herself as she raced for the back of the clearing, hunched low, breathing hard.

The dark trunks opened up and she fell into their cool protection. That was when she saw the boy. And in a hollow not three paces away from him crouched a wolf.

Pyotr Pashin didn't move a muscle, not even to blink, just stared at the creature. Its mean, yellow eyes were fixed on him and he didn't dare breathe. Never before in his young life had he stood so close to a wolf.

Pyotr had jumped at the chance to come hunting when Boris asked him. But it hadn't turned out to be a good day. Game was scarce and his other hunting companion, Igor, was tight-lipped as a lizard, so Boris had started in on the flask in his pocket which only sent the day tumbling from bad to worse. It ended up with Boris giving Pyotr a clout with his rifle, which had made Pyotr scoot off among the trees in a sulk.

Pyotr knew that what he was doing was wrong—it broke the first rule of forest lore, which is that you must never lose contact with your companions. Children of the *raion*, the district, grew up bombarded with bedtime stories of how you must never, never roam alone in the forest, a place where you will be instantly devoured by goblins or wolves or even a fierce-eyed axeman who ate children for breakfast.

But Pyotr was eleven now and he reckoned he was able to look out for himself.

He caught sight of the back of the cabin, covered in bright green moss. His interest was roused. He took one more step and immediately heard a low-throated sound at his feet that made the hairs rise on the back of his neck. He swung round, and that was when he saw the wolf.

He didn't dare breathe. Slowly, so slowly, he started to move his left hand towards the whistle that hung on a green cord round his neck.

Then, abruptly, a blur of moonlight-pale hair and long golden limbs hurtled into the stillness. A young woman was churning up the air around him, her breath so loud he wanted to shout at her, to warn her, but a wild pulse thudding in his throat prevented it. She stopped, blue eyes wide with surprise, but instead of screaming at the sight of the wolf, she gave it no more than a glance. Instead she smiled at Pyotr.

'Hello,' she mouthed. '*Privet.*'

She raised a finger to her lips and held it there as a signal to him to stay quiet, her mouth twitching as if in fun, but when he looked into her eyes, they weren't laughing. She was scared.

At that moment it dawned on Pyotr what she was. She was a fugitive. An Enemy of the State on the run. They'd been warned about them in the weekly meetings in the hall. A sudden confusion tightened his chest. No normal person behaved so oddly—did they? So he made his decision. He raised the whistle to his mouth. Later he would recall the feel of the cold hard metal on his lips and remember the hammering in his heart as the two of them stood, saying nothing, in front of those mean yellow eyes in the shade of the big pine.

The young woman shook her head, urgent and forceful, and once more pressed a finger to her lips and gave him a smile that seemed to steal something from inside him. It left a hole in a secret place, which previously only his mother had touched. His chest stung so badly he had to crush his hand against his ribs to stop the hurt, and by the time he looked back, she was gone. A faint movement of the branches, that was all that remained. Even the wolf had disappeared.

He stayed there with the whistle in his hand for what felt like for ever but which must have been no more than a minute, and gradually the sounds around him started to return. The dog whining; the hunters calling and cursing him. He knew he should shout to them, it was his duty as a Soviet citizen to alert them. *Quick, there's a fugitive running down to the river. Bring your rifle.* But something stubborn hardened inside his young chest when he thought of the moonlight hair, and the words wouldn't come to his lips.

The village of Tivil lay silent in the darkness and Sofia's heart lifted at the sight of it. This was the place she'd spent months searching for, and always with one person standing at the heart of it.

Vasily. Now she had to find him.

Was Tivil the right place? Or had she come all this way for nothing? She had staked everything on one woman's word. That woman was Maria, Anna's childhood governess.

How good was her word?

Maria had whispered to Anna when she was arrested that Vasily had fled from Petrograd after the 1917 Revolution and turned up on the other side of Russia in Tivil, living under the name of Mikhail Pashin.

But how good was her word?

Sofia had to believe he was here, had to know he was close.

'Vasily,' she whispered aloud into the wind. 'I need your help.'

The village was made up of a straggle of houses each side of a single central street, mixed up with an untidy jumble of barns and stables and patched fences. At the centre of the village stood the church. Now that in itself was strange. Throughout Russia most village churches had been blown up by order of the Politburo or were being used as storage for grain or manure—the ultimate insult. This one had escaped such shame but, judging by the abundance of notices pinned outside, it had been turned into a general assembly hall for the compulsory political meetings.

Sofia moved with the shadows into the doorway of the church. *Chyort!* The lock was a big old-fashioned iron contraption that would shrug off any attempts she made with her knife. With another muttered oath she skirted round the side of the building, her pulse missing a beat when the shadows abruptly grew paler around her. A light must have been turned on somewhere close. She edged to the corner of the building, her body becoming part of its solid mass, and, holding her breath, she peered into the street.

The solitary light gleamed out at her like a warning. It came from the window of a nearby *izba*. And, as she watched, a man crossed inside the rectangle of yellow lamplight, a tall figure moving in a hurry, and then he was gone. A moment later the *izba* was plunged once more into darkness and the sound of a front door shutting reached her ears.

What was he doing out so early? She hadn't bargained on the village coming to life before dawn. His determined stride and speed of movement made Sofia nervous, but still she crept forward to see more.

He was heading away from her down the street, picked out in detail by a brief trick of the moon. It allowed her to make out that his hair was clipped short and he was wearing a rough workman's shirt, which struck her as odd because he moved with the easy assurance and confidence of someone who was used to a position of command.

Could it be Vasily?

She almost stepped out into the street and called his name. Except of course it wouldn't be the name she knew, it would be *Mikhail Pashin*, the name Anna had said he was using. She struggled to subdue a wave of excitement and reined in an unruly surge of hope. Surely she couldn't be so lucky?

She saw him turn off the street up a steep rutted track that clung to the hillside, leading up to the vague outline of a long, dark building. She was tempted to follow his footsteps but there was an alertness about him that made her certain she would be discovered.

She sank to the ground, waiting, invisible in the black overhang of the church. Her patience was rewarded ten minutes later when she heard the sound of a horse descending the track, its hoofs lively on the dry earth. He'd obviously been up to a stable and saddled his horse for an early morning start.

But, to her surprise, behind him a man on foot was also trotting down the track. He was middle-aged but very nimble. They were talking in low voices but there was a certain curtness in their manner towards each other that spoke of ill feeling. Sofia's gaze remained fixed on the rider.

Anna. Her lips didn't move but the words sounded sharp as ice in her head. *I think I've found Mikhail Pashin.*

Just then the two men reached the point where the rutted track joined the road, and the rider turned abruptly to the left without a word.

'Comrade Chairman Fomenko,' the man called out sharply, 'don't push the horse too hard today. His leg is still sore and needs—'

In response the rider shortened the reins and pushed the animal into a canter and then a gallop. Steadily, man and horse disappeared towards the far end of the village and they were gone.

Sofia was shaking. She slid away into the blackness behind the church and rested her burning cheek against its cool bricks. The rider wasn't Vasily—or Mikhail Pashin—after all, but someone called Fomenko. Damn her stupidity! She'd got it wrong. As she wrapped her arms round herself, disappointment lay in her stomach.

What else had she got wrong?

Sofia was feeling light-headed. She hadn't eaten all day, and only a handful of berries had passed her lips yesterday. She needed to fill her stomach. She chose the last *izba* before the tangle of rocks and forest. From there escape into the trees would be easy if she was disturbed. She ducked low and slipped round to its vegetable plot at the back.

Searching among the rows of vegetables, she yanked up a couple of cabbages and thrust them into her pouch, then scrabbled from the earth whatever came to hand: a young beetroot, an onion, a radish. She glanced in the direction of the house, nerves taut, but the black shape of the *izba* remained solid and silent. She rubbed the radish against her sleeve and opened her mouth to bite off the end.

But before her teeth could close, a blow to the back of her head lifted her off her knees and sent her spiralling into blackness.

'Run, Pyotr, run.'

Pyotr Pashin tore down the dusty track, legs pumping, arms driving him on into the lead. Hot on his tail nine other boys panted and scrabbled after him. Suddenly he felt moist breath on his bare shoulder and turned his head just enough to catch a glimpse of its owner. One final burst was all it would take to beat Yuri and to get over the line in first place. But instead Pyotr put on the brakes, not hard enough to be obvious, of course, but enough to do damage. In ten strides Yuri had outpaced him and was hurtling past the winning post.

'Well done, Pyotr.' It was his class teacher, Elizaveta Lishnikova, who had come to stand beside him. '*Molodyets!* Congratulations.'

He looked up quickly. She was smiling, the wrinkles in her face re-arranging themselves. She was extremely tall with thick grey hair tied in a knot. Her long thin nose could sniff out a lie at a hundred paces.

'You ran well, Pyotr,' she said.

'*Spasibo*. Thank you.'

Instantly a flying body hurtled onto his back, sending him sprawling on to the dirt in a tumble of arms and legs.

'Yuri, get off me, *durachok*.'

'You were brilliant, Pyotr. Fantastic. But I knew I could beat you.'

'Shut up, Yuri.' But he couldn't help grinning.

There was something about Yuri Gamerov that made you want to please him. He was tall and strong with thick ginger hair and an easy way of always being the boss, something Pyotr envied. Pyotr was small and shy but around Yuri he felt more . . . well, more colourful. And for some reason he couldn't quite understand, they were good friends.

'Boys, you'll both be cleaning school windows after the races today if you behave so improperly.' The teacher's voice was sharp.

The grind of school term had finished for the summer and they were now into Young Pioneer Summer Camp, which Pyotr loved. But it was still held in the school yard each day and still organised by Elizaveta Lishnikova, so standards of behaviour were not allowed to slip.

'Take yourselves off the running track immediately. I am about to start the next race.'

The boys scuttled away, naked backs above their shorts tinged by the sun, and threw themselves down on the grass. It prickled their bare legs. Anastasia came trotting over at once.

Yuri groaned, 'Here comes the mouse.'

Yuri was right, of course, Anastasia Tushkova did look like a mouse: little pointed nose and chin; mousy hair that hung down her back in a skinny plait like a mousetail. But Pyotr didn't mind her really, though he wouldn't admit that to Yuri.

Anastasia plopped herself down on the grass in front of them and held out a hand. It was very grubby and on it lay a biscuit.

'It's your prize for winning,' she said to Yuri. 'Teacher sent me over with it.' She was eleven, the same age as Pyotr, but she looked younger. 'You should have one too, Pyotr. You almost won.'

'Almost is never good enough,' Yuri grinned and took the *pechenka* from her. Very precisely he broke it in three equal parts and handed one to each of them.

'No,' Pyotr said, pushing it away. 'You won it, you eat it.'

'I insist,' Yuri said. 'Equal shares for everyone. It's what we believe in.'

That was the trouble with Yuri. He believed in applying Communism to every corner of his life. Even when it came to biscuits.

'Mmm,' Anastasia mewed. '*Miod.* Honey.'

Before Pyotr could blink, her share of the biscuit had vanished into her mouth. Something about the speed of it embarrassed him and he looked out at the dense forest as it marched up the steep ridges of the valley and over the mountains beyond. She was up there, somewhere, the woman with the moonlight hair. Living in the forest. Maybe he would sneak back to that old cabin tomorrow to see if—

'Pyotr.' It was Anastasia.

'Yes?'

'Look.'

Her little bony hand was pointing beyond the broad cedar tree that marked the start of the village to a spot in the distance, where a ball of dust was rolling its way along the unpaved road towards them. Traffic on the road was always light, usually no more than a few carts a day and, on rare occasions, a car or truck.

Pyotr forgot the woman in the forest when he saw who was driving the cart that was trundling up the valley. It was Aleksei Fomenko.

The cart stopped outside the school yard. Yuri leaped to his feet, dragging Anastasia with him.

'It's Comrade Fomenko. Come on, let's wave to him.'

'No.'

Pyotr stood up beside her. 'Why not? What's wrong?'

'He took Masha last week.'

Pyotr didn't know what to say. Masha was the Tushkov family's last sow. All they had left. Without her . . .

'It's Comrade Fomenko's job,' Yuri said.

'To take our only pig?'

'Yes, of course it is,' Yuri replied with determination. 'We're a *kolkhoz*, a collective farm. It's his duty to do his job properly.'

'Then his job is wrong.'

Yuri shook his head fiercely at her. 'You mustn't say things like that, Anastasia. You could be put in prison for that.'

'Maybe it was a mistake,' Pyotr suggested.

'Do you think it might be?' Anastasia's eyes gleamed with hope and Pyotr was furious with himself for putting it there, but he couldn't bear to let her down now. He straightened his shoulders and ran a damp palm over his rumpled hair. He swallowed hard.

'I'll go and ask him.'

Aleksei Fomenko was the Chairman of Tivil's *kolkhoz*, the valley's collective farm, which was called *Krasnaya Strela*, the Red Arrow.

Though he was no more than thirty years old, he controlled it all: he was the one who decided the work rotas, made certain the work force was in place each day—and ensured the fulfilled quotas were sent off to the *raion* centre on time. He had arrived from the *oblast* Central Office four years ago and brought order to a haphazard farm system that was so behind on taxes and quotas that the whole village was in danger of being labelled saboteurs and put in prison. Fomenko had set them straight. Pyotr worshipped him.

He was talking to the teacher in front of the schoolhouse. Pyotr slunk round to the back of the cart where a skittish filly was tethered to the hinge of the rear flap. Pyotr tried to soothe her but she would have none of it and attempted to nip him, but the halter was too tight.

'Comrade Chairman.' This was the first time Pyotr had ever spoken to Aleksei Fomenko, though he'd seen and heard him often enough at the compulsory political meetings in the assembly hall.

'Not now, Pyotr,' his teacher said firmly.

'No, Elizaveta,' intervened Fomenko, 'let's hear our young comrade. He has the look of someone with something to say.'

Pyotr stared at Aleksei Fomenko, grateful for the warmth of his words. Deep-set grey eyes were watching him with interest. The face was strong. And despite wearing a loose work tunic he looked lean— and authoritative, exactly the way Pyotr longed to be.

'Well, what is it, young comrade? Speak up.'

'Comrade Chairman, I . . . er . . .' His palms were hot. He brushed them on his shorts. 'I have two things I wish to say.'

'Which are?'

'Comrade Chairman, last week you took a pig from the Tushkovs.'

The eyes narrowed. 'Go on.'

'It's just that . . . I thought that perhaps it was a mistake and if—'

'It was no mistake.'

'But they can't survive without Masha. Really they can't.' The words came out in a rush. 'They have eight children, Comrade Chairman. They need the pig. To sell her litters. How else will they eat?'

'Listen to me closely.' The Chairman placed a hand on Pyotr's bare shoulder. 'Who do you think feeds the workers in our factories? In the towns and cities, all the people making our clothes and our machines and our medical supplies, all the men and women in the shipyards and down the mines? Who feeds them?'

'We do, Comrade Chairman.'

'That's right. Each *kolkhoz*, each collective farm, must fulfil its quota. It supplies the *raion*, the district, and each district supplies the *oblast*, the province. That's how the great proletariat of this vast country is fed and clothed. So which is more important, young comrade? The individual? Or the Soviet State?'

'The Soviet State.' Pyotr said it passionately.

Fomenko smiled approval. 'Well spoken. So which one matters more, the Tushkov family or the State?'

Pyotr was caught unawares by this sudden twist and felt the inside of his stomach burn. How had he come to this choice?

'The State.' It came out as a whisper.

'That is why I took the sow. Do you understand?'

'Yes, Comrade Chairman.'

He released Pyotr's shoulder. 'And what was the second thing you wanted to talk to me about?'

'It's the filly,' Pyotr muttered. 'The halter is too tight.'

'You have good eyes, young comrade. The filly has thrown a shoe.' He reached into his pocket, pulled out a fifty kopeck coin and tossed it in the air. 'Here, catch. You're obviously a bright lad and know something about horses. Take her up to the blacksmith for me.'

Pyotr caught the coin and glanced at Elizaveta Lishnikova. She nodded. 'Take Anastasia with you,' she said.

It made his shame worse, knowing she'd heard every word. His cheeks burned. He ran from the adults, unhitched the filly and as he trudged up the street in the dust with Anastasia in tow, he threw her the fifty kopeck coin. 'You can have it.'

'Thanks, Pyotr. You're the best friend in the world.'

Sofia's eyes opened into darkness. She sat up. Mistake. The room splintered and lights flashed inside her eyes. She waited until the pieces slotted back together. She was on a bed, fully clothed, her fingertips told her that much. So far, so clear. She took a deep breath.

As her eyes grew accustomed to the darkness, she swung her feet to the floor, aware for the first time that she was not wearing shoes, and stood up. Not good, but not as bad as she expected. She took another breath and headed for the door. Her hands explored strong planks of wood, held shut by a wooden latch. Around the edge of it crept a whisper of daylight. Sofia put her ear to it and listened. No sounds. Just more silence and the thump of her own heartbeat.

She lifted the latch. It opened onto a low-beamed living room with rough split-timber walls, unpainted, a carved chest in one corner and in the centre a home-built table with two upright chairs. At one end stood the *pechka*, a large stove, and, more surprisingly, a big maroon armchair turned to face the stove. The air smelled heavily of herbs, which was hardly surprising as bunches of all kinds of dried leaves were pinned around the walls in a fragrant frieze.

More to the point, the room was empty. Over to her left was a window that revealed a dusty patch of road outside and next to the window was the door. She ran for it and breathed a sigh of relief as her fingers easily lifted the metal latch and she stepped over the threshold.

'You'll need shoes.'

She stopped dead. The voice had come from behind her, a man's voice. Slowly, she turned. At first she could make out nothing different in the room, but then a movement drew her attention to the maroon chair. There was a face, an upward curve of a gentle mouth, a shock of dense black hair swept straight back and an even blacker pair of eyes in a narrow face. He was watching her.

How had she not noticed him?

'Don't you want shoes?' He spoke quietly. He was leaning round the edge of the armchair, most of him hidden from view by the back of it

She had forgotten her feet were bare. She glanced over her shoulder at the sunlit slope that led up to the forest edge where safety beckoned.

Run, she told herself, *just run*. She'd come too far and worked too hard to risk losing her precious freedom now. She had to choose.

'Yes, I want my shoes.' Her tongue was dry in her mouth.

'I'll fetch them for you.'

He stood and moved away from the chair. He was shorter than she'd realised, not even as tall as herself, and older than his eyes and his hair indicated. Probably fifty, with the kind of skin that was swarthy.

He walked over to the oak chest by the wall, lifted the lid and extracted a pair of shoes. Slowly, so as not to startle her, he came forward and placed them on the table, then he backed off and stood next to the stove. He was tempting her back in, like you tempt a horse into a stall with an apple. She made her choice and walked back into the *izba*.

In some subtle way that she couldn't quite explain, the feel of the room had changed. The smell of herbs was no longer suffocating but refreshing, and the place seemed to possess a kind of enticing peace. Sofia looked at the shoes.

'Those aren't mine,' she said.

'Yours are worn through. Holes in both soles and tied together with string. I thought you might prefer these.'

He spoke about them as if they were a pack of cheap *makhorka* tobacco instead of possessions that some would kill for. Well-softened pigskin stitched onto double thickness rubber soles. New shoes. Who on earth could find new shoes these days? And then give them away? But she wasn't going to argue with him.

Instead she strode over to the centre of the room, snatched up the shoes and slipped them on her feet. They fitted perfectly.

'Thank you,' she said.

He gave her a warm smile. 'May they keep you safe.'

'What?'

'It seems to me you need help, that's all.' His voice was mild.

Sofia blinked, wary of this gentle-mannered little man.

'How long have I been here?'

'Two days.'

'I was attacked.'

'Yes. My daughter Zenia found you stealing our vegetables.'

'You kept me prisoner.'

There was a silence. The smile had gone and a stiffness altered the way he held his shoulders. Sofia knew she had offended him.

'I tried to heal you,' he pointed out quietly.

'Thank you. I'm grateful.' She recalled a voice murmuring strange words and the touch of cool hands on her burning forehead. 'But now I must leave.'

She turned towards the open door.

'You don't have to leave. You can stay here. You'll be safe.' This time his voice rumbled round the room and echoed inside her skull.

You'll be safe.

Out of nowhere came the realisation that she was desperately tired of being frightened. If she was going to reach Anna in time, she needed to be on the inside of Tivil, not struggling on the outside in the dead of night. Her thoughts became blurred, frayed round the edges.

'Sit down.' For the first time he came closer and stood with one hand on the table edge. She didn't move.

'Why? Why would you take me in? Without even asking why or how I came here? You must have realised that I'm . . . that it could make serious trouble for you and your daughter. So why take such a risk?'

'If the people of this country do not help each other,' he said fiercely, 'soon there will be no Russia. No people. They will all be in labour camps, as prisoners or prison guards. It makes no difference which. A whole nation condemned to a slow death. The only ones left will be the sleek Politburo in Moscow. I curse their rotten godforsaken souls. May they starve as we have starved. May they lose their wives and their children as we lose ours. Let the Devil take the lot of them.'

Sofia sat down on one of the chairs. She looked up into those intense eyes and the world became a smaller place, as though just the two of them in this room existed. There was something extraordinary about this man. She had survived this far because she'd learned that trust was as fragile as a moth's wings and you didn't give it lightly. But she gave him a smile instead.

He laughed, a warm sound, and held out his hand. 'My name is Rafik Ilyan. But they call me the Gypsy. You and I, we can help each other.'

'My name is Sofia,' she said.

3

Tivil
July 1933

'HAVE YOU SEEN HER?'

Elizaveta Lishnikova narrowed her gaze against the sun as she glanced up through the village towards the Gypsy's *izba*.

'*Nyet*. No,' Pokrovsky replied as he hammered the last nail into a well-oiled hoof and snipped off its metal tip with pincers.

The filly kept turning her head, pulling at the halter to inspect what he was doing back there.

'The Gypsy claims she's his niece by marriage,' Pokrovsky said.

'Do you believe him?'

'No.'

The blacksmith had been busy in the yard at the side of the smithy when the schoolteacher strode in with her usual forthright manner. The day was hot and humid and he'd been content at his work, but now he was suddenly aware of the sweat on his shaven head and the stink of horses on his leather apron. She always had that effect on him, making him feel big and clumsy instead of broad and powerful.

Elizaveta was wearing a long, black dress nipped in tight at her tiny waist, and everything about her was dainty and ladylike.

'Neither do I believe him,' she said.

'So why is she here?' Pokrovsky picked up a long file.

'Why do you think?'

His eyes met hers. She always made him think for himself, as if she didn't already know the answers. He ran the file over the filly's rear hoof, and said the words he was sure were already in her mind.

'She's an informer, sent by Stirkhov to spy on us. But why would Rafik, who loves our village so strongly, take in one of Stirkhov's spies?'

'He would if he wanted to keep an eye on her.'

'You think that's it?'

'It could be.' She let her eyes roam round the forge. Without looking at him she said, 'There's another package due in tonight, my friend.'

'I'll be there. You can rely on that.'

Sofia woke with a jerk. A ferocious banging on the front door of the *izba* yanked her out of a nightmare she was glad to leave, but before she could even begin to think straight, her body reacted instinctively. It leaped out of the makeshift bed at the back of the stove and raced across the living room, flattening against the wall behind the door.

'Rafik! Open up, damn you!' a man shouted outside. Its owner delivered a hefty kick that rattled the wooden planks on their hinges and made Sofia's heart jump.

The door to Rafik's bedroom opened abruptly and a candle advanced across the room. His black eyes took in her position of ambush and he spoke softly.

'It's all right, it's Mikhail Pashin. He is the *direktor* who runs the Levitsky factory in Dagorsk where Zenia works.'

Mikhail. He had come to her.

'Gypsy!' Another rap at the door. 'For God's sake, you're wanted.'

Sofia held her breath and reached out to lift the latch but, as she did so, Rafik's hand seized her wrist.

'You're safe here,' he said. 'So don't let your mind drown in your fear.'

'I'll remember that.'

'Good.' Rafik released her wrist and opened the door. 'What is it, Pilot?'

'It's the bay mare,' the voice outside replied. It was impatient.

'Foaling so early?'

'She's having a wretched time of it. Priest Logvinov is frightened we might lose her.'

Rafik's expression showed a spasm of pain, as if the thought of losing a horse wounded him physically. Sofia took the candle holder from his fingers to steady it.

'Wait in here, Pilot,' the Gypsy said and disappeared back into the darkness of his room.

Mikhail Pashin stepped over the threshold and closed the door behind him, firmly shutting out the wind and the night. In the wavering light, Sofia saw a pair of intelligent eyes, grey and private. Two lines ran from his nose to the corners of his mouth in deep furrows, though he was no more than thirty. They told of things kept unsaid. But in Russia now, who did not have words hidden behind their lips?

'I apologise for disturbing your sleep,' he said.

He treated her to a courteous bow of his head. She lifted the candle higher to see more clearly what it was about Mikhail Pashin that brought such energy into the house, and she noticed the way his long limbs kept flexing as though eager to be on the move. On his feet were black shoes, highly polished, and he was wearing a charcoal suit with crisp white shirt and black tie, all oddly incongruous in this rough and informal setting.

'Why does Rafik call you Pilot?' Sofia asked.

'It's his private joke. I'm not a pilot of anything.'

'Except the Levitsky factory?'

He laughed, but there was an edge to it that made it clear he was anything but amused. 'That's not piloting. That's crash landing.'

'Is it wise to say such things?'

She hadn't meant to startle him. But she saw one eyebrow rise and felt a subtle shift in the air between them.

'Thank you for the warning,' he said smoothly.

'It wasn't a warning, it was—'

At that moment Rafik hurried into the room, fully dressed and in a warm woollen jacket, with a coarse blanket over one shoulder and a large leather satchel slung from the other.

'Come, Mikhail,' he ordered. 'We must be quick.'

Mikhail Pashin spun round, opened the door and without even a farewell, the two men hurried away into what remained of the night. Sofia watched them go, one figure short and scurrying, the other tall and lean with the long easy stride of a wolfhound.

'It wasn't a warning, it was a question,' she finished.

He's real. *Anna, he's real. Real flesh. Real blood. Not just existing solely in our minds. He's solid, so solid I could have touched him had I chosen to.*

He'd come to her, coalescing out of the darkness just as he'd done a thousand times before when she'd summoned him, but never before had he been made of flesh and bone. Never before did he have a voice. Hair that smelled of early morning mists. Vasily.

Mikhail Pashin.

Her heart was pounding and she could still hear his voice: *I'm not a pilot of anything.*

'But you're wrong, Mikhail Pashin,' she whispered. 'You brought me here. You guided my footsteps to this village of Tivil.'

And what had she done with the precious moment? Wasted it. Her foolish tongue had frightened him off with a question that sounded to his ears too much like a threat. Damn it, damn it.

'Next time,' she murmured, angry with herself, 'I swear I'll touch you. I'll place my fingers on the muscles of your arm and feel your skin.' Abruptly she slumped down at the table and stared blindly into the shimmering flame. 'He's Anna's,' she whispered to the night.

Elizaveta Lishnikova felt sorry for the man seated in front of her in the chamber. His hand was shaking, but otherwise he was putting up a good show of confidence. His fair hair was combed and he was managing to keep his shoulders straight. She didn't like it when they arrived out of the darkness in crumpled rags, their bodies hunched with fear. She liked to see a bit of backbone on display. Though God only knew how desperately each package had good reason to be fearful.

'Now, Comrade Gorkin—that's your new name, by the way: Andrei Gorkin. Start getting used to it.'

He blinked, as if to seal the name into his mind. 'I won't forget.'

Elizaveta registered the refinement of his speech. Another intellectual, maybe a university lecturer who'd said one word too many in praise of the wrong kind of book or the wrong kind of music. She pulled her grey shawl round her to keep out the chill of such thoughts.

'Here,' she offered a small bundle wrapped in muslin, 'something to eat. It's only black bread but it'll start you on your way.'

'*Spasibo.*' His voice was shaky and he wiped a hand across his eyes.

'Do exactly as you're told and you'll get through it safely.'

'I can't thank you enough for—'

'Hush. Eat up. You'll be moving on any moment now.'

She rested a hand on the ancient iron latch of the door, ready to open it the second she heard the coded knock, and watched him force himself to eat. Clearly he had no stomach for food tonight. She didn't blame him. Nights like this set her own innards churning and she sighed at the thought of a whole generation of intellectuals being wiped out. Who was going to teach the next generation to think?

The candle hissed as a draught took the flame and she heard the rap of knuckles on old wood.

'Your guide is here,' she whispered.

She unlocked the door and the large figure of Pokrovsky slipped into the gloomy chamber.

'Ready?' Pokrovsky demanded of the man.

'Yes.'

'Then let's go.'

Elizaveta opened the door quietly and the man stepped out into the fresh night air. She laid a hand on Pokrovsky's massive arm.

'My friend,' she said softly, 'take care.'

'Don't worry, I'll deliver your package safely.'

Rafik stood in the privacy of his own room and held the stone in the palm of his hand. No larger than a duck egg and white as a swan's throat. He'd brought out the white pebble from its bed of scarlet because he could sense danger gathering, sabres rattling, like troops lining up for battle.

It grieved him deep in his heart to know his beloved Tivil was under threat once more tonight, and each time he closed his eyes he could see the blonde-haired one, Sofia, tall and slender. Behind his eyes a pin-point of pain began to throb. With a sudden urgent need, he rested his thumb on the smooth white pebble and felt its coolness against his skin. It brought to mind the ancient strength of his ancestors and cleared his mind. Now the Sight came to him more readily.

The stone had been passed down through his Gypsy line for generations, father to son, and was said to have come originally from the stone that was rolled aside from the tomb of Jesus Christ in the Holy Land. Each time it lay in the centre of his palm he was acutely aware that each person who owned it imparted a sliver of their strength to its tightly packed crystals. He could sense the vibration of white life inside them.

His thumb lingered over the pebble. Caressed its smooth carapace, traced a circle around it, a circle of protection.

'Zenia.'

His daughter came into the room at once. Her body was sheathed in a flowing red dress tied with a wide Gypsy waistband. He thought how beautiful she looked, how like her dear dead mother. She gazed at the stone in his hand with alert eyes, bright and black and curious. Yet for her it possessed no resonance. Whenever she handled it and turned it over and over on her palm, it was nothing but a white pebble with a faint web of silvery veins threaded through it, an ordinary stone. He knew it frustrated her that she could not sense her ancestors within it, and though he would never breathe a word of it aloud to her, his own disappointment was even greater than hers.

'Go with her tonight, Zenia. But don't let her know you are my sight.'

'Yes, Rafik.' She paused. 'Is she in danger so soon?'

'It comes from two directions. Make sure you guard her well.' Rafik closed his fist over the stone and swept it briefly through the candle flame. 'Darkness is coming to Tivil tonight. Fire and darkness.'

'You are prepared?' Zenia asked, her voice unsteady.

'I am prepared.'

'But will you fall ill?'

He smiled, a deep and tender smile. 'Don't be frightened. She is here.'

Pyotr liked the meetings. He loved to sit right at the front of the assembly hall, under the nose of the speaker. Every week he arrived early with his Young Pioneer shirt freshly ironed by himself, hair slicked down into temporary submission. His eyes shining.

'*Dobry vecher*. Good evening, Pyotr.'

A large figure with a smooth shaven head and a spade-shaped black beard took the place next to him.

'*Dobry vecher*, Comrade Pokrovsky.'

The blacksmith, too, invariably selected the front bench at these weekly meetings but for quite different reasons from Pyotr's. Pokrovsky liked to question the speaker.

'Your father not here again, Pyotr?'

'*Nyet*. He's working late. At the factory.'

'Hah! Tell me an evening that he's not working late when there's a meeting going on here.'

Pyotr felt his cheeks flush red. 'No, honestly, he's busy. Producing army uniforms, an important order. Directly from Moscow.'

'Proudly spoken, boy.'

'It's important work,' the boy said again and then feared he was insisting too much, so shut up.

But his mood was spoiled. He stared moodily around at the plain walls that had once been covered in colourful murals of Christ and the disciples; at the remains of the ornate icons on the pillars, though most of the carving and decoration had been hacked off, leaving behind jagged edges. All the religious images had been whitewashed into a clean and bland uniformity. This pleased Pyotr. As did the metal table set up on a low platform in front of him where the gilt altar had once stood, and the two sturdy chairs that waited for the speakers under the poster of the Great Leader himself. Beside it hung another, a bright red poster declaring: SMERT VRAGAM SOVIETSKOGO NARODA. Death to the Enemies of Soviet People.

This was as it should be. Plain. Real. For the people. Just like Stalin had promised. Pyotr and Yuri had read all the pamphlets, learned the

Party slogans by heart and Yuri kept telling him that this new world was for them. Pyotr so wanted to believe him, but sometimes a little worm of doubt wriggled through the slogans, making holes in his certainty.

He looked behind him to where the benches were filling up. Most of the villagers were still in their work clothes of coarse blue cotton, though some of the younger women had discarded their dusty headscarves and changed into colourful blouses that stood out in the drab crowd.

'*Privet*, Pyotr. Hello.'

It was Yuri. He arrived in a scramble of long limbs and squeezed himself in next to Pyotr at the end of the bench, immaculate in his white Young Pioneer shirt and red neckerchief.

'Have you heard?' Yuri bent his ginger head to Pyotr's. He was always one to know the latest news. 'Stirkhov is coming to address us tonight.'

Pyotr's chest tightened just for a second. 'Why? What have we done?'

'Don't be stupid. It's an honour for us to have the Deputy Chairman of the whole district here.'

It was the hands, Pyotr decided. The way they moved through the air, strong and controlling. Wide slicing gestures to underline words; sharp jabs to force a point home. The hands held the power. Aleksei Fomenko, as *Predsedatel kolkhoza*, Chairman of the collective farm, had been speaking for an hour, and Pyotr couldn't take his eyes off him.

So far he had been listing the recent quotas set by the Central Control Commission, naming the shirkers who had fallen behind on their labour days and urging them all to greater achievements.

'Beware of complacency,' Fomenko urged. 'We are nearly at the end of Stalin's First Five Year Plan that is building our country into the leading industrialised nation in the world. We have swept aside the superstitions of the past'—here his eyes turned to a tall man with fierce eyes, a lion's mane of chestnut hair and a straggly red beard, but his open shirt revealed the tip of a large wooden cross hanging round his neck—'and the concept of servitude has been replaced by the doctrine of freedom.'

He clenched both fists.

'A new world is emerging. One that will sweep away the mistakes of past centuries, and we are the engine that drives it. Yes, you and I. And collectivism. Never forget that. The grip of the *kulaks*—those rich bourgeois farmers who exploited you all—their grip is broken thanks to the inspired vision of our Great Leader.'

Fomenko turned to the giant poster of Stalin, swathed in the red banners that hung behind him. 'Josef Stalin, the Father of Our Nation, is the one who is carrying throughout this great Union of Soviets the torch that Vladimir Ilyich Lenin lit for us. Stalin is the one who is ridding us of the saboteurs and subversives, the wreckers and the spoilers who would destroy the drive forward of the great Five Year Plan.' The Chairman linked his hands together, fingers firmly entwined. 'We must unite in the great fight towards the Victory of Communism.'

'What about some great bread to eat instead of a great fight?' Pokrovsky the blacksmith demanded.

'Comrades.'

The man who spoke was seated next to Fomenko at the table, a stocky figure with a smooth well-fed face, wiry hair and strangely colourless eyes. He wore a sleek leather jacket, the cost of which even Pyotr could see would have fed Anastasia's family for a month. This man was the District Party Deputy Chairman, sent by the *Raikom*, and however much Yuri insisted it was an honour to have him at their meeting, it didn't feel like that to Pyotr. It felt more like a rebuke.

Fomenko eased back in his chair, yielding control to his superior.

'Comrades, I am proud to be here. With you, my brothers, the workers of Red Arrow *kolkhoz*. You all know me. I am Deputy Chairman Aleksandr Stirkhov from the *Raion* Committee. I am a man of the people. I bring a message from our Committee. We praise what you have achieved so far in this difficult year and urge you to greater efforts. The failure of the harvest last autumn was the work of wreckers and saboteurs, funded by foreign powers and their spies who plot to destroy our great new surge forward in technology. Throughout parts of Russia it meant we had to tighten our belts a notch or two—'

'Or three,' a man called out from somewhere at the back of the hall.

'Your own belt doesn't look so tight, Deputy Stirkhov.' Another voice.

'Listen to me, Comrade Deputy, I lost my youngest child to starvation.'

Stirkhov pursed his mouth. 'Admittedly shortages have occurred.'

'It's a famine,' Pokrovsky declared at Pyotr's side. 'People dying—'

'Comrade Deputy Stirkhov is a busy man,' Fomenko interrupted quickly. 'He is not here to waste time listening to your observations, Pokrovsky. There is no famine. That is a rumour spread about by the wreckers who have caused shortages through their sabotage of our crops.'

'That's a lie.'

Stirkhov rounded on the blacksmith. 'I remember you. You were a troublemaker when I was here before. Don't make me note you down as a propagator of Negative Statements, or . . .' He left the threat unsaid.

Everyone knew what happened to agitators.

Pyotr felt a moment's panic and glanced swiftly around him.

That was when he saw her, the figure at the back near the door, standing motionless. It was the young woman from the forest, the one with the moonlight hair, and her blue eyes were fixed right on him. Why was she here, the fugitive? A wrecker and a saboteur come to make trouble? Should he speak out? If only he possessed Yuri's absolute certainty of action in a black and white world. He dragged in a deep breath and jumped to his feet.

'Comrade Chairman, I have something to say.'

Sofia could see what was coming but she didn't blame the boy when he leaped to his feet. He was trapped. Enticed by burning zeal. She'd seen it growing in his face.

No, she didn't blame him. But that didn't mean she wouldn't fight him. Quickly she stepped into the aisle between the rows of benches.

'Comrade Deputy Chairman.'

She spoke out clearly, overriding the boy's thin voice. Instantly all eyes swung away from him and focused on the newcomer. A murmur trickled round the hall. 'Who is she? *Kto eto?*'

'State your name, Comrade,' ordered Stirkhov.

'My name is Sofia Morozova.' Her heart was kicking like a mule. 'I've travelled down from Garinzov, near Lesosibirsk in the north, after the death of my aunt. I am the niece by marriage of Rafik Ilyan.'

Heads turned to Zenia, who was seated next to the tall man with the lion's mane. She nodded, but said nothing.

'What is it you wish to say, Comrade Morozova?' Stirkhov asked.

'Comrade Deputy, I have come to this meeting to offer my labour for the harvest.'

It was Chairman Aleksei Fomenko who responded. 'We welcome labourers at harvest time when the hours are long and the work is hard. Have you done field work before?'

'Yes,' she said. 'I've done field work.'

Enthusiastic voices erupted along the benches.

'I could use her in my brigade.'

'We need her in the potato fields!' a woman shouted out.

'Very well, Sofia Morozova, we will find you work,' said Aleksei Fomenko. 'Have you registered at the *kolkhoz* office as a resident?'

'Not yet.'

For the first time he paused. She saw the muscles round his eyes tighten and knew he had started to doubt her. 'You must do so first thing tomorrow morning.'

'Of course.'

Pyotr felt his fear of her melt. One moment it was like acid in his throat, burning his flesh, and the next it tasted like honey, all sweet and cloying. He was confused. What had she done to him? She was an Enemy of the People, he was convinced of it. Why else would she be a fugitive in the forest? But when he looked around at the faces he couldn't understand why they couldn't see it too. What was she? A *vedma*? A witch?

'Comrades,' Stirkhov was saying, 'tonight I have come to inform you all of the quotas you are to fulfil with this year's harvest. The State demands that your quota of contributions be raised.'

A ripple of shock ran through the hall. Moans made a rustling sound like rats in corn stubble. Then came the anger. Pyotr felt it like a wave of hot air, thick on the back of his neck.

'Silence!' Fomenko rapped on the table. 'Listen to Comrade Stirkhov.'

'We're listening,' Igor Andreev, a brigade leader, said reasonably. His hunting dog whined at his knee. 'But last December the Politburo ordered the seizing of most of our seed grain and our seed potatoes to feed the towns and the Red Army, so we can't even fulfil the present quotas.' He stared dully up at Fomenko. 'Chairman, we'll be eating rats.'

'If you work hard,' Fomenko said, 'you eat. Stalin has announced the annihilation of begging and pauperism in the countryside. Work hard,' he repeated, 'and there will be enough for everyone to eat.'

It was Leonid Logvinov who stood up first, the ginger-haired man they still called the Priest, though his church was long gone. Logvinov's skeletal arm held his wooden crucifix out in front of him.

'God forgive your murdering ways,' he thundered, 'and the blaspheming lies of your Antichrist.'

'Too far, Priest, you've gone too far.' Stirkhov pounded his fist down on the metal table. But at the same moment the large oak door at the far end slammed open with a crash, rebounding on its hinges, and a wave of cold air swept into the hall. Mikhail Pashin strode into the central aisle, his brown hair windblown, his suit creased.

'Get out of here!' he shouted. He pointed a finger at the men behind the table on the platform. 'They've tricked you, those two. They've kept you cooped up in here while the forces of the Grain Procurement Agency are ransacking your houses, hunting out hidden stores of grain, stripping your larders and stealing your chickens to fulfil their quotas.'

Panic forced everyone to their feet.

'Go home!' Mikhail shouted above the noise. 'Before you starve.'

He stepped aside to let the panicked villagers pass. They were pushing and pressing, struggling and shouting, a hundred of them fighting to get through the door. Urgently he scanned the bobbing heads.

Where was Pyotr? He would be here somewhere. His son's seemingly infinite capacity for absorbing Communist propaganda made Mikhail clench his teeth, but right now all he wanted was to find him and get him safe. Tonight there would be violence.

Even as the thought entered his head, a stone abruptly exploded in through one of the side windows, scattering glass and drops of rain over the empty benches. Mikhail took a deep breath.

'Pyotr!' he roared.

'Papa!'

A huge wave of relief rushed through Mikhail as he caught sight of his son.

'You always seem to be the bringer of bad news.'

Mikhail glanced fleetingly at the person who had spoken. To his surprise it was the girl he'd met in that candlelit moment before dawn this morning, the Gypsy's niece. Her strange blue eyes looked at you as if seeing someone else, the someone you keep hidden from public gaze. She was standing in the aisle in front of him, still as stone, letting the flow of people break and reform around her.

'These days most news is bad news,' Mikhail muttered.

'Not always,' she said.

He wanted to push past to reach Pyotr but something about her held him there for a moment and, when an elderly *babushka* elbowed him against her, he found himself staring deep into her face, only inches from his own. He could smell the sweet scent of juniper on her breath.

She was painfully thin, bones almost jutting through her skin, and she had the bruised shadows of semi-starvation in the hollows of her face. But her eyes were extraordinary. Bluer than a summer sky, glittering in the light from the lamps, full of something wild. For one unnerving second he thought she was actually looking right into him and rummaging through his secrets.

Suddenly Pyotr's worried face appeared at Mikhail's elbow. He seized his son's arm in one hand and the girl's in the other and propelled them both through the door.

That night, Tivil was stripped naked. That's how it seemed to Pyotr.

'Stay indoors, Pyotr. And keep the house locked.'

Those were Papa's words. With a frown he lit himself a cigarette, ruffled Pyotr's hair and was about to disappear back out into the chaotic night when he stopped abruptly. He looked across at Sofia Morozova, assessing her. Mikhail Pashin had kept a firm grip on her arm, as well as on Pyotr's, when they left the assembly hall and had marched them both straight to the safety of his own home. Now he was leaving them.

'Will you take care of my son for me?' he asked her.

'Of course. I'll guard him well.'

Pyotr wanted to die of shame but his father nodded, satisfied, and stepped out into the road. A cold drizzle was falling as he pulled the door closed behind him and Pyotr tried not to be frightened for him. They were left standing in the tiny porch where boots were kept, the fugitive and himself, just the two of them alone in the house, eyeing each other warily. Pyotr picked up the oil lamp that Papa had lit on the shelf by the door and walked into the living room with it. He was hoping she wouldn't follow, but she did. Right on his heels.

Neither spoke. He placed the lamp on the table and headed straight for the kitchen. There he poured himself a cup of water, drank it down slowly, counted to fifty in his head and went back into the living room. She was still there. She was leaning over the half-constructed model of a bridge on the table, one of the tiny slivers of wood between her fingers.

'Don't touch,' he said quickly.

'It must take a lot of patience to make.'

'Papa is building it.' He shuffled nearer. 'I help.'

She gazed at it, very serious. 'It's beautiful. What bridge is it?'

'The Forth Bridge in Scotland,' he lied.

'I see,' she nodded. She put down the piece of wood and looked round the room.

'You have a nice house,' she said at last.

He wouldn't look at her. Of course it was a nice house, the nicest in the village. A huge *pechka* stove provided the heart of the *izba*, which had good-sized rooms, a large kitchen and furniture that was factory-bought, not hand-hewn. He glanced around proudly. It was a house fit for the director of a factory, with the best wool runners on the brown-painted floor and curtains from the Levitsky factory's own machines.

'May I have a drink?' she asked.

He scuttled back into the kitchen just as the cuckoo clock struck ten, and quickly poured her a few drops of water in the bottom of the same cup he'd used. He didn't bother washing it.

But when he hurried back into the living room she was crouched down in front of the three-cornered cupboard where Papa kept his private things. In one hand was an unopened bottle of vodka, a shot glass in the other.

'That's Papa's. Put it back.'

She smiled at him, a very small curl of her lips. Pyotr watched her unscrew the cap and pour into the glass some of the liquid. She carried the bottle and the untouched vodka over to the armchair and sat down in it. She raised her glass to him.

'*Za zdorovie!*' she said solemnly. She tipped her head back and threw the shot of vodka down her throat.

'I'm going to tell,' he said quickly.

'Tell what?'

'Tell Chairman Fomenko that you're a fugitive.'

'What makes you think I'm a fugitive?' she asked. 'I was just taking a break on my journey south, resting up in the forest.' Quietly she added, 'I don't want trouble.'

'If you don't want trouble, why did you go to the meeting tonight?'

'To find you.'

His stomach lurched.

'I had no idea when I met you in the forest that you were Mikhail Pashin's son.'

Pyotr just stared at his shoes. He'd forgotten to clean them.

'Where is your mother?'

He shrugged. 'She left. And never came back.'

'I'm sorry, Pyotr. How long ago?'

'Six years.'

'Six years is a long time.'

She leaned forward, chin propped firmly on her hand. 'Pyotr, please. We can be friends, you and I.'

He could sense the strands of her web twisting through the air towards him, so fine he couldn't see them but he knew they were there. She looked harmless, but he recognised the determination in her, the same way he recognised the coming of thunder behind the grey skirts of a storm cloud. He turned and ran out of the house.

Rafik fought them with his mind, one by one. He drew no blood, except in his own brain, but he raged.

The uniforms came. In ones and twos and threes. He manipulated their feeble thoughts. House by house he turned them back, bought time for goods to vanish from larders into the forest's sanctuary. Sacks of grain, haunches of pork, slabs of cheese, they all slipped away into the darkness. But the uniforms crawled everywhere, too many for him. The pain started when six faced him at once. Six was too many, they drained his strength, but when he saw the woman in the house weeping, entreating the stone faces to leave her family something to eat, he knew the cost the village would pay if he stopped.

So he didn't stop—and now he was paying for it. A red-hot pain erupted inside his brain. He staggered in the street, tasted blood.

'Zenia,' he breathed.

Before the sound was out of his mouth, his daughter was there at his side in the shattered darkness, a tiny vial of green fluid in her hand. Her gaze sought his and he saw her fear for him trapped in her eyes, but not once did she tell him to cease what he was doing.

'The potion won't stop the damage.' She soothed his temples with a cloth that smelled of herbs. 'But it will mask the pain, so you'll be able to continue. If you choose to.'

Her black eyes begged him not to.

He touched his daughter's cheek and tipped the dark green liquid down his throat.

Pyotr was running up to the stables when Sofia caught up with him. Her fingers fastened round his wrist and he was astonished at the strength in them.

'*Privet*,' she said, with no hint of anger that he'd run off. 'Hello again.'

'I was just going to check on Zvezda,' he said quickly. 'Papa's horse. To make sure he wasn't taken by the troops.'

She paused, considered the idea, then nodded as if satisfied and led him up the rest of the narrow track to where the stable spread out round a courtyard. Once inside the stables she released his wrist and lit a kerosene lamp on the wall. Pyotr wouldn't admit it but he had been frightened by the savagery of what was tearing his village apart tonight. Her eyes followed his every move as he refilled Zvezda's water bucket.

'Zvezda is growing restless,' Sofia said, lifting a hand to scratch the animal's nose.

The other horses were whinnying from their stalls and it dawned on Pyotr that something wasn't right, but he couldn't work out what.

'Listen,' she whispered.

Pyotr listened. At first he heard nothing but the restless noises of the horses. He listened harder and underneath those he caught another sound, a dull roar that set his teeth on edge.

'What's that?' he demanded.

'Pyotr!' The priest burst into the stables and instantly checked the dozen stalls to ensure the horses were not panicked. 'Pyotr,' he groaned, 'it's the barn, the one where the wagons are kept. It's on fire!'

His windblown hair leaped and darted about him as if the fire were ablaze on his shoulders.

'*I am a vengeful God, saith the Lord.* I tell you, this is the Hand of God at work. His punishment for the evil here tonight.'

Sofia hurried to the door of the stable. She looked out into the night and called out. 'Come here, Pyotr.'

Pyotr rushed to her side and gasped. The whole of the night sky was on fire. It sent Pyotr's mind spinning. Once before he'd seen an inferno like this and it had changed his life. He made a move to dash towards it but Sofia's hand descended firmly on his shoulder.

'You're needed here, Pyotr,' she said in a steady voice. 'To help calm the horses.'

Pyotr saw the priest and the fugitive exchange a look.

'She's right,' Priest Logvinov said. He flung out both arms in appeal. 'I'll need as much help as I can get with the horses tonight. Right now they have the stink of smoke in their nostrils.'

'But I want to find Papa.'

'No, Pyotr, stay here,' she ordered, but her eyes were on the flames and a crease of worry was deepening on her forehead. 'I'll make sure your Papa is safe.' Without another word she hurried away into the night.

Gigantic flames were ripping great holes in the belly of the night sky. Spitting and writhing, they leaped twenty metres into the air, so that even down at the river's edge Mikhail Pashin could feel the sting of sparks in his eyes, the smoke in his lungs. He was on his knees, crouched over the water pump on the riverbank, struggling in the darkness to bring it to life. It had so far resisted all his coaxing and cursing. In frustration he clouted his heftiest wrench against the pump's metal casing and instantly the engine spluttered, coughed, then racketed into action, sending gallons of river water racing up the rubber hose.

'The scientific approach, I see,' a voice said out of the darkness.

In the gloom he made out nothing at first, just the creeping shadows etched against the red glow of the sky, but then he saw a face close by.

'It's Sofia,' she said.

'I thought you were at my house, you and Pyotr.'

'Don't worry. Your son is safe in the stables with the priest.'

'Good. They'll be out of harm's way up there.'

She moved closer. 'The whole village is helping,' she said. Her words merged with the clanking of the engine.

'Yes, in an emergency the *kolkhoz* knows how to work together.' He glanced over his shoulder to the spot where a long line of men and women, clutching buckets, snaked up from the river all the way to the burning barn. Each face was grim and determined.

'Who the hell did this? Who would wish to burn down our barn?'

'Mikhail, look who's in the line.'

'In the line? The villagers, you mean?'

'And?'

'The troops helping them.'

'Exactly.'

'What about them?'

'Look at them,' she said urgently.

He frowned. What on earth was she talking about? All he could see was the blackness and the clawing flames. The effort of all those workers. Then suddenly it dawned. His pulse raced as he realised this was the moment when the troops' attention was totally diverted from the grain. Why the hell hadn't he seen it himself ? He leaped to his feet, abandoning the water pump to its own steady rhythm, and raced up through the drooping willows towards the centre of the village. Sofia matched him stride for stride.

'Wait here,' Mikhail ordered. 'And make no sound.'

The small group of villagers nodded, huddled silent and invisible at the side of the blacksmith's forge where the night wrapped them in heavy shadows. Four women, one of them sick, and two old men. Their backs didn't look strong enough to hoist the sacks but they were all Mikhail could find inside the houses. Everyone else was up at the fire, so they'd have to do. Plus Sofia, of course. Just as he was about to edge away, she leaned close to him, her breath warm on his ear as she whispered, 'Take care. I promised Pyotr I'd make sure you stayed safe.'

He couldn't see her eyes, so he touched her hand in reassurance. It felt strong and swept away his doubts about the handling of the sacks.

'I'll be back,' he promised and walked out into the main street.

It was dark and deserted now, except for an uncovered flatbed truck that was piled with more than a dozen sacks of various shapes and sizes. Beside the truck stood a soldier in the OGPU, the State Security Police, with a long coat flapping at his ankles and a Mauser pistol in his fist. Mikhail glanced around but there were no other troops in sight. This one was leaning against the tailgate, cigarette in hand, guarding the sacks on the flatbed and waiting for his comrades to return.

'*Oy moroz, moroz, nye moroz menya, Nye moroz menya, moego konya,*' Mikhail began singing, loud and boisterous.

The words slipped over each other in his mouth. He aimed himself in the general direction of the truck but his feet wove from one side of the road to the other, stumbling and tripping, only just correcting themselves in time. He threw back his head and laughed.

'Hey, Comrade, my friend, how about a drink?' His words came out slurred and he brandished a bottle of vodka he'd snatched from the smithy, at the same time looking around the dark street in a bewildered manner. 'Where'sh everyone?'

The man pushed himself off the truck, threw the cigarette in the dirt and ground his heel on it. He regarded Mikhail with caution.

'Who are you?'

'I'm your friend, your good friend,' Mikhail grinned lopsidedly and thrust out the bottle. 'Here, have a drink.'

'No. You're drunk, you stupid oaf.'

'Drunk but happy. You don't look happy, *tovarichch*.'

'Neither would you if you had to deal with such—'

'Here.' Mikhail thrust the bottle at the man again. 'Some left for you. You could be out here all night.'

The fire reflected in the man's spectacles. His hesitation betrayed him, so Mikhail seized the hand that had discarded the cigarette and wrapped it round the bottle. 'Put fire in your belly.' He rocked on his heels with laughter. 'Fire in your belly instead of in our barn.'

The man's mouth slackened. He almost smiled.

'Let's have it.' He took a mouthful. Smacked his lips.

'Good?'

'It's cat's piss. It's no wonder you peasants are mindless. This home-made brew rots your brains.'

'Come with me, Comrade Officer, and I will show you . . .' Mikhail lowered his voice in conspiratorial style, 'the real stuff. The good stuff.'

The man was drunker than a mule. But when Mikhail yanked him to his feet after an hour of pouring his best vodka down his throat, it came as a surprise at the door to find he still had a few wits clinging to him.

'You come too,' the man said, his head lolling on his thick neck.

'No, my friend, I'm off to bed,' Mikhail grinned.

He started to close the door of his house but the man put his shoulder to it. 'You come, my Tivil comrade. To the truck.' With astonishing speed of hand for someone swilling with vodka he produced the Mauser and pointed it at Mikhail. 'You come. *Bistro*. Quickly.'

So they stumbled up the road together, their path lit by the flames in the night sky. The truck loomed ahead. Even in the darkness it was obvious that the flatbed now held no more than a handful of sacks. The man stared at them and swallowed hard.

'Where's the grain?'

Shock was sobering him fast and with a grunt of effort he swung the pistol at Mikhail and held it against his temple. 'Tell me where the grain is, you thieving village bastard. *Right now*.'

Mikhail didn't move. 'Comrade,' he said with a slur, 'you've got me all wrong. I am just—'

'I'll count to three.'

'No, Comrade—'

'*Odeen*.' One.

'I know nothing about the grain.'

'*Dva*.' Two.

Mikhail's body tensed, ready to lash out, but a quiet voice from the side of the truck distracted them both.

'Comrade Officer, I think you have made a mistake.' It was Sofia. She and the Gypsy approached out of the darkness together as if it had been a cloak over their shoulders.

'Who are you?'

'I am Sofia Morozova. And this is my uncle, Rafik Ilyan.'

'You know where my grain is?'

'Of course. It's here.'

The gun released its pressure and Mikhail breathed. Rafik was so close to the man that their shapes seemed to merge into one. The Gypsy's black eyes were sunk like boreholes in his head and he was holding fiercely on to the man's arm, pressing his fingers into the flesh beneath the sleeve, and staring fixedly up into the narrow bloodshot eyes. And yet the officer made no word of complaint. What the hell was going on? The man was gazing back at the Gypsy with a slightly baffled expression, as though he'd forgotten where he'd left his cigarettes rather than more than a dozen sacks of grain.

'You made a mistake,' Rafik stated clearly and, as he said it, his other hand whipped out and fixed on Mikhail's arm. The Gypsy's voice was soft, but somehow it crept into Mikhail's head and crawled through the coils of his brain until he could hear nothing else. 'There were only ever four sacks in the truck, and you have them all there,' Rafik said. 'No grain is missing.'

Mikhail and the officer stared at the sacks. Sounds were tumbling around indistinctly in Mikhail's head as the Gipsy's words spilled into the night air. Of course there had only ever been four sacks. What had he been thinking of?

Sofia watched in disbelief. In some strange, impossible way Rafik seemed to take hold of the men's minds, first the OGPU officer's and then Mikhail's, and manipulate their thoughts.

'Sofia!'

She blinked and saw the Gypsy stumble in the darkness. Her hand shot out to steady him and she could feel the tremors shaking his body.

'Go,' he urged and his voice was weak. 'Run to the schoolhouse. Tell Elizaveta to bring the key to the chamber. Now. Run!'

The schoolhouse stood at the bottom of the village street, a modern box of a building with a neat low fence around it. A single window to the right gleamed brightly from within. So the teacher was at home. Sofia ran up the path, relieved, but couldn't help wondering why Elizaveta Lishnikova wasn't at the fire.

She banged on the door.

The door flew open immediately and Sofia was convinced the woman had been standing on the other side of it, listening for footsteps. Something about the tall, grey-haired teacher who observed her with such bright, hawkish eyes steadied Sofia's racing heart. This woman wasn't the kind of person who would take risks unnecessarily. That thought comforted her.

Sofia spoke quickly. 'Rafik sent me.'

'What does he want?'

'The key to the chamber. He needs you to bring it to him.'

There was a pause. Even in the darkness Sofia could feel the spikes of the woman's suspicion.

'Wait here.'

But the moment Elizaveta Lishnikova disappeared back into the hallway of her schoolhouse, Sofia followed her and shut the door. Standing outside on the path, spotlit by the lamp in the hall, was an open invitation to any troops who might decide they'd had enough of firefighting. Besides, the door Elizaveta had disappeared through had been left ajar, and the temptation to look was too great.

What she saw astonished her. The room was like something out of a St Petersburg salon, alive with colour: the deep maroon carpet covering the floor was of intricate Indian design; the table and cabinets clearly French from the last century, with ornate curlicues, gilt handles; the curtains wine-red swathes of heavy silk.

Sofia caught her breath and Elizaveta raised her head from what looked to be a secret drawer in the side of a fine satinwood desk. Her long back straightened and she faced Sofia with a sudden pulse of colour high on her cheeks. 'So I was right,' Elizaveta said quietly. 'You *are* a spy for Deputy Stirkhov, aren't you?'

'No.'

The two women locked eyes, the older woman's face growing ever more angular in her conviction, but Sofia said nothing more. If she did, she might say too much and not know when to stop.

'No,' she repeated firmly.

The schoolteacher didn't dispute it further. 'I did not invite you inside this room. Please leave.'

'I'll wait in the hallway,' Sofia said. 'Be quick.'

She left the beautiful room and a moment later Elizaveta Lishnikova joined her, with two keys in her hand. One she used to lock her private room, afterwards sliding it into the thick coil of grey hair at the back of her head. Sofia was impressed.

'You have the key to the chamber—whatever that is?'

'Of course,' the teacher nodded.

'Then let's take it to Rafik.'

'Not you.'

'What?'

'I want you to stay here. In the hallway. Don't leave it.'

'Why?' Sofia was impatient to return to Mikhail.

'In case the troops come searching. They most likely won't but . . . they might.' The older woman's careful brown eyes scanned Sofia appraisingly. 'You look the kind of person who could keep them out of my school. Guard it well. I'm trusting you.'

With a whisk of her grey shawl the teacher was gone, the door closing quietly behind her. Sofia paced the scuffed boards in frustration. She wanted to be out there, ensuring that Mikhail and Rafik were not tossed into the truck in place of the sacks. She hated being left behind to watch over some irrelevant little schoolhouse.

What was there to guard anyway, other than some pieces of fine furniture? And what did Elizaveta Lishnikova mean when she said Sofia was the kind of person who could keep the troops out of the school? That she was in league with the OGPU forces? Or that she had the youth and the feminine wiles to turn troops from their course?

It was some minutes later that she first heard the noise. A tiny, whimpering sound, like a mouse in pain. She wondered if it could be a creature that had fled from the barn fire.

It seemed to be coming from behind the other door in the hall, the one she assumed led into the schoolroom. Her breath grew shallow and she could feel the hairs rise on the back of her neck, but she wasn't going to stand here doing nothing. She lifted the oil lamp from its bracket and pushed open the door. The lamplight leaped in ahead of her, looping in great arcs though the pitch darkness, jumping off the windows and lighting up a clutch of small pale circles. It took her a second to recognise them as faces. Children's faces, pale and wide-eyed with fear.

Children from less than five years old up to ten or eleven were seated there, each one silent at a desk. Eleven pale moons in the darkness and, in front of each one on the desktop, a bundle of some sort, some large and lumpy, others small and strong-smelling. Nearly all the children had their thin arms wrapped protectively around the bundle of food they had saved from their homes.

The noise was coming from a tiny girl. She was sobbing, and an older girl had her hand clamped across the little one's mouth, but still the mouse-pain sound squeezed its way out. Quickly Sofia took the lamp back into the hall and replaced it in its bracket, so that no light showed in the schoolroom. She returned to the children and, as she shut the door behind her, she heard their collective sigh. She groped her way to the teacher's chair at the front and sat down.

'Now,' she whispered softly, 'I'll tell you a story. But you must stay quiet as little mice.'

4

Tivil
July 1933

'PAPA, WAKE UP. Please, wake up. You're late.'

Mikhail opened his eyes and a spike of morning sunlight lanced into them. He winced. He was on the floor of his own living room, curled up in his coat, a bottle nestled to his chest. An empty bottle.

'Papa, you got drunk!'

Mikhail sat up and scrubbed a hand through his hair. The ceiling swooped, then settled. His mind struggled. It felt oddly empty.

'I wasn't drunk, Pyotr.'

'You were, you know you were.' The boy's eyes glared, a long sulky beat. 'And now you're late for work.'

'What time is it?'

'Eight thirty.'

'*Chyort!*'

Mikhail rose to his feet and groaned. This was a hangover like none he'd experienced before. His whole brain felt dislocated and he stank of alcohol, and of something else. He sniffed the sleeve cautiously. Was it her? The scent of her skin on his arm? The sudden memory of Sofia's face in the darkness, her mouth soft and full as she whispered words to him. What words? Damn it, what words? He couldn't remember. He shook his head but nothing became clearer. Dimly he recalled Rafik being there last night. What had the Gypsy to do with it?

'Pyotr,' he said gruffly, 'you were right to wake me. *Spasibo.*'

He went into his room, shaved, changed his shirt and when he came out again Pyotr was waiting for him.

'Papa, what happened last night? What happened to the grain and the sacks, Papa? All the piles of them that the Procurement Officers stacked in the truck. People are saying it was stolen. That you were . . . involved.'

The boy's face was tense, as if he was frightened to hear the answer.

'No grain was taken,' Mikhail said firmly. 'There were only four sacks.'

'They say that's not true.'

'Then they're lying. Pyotr, stay away from the barns today. That fire didn't light itself and Fomenko will be looking for a culprit.'

The fresh air cleared Mikhail's head as he cantered down the dirt road, past the cedar tree that marked the village boundary and out into the valley that lay before him. The bushy green foliage of the potato crop rustled in the fields and stooped figures wielded hoes and rakes across the long mounds. The whole *kolkhoz* work force was already hard at it, striving to fulfil Aleksei Fomenko's labour quotas.

Above, a solitary skylark soared up into the brilliantly blue sky, its wings fluttering like heartbeats. Mikhail envied its effortless flight. He used to work at the N22 aircraft factory in Moscow and he missed that wonderful sense of freedom that came with flying, but freedom was a word that had no meaning these days.

He heeled Zvezda into a longer stride and the horse responded with ease. They were travelling fast, kicking up a trail of dust behind them, and it came as a surprise when he looked up and spotted a lone figure standing at the roadside some way ahead.

He recognised her at once, that distinctive way she had of cocking her head to one side, as if expecting something. She was watching him, one hand shielding her eyes. He reined Zvezda to a walk and approached with care, so as not to coat her in dust.

'Good morning, Sofia Morozova. *Dobroye utro.* You're a long way from home.'

She looked up with a wide smile. 'That depends where home is.'

The smile was infectious. 'Are you walking all the way to Dagorsk?'

'I was waiting for you.'

'I'm glad, because I have something to ask you.'

Mikhail slid off the saddle and landed lightly in front of her, the reins loose in one hand.

'Do you know what happened to the grain last night?' he asked.

Her eyes were an intense piercing blue, capturing his attention and holding it with their directness.

'You were there,' she said, shifting her gaze away from him and towards the village. 'You saw them.'

'That's what I don't understand. I *was* there, but somehow it's all mixed up in my mind and I can't make sense of it. I remember the fire, and you at the pump and a man with spectacles sweating over my best vodka but then . . .' He stepped closer. 'Just tell me, Sofia, how many sacks of grain were in the truck before everyone ran off to fight the fire?'

For a moment Mikhail thought she wasn't going to reply. Something in her eyes changed, a shutter slid down inside them. Before she even spoke, he knew she was going to lie to him. For some reason he couldn't quite understand, the thought made him feel sick.

'Mikhail, there were four sacks on the truck before the fire started and four sacks still there at the end of the night.'

He said nothing.

'Rafik is sick,' she said.

He tried to find a connection between Rafik and the truck, almost catching hold of it before it slipped through his fingers and vanished.

'I'm sorry to hear that Rafik is unwell,' he said.

'You don't look so good yourself.'

'That's because I need to know what went on last night. Please, tell me.'

She looked away.

He seized her arm. 'How many sacks, Sofia?'

'Four.'

A stab of anger made him drop her arm and in one easy movement he swung himself back up into the saddle, but whether the anger was at her for lying or at himself for not remembering, he couldn't tell.

Gathering the reins in one hand, and on the verge of urging the horse into a gallop, at the last second he looked down again at Sofia. And something in her held him. Something in her intent gaze, something he couldn't leave behind. He stretched out an arm. Instantly she seized it and he swept her up on to the horse behind him.

At first neither spoke. Sofia leaned forward and felt the hard muscles each side of Mikhail's ribs where she rested her hands to hold on. The moment her feet lifted off the ground as she swung up on the horse, she felt the past drop from her arms like a heavy bundle of dead sticks, and she left them there, lying in a spiky jumble in the dirt.

She'd have to pick them up. Of course she would, she knew that. But later. Right now she felt alert, happy and alive, and all that mattered was being here on his horse. With him so close she could smell the fresh clean male scent of him and study the strong curve of the back of his head. She wanted to wrap her arms around his body and hold herself tight against him, feeling his sun-warmed back against her breasts, and listen to his heart beating.

Instead she held on lightly and let her own body move with the rhythm of the horse beneath her. It was travelling at a good pace. Fields of potatoes dashed past, edged with a haze of clover flowers that drew the greedy bees to them. Was she a greedy bee? Drawn to her own personal flower?

But he wasn't hers. She was stealing him. An ache started up in her chest and her fingers fluttered involuntarily against his ribs, making him half turn his head to her.

'Are you all right back there?' he asked.

'I'm fine. Your horse must possess a strong back to carry the two of us so effortlessly.'

'You and I are no more than a gnat's wing to Zvezda. He's used to hauling massive carts all day round Dagorsk.'

'For your factory?'

'No, for a Soviet haulage business. You didn't think he rested in a stall with a net of hay and a young filly till sundown, did you?' He laughed. 'Like I'm sure Comrade Deputy Stirkhov spends his days.'

She could feel the laughter ripple under the tips of her fingers, vibrating his rib bones, and it echoed in a joyous rush through her own veins.

'Mikhail, you are too free with your insults. You should take care.'

He shrugged his big flat shoulder blades as if she'd laid an unwelcome weight on them. 'Of course you're right. You'd think I'd have learned by now. That's why I've washed up here in this backwater instead of . . .' His words trailed into a sigh.

'Instead of where?'

'Moscow.'

'Did you like Moscow so much?'

'I liked the Tupolev aircraft factory.'

'Is that why Rafik calls you Pilot?'

'Yes. But I was never a pilot. I'm an engineer. I worked on the engine designs and stress testing of the ANT planes.'

It wasn't hard to picture him soaring through the clouds, eyes bright with joy, up in the freedom of the clear blue sky. But she didn't ask the obvious question, made no attempt to search out the why or the how. Instead she laid her cheek against his shoulder. They rode like that in silence and she could feel the thread between them spinning tighter, drawing them together.

After several minutes, as though he could hear her thoughts, he said flatly, 'I was dismissed. I wrote a letter. To a friend in Leningrad. In it I complained that some of the equipment was agonisingly slow in arriving at the N22 factory because of incompetence, despite the fact that Stalin himself claimed to be committed to expanding the aircraft industry as a major priority.'

'Foolish,' she murmured and gently tapped his head. His hair felt soft.

'Foolish is right.' He leaned back a fraction in the saddle, so that his shoulder pressed harder against her cheek. 'I should have realised all employees in such a sensitive project would have their letters monitored. It was only because Andrei Tupolev himself intervened for me that I wasn't sent to one of the Siberian labour camps. Instead I was exiled out here. But I'm an engineer, Sofia, not a clothes merchant.'

'You were lucky.' Sofia sat up straight once more. 'You must be careful, Mikhail.'

'I admit I've had a few run-ins with Stirkhov and his *Raion* Committee already. I'm an engineer, and since all the big public show trials of the engineers he doesn't trust me.'

'What show trials?'

It slipped out. She wanted to cram the words back inside her mouth.

'Sofia, you must have heard of them, everyone has. The trials of the industrial engineers. The first one was the Shakhty trial in 1928. Remember it? Fifty technicians from the coal industry. The poor bastards were accused by Prosecutor Krylenko of cutting production and of being in the pay of foreign powers. Of taking food out of the mouths of the hungry masses and of treachery to the Motherland.'

She could feel his back growing rigid.

'Everyone clamoured for the deaths of these men, who were forced into confessing absurd crimes. They betrayed the whole engineering industry, humiliated us. Endangered us.' He paused suddenly and she wondered where his mind had veered to, but she soon found out.

It was in a totally different sort of voice that he said, 'You'd have to be blind and deaf and dumb not to know of the trials. They were a huge spectacle. Used by Stalin as propaganda in every newspaper and radio broadcast, in newsreels and on billboards. We were completely bombarded for months.' Abruptly he stopped speaking.

'I was ill,' she lied.

'Blind and deaf,' he murmured, ' . . . or not in a position to read a newspaper.'

'I had typhoid fever. I was sick for months and read no newspapers.'

'I see.'

He said it so coldly she shivered. They rode the rest of the way into town in silence.

The town of Dagorsk seemed to press in on Sofia as she walked its pavements. It used to be a quiet market town tucked away on the eastern slopes of the Ural Mountains, but since Stalin had vowed in 1929 to civilise the backward peasants of Russia and to liquidate as a class the *kulaks*, the wealthy farmers, Dagorsk had been jolted suddenly into the twentieth century.

Factories had sprung up on the edge of the town and were turning the air grey with the soot from their chimneys. The people had changed too, as new, forbidding, apartment blocks and tenements filled up with strangers looking for work; strangers who had been exiled to this remote region because of crimes committed against the State. Dagorsk was crawling with people avoiding each other's eyes.

As Sofia emerged from a gloomy *apteka* into the bright sunlight on Kirov Street, clutching Rafik's paper package in her hand, she saw Zenia. The Gypsy girl was standing in the shade under the spreading branches of a lime tree near the newspaper boards, with her bare arms draped around the neck of a young man, his hand curled snugly around her waist. He was wearing a uniform with a pale blue cap and epaulettes, the uniform of the State Security Police. Quickly Sofia whirled away in the opposite direction and ducked round a corner.

'Ah, what have we here? The beautiful Sofia Morozova from Tivil, I do believe.'

It was Comrade Deputy Stirkhov. And he was blocking her path.

Deputy Stirkhov's office was not at all what Sofia expected. It was stylish, with a spacious chrome-legged desk with shiny black top; a gleaming chrome clock and desk lighter; and curved tubular chrome chairs with pale leather seats. Of course it boasted the usual bust of Lenin on a prominent shelf and a two-metre-wide picture of Stalin on the wall, but Lenin with his pointed beard was carved out of white marble rather than plaster, and the portrait of Stalin was an accomplished original oil painting. This was a man who knew how to get hold of what he wanted.

Sofia sat in one of the chairs and crossed her legs, swinging one foot casually despite the pulse in her scarred fingertips pounding like a fresh wound—a sure sign of nerves. She accepted a glass of vodka, even though it was still only mid-morning.

'Thank you, Comrade Deputy. I didn't expect to find such a modern office in a town like Dagorsk.'

'Modern in mind, modern in body,' he said self-importantly and settled himself behind the expansive desk.

He flicked open a Bakelite box and offered her an elegant tan-coloured cigarette that didn't look Russian to her. Imported goods were not often to be seen these days, not openly in any case, though everyone knew they were available in the special shops that only the Party elite could enter. She shook her head and he lit one for himself, drew on it deeply and scrutinised her with an appraising look. She still hadn't worked out exactly what this pale-eyed man wanted from her when he'd suggested 'a talk in my office'.

'You are new to this area. And to Tivil?'

'Yes.'

'I am very interested in Tivil.'

She didn't like the way he said it. 'It's a hard-working village,' she pointed out, 'like any other. Of no particular interest, it seems to me.'

'That's where you're wrong, Comrade Morozova.'

Sofia waited, aware of the value of silence with a man like this, who would always be tempted to fill it.

'Tivil,' he said flatly, 'is not like any of the other villages in my *raion*. It keeps tripping up my officers and making fools of them. They go out there to ensure quotas are filled, that sufficient livestock and crops are handed over, that taxes are paid. But what do they come back with?'

He leaned forward in his chair and stared at her expectantly. Sofia sipped her drink and stared back.

'They come back with lists,' he snapped. 'Lists all neatly ticked, goods checked off, each page endorsed with an official stamp.' His fist came down on the desk, making the clock quiver. 'It's nonsense. At the end of each week there is a discrepancy between what is and what should be. That's why I went out there the other evening to settle matters myself. But it happened again. Everything went wrong. And I know who to blame.'

'Who?'

'That's not your business.'

'So why,' she asked with just the right touch of impatience, 'have you asked me here?'

'Because you are an outsider. You are not yet a part of that close-knit community. Instead of shitting all over each other to gain additional privileges for themselves like other villages do, the Tivil bastards keep their mouths shut. I can't find the crack in their shell.'

'A man like you would keep a Party spy in their midst,' Sofia said amiably, 'I'm certain.'

'Of course.' He waved a dismissive hand. 'But the *bedniak* is worse than useless except for petty tittle-tattle. Spends too much time inside a bloody vodka bottle.'

'So why have you asked me here?'

'To warn you.'

'To warn me? Of what?'

He smiled smoothly. 'Of danger.'

'What kind of danger?'

'Word is going round that it was you who started the fire.'

Her breathing grew tight. 'That's absurd,' she said. 'I had nothing to do with it. Why on earth would I set fire to the barn?'

'A grudge?'

'No, Comrade Deputy Stirkhov, I assure you I bear no grudge against the village. My uncle has kindly taken me in and I am grateful to him and to Tivil. Thank you for the warning, Comrade Deputy. I will take care. It's obvious that whoever torched the barn is trying to shift the blame onto me.'

He was observing her with shrewd eyes. 'Interesting,' he murmured softly. 'Let me see your *dokumenti*, Comrade.'

It was an offence not to carry identity papers at all times, papers that would state her place of residence, her date and place of birth and her father's name. And to leave the *kolkhoz* without official permission to do so was a second offence. She recrossed her legs, slowly, and watched his eyes follow the movement.

'Deputy Stirkhov, I have a suggestion to put to you first.'

He stood up, walked round to her side of his desk, perched his plump bottom on its edge and rested a hand on her knee. She refrained from slapping his wrist away.

'What kind of suggestion?' he asked.

'It seems to me that you need someone new in Tivil. Someone . . . with fresh eyes.'

His smile returned, a smile meant to charm, and the tip of his pink tongue popped out for a brief second. 'You will report to me only.'

'Of course.'

'And in exchange?'

'You pay me. Each week. One hundred roubles. And fifty now to seal the agreement.'

'Hah! You must think me stupid.' He leaned over her and she could smell French tobacco on his breath. 'Don't underestimate me, Comrade Morozova.' His hand tightened on her knee. 'You bring me information and then we'll talk money.'

She laughed and stood up, tipping his hand off her leg. 'An empty stomach dims one's eyes and ears, Deputy Stirkhov.'

She held out a hand, palm upwards. 'Fifty roubles now. It will be worth it to you.'

He narrowed his eyes. 'It had better be.'

'It will, I promise.' She gave him a dazzling smile.

I saw you watching me.' Zenia stepped out into Sofia's path as she left the *Raikom* offices. 'I'm supposed to be at work in the factory but . . .' her cheeks flushed and she looked away shyly.

The young Gypsy girl's wild hair was tamed under a bright yellow scarf tied at the nape of her neck, and her scoop-necked blouse, though old, was clean and showed more of her smooth olive skin than perhaps Rafik would approve of. A green cotton skirt swung from her hips. Sofia could understand why any soldier would come calling.

'Zenia,' she said, 'you look lovely. Who was your friend?'

The girl blushed deeper. 'His name is Vanya.'

'He works for the OGPU, I see. The Security Police.'

Zenia's black eyes darted defensively to Sofia's face. 'I haven't told him anything. About you, I mean.'

'Zenia,' she whispered, 'the Security Police are clever. You will tell him things without even knowing you're doing it.'

The Gypsy girl tossed her head. 'I'm not a fool. I don't say . . .' but she paused as though remembering something and her eyes clouded. 'I don't say anything I shouldn't,' she finished defiantly.

'I'm glad. Guard your tongue, for Rafik's sake.'

Zenia looked away again.

'It's all right, I won't say anything about Vanya. To Rafik, I mean,' Sofia said.

Zenia smiled, a sweet, grateful smile that made Sofia lean forward and brush her cheek against the girl's. 'But be careful. They will be stalking Tivil village after what happened with the Procurement Officer and you may be their way in.'

Mikhail's office was dark. He was often tempted to relocate to an office in the bright new extension he'd had built alongside the old factory, but always changed his mind at the last moment because he knew he needed to be here, overlooking the factory floor, visible to his workers.

His office was up a flight of stairs, but nothing more than a wall of glass divided him from his work force, which meant he could look down on the rows of hundreds of sewing machines and check the smooth running of his production line at a glance. He'd installed modern cutting machines in the extension but in here the machines were so old and temperamental that they needed constant attention.

He stood looking out at them now, hands in his pockets, feeling restless and unable to concentrate. Whatever it was that Sofia Morozova was up to, he was glad she'd arrived in Tivil like a creature from the forest, wild and unpredictable. She made his blood flow faster. In some indefinable way she had altered the balance in his mind, so that he was left with the feeling that he was flying high in the air once more. What was it about Sofia that had set this off? Just because she was fair-haired and blue-eyed and had a fiery spirit like . . .?

No. He slammed the door shut on it all and firmly turned the key. What good did looking back do? None at all.

A knock on the door distracted him.

'Come in,' he said but didn't turn. It would be his assistant, Sukov, with yet another pile of endless paperwork for his attention.

'Comrade *Direktor*, you have a visitor.'

Mikhail sighed. The last thing he wanted right now was an ignorant official from the *Raikom* breathing down his neck.

'Tell the bastard I'm out.'

An awkward pause.

'Tell the Comrade *Direktor* this bastard can see he's in.'

It was Sofia. Slowly, savouring the moment, he turned to face her. She was standing just behind his assistant, eyes amused, breathing fast as though she'd been running and, even in her drab clothes, she made the office instantly brighter.

'Comrade Morozova, my apologies,' he said courteously. 'Please take a seat. Sukov, bring some tea for my visitor.'

Sukov rolled his eyes suggestively, the impertinent wretch, but remembered to close the door after him. Instead of sitting, Sofia walked over to stand beside Mikhail at the glass wall and stared with interest at the machinists at work below.

'A pleasure to see you again so soon—and so unexpectedly.' He smiled and gave her a formal little nod. 'To what do I owe this treat?'

Instead of answering she looked out at the hundreds of heads bent over the machines. 'What nimble fingers they have.'

'They have to work fast to meet their quotas.'

'Of course, the quotas.'

'The curse of Russia,' he said and touched her shoulder, just on the spot where a tear in her blouse was mended with tiny neat stitches.

She didn't draw away. 'It looks to me,' she said, 'as though the machines are working the women rather than the other way round.'

'That is Stalin's intention. No people, just machines that do what they're told.'

'Mikhail!' Sofia hissed sharply and glanced towards the door. In a low whisper she warned, 'Don't talk so.' Her eyes met his. 'Please.'

The door opened and they stepped apart. Sukov entered with a tray that he set down on the desk with a show of attention that made Mikhail want to laugh.

'*Spasibo*,' Mikhail said.

Sukov rolled his eyes once more and tiptoed out of the room.

'I apologise,' Mikhail laughed as they settled down opposite each other at the desk, 'for my assistant's excessive discretion.' He picked up one of the glasses of tea in its *podstakanik*, a metal holder, noticed it had a picture of the Kremlin on it, swapped it for the other one with a picture of Lake Baikal and presented it to her.

'Shall I tell you a joke?' she asked.

Her words made him almost choke on his tea in surprise. 'Go ahead.'

She leaned forward, eyes bright. 'Two men meet in the street and one says to the other, "How are you?" "Oh, like Lenin in his mausoleum," comes the reply. The first man cannot work it out. "What do you mean? Why like Lenin?" The second man shrugs. "Because they neither feed us nor bury us."'

Mikhail threw his head back and roared with laughter. 'That is very black. I like it.'

She was grinning at him. 'I knew you would. But don't tell it to anyone else because they may not see it quite the way we do. Promise me.'

'Is that what we Russians are reduced to? Neither dead nor alive?'

'I'm alive,' she said. 'I move, I drink.' She sipped her tea. 'I'm alive.' But her blue eyes slowly darkened as she looked at him across the desk and said softly, 'I'm not dead.'

It was as if an electric shock hit him. Abruptly he stood up. 'Sofia, let's get out of here.'

His hands almost fitted round her waist as he swung her up onto the rusty iron perch of the freight wagon. She was so light he thought she might take flight in the clear bright air.

'It's a good view from here,' she said, shielding her eyes from the sun as she gazed out across the drab muddy waters of the River Tiva.

'And from here.' Mikhail was still standing among the weeds and dirt of the disused railway siding, looking up at her face.

She smiled. Was she blushing? It wasn't much of a place to bring her to but there was nowhere else, nowhere private anyway.

He leaped up easily and sat beside her, legs draped over the edge. He noticed her shoes were new and finely stitched, and when she bent to brush dust off them he saw the white scars on two of her fingers and wondered how they came to be there. He felt an absurd desire to touch their shiny, vulnerable surface. Somewhere out of sight the sound of a train wheezing its way into the station reminded him that a large consignment of army uniforms had to be freighted out today. He should be overseeing to ensure there were no slip-ups.

'To hell with it,' he said.

'To hell with what?'

'This crucible.'

Her gaze left the river and studied his face. 'Tell me what you mean.'

'I mean Russia. This Motherland of ours has become a crucible and we're all caught in it. Men and morals of every kind are being melted down and reshaped. No one can stay the way they were.' He looked at her fragile bone structure and wondered what kind of steel held it together. 'We all have to re-form ourselves.'

'Have you?'

'I've tried.' He tossed a stone in a high arc towards the river in front of them. 'But right now, I'm not interested in changing anything. Least of all you.'

A smile flickered to her lips but she looked away.

'Sofia, look at me.'

She turned back to him, shyly.

'Why did you come to my office today?' he asked.

'Because there's something I want to ask you.'

'Ask away.' He said it easily but he felt a part of himself tighten.

'Are you proud of your father? Of what he did?'

Mikhail had a sense of scaffolding falling away, leaving him unsupported, balanced precariously on a ledge.

'Why do you ask such a question?'

She looked at him with that odd directness of hers, head tilted to one side, pinning him down, and then suddenly she smiled and let him go.

'I wondered what kind of relationship you had with your father,' she said softly, 'because you obviously love Pyotr very much. He's a fine boy. I know people are reluctant to talk about the past these days because it's so dangerous but . . . I just wondered, that's all.'

Mikhail knew there was more to it but had no wish to push her in that direction. Besides, to talk of his son gave him pleasure.

'Pyotr and I are too alike. I see so much of myself at that age in the boy. That unshakeable belief that you can mend the world. It's enviable in some ways because it gives your life a rigid structure. Like the model bridge that I'm building, each girder firm and inflexible. Except believers' girders come from blueprints laid down by someone else, by Lenin or Stalin or God or Mohammed. It doesn't come from within.'

'So you no longer think you can mend the world?'

'No, I leave the world to take care of itself. I have no more interest in saving it.'

She let her gaze drift with the river. 'All right, so you cannot save the world. But would you save a person? One individual?'

This was the question. He could feel it. Although she asked it casually, this was the question that had brought her to his office.

'Save them from what?'

'From death.'

'That's a big question.'

'I know.'

'Would I save an individual? That would depend,' he said very deliberately, 'on the person. But yes, if it were the right person I would try.'

She lifted her hands to her mouth but not before he'd seen her lips tremble. The sight of that weakness, that momentary dropping of her guard, touched him deeply.

'That's a big answer,' she whispered.

'I know.'

Mikhail reached out and took her scarred hand in his, wrapped his own large hands around it to keep it safe.

'Why?' she murmured.

'It's just the way I see things,' he said, stroking one of her damaged fingers with the tip of his thumb. 'Someone has to fight back.'

'But you said you have no interest any more in changing the world.'

'Not the world, but maybe my small corner of it.'

He lifted her hand and brushed his lips along the back of it, feeling the pulse of her blood. She watched him intently as he spoke.

'When you let yourself become a cog in the vast machine that is the State, it's all too easy to forget that you are a person and you do things you later regret. But I'm Mikhail Pashin. Nothing can alter that.'

'Mikhail Pashin,' she echoed. 'Does the name Dyuzheyev mean anything to you?'

'No.'

The word came out too fast. Her shoulder, slender in the colourless little blouse, leaned against his and he could feel the heat of her seeping into his flesh.

'I've seen people, Mikhail, who have been robbed of who they were. By Stalin and his believers.' Her voice was no more than a murmur. 'Don't underestimate what they can do to you.'

He touched one of the scars on her fingers. 'Is this what they did to you?'

'Yes.'

Their eyes held and it was as though she threw wide the doors inside herself and let him in.

Gently, as if he might break her, Mikhail took her face in his hands, slowly studied the fine lines of her full lips, the tilt of her eyebrows and the flare of her nostrils, and felt something come alive deep within himself that he'd thought was dead for ever. He recognised it instantly. It was trust. Long ago he'd learned to exist without it, each day, each month, each year, dimly aware of the dull ache of loss. Now, suddenly, in this unlikely place, it had leaped back to life.

Softly, frightened that this magical creature might vanish before his eyes, he kissed her mouth. Her lips parted and a faint moan escaped as her body melted against his. His hands caressed the long line of her spine, fingers exploring each bone of it, sliding hungrily down to her narrow waist. Her arms twined around his neck with an urgency that set his blood racing, her mouth opened to his probing tongue, and the sweet taste of her flooded his senses.

5

Davinsky Camp
July 1933

AN IDEA CAME to Anna when she was drenched in sweat, labouring on the road construction, mashing up rocks into gravel with a hammer she could barely lift, and she wondered why she hadn't thought of it before. There was something she had to ask Nina.

As soon as the women were herded into their crocodile formation for the return trek, she couldn't stop herself whispering her question.

'Nina, there's a civilian worker in the Commandant's office, isn't there? The tall, dark-haired one.'

Her big-boned companion nodded her head. 'Yes. She lives in the civilian quarters and deals with the paperwork.'

'You talk with her sometimes, I've seen you.'

Nina laughed softly. 'I think she fancies me.'

Anna smiled. 'Would she know about any escapees and what happened to them? Surely there must be a record in the office.'

It wasn't much to go on. Just a flicker of Nina's eyes to one side, before she shrugged her broad shoulders and said, 'Knowing how drunk our beloved Commandant is most of the time, I don't think there's much chance of an efficient filing system in his office, do you?'

But the flicker of the eyes was enough for Anna.

'Nina,' she muttered, 'you're lying to me.'

'No, I—'

'Please, Nina. Tell me. What have you heard?' Anna pressed.

Nina spoke quickly. 'An unnamed female escapee from this camp was reported found at the railway station in Kazan.' She hesitated, then added. 'Found dead, shot in the head.'

Anna's feet stumbled, blind and boneless. White noise, the sound of pain, filled her head. Nina was still speaking but Anna couldn't hear her words.

'No,' she choked, 'it's not her.'

Her lungs closed up completely and she couldn't breathe. She stumbled, bent double, fighting to drag in air, and the crocodile behind her shuffled to a halt.

'Move yourself, *suka*, you bitch!' The nearest guard raised his rifle butt and brought it down with impatience on the small of her back.

She crunched to her knees on the dusty pine needles, but the shock of the blow jerked her lungs back into action. Nina yanked her onto her feet and into some kind of forward motion before the guard could strike again.

'It won't be her,' Anna whispered. 'It won't be Sofia.'

Beside her Nina nodded but she said nothing more.

As she walked, Anna had no ability to control what went on in her head. It took all her strength just to keep her feet and lungs working long enough to prevent a repetition of the rifle-whipping.

Throughout her years in the camp she had carefully steered her mind away from the razor-edged memories. But now, despite all her efforts, it returned again and again to the day in 1917 that she still thought of as Cranberry Juice Day.

The day had started well in the Dyuzheyevs' drawing room.

When Anna moved her bishop, Grigori Dyuzheyev had frowned and tapped his teeth with a long finger.

'Anna, my girl, you are becoming lethal. I've taught you too well.'

Anna laughed, looked out of the window at the snow drifting down from a leaden sky and tried to hide the ripple of pleasure she felt. Papa wasn't interested in chess, he was over by the fire buried in yet another of his dreary newspapers. But when she was young she had badgered Grigori to teach her and she'd learned fast. It seemed she had a natural flair for strategy and now, four years later, she was threatening to steal his king from under his nose.

But at the very last moment she saw his heavy eyebrows swoop together in a spasm of alarm at the prospect of losing to a twelve-year-old slip of a girl. She didn't want to humiliate this generous man, so she left the back door open for his king and let him win.

'Well done, my girl.' Grigori snorted his dragon sound. 'That was close, by God. Next time maybe you'll do better—if you're lucky!'

Papa glanced up from his paper. 'Got you on the run, has she, my friend?' But he leaned his head back against his armchair and stroked his whiskers the way he did when he was unhappy about something.

'What is it, Papa?'

He tossed the copy of *Pravda* aside.

'It's this damn war against Germany. It's going so badly for us because of sheer incompetence, and two more factories are on strike here in Petrograd. It's no wonder young men like Vasily are up in arms and on the march these days.'

'They should be horsewhipped,' Grigori growled. He blew out smoke from his cigar in a blue spiral of annoyance.

'Grigori, you can't hide yourself away among your Italian paintings and your Arab stallions and refuse to see that Russia is in crisis.'

'I can, Nikolai. And I will.'

'Damn it, man, these young people have ideals that—'

'Don't give me that tosh. Ideology is a word used to hide evil actions behind a cloak of justice. These Mensheviks and Bolsheviks will bring about the disintegration of our country, and then we can never go back.'

'Grigori, you are blind. The Romanovs' Russia is not an ordered Utopia and never has been. It's a doomed system.'

'Do these fools really think their Party membership card will be the answer to their problems? I tell you, Nikolai, they have a lot to learn.'

'Maybe it's we who have a lot to learn,' Papa said hotly.

'Don't be absurd.'

'Listen to me, Grigori. Do you know that Petrograd, this glorious capital city of ours, has the highest industrial accident rate in Russia? No wonder the unions are angry.'

'Papa,' Anna interrupted, quoting something she read herself in the newspaper the day before, 'this is the twentieth century, yet nearly half the homes in this city are without a water or sewage system.'

'Exactly my point. But does Tsar Nicholas care? No, no more than he does about the bread shortages.'

'That doesn't mean we have to face the downfall of the tsars,' snapped Grigori.

'I rather fear it does,' Papa retorted.

'Enough, gentlemen!' From her place on the sofa beside the fire Svetlana Dyuzheyeva scolded her husband and his friend. 'Stop your politicking at once and pour us all a drink, Grigori. Anna and I are bored to tears with it all, aren't we, *malishka*?'

'Isn't Vasily supposed to be here by now?' Anna asked, but was careful to keep her concern out of her voice.

'The infernal boy is late again,' Grigori grumbled as he went over to the drinks table and picked up the vodka bottle.

'Give him time,' Svetlana smiled, as indulgent as ever.

Anna abandoned the chess table with its inlaid squares of ivory and ebony and took up a new position on the padded window seat.

'Don't worry, he won't be much longer, I'm certain.' Svetlana smiled gently. 'Not when he knows you're here.'

Anna nodded to please Svetlana, though she didn't believe a word of it. She knew too well how strongly the activity in the streets drew Vasily into its coils. Her own mother had died when she was born, so her ideas of what a mother should be were all pinned on Svetlana, who was beautiful and kind.

On the other side of the window the lawns were covered in a crisp coating of fresh snow. The drive was still empty.

She couldn't remember a time in her life without Vasily's laughter and his teasing grey eyes, or his soft brown hair to cling to when he galloped her round those lawns on his back. But recently he had become more elusive and he was changing in ways that unnerved her. Even when he did sit quietly at home she could see his mind was rushing out into the streets. *Turbulent*, he called them.

Suddenly the door swung open and in strode a tall youth with grey eyes that sparkled brighter than the chandeliers. A dusting of snow still lay on his brown hair as though reluctant to be swept away, and his cheeks glowed red from the wind. He brought a great swirl of vitality into the room, but instead of his usual immaculate jacket and trousers he was wearing what looked to Anna like horrible workman's clothes, brown and baggy and shapeless. A flat cap was twirling in his hand.

There was a bustle of kissing cheeks and shaking hands, then Vasily bowed very stylishly to Anna.

'Don't look so fierce, Anna,' he chided her. 'I know I promised to be here earlier but I was . . . distracted.' He laughed and tugged at a lock of her hair but she was not ready to forgive him yet.

'I thought you'd had your head cut off,' she said accusingly.

'Annochka,' his voice was low and it made her scalp tingle, 'please forgive me for being late.'

'Vasily, I was so . . . ' but before the words *scared for you* rushed out of her mouth, something in her sensed he would not welcome her fears, so she changed it just in time, '. . . so tired of waiting. To dance.' She kissed his cheek. It smelled of tobacco. 'I want you to dance with me.'

With another elegant bow that made her heart thump, Vasily swept her up into his arms and twirled her round and round, so that her dress billowed out like a balloon.

'Mama,' he called, 'let's have some music for our ballerina.'

'Let me,' Grigori offered, moving over to the grand piano at the other end of the room. With a flourish he struck up a lilting piece.

'Ah, a Chopin waltz.' Svetlana sighed with pleasure and rose to her feet, as graceful as the swans on the lake. '*Doktor* Nikolai, will you do me the honour?'

'Enchanted.' Papa responded courteously and took her in his arms.

They danced round the room. Outside, the world was cold and growing colder each moment, but inside this room the air was warm and bathed in laughter.

Smiling down at her, Vasily held Anna tightly by the waist so that as she twirled in circles her cheek rubbed against the rough serge of his jacket. Every bone in her body was transfixed with joy. She blocked out all thoughts of workers and demonstrators and sabres. Vasily was wrong. This world would last for ever.

A knock. The drawing-room door burst open and Anna's governess, Maria, entered. Her voice was tight and pained. 'Excuse me, madam, but there's been an accident.'

All dancing ceased. The music stopped mid-phrase.

'What kind of accident?' Grigori Dyuzheyev asked at once.

'There's been trouble, sir,' Maria said. 'Down by the orchard. The head gardener is hurt. A bayonet wound, they say, a bad one.' She was punctuating each sentence with little gasps. 'By a troop of Bolsheviks. I thought *Doktor* Fedorin might be able to help.'

Instantly Papa was all business.

'I'm coming right away. I'll just fetch my medical bag from the car.' He was rushing to the door. 'Tell someone to bring clean water, Svetlana,' he called over his shoulder and was gone.

Svetlana hurried from the room. Grigori and Maria followed. Vasily was still holding Anna in his arms and she could feel the rapid pumping of his heart.

'Let's have one last dance, Anna,' he said, his eyes serious. 'There won't be any more dancing after today.'

He started to twirl her round the room again, even though the music had stopped and there were voices shouting outside. He kissed her on the forehead and she inhaled quickly to capture the scent of him. A single shot rang out. A scream outside. Instantly Vasily was pushing her to the floor and bundling her underneath the chaise longue.

'No, Vasily,' she whispered.

'Yes, Anna. You must stay here. Do you hear me?' The lines of his face had changed, sharper now and suddenly older than his fourteen years. 'Whatever happens, Anna, don't come out. Stay here.' He took her hand, kissed a fingertip, and was gone.

But she had no intention of being packed away like a china doll and immediately started to back out from under the chaise longue. She scurried across the floor on her hands and knees, to the window, where she placed her hands flat on the icy pane, nose pressed beside them, looking out. Why was there a pool of cranberry juice in the snow? Next to the pool lay Grigori Dyuzheyev. He looked asleep.

Anna ran out of the house, but her governess yanked her back onto the front steps, tight against her skirt. Maria was not going to let go.

'Say nothing,' she breathed, not taking her gaze from the group spread out on the drive in front of her.

Grey uniforms were everywhere, red flashes on their shoulders. Snow trampled and dirty under their boots. A circle of rifles, glinting in the sun, was aimed at the three figures in the centre of it: Vasily, Svetlana and Grigori. Grigori was splayed awkwardly on the snow in a sleep that Anna knew wasn't sleep and in a pool of red juice that she knew wasn't juice. Svetlana was kneeling beside her husband, a terrible moan escaping from her lips, her head bowed to touch Grigori's chest.

Vasily looked strange. He was standing stiff, his limbs rigid as he spoke to the soldier with the peaked cap, the one with a revolver still pointed at Grigori's motionless body. The words that rushed out of Vasily were hot and angry.

'You'll get the same, whelp, if you don't stop yapping.' The soldier's eyes were full of hate. 'You and your family are class enemies of the people. Your father, Grigori Dyuzheyev, was a parasite, he exploited the workers of our Fatherland, he had no right to any of this and—'

'No.' Vasily was struggling for control. 'My father . . . treated his servants and tenants well, ask any of them what kind of—'

The soldier spat on the snow, a jet of yellow hate. 'No one should own a house like this. You should all be exterminated like rats.'

Anna mewed.

The soldier swung his gun so that it was pointing directly at her. 'You. Come here.'

Anna took one step forward but that was as far as she could go with Maria still holding her tight.

'Leave her alone,' Vasily said quickly. 'She is only a servant's brat.'

'In that dress? What kind of fool do you think I am? No, she's one of your kind. One of the rats.'

'Leave her,' Vasily said again. 'She's too young to make choices.'

'Rats breed,' the soldier snarled. Without shifting the aim of the gun he turned his head to address a boy of about sixteen standing to attention at his shoulder, his cap low over his forehead.

'Son, fetch the rat.'

The boy looked directly at Anna. His pupils were so huge she feared they would swallow her up, black and bottomless. She glared back at the boy as he started towards her.

'No, Comrade.' It was Maria. Her voice was as cool and crisp as the snow. 'The girl is mine. My daughter. I am a servant, a worker, and she's a worker's child, one of the Soviet proletariat.'

'No worker wears a dress like that.'

'They gave it to her.' Maria gestured to the body of Grigori and to Svetlana bent over him. 'They like to dress her up in fine clothes.'

The soldier turned to Svetlana. 'Did you give the brat the dress?'

Svetlana ignored the soldiers but smiled lovingly at Anna.

'Yes,' she said quietly, 'I gave dear Annochka the dress. But you are the rats that will gnaw the heart out of Mother Russia until there is nothing left but blood and tears.'

The shot, when it rang out, made Anna jump. Her feet would have skidded off the step if Maria had not held her. She saw Svetlana hurled backwards off her knees. A red hole flowered in the exact centre of her forehead and leaked dark tendrils.

Vasily roared and ran to her.

Anna stared at the soldier boy in the too-big uniform and cap, rifle steady in his hand, and realised he was the one who had fired the bullet. The older soldier placed a proud hand on his shoulder and said, 'Well done, my son.'

The other soldiers murmured an echoing contented sound, passed from one to the other, so that rifles relaxed and attention lapsed.

Vasily came fast. It took no more than a second for the knife in his hand to sink into the soft throat of the older soldier in command, and for Vasily to leap up the steps and vanish into the house. Anna smelled the sweet familiar scent of him as he raced past her. The soldiers fired after him and a bullet grazed Maria's temple, but they were too slow. Their shouts and stomping feet echoed in the marble hall and up the stairs as they searched. There was the sound of glass shattering inside.

Anna barely moved her lips but she turned her eyes to Maria and whispered, 'Do you think he's safe now? Vasily has escaped, hasn't he?'

Her governess's face was grey as stone except for the small trickle of blood at her hairline. She was staring at the body of Svetlana. It was only then that Anna realised tears were pouring down her own cheeks. She dashed them away, scraping her cold fingers over her face, and that was when she saw Papa. He was running, his face twisted in anguish at the sight of his two dearest friends sprawled on the trampled snow.

'Stop there!' one of the soldiers shouted.

He was older than the rest, with troubled brown eyes that kept darting back to the body of his superior lying on his back in the snow.

'What happened?' Papa demanded. 'Why have you shot these people?' Anna could see the tick in his cheek muscle. 'I shall report you.'

'Who are you?' the older soldier raised his voice.

'I am *Doktor* Fedorin. I was tending to someone wounded by your men here.'

He stepped back and dropped on one knee next to Grigori. His eyes glanced over at Anna. Almost imperceptibly he shook his head. He touched first Grigori's wrist, then Svetlana's, his head bowed.

'The boy killed my comrade here,' the soldier growled.

Papa looked up. Slowly rose to his feet. 'What boy?'

'The Dyuzheyev son.'

Papa stood very still. 'Where is he?'

'My men are searching for him now.'

Papa looked at Anna but said nothing.

'I am taking over this house,' the soldier declared suddenly. 'I requisition it in the name of the Soviet people and—' He stopped abruptly and pointed at the black Oakland parked further along the drive, its headlamps sparkling in the sunshine. 'Whose is that vehicle?'

'It's mine,' Papa said. 'I'm a doctor. I need a car to visit the sick.'

'The rich sick,' the boy soldier spat.

'Tell me, *Doktor*,' the older man in command demanded sharply, 'do you also live in a big house? Do you also keep servants? Do you own horses and carriages and more silver samovars and fur coats than you can ever use?' The man took a step closer. 'Do you?'

Anna saw Papa's eyes go to the silent bodies of Svetlana and Grigori. Suddenly he yanked the handsome silver watch from his waistcoat pocket. 'Here,' he shouted, 'take this. And these.' He hurled his cigar case and his beaver hat on to the trampled snow at their feet. 'And take my house too, why don't you?' His heavy bunch of keys hit the boy's toecap. Papa's rage frightened Anna. 'Take everything. Leave me nothing, not even my friends. Will I then be fit to doctor your glorious proletariat? And are *you* fit to decide who is fit to be cared for and who isn't?'

The boy's eyes filled with loathing.

Anna watched Papa take four long strides towards her. *Odeen. Dva. Tri. Chetiri.* One. Two. Three. Four. Her heart leaped at the sight of his familiar, reassuring smile. His hand reached for her and she felt Maria's fingers uncurl.

There was a loud crack. Anna knew now that it was the sound a rifle makes when it's fired. Papa's mouth jerked open into a silent 'oh' and his eyes rolled up in his head, so that only their whites showed. And then he was falling, face first into the snow. The back of his head was blown open. The boy soldier was gripping his rifle proudly.

Anna ripped herself free of her governess and started to scream.

Anna had become a shadow after her father died in the snow, no longer a person, just a twelve-year-old shadow inside a cramped apartment that belonged to Maria's brother, Sergei, and his wife, Irina. She learned to call Maria *Mama* and she wore a plain, brown peasant dress and ate black bread instead of white. Yet still she wouldn't cry.

'It's not natural,' Irina said in a low voice. 'Her father has just died. Why doesn't she cry?'

'Give her time,' Maria murmured to her sister-in-law as she ran a hand over the silky blonde head. 'She's still too shocked.'

'A shock is what that girl needs,' Irina said and mimed a quick little slap with her hand. 'Well, child, it's time to snap out of it and give your poor Maria a chance to get on with her own life. She's starting a new job tomorrow and can't spend time fretting about you.'

Anna's eyes turned to Maria, panic fierce in them. 'Can't I come with you?' Her voice was barely a whisper. 'I can work too.'

'No, my love.' Maria kissed her forehead. 'I'm working in a factory, putting washers on taps. It'll be noisy and dirty and unimaginably boring. You'll enjoy it much more here with little Sasha and Aunt Irina.'

'You might die tomorrow. Among the taps.'

Maria put an arm around Anna and rocked her gently. 'Neither of us will die. You must wait patiently each day for me to return.'

They came for Maria in the middle of the night. They barely gave her time to pull a dress on over her nightgown, but she was quick to push Anna firmly against the wall.

'What do you want with my sister?' Sergei demanded. 'She's done nothing. We are a loyal Bolshevik family. I marched on the Winter Palace. Look.' He yanked open the front of his nightwear to reveal a livid scar across his chest. 'I am proud to bear the mark of a sabre.'

'I salute you, Comrade,' said the officer in charge. 'But it's not you we want to question, it's her.'

'But she's my sister and would never—'

'Enough, Comrade.' He held up his hand for silence. 'Take her outside,' he ordered two of his soldiers.

'Maria.' It was Irina who darted forward. 'Take this.' She thrust her own warmest fur hat onto her sister-in-law's head, a piece of cheese into her hand. 'Just in case,' she whispered.

Just in case? *Of what?* Anna wanted to scream.

After six days, Maria came home.

She said little and didn't go to work. She lay on her side on the bed hour after hour, eyes wide open. Anna sat on the floor beside the cot and twisted her fingers into the quilt because it was the nearest she could get to Maria without touching her. And she knew that if she touched the fragile figure, Maria would break.

So she sat still, made no noise, just fed tiny cubes of pickled beetroot into Maria's mouth. They turned Anna's fingers and Maria's lips the colour of cranberry juice.

'You have to go.'

Anna couldn't believe the words.

'You have to go, Annochka. Today.'

'No.'

'Don't argue. You have to go.'

Maria was holding a small hessian bag in her hand and Anna knew it contained her own few belongings.

'No, Maria, please, no. I love you.'

That was when tears started to slide down Maria's face and the bag shook in her hand.

'It's time for you to go, my love,' Maria insisted. 'Please don't look so terrified. Sergei is going to take you to the station and then a good kind woman will travel with you all the way to Kazan.'

Anna wrapped her arms around Maria's neck. 'Come with me,' she whispered.

Maria rocked her. 'I can't, little one. I've told you, the men who came here to the apartment want to ask me more questions.'

'Why?'

'Because they want to know where Vasily is. He killed one of their own when they shot his parents and they don't forgive that. They questioned me about where he could be hiding and I told them I know nothing but they . . . didn't believe me. Even though your papa is dead they have declared him an Enemy of the People and that means that you are in danger. You must leave. I'll come for you as soon as I can.'

'You promise?'

'Yes. In six months, when all this bloodletting is over, we'll be together again. You'll be staying with a distant cousin of mine but eventually I'll come and care for you. I love you, my sweet one, and now we both have to be strong.' Gently but firmly she detached Anna from her neck. 'Now give me a smile.'

Anna smiled and felt her face crack into a thousand splinters.

6

Tivil
July 1933

'I LIED TO MIKHAIL.'

'It was for his own good,' Rafik pointed out. 'The less he remembers about the sacks, the safer he is.'

'I know. But—'

'Leave it, Sofia.' There was an edge to his voice.

'Sometimes, Rafik, you scare me.'

'Good. Because you scare me, my dear.'

Sofia laughed softly and felt his answering smile strengthen the bond that had forged between them.

'Are you sure this is such a good idea?' she asked.

They were making their way down the dusty street to the *kolkhoz* office. It was by far the most conspicuous *izba* in the village, draped with placards and colourful posters listing the latest production figures and urging greater commitment from *kolkhozniki*. The smell of burnt wood and ash still hung between the houses like a physical presence.

Rafik was wearing a bright yellow shirt and was walking carefully, one hand lightly on Sofia's arm for support. He stumbled.

'You shouldn't be doing this,' Sofia told him. 'You should be resting.'

'Don't fuss. If you don't register as a member of this *kolkhoz* today people will start asking questions.' His black eyes sparked at her. 'You don't want that, do you?'

'No, I don't want that. But neither do I want to see you ill.'

'And I don't want to see you dead.'

The man behind the desk stood no chance. He was in his forties and was proud of his position of authority in the *kolkhoz*. His steel-rimmed spectacles reflected the bright lamp that shone on his desk.

'Identity papers, *pozhalusta*, please, Comrade Morozova,' he asked politely. He held out his hand and waited expectantly.

Sofia did exactly as Rafik had instructed her. She took a folded blank sheet of paper from her skirt pocket and placed it on the desk. The man frowned, clearly confused. He picked it up, unfolded it and spread its blank face in front of his.

'What is this, Comrade? A joke?'

Rafik rapped his knuckles sharply on the metal desk, making both Sofia and the man jump.

'No joke,' Rafik said.

Words in a language Sofia did not recognise started to flow from the Gypsy's mouth, an unbroken stream that seemed to wash through the room in waves, soft, rounded sounds that made the air hum and vibrate in her ears. A resonance echoed in her mind.

'No joke,' Rafik reiterated clearly.

He walked round the desk, his bright yellow shirt as hypnotic as the sun, till he was standing beside the man. He placed one hand heavily on the secretary's shoulder.

'Identity papers,' he purred into the man's ear.

Sofia saw the moment when understanding flooded the man's eyes.

'Of course,' he muttered in a voice that had grown unwieldy.

While Rafik returned to stand beside Sofia, the man rifled through drawers, yanked out forms, flourished the Red Arrow *kolkhoz* official stamp. But she barely noticed. All she was aware of was Rafik's arm in its yellow sleeve firm against her own. How long it was before they stepped out into the street again, Sofia wasn't certain, but by the time they did so, in her pocket was an official residence permit.

'Rafik,' she said quietly, 'what is it you do?'

'I wrap skeins of silk around people's thoughts.'

'Is it a kind of hypnotism?'

He smiled at her. 'Call it what you will. It kills me slowly, a piece at a time.' He could barely breathe.

'Oh, Rafik.'

With an arm around his waist and taking most of his weight herself, she walked him round to the patch of scrubland at the back of the office, away from watchful eyes. With great care she eased him to the ground. He sat there trembling, knees drawn up to his chest, eyes focused on the ridge of trees beyond the river.

'Better,' he gasped. 'In a moment I'll be . . . better.'

'Shh, just rest.'

Sofia wrapped her arms around him, drawing him on to her shoulder and accepting the guilt into her heart.

'Thank you, Rafik,' she murmured.

'Now,' he said in a voice held together by will-power, 'tell me why you are here.'

He didn't touch her. The piercing eyes were closed, no waves being sent to wash out the truth. He was leaving it up to her to tell him.

Or not to tell him.

Sofia hurried to the stables. She had come in search of Priest Logvinov and was nervous. He was the kind of person around whom someone always got hurt—and she couldn't afford to get hurt. Not now, not when she was so close.

The experience with Rafik in the office had made her doubt her own thoughts and it had taken an effort to drag her mind away from Mikhail. But it was her body that was less controllable. It kept reliving flashes of memory, the feel of Mikhail's mouth on hers, so hard it hurt at first and then so soft and enticing that her lips craved more. She walked harder, faster, driving herself to concentrate on other things.

'Is Priest Logvinov around?' she asked a youth who was sweeping the yard with slow, lazy strokes.

'In with *Glinka*,' he muttered, tipping his head towards one of the open stable doors without breaking the rhythm of the hazel broom.

'*Spasibo*,' Sofia said.

The gloom inside the stable came as a relief after the harsh glare in the courtyard. It took a moment for her eyes to adjust. She inhaled the smell of horse and hay, at first seeing no one. The horses were out working in the fields or hauling timber out of the woods, but the stamp of a hoof and a soft murmur drew her to the far end.

The priest did not turn at her approach, though Sofia was sure he knew she was there, his knuckles rhythmically kneading the forehead of a small bay mare whose eyes were half closed with pleasure. Close to her side stood a black colt on spindly legs much too long for him.

'That's a fine colt,' she said.

'He has the Devil in him.'

The colt thudded a hoof against the back board to prove the point.

'Priest, were you here in Tivil before the church was closed down?'

He twisted his head round to look at her. 'Yes, I was the shepherd of a God-fearing flock. In those days we were free to worship Our Lord and chant the golden tones of evensong as our consciences dictated.'

The sadness in his voice touched her. He was a strange man.

'So you were familiar with the church building inside? Before it was stripped of decoration and painted white, I mean.'

'Yes. I knew every inch of that House of God, the way I know the words of the Holy Bible. I knew its moods and its shadows, just as I had known the moods and shadows of my flock as they clung to their faith. Lucifer himself stalks the marble corridors of the Kremlin and he drags his cloven foot over the hearts and minds of God's children.' His gaunt face crumpled. 'An eternity of hell fire awaits those who forsake God's laws because they are stricken with fear.' His voice grew hoarse with sorrow. 'Fear is a stain spreading over this country of ours.'

'It is unwise to say such things aloud,' she warned. 'Take care.'

He spread his scarecrow arms wide, making the colt snort with alarm. '*Yea, though I walk through the valley of the shadow of death, I will fear no evil, for thou art with me.*'

'Priest,' she said softly, 'was there a statue of St Peter in the church before it was closed down?'

'Yes.'

'Where did it stand?'

'Why the interest?'

'Does it matter to you? I need to know where it used to stand.'

The colt suckling and the scratch of the hazel broom over the yard were the only sounds to be heard. At last Priest Logvinov scraped a hand across his fiery beard.

'They came one Sunday morning, a group of *Komsomoltsky*,' he said bitterly. 'They tore down everything, destroyed it with hammers. Burned it all in a bonfire in the middle of the street, tossed in all the ancient carvings and icons of the Virgin Mary and our beloved saints. And what wouldn't burn they took away in their truck to melt down, including the great bronze bell and the altar with its gold cross. It was two centuries old.' She expected him to shout and rage, but instead his voice grew softer with each word.

'The statue of St Peter?'

'Smashed.' His fleshless frame shuddered. 'It used to stand in the niche beside the south window. Now there's a bust of Stalin in its place.'

'I'm sorry, Priest.'

'So am I. And God knows, so is my flock.'

'Stay alive. For them at least.'

Quickly she thanked him and left the stables, but as she retraced her steps down the rutted track back to the street she became uncertain as to why she felt so upset.

What was wrong? Was it fear for Rafik? Or was it because of Mikhail? The wind seemed to ripple through her mind, stirring up her thoughts, and it carried to her again Priest Logvinov's words. *Fear is a stain spreading over this country.* And then she understood. She'd heard almost the same words months ago from Anna's mouth.

Anna. Whose fragile heartbeats would fade away if she didn't reach them soon.

The church—or assembly hall, as it was now called—was the only brick-constructed building in Tivil. The walls were divided by rows of narrow, tapered windows set with plain glass, though one was boarded up. A reminder of the violence on the night of the meeting. A stubby open-sided tower sat above the door. Presumably where the bell had once hung. Sofia tried the large iron handle but the door didn't budge.

She cursed and pushed harder. *Chyort!* But she was beginning to realise that Chairman Fomenko was not the kind of person to leave anything to chance, certainly not the safety of his assembly hall. She took a good look up and down the street but at this hour there wasn't much activity, just a child and his goat ambling out to the fields, but closer in the shade sat two old women. They wore headscarves and long black dresses, despite the heat, and seemed almost to be part of the landscape. As Sofia approached them she realised one was reading aloud from a book on her lap.

'*Dobroye utro, babushki,*' Sofia said with a shy smile. 'Good morning.'

The old woman with the book reacted with surprise. Her ears were not good enough to have heard Sofia's soft footfalls. The book slid instantly under a handwoven scarf, but not before Sofia saw it was a Bible. It was not against the law to read the Bible but it labelled you, if you did, as someone whose mind was not in line with Soviet doctrine, someone to be watched. Sofia pretended she hadn't seen it.

'Could you tell me who has a key to the assembly hall, please?'

The woman who had not been reading lifted her chin off her chest. Sofia saw the milky veil of blindness over her eyes.

'The Chairman keeps it,' she said. She tilted her head. 'Is that the new girl?'

'*Da*, yes, it's her,' responded the other. She puffed out her lined cheeks into a warm smile. 'Welcome to Tivil.'

'*Spasibo*. Where will I find Chairman Fomenko?'

'Anywhere where work is being done,' said the blind *babushka*. 'But his house isn't far, just the other side of the chu . . . of the assembly hall. His is the *izba* with the black door. You could try there.'

'Thank you. I will.'

The black door didn't respond to her knocks, but as she turned to retrace her steps, she saw Fomenko striding up from the low field by the river, a net of cabbages over his shoulder and a long-legged wolfhound at his side. He didn't look pleased to see her idling on *kolkhoz* time.

'Have you registered?'

His manner was curt, but the look he gave her was one of sharp interest. It occurred to her that he was a man more curious about others than he was willing to admit. Zenia had told her he wasn't married, so Sofia wondered what his home was like. It was clear that he expected her to wait outside, but she didn't. After the dog entered, its claws clicking on the wooden flooring, she followed him in.

'Yes, I have registered,' she said.

Her eyes darted quickly round the room. *Know your enemy.* She'd learned that lesson well. *Know him. And seek out his weak spot.* More than anybody in the village, Aleksei Fomenko was the greatest threat to her. But his weak spot was well hidden.

What did this lair tell her about the man? It was startlingly barren. Nothing on the walls, strictly no bourgeois frills or pretensions. A chair, a table, a stove, some shelves, and that was it. Chairman Fomenko obviously didn't believe in pampering himself. Instead of a property of distinction worthy of a *kolkhoz* Chairman, the house was indistinguishable from any of the other village *izbas*. It was the house of a tidy mind. Or a secretive one.

No clues, except the dog. Sofia extended her hand. The animal touched her fingers with its damp black nose. It was an elegant Russian wolfhound, a bitch with soft brown eyes that gazed up at Sofia with an expression of such gentleness that she felt herself fall a little in love with the creature. But it was no more than a minute before the hound returned to its position next to Fomenko's thigh and stayed there.

'She's beautiful,' Sofia said. 'What's her name?'

'Nadyezhda.'

'Hope. An unusual name for a dog.'

He rested a hand on the hound's head, fingers instinctively fondling one of its ears. He looked at Sofia as though about to explain the name, but after a second's thought he made an abrupt turn and picked up a large iron key from a shelf of books at the rear of the room. He moved briskly now as though pressed for time, but when it came to handing over the key, he paused.

'You lost something in the hall, you say?'

'Yes. A key.'

'I can't spare time to help with a search myself, Comrade, but if I give you the key to use, you must return it to the office as soon as you've finished with it.'

'Of course.'

'Then report immediately to the potato brigades.'

'I'll work hard.'

Still he weighed the key in his hand, subjecting her to careful scrutiny, his grey eyes so intent that she had a sudden sense of the loneliness inside this man and of the effort he put into hiding it.

He lifted the key and tapped it against the line of his jaw. 'Come to the office at noon tomorrow. I'd like to ask you some questions.'

'Questions about what?'

'About where you've come from. Who your parents were. About your family.' He paused again and observed her closely as he added, 'About your uncle.'

'Uncle Rafik is not well.'

'It's interesting how often the Gypsy is sick after the Procurement Officers have come calling in Tivil.' He gave an ironic half-smile. 'So often, in fact, that I'm beginning to wonder if there is a connection.'

'I believe he grows sick at heart when he sees the village suffer.'

Fomenko didn't like that. 'He should be sick at heart at the thought of the men and women and children going hungry throughout our towns and cities. It is my job to make sure they don't, by making this *kolkhoz* productive. We must help fulfil our Great Leader's Plan.'

The pause he left demanded a patriotic response, but the words wouldn't come to her tongue. Instead she held out her hand for the key.

The church was cool, hushed, as Sofia locked the door behind her. She breathed deeply, shocked to find she was shaking.

How could Fomenko have that effect on her, just by breathing the same air? She stared down at her palm and almost expected to see the imprint of his fingers there. But the thought was foolish, so she pushed it aside and looked around her. *You're here for Anna. Now search this barren place, just like she told you to.*

Quickly, she sought out the bust of Josef Stalin's head. It was easy to find, displayed prominently in a niche on the side wall, as Priest Logvinov had said. She stared with dislike at its lifeless eyes and arrogant chin, wanting to climb up there to give it the same treatment the *Komsomol* thugs had given St Peter.

No risks. Not now. Get on with the search.

First she examined the bricks beneath the niche. Her fingers traced the outline of each one, seeking a loose corner or some disturbed mortar that would indicate a hiding place. But, no, the bricks were smooth. She traced them all the way to the floor with no success and then knelt on the boards and set to work, running a hand along each one, tapping it, picking at its edges, testing if it would lift or rock unevenly. Nothing. Nothing at all. Except the cold lead of disappointment in her stomach. Frustrated, she crouched on the floor, elbows on her knees, and stared at the white wall. Where? Where was the hiding place? Maria had whispered to Anna that a secret box was concealed here, but where, damn it, where? Where would someone hide something they didn't want found?

She scanned the wall beneath the head of Stalin again. *A box buried at St Peter's feet.* That's what she'd been told, but it was so little. Abruptly she dropped to her knees.

'St Peter,' she whispered, 'grant me inspiration. Please, I'm begging.'

Nothing came. No shaft of sunlight to point the way. Sofia nodded, as though she'd expected no less.

She made her way up the central aisle and inserted the key in the lock. As she did so, a longing for Mikhail came with such force it took her breath from her.

'Mikhail,' she whispered, just to feel his name on her tongue.

He could help her. But would he? If she told him all she knew about Anna and his past and about what was hidden in the church, would he turn her away like a thief? He'd said he would help the right person but was she that right person? Was Anna? He was in a position of authority now and worked for the Soviet State system, he had a son whom he loved. Would he risk it all if she asked?

Would you, Mikhail, would you? You'd be insane to do so.

She straightened her shoulders and turned the key. If she asked for his help, she risked failure. And failure meant death. Not just her own.

'That's it for today,' the woman tending the next potato row called across to her. 'Come on, you can finish now. Enough for today.'

Sofia shouldered her hoe. 'So Chairman Fomenko does allow us to stop work eventually, then?'

The woman chuckled and together they trudged up the valley, talking about the condition of the crop this year, while the evening sun sent their long shadows ahead of them. It was as they approached the cedar tree that Sofia spotted the two children crouched in the dust at the base of its wide trunk, playing a game of some kind with small stones and a rubber ball. A pair of brown eyes met hers and looked away quickly. It was Pyotr. Sofia felt an unexpected tug at her heart at the realisation that he was nervous of her. She was just as nervous of him, that's what was so stupid. They were too aware of each other's weakness. He knew she was a fugitive, and she knew he hadn't reported her. Not yet, anyway.

'Hello.'

Sofia halted, and her companion from the field nodded pleasantly and walked on. It took Sofia a moment to recognise the narrow face and uncombed hair at her side. It belonged to one of the girls from inside the schoolroom last night, one of the silent little mice.

'It's me, Anastasia.'

'Hello, Anastasia.'

'My mother said to thank you.'

'For what?'

Anastasia glanced furtively around with exaggerated care, though no one except Pyotr was within earshot. 'For the story.'

'It was my pleasure.'

'We asked our teacher if you can come in again. Will you?'

'*Da.*' Sofia smiled. 'Yes, I'll come in again. If I'm invited.'

'Did you hear that, Pyotr? Comrade Morozova might be coming into our school!'

The boy shrugged and tossed a stone high into the cedar branches.

'Don't take any notice of Pyotr.' Anastasia sighed apologetically. 'He's sulking because his father is leaving Tivil.'

Leaving. Sofia's heart knocked against her ribs.

'Pyotr, is your father leaving Tivil?' she asked softly.

Reluctantly he nodded. 'He's going to Leningrad.'

'When?'

'Tomorrow.'

One word. That's all it took, and the evening sky grew dark.

Why didn't you tell me?'

'Would it have changed anything?'

'No. Except . . .'

'Except what?'

'Except make me . . . more aware of what I had and . . . of what I was losing.'

The look Mikhail gave her in response made her pulse quicken. It made the long wait alone in the dark worth every minute. The sun had set several hours ago but she had sat patiently on the edge of the stone water trough in the stableyard, listening to the contented sighs and snores of the horses. She was growing used to waiting for him.

'Did you get my letter?'

'What letter?'

'I gave a letter to Zenia to deliver to you. I knew I wouldn't be back until late tonight because I had to finish writing a report. Didn't you receive it, the letter?' He swung round and gazed intently at her face.

'No. I came here straight from working in the fields.'

'Oh, Sofia! You must be cold after waiting so long.'

He took off his jacket and draped it over her thin blouse, his hands lingering on her shoulders. She could smell the scent of him wrapped round her body and it released some of the tension from her skin.

'Tell me what was in the letter, Mikhail.'

'It's about tomorrow.'

'You're going to Leningrad.' Her voice sounded flat.

'Yes, I am.'

'Weren't you going to say goodbye? Or is that what the letter was for?'

'If you haven't yet read my letter, how did you know I was leaving?'

'Pyotr told me.'

'Ah, yes, Pyotr. The boy is unhappy at being left behind in Tivil.'

She stared at him aghast. 'You're abandoning your son?'

There was an odd little pause, a kind of blink in time, then Mikhail placed a hand on her arm and shook it hard. The movement shocked her, as did his rough laugh.

'The boy will survive. The delegations meet for only a few days.'

'Delegations?'

'Yes. It's the summons to report to the Committee of Soviet Production and Distribution. An annual chore that . . .' He stopped, removed his hand from her arm and stepped back. 'You thought I was going off permanently to the bright city to enjoy myself without my son and without saying goodbye . . . to you.'

Sofia nodded. Then the fact that Mikhail was coming back to Tivil in just a few days sank in and got the better of her. She looked up at him with a wide grin.

'It wasn't your going away that I minded. It was that I wouldn't get to ride on Zvezda any more. I'd have to walk all the way to Dagorsk.'

He threw back his head and laughed, and the unfettered joy of it made her blood pulse.

'Shall I tell you a story?' he asked.

'If it's a funny one. I'm in the mood to laugh.'

'Well, you recall the flight of stairs up to my office at the factory?'

'Yes.'

He chuckled and she found herself smiling in anticipation.

'My assistant, Sukov—remember the cheeky bastard who brought us our tea?—he fell down them today. All the way from top to bottom and broke his leg in two places.'

Sofia stared at his delighted smile. 'What is funny about that?'

Mikhail's smile widened, but his eyes were dark and serious. 'He was coming to Leningrad with me in the morning. Now it means there's a train seat and a travel ticket going spare.'

The river gleamed like polished steel in the moonlight. Sofia waded into it, naked. Even the touch of the chill water on her skin couldn't cool the heat in her blood.

One week with Mikhail. She was to have one whole week. It was more than she'd ever dared hope for, much more. Just the thought of it set her heart drumming in her chest and she gazed up at the dazzling array of stars above as if they'd been put there tonight just for her. She laughed out loud. The happiness wouldn't stay inside, it just bubbled out into the silent night.

Anna, are you looking at this same moon? These same stars? Waiting for me. Oh, Anna, I'm coming, I promise. Hold on. By the end of this week together I'll know if I can ask him to help. Your Vasily. She hesitated, then spoke the words aloud this time so that her ears would have to hear them.

'*Your* Vasily. Don't hate me, Anna. It's for you. I swear it's for you.'

A shadow, among many shadows.

Sofia was dressed and standing on the riverbank when the narrow track across the river changed fleetingly from silver to black, then again further along. Instantly she was alert and retreated into the overhanging curtain of a willow tree. From there she watched the shadow and quickly made out that it was a man, and that he was walking away from her. The moonlight painted the back of his head and sketched his long limbs, and a wisp of light caught the long back of the ghost-dog at the shadow's side and she realised it was Aleksei Fomenko with his hound.

Fomenko? What was the Chairman doing prowling the night?

There was just enough breeze to rustle the night and hide the crack of a twig underfoot as she followed them. The dog worried her. The animal's ears were sharp, but it seemed intent only on what lay ahead. Sofia stayed a good distance behind They were tracking up over the ridge and her mind raced for an answer to explain Fomenko's surprising night-time wanderings.

A lover? In the next valley?

The dog whined as its claws scrabbled up a gulley. The sound of it was so familiar it made the hairs on the back of her neck rise. She became convinced she knew where they were heading.

The hut.

Sofia sheltered in the undergrowth, tight against a tree trunk, and watched a flame flare into life in the small window of the hut after Fomenko had entered with the dog.

Was he meeting someone?

Ducking low, she crept out into the clearing, aware that she was now visible to watchful eyes. She moved silently to the window and with caution peered in at one corner, but she needn't have worried. Aleksei Fomenko was kneeling on the dusty floor, totally engrossed. His long back in the familiar work shirt was angled towards her, but she could just see that he was bent over a hole in the flooring. A hole? She hadn't noticed one when she slept here. It was explained by the sight of two wooden planks lying to one side, the floorboards, and next to them a candle, its flame casting uncertain light round the room. Sofia eased further along the window frame and, over his shoulder, she caught a glimpse of what was holding his attention so seriously. A khaki-green square object. It took her a moment to recognise it for what it was.

A two-way radio, all dials and pointers and knobs. A sudden burst of static took her by surprise and she ducked down below the sill, her breath raw in her throat. A secret radio. Why did the Chairman need a secret radio?

As she crouched low to the earth, her mind struggled to find an explanation. Was it to connect him directly to the OGPU, to give him a direct line to the Security Police where he could betray the secrets of his *kolkhozniki* in private? But what was wrong with the office telephone? Did this radio bypass the normal channels and take him straight to the man at the top? She decided to risk another glimpse and slid up slowly till her eyes were again on a level with the cobwebbed glass. This time she took in more of what was in front of her: the stillness of Fomenko's powerful shoulders, the earphones on his head, the mouthpiece he was murmuring into, the notebook open at his side and covered with lines of dense writing.

With a small sense of shock she became aware of the dog. It gazed at the closed door and, making no sound, it raised its lips to show its teeth in a silent snarl. Sofia didn't know what its quick ears had picked up but she wasn't going to hang around to find out. She pushed herself away from the hut and raced away back down the track to Tivil.

7

Leningrad
July 1933

THE TRAIN JOLTED TO A HALT. Mikhail reached across and pulled the leather strap, so that the window slid all the way down. Sluggish air drifted into the carriage from outside, hot and heavy and laden with smuts from the engine. On the platform vendors fought to peddle baskets of food.

Sofia was seated in the corner next to the window, looking out at the crush of bodies on the platform. During the two-day journey she had spoken very little, but could Mikhail blame her? From the start things had gone wrong. On the platform he had introduced her to Lev Boriskin, his chief foreman from the factory, and to Alanya Sirova, Boriskin's secretary, a woman of about thirty with ambitious eyes behind thick tortoiseshell spectacles. It was only when he saw Sofia's face grow rigid with dismay and her gaze turn to him questioningly that he realised he'd forgotten to mention their travelling companions. He'd ushered her into the seat by the window.

'I thought,' the foreman had said, with a shift of his eyes to Sofia, 'that as *Direktor Fabriki, you* should have the best seat. Instead of—'

'Comrade Morozova has been commissioned to write a report,' Mikhail cut in sharply, 'on this delegation. She will cover our contribution to the Committee. So I think she is entitled to the window seat, don't you?'

Boriskin paled, pulled at his lip and shook open a copy of *Pravda* with a show of indifference. Mikhail sat himself next to Sofia, a barrier between her and his foreman. She looked at him with stern blue eyes, but in their depths he could see a ripple of laughter.

How do they do it? Sofia gazed around at the sea of faces, at the concentration on them. Did they really care so much or was it all an act?

The great dome above the hall was supported by massive pale marble pillars. Beneath it rows and rows of packed seats curved in a wide sweeping arc. Sofia tried to concentrate on the speeches, but boredom invariably seeped in, as lists of production figures and target levels were recited for each *raion*. The only rousing moments came when Party slogans were hammered out with fists on the lectern and a thousand voices roared back from the floor as one.

The pillars. Her eyes were drawn to them, instead of to the pad on her lap. Bone-white pillars. She couldn't keep her eyes off them. Each one made her think of Anna, still out there in the forest, her blade slicing through the flesh of a tree. *Don't stop, dear Anna. Breathe, my friend, breathe.* She swallowed the rage that rose in her throat at the injustice of it, but she must have made some noise because in the next seat Alanya Sirova turned and studied her.

'Are you all right?' Alanya asked.

'I'm fine.'

Still Alanya stared at her. 'You haven't written down anything for the last half an hour.' She nodded at Sofia's blank page.

Sofia turned her head to look into the suspicious brown eyes. The two women's communication had so far been stilted, despite sharing a bedroom at night and being seated next to each other for the last six hours in the conference hall. Sofia could feel Alanya's curiosity like something palpable crouched between them.

'Comrade Sirova,' Sofia said in a muted tone, giving it just the right touch of condescension, 'I am listening. But it is essential to think things through first and write afterwards.' She narrowed her gaze. 'I advise you to bear that in mind—if you want to progress further than a lowly secretary. I'm sure you have the ability to do so.'

Alanya's ambitious eyes gleamed behind the thick lenses of her spectacles. '*Spasibo*, Comrade. I promise I will in future.'

Sofia allowed herself a faint smile. That was Comrade Sirova dealt with. She turned back to the pillars, to the pine trees.

It was out among the pine trees one hot, mosquito-ridden afternoon that Sofia had learned from Anna about her visit to Maria, the woman who had been her governess. Maria who, during all those years when Anna was living with a distant cousin in a village hundreds of miles away near Kazan, had never come for her. Had never once written. Nothing. Anna had waited, always believing that one day Maria would come. Her lonely young heart clung to Maria's words: 'I promise I'll come for you.'

But she didn't come.

Now in the damp forests of a Siberian Work Zone, Anna shook her head sadly. 'I was foolish. I wouldn't let it go. So when the woman who had taken me in suddenly died, I took the small amount of money she left me in her will, bought myself a train ticket and travel permit and went in search of Maria in Leningrad.'

Sofia was honing Anna's axe, squatting down among the wood chippings with a flat stone in front of her, keeping down below the eyeline of the guards. Anna was leaning back against a tree trunk, each breath wheezing as she spoke.

'Don't talk, Anna. Rest your poor lungs.'

'No, you must know this. For when you go.'

'Very well, tell me,' Sofia said, one eye on the nearest guard. His back was turned to them for the time being.

Anna sighed with satisfaction. 'I found the house in Liteiny district, the one where Maria's brother, Sergei Myskov, and his wife, Irina, lived. It was only round the corner from the tap factory.' She paused, resting a moment, her sunken blue eyes on Sofia's face. 'I remembered the iron staircase and a courtyard with a well at its centre. And there was a lion's head carved above the archway. It frightened me when I was young.'

'You two!' The guard had caught sight of them. 'Get back to work.'

'*Da*,' Sofia called out, 'right away.' She started to move, as if to do as ordered, and the guard turned away.

'Anna, there's no time now and you're not—'

But Anna seized Sofia's wrist. Her grip was still strong. 'Listen to me. It's important. You must remember this, Sofia. It will help you.'

Sofia lifted her hand to wipe the sweat from her friend's gaunt face, but Anna swept it aside impatiently. The flash in her blue eyes reminded Sofia of the old Anna.

'I'm fine,' Anna hissed. 'Just listen.'

Sofia laid aside the axe and crouched beside her, attentive.

'By the time I found the apartment building it was raining. I was wet through but I barely noticed. I was so excited at the prospect of seeing Maria again after nine years. When I knocked, the door to the apartment on the first floor was opened by a youth with wavy brown hair and ears that stuck out like a baby elephant's. I recognised him at once.

'"Sasha?" I gasped. It was Sasha, Irina's son. He was about eleven then. "I'm a friend of your Aunt Maria."

'"*Tiotya* Maria doesn't have friends."

'What did he mean? Why didn't Maria have friends?

'"Where does she live now, Sasha?"

'"Here."

'"Here?" This was too easy. "May I come in and see her?"

'He stepped back and called over his shoulder, "*Tiotya* Maria, a visitor for you."

'"Who is it, Sasha?"

'It was Maria's voice. I rushed into the room and a pale-faced woman with white hair was sitting in a chair by the window. It was a much older Maria, but still my dearest governess.

'"Maria," I breathed, "it's me."

'A tremor ran through the silent figure, then tears started to slide down her cheeks. "My Anna," she sobbed.

'I clasped my arms around her neck, while she touched my wet hair and murmured soft words against my cold skin.

'"Why didn't you come?" I whispered the words. "I waited for you."

'Maria placed a shaky hand over her eyes. "I couldn't."

'"Why didn't you write?"

'"Aunt Maria had a stroke." It was Sasha's voice. I had forgotten he was even still in the room. "It happened when she was tortured."

'My thoughts beat panicked wings in my head. White hair? Maria could not be more than forty. Why white hair? Her eyes were still beautiful, still luminous brown, but over them hung a veil, gossamer-fine, and behind it lay a world of bafflement and confusion. And she hadn't risen to her feet to greet me. It all made agonising sense.

'"Oh, Maria, my poor dearest Maria. Why didn't you ask your brother Sergei to write to me? I'd have come . . ."

'Maria's eyebrows gathered in a lopsided frown and she murmured,

"Hush." She glanced quickly in Sasha's direction and then back again to my face. "It's not important."

'"Of course it's important. I would have taken care of—"

'"No, no, not you, Anna Fedorina," Sasha interrupted roughly. "My parents would never have written to you or wanted you in this house." He stood with his hands on his hips and his chin jutting forward. "Aunt Maria suffered the stroke when she was tortured on account of her connection with you and your father and your father's friends. I grew up on the story of how her hair turned white overnight in the prison cells. Your father was declared a Class Enemy and—"

'"Shut up!" I shouted.

'"Leave us, Sasha," Maria moaned. "Please."

'He glared at me for a long moment before marching out of the room, slamming the door behind him. Quiet settled after that. Maria dismissed my apologies for what she'd suffered, so instead I kissed her, told her I loved her and would take care of her now that I had found her again. I made us tea from the samovar in the corner of the cramped room, then I pulled up a stool and told tales of my long years in Kazan. As the daylight started to fade from the room, I risked the question that burned inside me.

'"Did you ever hear what happened to Vasily?"

'Maria laughed, soft and low like in the old days. "How you worshipped that boy! You used to trail round after him like a little shadow. Do you recall how you used to make him dance with you? Or maybe you've forgotten that."

'"No, I haven't forgotten."

'"And he adored you." She chuckled again. "He came looking for you, you know."

'"When? When did he come?"

'"I'm not sure, I can't . . . Think, stupid brain, think." Maria rapped her knuckles against her own forehead. "I forget everything now."

'I stroked the skin soothingly. "It's all right, there's no rush. Take your time. Can you remember what he looked like?"

'The crooked mouth smiled its crooked smile. "Oh, yes, he was tall. Grown into a man."

'"And still as handsome?"

'"Yes, still as handsome. He came twice and told me he'd changed his name for safety."

'"To what?"

'Again the look of bewilderment.

'"Did you tell him where I was, Maria?"

'"No, my love. I'm sorry. I couldn't remember where you were."

'"Was he . . . disappointed?"

'"Oh, yes. That's why he came twice. To see if I had remembered." Tears filled her eyes. "But I couldn't."

'I hugged her close and whispered without hope, "Where is he living now?"

'To my surprise Maria nodded. "He wrote it down."

'From a large battered canvas bag that lay at her feet she withdrew a Bible, its cover well worn to a faded black. Tucked inside its pages was a scrap of grey envelope and on it printed in black letters: *Mikhail Pashin, Levitsky Factory, Dagorsk. Home: Tivil Village, near Dagorsk*. But just as I was holding the piece of paper in my hand, the door to the room crashed open and uniforms marched into the small space, their leather boots and broad shoulders swallowing up the air around us. Five stern faces turned on me. Behind them, with the sternest face of all, stood eleven-year-old Sasha.

'"Anna Fedorina?" The officer had a black Cossack moustache that seemed to bristle and threaten, but his eyes were calm. "You are Anna Fedorina, daughter of *Doktor* Nikolai Fedorin who has been declared an Enemy of the People."

'"But that was years ago."

'The officer gave me a smile that was not a smile. "We don't forget. Or forgive."

'Strong hands seized my arms and dragged me off my feet.

'"Anna!" Maria screamed, with all the power of her frail lungs, her one good hand clawing the air again. "Let me kiss her, let me kiss my Anna goodbye."

The soldiers hesitated, then thrust me at Maria's chair. Maria clamped her arm fiercely around my neck and buried her face in my hair, kissing my cheek, my jaw, my ear, all the time whispering, whispering, whispering. So that when the rough hands stole me from Maria's grasp, I was aware of nothing but those words:

'"His mother's jewels. In a box. He buried them in the church under St Peter's feet. He told me. In the village where he lives."'

'**W**here are you going, Comrade Morozova?'

Sofia had risen to her feet in the conference hall. She couldn't bear it inside this hothouse of lies and paranoia a moment longer.

Alanya Sirova's expression was poised halfway between curiosity and suspicion. 'Are you leaving?'

'*Da*. Yes, I have work to do.'

'But I thought—'

'While Comrade *Direktor* Pashin and Comrade Boriskin are reporting to the Committee,' Sofia tossed her pad and pen on the lap of Alanya's navy blue suit, 'I want you to take notes of everything that goes on here.'

The secretary's cheeks glowed pink with pleasure. '*Spasibo*, Comrade. I won't let you down, I promise.'

It made Sofia want to cry.

The streets of Leningrad had changed The tall pastel-painted houses with ornate window frames and balconies had been transformed into sooty, drab buildings crammed full of sooty, drab people, who scurried to the bread queues and the candle queues and the kerosene queues, where they waited for hours like sheep in a slaughter house.

Sofia was here to search out the apartment where Anna had lived briefly with Maria and Irina, but had no exact address to go on. Once in the Liteiny district she set about combing the spider's web of streets with their dismal tenements, but it took her an hour to find it. The tap factory. It was still there.

What else had Anna told her?

An iron staircase. A courtyard with a well at its centre and a lion's head carved above an arch. But the dark rows of crumbling tenements all seemed to have iron staircases to the upper storeys and courtyards where ragged children crawled among the woodpiles. It was only when she spotted the lion's head above one of the arches that Anna's voice pulsed in her ears. *'You must remember this, Sofia. It will help you.'* She approached the entrance. She lifted the big knocker and rapped it.

A woman's wrinkled face peered round the door. 'Yes?'

'I'm looking for Maria Myskova. I believe she used to live here with Comrade Sergei Myskov and his wife and child. On the first floor. Do you know where they are now?'

'At work.'

'You mean they still live here? When will they be home?'

'Who wants to know?'

The crash of a piece of crockery followed by a man's voice raised in a curse erupted from somewhere at the back of the hallway. The woman swivelled round with a squeal and scurried back into the shadows towards a door that was half open. Sofia didn't hesitate. She stepped inside and leaped up the stairs two at a time, trying not to inhale the smell of boiled cabbage and unwashed bodies that seemed to breathe out of the fabric of the building. It brought the stink of the barrack hut at Davinsky Camp crashing into her head.

When she reached the first-floor landing she turned to her left, where a boarded window let in a few dim streaks of light.

To her surprise, packed tight against the wall of the dingy corridor, were three beds, low and narrow. One was tidily made with a folded quilt, the second was a jumble of stained sheets and the third was occupied by a bald man whose skin was yellow as butter. This was Sofia's first experience of the *kommunalka*, the shared apartments where several families were crammed into the space that had once belonged to only one.

On tiptoes, so as not to wake him, she crept to the door at the end of the landing and knocked quickly. The door opened at once. A dark-haired woman stood in front of her, shorter than herself but broad across the bust. Sofia smiled at her.

'*Dobriy vecher*,' she said. 'Good evening. I am Anna Fedorina.'

'**S**he's dead. Maria died two years ago. Another stroke.'

The words were stark, but Irina Myskova spoke them gently. 'I'm sorry, Anna, it's so sad that she didn't live to see you released.'

'Tell Sasha that.'

The woman's face stiffened at the mention of her son. His part in Anna's arrest seemed to sit uneasily in Irina's heart and she ran a hand across her large bosom, stilling whatever turmoil simmered there. Her clothes were neat but old. The apartment was the same, clean and tidy with striped homemade *poloviki* rugs on the floor. Everything looked old and well used. Only the white plaster bust of Lenin gleamed new, and the bright red posters declaring: *Forward towards the Victory of Communism* and: *We swear, Comrade Lenin, to honour your command.*

'Sasha was only doing his duty,' Irina insisted loyally.

Sofia hadn't come here to argue. 'What's done is done, Irina. We can change the future but we can't change the past.'

'*Nyet*. And I wouldn't wish to. But . . . if I can help you . . . I know from Maria that you were always fond of the Dyuzheyevs' boy.'

'Vasily?'

'Did Maria tell you he came here once? He's going under a different name now.'

'Yes. Mikhail Pashin. She said he came twice.'

'I wasn't here, but I believe it was only once. Maria got confused sometimes. The other time it was a different man who came to see her.'

'Do you know who?'

'Anna, I think you should know that the man had come trying to find you.'

'Me?'

'*Da.* It seems he was the young Bolshevik soldier, the one who shot your father and Vasily's mother. He was searching for you.'

Sofia's heart seemed to hang loose in her chest. 'Who was he?'

'That's the odd thing. He said he'd been sent to work in a village in the Urals.'

'His name?'

'Maria wasn't any good at remembering, but she told Sasha the name and he remembered it.'

'What was it?' She held her breath, and a sense of foreboding chilled her, despite the heat in the apartment.

'Fomenko. Aleksei Fomenko.'

8

Tivil
July 1933

EACH PERSON MUST BE REBORN. Each person must be taught to rethink. Everyone will have a new heart.

Yes, Pyotr understood that. Unless you erased the old and the bad, how could there be room for the new and the good? Which was why he was knocking on Chairman Aleksei Fomenko's door. She'd be grateful in the end, the fugitive woman. When she had her new heart.

'Hey, Pyotr, what you doing?'

It was Yuri, his face flushed from running.

'I'm waiting for the Chairman.'

'What for?'

'I've something to tell him.'

Yuri's eyes brightened with interest. 'What's it about?'

Pyotr almost told him. It was on the tip of his tongue, the words that would betray Sofia. *She's dangerous*, but a strange, quivering feeling in the depth of his stomach held him back.

'Well?' Yuri urged. 'What is it—'

At that moment Anastasia came hurtling down the dusty street and skidded to a halt in front of them.

'What are you doing here, Pyotr?' She grinned at him. 'Not in trouble, are you?'

'Of course not,' Pyotr objected.

'He's got secret information to tell the Chairman,' Yuri said grandly.

'Really?' The girl's eyes widened. 'What is it?'

Pyotr felt himself cornered. 'It's about a girl in this village,' he said in a rush. 'About her anti-Soviet activity.'

To his astonishment, tears leaped into Anastasia's eyes and she started to edge fearfully away from him.

'I must go home now,' she blurted out and ran off down the road, her hair flying out behind her. Quite clearly Pyotr could see the four bulges under her faded blouse, at the back where it was tucked into her shorts.

Anastasia had stolen potatoes. Only two weeks ago a woman in a village the other side of Dagorsk was sentenced to five years in one of the labour camps for stealing half a *pud* of grain from her *kolkhoz*. Suddenly dismay spilled into his mind. If he told Chairman Fomenko about Sofia, wasn't it his duty to tell about Anastasia too? He looked up and saw his father striding up the street towards him.

'What are you up to, boys?'

'Nothing much.'

'You're standing on the Chairman's doorstep for nothing much?'

But instead of being annoyed Papa was laughing and his face was free from the usual shadows it wore after a day's work. Ever since he'd come back from the conference yesterday, he'd been in a good mood. It must have gone really well in Leningrad.

'Good evening, Comrade Pashin. *Dobriy vecher*,' Yuri said. 'Have you heard if there's any news about the sacks of grain that went missing?'

That was typical of Yuri, always digging around for information. But Papa wasn't pleased and his face lost its smile.

'I know nothing at all about that. Come, Pyotr,' Papa said firmly, taking hold of his son's arm. 'We're going to Rafik's house.'

They walked up the road in an awkward silence.

'Why do you dislike Yuri, Papa?'

'Because I don't want the young fool turning you into him.'

'No, Papa. I think for myself.'

His father halted in the middle of the street and turned to him. 'I know you do, Pyotr. I've seen the way you make your choices after working out what's right and what's not.' He smiled. 'I admire that.'

It was the first time Pyotr had ever been inside the Gypsy's *izba*. It smelled funny and half the forest appeared to be dangling from the roof beams. He hung back near the door, unwilling to go too deep.

'*Dobriy vecher*,' Papa said to Rafik. 'Good evening.'

'*Dobriy vecher*, Pilot. And good evening to you too, Pyotr.'

The Gypsy was swallowed up by a huge maroon armchair. 'How's the colt up at the stable?'

'He bit Priest Logvinov today.'

Rafik laughed. 'He has spirit, that one. Like you.'

Pyotr gave a quick nod. The fugitive woman was seated opposite Zenia at the table.

'I'm pleased to see you're feeling better, Rafik,' Papa said.

'Much better.'

Then his father turned to the two women at the table and gave them a small old-fashioned bow, which surprised Pyotr. What was going on?

'Good evening, Sofia.'

Pyotr had avoided looking at her face so far, but now he risked it. Immediately he wished he hadn't, because he couldn't look away. Her eyes were shining, deep blue and swirling with light the way he imagined the sea to be. Her lips opened a fraction when she looked up at Papa, just as Anastasia's did at school when she looked at Yuri's slice of bread and honey. And Papa was doing the same. Pyotr felt a flutter of panic in his stomach. *Look away, look away.*

'I have a surprise for you all.' His father turned to him.

'What is it, Papa?'

'The *Krokodil* is coming to Dagorsk next week.'

All sense of danger and fugitives vanished right out of Pyotr's head and he gave a shout of delight that filled the room. 'Can we go and see it, Papa? Which day? How long will it be here? Can we take Yuri—'

His father chuckled. 'Slow down, boy. Yes, of course we'll go and see it.' He turned back to the others in the room and said with that formal little bow again, 'You're all invited.'

Rafik shook his head and ran a hand through his thick black hair. 'I don't ever leave Tivil, but the rest of you go and enjoy yourselves.'

'What is the *Krokodil*?' Sofia asked.

'It's an aeroplane,' Pyotr explained excitedly. 'One that's painted to look like a crocodile.'

Mikhail nodded and sketched its outline in the air. 'It's one of the squadron of Tupolev PS-9s—they're part of Stalin's propaganda drive. It flies round the country to demonstrate Soviet progress to the people. The idea is to give film shows and hand out leaflets and things like that. One of the Politburo's better ideas we think, don't we, Pyotr?'

'Yes.' Pyotr grinned.

'Pilot.' It was the Gypsy.

Something in the way he said it made everyone turn to look at Rafik. He'd left the chair and was standing rigidly in the centre of the room.

His hands were pressed to his temples as though holding in something that was trying to get out. His black eyes looked sick.

'Pilot!' This time it was a shout. 'Get out of here, now, quickly! Run!'

Instantly Zenia was at his side. 'Tell us, Rafik.'

'They're coming for him, to seize him. Run, Mikhail!'

'Papa?' Pyotr cried out.

Sofia leaped to her feet. 'Go, Mikhail. *Go*.'

But his father didn't move. 'What the hell do you mean, Rafik? Who on earth is coming for me?'

The door burst open with a crash. Uniforms streamed into the room.

The cell door slammed shut behind Mikhail. The stench hit him like a blow to the face. How many men were in here? Twenty? Thirty? In the semi-darkness he couldn't tell, but there was no air to breathe, no place to sit.

This was the new reality and he'd better get used to it. Stuck in this wretched hole. He would still be here tomorrow, and the next tomorrow and the tomorrow after that. He spat on the floor, spitting out his fear, and he searched his mind for something clean and cool and strong to hold on to. He found a pair of eyes. Eyes that looked at him straight, blue as a summer sky and bright with laughter. He drew them to him and filled every part of his mind with them, even the dark rotten places where he didn't like to look.

'Sofia,' he whispered. 'Sofia.'

'Name?'

'I'm enquiring about Mikhail Antonovich Pashin. He was taken from Tivil last night but—'

'Who are you?'

'I'm here with his son, Pyotr Pashin.'

'Papers?'

'These are Pyotr's.'

'And yours?'

'I'm just a friend. I'm helping Pyotr to find out what—'

'Your name?'

'Sofia Morozova.'

'Papers?'

Sofia hesitated. 'Here. It's my resident's permit at the Red Arrow *kolkhoz* in Tivil, though I don't see why I—'

'Wait.'

The shutter slammed shut.

'**S**ofia.'

'No need to whisper, Pyotr. It's all right, we're outdoors now. No one can overhear.'

'I know what happens when a person is arrested.'

'Do you?'

'Yes. It happened to Yuri's uncle. The person is interrogated, sometimes for months, and if he's innocent he's freed, so . . . Why are you laughing?'

'No reason. Go on.'

'So do you think Papa will be freed?'

Sofia's heart went out to the boy. She swung him to face her, her hands pinning the slender bones of his shoulders.

'He'll be set free,' she told him fiercely. 'Your father is a good man.'

'He's not my father.'

'Pyotr, don't you dare say such a thing.'

Brown eyes stared miserably into hers. 'He's not. Ask Rafik. My father was the miller in Tivil. Six years ago my mother ran off with a soldier to Moscow and my father burned down the mill with himself inside it.'

'Oh, Pyotr.'

'I had no one, no family. My father was labelled a *kulak* even though he was dead, so no villager would help me. The authorities were going to send me to an institution.' He stopped and dragged a hand across his eyes. 'But Mikhail Pashin adopted me. He was new to the village and he didn't even know me, but he took me in.'

Sofia drew Pyotr to her and gently stroked his hair.

'He'll be set free,' she whispered.

'**N**ame?'

'I am Mikhail Antonovich Pashin.'

'Occupation?'

'*Inzhenir*. Engineer First Class. And *Direktor Fabriki*. Factory manager.'

'Which factory?'

'The Levitsky factory in Dagorsk. We make clothes and military uniforms. It is a loyal factory with dedicated workers. This month we exceeded our quota of—'

'Silence.'

The peremptory order made the small interrogation room shrink further. There were no windows, just a bright naked light bulb dangling from the ceiling. A metal table stood in the centre, two chairs behind it, another one alone and bolted to the floor in front of it. Mikhail stood very erect, focused on what he intended to say, and forced himself to swallow his anger. He felt it burn his throat as it sank to his stomach.

'Sit.'

He sat.

'Place of birth?'

'Leningrad.'

'Father's name?'

'Anton Ivanovich Pashin.'

'Father's occupation?'

'Wheelwright.'

'Why did you leave the Tupolev aircraft factory?'

'I'm damned sure you know why I had to leave. It'll be written down in that fat file in front of you. So why bother to ask me?'

For the first time the man behind the desk showed a flicker of interest. He was tall and elegant, in a uniform that bore a row of medals.

'Answer my question.'

'I left because I was forced to.'

'And why was that?'

Keep it calm. Wrap the anger in a tight shell of control. Play it their way.

'Because I made an error. I criticised the system of delivery. I was so eager to build the ANT-4 aeroplane for our Great Leader that I allowed my disappointment at the delay in the arrival of some essential items of equipment to cloud my judgment.'

'You admit you were wrong.'

'I admit it freely. I didn't consider the magnitude of what our Leader had undertaken. I know now that the railways had to be expanded first before they could deal with the loads they had to carry.' He lowered his voice. 'I was young and foolish.'

'Don't lie to me, you filthy wrecker.'

'I am no wrecker.'

'Don't lie to me. You tried to wreck the Tupolev factory and now you are wrecking the Levitsky factory. Working against the forces of progress outlined for us all in the First *Piatiletka*. It is people like you who cause the shortage of goods.'

'No, I told you we exceeded our targets.'

'Who is paying you?'

That came as a shock. 'Nobody.'

'You were seen to wreck the Tivil Red Arrow *kolkhoz* Grain Procurement system.'

'No.'

'Yes. There are witnesses.'

'Who?'

'Silence, scum. Who is paying you? Foreign powers are frightened of our great success. It is well known that they employ subversives to destroy our industry. Subversives like you who commit treason and deserve to be shot.'

Mikhail's blood was pounding. This was worse than he had expected.

'I am innocent of these charges. I am a Communist, loyal to Russia.'

The interrogator sighed and shook his head. 'Let's start again.'

'I've told you everything.'

'Not yet, but you will.'

The cement floor was wet, freshly hosed down. Barefoot, Mikhail was marched into the empty cell by two warders, hands cuffed behind his back. The door swung shut with a heavy metal clang. The warder with the lean face and impatient eyes locked it with an iron key that was attached to his belt by a chain, then he turned a smile on Mikhail. Except it wasn't a smile, it was a baring of the teeth. The second warder sniggered in anticipation. He was a solid, big-muscled ox of a man with almost no forehead, and broad beefy fists that flexed and unflexed. An objective part of Mikhail's mind registered that these two men were well chosen for the work.

Fight or yield? It would make no difference. Two brick-hard rubber sticks and a metal bar would be the victors. Fists that were chained behind your back were no fists at all.

The metal bar swung. He ducked and it whistled past his ear, but from the other side a fist sledgehammered into the centre of his chest. He made no sound. A rubber stick slammed onto his mouth, blood exploded on his teeth and he spat out a sliver of something white.

'Is that all you've got?' he taunted.

The next blow crashed down on the spot between his neck and his arm, sending pain searing through his skull. Neither his shoulder nor arm would move. A crunch from the metal bar to the back of Mikhail's legs brought him buckling to his knees. Then it came, the real pain. Again and again, blows like rain. To his back. His ribs. Knees. Kidneys. The nape of his neck. The soles of his naked feet. Worse. To his testicles. That pain was special. White hot. A steel furnace, flames leaping and scorching his every nerve-end, a throbbing, sickening agony.

'Confess!' one of the warders roared in his ear.

'Devil curse you, you bastards,' he spat through blood.

An explosion of pain registered in his brain, but he could no longer tell where it came from in his body. At long last, he let go. He stopped holding the parts together. He couldn't breathe.

Sofia left Pyotr outside the *kolkhoz* office. She hurried past the pond where two boys were making a lot of noise trying to capture a duck, and up to Rafik's *izba*. She burst into the cottage, calling his name.

'Rafik?' Where was he? She had questions to ask and time was trickling through her fingers too fast.

She sat down in Rafik's maroon chair, dropped her head in her hands. All the misery and suffering of the last four months when she'd battled halfway across Russia, footstep by footstep, crushed her so that she could barely breathe. She remained like that for a long time, till her fingers grew stiff in her hair, and the whole time she thought hard. About Mikhail. About Anna. About what she was about to lose. And at last, when the pain became manageable once more, she rose and walked over to Rafik's carved wooden chest against the wall, the one he had drawn her shoes from. The lid was carved with serpents. She lifted it.

She didn't know what she'd expected but it certainly wasn't what stared up at her.

Two bright black eyes and fur whiter than snow, sparkling like ice. She touched it. It was the complete pelt of an Arctic fox, beautifully tanned to such perfect suppleness it was hard to believe the animal wasn't still alive. She stroked the soft fur and gently lifted it out. Underneath lay a folded pile of white sheets, and beside all this whiteness a bundle in the corner sang out. It was a bright red piece of material.

She snatched it up, and could feel something weighty inside. Cautiously she unwrapped it. A single pebble tumbled onto her lap and she felt disappointed. She'd expected something . . . more revealing, but she picked it up and examined it anyway. The pebble was bone-white with silvery veins running through it, but otherwise quite ordinary. What on earth did Rafik use it for? It was absurd but the more she stared at the stone, the less she wanted to relinquish it back to the chest. It felt oddly comforting in the palm of her hand, so that she lifted it to her cheek, running its milky surface along her skin.

Her mind grew calm and she breathed more easily. Whatever was going on here, the fear and weakness of a few moments ago had drained away. It was strange. Maybe Rafik had handled this stone so often that he'd left a small piece of himself in its silvery veins. Was it Rafik's strong spirit that was steadying her, or was it something rising to the surface from within herself ? She was uncertain.

With a shake of her head she bundled the pebble inside the red cloth again and returned it to its position in the chest. She needed to find Rafik but, as she stepped out of the house, she heard the sound of hoofs and glanced up to see Chairman Fomenko astride a long-boned black horse heading down towards the *kolkhoz* office. He reined the animal to a halt in front of her.

'Good day, Comrade Morozova.'

Sofia gave him a cold, hard stare. This man was the young boy soldier who had killed Anna's father in cold blood sixteen years ago and also shot Svetlana, Mikhail's mother. She wondered for the thousandth time whether Mikhail was aware of the truth and whether she should tell him.

'You haven't yet attended my office, as I requested.'

'I was in Dagorsk today. Mikhail Pashin has been arrested—'

'I am aware of that,' he interrupted.

'Arrested wrongfully,' she continued. 'He had nothing to do with the sacks of grain that went missing.'

'That is for the interrogators to establish.'

'But if a person in authority, a powerful man like yourself, reported to these interrogators that their prisoner was a loyal Communist who at the time of the theft was drinking inside his home with an OGPU officer and was clearly innocent of any . . . sabotage, then they would release him. They would believe your word.'

His face changed. It lost the tautness that usually held it together and curved into a wide smile. 'Comrade,' he said with a soft laugh, 'I am concerned. I think your brain must be addled.'

'No, Chairman, I think not. No more than listening to a radio in the forest has addled yours.'

It was as though she'd slapped him. A dull flush rose to his cheeks while one fist clenched and unclenched on his reins.

'Don't let me keep you,' he said, and rode away.

'**I**'ve been waiting for you.'

Rafik was seated at the rough table when Sofia returned to the *izba*. He was wearing his bright yellow sunshine shirt. His black eyes were half hooded, his olive skin seemed darker and his black hair was hidden from sight under the pelt of the white fox. His shoulders were hunched over like an old man's. This was not a Rafik she recognised. Her mouth grew dry. The room was dim despite the daylight outside, the air scented and heavy, and the moment Sofia breathed it in she could sense a strangeness in it.

Warily she sat down opposite him.

'I have been searching for you,' she said. 'Why didn't you help Mikhail when he needed it?'

'Oh, Sofia, don't look so angry. You have to understand that there were too many troops swarming round him and it was impossible. The time was all wrong, but now . . . the time has changed. Tonight is the moment when your eyes will open.'

She didn't know what he meant. There was a strange formality in the way he spoke, his tongue clicking against his teeth. His gaze was distant and she was not sure he was even seeing her at all.

'Rafik,' she whispered. 'Who are you?'

He didn't answer. The whistle of his breath grew louder in the room and a movement of his hands made her look down at the table where they'd been clenched together. Now they lay apart, and between them lay the white pebble. It seemed to draw all light from the room deep into itself. Sofia felt her skin grow cold.

The stone was the one she'd found earlier in the chest. Then it had seemed harmless but now, for some unknown reason, it made her nervous. And yet her eyes refused to turn away from it.

'Sofia.' Rafik's voice was deep. He reached out and rested a heavy hand on her head.

Instantly her eyelids drifted shut. For the first time in the darkness of her own skull she became aware of a powerful humming sound, a vibration that rattled her teeth. To her dislocated mind it seemed to be coming from the stone.

She opened her eyes. She had no idea where she was or how she'd arrived there, just that she was standing upright in the dark, arms outstretched to each side. White figures circled her, four of them. Flickering lights in their hands, candle flames and the scent of cedarwood. Rising from the floor, a mist wove around her. She inhaled, a short sharp breath, and tasted the tang of burning pine needles. It made her look down.

At her feet stood a small iron brazier. In it were things she could only guess at but which were alight; all of them crackled and writhed. Her feet were bare. Outside the circle of light all was darkness but she could sense instantly that she was indoors. The four figures stood silent and unmoving around her, one at each point of the compass, a loose white gown covering each of their bodies.

'Rafik,' she murmured to the one directly in front of her.

As she did so she became aware that her own body was draped in a white gown, which rustled when she lowered her arms.

'Sofia.'

Rafik's single word was like a cool touch on her forehead.

'Don't be afraid, Sofia, you are one of us.'

'I'm not afraid, Rafik.'

'Do you know why we have brought you here tonight?'

'Yes.'

She didn't know how she knew but she did. Her mind struggled to clear itself but it was as if her thoughts were no longer her own.

'Speak it,' Rafik said. 'Why are you here tonight?'

'For Mikhail.'

'Yes.'

There was a prolonged silence while words pushed against her tongue, words that didn't seem to rise from her own mind.

'And for the village, Rafik,' she said clearly. 'It is for the village of Tivil that I am here, to make it live a life instead of die a death. I am here because I need to be and I am here because I am meant to be.'

She barely recognised her own voice. It was low and resonant and each word vibrated in the cool air. She shivered beneath her gown, but not with fear. She gazed round at the four figures, their eyes steady on hers, their lips murmuring silent words that drifted into the mist, thickening it, stirring it, causing it to linger as it brushed Sofia's cheek.

'Pokrovsky,' she said, turning her eyes on the broad bear of a man, whose wide shoulders stretched the white robe to the edge of its seams. 'Blacksmith of Tivil, tell me who you are.'

'I am the hands of this village. I labour for the working man.'

'*Spasibo*, Hands of Tivil.'

She lowered her eyes from the blacksmith to the slight figure with the full lips and bold gaze. 'Zenia, who are you?'

'I am a child of this village. The children are the future and I am one of their number.'

'*Spasibo*, Child of Tivil.' Sofia swung round further to face the figure to the east of her. 'Elizaveta Lishnikova, schoolteacher of Tivil, tell me who you are.'

'I am the mind of this village. I teach the children who are its future and bring knowledge and understanding to them the way the dawn in the east brings each new day to our village.'

'*Spasibo*, Mind of Tivil.'

Finally Sofia stepped round to look, once more, deep into the intense black eyes that burned with their ancient knowledge.

'Rafik,' she asked, softly this time, 'who are you?'

Ten heartbeats passed before he spoke. 'I am the soul of this village, Sofia. I guard and guide and protect this small patch of earth. All over Russia villages are destroyed and trampled by the brutish boot of a blood-addicted dictator who has murdered five million of his own people, yet still claims he is building a Workers' Paradise. Sofia,' he spread his arms wide to include all the white robes, 'the four of us have combined our strengths to safeguard Tivil, but you have seen the soldiers come. Seen the food stolen from our tables.'

'I have seen this.'

'Now you have come to Tivil and the Pentangle is complete.'

Sofia observed no signal, but the four white-clad figures stepped forward out of the shadows as one, until they were so close around her that when they each raised their left arm it rested easily on the shoulder of the person to their left. Sofia's heart was racing as she felt herself enclosed inside the circle. Rafik scattered something into the brazier at her feet so that it flared into life and the mist thickened into a dense fog. She could feel it crawling far down into her lungs every time she breathed. She swayed, her head growing too unwieldy for her neck. A pulse at her temple throbbed in time with her heartbeat.

'Sofia, take the stone into your hand.'

Rafik was holding out the white pebble to her and without hesitation she took it. She expected something from it, some spark or sign or even a pain shooting up her arm, but there was nothing. Just an ordinary warm round pebble lying in the palm of her hand.

At a murmur from Rafik the circle sealed itself tighter and a slow rhythmic chanting began, the language unknown to her, until it was a rushing wind that tore at her mind, ripped out her conscious thoughts and swept them away until only a great echoing chamber remained inside her head. Only one word leaped out of it.

'Mikhail!' she cried out. '*Mikhail!*'

'Mikhail,' the circle echoed.

'Mikhail,' she intoned into the shadows. 'Come to me.'

'**W**hy me?' Sofia asked.

'Don't you know?' Rafik asked in a low voice. He was pacing with a smooth unbroken stride over the uneven tangles of roots and soil, skirting round the fringes of Tivil. 'Don't you know now who you are?'

'Tell me, Rafik, who I am.'

'Feel for it, Sofia, stretch your mind back to the beginning and to before the beginning. Reach deep into yourself. You are strong.'

Together they were pacing out the circle that the Gypsy trod nightly around Tivil. Through the fields, past the pond and round the back of each *izba*, weaving what he called a protective thread. When he led her out of the ritual chamber she was not surprised to discover the mysterious ceremony had taken place inside the church, not in the main hall but in an old storeroom at the back.

'Now,' Rafik had said with his hands on hers, a prickling sensation growing between their palms as if they were being stitched together, 'now you shall tread the circle with me.' His eyes probed hers and she was certain he could see clearly even in the moonless night air. 'Are you ready, Sofia?' He'd wrapped a hooded cloak around her shoulders and tied it securely at her throat.

'Yes, I'm ready.'

Her blood was pounding in her ears. Ready for what? She didn't know, but without anything being said, she understood that this was the bargain she had struck with Rafik. His help with the safety of Mikhail in exchange for her help with the safety of the village. She had a feeling that the cost of this bargain to both could be high.

'I'm ready,' she said again.

Suddenly he smiled a gentle smile and softly kissed her cheek. 'Don't fear,' he whispered in her ear. 'You are strong and you have the power of generations within you.'

Sofia waited in the dark, tense and breathing hard. She was standing by the cedar tree at the gateway to Tivil. He would come, she was certain he would come. In the silence, in the cold, she heard Rafik's words again: *Reach deep into yourself. You are strong.*

Strong?

She didn't feel strong, she felt battered and exhausted. She wanted to weep with need. Would Mikhail come? She had to believe he would, whether as a result of Rafik's ceremony or simply because Fomenko had responded to her threat and decided to throw his weight around in the right places. Whichever it was she didn't care, so long as he came. She took a deep, slow breath to calm her quivering mind and felt the night breeze wash through her lungs, flushing out the panic.

Mikhail, my Mikhail. Come to me.

Her eyes scoured the blackness for a long time and saw nothing. And then a tingling sensation started in the soles of her feet, spreading to the palms of her hands, and suddenly her heart tightened in her chest. Her legs started to move and she was flying down the road, racing towards him, arms outstretched.

Mikhail was in her arms, warm and safe and alive. For a second she was frightened her senses were betraying her. This wasn't real, just her desire unfolding inside her head. But his clothes stank, dried blood lay stiff on his collar, his unshaven jaw felt rough against her skin. His lips were swollen. But not too swollen to press hard on hers or to whisper into her mouth over and over, 'Sofia, my love, Sofia.'

He washed in the yard at the back of the house. A dim pool of light spilled from the room's oil lamp but most of the yard lay in shadows. She watched him from inside as he stripped off every filthy scrap of clothing, threw it in a pile on the ground and set light to it. The flames were small and smouldering in the damp air but they sent golden fingers of light shimmering up his long naked thigh and gleaming over the strong curve of his buttock. Sofia felt a surge of desire but, as the shadows shifted and draped themselves over him like a cloak, she moved away from the window to give him his privacy.

When he eventually entered the room he was wearing a clean black shirt and trousers. At the sight of her tucked into his big wing chair his face broke into a smile of relief, as though he feared she might have gone. His eyes were a dull and damaged grey that bruised her heart. One eye and his lips were swollen, a tooth chipped, and he was moving awkwardly, something hurting inside, but when she started to ask he dismissed it as nothing.

She rose, kissed his mouth, gently soothing it with her tongue, and eased him into the chair. She curled up at his feet with her chin resting on his knee. Her hands began to stroke the calves of his legs, drawing the anger from his muscles, willing her strength into him.

'You look wonderful,' he said and tenderly touched her cheek. His finger traced the line of her lips. 'You shine.'

She kissed the tip of his finger. 'I missed you.'

He twisted a lock of her blonde hair around his forefinger as though attaching her to himself. The silence between their words dropped away. He cupped his hand round the back of her head, cradling it.

'You were with me,' he whispered, his gaze intent on her face. 'All the time you were with me.'

He held out a hand to her and, when she slipped hers into it, drew her to him on to his lap. He rested his head against hers, holding her so close she could feel the beat of his heart.

'Sofia,' he whispered into her hair, 'tell me what the hell is going on.'

She was silent.

He tipped her chin up to look at him, his eyes lingering on her face. 'You were waiting for me. How did you know I was coming?'

'I didn't, not for certain.'

'Sofia, I was in prison being bounced from interrogation to beating and back to interrogation, no food, no water, no sleep. Then suddenly in the middle of the interrogation an OGPU officer marched into the room, waved around a signed release order and I was out on the street in the rain in the middle of the night before I could say: *Chto za chyort!*'

He knocked back a shot of vodka and shuddered. 'And then I found you waiting for me.'

'You're safe,' she whispered. 'That's all that matters.'

'Sofia, I need to know.'

Tenderly she took his face in her hands. 'Mikhail, my dearest Mikhail, I honestly don't know what happened. Your release could have been caused by Rafik—the Gypsy has amazing powers to move thoughts—or by . . . someone else. Let's leave it until tomorrow, my love. You've been through enough.'

Mikhail frowned, his dark gaze searching her face. Their eyes held fast on each other until suddenly something deep within him seemed to open, some emotion shaking his strong frame so violently that his limbs trembled under her. He groaned, and Sofia hungrily pressed her lips to his throat. When Mikhail rose from the chair with her in his arms and bore her from the room, she shut her ears to the accusing voice in her head, the one that said she was stealing.

9

Tivil
July 1933

'THIS IS AS IT SHOULD BE.' Sofia whispered the words to the darkness. A glorious outburst of joy that transformed her body into something wonderful and vibrant, something she barely recognised. She brushed her lips on Mikhail's wrist, tasting his skin once more. 'This is as it should be,' she whispered, again.

She sighed, unable to make herself leave him. The kerosene lamp in the living room had burned out so that the night's darkness was complete, denser now as dawn approached. She knew she had to move. But instead she nestled closer in the crook of Mikhail's arm, rubbing her skin against his, feeling the warmth of him as he slept wrapped around her. She loved the weight of his body against hers. She listened to the rhythm of his breathing and wished sweet dreams into whatever life he was leading behind his flickering eyelids.

She dressed quickly and quietly, then brushed her lips against his forehead. Even in the dark she knew his mouth had curled into a smile as he slept.

She longed to keep him like this, hers for ever, hers alone, to love and to cherish. To live a whole life together till they were old and grey and could look back on these days with laughter and say that magical phrase *Do you remember when . . .?* Why not? She could. It would be so easy to say nothing and start a new life here and now with Mikhail.

Oh, Anna, I can't.

She stepped back from the bed and tears filled her eyes.

Today everything would change.

'**A**n unanticipated pleasure, my dear. I didn't expect to see you so soon.' Deputy Stirkhov exhaled a grey snake of smoke that coiled round the room as he waved Sofia into a chair in his gleaming chrome office. A vodka bottle sat on his desk without its lid. It was half-empty but the glass beside it was full.

Sofia slid on to the leather seat in front of the desk. 'You underestimate me,' she smiled.

'You have information for me?'

'Of course. It's what you paid me for. Didn't I promise it?'

A satisfied smile split his smooth moon face in half. 'Not everyone does what they promise in this world.'

'I do. If you think otherwise, you don't know me.'

'I intend to get to know you much better,' he said smoothly and reached into his desk drawer. He drew out another shot glass, filled it and pushed it across to her.

'Thank you,' she said, but didn't pick it up.

She felt his gaze on her blouse. It was one of Zenia's, a dusky rose-pink with embroidered woodland flowers on the collar and cuffs.

'I am informed that a member of your village is in prison right now.' He seemed to be talking to her breasts.

'If you mean Comrade Pashin, he has been released.'

His eyes shot up to hers. 'Indeed? When?'

'Today.'

'That's a shame, I was sure they'd hold on to our wayward Factory Director. Dagorsk is better off without the likes of him.'

'Why?'

'Because he's a troublemaker. Oh, yes, I grant that he knows his stuff as an engineer and has shaken up those lazy imbeciles who work in his factory, but he's one of those arrogant bastards who think they know better than the Party line.'

Sofia scooped up her drink from the desk, raised her glass to the portrait of Stalin and drank it straight down.

'So what's this information you've brought me from Tivil? A *kolkhoznik* been late to work, has he? Or did one of your hamfisted peasants get into a drunken brawl and is now being denounced for singing obscene words to the tune of the *Internationale*?'

'No, nothing like that.'

'Then what?'

'Someone in Tivil is hoarding large quantities of potatoes and grain.'

It was like throwing a grenade. In her mind she heard the explosion rip through the quiet office. Comrade Stirkhov's mouth hung open.

'Now I'll grab Tivil by the throat,' he growled, 'and shake it till it begs for mercy. Who is this Enemy of the People?'

Sofia slipped into the bedroom where Mikhail was sleeping. One arm was thrown out in a gesture of abandon as if letting go in his sleep of what he couldn't release when awake. Sofia moved silently to the bed.

She stood there quietly and absorbed every detail of him, not just into her mind but into her body, deep into her blood and her bones. The fineness of him, the line of his cheekbone, the thick fan of his dark lashes, even the black and swollen bruise around his eye. She imagined him laughing in the snow and building a sleigh of ice. All the things she knew he'd done, and many more when he was Vasily. But then he stuck a knife in the throat of his father's killer and Vasily died. Mikhail was born. It made no difference to her.

Vasily.

Mikhail.

She loved them both. Her body ached with loving him, but it was nothing compared with the desperate ache at the knowledge that she was about to lose him. So softly that he didn't break the rhythm of his dreams, Sofia dropped her clothes to the floor and slid in beside him between the sheets. She curled her body around his and lay like that for an hour, maybe two. When eventually his hand found her in his sleep, she smiled. Slowly, without opening his eyes, he started to caress her breasts till a moan crept from between her lips and she heard his breath quicken.

'Ssh,' she whispered, 'you need sleep.'

'No, I need you.'

'I've been waiting for you.' Rafik was seated at the table in his *izba*. He indicated the two chairs opposite him.

Sofia and Mikhail sat down. Sofia's eyes focused immediately on the white stone that lay on the surface of the table.

'Sofia,' Rafik said and smiled at her. 'It is time for you to know more.

But first,' his gaze shifted to Mikhail, 'what is it you want of me, Comrade Pashin?'

Mikhail gave the stone no more than a cursory glance, but he draped a protective arm along the back of Sofia's chair. 'Rafik,' he said, 'yesterday I was incarcerated in a filthy cell looking at a future in a labour camp—at best. Today I am here in Tivil, a free man.' He leaned forward, searching the Gypsy's face. 'It's a miracle, and I don't believe in miracles.'

'No, it's not a miracle. You were saved by Sofia.'

Mikhail thumped a hand on the table, making the stone leap from its place. Rafik flinched but didn't touch it.

'Rafik, you say Sofia saved me but she claims that you did. I need to know what is going on here. People have always whispered that you have mystic powers but I dismissed it as village tittle-tattle. Yet now . . .'

'Mikhail,' Rafik said in a soothing tone, 'I'm going to tell you a history.' With his words the thoughts in Sofia's head seemed to grow heavy. 'For centuries,' he continued, 'generations of my family were advisers and astrologers to the Kings of Persia. Their knowledge and intimacy with the Spirits made them a force that guided one of the greatest Empires in history through times of war and times of peace. But nothing . . .' he brushed a finger over the stone and eased it back into its position, 'nothing lasts for ever—not even Communism.'

He frowned, drawing his heavy black brows together. 'My ancestors were driven from their Land of Honey and fled throughout the known world, some escaping to Europe, others to India and further into the Orient, as the Empire crumbled.'

Sofia closed her eyes for a moment. 'I feel it,' she murmured.

Mikhail's solemn gaze scrutinised her face, then he passed a hand in a gentle caress over her forehead.

'What does she mean?'

Rafik took Sofia's hands between his own, palms together as in prayer. 'She is like me,' he said.

'She's not a Gypsy.'

'No. I am the seventh son of a seventh son, going back through generations of seventh sons all the way to Persia. That's where my power comes from, passed on in a connection of blood. Sofia is the same.'

'What do you mean? Is she the daughter of a seventh son?'

'No. She is the seventh daughter of a seventh daughter, going back through generations. Because her mother died when Sofia was so young, she never learned from her mother what she should have been told about the power that is centred in her, drawn from the strength and the knowledge of others before her.' He pressed Sofia's hands tight together. 'My will is strong, and so is hers. But together,' Rafik continued, his black eyes searching hers, 'we are stronger.'

'But my father was a priest of the Russian Orthodox church,' she pointed out. 'Murdered for a faith that surely would have clashed with my mother's . . . if what you say is true.'

'Faiths can work together. The bond they create can be a powerful force.'

She nodded. 'Have you ever spoken to Priest Logvinov here in Tivil? About working together?'

'He's not ready. Until he is, I protect him.'

Mikhail leaned forward, intent on Rafik. 'That explains why the crazy fool still has his life in one piece. I've never been able to understand why he wasn't shot or exiled long ago by the authorities. He takes risks, big risks.'

Rafik looked at Mikhail. 'So do you.'

A shout in the street shattered the moment. They heard the sound of boots pounding outside, the growl of a truck engine revving impatiently. Children were bounding up from the school, voices in the street raised in dispute. Rafik and Mikhail hurried to the door.

Only Sofia remained where she was. She was staring at the white pebble. She touched it and it was ice cold.

'Sofia,' Rafik demanded harshly behind her. 'What have you done?'

Aleksei Fomenko, the Chairman of the Red Arrow *kolkhoz*, stood in the grip of two burly soldiers outside his house. Around them swarmed the *kolkhozniki*. News travelled fast in the fields.

Sofia forced herself to watch. The way the uniformed soldiers manhandled him as though he was dirt. The erect manner with which he carried himself in his checked shirt and work trousers as though proud of them, the straight back, the accusing grey eyes that swept the crowd. At his feet lay a sack packed with secret plunder.

'Hoarder!'

'Thief!'

'You disgusting hypocrite, after all the food you took from us—'

'Liar! All the time you were stealing for yourself.'

A stone flew from a woman's hand and then another, which hit its target. Sofia could see the blood trickle along Fomenko's scalp. She made herself watch, but where was the sense of satisfaction she had expected? Why wasn't she enjoying the gloating and the triumph? This was what she'd wanted, wasn't it? This was what she'd sworn to do. So why did revenge taste so sour?

'**W**e were all shocked,' Mikhail said and shook his head. 'I'd never have believed it of Fomenko.'

Sofia was quiet. All afternoon she'd been subdued.

'Sofia, what is it, my love?'

She took a deep breath, quivered, but said firmly, 'I want us to talk.'

'What is it you want to talk about?'

'I want to talk about . . . the Dyuzheyevs.'

He stopped breathing.

'You know the name?' she asked.

'Yes.'

'When I asked before, you claimed you didn't.'

'I lied.'

'Why would you lie about it?'

'Because . . . oh, Sofia, I don't want to think back to those times. They're . . . over, locked in the past. Nothing can change what happened back then.'

In the silence that followed, Mikhail had a sudden sense of things slipping away. Just the same as that day so long ago in the snow, when his whole life slipped from his icy fingers. Not this time, not again, he refused to let it happen again.

'Why are you doing this, Sofia? What are you trying to get out of me? Yes, I knew the Dyuzheyevs. Yes, I saw them die. A day etched into my brain in every detail, however hard I try to forget it. So I've answered you. Now leave it, my love, leave it alone. Whatever your connection is with that dreadful day, don't drag it in here.'

'I must.'

'I love you, Sofia.'

'I love you, Mikhail.' Her eyes shimmered in the shaft of light.

'Very well, my sweetest, what is it you want?'

'Anna Fedorina is still alive.'

Mikhail was angry. Not with Sofia, but with himself. Something that happened sixteen years ago should not still have this power over him.

'Where is she?' he'd asked.

'In a labour camp in Siberia.'

He stood in the middle of the room and stared down at the half-built model of the bridge on the table. 'It's the Brooklyn Bridge,' he said flatly. 'In America. It spans the East River between New York and Brooklyn.'

'I thought it was the Forth Bridge.'

'No.' He frowned. Why was he talking about bridges? 'The Forth Bridge is cantilevered, this one is a suspension bridge.' He ran a finger along the top of one of the towers, picking out the intricate woodwork. 'What was I thinking? That one day I could become an engineer again instead of a miserable factory manager? I was a fool.'

With a sudden jab of anger he hammered his fist down on top of the bridge, bringing it crashing down in a thousand pieces.

'Mikhail!'

'I've been living in a dream-world,' he said sourly. 'I thought that I could rebuild the past, I could create a new family with Pyotr and you and that one day my dedication to the State's demands would win me the reward of a job that I could love again.' He placed his foot on one of the replica masonry anchorages lying on the floor and crushed it. 'No more dreams.'

'Why should knowing that Anna is alive destroy your dreams? Is your life so unbearable without her?' Her eyes were fierce. 'She still loves you.'

'Loves me! She should loathe me.'

'Why? Because you never came for her? Don't worry, she knows you tried. Maria told her when she went to the apartment in Leningrad.'

'She saw Maria?'

'Yes. That was where she was captured. But Maria showed her the name and address you'd written down, so that's why I came here to Tivil, to find you.' She paused, her voice briefly unsteady. 'Anna loves you . . . Vasily. She always will, till her dying breath.'

Mikhail strode across the room, seized her wrists and yanked her to her feet.

'I'm not Vasily,' he said coldly.

He felt her go rigid, but he couldn't stop now.

'Vasily Dyuzheyev knifed my father to death that winter's day in 1917 on the Dyuzheyev estate. My father was the soldier in charge of the patrol, but my contribution to the massacre was twice Vasily's. I shot his mother and I shot Anna Fedorina's father in cold blood.' He shook Sofia, shook her hard. 'Now tell me,' he demanded, 'that she loves me. Now tell me . . . that *you* love me.'

It took them time to untangle the truth. Again and again they came back to Maria to discover that she lay at the heart of the confusion.

'You say Maria told Anna that Vasily visited her twice. That he wrote down the name Mikhail Pashin with an address in Tivil and the Levitsky factory. But that wasn't Vasily. That person was me. And according to your talk with Maria's sister-in-law, the second man was Fomenko. You see, I only went to see her once.' Mikhail recalled the day. The tiny apartment, stiflingly hot, and the white-haired woman so eager to please and so damaged by the stroke. 'I had no idea she believed I was Vasily Dyuzheyev. I'd been searching for her for years.'

'Why?'

Mikhail stopped pacing. 'Isn't it obvious? Because I killed the child's father. I wanted to find Anna Fedorina and do what I could to make amends for what I'd done to her family. I discovered that her mother had died years earlier and that the woman with her was her governess. But . . .' he spread out his arms in a gesture of despair, 'both vanished off the face of the earth. It was a time of chaos and disappearances were common. The civil war started and normal life became . . . impossible.'

'Mikhail,' Sofia asked quietly, 'how old were you when you shot Svetlana Dyuzheyeva and *Doktor* Fedorin?'

'Fourteen.'

'Only three years older than Pyotr.'

'I was so like him at that age. So convinced that Bolshevism was the universal truth that would cleanse the world. All else was lies.'

'Tell me what happened.'

'I stood shoulder to shoulder with my father that day and mowed down the idle bourgeoisie like rats in a barrel.' He turned his back on Sofia. 'Why torment ourselves? You cannot despise me more than I despise myself for what I did. And the ultimate irony is . . .' he gave a bitter laugh, 'that all this time the boy who cut my own father's throat that day has been living right here beside me in Tivil. Aleksei Fomenko turns out to be Vasily Dyuzheyev under another name.'

He slumped down in a chair at the table. 'Neither he nor I recognised each other after all these years, but I hated him anyway for being the kind of person I used to be. And he hated me for having lost my faith. I was a threat. It didn't matter how many quotas I exceeded at the factory, my mind wasn't a Bolshevik mind and Fomenko wanted me to relearn the faith. He is a blind idealist.'

'Don't,' Sofia said.

Mikhail looked at her and something wrenched in his chest. She was perched forward on the edge of his big armchair, her hair bright in a splash of sunlight.

'Sofia,' he said gently, 'until you came into my life I was incapable of loving anyone. I didn't trust anyone. I despised myself and believed that others would despise me too, so I was wary in relationships. I went through the motions but nothing more. Instead I gave my love to an aircraft or a well-turned piece of machinery or . . .' he gestured at the mess of wooden struts on the floor.

'And to Pyotr.'

'Yes, and to Pyotr.' The hard muscles round his mouth softened. 'When I came to this village six years ago, riding up the muddy street into my exile from Tupolev, and spotted this scrap of a child being tossed into a truck about to be carted off to some godforsaken orphanage, I saw Anna Fedorina in him, as she was on the doorstep all those years before—the same passion, the same fury at the world. So I carried the fierce little runt into my house and I petted and protected him the way I couldn't protect her. I grew to love him as my own flesh and blood.'

'But you still kept trying to find her.'

'Yes. One day I did a favour for an officer in the OGPU and in return he tracked down Maria for me. But I swear I only went there once, Sofia.'

Sofia nodded. 'Maria muddled the two of you up in her head.' Her words were heavy and lifeless. 'Both tall with brown hair and grey eyes. She got it . . . all wrong.' Her gaze fixed on his face. 'Like I did,' she whispered.

'No matter what happens now, I want you to know I love you and will always love you.'

She leaped to her feet, shaking her head violently. 'No, Mikhail. I came here because I swore an oath to Anna. To find Vasily and to destroy the killer of her father if I could. Instead I've destroyed Vasily.'

'**P**lease, Rafik, please. I implore you.'

Sofia was on her knees on the wooden floor before the Gypsy, clutching his brown hands in her pale ones, her eyes unwavering on his face. The white stone lay on the table before him.

'I beg you to do for Aleksei Fomenko what you did for Mikhail.'

The Gypsy again shook his head. 'No.'

'Why, Rafik?' Sofia demanded. 'It was my mistake, not Fomenko's. I was the one who hid one of the stolen sacks of food under his bed when he was out in the fields. You know no one locks their doors during the day here in Tivil. I denounced him to Stirkhov. It wasn't his dishonesty, Rafik, it was mine, I swear it.' She pressed her forehead to his hands.

Rafik removed his fingers from her grasp.

'Sofia, I will tell you this. Chairman Aleksei Fomenko has taken from Tivil everything that belonged to the village by right and he has left us gaunt and naked. He has stripped the food from the mouths of our children to feed the voracious maw that resides in the Kremlin in Moscow. Above all else on this earth it is my task to protect this village of ours and that's why I never leave it. If that means protecting it from Aleksei Fomenko at the cost of his life, so be it.'

Sofia rose to her feet. She begged no more. Instead she moved to the door and Mikhail loved her for the proud way in which she walked.

'Rafik,' he said fiercely. 'She needs help.'

The deep lines on Rafik's face were etched white. He shook his head. Mikhail seized the stone. 'Give her this.'

For a long moment the Gypsy scrutinised the stone in Mikhail's hand, then slowly he nodded. 'Yes. Give it to her, Mikhail.'

Sofia's eyes grew wide. He placed the white stone cautiously on her palm, as if it might burn her, but the moment it touched her skin something in Sofia's eyes changed. Mikhail saw it happen. Something of the wildness vanished and in its place settled a calm determination.

Please God, Mikhail prayed to the deity he didn't believe in, *don't let her be harmed by it.*

Pyotr was halfway through scraping burnt clinker off a big flat shovel when he saw his father in the street.

'Papa,' he said, throwing down the spade. 'I've been thinking.'

His father smiled but it wasn't a happy smile. 'About what?'

'About Chairman Fomenko.'

The smile vanished. 'Don't concern yourself, Pyotr. Finish up here and come home.'

'I've worked it out, Papa. Chairman Fomenko would never steal from the *kolkhoz*. He's innocent. Someone else must have put that sack under his bed, someone vicious who wanted to—'

'Leave it, Pyotr. The interrogators will have thought of that, I assure you. So forget it.'

Just then Sofia hurried over to them, her skirt tangling round her legs in her haste, her hair bobbing loose. 'Mikhail, Pyotr,' she whispered, 'I need your help.'

'What are we searching for?' Mikhail asked.

'A box of jewellery.'

'Whose jewels?'

'Svetlana Dyuzheyeva's,' she answered, without turning.

Mikhail stiffened.

'Are we stealing them?' Pyotr asked quickly.

'Not if we use them to do good,' Sophia answered. 'We need to find them and use them to help Chairman Fomenko.'

They explored even the faintest nook or hint of a crevice, trailing fingers around bricks and behind beams. Mikhail searched in a methodical manner at one end of the hall, Sofia at the other, but her shoulders were hunched, her skin almost blue in the strangely discoloured light.

A fist banged outside on the oak door. Pyotr's tongue tingled with fear. Soldiers? He swallowed hard and knew in his heart that what they were doing in the hall was wrong.

'Pyotr,' his father whispered urgently. 'Come here.'

Pyotr scampered over a bench and was seized by his father's strong hands. Immediately he felt better. Sofia appeared at Papa's side, though Pyotr hadn't heard or seen her move. And for the first time the two of them looked at each other, really looked, speaking only with their eyes in a language Pyotr couldn't understand. Sofia pointed to Pyotr and then to a spot by the entrance. Mikhail nodded, whisked Pyotr over there and pressed him against the wall behind the heavy door, its rough surface cold on his bare arms. The knock came again, rattling the iron hinges. Pyotr watched in astonishment as his father took Sofia's face between his hands and kissed her lips. For half a second she swayed against him and Pyotr heard her murmur something, then just as suddenly they were apart again.

'Who is it?' his father demanded in the big voice he used for his factory workers.

It was Priest Logvinov.

'What is it you want, Priest?' Mikhail asked curtly.

'Mikhail, my friend, I'm looking for the girl.'

'Which girl?'

Sofia stepped into view. 'This girl?'

The priest nodded, his expression uneasy. 'You asked me before about a statue of St Peter.'

'I did.'

'I've come here because . . .' Logvinov paused, looked wistfully out into the street, 'because . . .' He sighed deeply. 'Dear Lord of Heaven, I don't know why I've come. Just that I felt . . . drawn here.'

Pyotr noticed the pebble then. He couldn't see Sofia's face on the other side of the door but he could see her hand at her side and in it she held a smooth white stone.

She spoke softly. 'Tell me, Priest, what have you come to say?'

'I told you of the statue of St Peter inside the church.'

'Yes.'

'But there used to be another.'

'Where?'

'Outside, at the back of the church. It was a magnificent marble statue that the *Komsomol* devils smashed to pieces and used as hard core under the *kolkhoz* office building.' He pointed a finger out into the gloom that had enveloped the village. 'Round the rear of the church beside the buttress, you'll see the old plinth where it used to stand, covered in moss now.'

'Thank you, Priest.'

Logvinov carved the sign of the cross in the air and left.

Pyotr squirmed round the door and raced down the path that led round the building, the damp evening air cool in his lungs. The plinth was there, just where the priest had said.

'You dig,' Sofia urged.

Pyotr scrabbled like a dog in the dry crumbling earth, using his hands and Papa's knife to make a hole a metre deep. His breath came fast with excitement.

'I feel it,' he cried when the blade touched something solid.

It was a box made of rough pine and wrapped up in sacking. Inside it, enveloped in a sheet of leather that had gone stiff with age, lay a small enamelled casket. It was the most beautiful object Pyotr had ever set eyes on, its surface inlaid with ivory peacocks and green dragons that Papa said were made of malachite. He lifted it carefully and placed it in Sofia's hands.

'*Spasibo*, Pyotr.'

She slid open the gold catch and lifted the lid. Pyotr gasped as he caught sight of colours he'd never seen before, molten glowing stones.

'Sofia,' he whispered, 'these could buy you the world.'

Sofia stood in Deputy Stirkhov's office. Svetlana's pearls hung from her hand like a string of snowflakes, each unique in itself, yet perfectly matched to its fellows.

'Comrade Deputy, I think these might help you decide.'

She dangled the triple strand of pearls over his desk and set them swaying slightly, wafting the sweet smell of money in the direction of his wide nostrils. Behind his spectacles his eyes had grown as round as the pearls themselves and his lips had parted, as if preparing to swallow them. He held out a hand.

'Let me see them. They may be fake.'

He tried to take the necklace from her but Sofia stepped back and lifted them out of his reach. He was seated behind his desk and half rose from his chair, but one look at her face made him change his mind. In front of him on a soft square of white cotton lay a brooch. It was made of silver gilt in the shape of a long-legged Borzoi hound and in its mouth it carried a dead pheasant that was studded with emeralds. Stirkhov's eyes slid from the pearls to the brooch and back again. Sofia could see his greed grow the more it fed on them.

'Half now,' she said, 'and half when the job is done.'

Stirkhov puckered his smooth forehead, not understanding.

'I'll make it easy for you.' She drew a small pair of sewing scissors from her pocket.

Comprehension dawned. 'No.'

'Yes,' she said and snipped through the strands. Pearls cascaded on to the desk, bouncing and skidding off its glossy black surface like hail-stones. Stirkhov scrambled to collect them.

'I could have you arrested,' he snarled.

'But then you'd lose these, wouldn't you?' She smiled coolly.

She slipped the pearls into her pocket and was out of the building before he could change his mind.

'**P**atience.'

Sofia was inside Aleksei Fomenko's house. The *izba* was so bare inside, it scarcely looked lived in. She saw no reason not to be here, as she'd invaded his privacy once already—more than invaded it when she'd stuffed the sack under his bed. She'd violated it.

'He'll come,' she told herself and curled her fingers round the stone in her pocket. It lay there, cold and stubborn.

Vasily, oh, Vasily. How could I have got it so wrong? How did you become Fomenko? What happened to you?

She touched the board where he cut his bread, the skillet in which he fried his food, the towel where he dried his hands, searching for him. She walked into his bedroom, but it was like entering a dead person's room. A bed, a stool, hooks on the wall for his clothes.

She went over to his plain pinewood bed. It was covered by a patch-work quilt over coarse white sheets. She touched his pillow and it felt soft. That surprised her. She had expected it to be hard and unyielding like his ideas. She bent over and placed her cheek on it, sank into its feathers and closed her eyes. Did he ever dream of Anna? Her hand slid under the pillow, feeling for any secret talisman, but found nothing. When she stood upright she felt a dull kind of anger rise to her throat.

'You've killed him!' she shouted into the dead air of this dead house. 'You've killed Vasily!' She picked up the pillow and shook it violently. 'He was Anna's. I know I borrowed him, but he was always Anna's and now you've killed her as surely as you killed him.'

She hurled the pillow across the room. It hit the log wall and slid to the floor, but as it did so something tumbled out of the white pillow-case. Something small and metal rattled into a corner as though trying to hide. Sofia leaped on it. She picked it up, placed it on the palm of her hand and studied her find. It was a pill box fashioned out of pewter.

A dent on one side. It reminded her of the pebble in her pocket. She opened it and inside lay a lock of blonde hair, bright as sunshine.

She waited, her skin prickling with impatience. She watched the sun march slowly across the room from one side to the other. And all the time she brooded about Mikhail Pashin and about who he really was. About what he'd done. About what she, Sofia, had sworn to do to him.

Oh, my Mikhail, you made yourself suffer for what you did. You constructed a life for yourself that tried to atone and you did it with as much care as you built your bridge. I don't want to smash my fist on it and bring it crashing down now. But . . . you killed Anna's father.

She took out the pebble and placed it on her lap but it lay lifeless, a dull white. Yet as she stroked its cold surface, she felt herself change. A vibration rippled through her body and she almost heard the stone hum, high-pitched and faint inside her head. Its colour seemed to gain a sheen, just like a pearl.

Was she imagining this? Was Rafik imagining it all? The seventh daughter of a seventh daughter. Was it true? And if it was, did it mean anything at all? She wrapped her fingers tight round the stone.

'Anna,' she said firmly, 'wait for me. I'm coming.'

'What are you doing in my house?'

Sofia felt a wave of sorrow for the tall, arrogant man who she had wronged. He stood in the doorway with no marks on him, none that showed anyway, but something about him looked bruised.

She remained seated. 'Comrade Fomenko, I am here to tell you something important.'

'Not now.'

He walked over to the jug of water on the table and drank from the glass beside it, greedily, as if to flush away something inside himself.

He turned to her, his voice cold. 'Please leave.'

'I've been here all day, waiting for you.'

'Why on earth did you assume I would return from prison today?'

'Because of these.'

She held up the remains of the pearl necklace. They shimmered in the last of the evening light that streamed through the window. He drew in a breath, then fixed his gaze on her face.

'Who are you? What are you doing here?'

'I am a friend.'

'You are no friend to me.' He put down the glass. 'So why the pearls?'

'I used half of them to bribe an official to set you free. These,' she cradled the pale beads in the palm of her hand where they chittered softly against each other, 'are promised to him now you are home again.'

He stood staring at the pearls. She thought she could see a spark of recognition in his eyes, but maybe she was wrong. He was hard to read.

Abruptly he walked to the front door and held it open. Outside, the wolfhound lazed in the sun. 'Get out before I throw you out.'

Sofia rose and moved closer. He was in need of a shave. Her heart went out to him, this man she'd both loved and hated.

'Vasily, I am a friend of Anna Fedorina.'

She saw the shock hit him. A shudder. Then so still, not even his pupils moved. 'You are mistaken, Comrade.'

'Are you telling me that you are not Vasily Dyuzheyev, only son of Svetlana and Grigori Dyuzheyev of Petrograd? Killer of the Bolshevik soldier who murdered your father, protector of Anna Fedorina who hid under a chaise longue, builder of snow sleighs and agitator for the Bolsheviks. That Vasily. Is that not you?'

He turned away from her, his back as straight as one of his field furrows. For a long time neither spoke.

'Who sent you here?' he asked at last without looking at her. 'Are you an agent for the OGPU, here to entrap me? I believe it was you who placed the sack under my bed. I could see the hate in your eyes when the soldiers came for me.' He breathed deeply. 'Tell me why.'

'I thought you were someone else. I am not with the OGPU, have no fear of that, but I did make a terrible mistake and for that I apologise.'

'Who did you think I was?'

'The boy soldier who shot Anna's father and Svetlana Dyuzheyeva.'

No response.

'Vasily, speak to me. She's alive, Vasily, Anna Fedorina is alive.'

It was like watching an earth tremor. His shoulder blades shifted out of alignment and his muscular neck jerked in spasm. He tightened his folded arms around himself as though holding something inside.

'Where?'

'In a labour camp. I was there with her.'

'Which one?' Barely a whisper.

'Davinsky Camp in Siberia.'

'Why?'

'For nothing more than being the daughter of *Doktor* Nikolai Fedorin, who was declared an Enemy of the People.'

No more words. Neither of them could find any. The black shadow of Vasily lay across the wooden floor between them like a corpse.

They drank vodka. They drank till the pain was blunted and they could look at each other. Sofia sat in the chair, upright and tense, while Fomenko fetched a squat stool from the bedroom and folded himself onto it, his lean limbs orderly and controlled once more.

After the initial shock, he snapped back from the edge of whatever abyss had opened up and his strength astounded her. How could he hold so much turmoil within himself, yet seem so calm?

'Comrade,' he said, 'I am glad Anna has a friend.'

'Help me, Vasily, to be a true friend to her.'

'Help you how?'

'By rescuing her.'

For the first time the firm line of his mouth faltered. 'I have no authority to order any kind of release in—'

'Not with orders. I mean together, you and I, we could go up there. You could authorise travel permits and we—'

'No.'

'She's sick.'

'I'm very sorry,' he said quietly.

'Sorry means nothing. She's going to die. She's spitting blood and another winter up there will kill her.'

A dull mist seemed to settle behind his eyes, blurring them. 'Anna,' he whispered.

'Help her.'

He shook his head slowly, full of regret.

'What happened to you?' she demanded. 'When did you lose your ability to care for another human being? When your parents were shot? Did that moment smother every feeling in you for the rest of your life?'

'You don't understand, Comrade.'

'Make me, Vasily, make me understand.' She leaned forward. 'How can you abandon someone you loved, someone who still loves you and believes in you and needs you? How does that happen? Tell me.'

'Comrade Morozova, my feelings are my own business, not yours. Now please leave.'

'No, Vasily, not until you tell me—'

'Listen to me, Comrade, and listen well. Vasily Dyuzheyev is dead and gone. Do not call me by that name ever again. Russia is a stubborn country, its people are hard-headed and determined. To transform this Soviet system into a world economy—which is what Stalin is attempting to do by opening up our immense mineral wealth in the wastelands of Siberia—we must put aside personal loyalties and accept only loyalty to the State. This is the way forward—the *only* way forward.'

'The labour camps are inhuman.'

'Why were you sent there?'

'My father was a priest who was whipped to death. I then went to live with my uncle, but he was too good at farming and acquired the label *kulak*. They thought I was "contaminated".'

'Do you still not see that the labour camps are essential because they provide a work force for the roads and railways, for the mines and the timber yards, as well as teaching people that they must—'

'Stop it, stop it!'

He stopped. They stared hard at each other. The air between them quivered as Sofia released her breath.

'You'd be proud of her,' she murmured. 'So proud of Anna.'

Those simple words did what all her arguments and her pleading had failed to do. They broke his control. This tall powerful man sank to his knees on the hard floor like a tree being felled, all strength gone. He placed his hands over his face and released a low stifled moan. It gave Sofia hope. She could just make out the murmur of words repeated over and over again. 'My Anna, my Anna . . .' The dog stood at his side and licked one of its master's hands, whining gently.

Then, in a quiet voice, she started to tell him about Anna. What made Anna laugh, what made her cry, how she raised one eyebrow and tipped her head at you when she was teasing, how she worked harder than any of his *kolkhozniki*, how she could tell a story that kept you spellbound and carried you far away from the damp, miserable barrack hut into a bright, shining world.

'She saved my life,' Sofia added at one point. She didn't elaborate and he didn't ask for details.

Gradually Aleksei Fomenko's head came up and his eyes found their focus once more, his limbs rediscovered their connection and his mind regained control. As Sofia talked, a fragile smile crept onto his face. When finally the talking ceased he took a deep breath, as though to inhale the words she had set free into the air, and nodded.

'Anna always made me laugh,' he said in a low voice. 'She was always funny, always infuriating. She drove me mad and I adored her.'

'So help me to rescue her.'

The smile died. 'No.'

'Why not?'

'You have to understand, Comrade,' he said. 'Sixteen years ago, to satisfy my own anger and lust for vengeance, I slit a man's throat. As a result Anna's father was shot and her life was destroyed. That taught me a lesson I will carry to my grave.'

His grey eyes were intent on Sofia's face. She could feel the force of his need to make her understand.

'I learned,' he continued, 'that the individual need doesn't matter. The individual is selfish and unpredictable, driven by uncontrolled emotions that bring nothing but destruction. It is only the need of the Whole that counts, the need of the State. So however much I want to rescue Anna from her . . . misery'—he closed his eyes for a second as he said the word—'I know that if I do so . . .'

He broke off. She could see the struggle inside him for a moment as it rose to the surface, and his voice rose with it.

'You must see, Comrade, that I would lose my position as Chairman of the *kolkhoz*. Everything that I have achieved here—or will achieve in the future—would be destroyed because they would revert back to old ways. I know these people. Tell me which counts for more? Tivil's continued contribution to the progress of Russia and the feeding of many mouths or my and Anna's . . .?' He paused.

'Happiness?'

He nodded and looked away.

'Need you even ask? You're blind,' Sofia said bitterly. 'You help no one, nor do you think for yourself any more.'

Something seemed to snap inside him. 'Thought,' he said, his face close to hers, 'is the one thing that will carry this country forward. At the moment Stalin is pushing us to great achievements in industry and farming but he is at the same time destroying one of our greatest assets—our intellectuals, our men and women of ideas and vision. Those are the ones I help to . . .' He stopped and she saw him fighting for control.

'The radio in the forest,' she said in a whisper. 'It's not to report to your OGPU masters. It's to help—'

'It's part of a network,' he said, angry with her and with himself.

'You help them escape.'

'Yes.'

'Does anybody else in Tivil know?'

He drew in a harsh breath. 'Only Pokrovsky, and he is sworn to secrecy. No one in the network knows of more than one other person within it. That way no one can betray more than one name. Pokrovsky provides . . . packages . . . and forged papers for them. Where he gets them, I don't ask.'

Sofia recalled the secret drawer in Elizaveta Lishnikova's desk. She could guess. She walked over to the open door, where she stood looking out at the village.

'Chairman Fomenko,' she said softly, 'I feel sorry for you. You have hidden from yourself and from your pain so deeply, you cannot—'

'I do not need or want your sorrow.'

But he came up behind her and she could feel him struggling with something. She turned and looked into his grey eyes, and for a moment caught him unawares. The need in them was naked.

'Tell her I love her. Take my mother's jewels, all of them, and use them for her.'

She slid the damaged necklace from her pocket and slipped a single perfect pearl off its strand, took his strong hand in hers and placed inside it the pale sphere that had lain next to his mother's skin. He closed his fingers over it. His mouth softened and she felt the tremor that passed through him. In the same moment she replaced the necklace in her pocket and removed the white pebble. With her other hand she rested her fingers on Fomenko's wrist and pressed deep into his flesh as she'd seen Rafik do, touching the hard edges of his bones, his tendons, his powerful pulse, seeking him out.

'Vasily,' she said firmly, fixing her gaze on his, 'help me to help Anna. I cannot do it alone.'

Something seemed to shift under her fingers. She felt it, as though his blood thickened or his bones realigned. A tiny click sounded in her head and a thin point of pain kicked into life behind her right eye.

'Vasily,' she said again, 'help Anna.'

His eyes grew dark but his lips started to curl into a soft acquiescent smile. Her heart beat faster.

'Chairman Fomenko!' A boy's voice shouted out from the street and footsteps came hurtling up to the doorway. It was a clutch of seal-haired youths still wet from the pond. 'Is it all arranged for tomorrow?'

Fomenko jerked himself back to the present by force of will and wrenched his wrist from her hold. His eyes blinked again to refocus on the world outside his head.

Sofia stepped out into the street. She'd lost him.

'Is what arranged for tomorrow?' he demanded.

'The wagons to take everyone to Dagorsk to see the *Krokodil* aeroplane and hear our Great Leader's speech.'

Fomenko gave a harsh cough, as though trying to spit something out. 'Yes, of course, it's all arranged.' With a brisk nod of his head he moved back into the house and shut the door.

The night was unbearable without her. Mikhail spent the dark hours wrestling with the knowledge Sofia had given him.

Aleksei Fomenko. The name was branded into his brain. Fomenko was Vasily Dyuzheyev, the killer of his father. Yet at the same time Fomenko was the son of Svetlana Dyuzheyeva, the woman Mikhail himself had killed in cold blood.

They were bound together, Fomenko and himself, bound in some macabre dance of death. Both servants of the State and both sent to the same peasant *raion* to drag it into the twentieth century. So similar, yet so different. Mikhail hated him as much as he hated himself. And he hated the hold that Fomenko—as Vasily—seemed to have on Sofia.

'Sofia,' he said, as the moon slipped out from behind the clouds, its light trickling into his bedroom, 'don't think I will let you go so easily.'

His decisions started to harden. He owed Fomenko, an eye for an eye. He owed Anna, a life for a life. But most of all, he owed himself.

10

Dagorsk
July 1933

THE WIDE GREEN meadow stretched out, lazy in the sunshine on the far side of Dagorsk. From every direction carts and wagons were descending on it, tents springing up all over its surface like mushrooms. Men in red armbands were running around blowing whistles, shouting orders and waving batons, but nothing could subdue the spirit and energy of the crowd that surged into the field.

Pyotr loved every single second of it. Even the journey in the ramshackle old wagon had been fun. It had been packed with villagers from Tivil and he'd sat squashed close to Yuri at the back, legs dangling over the tailboard. Dust had swirled up from the track into their mouths, coating their tongues, but everyone began to sing to the playing of an accordion, loud and boisterous. It was like going to a party. Somewhere up ahead in the first wagon were Papa and Sofia and Zenia, but the children of the village were bundled into the second one with their teacher. Even Comrade Lishnikova was laughing and wearing a bright-red flowered shawl instead of her usual grey one. Today was going to be special. Today he wasn't going to think about the jewels they'd found yesterday. He wanted desperately to tell Yuri about them but knew he couldn't. When he'd stared into the casket at the fiery jewels, he'd felt their power in a way he'd never expected, so strong it had made him nervous. Where had it come from, this greed squirming inside him? Chairman Fomenko had been released and Pyotr knew for certain it was because of the pearls. That meant corruption. So he should speak out, loud and clear. It was his duty. Speak out about the existence of these corrupting jewels, that's what Yuri would say.

But how could he without denouncing Papa and Sofia? And without putting Chairman Fomenko's freedom at risk?

At the meadow they tumbled from the wagon in a flurry of pushing and shoving and high-pitched squeals.

'The aircraft isn't due for another half-hour,' Elizaveta Lishnikova announced.

'Can we look inside the film tent?' Pyotr asked.

'Yes, you may go and explore, but when I blow my whistle I expect you all to line up just the way we practised.'

'A guard of honour,' Yuri whooped.

She smiled and her long face creased in amusement. 'That's right. And I'm relying on you Young Pioneers to make me proud of you.'

'We will! For our Great Leader!' Pyotr shouted, and everyone gave the Pioneer salute. *'Bud gotov, vsegda gotov!'* Be ready, always ready!

'I'm going to be a fighter pilot,' Pyotr announced as he and Yuri emerged from the film show. They had just sat wide-eyed through the footage of the May Day Parade in Red Square and their pulses were still beating to the powerful rhythm of the martial music. Pyotr began to swing his arms in imitation of the soldiers on screen, his legs striding out in a stiff-kneed goose step.

Yuri giggled and copied his military bearing, puffing out his chest and grinning. The boys marched round the field in unison, swerving to avoid a bald man rolling a wooden cask over to one of the tents. Yuri was clutching a pamphlet in his hand and on the front of it was printed in big red letters: *Beware of Enemies of the People Among You.*

'I wonder,' Yuri said, flapping the pamphlet as he marched, 'who are the enemies in Tivil.'

Pyotr missed his step. His cheeks flushed. 'Maybe there aren't any,' he said quickly.

'Of course there are. They are everywhere, hiding among us. Most of them employed by Foreign Powers to—'

'Why on earth would a Foreign Power be interested in what goes on in our village?'

'Because we provide the food to feed the factory workers, stupid,' Yuri scoffed.

Pyotr was stung. 'I bet I know more about enemies in Tivil than you do.'

'You don't.'

'Yes, I do.'

They stopped in the middle of the field and glared at each other.

'Name one,' Yuri challenged.

'I could if I wanted.'

'You're lying.'

'No, I'm not.'

'I knew it. You don't know.' He gave Pyotr's shoulder a scornful shove.

It was the shove that did it, as if Pyotr were a stupid child to be pushed around. His cheeks darkened and he gave Yuri's chest a thump with his fist. Not hard, but hard enough to show he was serious.

'I'll tell you only if you promise to keep it secret.'

Yuri's eyes gleamed. 'Go on, tell me,' he urged. But he didn't promise.

Pyotr was desperate to find Sofia. He had to talk to her, to warn her. His heart was squeezed tight inside his chest as he scoured the field, trying to catch a glimpse of white-blonde hair. How could he have done it? Betrayed her, just because he was annoyed with Yuri? He scuffed his shoe furiously in the dusty soil. His skin was sticky with sweat because he knew he had to face her. And quickly.

He raced past a group of men tossing iron horseshoes onto pegs, and was relieved to spot Yuri among them. Maybe he wouldn't tell . . . Then Pyotr saw her down the side of one of the large tents. She'd know what was best to do. He started to run towards her but skidded to a halt when he saw she was talking to someone. With a funny twist in his stomach he recognised her companion. It was Deputy Stirkhov, the one who had given the address at the meeting, Deputy Chairman of the whole *raion*. Deputy Stirkhov was a man of the Party, a man who knew right from wrong.

Sofia was handing him something small wrapped in material and Pyotr's heart skipped a beat. He knew without even looking what was inside it. It would be the diamond ring or maybe the pearls. Stirkhov stuffed it deep in his trouser pocket. What had Sofia done to the man? Was she corrupting Stirkhov, too?

Up in the blue sky a thin trail of noise like a distant buzz-saw started to drill into his mind. He recognised it as the *Krokodil* approaching. He wiped his palms on his shorts, his mind spinning. He'd been right all along. Sofia wasn't just a fugitive, she really was an Enemy of the People. That realisation sent sorrow into his heart because Papa loved her. Papa, he must find Papa and speak with him. He started to run.

'**S**he's beautiful.'

Mikhail's eyes shone with pleasure as he squinted up at the aeroplane's wings glinting in the midday sun. 'Just the sight of her so close makes my hands itch to touch her.'

'It's a brilliant propaganda weapon,' Sofia admitted, shielding her eyes with her hand.

The high-winged silver-skinned aeroplane swooped down from the sky like a giant bird of prey. On each side of the makeshift runway Sofia could see the Young Pioneers lining up, backs stiff as soldiers'. Behind them stood the real soldiers, the ones with rifles to keep the spectators away from the plane.

'The *Krokodil* is one of the Maksim Gorky Agitprop Squadron,' Mikhail informed her, 'designed to fly from town to town across Russia. It distributes pamphlets and gives film shows to demonstrate what great strides Communism is making. It shows off Stalin's grandest projects, like the building of the White Sea Canal. It was named after the *Krokodil* magazine and differs from other ANT-9s by having aerodynamic fairings over the wheels and struts.'

'Interesting. But what about its engines?'

'Well, it has two M-17 engines instead of the original three . . .' He dragged his gaze away from the plane, looked at her and grinned. She loved his grin. 'You're making fun of me, aren't you?'

'Yes.'

'So what else shall I tell you? How Stalin intends that Russia will soon outstrip the West or . . .' his mouth twitched with mischief, 'that you have the most beautiful eyes on earth and that I want to kiss you?'

'Hmm, let me think. That's a hard one to choose.'

She stepped closer, leaning in towards him, but at that moment the guttural growl of the twin engines roared across the field.

'Look!' He pointed over the heads of the crowd. 'Look at its teeth!'

The plane dropped down onto the grass where, as it rolled and bounced to a stop, the crowd broke into cheers, the Young Pioneers saluted and the brass band struck up the *Internationale*.

'It's smiling,' Sofia laughed in astonishment.

Painted on the long reptilian plywood nose that designer Vadim Shavrov had specially added were the jaws and sharp teeth of a crocodile, curved into a disarming smile. Down the spine of the fuselage a row of bumps rose like the scaly ridges of a crocodile's back.

'It's inspired,' Mikhail exclaimed. 'The most famous aeroplane in the country.'

'It makes me proud to be Russian,' Sofia said solemnly.

He gave her a wide smile. 'Then let's go and inspect it.'

He took her hand in his, led her across the field through the milling throng, but the look in his eyes was so serious and so determined, it didn't match the smile on his lips. It made her uneasy.

The afternoon was measured by how many times the propellers swung into action. A collective intake of breath from the crowd whispered on the hot summer breeze as the aircraft shook off its lumbering attachment to the ground. It soared up into the air and at once, in its natural element, it possessed all the grace of a dancer. It dipped one wing and banked smoothly into a circle above the field, climbing higher and higher with each circuit.

'Sofia, have you seen Yuri?' Mikhail asked, as he found her again in the crowd.

'No. The races are about to start, so he's probably over by the flags.'

Mikhail's gaze scanned the sea of faces on the field. 'I can't see him.'

Sofia rested a hand lightly on his forearm. 'What is it, Mikhail?'

'Pyotr came to see me.' He released a harsh breath. 'He said things about you to Yuri that he shouldn't have said, and he's frightened that Yuri will go to Stirkhov with it.'

Despite the warmth of the sun, Sofia's face froze.

The voices and the laughter all around them, the band's incessant drumming and the throb of the heavy M-17 engines, all faded to nothing. Silence seemed to fill the whole wide arc of sky.

Mikhail stared at her, grim-faced. 'It's time to leave.'

'Zenia, wait a minute.'

The Gypsy girl was emerging from a tent. Each tent contained a different machine or process on display to indicate the modernisation of industry, but the most popular by far was the one full of the latest shiny sewing machines. Every woman in the field coveted one. Sofia caught the Gypsy girl's arm and drew her aside behind a heavy Gaz truck that had transported the benches and chairs.

'What is it, Sofia? You look . . . unhappy.'

'I saw you with your friend Vanya earlier. He isn't in OGPU uniform today.'

'No, he's off duty.' Zenia smiled as she talked of him.

'But he'd hear what's going on, wouldn't he? He'd know if there's any trouble today.'

'What kind of trouble?'

'A search for someone.'

Zenia studied Sofia hard. 'Wait here and stay behind the truck. I'll be back as quickly as I can. Don't move.' She hurried away.

Sofia didn't move. She remained behind the truck and knew this was the end. The end of everything. The choice was already made.

And at that moment she hated Anna with a hatred that took her breath away.

'*Bistro!*' Zenia was back. 'We must swap clothes.'

She was already untying the red scarf from her neck and yanking off her skirt to reveal thin, childish legs. Sofia didn't ask why. It was obvious they were searching for her and had her description.

'*Spasibo*, Zenia,' she said as she stepped into Zenia's black skirt. It had felt flowers in bright colours round the hem. She buttoned up the white Gypsy blouse. But the words *thank you* were nowhere near enough.

'I asked Vanya. You are to be arrested as an escaped fugitive the moment they find you.'

Sofia tied Zenia's triangular scarf over her head to disguise her blonde hair and knotted it at the back.

'Take care, Sophia.'

'**Z**enia told me you were here,' Mikhail said as he stepped round the rear flap of the Gaz truck and gathered her into his arms. He caressed the nape of her neck and she wanted to stay on that spot with him for the rest of her life. She laid her forehead against his chest and listened to the rapid beat of his heart.

'I thought you weren't coming back,' she whispered.

He took her face in his hands and tipped it up to look into his eyes.

'I'll always come back, my love,' he promised. 'Always.'

He kissed her mouth. Soft and tender. She clung to him, imprinting the feel of him into her muscles, then she stepped out of his arms and kept her voice steady.

'Did you find Yuri? Or Pyotr?'

'No. Pyotr seems to have vanished, but I learned that Yuri is up in the plane.'

'It's Stirkhov's reward to him,' Sofia moaned. 'For information.'

Mikhail nodded, silent and severe. 'I'm so sorry, Sofia.'

The aircraft was coming in for its final landing of the day, its engines drowning out the chorus of cheers hailing its return.

'They're hunting for you, my love. Our best chance of hiding you safely is in the middle of the crowd where you can keep on the move, until you—'

'Mikhail, Pyotr idolises the Party. Don't blame him.'

'I do, Sofia. I blame him, and I blame myself.' He looked at her, noticed her change of clothes, and the anger in his eyes softened. Gently he cupped her cheek in his palm and she tipped her head sideways into it.

'Well, what have we here?' An officer in khaki uniform was standing beside the front wing of the truck, staring at them.

'Comrade,' Sofia smiled and slid an arm around Mikhail's waist, 'you wouldn't deny us five minutes away from the sharp eyes of my friend's wife, would you?'

The soldier laughed. His trousers were already half unbuttoned and it was obvious he'd come to relieve himself behind the truck.

'Don't mind me, Comrades,' he said easily. But just as easily the Tokarev pistol flew from the holster on his hip into his hand, its business end pointed straight at Sofia. 'Just show me your papers first.'

'Of course, Comrade.'

Sofia made a show of rummaging in her pocket for her papers, but instead her hand touched the cool surface of the stone and instantly she cleared her mind, stilled her breath. She moved forward towards the *soldat*, her eyes locked tight on his, and she saw him frown and glance down at the gun in his hand with sudden confusion

That was when Mikhail struck. Two strides and the edge of his hand to the man's throat, followed by a sharp blow to his jaw that sent the soldier's head snapping back against the side of the truck with a loud metallic thud. The body crumpled onto the grass. They took no chances. In seconds Sofia had the soldier's belt off and Mikhail had used it to truss his hands and feet together behind his back, then they stuffed his handkerchief in his mouth and pocketed his gun.

'Now,' Mikhail said. 'Time to leave.'

As soon as the *Krokodil* touched down, everything happened fast. The two crewmen and their two assistants bundled projection equipment and cardboard boxes back onto the plane, while final but mercifully brief speeches were made and the band struck up the *Internationale* for the last time. Clouds began to drift across the sun like curtains drawing a performance to a close. The mood in the field was one of exhilaration, as noisy huddles of men started to gather round bottles of vodka.

But none of it stopped those in uniform going about their job efficiently, and every blonde young woman was ordered to show identity papers. Sofia dodged several, but time was running out. Any moment now the soldier behind the truck would be found, but Mikhail had gone once more in search of Pyotr.

'Don't attempt to leave until I return,' he'd said sternly.

She'd kissed him farewell, a light brush of the lips, and with it every-thing cracked inside her. She breathed, but only because she had to. She stood in the middle of a dense gathering close to the aeroplane and became aware of the tall figure of the blacksmith, Pokrovsky, on her right, and Elizaveta Lishnikova over to her left. They were keeping watch, extra eyes seeking out danger, and Sofia was certain it was Rafik who had told them to guard her. She was just edging in Pokrovsky's direction when a hand fell on Sofia's shoulder. She spun round.

It was a khaki uniform but not the one from the truck. This man was older, alert eyes under heavy bristled brows.

'*Dokumenti*,' he ordered.

Four men in uniform stood around her, like wolves, and from the corner of her eye she saw Pokrovsky pushing his way through the crowd towards her. *No, don't come near*. She willed him to keep away because she didn't want him hurt too. Time slowed down as she reached into her pocket and slid out her residency permit. *Anna, forgive me. Forgive me, my friend, forgive me for failing.*

'Ah, there you are.' Mikhail's hand suddenly slotted under her elbow, almost jerking her off her feet. Pyotr was pressed close to her other side, his brown eyes dark with misery.

'I'm sorry,' he whispered.

'It's all right, Pyotr, you did what you believed was right.' Gently she touched his hand and felt his fingers cling to hers.

'Your papers?' The soldier raised his voice.

'Comrade,' Mikhail said sharply, 'this woman is with the crew of the—'

But already the soldier was reaching forward to pull her from Mikhail's grasp. Rifles rattled around her.

'Stop that at once.'

Sofia swung round and was astonished to find herself staring into the face of Aleksei Fomenko. He gave her no more than a fleeting nod, then flashed some identity in front of the uniformed officer. A space immedi-ately cleared around her.

'I can vouch for this woman,' he said brusquely. 'What the hell are you and your men doing wasting your time here when you should be searching for the fugitive?'

The space around Sofia grew even larger as the soldiers backed off and she felt Mikhail's grip tighten on her arm.

'This woman and I are to leave with the aeroplane crew,' Mikhail protested angrily.

'I'll need to see proof of that,' the officer responded, but already the aggression had waned and his manner was hesitant.

Fomenko put himself between Sofia and the uniform, his authority taking easy control. 'Don't be bloody foolish, *soldat*. The cloud base is lowering every minute, so they need to leave right now, or shall I report you for causing delays, too—'

'No, Comrade Chairman, that won't be necessary.'

Sofia felt Mikhail jerk her into action. Her feet remembered to move as, heart hammering, she was propelled forward and into the aeroplane. The flimsy corrugated door closed behind her.

Rivers meandered lazily below as the aircraft flew due north. The threads criss-crossed through a vast water-filled landscape, emptied of all colour by mists that shrouded them in secrecy. The M-17 engines throbbed and as Mikhail sat in the passenger cabin he could feel every beat of the pistons, driving his blood through his veins. They powered a wonderful sense of being cut free from the earth.

It was a long time since he'd felt like this, as good as this. Which was crazy because he knew he was in serious trouble whichever way he looked, but somehow that all faded into insignificance up here. He was with Sofia and he was flying again, and he was determined to find Anna Fedorina. Reality on the ground seemed a long way down.

'Are you all right?'

Sofia turned her face from the window and gave him a smile, that crooked little curve of her lips that he loved.

'I'm fine.'

'Not nervous on your first flight?'

'No, I love it. How high are we?'

'Around three thousand metres.'

She nodded but looked tense. He put out a hand across the narrow aisle that divided them and stroked her arm, soothing her.

'How far will we fly?' she asked in a low tone.

'The *Krokodil's* range without refuelling is seven hundred kilometres.'

'We'll go that distance?'

'Yes.'

Her eyes changed as they stared at him in disbelief. Then she tipped back her long throat and released a silent shout of joy.

'I thought,' she said, struggling to sound casual, 'that we would just be taken . . . out of that field and put down somewhere nearby.'

'No.' He laughed for the benefit of listening ears. 'The Captain is taking us on quite a little jaunt. He wants me to give my professional

assessment of how these propaganda trips are working out. As my secretary, you must take notes.'

'Of course,' she responded in a demure secretarial kind of voice, but
she rolled her eyes and mimed typing in the air, so that Mikhail had to
bite his tongue to stop a laugh. As the shadows of the clouds chased each
other over the flatlands below, she whispered, 'Did you know when we
set off for the *Krokodil* display, we would fly north in the aeroplane?'

'I intended to try, but I wasn't certain it would happen. That's why I
said nothing to you.'

'Did the Captain agree to help us for money?'

'No.'

'Why then?'

'I used to work with his brother Stanislav at the aircraft factory in
Moscow. He got into trouble once and I helped him. That's all.'

'Thank you,' she whispered.

She gazed intently out of the small window. Eventually she turned to
him again. 'Mikhail, what about Pyotr?'

'He'll be all right. Zenia is going to take care of him while I'm away.'

'I didn't expect that from Fomenko,' she murmured.

He gave her a long look. *Chyort!* Was that man still in her mind? He
put his head back and shut his eyes. Concentrate on Anna Fedorina, he
told himself, this is your one chance. Concentrate on her.

The *Krokodil* touched down. The surface of the landing field gave them
a bumpy ride but the plane rolled quickly to a stop and they climbed
out. After hours of almost nothing but forests of massed pine trees and
shimmering, silver waterways with an occasional village clinging to the
banks, the squalor of the streets of the northern town of Novgorki came
as a sharp reminder of how easily people could make a place ugly.

It was a purpose-built town dedicated to minerals, with belching
chimney stacks that soared into the grey sky, thickening the air with
chemicals. Yet Mikhail liked it. It was an unpretentious place—he could
sense an undercurrent of wildness as strong as the stink of the sulphur, a
town on the very edge of civilisation. That suited him just fine.

He thanked the pilot of the *Krokodil*, a handshake was enough.

It was evening when they reached the centre of Novgorki, but in July
the days were long and the nights no more than a darker shade of
white. The main road was called Lenin Street, as was usual, and held a
crush of shabby concrete buildings. Rain-filled potholes littered the
road—even at this hour it was busy with trucks and cars making the
most of daylight hours.

'What now?' Sofia was looking round warily.

'A bed and a meal.'

Groups of men stood around on street corners, cigarettes hanging from their lips and bottles in their pockets. Mikhail approached one man with a thick Stalin moustache who directed them to a workers' dormitory, a bleak building where they showed their identity papers and paid a few roubles in advance. They were allotted a couple of camp beds and soiled quilts, in separate communal sleeping areas.

They walked up the main street, aware of eyes watching them.

'More of Stalin's economic boom times,' Sofia muttered under her breath, with an ironic nod towards the empty shop windows.

Even at this hour many of the shops were still open and they chose a prosperous-looking hardware shop for their purpose. It smelled of pine resin and dust inside, where a short man with a broad northern face greeted them from behind the counter.

'Evening,' Mikhail said and let his gaze roam the shop. 'Busy, I see.'

The place was empty of other customers but did at least have a few goods on display. A sack of nails and screws, a box of hinges, some kerosene cans and paint brushes—but no paint, of course. Behind the shopkeeper's head were shelves holding a row of cardboard boxes, unlabelled, and Mikhail suspected they contained the better stuff for the better customers. He picked up a roll of canvas and tossed it onto the counter. Beside him Sofia stood silent.

'Is that all?' the shopkeeper asked, scratching his armpit with relish.

'No.'

'What else?'

'I have something to sell.'

The storeman's eyes brightened and slid to Sofia.

'Not me,' she said fiercely.

The man shrugged. 'It happens sometimes.'

Mikhail placed a fist on the counter between them. 'Who in this town might want to buy an object of value?'

'What kind of object?'

'One that is worth real money, not . . .' he gazed disdainfully round the shop, 'not Novgorki kopecks.'

The man squinted at Mikhail, his tobacco-stained teeth chewing on his lower lip. 'Very well,' he said, pointing to a curtained doorway at the back of the shop. 'You, Comrade, come with me. You,' he pointed at Sofia, 'wait here.'

Before the storekeeper could draw breath Mikhail had leaped over the counter and pinned him against his boxes, a hand crushing his throat. He could feel the man's windpipe fighting for air.

'Don't mistake me, Comrade,' Mikhail hissed in his face. 'I am not one of your peasant fools. I do not walk blindly into your backroom to be ambushed and robbed while my woman is stolen. Understand me?'

'*Da.*' The man's voice was a gasp, his eyes popping in his head.

Mikhail removed his hand and let him breathe.

'Now,' Mikhail said, keeping the man jammed against his shelves, 'tomorrow morning I will return here at eight o'clock for no more than five minutes. If you know a buyer for a jewel worth more than you'll earn in ten lifetimes, bring him here. Got that?'

The man blinked his understanding.

'So you're not just a handsome face after all,' Sofia said.

She was teasing him, but her smile didn't reach her eyes.

'I had to do it, Sofia. It was the only way of showing that man I'm serious. Don't look so reproachful.'

'He might have pulled a gun on you.'

Mikhail patted the loaded pistol hidden under her slender waistband, the one he'd stolen from the officer behind the Gaz truck. 'Then you'd have shot him,' he said and kissed her nose.

She shivered nevertheless. He wrapped an arm around her to keep her warm, as neither of them was dressed for a cool northern evening, but she pulled away.

'Don't,' she said angrily. 'Don't take risks.'

He burst out laughing and felt her fist smack into his chest. He caught it in his hand and pulled her tight to him. 'This is all one huge risk, my sweet love, so what's an extra little one or two along the way?'

'Don't die,' she whispered.

'I intend to live till I'm a hundred, as long as you promise to live to a hundred with me.'

'To darn your socks and cook your meals?' she teased.

'No, my precious, to warm my bed and let me kiss your sweet neck.'

She nestled her lips in the hollow of his throat. 'I'll warm your bed and let you kiss my neck,' she crooned, 'if you darn my socks and cook my meals for a hundred years.'

He laughed. 'Agreed.'

'No, Mikhail, we do this together. We agreed.'

They were standing in the street and heavy rain was lashing down, soaking them to the skin. A stray yellow hound crouched shivering in the gutter, its mournful eyes following their every move.

Mikhail pushed open the door to the hardware store and Sofia positioned herself silently just inside the entrance, leaning against the timber wall where she casually laid one hand on the gun at her waistband. Her eyes followed Mikhail as he approached the stranger who was waiting next to the counter with folded arms. The man was built like a series of boxes balanced on top of each other: square hat, square head, square shoulders, a sharp square suit. His face displayed the broken veins of a drinker and the shrewd eyes of a man in authority. The shopkeeper hovered in the background, as brown and dusty as his boxes.

'So, Comrade, what have you brought for me to see?' the square man said without preliminaries. 'It had better not be shit. No *gavno*.'

Mikhail didn't speak, just took a small piece of green material from his back pocket and opened it on his palm. The man's eyes widened, then narrowed to half shut like a lizard's, because even in the dim light of the hardware shop the diamond on the green cloth winked at him.

For the first time Mikhail spoke. 'It's worth more than you possess.'

'Comrade, there's something you need to learn. A jewel like that is only worth what someone will pay.'

'And . . .' Mikhail gave him a cold smile, 'how quickly they will pay for it.'

The man nodded his square head, took out a handkerchief and blew his veined nose in it. This seemed to be a signal of some kind because another man stepped out from behind the curtain to the backroom, a great bearded ox of a man with a badly scarred face. Instantly Sofia pulled the gun out of her waistband and, clutching it with two hands, pointed it directly at the square stranger. His lizard eyes stared at her for a second, assessing the danger, then he waved a hand dismissively and his henchman lumbered back into his curtained den.

Nothing was said, no mention was made of the short-lived intrusion, but Sofia didn't lower the gun. Mikhail took a slow and deliberate step forward, then spoke in a voice that crowded the dismal room.

'Now that we understand each other . . . *Comrade*,' he made the word sound like something he'd scraped off the bottom of his shoe, 'let's get down to business. My time is short.'

'Of course.' The man's gaze focused on the diamond. 'Let's talk money.'

'No, Comrade. Let's talk horses.'

Sofia waited alone in the rain. Zenia's scarf on her head was soaked, but a few metres of canvas with a hole cut in it for her head was keeping the worst of the downpour off her body. The black earth beneath her feet had turned to a quagmire but she barely noticed the squelch of mud as she prowled soft-footed among the trees, her eyes scanning the road that ran straight as a rifle barrel into Novgorki.

Where was he? He should be here by now. Her head swarmed with fears for Mikhail.

The square man with the smile that stretched too tight had insisted on a one-to-one deal, with no guns and no henchmen. So Mikhail had kissed her, a light touch of lips that she committed to memory, and left the hardware store. Sofia had watched them disappear up the street, the yellow dog trailing behind them, then she had retreated to the spot on the edge of town where Mikhail had told her to meet him.

Hidden from curious eyes, she waited for him. She felt as if she'd been waiting for him all her life.

When he finally emerged through the grey curtain of rain, Sofia wanted to throw herself into his arms and yell at him for putting her through such hell. But instead she stood quietly under a dripping poplar tree and let him come to her. He was riding a big chestnut horse and leading two others, one of which was carrying quite a load on its back, strapped down under a canvas sheet. Mikhail slid to the ground in one easy movement, placed his hands on her shoulders and looked carefully into her face.

'You were a long time,' she said simply.

'I'm sorry. Were you worried?'

'No.'

'Good. You must trust me.'

'I do.'

He smiled, the wide smile he kept just for her, and she wrapped her fist into his sodden shirt in an effort to hold on to that smile.

'I hope one of those horses is for me.'

'Always thinking of taking it easy, aren't you?'

She laughed and the unexpected relief of it doused her fears. 'Did you get a good deal?' she asked and released his shirt.

'Svetlana Dyuzheyeva would turn in her grave if she knew how cheaply her diamond ring had changed hands, but, yes, for us it was a good deal.'

From inside his wet shirt he pulled out a fistful of large rouble notes, lifted the front of her canvas cape and slipped the money into the pocket of her black skirt.

'That'll keep you safe.' He smiled and suddenly took her in his arms, as though frightened of losing her.

They stood like that, Sofia had no idea for how long, heads together.

But when their hearts had finally stilled, they swung up onto the horses and headed off through the forest. Behind them the yellow dog skulked in their tracks.

It was the dog, warning her with its low throaty growl, that raised the hackles on her own neck. They were riding through the forest with just the pattering of rain for company and the soft shuffle of horses' hoofs through the undergrowth. Mikhail was leading the way, Sofia close behind, but her horse had a shorter stride and kept hanging back. They had been weaving their way through the trees for more than an hour when the attack came.

But the dog had warned her, so the gun was ready in her hand.

Two bulky figures leaped out from the trees with a great roar as they launched themselves at Sofia and a rifle shot rang out, ricocheting off the trunks. Her horse screamed a shrill shriek of fear that split the air and the dog snarled, loud and menacing. A man's face appeared next to her horse's head, bellowing threats and insults and crude curses. Sofia raised the gun and shouted a warning. Her attacker yanked hard on the horse's mouth, drawing blood. In terror the animal jinked sideways and reared up, its front hoofs slicing through the rain, its wet head thrashing violently from side to side, tumbling Sofia from its back.

As she fell to the ground, she pulled the trigger.

'Sofia.'

Mikhail's voice was drifting in and out of her head. Sometimes near and sometimes so far away she could barely hear it. She flicked open her eyes. Her head hurt.

'Mikhail,' she murmured.

'My Sofia.' At once his head bent over her and his lips touched her temple. 'Don't move, my love. You've taken a bad knock on the head.'

Slowly things came to her, thought by thought, and she realised she was lying on her side, her head on Mikhail's lap. He was sitting with his back against a pine tree, one hand holding her, the other holding the gun. Above them he'd rigged up a canopy of canvas and under it he'd lit a small fire that hissed when a splash of rain blew into it.

'Help me up,' she said.

He sat her up and held her steady while the world swooped around her. He placed a metal cup of hot tea in her hands and sat quietly while she sipped it.

'Where are they?' she asked at last, leaning against him.

'Over there.' He gestured off to the left. 'They're dead. Both of them.'

'Who were they?'

'His henchmen. Come to retrieve the money and the horses.'

'You're not hurt?'

'A bruise or two, nothing much.'

When she was ready, he helped her stand. She insisted on going over to check on the bodies of their attackers because only seeing them with her own eyes would convince her that she and Mikhail were safe. For now, anyway. Together they threw a few branches over the bodies and left them to the wolves, then they struck camp, mounted their horses and rode on.

They rode the rest of that day and most of the night. At times they walked, allowing the horses a break, ears alert for sounds of pursuit. To navigate, Mikhail used a small hand compass, and most of the time the terrain forced them to travel in single file with the packhorse trailing behind Mikhail's mount. They were too far apart to whisper any conversation, so they slid into silence and into their own thoughts. But just before dawn, when the new morning was nothing more than a blush of gold on the topmost branches of the trees, Mikhail called a halt.

'Is it safe?' she asked.

'We have to sleep, my love, and the horses need rest. We'll do best to hole up here for two or three hours.'

'No longer.'

Her impatience to keep moving was always there. Mikhail walked over to her and slipped an arm around her waist, loving the way her immediate response was to lean the whole length of her body against him. What was it that gave this extraordinary woman such strength? Gently he stroked her hair, but later, when they were stretched out on a blanket under the tall columns of the trees, there was nothing gentle about their lovemaking.

Sofia sat on the riverbank in the early-morning sun, her feet trailing in the strong current, and watched Mikhail splash water over himself. They had travelled relentlessly for ten days and were stealing an hour to bathe before moving on. The yellow dog ambled past her on the grass, brushing its wet pelt against her shoulder, and went to lie nearby.

'What kind of man are you, Mikhail?'

He looked over his shoulder at her, surprised. He smiled at her.

'A fortunate man,' he said at last.

'Really? Is that what you believe?'

'Yes, with all my heart.'

'Mikhail, for heaven's sake, think straight! Here you are in the middle of a forest, with no home, no job, no travel permits, your life in danger every moment. So why say a *fortunate* man?'

He scooped up a double handful of sparkling river and emptied it over his face.

'Fortunate because I have you. You've granted me a second chance.'

'What kind of second chance?'

'A chance to right a wrong.'

'You mean . . . when you killed Anna's father.'

She'd said it. She had finally dragged the words from their hiding place and shaken them loose in the bright golden air.

'Yes. That's exactly what I mean.'

'And Fomenko? What about your killing his mother? Is that a wrong you intend to right as well?'

A pulse ticked in Mikhail's jaw and he smacked his palm on the surface of the water, sending up a rainbow of droplets.

When he spoke, his single word was calm. 'No.'

'Why not?'

'Because he put a knife in my father's throat. Tell me how I forgive that.'

'I see. So when we've done this, will you stop hating yourself?'

'You know me too well, Sofia.'

She laughed and, before she knew it, he was charging at her through the river, sweeping sun-bleached waves in every direction as he rushed at her in a roar. She shrieked with astonishment and leaped to her feet but he was too fast. His hand caught her wrist, and pulled her to him. His body pressed hard against hers, his lips finding her mouth.

Behind her the dog barked, two sharp high-pitched notes.

'Quickly.' She threw herself into the water, dragging Mikhail with her.

'What is it?'

'Danger.'

Together they let the current sweep them rapidly downstream, before striking out for the shore at a spot where a cluster of bushes reached down to the river. They crouched there, listening.

'Our horses,' Sofia grimaced.

'I tethered them for shade where the trees are thickest. If it's a wolf, they'd already be panicking.' Mikhail brushed a strand of wet hair from her face. 'What warned you of danger?'

'It was the dog—'

Suddenly the sound of men's voices reached them and the whinny of thirsty horses sighting water. Upstream, on the same stretch of beach where Sofia and Mikhail had been standing, a patrol of soldiers tumbled out of the forest.

They rode hard the rest of the day. The pine trunks whipped past in slender shadows and the blades of sunlight sliced between them like knives. They had waited in the undergrowth by the river until they were certain the patrol was long gone. The soldiers had missed Mikhail's horses, tucked away deep among the trees, but their clothes lying at the water's edge must have caused some comment. Sofia and Mikhail rode in silence, wary of further patrols.

A thickset old man sat half asleep in the late-afternoon sun, leaning back against the timber wall of his solitary *izba*, a picture of contentment in the middle of nowhere. He wore patched trousers and a threadbare shirt, a twist of smoke rising from the carved pipe in his mouth, keeping the mosquitoes at bay.

Mikhail greeted him pleasantly. '*Zdravstvuitye*, Comrade.'

'What can I do for you, Comrade?'

'My saddle girth has snapped and I need—'

'In there.' The old man jerked a thumb at the barn beside the house, which was well built but slowly turning green with moss. 'You'll find plenty of tack hanging on the hooks. I've not much use for it now. Old Ivan is all I've got left to pull a plough.' He scratched his beard. 'Who's she?' He smiled a welcome at Sofia.

'My wife.'

The man blew out an appreciative billow of fragrant smoke. 'She can talk to me while you fix your girth. I don't get much conversation these days, not since my Yulia died.'

Mikhail took the reins from Sofia's hand and headed for the barn.

'What would you like to talk about?' Sofia smiled and sat down on the bench beside him, stretching her legs out. The word 'wife' had taken her by surprise and to her ears it sounded good. Several scrawny chickens paused in their dustbaths to bob their heads at the intruders.

'Do you know Moscow?' the old man asked.

'I've never been there, I'm afraid,' she said.

'Is it true Stalin dynamited the sacred Cathedral of Christ the Redeemer and is planning to build a Palace of the Soviets in its place?'

'So I believe. You're well informed.'

'*Da*. I read *Pravda*. My son comes to see me every three months and brings me all the newspapers I need.' He nodded his head proudly and chewed at his tobacco-stained moustache. 'He's a good son to me.'

They talked further, about bread rationing, the high prices in shops, the increase in educational places for girls and Kirov's plans for Leningrad. None of it could touch the old man out here in the wilderness, yet he was passionate about seeing the rebirth of Russia. Alongside a steady flow of chatter, he provided a welcome meal of chicken, boiled potatoes, salted cabbage and cucumber with *smetana*, and in return Mikhail took an hour to split logs while Sofia stacked them up against the wall. It was almost like normal living again. Even the dog lay in a patch of shade and snored contentedly, its stomach sated with some chicken scraps.

'Time for us to leave,' Mikhail finally announced. 'Thank you for your hospitality. *Spasibo*.'

'I've enjoyed the company.' He smiled at Sofia and patted her hand, pulling a face at the scars on her two fingers. 'Been in the wars, have you, girl?'

'Something like that.'

'You should take better care of your wife in future, young man.'

Mikhail gave Sofia a pointed look. 'She's not the easiest of women to take care of.'

Their gaze met and Sofia suddenly saw, for the first time, his fear for her. A rush of longing hit her. She wanted to rid this man she loved of those dark, tense shadows, to make him as content and relaxed as the dog in the dust.

'When this is over,' she promised, and tipped him a crooked smile.

He nodded and returned the smile. It was only a moment but it was one she would keep safe.

She thanked the old man and Mikhail started to lead the horses forward, reins loose in his fingers. That was when she slid her hand into her pocket to tuck a couple of biscuits in there, provided by their host for the journey. One of her fingers brushed against the white stone where it lay, warm from the heat of her body, and she felt something change. Startled, she looked around her, expecting to see something different, but still the silver birch branches shimmered gently in the breeze. The *izba* looked as peaceful as ever, its windows blinking in the sun.

But something had definitely changed. She didn't know what, but she could sense it. Then, slowly, like the echo of distant thunder, in the soles of her feet she felt the vibration of horses' hoofs.

'Mikhail!' she called. 'They're here.'

'Who?'

'The soldiers.'

They prepared quickly, dismantled their packs and turned the horses into a field down by the river. Mikhail would be splitting logs in the front yard and the old man was to remain seated on his bench outside the house, this time with a wooden chess set at his side. Sofia was banished with a hoe to the vegetable patch at the other side of the barn.

'Sofia, take no chances, do nothing . . . foolish. Promise me.' Mikhail took her face between his hands. 'Promise me,' he said again.

'We're a happy peasant family just going about our chores.' She smiled at him and touched her hand to his chest, but he didn't smile back. His eyes were serious.

'I promise,' she said.

But he knew her too well.

The rattle of rifle bolts surrounded the house. Sofia felt the hairs rise on her neck.

'Who's in charge here?'

The demand came from the soldier at the head of the troop: a lean figure with dark hair swept off his face and quick, intelligent eyes. Around him the men fanned out.

'This is my home,' Mikhail said, polite but unwelcoming. He hung the axe from one hand and stood with legs wide and a thumb tucked into his belt.

'And who are you?'

'Mikhail Pashin.'

'The others?'

'My father-in-law and my wife.'

From where she stood beside the barn Sofia held her breath.

A brush of fur on her leg made her look down. The yellow hound was pushing its shoulder against her knee, a faint whine in its throat. What was the matter with it?

'Look what I've found.'

The words came from one of the soldiers, a short, well-built man with a neck almost too thick for his shirt collar. He was leading the three horses into the yard and grinning broadly.

'They were down by the river and there's another old wheezer in the barn, but he's not worth bothering with.'

'Four horses,' the officer said sourly. 'That makes you a rich *kulak*.'

Sofia's throat closed.

Mikhail laughed. 'No, Comrade.' He waved a hand around the primitive home and barn. 'Do I look like one of the wealthy bourgeoisie?'

Sofia's fingers found the white pebble and drew it from her pocket.

In her head she pictured the officer's thoughts as grains of sand, then she left the barn and the hoe, and stepped forward. Immediately came the metallic ring of the axe as Mikhail barked it against a log in warning, but still she fixed her eyes on the officer.

'Comrade, my husband is no *kulak*.'

'We shoot *kulaks*.'

'So there is no reason to shoot my husband.'

She kept moving closer till she was only two paces from the officer, where he was leaning forward in the saddle. Tightening her grip on the pebble, she took a breath, reached out her hand and touched his boot in the stirrup. She shifted the sand.

'No reason at all, is there?' she asked in a soft, persuasive voice.

His eyelids quivered, thick and greasy, then settled. 'No,' he muttered. 'But the horses will come in useful.'

'Not this one.' Sofia entwined her hand in their grey's thick mane. *Without a horse, Anna cannot travel.*

'Get your hand off it.'

'No.'

The soldier leading the horses raised his rifle. 'You heard. Let go.'

From nowhere a fist slammed into the side of Sofia's face, sending her sprawling to the ground.

'How many times have I told you to do as you're told?'

It was Mikhail's voice. He was standing over her, silhouetted against the pale sky. For a moment she couldn't believe Mikhail had hit her and she stared up at him in dismay, but his eyes remained harsh.

'Mikhail . . .' she whispered.

'Get in the house.'

She gave a moan and a soft warm tongue licked her cheek. She shivered, struggled to her knees and onto her feet, her head stinging. As she touched the dog's coat, she had an odd sense of Rafik being at her side. She thought she heard his voice whispering in the clearing.

'Don't die for nothing, Sofia. You are needed.'

She hesitated.

You are needed.

The grey horse was moving away, its tail twitching.

Needed.

The word pounded in her mind.

Anna needs me. Anna needs the horse.

She reached out and seized the tail. The horse reared, the metal edge of its front hoof clipping the soldier's shoulder. He cursed fiercely. Without hesitation the officer aimed his rifle straight at Sofia and fired.

11

Davinsky Camp
August 1933

THE WORKDAY WAS FINALLY OVER. The grate of saw and the bite of axes ceased, backs were flexed and muscles coaxed back into life as daylight trickled away behind the trees. It was at that time of day that the forest began to change, its black depths wreathed in mist and edging closer, its earthy breath more rank and menacing. Prisoners averted their eyes and guards didn't turn their backs on it—it made them nervous. That was when the rifle shots shattered the silence of the Work Zone and two guards dropped dead among the wood chippings.

The crack of another shot rang out, then three more in quick succession. Another uniformed body crumpled and a brigade of women prisoners started to scream. Panic flared. No one knew where the shots were coming from and people started to flee for cover in all directions. Guards fired wildly into the trees but four more grew scarlet flowers on their chests. Voices shrieked orders, heads ducked, arms flailed.

Anna stood and stared into the forest. Using all her strength she started to shuffle towards it.

'You!' Anna took no notice and pushed herself through the trees.

'You!' The voice came again. 'Stop!'

Only death would make her stop. All around her prisoners were taking advantage of the chaos and seizing their chance at freedom, their skeletal figures flitting into the forest like fleeing ghosts into the grey mist that enveloped it. She caught sight of Nina and Tasha disappearing far ahead of her and she envied them their speed.

Suddenly, a hand yanked her almost off her feet and she lashed out, but her blows were weak. Her captor was a guard, his face a mixture of fury and terror, his mouth working in an effort at control. Without hesitation Anna pointed a finger at the sinister depths of the forest and screamed.

'He's there!'

That's all it took, one brief second. The guard turned his head and she swung the hand axe that was still in her grasp. The flat of the blade connected with his skull. His fingers slid from her arm and she hurried on into the mist.

Anna had no idea how he found her when there were so many fleeing women in rags. So little visibility among the trees and so much panic. She could barely breathe and in her haste she had stumbled and fallen. She was forcing herself to stand when he called her name.

'Anna Fedorina?'

She peered through the dank curtain of mist and a tall man in dark clothes rose out of it. His long-fingered hand was extended towards her and she saw a white stone balanced on its palm. It was Death drawing her into its embrace.

'Anna Fedorina? I've been shouting for you. Someone told me you were back here.'

'Yes. I'm Anna Fedorina.'

'Come with me.'

'No.'

'Sofia sent me.'

Anna started to shake. '*Sofia!*' she shouted.

She looked frantically among the shadowy trunks. Was Sofia dead? Had she sent Death's Messenger to fetch her too?

'*Come quickly,*' Death's Messenger whispered in her ear.

Without knowing how, she found herself on his broad back being transported at speed through the shadows. She rested her head on the Messenger's damp head and it occurred to her how like a human's was the hair of an angel.

Sofia was waiting for her. She was so beautiful. Anna didn't remember her being so bewitchingly beautiful. She was propped up against a small grey horse, a pistol in her hand to defend the animal against all would-be thieves and on her face a look of grim determination.

Anna felt a fierce eruption of joy flood through her body at the realisation that Sofia wasn't dead.

Thank God, she isn't dead.

Sofia opened her arms and Anna fell into them.

Neither spoke.

The two women clung together. Inhaling each other's breath and letting their hearts hammer against each other's. Dimly Anna was aware of voices shouting in the distance but she took no notice, just held Sofia tight and felt tears hot on her skin.

'You're free now,' Sofia whispered.

The familiar sound of her voice gave Anna a sudden surge of strength that cleared her mind. She lifted her head and, without releasing her hold on Sofia, asked desperately, 'Where's Vasily?'

Death's Messenger was called Mikhail. Even so, Anna would always think of him as Death's Messenger in her own mind because he'd killed her father. Mikhail confessed that fact to her himself at their first stop for rest in the forest, and she wanted to tear out his heart there and then. To slice it into forty-one ragged pieces, one for each year of Papa's life, but she couldn't. It was clear he'd given that heart to Sofia and Anna would steal nothing from her friend.

'Thank you for rescuing me, Mikhail,' she said with cool politeness. 'The debt is repaid. A life for a life.'

But she was glad to see the Messenger's grey eyes remain tormented, and pleased that he felt the need to ask, 'How many guards were killed back there?'

'A handful compared to the number of prisoners you released.'

'Still too many.'

'No, Anna's right,' Sofia said, brushing her hand against his in a gesture of comfort. 'You've given those women a chance at life.'

'If they make it to freedom.'

'Some will, some won't. We will.'

Mikhail nodded stiffly. He lifted both women on to the grey horse's back once more and set off with a long loping stride.

'What does Vasily look like?'

They were lying on a blanket together, but Anna couldn't sleep. Her thoughts wouldn't stop. The moon was a giant disc in the sky, bigger than any moon she'd ever seen in the camp, the night breeze was full of secrets instead of stale and fetid, and the fresh smell of forest creatures made her giddy. It swamped her senses. She muffled her cough in her scarf and kept her eyes wide open. To miss even a single minute of her freedom would be a sin. They had travelled all night and hidden unseen among the trees by day under a green canopy of branches. They heard tracker dogs in the distance but none came near.

'Is he still as I described to you?' Anna asked.

'He's tall,' Sofia said gently. 'He stands very upright and swings his shoulders when he walks as if he knows exactly where he's going. You feel he's in control. Not just of the *kolkhoz* but of himself.'

'Is he still handsome?'

'Yes, he's still handsome.'

'Tell me more.'

'Well.' Sofia smiled and Anna could hear her picking her words carefully as she gazed up at the stars. 'His eyes are the kind of grey that changes shade with his mood and they are always observant. He's

watching and thinking all the time. He can be quite unnerving sometimes. But he gleams, Anna.'

'Gleams?'

'With belief. His certainty of the future he's building gleams like
gold.'

'Tell me again what he said.'

'Oh, Anna.'

'Tell me.'

'Why? It only hurts.'

'I want to hear it again, what he said.'

'He said Vasily is dead and gone . . . We must put aside personal loyalties . . . This is the way forward, the only way forward.'

Anna closed her eyes. 'He's right. You know he is.'

'There's something else,' Sofia said. 'Something I kept to myself
because I didn't want it to hurt you by raising your hopes.'

'Tell me.'

'Vasily keeps a lock of your hair under his pillow.'

Anna's breath stopped. She coughed, wiped blood from her mouth
with her sleeve and felt something roar into life inside her.

'**A**nna.' Mikhail spoke in a low voice so as not to wake Sofia. 'She is not
as strong as she pretends.'

'You mean the wound in her stomach.'

'Yes.'

'She won't tell me how it happened.'

Mikhail sighed. 'It was a group of soldiers. They were taking our
horses and she . . . tried to stop them.'

A soft rain was falling, muffling their voices as it pattered on the
canvas stretched over their heads. Anna was sitting upright in her effort
to breathe quietly beside Sofia, who was fretful and restless in her
dreams. Mikhail stroked her shoulder, a gentle touch so tender that it
made Anna want to cry.

'Sofia mentioned a dog,' she prompted.

Mikhail nodded. 'Yes, there was one, an unwanted stray that she
adopted and fed. It was extraordinary. When the shot was fired, it
leaped in front of her and died from the bullet.'

'Maybe it just jumped up with excitement.'

'Maybe.'

'But she was hit in the stomach anyway.'

'Yes, but only a shallow wound. The bullet went through the dog
first and then into her. An old man we were with at the time—the one

who let us take one of his rifles—removed it and stitched her up. He said she was very lucky because at that range the bullet should have ripped holes through her vital organs but . . .' He brushed the tangle of pale hair off Sofia's sleeping face and the lines of his mouth softened.

'But what?'

'But I don't believe it was luck.'

'So what was it?'

'Something more than luck.'

For a while they were silent, watching the rain, then Anna whispered, 'Mikhail, where are we going?'

A shadow crossed his features. 'To Tivil, because I have a son there. Sofia and I have it all planned . . . we'll collect him and after that we'll use the remaining jewels to buy tickets for all four of us, as well as travel documents and new identities. And medicines for you. We'll go somewhere safe and start a whole new life down by the Black Sea, where it's warm and your lungs can heal.'

'Will we make it, Mikhail? To Tivil?'

'The truth is . . .' he paused and leaned closer, 'it's unlikely, Anna. But don't tell that to Sofia. She is so determined to make it and I'll do everything in my power to get us there, I swear, but we're fugitives. Our chances are . . .' He didn't finish.

'Poor?'

'I have only four shells left for the rifle.'

'And the pistol?'

'Two bullets.' Something seemed to loosen inside him and he shuddered. 'I'm saving them.' He looked at Anna and then at Sofia, and it was obvious what he meant. 'Just in case,' he murmured, lowering his head to kiss Sofia's hair.

Nights merged. Anna could no longer separate them from days, as darkness settled in her mind and refused to lift. She could feel her body shutting down and she fought it every breath of the way.

'She can't travel any further, Sofia. It's killing her.'

'Mikhail, my love, we can't stop. It's too dangerous.'

'Dangerous to stop and dangerous to go on. You choose.'

Sofia's voice dropped to a fierce whisper, but Anna heard the words as she lay strapped to the horse's back.

'She's dying, Mikhail. I swear on my love for you that I won't let her go without seeing him one last time.'

The horse walked on and each step jarred Anna's lungs, but she didn't care. She was going to see Vasily. Sofia had sworn.

12

Tivil
January 1934

'A HORSE IS COMING.'

Pyotr stamped his *valenki* in the snow. 'I can't see any horses,' he complained, screwing up his eyes to peer into the white fog.

'They're coming,' Rafik repeated.

'Is it Papa?'

Rafik frowned, his black eyebrows twitching under his *shapka*. 'It's him—and he's not alone.'

'How do you know, Rafik?' Pyotr asked.

But Rafik didn't answer. He and Zenia were standing with hands linked, muttering strange words that made no sense to Pyotr.

Pyotr was the first to hear the whinny of the horse. He straightened up and stared into the shifting banks of fog where the road should be. It was like floating into another world, unfamiliar and unpredictable.

'Pyotr.'

The word drifted, swirling and swaying towards him through the air.

'Papa!' Pyotr yelled, 'Papa!'

Out of the wall of white loomed a tall figure in a filthy coat. At his side hobbled a small grey horse.

Pyotr flew into the outstretched arms, burrowed his face into the icy jacket and listened to his father's heart. It was real. Beating fast. The cloth of the jacket smelled strange and the beard on his face felt prickly, but it was his papa. The big strong familiar hands gripped him hard; held him so close Pyotr couldn't speak.

'What's going on here?' his father demanded over his head.

'We've been expecting you,' the Gypsy responded.

Mikhail disentangled himself from his son and held out a hand to Rafik. The Gypsy grasped it with a fervour that took Pyotr by surprise.

'Thank you, Mikhail,' Rafik murmured. Not even the chill moan of the wind could conceal the joy in his voice.

Then for the first time Pyotr noticed the person behind his father.

'Sofia!' he gasped.

'Hello, Pyotr.' She smiled at him. Her face was painfully thin. 'You look well,' she said.

In her voice he could hear no trace of anger at what he'd done, just a warmth that defied the cold around them.

His father ruffled Pyotr's hair under the fur hat, but his look was serious. 'Pyotr, we've brought Sofia's friend back with us.'

He gestured at a dark shape lying on the horse. It was strapped on the animal's back, skin as grey as the horse's coat, but the figure moved and struggled to sit up. At once Pyotr saw it was a young woman.

'We have to get her out of the cold,' his father said quickly.

Sofia moved close to the horse's side. 'Hold on, Anna, just a few minutes more. We're here now, here in Tivil, and soon you'll be . . .'

The young woman's eyes were glazed and Pyotr wasn't sure she was even hearing Sofia's words. She attempted to nod but failed, and slumped forward once more on the horse's neck. Sofia draped an arm around her thin shoulders.

'Quickly, *bistro*.'

Rafik and Zenia led the way, heads ducked against the swirling snowflakes that stung their eyes. Pyotr and Mikhail started to follow as fast as they could, with Mikhail leading the little grey mare. Sofia walked at its side, holding the sick young woman on its back.

Pyotr could hear his father's laboured breathing, so he seized the reins from his hand and tucked himself under Papa's arm, bearing some of his weight. The horse dragged at every forward pace and Pyotr was suddenly frightened for it. *Please, don't let it collapse right here in the snow.*

The sky was darkening. Pyotr could sense the village huddle deep in its valley, shutting out the world beyond. Something stirred inside him, something strong and possessive, and he tightened his grip on his father. The snow underfoot was loose and slippery but, instead of stopping at his own house, the little procession continued right past it.

'Where are we going, Papa?'

His father didn't speak, not until they stood outside the *izba* that belonged to the Chairman.

'Aleksei Fomenko!' Mikhail bellowed against the wind. He didn't bother knocking on the black door. 'Aleksei Fomenko! Get out here!'

The door slammed open and the tall figure of the Chairman strode out into the snow, dressed in no more than his shirtsleeves, the wolfhound a shadow behind him.

'Comrade Pashin, so you've decided to return. I didn't expect . . .'

His eyes skimmed over Mikhail and Pyotr, past the Gypsies, and came to an abrupt halt on Sofia. His jaw seemed to jerk as if he'd been hit. Then his gaze shifted to the wretched horse. No one spoke.

Fomenko was the first to move. He ran over to the horse and, working fast but with great care, he untied the straps.

'Anna?' he whispered.

She raised her head. For a moment her eyes were blank and glazed, but snowflakes settled on her lashes, forcing her to blink.

'Anna,' he said again.

Gradually life trickled back into her eyes. She pushed herself to sit up and stared at the man by her side.

'Vasily, are you real?'

He took her mittened hand in his and pressed it to his cold cheek. 'I'm real enough, as real as the sleigh I built for you and as real as the songs you sang for me. I still hear them when the wind blows through the valley.'

'Vasily,' she sobbed.

She struggled to climb off the horse but Fomenko lifted her from the saddle as gently as if he were handling a kitten, cradling her in his arms. Her head lay on his chest and he kissed her dull, lifeless hair. He turned to face Sofia and Mikhail.

'I'll care for her,' he said. 'I'll buy the best medicines and make her well again.'

'Why?' Sofia asked. 'Why now and not before?'

Fomenko looked down at the pale woman in his arms and his whole face softened. He spoke so quietly that the wind almost snatched his words away. 'Because she's here.'

Fomenko turned away from the watching group. At a steady pace so as not to jar her fragile bones, the dog walking ahead of him over the snow, he carried Anna into his house in Tivil.

The air was warm. That was the first thing Anna absorbed. Her bones had lost the agonising ache that had pulled at them for so long and seemed to be melting from inside, they felt so soft and heavy. She opened her eyes.

She'd forgotten what it was like to feel like this, so comfortable, so cosseted, a downy pillow under her head, a clean-smelling sheet pulled up to her neck. No brittle ice like jagged glass in her lungs. She tried breathing, a swift swallow of the warm air.

Bearable.

Her gaze explored the room, sliding with slow consideration over the curtains, the chair, the carpet, the shirts hanging on hooks, all full of colour. Colour. She hadn't realised how much she'd missed it. In the camp everything had been grey. A small sigh of pleasure escaped her, a faint sound, but it was enough. Instantly a whining started up outside the bedroom door and brought her back to reality.

Whose house was she in? Mikhail's? Or . . . No. She shook her head. No, it wasn't Mikhail's. Only dimly did she recall being carried in a pair of strong arms, but she knew exactly whose bed she was lying in and whose dog was whining at the door.

The latch lifted quietly. Anna's heart stopped as her eyes sought out the figure standing in the shadows. He was tall, holding himself stiffly, and in a flash of anxiety she wondered whether the stiffness was in his mind or his body. His shirt fitted close across his wide chest, and his hair was cropped hard to his head.

Vasily. It was Vasily, with the Dyuzheyev forehead, the long aristocratic nose—and the eyes, she remembered those grey swirling eyes. But the once generous mouth was now held tight in a firm line. At his heel stood a large rough-coated wolfhound; Anna recalled Sofia telling her its name.

'Hope,' she breathed. It was easier than saying *Vasily*.

The dog loped towards her, its claws clipping the wooden floor, and nuzzled her hand. The simple display of affection seemed to persuade Vasily at last to walk into the room, but there was something deliberately formal in his step and he came no nearer than the end of the bed.

He spoke first. 'How are you feeling?'

His voice was deeper than it used to be, but she could still hear the young Vasily in it. A shiver of pleasure shot through her.

'I'm fine.'

'Are you cold? Do you need another quilt?'

'No. I'm warm, thank you.'

Another awkward silence.

'Are you hungry?'

She smiled. 'Ravenous.'

He nodded and, though he didn't move away, his eyes did. They looked at the dog's shaggy head now resting on the quilt, at the window and snowflakes sweeping across the yard outside. Anywhere but at her.

'You look well, Vasily,' she said softly.

He studied his own strong hands, but didn't comment.

This time she let the silence hang. She didn't know what was happening and her mind felt too weak to struggle with it. Was he angry at her for coming here? For risking his position as Chairman of the *kolkhoz*? Who could blame him? She didn't want him to be angry, of course she didn't, but at the same time, in some strange way, it didn't matter if he was. *This* was what mattered. *Being here*. Seeing the way his grey eyes had sparked as he stepped into the room.

She studied the long, lean lines of his body, the familiar set of his head on the broad shoulders. The only thing she missed was his hair, the way it used to fall in a soft brown tumble across his high forehead and make him look . . . what? She smiled. Look lovable. These shorn hard spikes of hair belonged to a different Vasily.

He saw the smile. Even though he wasn't looking at her, still he was aware of the smile and she saw him move closer. She felt choked by the wave of love that engulfed her. So much was unsaid. And she felt no need to say it. Just looking at him was enough.

Abruptly, when she least expected it, he turned and disappeared from the room. She had no idea whether he was gone five minutes or five hours, but when she opened her eyes again he was sitting in a chair beside her bed.

'Here, time to eat.' In his hands lay a bowl of soup.

She tried to sit up and failed, so struggled instead to lift her head higher on the pillow. She was shocked to find herself so weak. Even that little movement of her head set off more coughing, and when she'd finished gasping for breath he wiped a damp cloth across her lips, studied the red smear on it with a frown and put the cloth aside.

He lifted a spoon from the bowl and raised it to her lips. Willingly she parted them and felt the thick aromatic liquid flow down into her starved stomach.

'It's wonderful,' she murmured.

'Only a few mouthfuls now. More later.'

'But I'm—'

'No. Your body can't take much yet, Anna.'

Anna. It was the first time he'd spoken her name. She badly wanted him to say it again.

'Thank you . . . Vasily.'

'My name is no longer Vasily. I am called Aleksei Fomenko now. It's important that you call me that. I'm putting it about in the village that you are . . .'

But he stopped, unable to finish. His eyes were fixed on her face and she could see a thousand thoughts and questions racing through their grey depths, but none that she could decipher. She was acutely conscious of what she must look like to him, a skeletal jumble of bones in a nightdress, her skin as lifeless as ash and weeping sores on . . .

Nightdress?

Who took her out of her filthy rags? Who clothed her in this pure white nightgown? Instantly she was sure it was Vasily himself. He'd undressed her and bathed her and seen the sickening state of her, and the thought surfaced with a hot surge of shame. He seemed to read her thoughts and put down the bowl, reached out a hand and rested the tips of his fingers on her bare throat.

'Anna,' he said in a low voice, 'I can feel your heart racing. You . . .' His breath caught. For a long moment there was only the wind rattling the window pane and Vasily's finger brushing her throat. 'You are even more beautiful than I remembered.'

'Vasily!'

As his name burst out of her mouth she saw something break inside him. And suddenly his arms were around her and he was sitting on the bed holding her to his chest, rocking her, crushing her tight against his own body, as though he could press her deep in his bones.

'Anna,' he whispered over and over, 'Anna, my Anna.' He kissed her hot forehead and caressed her filthy lank hair. 'Forgive me.'

'For what?'

'For not coming.'

She brushed the line of his jaw with her lips. 'You're here now.'

'I made a promise,' Vasily explained.

'To whom?'

'To Lenin.' He shook his head. 'To the bronze statue of him in Leningrad. After I came back from the Civil War'—a tremor shook his voice—'and couldn't find you—though I scoured the city endlessly for news of you—I swore I would become the perfect Soviet citizen, dedicating my life to Lenin's ideals, if—'

She lifted a finger to his lips. 'Hush, Vasily, there's no need to explain.'

'Yes, there is. I want you to understand. I dedicated my life to Communism, in return for Lenin's spirit keeping you safe.'

Anna gasped.

'I kept my word,' he murmured into her hair, 'all these years. When I did help people escape from the authorities, it was because they were the intellectual building blocks who would be needed to strengthen Russia.' He drew in a deep breath and repeated fiercely, 'I kept my word.'

'Even when Sofia came and begged.'

'Yes, even then.'

'To make sure my heart kept beating?'

'Yes.'

'Oh, Vasily.'

They clung to each other, motionless, his arms cradling her. Neither spoke for a long while.

Anna slept. She had no sense of time. Just moments that sl
one into her feverish mind. At intervals she woke and Vas
always there, feeding her spoonfuls of soup and finely sm
meat, or dosing her with foul-tasting medicines. He talked to her b,
hour and she listened.

'Wake up.'

Anna had dozed off again into a world of nightmares, but opened her eyes swiftly the instant she heard Sofia's voice.

'Wake up,' Sofia said again. 'Every time I come to see you, you're asleep.' She was perched on the side of the bed, wearing a wool dress the colour of dark lavender, and there was a smile on her face.

'I can't believe how much better you look already,' Sofia announced. 'And you've only been here a week. How's the coughing?'

Anna pulled a face. 'Give me time. I know you planned for us to move somewhere safer but . . .'

Sofia took her friend's hand in hers and gently chafed it. 'You have all the time in the world now.'

'Thanks to you.'

'And to Mikhail. I couldn't have done it without him.'

'Yes. And to your Mikhail. Thank you both.'

Their eyes met, two different blues, and something passed between them; a knowledge of what Sofia had done but also an agreement never to talk of it again. Words were too small to voice what lay deep inside them both.

Instead Anna asked, 'Has Mikhail spoken to Vas—, I mean Aleksei, about the killings . . . that day at the Dyuzheyevs' villa?'

'Yes. They'll never be friends. But now they're prepared not to be enemies. It's a first step.'

'That's wonderful.'

Sofia nodded and smiled. 'Give me a hug, you skinny lazybones.'

Anna struggled to sit up and immediately a spasm of coughing racked her chest. Sofia held her close until the shuddering subsided, and Anna could smell the clean soapy fragrance of her blonde hair. When the spasm was finally over she insisted on sitting up.

'Wash my hair, Sofia.'

'It'll exhaust you.'

'Please, Sofia. For me.'

'For him, you mean,' Sofia said with a ripple of laughter that set her eyes alight.

'Yes,' Anna whispered as she entwined her arms around the young woman on her bed. 'For Vasily.'

Sofia was in the icy back yard of Mikhail's *izba* when Priest Logvinov arrived. It was just as she was collecting logs from the woodpile that he appeared round the corner of the cottage and called her name.

'Sofia.'

She'd always known this day would come. That this man would somehow be involved in the disaster that she could sense breathing, snarling, circling round the village of Tivil.

She dropped the logs to the ground and turned to face him.

'What is it, Priest?'

He was draped in a threadbare coat that reached down to his ankles and a black *shapka* with ear flaps, his green eyes flashing like summer lightning. He was breathless. He'd been running.

'They're coming!' he gasped.

'Who? Who are *they*?'

'Ask Rafik.'

'Where is he?'

The priest waved a long scarecrow arm. 'Out there.'

'Show me.'

She ran into the house and pulled on her coat. 'Mikhail,' she called urgently, 'someone is coming. Rafik is waiting outside.'

Mikhail lifted his head from the intricate work of rebuilding the model bridge, his calm gaze immediately steadying her. One look at her face and he rose to his feet, two strides and his arms were around her.

'You don't have to go, Sofia.'

'I do.'

'You have a choice.'

She nodded. 'Yes. We could leave. You and I, with Pyotr. Right now. We could grab a few things and escape into the forest and head south like we planned and—'

'Is that what you want, my love? Is that what you came back for?'

Their eyes held, then she leaned against him, her whole body moulding itself easily into his, her forehead resting on his cheekbone, and she felt the fear drain away.

'Hurry, Sofia.' It was the priest's voice outside.

She tilted her head back to look up into Mikhail's face. 'Will you come?' she asked.

'You don't have to ask.'

He kissed her, hard and protective.

'We'll do this together,' she whispered.

A figure in a fur coat appeared at her side.

'And me.' It was Pyotr.

'**M**ore horses are coming,' Rafik's black eyes closed as he searched for them inside his mind. 'Four of them.'

The group was gathered on the packed snow. Above them spread the large cedar tree. Fingers of white fog wreathed its branches and crept down to the eight figures beneath it, brushing their chill cheeks and soaking their hair. By the time Priest Logvinov led Sofia and Mikhail, with Pyotr determinedly rushing ahead of them, to where Rafik and his daughter were staring out into the shapeless distance, the sky had slid down from the ridge and closed in around them. The fog had claimed the valley for itself.

Sofia was surprised to find Elizaveta Lishnikova and the black-smith standing shoulder to shoulder beside the Gypsies. Their silent presence here meant only one thing: Rafik was going to need help. Sofia slipped her hand into her pocket and let her fingers fret at the white stone. The priest raised his arm in the freezing air and painted the sign of the cross.

'Four horsemen,' he announced. 'You understand what that means? May God have mercy on our souls.'

'What does it mean, Sofia?' Pyotr asked impatiently. 'What does it mean? Who are the four horsemen?'

'They're soldiers,' Rafik said.

'Why are soldiers coming to Tivil?' Pyotr asked.

Instead of replying, Rafik fixed his gaze on Zenia and he asked her softly, 'Is it you who brings them here?'

'No, Rafik!' she cried out. 'I didn't, I swear I didn't.' Her black eyes glittered and her hands stretched out to her father.

Gently he enfolded them in his.

'I always knew it would happen.' The sorrow in Rafik's quiet voice melted the air around him. 'I knew that betrayal would come, but . . .' his lips smiled at her tenderly and he raised her hands to them, 'but I could not see it would be you, my daughter. My love for you stood in the way of my Sight.'

'Rafik, no. *No*.'

He pressed his lips to her cold forehead just as the jangle of horses' bridles and the creak of stiff leather came upon them.

'Rafik, forgive me. I meant no harm.' Zenia clung to him. 'A careless word to Vanya, that's all it was, I didn't mean it. You know how I love you. I even torched the barn last summer to distract the troops from ransacking Tivil and causing you pain. Please forgive me, I—'

'Hush, my beloved daughter. There's nothing to forgive.' He opened his arms to her.

Four shapes emerged from the white confusion of the fog. Men on horseback, bulky in their greatcoats and high leather boots, determined men who knew their own power. They were OGPU. The officer in the lead was scanning the group standing in the snow with a hard, arrogant scrutiny, his collar turned up against the cold and a calming hand laid on the neck of his pale-coated horse.

'Do you know the man named Rafik Ilyan?' the officer demanded.

'I am Rafik Ilyan.'

The other three horsemen dismounted. Sofia saw the teacher immediately link hands with the blacksmith and with the priest. Zenia joined them and they stood facing outward in a circle around Rafik.

'We are here to arrest you, Rafik Ilyan.'

'Comrade,' Elizaveta spoke calmly, 'I think there has been some mistake. Rafik Ilyan is a loyal member of our village.'

'No mistake.'

'Why is he under arrest?' Pokrovsky demanded.

'My father has done nothing wrong.' Tears were running down Zenia's cheeks.

The priest glared at the intruders, his lips moving in silent prayer.

The officer nodded at his men. 'Arrest the Gypsy, then search his house.'

They came for him, and it was Zenia who broke the circle first. She threw herself towards the officer, clung to his horse's bridle and begged.

'Please don't. This is all wrong, a mistake. I didn't mean to tell Vanya anything—'

The horse tossed its head viciously, sending Zenia flying onto the trampled snow. Sofia ran to her, crouched down and put an arm around her shoulders, despite the sharp hoofs dancing close.

'This isn't right,' she accused.

'Not right?' The officer chuckled, his expression so amiable she thought for a moment he was agreeing with her, but the chuckle ceased abruptly. 'We have information that Rafik Ilyan has been conducting anti-Soviet activities. Arrest him.'

'That's nonsense,' Sofia said sharply. But she turned in a swift movement away from the officer, closing the gap between herself and the Gypsy. Her eyes pleaded with him.

'Rafik, help yourself,' she murmured.

He shook his head. 'I have no power to help myself, Child of the Stone. I can only help others.'

Sofia reached quickly into her coat and drew out the white stone.

'Help me to help you,' she begged.

His eyes locked on the pebble. Its milky surface seemed to pull at him so that he stumbled towards it, but suddenly the uniforms surrounded him. With a bellow of rage the big blacksmith charged forward, Zenia at his side.

'If you take one more step, it will be your last.' The officer's voice rang out through the bleak landscape.

Rafik shook his head. He laid a gentle hand on each of his companions in turn; on Pokrovsky's barrel chest, on Elizaveta Lishnikova's proud shoulder, on Zenia's pale damp cheek. He caught hold of the priest's hand for a moment, staring deep into his eyes. 'You are ready now,' he said, and then released him in a mute farewell. When finally he stepped away from them, the three uniforms moved with him.

'Comrade,' he called to the officer, 'leave my friends in peace. I am the one you—'

Before he'd finished speaking Sofia stepped forward, her hands on the wrists of two of the OGPU men. She was pressing their flesh and murmuring to them. Time hung lifeless in the white fog. The metallic click of a rifle bolt sounded loud in the silence.

'Get away from her. Come over here.' The officer was gazing fixedly at Sofia but he was speaking to Rafik.

'Sofia, don't.' It was Mikhail. 'I love you, Sofia.' His voice was urgent. 'Don't risk it all. You are needed.'

The two men were standing slumped, their jaws slack, their spines soft. Rafik was smiling strangely at Sofia.

'Mikhail is right,' he said. 'You are needed.' He placed his thumb in the centre of her forehead. 'I have faith in you, Daughter of my Soul.'

'I'll say it only once more. Come here,' the officer snapped.

Instead of obeying the order, Rafik turned and walked in the opposite direction towards the village.

'Rafik!' It was Zenia's desolate cry.

'I cannot leave Tivil.' His voice carried to them through the fog and Sofia heard the Gypsy's words echo, resounding in her head, a split second before the shot rang out in the still air. Rafik's wiry frame jerked. His arms flew out like wings, then he crumpled to the snow and a stain spread from under him.

'Run, Pyotr, run! Fetch Chairman Fomenko.' Mikhail's voice sliced quick and decisive through the heavy air.

Pyotr ran. Sofia couldn't feel the ice freezing her cheeks or the snow treacherous under her feet—all she could feel was the hole in her heart.

'Rafik, don't leave me.'

The words trailed desperately out of her, but Rafik was gone. The pain of it pooled in her chest and she closed her eyes, but dark places had started to open up in her mind, lonely places she didn't want to visit. She shivered uncontrollably.

Then warm arms were around her and the air rushed back into her lungs. Mikhail was speaking to her. She didn't hear the words but she heard the love in them, felt the strength of them banish the loneliness.

He led her to where Rafik lay in the snow. Zenia had turned over her father's body. The Gypsy girl lay across Rafik's chest, her wild tangle of black hair writhing, dry sobs shaking her. Around her stood the teacher, blacksmith and priest, their faces grey with shock.

Snowflakes had started to come spinning down in great white spirals, the first icy blast of a *purga*, a sudden snowstorm, and dimly Sofia became aware of angry voices behind her. She turned to see Aleksei Fomenko, a tall and broad figure in his *fufaika* coat, arguing with the OGPU officer. As always, the wolfhound was at his side.

'You had no right to come into my village to arrest a *kolkhoz* member without informing me first.'

'I am not answerable to a village Chairman.'

'It looks like you've more than done your job,' Fomenko growled with fury. 'Now leave.'

'My men will search the Gypsy's house first.'

'No,' Sofia whispered. The strange mystical contents that lay therein would condemn the whole village.

Mikhail stepped forward to stand beside Fomenko, eyes narrowed against the falling snow. 'Look, he was just a Gypsy who was good with horses, nothing more. And now he's dead. You'll find nothing in his house except a few pots of stinking grease for softening bridles.'

'So you knew this Enemy of the People?' the officer demanded with interest.

Sofia's heart slid somewhere cold.

But Mikhail was careful. 'I knew him only as someone who lived in Tivil. We didn't share a glass of vodka together, if that's what you mean.' He nodded at the officer and banged his hands on his arms in a noisy show of the shivers. 'It's cold, Comrade. The coming storm will trap you here in Tivil if you don't hurry. Get back to Dagorsk with your men, this business is finished.'

Sofia could feel an uneasy suspension of breath around her and, barely noticeable in the darkening of the light, she moved close and touched the officer's pale horse on its big shoulder muscle. It bared its teeth but didn't bite, though the white threads of its tail twitched like serpents. *Leave. Just leave.*

After a long thoughtful moment the officer swung his horse's head and, hunched against the wind, cantered off through the snow at the head of his troop. The *purga* swallowed them.

The figures stood motionless in the moment of shock that followed, then Mikhail quickly wrapped one arm around Sofia, the other around Pyotr. 'We must get Rafik's body out of the storm.'

But before they could move, Elizaveta spoke out in a voice that was powerful against the rising wind.

'Listen to us, Sofia.'

Four figures stood in a line, blocking the path into the village. Priest Logvinov, Elizaveta Lishnikova, Pokrovsky and the weeping Gypsy girl. The blacksmith had lifted Rafik's limp body into his arms and Zenia's hand rested on her father's dark head.

'Sofia,' Elizaveta said, 'we ask you to take Rafik's place.'

'No.'

'Sofia,' Pokrovsky said, 'you are needed.'

You are needed. Rafik's words.

Sofia recoiled. 'No.'

'Sofia.' The priest raised a hand into the snow-laden air between them but carved no cross this time. 'God will grant you strength. You are the one who can help care for our village. Rafik knew it. He believed in you.'

I have faith in you. His final words to her.

'*Nyet.* No.' She inhaled deeply, ice stinging her lungs. 'Mikhail, it's dangerous. Tell them.'

Fomenko was standing to one side, observing them in silence, his eyes intense and curious. But Sofia's eyes were drawn to the road into Tivil and she felt it pull at her, as powerfully as the moon pulls the tide.

Mikhail took her hand in his. 'My love, it has to be your decision. Yours alone.'

'I don't have the strength. Not like Rafik.'

'We will help you.'

Sofia looked at the circle of people around her. With a rush she knew that the life she'd been pretending she and Mikhail could lead elsewhere was never destined to happen.

'I'll be with you,' Mikhail said, his hand tightening on hers.

The sound of Tivil breathing came to her. She didn't want it to die, and somehow she sensed that the decision had been made long ago, before she was born. Was there any truth in what Rafik had told her, that she had inherited a special gift as the seventh daughter of a seventh daughter? She didn't know. She knew only that from him she had started to learn a way of applying her mind, a way of shifting sand. She looked around her in the swirling snow, at these people who believed in her and who cared so passionately for their village, and she felt for the first time a huge sense of belonging. Here was a place that pulled at her heart, a place that was home. And she owed it to Anna. *My dear Anna, grow well and strong again. It's because of you that I am here, with this man at my side.* Spasibo.

'I'll stay,' she said simply.

13

Tivil
Spring 1934

THE AIR WAS crystal clear, and high above Tivil the trail of an aeroplane skimmed across a blue sky. Mikhail gazed up at it, shading his eyes.

'It's an ANT-9,' Pyotr said confidently. 'The same as the *Krokodil*.'

'You're right,' Mikhail grinned. 'You'll be a pilot yet.'

They were in the graveyard at the back of what was once the church, the grass still fragile with frost where the building's shadow lay, but the spring sunshine was tempting out the first buds. Sofia was kneeling beside Rafik's grave. In her hand she held a bunch of *podsnezhniki*, snowdrops, their delicate heads softly swaying as she placed them in a jar on the grave.

'Where did you find the flowers so early?' Mikhail asked.

She smiled up at him. 'Where do you think?'

'Beneath the cedar tree.'

'Of course.'

She and Anna had picked them together. It was there that Anna had shyly whispered the news that she was pregnant.

'It's a secret,' Anna smiled, 'but I can't keep it from you. Now that I'm so much better, it'll be safe.'

'Have you told your husband yet?'

'Yes.'

'And?'

Anna touched her stomach. 'We're naming him Vasily.'

Sofia had laughed. 'Let's hope it's a boy then.'

Now she took the white stone from her pocket and rested it on Rafik's grave.

'Why do you always do that?' Pyotr asked.

He'd grown taller in the winter months, his shoulders suddenly broader and his eyes more thoughtful. Sofia had found herself watching him and wondering.

'I do it because this stone connects Tivil to Rafik.'

She picked it up. Neither Communism nor the Church had brought peace to Tivil, but this was something different, a strength that seemed to rise from the heart of the earth itself. She looked into the boy's eyes.

'Hold the stone,' she said.

Pyotr didn't hesitate, as if he'd been waiting a long time for this moment. His hand grasped the stone and immediately his young eyes filled with light in the bright spring morning.

'Pyotr, before your papa adopted you, did you have brothers?'

'Yes, but when I was three,' his eyes were studying the milky stone, 'they all died in the typhus epidemic.'

'Six older brothers? Making you the seventh son.'

'Yes. How do you know that?'

She didn't answer his question.

'Pyotr, would you like to come for walks with me sometimes when it's dark? And learn to shape the thoughts that form in your mind?'

Pyotr looked to his father. Mikhail gazed at his son with gentle regret and nodded. 'Take care of my son, Sofia.'

'I will, I promise.'

Pyotr stood, still fingering the stone. 'When will we start?' he asked.

Sofia gazed round at the village that was her home, at the houses so sturdy and yet so fragile in the sunshine.

'Tonight,' she murmured. 'We'll start tonight.'

Kate Furnivall

Have you always wanted to be a novelist?
Not always, no. For many years I worked in publishing and advertising, until my husband, Norman, decided to sell his London advertising agency and we moved to Wiltshire, where he began to write. He has now had thirteen crime novels published under the name of Neville Steed. Over the years I helped out with plot lines and editing and during that process I observed the mechanics of creating a book, the patience you have to have—it's as intricate as making a galleon out of matchsticks! It was not until I learned more about my family's past, however, that I decided to start writing myself.

So what was the spark that persuaded you?
Years ago I was going through boxes of sepia photographs with my mother, Lily, as I wanted to record on the back of them where they were taken and who was in them. Looking at a photograph of herself as a child with her parents, my mother said, 'Of course, I was known as Lydia then.' She went on to talk about her past: how her family had fled from the Bolshevik Revolution across the wastelands of Siberia; how she had grown up in an International Settlement in China before moving to India and finally to England—and I was spellbound.

After her death, my family asked me to write her story and I just couldn't walk away from it. So my first novel, *The Russian Concubine*, was born. It was set in China but I knew that inside me, there burned a story about Russia itself. That's when Sofia, Anna and the village of Tivil came to life in *Under a Blood Red Sky*.

What made you want to incorporate an element of mystery and magic?

One of the main themes in *Under a Blood Red Sky* is the human need to believe in something greater than ourselves. This may take the form of a religious faith, like Christianity, or of a rigid political and social belief system, like Communism. Or it may be something less precise, more mystical and magical, like superstitions that have been handed down from generation to generation, as represented by the Gypsies in the novel, Rafik and Zenia. I wanted to see what would happen when all three belief systems—Christianity, Communism and superstition—were forced into contact and how this clash would affect each of my characters in the microcosm that is the village of Tivil.

How do you begin researching your novels?

My problem is that I love doing research and could quite happily go on delving for ever. At some point I have to say 'enough is enough' and start writing. I read every book I can lay my hands on about the particular place or period I'm writing about. For *Under a Blood Red Sky* the horrors of the Siberian Gulag camps and the human cost were brought home to me through deeply moving accounts by writers such as Alexander Solzhenitsyn. I am fascinated by what makes a person a survivor and also read the personal stories of the Beirut hostages: Terry Waite, John McCarthy and Brian Keenan. I went to Russia and travelled through large tracts of countryside where rural villages have barely changed since the 1930s— and where there is nothing but trees and more trees for miles and miles!

Do you have a writing regime?

When I'm writing I don't sleep very well. All night my subconscious is whirring and when I wake in the morning, the first thing I do is write down all the ideas that have come to me in the night. If I shower, go downstairs to make a cup of tea, feed the cat—the ideas and the story just evaporate. So—and this is going to sound really lazy and decadent—I stay in bed for an hour or so and just let the thoughts flow. Once that's done, I get up and meet the day.

What is the best thing about being an author?

Living so many different lives through my characters. An author has the chance to be a Russian aristocrat one day, a headstrong young girl the next, a Gypsy, a Chinese revolutionary, a doctor, a prison guard—the list is endless.

What do you do to relax?

I love to walk. We now live in a 300-year-old cottage in Devon, just ten minutes from the sea. I like to stop writing around 4 p.m. and head for the beach. But just to paddle—it's too cold to swim, even in the summer!

Jane Eastgate